ASH WEDNESDAY '45

ASH WEDNESDAY '45 by Frank Robert Westie

Ash Wednesday '45 is a vivid account of what the air war was like, *as experience*, for those American men who flew into battle over Germany in World War II, knowing each time that this day might be their last. And yet *Ash Wednesday '45* is not a saga of unremitting tragedy or gloom. A small group of close friends—men and women—come to know a joy of friendship such as few ever experience in peacetime.

If there is a quality that distinguishes *Ash Wednesday '45* from other books on the air war in World War II, it is a *"you are there"* feeling. The reader flies into battle in the cockpit of a B-17 Flying Fortress, experiencing the air war as the author experienced it flying out of England as a pilot in World War II.

In the shadow of war, Robb Robertson, an American pilot, and Cynthia Allsworth, an English woman, discover the joys of *living in the now*, savoring their existence as they blot out the past and future.

- **Michael Norell, Emmy award-winning screenwriter:** *"The best war novel I ever read and one hell of a romance as well. A masterpiece."*

- **Hollis Alpert, author and critic:** *"I have yet to read air-combat scenes of World War II as vivid and as pit-in-the-stomach exciting as those in Frank Westie's* **Ash Wednesday '45***".*

- **Ulf Mörling, Senior Correspondent and former Editor-in-Chief,** *Sydsvenska Dagbladet,* **one of Sweden's largest newspapers:** *"...the best war book I have read since* **All Quiet on the Western Front."**

- **Delbert Mann, Academy Award-winning film director:** *"... I couldn't put it down until I finished it today"*

- **Kenneth Thurston Hurst, former president, Prentice-Hall Publishing Company:** *"Frank Westie evokes the real air war of World War II—hard, unromantic, gruelling, deadly ... so tighten your seatbelts, reader, and you'll be caught up in the lives of the brave aviators who daily endured hell at 30,000 feet."*

- **Sylvia La France, radio talk-show host:** *"Your book moved me emotionally more than any book I remember. It should be put into a time capsule."*

Frank Robert Westie

ASH WEDNESDAY '45

The front cover is the creation of
Bruce Unwin, distinguished artist, ex-Eighth Air Force B-24 pilot,
and German prisoner of war.

George Wahr Publishing Co.
Ann Arbor, Michigan
Established 1883

George Wahr Publishing Company
304½ South State Street
Ann Arbor, MI 48104
© 1995, George Wahr Publishing Company
All rights reserved.

First Published 1995
Second printing 1996

Printed in the United States of America

Library of Congress Catalog Card Number: 95-60995

This novel is a work of fiction. Any references to real people, events, establishments, organizations, or locales, are intended only to give the reader a sense of reality and authenticity. Other names, characters, places and incidents are either the products of the author's imagination or are used fictitiously. The 990th Heavy Bombardment Group, its airfield, and the people who inhabited it, never existed.

Acknowledgement is made to Harcourt Brace & Company for permission to reprint an excerpt from "Ash Wednesday" in COLLECTED POEMS 1909-1962 by T.S.Eliot, copyright 1936 by Harcourt Brace & Company, copyright ©1964, 1963 by T.S.Eliot, reprinted by permission of the publisher.

Acknowledgment is made for permission to reprint lyrics from the song *TOGETHER*, by Ray Henderson, Lew Brown, B.G.DeSylva
Copyright © 1927 (Renewed) Chappell & Co. (ASCAP) All Rights Reserved. Made in USA. Used by Permission of WARNER BROS. PUBLICATIONS INC., Miami, FL. 33014

This book is about deviance and so it is not inappropriate that it be dedicated to the memory of my brother,

Charles Matt William Westie

who lost a leg to a strafing Messerschmidt along a hedgerow on the road to Saint - Lo, in Normandy on July 28, 1944, and in that moment became forever deviant, a one-legged man in a two-legged world, joining a host of other deviants who, by the very nature of their estate, offend: among them blacks in a white world, the blind in a sighted world and, if you like, left-handed people— sinistri in Italy, gauche in France— in a right-handed world. That he "gave his leg", as people used to say, was once offensive. Now it is merely irrelevant, not only because he died eventually of his wounds, but because all of that was so long ago. Besides, he could have stayed home. After all, many other fathers did.

I wish to make two acknowledgments:

Margaret Westie, my wife and partner in this and numerous other writing projects across the years.

Elizabeth K. Davenport, Editor-in-Chief at George Wahr Publishing Company, who brought her years of experience as writer and editor to bear on this project in more ways than I can possibly enumerate.

Author's Preface to the Second Printing

Ash Wednesday '45 is a novel of love in war. Flyers stationed in England in World War II moved in and out of the war—from weekends in London to combat over Germany—with mind-bending suddenness. A small group of deeply committed friends—Robb, Evelyn, Stosh, Merrie, Sam, Bradley—all accept the fact that, for them, life's timetable is severely distorted, and in this acceptance their lives and loves acquire a special poignancy.

Ash Wednesday '45 speaks to the collision between an individual's conscience that will not yield, and a military system, that, like all large social systems once set in motion, becomes an inexorable tide that can not be stayed or re-directed by individuals, however great their social power or noble their intentions.

This novel is not military history or autobiography. The 990th Heavy Bombardment Group, like its airfield, the people who inhabit it in this story, and the English village Allsford Lynn, never existed. The characters, where they aren't purely products of my imagination, are composites of attributes borrowed from many persons. Like the characters in the novel, descriptions of bombing missions and events during the missions are composites drawn from my imagination and my experiences during missions as I flew out of England in World War II, but they rely even more on the experiences of other flyers who flew with the Fifteenth Air Force out of Italy and with the Eighth Air Force out of England. But the events in this story are no less real, as experience, than those that occurred throughout the American Eighth Air Force. There were dozens of 990ths, each with its own airfield, scattered throughout southern England. Each had its tragedies, triumphs, and loves, as did the 990th in this novel.

Many readers of the first printing found the flyers' experiences hard to believe. They asked, "Was it *really* like this?" The answer: ***Yes, it really was like this.***

Frank Robert Westie
November, 1996

BOOK I

Cambridgeshire
Autumn

Because I know that time is always time
And place is always and only place
And what is actual is actual only for one time
And only for one place
                    T.S. Eliot
                    Ash Wednesday

The wind seemed to gain momentum as it swept across the airfield before spending its fury on the bare branches of the forest that separated the air base from the rest of the world. It shrieked through the upper branches of the trees, but only moaned as it swept the arched, corrugated roofs of the buildings huddled in the night around Headquarters, as though offended by their strange shapes.

Small, hard snowflakes stung Sam Prentice's cheeks as he trudged along the gravel path. Snow? In mid-October? Hail, perhaps. Whatever, there was a winter crunch in the gravel beneath his feet. He pulled the visor of his cap lower over his glasses and pressed the collar of his trench coat tighter against his ears, keeping his flashlight beam focused on the edge of the path. He watched in fascination as crystalline drifts of tiny hailstones formed against the dead grass at the gravel's edge. As he contemplated the minuscule drifts, they became full-blown snow-drifts, not in England but in rural Massachusetts. Winter's first surprises, promises of white hillsides and village streets lined by elms, their bare branches snow-laden, houses blue-white in the winter night, and warm windows whose glow seemed to say that all was as it should be in a friendly world.

But for Sam Prentice this cold, dismal English night held no such cozy promises but, rather, dark forebodings; not for himself, a ground officer, but for his friends who soon would fly in weather far worse than this. Sam Prentice was not only the chief intelligence officer of the 990th, he was its chief worrier. He worried for every crew on the base, but he worried most of all for Robb Robertson and Stosh Kovacs and Monk Bradley, his best friends in the Group. Actually, his best friends anywhere, ever.

Winter was short-lived. By the time he turned up the path to the officers' club the hail had given way to a cold, driven rain. The shadows of the two arched, hangar-like buildings loomed large ahead of him. The one to the right was the officers' mess, the left one the officers' club. Together they formed an "H"-shaped structure, with the entrance vestibule and connecting hallway forming the crossbar of the "H".

A rush of warm air hit him in the face as he opened the door. Not only did the officers' club have a furnace that maintained an internal temperature in the 60's Fahrenheit, it had a dropped ceiling that hid the ugly corrugated steel arch that made most other buildings on the base cold echo-chambers. And the club's furniture—overstuffed artifacts and threadbare rugs of the English Twenties and Thirties—lent a warmth to the club even though the decor was the product of pure chance.

Sam smiled when he spotted Robb seated in the most remote corner of the club, as far as possible, a hundred feet at least, from the bar and the crowd of men gathered there. and as far as possible from the "Old Timer's Corner", off to the right of the bar, where the top brass and the lead pilots congregated. Robb's six foot three inch frame seemed to drape over rather than occupy the easy chair. His garrison cap was tilted forward so that its visor covered his eyes.

Sam hurried across the room. He was about to speak when he saw that Robb was asleep. He lowered himself silently into a chair and sat quietly, studying his friend. Alvin G. " Robb" Robertson, 27 years old, was nine years younger than Sam—and three or four years older than the average pilot—yet a stranger would have thought Robb older than Sam. Robb had a youthful, boyish look about him—a mop of thick, dark brown hair that was often unruly and, by Army Air Force standards, quite long, and the broad-shouldered, thin-waisted physique of a well-proportioned young man.

But Robb had been flying in combat for more than two years, and it showed. No one could say how—perhaps it was under the eyes or in the eyes themselves or around the corners of the mouth, or perhaps it was a certain grayness of skin-tone—but one could see it in every veteran combat flyer. They not only looked older, they *were* older.

Sam had seen these changes in Robb over the past two years. He didn't like it, but that wasn't what worried him now. Robb had become a different person over the past two or three months. Colonel Strang must have seen it too. In fact, even though Robb was, next to Stosh Kovacs, the most experienced lead pilot in the 990th Heavy Bombardment Group, the C.O. no longer used him as a lead pilot. He still flew as deputy lead quite often, but never as the primary leader of his squadron or the Group.

Sam had seen many Eighth Air Force flyers fold over the past couple of years. Robb was showing unmistakable signs that he might be on the edge, retreating into a dream world. He was melancholy much of the time, and he appeared to have lost all interest in the world around him. Except for classical music, which seemed his only solace.

But Tony Rizzo, the Group Flight Surgeon, had seen countless flyers fold, and he told Sam he was almost certain Robb's emotional decline wasn't due to combat fatigue. He didn't fit the syndrome. Tony had said, sure, Robb was tired after having flown a full tour and a half—some forty to fifty combat missions—but he wasn't flying terrified and, according to Monk Bradley, his co-pilot, he was still one of the coolest pilots imaginable under fire. Sam wondered, if it's not combat fatigue, then what is it? He'd asked Robb on many occasions what it was that was eating at him, but the answer was always the same: "Nothing."

Robb must have sensed Sam's presence. His eyes opened slowly. He stared at Sam for a moment. He pushed up the visor of his cap, looked around the room and then back at Sam.

Sam said softly, "Hi, Robb."

"Why didn't you wake me up?"

"You were sleeping the sleep of the righteous."

Robb smiled wanly, "Sleeping under false pretensions."

"Pretty sharp for a guy half awake." Sam stood up. "I'll get us a cup of coffee."

Robb watched Sam as he headed to the mess hall: tall, skinny Sam extending his long legs full out as he hurried across the room. Robb stood up and stretched. He sat down as Sam returned with two cups of coffee.

Robb felt a wave of affection for his friend as he watched him place the coffee on the low table between them. "What would I do without you, Sam?"

Sam stirred his coffee absently for a time. Finally he said, "Actually, you're not doing too well *with* me."

"What are you talking about?"

"We've been close friends ever since Walla Walla, going on three years."

"What's your point?"

"Have I ever kept anything important from you?"

Robb smiled, but without humor. "I see where this conversation is going."

"Goddamn it, Robb! Don't you think it's about time you told me what's going on? Maybe I can help."

Robb stared at the table. Finally he spoke, just above a whisper. "No one can help."

Sam was encouraged. This was as close to a response he'd gotten on the subject. "You can never tell. Tell me about it."

Robb pulled a cigarette out of his package, lit it, and inhaled deeply. "It's pretty stupid, childish. I should say adolescent."

Sam leaned forward slightly. "Go on."

Robb said, "I met a woman a couple of months ago. I didn't really meet her for some time after I first saw her. The first time I saw her she didn't see me. At least I don't think she saw me. I sure hope to hell she didn't see me that first time."

Sam was mystified, but Sam was a patient man. He remained silent.

"Sorry. I'm doing a lousy job of telling this. I'll start over. I went trout fishing—this was late last August—on the stream that runs along the south boundary of the air base."

Sam nodded. "I know the stream. It runs through the Allsford estate, not far from the manor house."

"That's it. I was fishing pretty close to the house, without knowing it at the time. I couldn't see the house because the stream runs through a thick forest. That's when I saw her . . . the most beautiful woman I'll ever see if I live to be . . ." He smiled ruefully. There was an unwritten understanding among the flyers not to talk about themselves in the long-range future tense. "I mean I don't expect to ever see a more beautiful woman."

"Was she fishing, too?"

"She was lying on her back, sunbathing on a little sort of dock, a small wooden platform that juts out over the edge of the stream. The place is quite secluded, with trees all around a little clearing. I came wading around a bend in the stream and there she was, maybe fifty feet or less from me. She was asleep. At least she appeared to be asleep. She was lying on her back, with her head turned to one side, facing me."

"Did she hear you? Did she wake up?"

"Not as far as I could tell. I looked at her for ten or twenty seconds, maybe thirty, holding my breath for fear I'd awaken her. Then I slipped back around the bend as quietly as I could. I felt like a goddam Peeping Tom."

"I think you're making too much of this."

"There's one thing I didn't tell you." He shot a glance at Sam. "She was naked."

Sam sat up straighter. He looked at Robb curiously, his eyebrows raised. "Naked?"

"Yes."

Sam grinned broadly. His grin gradually metamorphosed into a bemused expression. "Hmm. Naked. I'll be damned. I see why you felt like a Peeping Tom. But who cares? Why don't you just chalk it up to good luck?"

"It's not that simple." He smiled his humorless smile. "I went back."

Sam's eyes lit up, as if to say, "Aha!" Finally he said, "Oh, I see."

Robb smiled, this time genuinely. "I didn't go back for another peep, or anything like that."

"You went back hoping to meet her."

"Yes. I went fishing again."

" Did you meet her?" Sam inched forward in his chair.

"In a way. You know we take off practically over the manor house when the wind is right. Actually the house is maybe five hundred feet to the left of the takeoff path. Anyway, I shot landings and takeoffs on sunny days, keeping the rate of climb low on takeoffs so I wouldn't be too high—about 300 feet—when I got to the house."

"I remember when all that was going on. Monk told me you were pretty upset one afternoon when one of the other guys got permission to use the Colonel's retired B-17 before you put in your request."

Robb smiled. "I guess I was starting to think of 'The Colonel's Lady' as my own private plane. But that worked out all right because after that the Colonel let me use his P-47 when The Lady wasn't available."

"You flew 300 feet over the house in the Thunderbolt? I'll bet you damn near broke out the windows in the house."

"I eased back on the power as much as I could."

"Go on with the story."

"Well, as you put it, I got lucky on one of those practice takeoffs. I banked over the house on a beautiful summer afternoon and there she was on the platform. I landed as quickly as I could and went fishing."

Sam started to laugh, but he stifled it when he saw that Robb was serious. "Then what happened?"

"Well, things started out pretty much the same as the first time. I rounded the bend and there she was. But this time she saw me about the same time I saw her."

Sam leaned forward. "Was she naked?"

"No. Actually, I don't know. What I mean is I don't know if she had been naked just before I rounded the bend. She had a robe pulled around her by the time I saw her."

"What happened? Did you talk to her?"

"Yes."

"Who is she? What's her name?"

"Cynthia Allsford."

"I'll be damned. Cynthia Allsford, as in Allsford Lynn, and Allsford Hall. The daughter, perhaps, of the family that owns the land our base is on."

"That's right. At least I think so. She . . ."

Sam looked up at the bartender who suddenly appeared. "Yes?"

"Phone call for you, sir."

Sam sighed. He knew what a phone call for him at this hour always meant. And Robb and every other flyer in the room knew what a phone call to the Group Intelligence Officer meant: the Group was alerted. The only question: would the mission be a short, sweet milk run? Or a journey into hell?

Sam said, "I guess you'll have to finish the story later, after you get back from wherever you're going tomorrow. I can't wait for the rest of it."

Robb saw Sam's disappointment. "It'll keep."

Sam negotiated the 100 feet or so to the bar in short order. He picked up the phone and listened. He put the receiver on the hook and said something to the bartender. The bartender moved to the center of the back bar and turned the face on the English Toby mug to the wall. As of that moment the bar was closed. It was now official: the 990th Heavy Bombardment Group was alerted.

Robb watched Sam carefully as he strode back toward him. He could tell by Sam's expression that the news was not good.

Robb said, "Where to?"

Sam said, "Don't ask."

———2———

At precisely 0155 hours on the morning of Saturday, October 13, 1944, two alarm clocks went off simultaneously on the floor on either side of a figure curled up, fetus-like, in a wooden swivel chair behind the stove in the orderly room of Amber Squadron. The little soldier sprang into action. He rushed out the door and into the squadron washroom next door, splashed water on his face, and hurried back into the orderly room, where he shut off the alarm clocks, donned his rain parka, and picked up his flashlight. He looked at his watch as he grasped the door knob. Exactly one minute had elapsed since the alarm clocks went off.

Anyone unaware of the circumstances might have wondered, what's the emergency? This morning, like all mission mornings, was in fact an emergency in the life of Private Milan Swovik. If Private Swovik overslept or for any reason failed to wake up the flyers on time, he'd be buying a one-way ticket to the front lines in France, and he knew it.

A sheet of driving rain blinded Swovik momentarily as he stepped into the night. He pulled his parka hood tightly around his face and followed his flashlight beam to the first Nissen hut in "officers' row." He entered the barracks quickly, shutting the door behind him. He took his watch out of his pocket and focused his flashlight beam on the watch: 0158. He stood looking at his watch for one minute and 55 seconds. He then moved quickly to the side of the bunk of the officer who would lead the squadron today. He spoke in a loud stage whisper. "Captain Kovacs! Time to get up, sir!" No response. He pushed gently on the mound of blankets and coats. "Time to get up sir! Briefing at O three hundred, sir!"

A hand emerged from under the mound and reached under the bunk, turned a valve on an oxygen bottle and came up with an oxygen mask. The mask disappeared under the mound.

Private Swovik moved to the adjacent bunk and said, "Captain Robertson! Time to get up, sir! Briefing at O three hundred, sir!"

Robb threw back the covers and retrieved an oxygen mask from beneath his bunk. "Okay, Swovik. Turn on the lights." He sat on the edge of his bunk and sucked oxygen and watched Kovacs' mound. Kovacs sat up suddenly. Six-foot four, raw-boned, hard-muscled Stosh Kovacs in his dark green G.I. winter underwear, twenty pounds under his football-playing days at the University of Detroit, but still big by any standard.

Kovacs slipped his feet into a pair of leather flying boots and reached under his bunk and shut off the oxygen valve. He came up with a half-gallon can of army grapefruit juice and a bottle of vodka. He cut two holes in the top of the can and handed the can to Robb. Robb took a long pull on it and handed it back.

Kovacs raised the can to his lips and drank thirstily. He grimaced and said the words that were his first words on the morning of every mission Robb could remember: "This battery acid could kill you." He poured small amount of vodka into the can—enough to alter the taste of the battery acid—and rotated the can slowly, the way one mixes cream into a cup of coffee without a spoon. He held the can out to Robb. Robb took a symbolic swig. Kovacs raised the can to his lips and took another drink, longer than the first. He uttered a long "Ahhhhh," and wiped his full, black moustache with the back of his hand. "That's more like it."

The officers mess was crowded by the time Robb and Kovacs arrived. The air was pungent with steam table army food and wet clothing. Kovacs piled the plates on his tray high with Spam, hash- brown potatoes, scrambled powdered eggs, and toast. The two fresh fried eggs issued to each flyer before a mission—the Eighth Air Force's special reminder that this meal might well be his last—seemed small and inadequate on Kovacs' tray. With solemnity worthy of a Croix de Guerre, the private behind the line handed Robb his two fried eggs on their little plate. Robb nodded to the man and proceeded to serve himself more public food: a couple of slices of fried Spam and two pieces of toast.

They joined Second Lieutenant Malcolm "Monk" Bradley, Robb's co-pilot, at a table at the rear of the room. Greetings were perfunctory. No one was ever cheerful at this time of the morning before a mission, but the gloom seemed to Robb heavier than usual. Maybe it was the rain—for the others anyway—but he knew his own mood was born of his frustration at facing this damned mission, which Sam had implied would be a bad one, before he'd managed to establish contact with Cynthia Allsford.

Robb made a sandwich of his toast and Spam. Stosh Kovacs ate everything on his tray and went back for more of everything—except for the fresh eggs.

Robb and Kovacs sat on the aisle in the last row at briefing. Lieutenant J.P. "Gib" Hawkins, the Group Meteorologist, presented the weather predictions, always a joke because there was general agreement among the flyers that anyone could do as well flipping a coin. This morning Hawkins began his predictions by announcing that they would encounter heavy rain in the climb to formation altitude. He had to raise his voice to make himself heard over the din of the rain pelting the corrugated steel roof of the briefing room. The hoots this brought forth were the closest thing yet to a laugh in the briefing room this morning.

The meteorologist's other predictions were not unexpected: the weather over the target—still unannounced—would be clear, but there was a good chance of a low ceiling and precipitation over England by the time they got back. This brought forth another wave of hoots from the gathered flyers. Everyone always hoped for the opposite: clear weather over England and a thick, protective undercast over the target, but it seemed that in fall and winter they almost always got what Hawkins promised them today.

The pilots, navigators and bombardiers talked in muted tones as they waited for the next presentation. Their jumbled voices produced a hollow, echoing rumble as the sounds bounced off the bare steel arch of the oversized Nissen hut. Captain Sam Prentice stood up. The rumble stopped abruptly, as quickly as if the assembly of flyers were a highly trained choir whose conductor had flicked his baton. All eyes followed Prentice as he moved to the map on the front wall of the room.

Every man in the room knew the range of possibilities. If the string on the map leads to the German submarine pens at Brest or St. Nazaire, the mission will be short and sweet, a milk run. But if the target is the Leuna Oil Refinery at Merseburg, one-fourth of them, more or less, could be dead by noon.

Sam pulled back the curtain from the map and declared in his high, reedy, public speaking voice, "Today's target is Merseburg!"

All human sounds ceased. The din of the rain on the roof became a roar in Robb's ears, declaring that this was the real world, that he was awake and he had heard Sam say what he thought he heard.

Someone moaned, "Oh my God!" A chorus of moans and groans and curses erupted, diminishing gradually until only hushed entreaties and whispered prayers could be heard from those close by.

Robb wasn't unprepared; Sam's hint last night had steeled him for the announcement, yet when Sam uttered the dreaded name just now he felt as if he had been kicked in the stomach. He glanced at Kovacs. Stosh's face was impassive. He looked at the man on his left, a young second lieutenant. All color drained from his face, he looked as if he had died sitting up. Robb put his hand on the young man's arm. The lieutenant turned toward him.

Robb said, "Which one is this for you?"

"Fourth." His tone was flat.

"I don't know exactly which one this one is for me—I'm on my second tour—but it must be forty something. I've been to Merseburg three times and I'm still here. Merseburg is a symbol around here. It's not as bad as the guys make it out to be."

The young man's face relaxed slightly. Robb wondered if the lieutenant believed his lie, or if his true statement, that he had survived three trips to Merseburg, was more comforting.

Sam Prentice continued his presentation. "At Göttingen, which is approximately one hundred miles west northwest of Merseburg, the bomber stream will make a feint toward Berlin to draw out the German fighters. Be ready for fighters, and stay ready even after the course is corrected back toward Leipzig."

It seemed to Robb that Sam's words were now reaching very few of the men, yet when he announced that flak over the target would be heavy, a rumble of derisive, angry sounds flowed from the rear to the front of the steel half-tunnel like a tidal wave. The men hated Sam Prentice in this moment.

Sam continued, "We turn on the Initial Point on to the bomb run at 1205 hours; we drop our bombs at precisely 1207. Remember now, we have to keep our eyes peeled for fighters in the Göttingen area." Sam peered at his audience through the thick lenses of his glasses. "Any questions?"

A first lieutenant sitting in the back row, on the aisle directly across from Kovacs, stood up. He shouted above the clatter of the rain. "Captain, I heard you say 'We have to watch for fighters, we turn on the IP at 1205, we drop our bombs at 1207'. My question is this. Where are you going to be at 1207 today?"

There was a sudden roar of laughter, as though all of the pent up tension of this morning was released at once. Sam's face turned dark red. Stosh Kovacs, all six foot four, two hundred twenty pounds of him, leaped across the aisle in a single stride and grasped the fleece collar of the lieutenant's flight jacket. He jerked the man from his chair in a quick, single motion, flipped him around in his arms so that he held him from the rear, his feet a foot above the floor. All heads turned to the rear of the room.

Robb sprang to the door and opened it. Kovacs threw the man out into the torrential rain and slammed the door shut. Sam's audience of more than one hundred officers broke into loud laughter and applause. The Merseburg paralysis was broken.

Colonel Strang stood up to give his standard pep talk. He had a hard time keeping a straight face. He began by shouting to the back of the room. "Captain Kovacs, I don't think we need you to guard the door. Sit down please." More laughter. Kovacs complied. The C.O.'s remarks were perfunctory. He ended with his predictable conclusion. "Remember men. There's no such thing as a too-tight formation when we're under attack! Dismissed!"

Robb waited in the vestibule of the equipment room where Stosh Kovacs and Monk Bradley took Communion with the line of flyers kneeling before Father Paul Miller. Captain Miller, a cassock draped over his uniform, moved rapidly along the line, laying a wafer on the tongue of each man, repeating a Latin phrase. The priest gestured to the men to rise. He turned to Robb and held out his hand. "God bless you, Robb." Robb shook hands with the priest. Kovacs and Bradley exchanged glances.

Robb stepped out into the night and the torrential rain and ran toward the nearest truck in the line of canvas-covered personnel carriers. He moved awkwardly, weighted down by layers of flying clothes, parachute harness, Mae West life preserver, forty-five caliber automatic, first aid and escape kits, maps, and various other paraphernalia. He leaped up the steps at the rear of the truck and held the canvas flap back for Kovacs and Bradley. The truck ride was short. Robb's plane, "Brillig", like the planes of all the lead pilots in the Group, was assigned a hardstand close to Operations. The truck stopped and Robb and Bradley stood up.

Kovacs said, "See you tonight. Keep a tight asshole."

They ran through the downpour to the rear door of the plane and hoisted themselves in. They stood in the plane's waist and took off their rain parkas, careful not to shower water on Sergeant Marconi and Sergeant Broz, the waist gunners sleeping on the floor. Robb marveled that they were able to sleep, knowing today's target was Merseburg. He looked toward the tail of the plane. He could see the glow of two cigarettes. As his eyes adjusted to the darkness, the barely discernible silhouettes of his Tailgunner and ball turret gunner, Sergeants Hoyt and Bohall, came dimly into focus. The two gunners from the hills of eastern Kentucky always lurked in the shadows, as though their lives were dark secrets. They were fiercely independent and proud and, when crossed, dangerous. Robb had known them for two and a half years—they had flown with him on his first tour—and in all that time he had never known either of these furtive, nocturnal creatures to fall asleep in the plane.

The pilot and co-pilot moved forward through the long, bare, tubular fuselage. Robb turned into the radio room. Sergeant Billy Blum— known as "Brain Child" by all the enlisted men in Amber Squadron— looked up from his radio console. "We drew the ace of spades today, Robb."

Robb said, "You can never really tell, Billy. I've been on a couple of trips to Merseburg that weren't too bad." The radio operator turned back to his console and adjusted his ear phones. Robb was disgusted with himself; he should know better than to try to soften today's harsh reality for Brain Child.

The name "Brain Child" had stuck because Blum's mental quickness was legendary, and all the more remarkable because he was very small and ingenuously open-faced. He looked more like sixteen than twenty. Despite his youth and modest education, he was a fountain of knowledge. In the barracks, arguments over factual issues often ended with the remark, "Go ask Brain Child". His knowledge was encyclopedic because that was where he got it. If he didn't know the answer to your question, he had a set of encyclopedias at hand to check it out. If the answer wasn't in his head or the encyclopedia, he'd wing it. Robb had never heard him say "I don't know." Some of the squadron's enlisted men said Brain Child was the biggest bullshit artist there ever was, but to most of the men his vast store of knowledge was impressive. In any event Sergeant Billy Blum was a friendly, generous young man who stood ready to share his half-knowledge on any subject with anyone who asked. Hardly more than five feet tall, he had hit upon a formula for increasing his stature.

Brain Child's knowledge of Merseburg wasn't half-knowledge. He'd been there and he remembered everything. Robb put his hand on his radio operator's shoulder and gave it a slight squeeze. He left the radio compartment and entered the bomb bay, placing one foot carefully in front of the other as he felt his way along the narrow catwalk. He didn't turn on his flashlight but the deadly cargo was revealed by the dim light admitted through the open door to the flight deck. He stared straight ahead yet he could see the bombs peripherally and he knew they were one-thousand pounders.

In the cockpit, Lieutenant Monk Bradley, his co-pilot, and Sergeant John Wieriman, his flight engineer, were discussing an item on the Airframe and Engine form that their ground crew chief, Sergeant Scroggins, had filled out. Wieriman turned and pointed to an item on his clipboard. "Robb, we still have the oil leak in Number Two engine, and its cowl flaps still won't open more than one-fourth."

"Did you talk to Scroggins about it?"

"He says no B-17 is perfect in wartime. He says those are our imperfections, or something like that. 'Imperfection' is too big a word for him."

"I'll have to have a talk with him when we get back." He added a silent qualifier: *if* we get back. "Monk, I'm going down below for a minute." He dropped through the hatch from the flight deck into the nose compartment. Second Lieutenant Fritz Carlson, the navigator, sat hunched over his desk. He was writing a letter. Second Lieutenant Will Richards, the bombardier, was asleep, his back against the rear bulkhead.

Robb squatted next to Carlson. "How's everything, Fritz?"

"Perfect. My wife is expecting a baby and I'm going to Merseburg."

"We've been there before, and we're still here."

Carlson nodded, "I've been there once, but this is your fourth time, isn't it? Doesn't that make you nervous—like you're mocking the laws of probability?"

"Whatever happened before doesn't count. If you had five sons already, the chances now would still be fifty-fifty that your wife will have a boy."

"So it's still Russian roulette with a four-shooter, one bullet in the magazine."

"The target may be obscured by an undercast, in which case our chances improve considerably. And I'm told we have new developments in our radar jamming devices."

Richards woke up and yawned. "Nice try, Robb. Rumors about our new jamming devices fly around the base on the morning of every Merseburg mission."

"They're bound to improve it from time to time. Maybe the story is true today. How's the knee?" Richards had been laid up by a piece of flak early in their tour.

The bombardier smiled ruefully, "About the same, like a good case of rheumatism. Our distinguished flight surgeon says a guy's gotta expect this sort of thing when he reaches twenty-four. Let's face it, Robb, we're not getting any younger."

Carlson said, "Cheer up, Will. You may not get any older after today."

Robb stood up and moved to the upper hatch. "I'm getting out of here. You guys are undermining my morale. Don't forget to watch for fighters around Göttingen."

Robb slipped into his seat, clamped on his earphones, and snapped his throat mike garter around his neck. He sat still for a minute, his eyes closed. Bradley was used to the ritual. Robb finally turned toward him. He placed his right earphone above his ear so he could hear Bradley while he monitored the command channel.

Bradley said, "Time to pull 'em through." He checked the ignition switches. He slid his window open and motioned for Sergeant Scroggins to start rotating the props. The ground crew chief and his assistant stepped out from under the wing and began the slow process of rotating the huge propellers to clear the cylinders of accumulated oil.

Bradley began their checklist. Robb tested and tapped the various instruments, switches and controls as Bradley called out the items. The co-pilot placed his hand on Number One energizer switch and called out, "Energizing Number One!" He lifted the switch. When the sound of the spinning flywheel reached a high, steady pitch, he looked at Robb and called out, "Engaging Number One!" The engine roared to life. Robb adjusted the throttle, fuel mixture and prop controls. They repeated the ritual for the other three engines. They completed the engine run-ups and awaited orders to taxi, the engines idling at 800 RPMs. Robb hoped they'd get the go-sign soon. Each minute of engine idling cost them precious gallons of fuel, fuel that might at the end of the day spell the difference between landing in England or in the English Channel. Merseburg was a long haul and they were carrying a maximum load. He hoped the mission would be scrubbed, but if not he'd as soon get going right away.

After ten minutes of idling, Robb decided to shut down the engines. Amber Squadron was Number Three Squadron today, so he'd have time to start up again while Barnstorm and Dagger Squadrons were taxiing. They had no sooner completed the shutdown procedure when Colonel Strang's voice crackled from the tower. "Upshaw Command to Barnstorm Squadron! First echelon: Roll!" Robb shook his head in disbelief and motioned for Bradley to energize Number One.

Five minutes later the word came from the tower, "Amber Squadron: Roll!" Stosh Kovacs' plane, 'Dogbreath', lumbered past Brillig's windshield almost as soon as the echo of the colonel's voice died. Robb gave his outboard engines a blast and the huge plane lurched forward. He hit the right brake and gave Number One a full shot of power and Brillig swung neatly into place behind Kovacs' plane. Kovacs taxied into the blinding rain as though it didn't exist. They taxied the mile of parking aprons and taxi strips in less than five minutes—about the same time it would have taken on a clear day.

When all twelve planes of Amber Squadron were tightly bunched at the head of the runway, Kovacs' standard call to battle rang out over the command channel. "Okay, men, here we go. Keep it tight!" And, as always, Robb wondered if he was talking about tight formations or tight assholes. A good idea in either case. Kovacs' exhausts grew brighter and brighter as he opened his throttles, holding his brakes. Kovacs let go his brakes and Bradley started counting out loud, "Twenty, nineteen, eighteen . . ." Kovacs' lights became a blur for a brief instant and disappeared completely before Bradley said "eighteen." He fell silent until he picked up the count again. "Ten, nine, eight . . . "

Robb and Bradley pressed their feet more firmly on the brakes. Robb pushed the four throttles all the way forward. Bradley continued,

"... six... five... four..."   The plane shuddered violently, threatening
to tear itself apart under the harnessed thrust of its four engines straining
full blast. "... three, two, one, *go!*"

They released their brakes simultaneously and the big plane lurched
forward into the night. Robb could see nothing straight ahead—neither
the runway nor the string of amber lights at the sides of the runway—but
he could see each individual light as it flashed past the corner of his left
eye. He kept his eyes on his gyrocompass and registered the amber
lights peripherally, estimating the distance between the plane and each
light as it flashed past. He made hair-trigger corrections as the lights got
closer or farther away. The airspeed indicator reached sixty miles per
hour—half way to takeoff speed. Seventy... eighty... eighty-five. He
pushed hard on the throttles even though they were against the stop. As
always, he wondered, would they get off before they ran out of runway?
Finally, 120 miles per hour! Robb eased back on the control column.
The loud rumbling of tires against concrete ceased, just as the last amber
light flashed past.

Bradley raised the landing gear and then, like a victorious boxer,
clasped his hands over his head and grinned. Robb smiled. Taking off
blind in a loaded bomber was an act of faith, and the relief was propor-
tionate to the faith required.

They were in the soup, the windshield opaque. Robb, his eyes glued
to his instruments, was ever aware that there was no room for error with
a plane twenty seconds ahead of him and another twenty seconds behind
on precisely the same flight path. He held his heading steady on 310
degrees, indicated air speed 140, rate of climb 300 feet per minute. The
beam came through unbroken in his earphones. Precisely thirty seconds
after they broke ground he heard the fan marker beacon code override
the beam sound. He banked into a procedural turn to the left, three degrees per second, and held it for thirty seconds, airspeed and rate of
climb steady. The steady beam sound changed to dit daah, dit daah, and
soon faded out altogether. Thirty seconds after leaving the solid beam
sound he banked to the left into another procedural ninety degree turn.
He rolled out on a heading of 130 degrees, the downwind leg parallel to

the runway below. He held it for 90 seconds before he banked to the left again. He was now flying the crosswind, base leg of the pattern, perpendicular to the runway. As soon as the dit daah, dit daah of the near side of the beam sounded in his ears, he began a three degree per second turn to his left. The dit daah merged into a solid, continuous daaaaah as he rolled out of his turn. He was lined up with the runway again. His altimeter indicated precisely three thousand feet as he passed through the Allsford Lynn cone of silence. On the money.

Pray everyone else is on the money! If someone begins a turn a second or two too soon, or makes a four degree per second turn, or lets his rate of climb or airspeed wander: a midair collision. No room for error, yet errors occurred with a certain regularity. Robb dwelled on the simple fact that there was no way thirty-six airplanes could climb through the soup, day after day, twenty seconds apart without planes running into one another from time to time. It happened with a certain regularity. Robb wondered how many of the thousands of crosses in the Eighth Air Force Cemetery outside of Cambridge were monuments to mid-air collisions. In his mind's eye he saw the white wooden crosses marching in neat rows over the gently rolling landscape, as far as the eye could see.

Seven thousand feet. Kovacs' lights! But in a moment they disappeared. He found the brief glimpse comforting. At least two planes were where they were supposed to be. The windshield was solid black again. He looked up. There were no stars overhead so they must have been between layers of clouds when he saw Kovacs.

The B-17 Flying Fortress clawed its way upward, slowly, painfully, its engine head temperatures just under the redlines. As always in a blind climb, Robb wallowed in a crazy state of anxiety and boredom. At last! The first glimmer of stars flickered through the top of the overcast, and then suddenly, though it was still night, the world seemed light. The stars shone brightly in the pristine atmosphere above the clouds. Robb felt his spirits lifting, his body relaxing.

Eleven thousand feet. Thirty-six minutes since takeoff. He switched to intercom and told the crew they could smoke. They'd be circling at

11,500 feet. It would be about a half hour before they would have to go on oxygen.

Robb had climbed through crap like this a hundred times, yet when they broke into the clear, he never failed to gaze in awe at the wonderland above the clouds. Who among those below, those who had never flown, would believe that above the dismal pall of rain and smoke now smothering them there existed this canopy of stars, stars shining as brightly as they had on the clearest nights in England's pre-history, when Druids worshipped strange gods beneath the trees?

Kovacs, now circling a quarter mile or so off to their left, must have seen Brillig break out of the undercast; two flares, a red followed by a green—the Christmas colors of Amber Squadron—shot upwards in soaring arcs above his plane. A mile or so ahead of Kovacs and two or three hundred feet higher, Barnstorm and Dagger Squadrons flew in formation with one another, patiently waiting for Amber Squadron to form.

Robb began a leisurely turn to his left and intercepted Kovacs without increasing his manifold pressures. More gas saved. He had no sooner slipped into the number two, deputy leader position on Kovacs' right wing when number three plane dropped into position on Kovacs' left wing. He checked the formation chart taped to his leg. Skip Andrews. He must have cut a few corners too tight or else let his airspeed wander upwards. Nine minutes after Kovacs fired his first flares, the last plane of Amber Squadron joined the formation. Major Red Hammersmith, flying Group Lead with Barnstorm Squadron, ceased circling and pointed his plane due east, toward the pale pink glow on the eastern horizon, toward Merseburg.

Twenty minutes later, just as the sun broke the horizon, the 990th joined three other Bombardment Groups to form a Wing, and fifteen minutes later, off the eastern coast of England, their Wing joined other Heavy Bombardment Wings to form Task Force Carthage. Task Force Carthage, a mile or two wide and God only knows how long, stretched ahead of Brillig's windshield as far as the eye could see. The monstrous silver snake crawled inexorably eastward, incongruously sparkling as the silver planes took turns catching the sun's rays and bending them sky-wards.

Robb pushed his intercom button. "Pilot to crew. The smoking lamp is out. Everyone on oxygen now. Over and out."

The pilot and co-pilot shed their earphones and donned their leather helmets and oxygen masks. They plugged in their helmet earphones, removed their throat mikes and plugged the mike wires into their mask microphones.

Robb saw the bomber stream stretching ahead of them as farther than he could see. He wondered how near they were to the end of the parade. He pushed his intercom button. "Pilot to Tailgunner. Over." Hoyt's nasal twang came back, "You got 'em, Cap'n Robb."

"Tailgunner. How many Bomb Groups are there behind us?"

"Cap'n Robb. They ain't nobody behind us. We gets to be Ass End Charley today."

"Roger Tailgunner." Christ! Of all times to be stuck with Tail End Charley position! Tail End through the gauntlet at Merseburg! Damn! Damn! Damn! Of all the lousy luck! By the time they ran the gauntlet the German anti-aircraft gunners would be zeroed in on the correct altitude, and the 990th, as Tail End Charley, would probably suffer the greatest losses of any Group.

Robb didn't know that the generals who designed this monstrous silver snake had decided that it would shed its tail halfway between Göttingen and Halle. The front portion of the snake would drone on eastward to targets on the Eastern Front, but the back half would whip sharply to the southeast, to Merseburg. So it wouldn't be as bad as if they had to follow the entire Task Force across the target. The first planes of the creature's tail would achieve an element of surprise and might make it across the target before the anti-aircraft gunners got their fuse lengths set properly. But the 990th was the end of the tail, and Amber Squadron was the last squadron in the 990th, the very tip of the end of the tail running the gauntlet over the Eighth's worst target by far in Europe. He wondered how Fritz Carlson was reacting to Hoyt's announcement. Poor Fritz, his wife expecting.

Twenty-two thousand feet now. The undercast was breaking up. He could see the Dutch coast here and there through holes in the clouds, and he caught a glimpse of the Zuyder Zee off to the north of their course. The top edge of the sun, now dead ahead, made its first appearance above the bomber stream. Its rays, barely filtered by the earth's atmosphere, drilled mercilessly into his eyes. Bradley snapped layer after layer of dark green plastic inserts into his goggles. He gestured to Robb that he was ready to take over. He slapped Robb's throttle hand firmly, and Robb relinquished the controls. Robb removed his goggles and snapped several plastic inserts into them. When he put them back on, the blinding sun became a bright orange ball. Kovacs' plane was now a dull shadow highlighted by occasional flashes of red and yellow and orange as the sun's rays glanced off wings and fuselage.

Robb switched to intercom and motioned to Bradley to monitor the command channel. He leaned back in his seat and let his head fall forward. They were less than one-third into the mission and he was already exhausted. He fell into the delicious half-sleep the army, without intending to, taught every man to achieve effortlessly.

The silver monster climbed relentlessly, hour after hour into the morning sun. At Göttingen, the lead Group of the task force made its abrupt turn toward the northeast, toward Berlin. The lead Group had been on the new heading for fifteen minutes or so when the call rang out. "Bandits! Nine o'clock high!" Robb awakened with a start. He shook his head back and forth quickly and reached under his goggles and rubbed his eyes with his gloved hands. He looked to the north. He saw them: an incredibly large number of fighters—a hundred or more— bearing down on the bomber stream. As he watched the fighters, now some five or six miles away, he saw them alter their course to the right— straight at them. *Straight at Tail End Charley.*

Red Hammersmith's voice came across the airwaves. "In case anyone isn't aware of it, there's about a hundred fighters bearing down on us. Nine o'clock high. Tighten it up and get ready for a sharp turn to the left." In a sudden process of involution the twelve planes of Amber Squadron became a single entity, coalescing into single mass as though drawn together by a powerful magnet: wing tips moved within thirty feet of waist windows, echelons stacked themselves neatly one under the other, each echelon twenty or twenty five feet below and behind the one ahead of it. Amber Squadron had become a single, huge airplane, as had Barnstorm and Dagger squadrons.

Robb switched to intercom. He spoke calmly. "Pilot to crew. Bandits coming at us nine o'clock high. Hold your fire until they are well within range. Keep cool. Make your shots count."

Hoyt and "Boo" Bohall started their inevitable chatter. "Come on you yellow-livered bastards! Come on you bastards. Come on! Come on!" Robb usually let them go on like this for a half minute or so. It helped to dissipate the fear in the hearts of the other gunners—and in his own heart.

Amber and Dagger squadrons moved in tightly on either side of the lead squadron. Hammersmith executed Colonel Strang's favorite maneuver: He swung his plane into a steep left bank, directly toward the oncoming swarm of fighters. The Group followed him as one. The tight cluster of thirty-six huge planes flew on its side for a moment before Hammersmith rolled out of his turn on to a head-on collision course with the onrushing Messerschmitts and Focke-Wulfs.

Hoyt and Boo rattled on, their voices jumbled as their yells intermingled. "Come on you bastards! Come on! Come on!"

Robb climbed ten or fifteen feet higher to give his gunners a clear shot over Kovacs' plane. The swarm, almost within range now, swung sharply to its left, parallel to the bomber stream. Bradley made a brow-wiping gesture. Robb nodded. The Luftwaffe commander had decided, clearly, to look for a less disciplined bombardment group to attack. Boo took a parting shot at them from his ball turret—a futile gesture. Boo yelled, "Come on you yellow-livered sombitches!" But his tone had lost its excitement. He sounded angry and disappointed. His buddy's twang rang out from the Tailgunner's turret. "You shouldn'a shot at 'em, Boo. You skeered 'em off."

Major Hammersmith and the 990th swung back on course, but they had lost a precious three or four miles, maybe more, to the outfit ahead of them. The 990th would be alone, a sitting duck when it made its Tail End Charley run on Merseburg.

There was a sudden commotion over the command channel; some outfit farther up the line was catching the fighter attack that the 990th so narrowly escaped. The air was filled with urgent yells of command, anger, and screams of terror, all punctuated by machine gun fire and explosions. And then Robb heard the call, "Little Friends six o'clock high!" The American P-51 fighters had arrived. The war-sounds subsided and soon all was silent except for the fighter commanders' directions to their pilots on who was to chase the German fighters and who was to remain to guard the bombers. Robb knew that it was unlikely that the German fighters would return. The German high command had decided some time ago that their precious fighters and fighter pilots must be used to attack American and British bombers, not to engage in aerial dogfights with the American Mustangs or RAF Spitfires.

Robb slapped Bradley's throttle hand and took over the controls. His eyes scanned the panel: Thirty-one thousand feet—mission altitude. Indicated air speed 150 miles per hour. Number Two cylinder head temperature was hovering at the redline. He enriched the fuel mixture to Number Two. And then he saw the clock. 1144—twenty-one minutes to the Initial Point! How long had he dozed? He pushed his intercom button. "Pilot to navigator."

"Go ahead, Robb." Carlson's voice was steady. Good.

"Fritz, our little maneuver just now is going to cost us some time. Give me a new ETA for the Initial Point."

"Navigator to pilot. I figured it out just now. We'll be three minutes late, unless Upshaw Leader decides to trade altitude for speed, in which case we could catch up, but we'd be a thousand or two thousand feet lower than everybody else. I hope he doesn't do it. We need all the altitude we can get."

"Roger, Fritz. I agree. Over."

3

The back half of Task Force Carthage split off from the front half soon after the German fighters departed. Task Force Carthage Two picked up a course slightly south of due east.

They were ten or fifteen miles from Merseburg when Bradley nudged Robb's shoulder. He pointed ahead and to their right. A huge mottled gray-black cloud, more a dirty smudge in the sky than an opaque cloud, hovered on the otherwise clear horizon. Both pilots knew what it was: the Merseburg cloud, the man-made cloud produced by the black smoke of thousands of exploding anti-aircraft shells. He watched as squadron after squadron, Group after Group, emerged from the other side of the cloud and dove off to the right to escape the flak. The lucky ones. They had attacked Merseburg and they were still flying. Robb knew that many men aboard those planes were wounded, but for those who emerged unscathed this day's hell was over, provided their planes made it back. Sergeant Weiriman, a portable oxygen bottle attached to his parachute harness, appeared behind the pilots' seats. Bradley leaned forward and Wieriman lowered a heavy flak vest over Bradley's head and on to his shoulders. Wieriman placed a trench helmet with large metal ear-phone flaps over Bradley's leather helmet. Bradley slapped Robb's throttle hand and took over while Wieriman helped Robb get into his flak gear.

Wieriman returned to his top turret. He had long since resigned himself to the irony of the situation: he had just dressed the pilots in flak gear, but all that stood between his own head and the hail of shrapnel they were about to enter was his leather helmet and his highly penetrable plexiglass turret.

Robb recalled vividly his discussion with Sam about the flak cannons at Merseburg. Sam said the Germans were determined to save the I.G. Farben Leuna Oil Refineries at all costs. Most of the fuel for the Luftwaffe and the Germans' armored divisions on the Western Front came from the Merseburg refineries, just as their Eastern Front was supplied largely by the oil fields and refineries at Ploesti in Romania. Sam said this was why Merseburg and Ploesti were the most important Axis targets in Europe, each of them far more heavily defended than even the Reichstag in Berlin. Sam may not have exaggerated when he said Merseburg and Ploesti were the most heavily defended pieces of real estate in history. Thank God Ploesti is the special target of the Fifteenth Air Force flying out of Foggia in Italy, not ours!

He watched the mottled cloud darken and expand. He wondered if Sam could imagine the significance of the knowledge he imparted that evening not long ago. Sam said he'd seen reports of aerial photography studies which tried to estimate the number of anti-aircraft cannons firing at one time at the height of an attack on Merseburg. The photo-interpreters estimated that the Germans had more than one thousand anti-aircraft cannons there, but no one knew how many of them were the big 88 millimeter "wonder guns" that could reach mission altitude easily, and how many of them the smaller anti-aircraft cannons which, while they fired hundreds of rounds per minute, couldn't reach thirty thousand feet. Sam said that each German 88 fired twenty rounds per minute. Robb did some quick calculations. Say they have only one hundred 88s. That means two thousand explosions per minute on the bomb run. Having run the Merseburg gauntlet three times, Robb wondered if there weren't a lot more than a hundred 88s in that one thousand. An Eighth Air Force cliché had it that the flak was so thick over Merseburg you could practically get out and walk on it. However inept the figure of speech, that was about the size of it.

Robb checked the clock on the panel against his watch. Five minutes to the IP and the turn onto the bomb run. The black smudge was getting bigger by the minute. Robb figured it must be at least ten miles wide now, its bottom at 25,000 feet or so, its top soaring up to 33,000 feet or more—higher than a loaded B-17 could fly. He slapped the back of Bradley's throttle hand. Bradley relinquished the controls.

The bombardment group in front of them, now four or five miles ahead, wheeled sharply to the right on the IP. Two minutes to go for the 990th. Robb switched to intercom. He pushed the button. "Pilot to Navigator. Over."

Fritz Carlson responded. "Navigator."

"Fritz, give me a countdown to the Initial Point, starting at minus ten seconds."

"Roger, Robb. We're approximately ninety seconds from the IP now."

"Roger, navigator. Pilot to bombardier. Over."

"This is the bombardier."

"Bombardier, give me a thirty second countdown on bombs away. Over."

"Roger, Robb."

They would simply follow Stosh Kovacs today, turning when he turned and dropping their load when he dropped his. But Robb had to be ready to take over if Kovacs bought it.

He looked off to his right, toward the target, and he saw a sight that would remain etched on his brain for as long as he lived. The Merseburg cloud was disgorging B-17s, some diving straight down, others spinning out of control, many of them on fire. As he watched, one of the burning planes exploded, wildly scattering bodies, bombs, engines, machine guns, gas tanks, and pieces of aluminum and steel and, he surmised though he couldn't see it, human flesh. And behind and above it all, airfoil remnants floating gently earthward like huge, silver falling leaves.

He gave his head the quick one-two shake. There must have been a half dozen planes falling at once, but he couldn't be sure; there were large parts of planes as well as whole planes falling. He raised himself in his seat and looked downward. Far below parachutes billowed as the flyers, free-falling to oxygen level, now pulled their rip cords. Some of them would land in the inferno they helped create.

He guessed what had happened. A plane in the middle of a squadron had taken a direct hit in its bomb bay before releasing its load. The single plane's explosion had taken several nearby planes with it.

He felt sick for a moment, and then he began to feel it coming on, the beginnings of the narcosis, the narcosis the first shock always brought on, the built-in narcotic that transformed him from a frightened victim into detached spectator, the narcosis that came with the first death-convincing shock, the narcosis born of his acceptance of his death as fait accompli. But it fell short. It didn't come all the way on. Damn! A wave of fear engulfed him; he felt sick to his stomach. What if it didn't come today! Would he be able to do his job? Why didn't it come on? He yelled into his mask. "Why? Why? Why, damn it!" He knew the answer. "Cynthia . . . Cynthia! God damn you, Cynthia!" He had accepted his death long ago; a fact waiting to happen. But now, with the hope of seeing her again still lurking within him, the future was again part of him, and he couldn't bring himself to accept his death. Without that acceptance the narcotic didn't work. He should never have met her! He should never have looked for her!

Fritz Carlson's voice, "Ten . . nine . . . eight. . . seven . . ."

Kovacs' right wing dropped slightly—his warning to get ready for a quick, steep turn. Robb lowered his right wing.

". . . four. . . three . . . two . . . one!"

He was ready for the turn, but not quite ready for the violence of it. Kovacs whipped his plane steeply to the right. Robb hit right rudder and hard right aileron, hauling back on the column with all his might to keep from running into Kovacs. As they rolled out of the turn the bombardier called out to Robb, "Opening bomb bay doors." Robb added power on all four engines as the gaping hole dragged at the bottom of the plane. The needles of all four manifold pressure gauges climbed beyond the redlines. The cylinder head temperatures rose rapidly far beyond the redlines, but they finally stopped, well short of the needle-stop. All except number two. Number two engine's head-temperature kept on climbing all the way to the stop on the gauge. Bradley opened number two's cowl flaps but they stuck at one-fourth open. He pulled number two's fuel mixture lever to full rich.

Will Richard's voice: "Thirty, twenty-nine, twenty-eight, twenty-seven . . ."

Robb pushed his intercom button. "Pilot to waist gunners."

"Waist gunner. Waist gunner."   Broz and Marconi walked on each other's transmissions.

"Waist gunners. Start throwing the chaff."

Broz and Marconi, like seventy other waist gunners in the Group, began throwing bushels of Christmas tree tinsel out the waist windows to jam the German radar. Though it was a clear day, the German artillery-men would be using radar now to bring their guns to bear on the Flying Fortresses in the gray-black cloud of their own making.

"Nineteen. . . eighteen . . . seventeen . . ."

Robb felt a jolt. He looked to his left. Brillig's left wing seemed to explode. Number two engine had blown itself to bits. The entire cowl of number two engine went flying along with the engine parts that blew it off. Bradley hit number two fuel cutoff valve and number two feathering button simultaneously. Robb pulled the mixture control to idle cutoff and flicked off the ignition. Bradley hit the engine fire extinguisher selector control and the extinguisher button. Robb pushed the remaining throttles full forward, lest someone behind them chopped off their tail. He stole a quick glance at number two engine and quickly re-fixed his eyes on Kovacs' plane. Good! No fire!

The plane shuddered. There was a moment of smoothness followed by another shudder. And yet another. The cockpit dimmed as though someone was turning down the lights; they were into the edge of the smoke cloud now. The plane shuddered constantly now. The concus-sions from the heart of the cloud hit them head-on.   Kovacs' running lights came on. Bradley switched on Brillig's running lights and instru-ment panel lights.

Kovacs' plane bounced as though the weather had suddenly turned rough. Brillig's bounces were out of sync with Kovacs'.   Andrews in Number Three position pitched and twisted worse than Kovacs. A shaft of light penetrated the top of the smoke cloud for a brief moment, and then it was gone and an eerie half-darkness enveloped them. Robb had never seen it this dark over Merseburg on his previous runs, but then he had never flown tail-end Charley over Merseburg before. He swung off to his right, another plane width away from Kovacs. Andrews, his plane a shadow now, took the cue and followed suit, swinging wide to his left, perhaps two plane widths farther yet from Kovacs.

And then the world exploded! In a split second, a totally insane inferno, a wildly unimaginable hell blasted itself into minds and bodies and planes. Red, yellow, orange and white flashes exploded ahead and above and below and on either side of the shuddering, lurching, twisting airplanes. Each blinding flash, each flash one of a hundred flashes at any moment, shot steel missiles in all directions with the speed of bullets. And on the airwaves wild commands and horror-filled man-screams cut through the cacophony of booming shell-explosions and the crashing, tearing sounds of steel smashing through aluminum.

Holes, rips, and gashes appeared in aluminum fuselages and wings. Engines blew themselves to pieces as oil lines severed. Pieces of tails and wings flew wildly into the slipstream, and whole tails and whole wings exploded off fuselages. Exploding planes disgorged bombs and guns and human bodies, bodies inhabited a second ago, now mere flesh. And the unlucky ones, men still alive: living, breathing, seeing missiles, clothes and parachute harnesses torn away by the blast, breathing and seeing until, in a minute or two six miles below, they would become in a red flash part of the rubble of the Leuna Oil Plant.

The smoke cloud didn't blot out the sun completely: Robb could see Kovacs and Andrews plainly by the natural light, now augmented by constant red, orange, yellow and white flashes. A vision of the black interior of a surreal night club in Chicago flashed through his mind, an eerie room lit by flashing red and orange and yellow lights.

Will Richard's voice: ". . . six . . . five . . . four . . . three . . . two . . . one. . . bombs away!" Each plane leaped upwards as it disgorged its bombs. Robb and Bradley pushed forward on the column. Richards hit the bomb-bay door switch to "closed".

Andrews' right wing burst into flames. An incredibly eerie sight: an airplane brightly burning and illuminated by blinding flashes on a level of hell Dante never imagined or matched.   Andrews started to swing off to his left.   And then, in a flash much brighter than the others, the plane was gone, now part of the Merseburg cloud's fallout of wings, fuselages, engines, and human bodies. And beyond Kovacs' plane, where Andrews' plane had been, nothing but a hole in the sky lit by eerie flashes.

Robb felt nauseous. Hoarse screams over the intercom. One of his crew hit! Who? What position? He pushed his intercom button and yelled, "Wounded man report . . . " He never finished the sentence. The left half of his windshield blew away. Bradley grabbed the controls. Robb's mind went blank for a moment. He shook his head violently and leaned to his right to get out of the air blast. He wiped his goggles with his hand. His lap was covered with pieces of plexiglass. He took off his outer glove and felt his oxygen mask. He looked down and examined his oxygen hose. He felt his forehead and neck and looked at his silk inner glove. He ran his hand over his flak helmet. He turned up the current to his heated flying suit.

He felt the narcosis coming on again, the sudden, soothing, pain-killing, fear-killing shot that came with sudden trauma. He hadn't lost it! Thank God! It wasn't Cynthia!   The earlier shock of the falling B-17s hadn't been strong enough to bring it on!

He shook his head violently. Get with it! Watch Stosh! He checked his oil-pressure gauges and head-temperatures.

He watched Bradley wrestling with the controls.   The shot was coming on good now. He felt it flowing through his veins. Heavenly, blessed, warm flow of . . . of . . . of what? He waited with intense curi-osity. He waited with fascination. He waited with fascination for his death to happen. He waited without fear.

He watched himself watching Kovacs. He watched himself watching Bradley pushing and pulling and twisting the controls and kicking the rudder pedals. For a moment he was outside his body, now outside the plane, now above the plane. He watched himself watching himself and Bradley in the cockpit, and Carlson and Richards in the nose compartment, and Marconi and Broz in the waist, and Brain Child in the radio room bent over his console, praying. And he saw Hoyt in the tail, grinning from ear to ear, enjoying the adventure of his life. And Boo, a fetus curled up in his aluminum and plexiglass womb hanging below the plane, watching the red and yellow and orange and white explosions, enjoying the show from the best seat in the house. He returned to the cockpit and he watched himself watching Monk Bradley. He smiled at Bradley benignly beneath his mask and he felt a strong love for Bradley in this moment.

The plane pitched and twisted and Bradley fought it pitch for pitch, twist for twist. The nose of the plane began to drop. Robb grabbed the column and he and Bradley hauled back together. The plane leveled, but they were flying level with the control column all the way back into their guts. Something wrong with the cables or the elevator. Robb reached down and spun the elevator trim tab control to full up position. He felt the trim tabs take hold. They climbed slowly back to Kovacs' level. They eased forward on the column. He slapped Bradley's hand and took over control of the plane.

But he remained a spectator. He watched with fascination as the plane shuddered and bounced and twisted and he stared curiously at the strange half-night filled with the flashes of the massive artillery barrage. He calmly summarized the total insanity of it all. Here he sat at noon on a bright October day, flying an airplane through a man-made twilight filled with thousands of flashing artillery explosions. He was going to die. That was certain. He was going to die *now*, in the very next moment. They all will die in the next moment. And it was fascinating. He knew it had happened long ago, but now it was about to become official, and in his acceptance of it he knew a serenity the depths of which no one on this earth *who had not died before he died* could ever know or imagine. And as he said these words to himself another surge of narcosis swept over him. The warm, soothing wave surged over him and around him and through him. He felt it in his abdomen and in his chest and in his head. He felt it running out into his arms and legs, to his toes and fingertips. A thing of substance coursing through his veins, a thing of peace, complete peace, a peace he could never describe. A peace he wouldn't try to describe even to himself. To talk about it would be to destroy it, and he would be left naked, unprotected, screaming amidst the explosions, screaming in the hell six miles over Merseburg.

The concussions ceased. Thank God! Clear sky ahead! In ten or fifteen seconds there will be pure sunlight! Beautiful, unblemished sunlight! How lovely the world! How lovely the light of the whole world!

And the cockpit was filled with the glorious light. He beheld the light in wonderment. He beheld the light with the awe of a blind man to whom light, forever forfeit, is suddenly returned.

*　*　*　*　*　*　*　*

The last vestige of daylight lingered beneath the heavy overcast that hung three or four hundred feet over the United States Army Air Force base at Allsford Lynn. Some twenty or twenty-five officers stood along the pipe rail on the roof of the small, two-story building that served as the tower, each man peering intently eastward. Red Hammersmith had made his first transmission minutes ago and everyone had rushed to the roof. Hammersmith hadn't said anything about losses, but the Group was returning from Merseburg and everyone knew the losses would be high. They would have known it even if Hammersmith hadn't asked them to have all available fire-fighting equipment and all ambulances standing by.

A lieutenant standing between Colonel Strang and Captain Prentice held a pair of binoculars to his eyes. Sam Prentice had a notebook in his hand. The lieutenant with the binoculars called out, "I see them now! First squadron . . . wait . . . let me count 'em again. Eight! That's right. Eight! Lots of feathered props. Better warn the crash crews.

"I'm on the second squadron now. Second squadron . . . let's see now . . . second squadron . . . nine!

"Third squadron . . . third squadron, nine!"

The drone became a roar as the first squadron flashed past, three hundred feet above the tower. The planes peeled off one by one, steeply to the left as they entered the landing pattern, most of them shooting off flares indicating wounded on board or damage to the plane. Planes with more than one engine out or with control problems came straight on in without circling. The circling planes turning on to the landing approach squeezed between the severely damaged planes. Nobody went around the pattern a second time, regardless of how tight the situation. The object was to get on the ground. Now!

Ambulances sped to the planes in response to requests radioed by pilots. Personnel carriers, trucks, and jeeps doubled as ambulances. The wounded were taken to the base hospital, the dead to the morgue. The survivors headed for the whiskey tables.

Robb, Bradley, Carlson and Richards watched as the medical corpsmen, assisted by Brain Child, Hoyt, and Boo, slid the stretcher bearing the 240-pound hulk of Bruno Broz into the rear of the ambulance, next to the stretcher on which Tony Marconi lay, a victim of the same shell that caught Broz, his fellow waist gunner. As a corpsman closed the ambulance door, the four officers turned and walked toward the waiting personnel carrier.

Robb stopped suddenly. "You men go on. I've got something to settle with Sergeant Scroggins." He nodded toward Scroggins who was at that moment entering his wall tent.

Bradley said, "What's the plan for Scroggins? He damn near killed us today."

"I'll tell you later. You men go on to the whiskey tables. I'll meet you there before we go in to de-briefing."

Robb went to Hoyt and Boo who were standing near the rear door of the plane. He asked them to stand guard and not let Scroggins or anyone who worked with him near the plane.

Hoyt said, "You unloadin' that sombitch, Cap'n Robb?"

"He's taking a trip to France."

Hoyt exclaimed, "Good!" Boo yelled "Whooie!" Both men grinned broadly. Hoyt's grin was more a leer.

Robb climbed into the cockpit and called the tower and asked them to send the Engineering Officer of the Day and two MPs to his hardstand immediately. He climbed out of the plane and went to Scroggins' wall tent. He found Scroggins reading a comic book amidst a rubble of food, dirty clothing, and aircraft parts. "Howdy, Cap'n."

"Stand up, Sergeant!"

Scroggins' comic book dropped to the floor. His mouth dropped open. He stood up slowly.

"Start packing. You're taking a trip to France."

"What you talking 'bout, Cap'n?"

"You're under arrest for gross dereliction of duty."

"You doing this just because of a little old oil leak and a set of cowl flaps?"

"And stay away from my plane. I don't want you or your assistant anywhere near my plane. Do you understand?"

Scroggins stared dumbly about the tent, his mouth hanging open.

"Answer me, damn it!"

"Yes, sir."

Robb turned and left the tent. The MPs' jeep was pulling to a stop under Brillig's wing. He told the MPs that Sergeant Scroggins was under arrest, and that he wanted him in the stockade until he left the base. There must be no chance of him getting anywhere near the plane under any circumstances. The MPs nodded. They knew, like everyone else, that a seriously disaffected crew chief or mechanic could be dangerous to have around the plane of the object of his disaffection.

The assistant engineering officer, Lieutenant Hensley, pulled up in his jeep. Robb told him he had fired his ground crew chief and his assistant. He'd need replacements immediately. Hensley said he'd send over replacements, but that the first order of business was to tow Brillig to the engine hangar right away and to start replacing number two engine. He gave Robb a ride to debriefing.

Flyers crowded around the whiskey tables that stretched some forty feet along the concrete apron in front of the debriefing room. Robb joined his crew and Kovacs and Stew Adams, Kovacs' co-pilot, at the far end of the table. No greetings were exchanged.

Robb saw that Linda Emerson, the young Red Cross woman who always greeted him warmly after each mission, seemed on the edge of tears. Her eyes were red-rimmed, her lips compressed. He had known her since his first tour. He wondered, was one of the men lost today a special friend of hers? He walked around the end of the table and put his arm around her shoulders. "You don't have to do this today. We can serve ourselves."

"It's my job, Robb. I'll be all right." She moved down the table filling double shot glasses with rye whiskey, placing a glass before each man as he approached the table. Each man was allotted one double shot, but after a mission like today's no one was keeping score.

Kovacs looked at Robb and Bradley, their faces white where mask and goggles had protected them, but near-black where the soot and smoke of Merseburg had penetrated their broken windshield and stuck to their faces. They looked like wide-eyed gargoyles, actually comical, but Kovacs didn't say anything.

Robb said, "I saw your nose turret catch it. I was hoping maybe Harold was away from his turret when that shell hit."

"He was, but he caught a lot of blast. He was alive when we landed, but I'm praying he dies. His eyeballs froze and fell out of their sockets. Tony Rizzo said that if he survives he'll be blind and a quadruple amputee."

Robb whispered, "Oh my God." He decided not to mention Broz and Marconi. He tossed back his drink. "How many planes did we lose?"

"Ten. Amber lost four and the other two squadrons three apiece."

"Christ, no!"

Kovacs said, "The high cost of flying Tail End Charley through the Merseburg gauntlet. I'm going to tell the C.O. to never let Division forget we flew Tail End Charley to Merseburg. The way I see it, the 990th paid its dues today. We should never be Tail End Charley again, anywhere! Never again for the whole fucking war!"

The debriefing room was packed. Air crews sat or stood around the half dozen tables arrayed around the perimeter of the room. Sam's interviewers sat behind the tables recording each crew's story. A crew was gathered around Sam's table at the center of the rear wall of the room. Other interviewers became available, but Robb's and Stosh's crews waited for Sam.

As the crew he had been interviewing departed, Sam stood up and walked around his table. His face was ashen. He shook Robb's hand. He didn't say anything. He just shook his hand. Then he shook hands with the rest of Robb's men and with Stew Adams, and finally with Stosh Kovacs. Sam said, "I just got a call from Tony Rizzo. He told me to tell you Harold died. I'm sorry, Stosh."

Kovacs crossed himself. He whispered, "Thank God."

There was an awkward silence. Sam said, "Sit down, please."

They sat in a circle around Sam Prentice's table and began their grisly story.

After mess, at about 10:00, Robb called the hospital from the telephone in the vestibule between the mess hall and the club. Marconi was fine, and Broz was going to make it. Broz had been transferred to the big hospital and they had just called to report that he was out of danger. Robb's relief drained from him whatever remaining strength he had. He swayed slightly and grabbed onto the telephone box on the wall to steady himself.

Kovacs gripped Robb's arm firmly. "Hang in there, pal."

Robb and Kovacs went into the officers' club for a drink. The bar was closed, the club deserted. The 990th was alerted.

They stood in the center of the room staring at the darkened bar.

Robb whispered, "I don't believe this!"

"I've heard you say that line every time we're alerted after a rough mission."

"I still don't believe it. Where are they going to get the planes and the men?"

"Camelot Squadron stood down today. They'll use Camelot's planes and crews and to fill out the other three squadrons, and they'll fill out your crew and mine and the others from the replacement pool. They'll have your blown engine and windshield replaced in a few hours.

The ground troops don't get a day off after a tough battle. Neither do we.
Hell, you know that as well as I do."

"I still don't believe it."

————4————

On the afternoon of Thursday, October 19—six days after the Merseburg massacre—Robb sat alone in the officers' club, waiting for Sam. Patches of sunlight marched along the floor opposite the row of windows on the south wall of the room. The threadbare imitations of Persian rugs captured a suggestion of their past brightness, a brightness that had faded long before they were appropriated   for this, their final duty.

Robb had slept until noon, their first day off since last Saturday. They had three hours of drugged sleep on Saturday night, the night of the Merseburg massacre, before Private Swovik awakened them at 2:30 a.m. to go back to their hell six miles in the sky. Thirty-four of the thirty-six planes that went out on Sunday's fourteen-hour haul to the Russian Front made it back. One of Dagger's planes went down over the target, and one of Amber's ditched in the North Sea—not really one of Amber's, but one of the planes pirated from Camelot Squadron to make up for the previous day's losses.

They were awakened between 2:00 and 3:00 a.m. on Monday, Tuesday, and Wednesday, and on each day, after suffering the myriad preparations, from Swovik's gentle nudge to taxiing to the head of the runway, the mission had been scrubbed. The clearing weather predicted over the targets in eastern Germany failed to materialize, so it was back to the sack after putting in several hours getting ready. They finally got off yesterday morning. It was practically a milk run. No casualties. An exhausting, fourteen-hour haul to the Eastern Front in crappy weather, but a milk run nonetheless.

He hit the sack just past eleven last night, after swallowing two of Swovik's happy pills. He awoke around 5:00 a.m., screaming. As always in his nightmare, Brillig was a sitting duck, separated from the Group over Germany. Hoyt and Boo kept yelling on the intercom, "Come on you bastards. Come on! Come on!" Robb screamed at them to shut up, but the German pilots must finally have heard them, for they came streaking at him, machine guns and 20mm cannons blazing. The cockpit was full of blood and gore and arms and legs and smoke and fire when Robb threw his mound of blankets and coats to the floor, screaming at Hoyt and Boo, "Shut up! For God's sake shut up! They'll hear you!"

He had screamed out loud, yet there was no indication that the other men in the barracks heard him. They would yell and swear at anyone whose alarm clock rang on a morning off, but no one would let a screaming comrade know he had heard him.

Having "slept in" until 5:00 a.m., Robb knew there wouldn't be a mission that day, so he retrieved two phenobarbitals from his shaving kit and swallowed them without benefit of Swovik's canteen and went back to sleep. He joined the world of the living around 1:00 p.m.. He had a Spam sandwich and four mugs of coffee in the mess around 2:00 and arrived at the club in time for his 3:00 P.M. get-together with Sam, whom he hadn't seen except at briefing for a week.

Sam arrived at the club to find Robb sound asleep again, in his easy chair. And again, as last time, Sam eased himself silently into a chair opposite his friend.

Robb stirred. His eyes opened slowly. "Hi, Sam."

"You're becoming a light sleeper."

"Fourteen hours of sleep will do that to you." Robb yawned.

"Something big must be cooking at Division." Except for briefings and de-briefings, Sam had spent his every waking hour at Division for the past week.

Sam ignored Robb's implied question. "Funny thing. I've been thinking a lot about your strong attraction to Cynthia Allsford—sort of obsessed with your obsession.

"A good choice of words. She really is an obsession."

"Let's have the rest of the story. Start where you were when we were interrupted by Merseburg. I remember exactly where you were in the story. I had just asked you if you talked to her that second time on the stream, and you said you had, but you didn't say what you talked about."

Robb smiled. "You really have been thinking about this." He exhaled audibly. "This is the part I don't like to think about. I mostly listened while she talked. She gave me the devil for trespassing on her property. For violating her privacy."

"What a heck of a note!"

"I wanted to drown myself right then and there. After she told me off she stomped off—to the house, I suppose—and I slunk back around the bend and came back to the base."

"Didn't you say anything to her before she left?"

"I said I was sorry, and I hoped that after she had time to think about it maybe she'd find it in her heart to forgive me."

Sam pulled in his chin. "Did you really say that?"

"That's exactly what I said."

"Quite a speech on the spur of the moment. That doesn't sound like you."

"I know. It even surprised me. It just came out that way."

"This thing is really burned into your memory, isn't it?"

"I remember what I said because she told me later what I said at the time. I saw her in Cambridge, by accident, at one of those Sunday after-noon chamber concerts we sometimes go to. I just happened to look over at the audience across from me—you know how the seating is arranged there in a semicircle—and there she was."

"I'll be damned!"

"I never had anything hit me so hard." He stared blankly for a time. "She was there the next Sunday, too. I thought I caught her looking at me a couple of times."

"Or she caught you. When did you finally talk to her?"

"That night, after the concert. When people were applauding after the last number I hurried back into the lobby and over to the door to the aisle she was seated on and waited for her. When she came out I fell into step beside her. I was going to tell her I'd like to talk to her but, would you believe it, before I could say anything she said she'd like to talk to me."

Sam said, "Another surprise."

"You can say that again. Anyway, she suggested we go to a pub nearby. We went over there and talked. It turns out she wanted to apologize for treating me so badly on the stream. She said that when she saw me on the stream she didn't know I was a flyer."

"What's that got to do with it ?"

"I'm not sure. Well, we really hit it off. Sam, believe me, she's the most beautiful woman I've ever seen—like the most beautiful women you'd ever see in one of those cigarette ads. Short, wavy hair—auburn, I think—brushed-back, flawless complexion, perfect features, beautiful eyes with a sort of inquiring expression, as though she wants to know as much as possible about you or what you're talking about. Very poised and dignified, and bright as hell. And best of all, Sam, she loves chamber music as much as you or I do, and she really knows music, especially chamber music."

"Almost too good to be true."

"I couldn't believe it. We got to talking about different quartets — the Budapest, the London and the rest, and their renditions of particular works. It turns out she's as crazy about the late Beethoven quartets as I am. We were so enthusiastic about our shared love of Beethoven we sort of got carried away. The first thing I knew I had my hand on top of hers on the table, and pretty soon she was squeezing my hand, without seeming to realize it. Sam, if I could have designed the perfect woman for me I would have designed her. Actually, she exceeds any design I could have imagined."

"You're really gone on her, aren't you?"

"That's putting it mildly."

"Go on with the story."

"Well, not much happened except for our wonderful talk together— almost entirely about music. We must have been there an hour and a half, maybe two hours, when she said she had to get home. I was really knocked on my ass by her beauty, her charm, and especially her enthusiasm for the kind of music I love more than anything in the world. Hell, you know what I mean. You love the same music."

"What happened next?"

"I offered to take her home in a cab, but she said she'd prefer to go home alone. She asked the proprietor of the pub to call a cab for her. She left when the cab came."

"When did you see her again?"

"Before she left I asked her if I could pick her up at her house the next Sunday—I was hoping to use your jeep—and go to the concert together and then to the pub afterwards. She said she'd rather not go together or sit together, but that she'd meet me at the pub afterwards.

"Have you seen her a lot since then?"

"Here's where the story gets pretty strange. I only saw her one more time after our first meeting."

"What?"

"She disappeared after that."

"Disappeared?"

"That's right. Vanished from the face of the earth."

"I don't get it."

"I don't either. I'll tell you about it, but first let me tell you how things worked out after the second concert. Then I'd like to see if you have any ideas on how I can go about finding her."

"Why don't you just go to her house—the manor house at the end of the runway—and ask to see her?"

"I did, but the butler there says no Cynthia Allsford lives there or ever did. Look, Sam, this whole thing is pretty weird, but let me tell you exactly what happened, so you can help me."

"It really is strange."

"I missed the next concert when we were supposed to meet in the pub. We flew to Kiel that Sunday, the time we tried to bomb that German battleship—the Prince Ruprecht—in the harbor there. Remember that one? We missed it."

"Not nearly by much, but go on. I want to know about Cynthia Allsford." Sam obviously didn't want to be reminded of their failure.

"That was the day I picked up that little piece of flak in my elbow. But I did get to the concert on the following Sunday. She was there again, of course, and when the concert was over she was waiting for me when I came out of the main hall. We went over to the pub together. As you can imagine, I was damned glad to see her. I greeted her pretty enthusiastically, but she didn't say anything and hardly smiled."

Robb lit a cigarette and blew out a blue cloud of smoke. He seemed lost in thought.

"Get on with it, Robb. Don't leave me hanging like this."

"She was like a different person this time. Still as beautiful as ever, but very sad, morose. She told me she was terrified, afraid I'd been killed—when I failed to show up for the previous week's concert. She said she was relieved to see me at the concert that day, but terrified all over again when she saw my arm in the sling."

Sam took off his glasses and began polishing them with his handkerchief. "How do you figure she got this idea you might be killed?"

"She said she hears the Group taking off for Germany in the early mornings, and she hears us when we come back at night."

"Of course. She lives just off the end of the main runway. She hears us all right."

"She told me she counts the planes as we go out, almost over the roof of her house. She said the number that comes back is often smaller than the number that went out. She started crying right about then. She really came apart. She put her head down on her arms on the table and cried. You know, sobbing quietly, but really unable to stop for a long time."

"Did she say anything about why she was crying?"

"Not really. I waited quite a while—until she stopped crying—before saying anything to her. Then I asked what I could do to help her. She told me to go away. Can you believe that? Right out of the blue, she told me to leave. I asked her when I could see her again. She said never. She said it without raising her head from her arms. She said I would never see her again. Ever."

"But you couldn't leave her like that, could you? What did you do?"

"I asked her if I could take her home. She said she'd get a cab. No matter what I said to her, she just kept saying, 'Please go.' Even though she never again raised her head. I stayed there quite a while after she put her head down. There was no way she was going to even look at me. I finally left. I had no choice. But before I left I asked the pub proprietor to look after her, and to get her a cab. He said he'd make sure she got home all right."

"What happened the next time you saw her?"

"I never saw her again. As I said, I went to her house a few days later and told the butler I wanted to see Cynthia Allsford and he said no such person lived there or ever did. Then I asked to see the man of the house. He said he wasn't home and would be gone indefinitely. When I asked him if the Allsfords lived there he didn't even bother to answer. He closed the door in my face."

"Hell, Robb, that manor house is called Allsford Hall, and has been for centuries. They're the most prominent family in the area. They own the land the base is on and thousands of acres beyond. The village is named after them and I happen to know they still collect land rents from most of the business places in the village. What are they trying to hide? Why the lies?"

"I wish I knew. We know she lives there, or did live there. She told me her name is Cynthia Allsford. I saw her on the stream there, and she said sometimes it sounds like the planes are about to come right through the roof into her bedroom. And she told me the base is on her family's land. The butler was lying, obviously. I wish to hell I hadn't gotten so caught up in discussing music with her that first time and had spent more time learning more about her—what she does, where she lives when she's not at their place here. I blew it."

"The butler is obviously lying, and he knew that you knew he was lying. And he didn't care if you knew it or not. I find this fascinating. I'll bet Stosh would too. Does he know about all this?"

"No."

"Would you rather he didn't know about it?"

"I'll tell him about it one of these days."

"Do you mind if I tell him?"

"That's a great idea. You tell him."

Sam said, "Of all the people I know, I'd bet on Stosh Kovacs to figure out how to find Cynthia Allsford. I meant to ask you, have you tried phoning her?"

"They're not listed."

"What about the pubkeeper? You did say he said he'd take her home, didn't you?"

Robb nodded. "Not exactly. He said he'd see she got home all right. I 've gone back and talked to him. Several times. I get a feeling he knows more than he's letting on. When Cynthia and I came into the pub that first time, the pub man—actually he's the proprietor—greeted her like a long-lost friend, but Cynthia said he must have her confused with some-one else. The man was miffed, actually crushed. And then when I told Cynthia I couldn't leave her like that, she said the proprietor would call her a cab, and when I asked him to look after her and get her a cab, he said he'd see she got home all right. He sounded like he knew her and she sounded like she knew him."

"Has he ever wavered when you've questioned him?"

"Not really, but he seems terribly upset when he sees me come into his place, and when I question him he seems even more upset. Not hostile-upset. More like confused, morally torn."

"Would you mind if I had a talk with him?"

"I'd be delighted. I'm sure as hell not getting anywhere.

"I'll go tomorrow."

"Great! I'd just about given up."

Sam stood up and put on his trench coat. "I've been meaning to ask you, how do you understand your fascination with this woman, this obsession of yours? It's not like you, no matter how attractive she may be. You only met her twice, only once to really talk to her."

"All I can say is I just can't get her off my mind. After that first time I saw her there on the stream, in the sunlight on that summer afternoon, I carried that picture in my mind, almost like an impressionist painting. I guess you could say I fell in love with a picture. Then, when I met her, I felt like there was something between us. A sort of chemistry, I guess. A really powerful chemistry." He smiled sheepishly. "Christ, this sounds idiotic."

Sam said, "That's about the way I had it figured."

"What do you mean?"

"Quite obviously, you've fallen for her, however strange that may seem, given the brevity of your acquaintance. And, equally strange, I think she's afraid of falling for you, if she hasn't already." He waited for his friend's response. None was forthcoming. Sam said, "Say something."

"Let's say you're right. What's she afraid of?"

"She said in the pub she was afraid you'll be killed. I think that's why she's afraid of falling in love with you."

"Why doesn't she simply tell me why she doesn't want to have anything to do with me?"

"That's what makes me think she may already have some feelings for you. It would be easy for her to brush you off otherwise." He turned to leave. "I'll tell Stosh tonight."

That evening Sam told Stosh "the Cynthia Story"—as he'd come to think of it—pretty much as Robb had told it to him that afternoon. Stosh said, "That's one hell of a story. As good as anything I ever read."

Sam said, "Don't you find the whole thing kind of strange, I mean Robb falling that hard over someone he hardly knows?"

"Hell no. I fell in love with Stella Diptula head over heels when I was in the ninth grade the first day when we moved from Hamtramck to Dearborn. I tried to talk to her in school but she wouldn't have anything to do with me. But I rode my bike around the block she lived on every night, maybe fifty times, just to look at her house. I got a big charge just looking at her house. It happens, pal."

"Robb's not an adolescent. I'm worried about him. I think he's had much too much combat. He was slipping before he met this woman, but he's a lot worse since he met her. It wasn't too long after last August that the C.O. quit using Robb as a lead pilot. He saw the change in Robb too."

"I think you and the colonel are making too much out of Robb's little quirks."

"Little quirks? Come on! Have you heard that wild, crazy laugh of his lately? Not that that's serious in itself, but look how he's in a fog much of the time. Look, Stosh, he slips into his daydreams right in the middle of a sentence. Not only your sentence. His own! Right in the middle of something he himself is saying. He's out of touch a lot of the time. That's why he shakes his head like that—to bring himself back to reality. I'm really worried about him."

"I still think you're making too much out of it. I talked to Monk about his flying and Monk says he's quick as a cat in the cockpit and always on top of everything on a mission. He runs a tight ship and he's still as good a pilot as they come. Let him daydream as much as he likes when he's not flying."

Sam said, "I wonder why Robb became a flyer in the first place. Here he is, a fine musician, a really sensitive, poetic sort of personality, a scholarly guy just a dissertation away from the Ph.D. in psychology when he enlisted. He should be in a job like mine, flying a desk."

"Sam, you got it all wrong. You make him sound like some goddamned professor. He doesn't look like a professor, he doesn't act like a professor or a long-haired musician or anything else like that. He looks like a pilot, he acts like a pilot, and he is in fact one of the best pilots to ever climb into a B-17. You and the C.O. are going to have to get over that shit about Robb."

"You have a right to your opinion, but regardless, this obsession of his isn't doing him any good. I'm sure you'd agree with that."

Kovacs stood up. "I'd like to see him happy, if that's what you mean, and this Cynthia Allsford thing is making him pretty unhappy. I can see that."

"So what do we do about it? Do you think perhaps we should try to convince him that he's barking up the wrong tree? That she's obviously a pretty unstable woman—the way she put her head down and wouldn't talk to him—who can only mean trouble for him, even if he could find her?" Sam shrugged. "Hell, I don't know what to do."

Kovacs said, "I've known some pretty neat unstable women. All we got to do is find this Cynthia Allsford for him."

"That's all?"

"That's all. Duck soup. Like falling off a log."

"I forgot to tell you. I told Robb I'd go to Cambridge and talk to the pubkeeper to see if I can squeeze something out of him"

"Good idea. That's where I'd start. Good luck, pal."

—5—

Sam Prentice had difficulty finding the White Horse Public House on the evening of Friday, October 20, even though he had been there earlier in the day. Cambridge, like every other city and town in England, was blacked out completely, and the steady rain all but obscured the tiny, blackout-shielded sign.

He had looked in the door of the White Horse earlier to determine if a "stout, red-faced, sixtyish man with a full, white moustache"—Robb's phrase—still worked there. He did. But the place was crowded, and it was obvious he would have no opportunity to talk to the man. He decided to return shortly before 10:00, the pub's closing time as announced on the door. There were a dozen people in the pub when Sam returned, all of them standing at the bar except for an elderly couple at a table. Sam sat down in a booth to the right of the door to the street. A heavy blackout curtain was drawn across the window at his shoulder. He could hear the rain striking the panes behind the curtain.

He contemplated the elderly man sitting with his wife at the table. The old gentleman symbolized England itself at war, sapped of her energy and resources by the voracious appetites of the machines of war that left so little for the hands that fed them. The old gentleman's determinedly erect posture could not camouflage the gray fatigue written on his face, nor could his stately manner conceal the fact that his meticulously neat, proper attire was now threadbare at elbows and cuffs. But, for all of that, he still communicated, like England herself, a resolute courage and dignity that five years of war and deprivation could not extinguish.

A young woman's voice startled Sam. "Excuse me, Captain." The overweight, round-faced barmaid made no effort to conceal her amusement at his startled reaction. Sam smiled up at the pleasant countenance.

"And what will be your pleasure tonight, Captain?"

"Let me see. I hadn't thought about it. Oh, let me have a pint of bitter, please."

"May I ask you, sir, if you don't mind, what would you ask for if you really had a choice? You know, if there wasn't the war and the shortages."

He found this warm young person amusing. The English were supposed to be reserved but perhaps barmaids were an exception. "Well, if I had my choice, I'd say Scotch and soda."

"I knew it! I knew you were a Scotch and soda man! Well sir, we happen to have a bottle of fine Scotch whiskey back there tonight. One Scotch and soda coming up!"

Sam smiled. She surely couldn't have been announcing that bottle of Scotch all evening. By now there wouldn't be any left.

He sipped his drink slowly, relishing the taste of good Scotch as he studied the rotund, red-faced man behind the bar.

The knot of people at the bar dwindled to two middle-aged men now draining the last dregs of their warm English beer. When they turned to depart, Sam got up and walked quickly to the bar. He placed his glass on the counter and smiled at the bartender. "That, sir, is the best drink I've had in years. May I ask just what brand of Scotch that was? I'd like to know so I can make a point of getting some when the war is over."

The ruddy face brightened. The thick, white moustache stretched wide above the broad smile. "You liked that, did you, Captain? You are a man of taste, sir. A discerning man."

Sam noted that his inflection matched the barmaid's. He too probably just missed being a Scotsman by an accident of geography or warfare in the distant past. Northumberland, without a doubt. "It doesn't take too much discernment to recognize that as a fine Scotch whiskey. With a bit of age on it, I might add." He had mimicked the man's inflection without intending to. He felt a surge of embarrassment. "It does seem to have aged a bit," he continued, pleased that his phraseology was more his own.

The pubkeeper reached under the bar and came up with the bottle of Scotch. Chivas Regal. "This, laddie . . . oh, I beg your pardon, I mean Captain . . . is *real* Scotch whiskey!"

"That it is, sir. That it is!" Sam's inflection was leaning northward again. He quickly added, "There's no finer Scotch than Chivas Regal."

"Have another, Captain, on the house. And I'll have a wee one on the house." He laughed at his little joke. Sam felt his spirits rising with those of this cheerful man.

"That's very kind of you, sir, but I'll have another one with you only if you will allow me to pay for both yours and mine."

"I'll not hear of it, sir!" The proprietor started to tilt the bottle over Sam's glass.

Sam quickly put his hand over his glass. "In that case, sir, I can't accept your fine whiskey." He looked directly into the man's eyes. "It's a matter of honor, America's honor." He tried to keep a straight face, but failed. He grinned broadly, but he remained resolute. "It really is a matter of honor, sir."

"All right then, seeing as you put it like that." The proprietor poured generously and raised his glass. "To the American Eighth Air Force!"

Sam had drunk many such toasts in the officers' club. They were always offered as a joke. Sam quickly erased his grin when he saw the man's solemnity wasn't mock. He repeated solemnly, "To the Eighth Air Force!"

Each man took a generous draught and each sloshed the whiskey around in his mouth before swallowing. And each uttered a breathy "aah!"

"That, sir, is how fine whiskey is supposed to taste. And now," he continued, raising his glass, "I give you the Royal Air Force!" He squirmed inwardly. He respected the RAF immensely but he was embarrassed at the thought that he was manipulating this genuinely friendly man.

"To the Royal Air Force!" The Englishman intoned the toast in a deep baritone, rich with pride. Again they drank ceremoniously.

Sam extended his hand across the bar. "My name is Prentice. Sam Prentice."

"Mosely, sir. A pleasure to meet you."

Sam wondered how to go about bringing up the Cynthia Allsford matter. He knew that if he began quizzing the man right now, his own conviviality and his toast to the RAF would be reduced to a sham. He hated the thought that he really was manipulating this man.

Mosely said, "I never think of the RAF without thinking of Mr. Churchill's words at the time of the Battle of Britain."

Sam pretended he didn't know the quote that was coming. "Oh?"

The proprietor, still gripping the edge of the bar, seemed to become taller as he replied. "Sir, Mr. Churchill said, 'Never in history have so many owed so much to so few.' And I agree with Mr. Churchill. We owe them more than we can ever repay, I say!"

"I agree. I often think of Mr. Churchill's words when I see our B-17s taking off for Germany, knowing some of them won't return."

"We owe your pilots, too, Captain, and the other people on their crews, more than we can ever repay. There's nothing we could do for them that would be too much."

"I couldn't agree with you more, as regards both the RAF and the Eighth Air Force flyers." The time had come for him to lay it on the line. He tossed back the double shot in one motion. "Mr. Mosely, I must tell you it wasn't an accident that I came in here tonight. I came here with a purpose, so that I could perhaps find help with a big problem we have in the 990th."

Sam watched the man's bewilderment slowly shade into wariness. "Just what sort of problem are you talking about, sir?"

"Do you remember the American pilot, a captain, who came here about two months ago with a young English lady? They sat in that booth by the window."

"We have quite a number of American pilots coming in here with English ladies, don't you know. You'll have to be more specific, sir."

"This particular young lady put her head down on her arms on that table and cried. And she sent the American pilot away. Perhaps you remember now?"

Mr. Mosely pulled thoughtfully at the end of his broad moustache. He looked up at Sam and then looked down at the bar again. Finally, he nodded. "Yes. I remember her, and the American pilot."

"Perhaps you also remember that the American pilot—his name is Robertson—came in here on several occasions to ask if you could help him find this young lady, whose name, incidentally, is Cynthia Allsford."

The proprietor nodded, slowly, sadly. "I remember that very well. He struck me as a nice sort of chap. Soft spoken, you know. A real gentleman. But very sad, I'm afraid. I wanted to help him. I wanted to very much, but I couldn't."

"Captain Robertson is one of the most important pilots in the entire Group at Allsford Lynn. He's a lead pilot, very experienced and very skilled. And, of course, very brave, but some of us are quite worried about him now. His health is declining. He hardly eats anything these days, and my own guess is that he doesn't sleep much either. He's lost quite a bit of weight. He may have to be grounded."

"You don't say! I *am* sorry to hear that."

"I'm sure you surmised that Captain Robertson has a rather strong emotional attachment to Miss Allsford."

The proprietor nodded slowly. He picked up a glass from the back bar and began polishing it with a white towel.

"Now it could well be that Captain Robertson's malady is combat fatigue. But I doubt it's simply that. Frankly, sir, I think this young lady's disappearance has contributed much to his illness, along with combat fatigue, of course. Captain Robertson and I are convinced that you know this young lady." Sam's tone was firm but in no way unfriendly or accusing. "You greeted her as a friend, but she decided not to acknowledge your acquaintance, or friendship, because she knew from the time she came in here that day that she was going to send Captain Robertson away and that she didn't want him to find her again. At least that's our guess."

The proprietor turned to the array of sparkling glasses on the back bar. He put down the glass he had been polishing and picked up another. He turned back to Sam, studying the glass as he resumed his polishing motion. "Well, Captain, I hardly know what to say." He looked up at Sam, clearly waiting for some sort of response, but Sam remained silent, his eyes on his empty glass. The proprietor sighed again. "Captain Robertson is in declining health, you say? Is that a fact, sir?"

"You have my word on that. I would have to say that if he doesn't resolve this Cynthia Allsford obsession, his career as a military pilot will soon be finished."

The proprietor stared into space for a time. He sighed. "All right, then, Captain. I suppose it is possible that circumstances can change so as to release one from a confidence, or a promise. Right now it seems to me the most important thing is that we do all we can to keep Captain Robertson healthy and leading your people to Germany to give them

what they gave us in '40 and '41.   I'm sure Miss Allsford would forgive
me under the circumstances." He looked at Sam quizzically.

"Please go on."

"I've known her since she was a little girl. Cynthia and her father
and mother used to come in here after the Sunday afternoon concerts.
Then, later, just the two of them. Thick as thieves they were, her and her
father.   She couldn't have been more than eight years old when her
mother died.   After that . . . after the sadness . . . her and her father
would come in here after a Sunday concert, and you should have heard
the two of them talking. Just like two adults, it was.

"They would talk about the performers at the concert, and the com-
posers of the music, people long dead, as though they were still living
today. After a while you came to think of the little girl as an adult in a
funny sort of way, don't you know.

"And they would often talk about archaeology. That little girl would
talk about Egypt and Greece and God knows where as though she knew
them like her own town. I guess they must have gone to such places a
good deal. And they would talk about the books the father was writing.
Maybe the little girl was a genius, or maybe it was just that the father had
no one to talk to at home, so he talked to the little girl like she was an
adult, and she sort of became one."

Sam nodded, slowly, thoughtfully. "That could very well be.   What
else do you know about her?"

"Not much, I'm afraid. I knew them only here in the pub."   He
stopped polishing and stared into space. When he resumed talking, he
talked more to himself than to Sam. "She took a fancy to me, she did, if
I may say so. I and the missus—my wife was living then—took to
looking forward to the little girl's visits, and we would prepare a little
surprise for her now and then. Sometimes a sweet, sometimes a little
child's drink we'd fancy up a bit.

"First thing she would do when she came in—when she was very
little—she would run up to me and throw her arms around me. And I
would pick her up and she would kiss me on the cheek. And then she
would ask, very adult-like, 'And how are you today, Mr. Mosely?' This
was when she was very little, before her mother died. After that she
would greet me like a polite little lady, but she still liked my little sur-

prises. But the joy was gone. The sparkle. Like she suddenly grew up. Do you know what I mean, Captain?"

"Yes, I do," Sam replied solemnly. "What do you know about her father?"

"Not a great deal, I'm afraid. I felt I knew him very well, after them coming in here so many years. But I really didn't know him at all, Doctor Allsford and me being of different stations in life."

"You called him Doctor Allsford. Was he a professor of archaeology?"

"Well, Captain, I always assumed he was a professor, but I really don't know. I know he was a doctor because I heard him called that now and then by people who came in here. All of the professors here are doctors, aren't they? Not doctors of medicine, but another kind."

"When was the last time you saw Doctor Allsford? Or Cynthia?"

"Eight or ten years ago, I would guess. Not until that afternoon. I suppose that's why she figured she could get away with telling me I must be mistaken. But I wasn't fooled for a minute. I would have known it was her even if I was blind-folded, just hearing her talk."

"Do you know where she lives now?"

"I do indeed, if she still lives in the flat I took her to that evening."

"You actually took her home?"

The pubkeeper nodded. "The captain asked me to look after her when he left, to see she got home all right. He didn't have to ask me to do that. No sir. Not to look after Cynthia. I would never let her wander out into the street that night. Not with her so upset and it raining so hard and all."

"What did you do after Captain Robertson left?"

"Well, sir, I waited a little while to see if she would collect herself. When she didn't raise her head after quite a long time I went over there with a cup of hot tea for her. And I told her I knew she was my old friend Cynthia and she should let me help her."

"What did she do then?"

"I sat there across from her for a while, and presently she raised her head and she reached out and took my hand, and she said how sorry she was for trying to fool me. Then she asked me how Mrs. Mosely was, and I told her the missus had passed on, and then she broke down again and put her head back down on her arms and began sobbing again. I kept asking if I could help her, and she didn't respond. So I finally went out and got a cab and came back here and closed up the place and turned out the lights, except for the little one I keep on all night. Then I told her I was going to take her home, which is what I did. I went up the stairs with her, to the door of her flat. That's when she made me promise not to tell Captain Robertson, or anyone else, where she lived. She told me how much me and the missus meant to her when she was growing up. I don't mind telling you, sir, right now I feel a bit of a traitor to Cynthia, me telling you all this."

"I understand, but sometimes we have to violate one commitment in order to serve another commitment, a higher commitment."

The proprietor nodded.

"Where does she live?"

"In High Street. At the corner of High Street and Brook Street, above the chemist's shop there on the corner."

"I would like to tell Captain Robertson where she lives. Perhaps he can persuade her to see him, or at least tell him what this is all about."

"I don't think that would be a very good idea. Don't you see, sir, I've broken my promise, and she specifically said I shouldn't tell Captain Robertson. And here I would be telling the very person she didn't want me to tell."

"What do you think I should do?"

The proprietor gazed across the room, pulling at the end of his moustache. After a time he said, "Perhaps you should go there yourself, sir, and tell her about him losing his health and maybe being grounded, and him being so important to his people. Maybe she will agree to see Captain Robertson. Or if she won't, then maybe she'll at least explain to you just why she doesn't want to see him."

Sam took out a package of Luckies and offered one to the proprietor. They smoked in silence while Sam considered the possible consequences of his further intervention. Wouldn't Robb's chances be better if she saw Robb in person? Perhaps she could reject him in the abstract, while she might not be able to do so with him standing at her door. But he knew he must honor Mr. Mosely's wishes. He looked at his watch. Almost 10:30. Too late to call on Miss Allsford tonight. No, damn it! As Stosh would say, what the hell, there's a war on. If he hurried he could get to that apartment over the chemist's shop by 10:45.

—6—

Robb sat in his remote corner of the club on Saturday, the day after Sam went to Cambridge. Sam had left a telephone message for him this morning, saying he'd join him for lunch, around two, if his meeting let out in time. Robb got there an hour early. Slouched down in his chair, the visor of his garrison cap low over his eyes, legs stretched out. He looked as if he was asleep, but his eyes never strayed from the club entrance for more than a few seconds. He knew that if anyone could pry information out of that pubkeeper, Sam could. After all, as an intelligence officer he was an expert at squeezing information out of people.

Robb couldn't remember when he'd been more anxious about anything. He spoke out loud to himself, his voice almost a hiss. "Why the hell does Intelligence have to have meetings every day?" He didn't see Stosh approaching at right angles to his chair.

"Hi, pal."

Robb reacted like a coiled spring. His head hit the high back of his chair. "Damn it, Stosh! Don't ever do that again!"

"You sure are wound up."

"I wasn't that tense. It's just that I was far away."

"Dreaming about the mysterious Lady X, no doubt."

Robb smiled sheepishly. "So Sam told you about her."

Kovacs grinned, his thick black moustache stretched wide. "He sure did. That's some kind of story, pal. Beats anything I ever read. I can't wait for the next chapter."

Robb stood up. He nodded toward the doorway where Sam Prentice stood surveying the room. "We'll find out now if there's going to be a next chapter. Sam went to Cambridge yesterday."

Sam came striding across the room. He grinned. "As you were, men."

Robb studied Sam's face as he sat down. "Well?"

"I'm glad you waited for me. I was afraid you might have gone to your barracks, Robb."

"Let's have it. I gather by your grin you found out something. Let's have it."

"Mr. Mosely told me where she lives."

Robb stared at him, for a moment speechless. "I'll be damned! I can't believe it!"

Kovacs said, "Good job, Sam."

"I got lucky. Things fell into place. A solution to the problem, how to approach the pubkeeper—his name is Mosely—fell into my lap."

"Where does she live?"

"In Cambridge. Mr. Mosely took her home that night."

"I knew he knew more than he let on! I'm going to Cambridge to-morrow."

"No need for that. I've already been to her apartment. I went there last night, after I saw Mosely. Cynthia wasn't there. She moved out the day after you saw her."

"Damn!"

"But I've got a great lead. We'll find her, I have no doubt."

"Do you know where she moved to?"

"Not really. But I have the address of someone who will most certainly know where she is." Sam smiled a pleased smile. "The young woman who lives there now—actually I woke her up but she was awfully nice about it considering . . . "

"Get to the point!"

Sam smiled. "The woman there now showed me a letter addressed to Cynthia that the postal people failed to forward and which the woman hadn't yet given back to the postman. It was addressed to Cynthia Allsford, Manuscript Editor, The Journal of Social Anthropology. I went to the Cambridge University library and found the current issue. It's a quarterly. The October issue just came out."

Robb said, "Is Cynthia still listed as the manuscript editor?"

"No, but . . ."

"Damn!"

"Wait a minute. It's not all that bad. I've got the name and address of the head editor, the same man who was editor when Cynthia was manuscript editor. He'd have had to be in touch with her to put out the October issue, even though they have a new manuscript editor now. He's a professor at the University of London. I got his address from the journal." Sam looked up quickly at Robb. "I phoned him from Cambridge."

Kovacs said, "Nice going, Sam. Don't screw around."

"I told him an American pilot and I would like to call on him sometime in the next week or two, the war permitting."

Robb stared warily at Sam.

Kovacs grinned. "Good move. I like that 'war permitting' approach. How could he refuse? He said he'd be delighted. Right?"

"That's exactly what he said, but I wasn't quite as manipulating as all that."

"Who cares? You did the right thing. Now if he clams up, you give him the old Battle of Britain bit. He'll come around. Ten to one he's an air raid warden."

Sam sighed. "Knock it off, Stosh."

Robb said, "Let's go see him the first day the Group stands down and there's no alert in the offing."

Sam nodded. "It's liable to be a while. We have to wait until we have a prediction of a stretch of two or three days of bad weather over the continent."

7

The 990th Heavy Bombardment Group went out on Saturday, October 28, but Amber Squadron stood down. Robb sat alone in his remote corner of the officers' club. His eyes followed the print in The London Times, but his mind wandered between an imaginary interview with a professor in London and the 990th Heavy Bombardment Group. It was 1830 hours and the Group was still out. The weather was rotten and getting worse.

He looked up and saw Monk Bradley walking toward him. "Robb! Am I glad to find you! I was afraid you might have gone to Cambridge."

"What's up?"

"Hoyt and Boo are in the stockade."

Robb's face fell. "Another fight?"

"A dilly. Hoyt hit a mechanic over the head with a lead pipe last night, and Boo worked over another man who stepped in to help the first one. The guy who got it with the pipe is in the hospital."

"God damn those crazy bastards!" Robb stared across the room. After a time he looked up at Bradley. "How bad off is the guy? Is there any chance he might die?"

"He has a concussion and they had to sew up his scalp. Rizzo says he'll be all right in a few days, but the Provost Marshal is convinced Hoyt tried to kill the guy. What do you intend to do?"

"With those two on the crew we've got a great crew. Without them, and with Broz and Marconi laid up . . . well, we're . . ." Robb heard the drone of the bomber formation as it approached the air base. Good. They're back. The crescendo increased and then faded slightly before settling down to a constant level. It sounded as if they were at least 20,000 feet up. They'd be peeling off into the overcast now. A very long instrument letdown in a crowd. He hoped to God they'd all make it down.

Bradley said, "I'd hate like hell to find out we're alerted for tomorrow with those two locked up. I don't even want to think about it."

Robb stood up. "I'd better get over to the stockade."

"Okay, let's go."

"I'd rather handle this by myself. Do me a favor. Stosh and I were going into the village, to the hotel to take a bath. Wait for him and tell him what happened."

"I'll do better than that. I'll go with him to the hotel and I'll take your bath for you."

The MP inside the front door of the stockade jumped to his feet as Robb entered. He snapped to attention, shouting, "Attenhut!" His colleague at the far end of the aisle joined him in the ritual.

"As you were, soldier. I'm here to talk to Sergeants Hoyt and Bohall."

"Yes, *sir!*"

The MP led him down the aisle.

The interior of the stockade—two Nissen huts stuck together end to end—was partitioned into rows of cells on either side of a center aisle that ran the length of the building. The cells were made from oak planks bolted to heavy vertical beams. The one inch space between the horizontal planks gave the interior of the building the appearance of an elongated corn crib.

The MP stopped opposite a cell half way down the aisle, on the left.

"Open the door, private."

"It's against regulations, sir. You'll have to talk to him through the hole in the door, sir." The soldier opened a tiny aperture in the door and stood to one side.

Robb looked at the MP. "I intend to talk to him alone."

The MP hesitated. Robb stared at him. The MP marched off to his place at the front door. Robb looked into the hole in the door, squarely into the eyes of Sergeant Clovis Hoyt.

"Evenin' Cap'n Robb. Me 'n' Boo's been 'spectin' you." His tone was soft, liquid, yet matter of fact.

Robb couldn't see Hoyt's mouth, but Hoyt's eyes were smiling and he knew he had to be grinning his self-deprecating, shit-eating grin. "Where's Sergeant Bohall?"

"Ole Boo's down at the back end of this here jayul, Cap'n."

"All right, Sergeant. First of all, are you all right? Are you injured in any way?"

"Why hayell no, Cap'n. Ah ain't the one what's hurt. It's that no good sombitch mechanic what's hurt. They tell me he's hurt purty good."

Robb's eyes held Hoyt's. The gunner finally looked away. "Tell me exactly what happened."

"Wayell, Cap'n, me and Boo we drink a lotta beer and we was goin' fix us up a couple a pissin' hoses so we could take a leak without gettin' outa the sack at night. You know, run a hose from our bunk outside through a lil hole we was goin' knock in the side of the barracks. So we went down to the engine repair hangar last night to see if we could find us some hose and a coupla funnels, when this here mechanic. . ."

"How did the fight start?"

"I was jus' comin' to that. It wern't really no fight, not to start with."

"Why did you hit the mechanic on the head with a piece of pipe?"

"I was coming to that, Cap'n. Me and Boo was jus' kinda walking around this here hangar. Wayell, this PFC come over and he asks us what we was doing and we told him we was looking for some hose for a pissin' hose. So he said he'd help us find some. And then he did, just about the right size and . . . "

"Why did you get mad at him?"

"Well, Cap'n, I was comin' to that. After he found us the hose, we was walkin' round that hangar lookin' for some funnels, and this PFC flunky he asks us what plane we was gunners on. I told him Brillig. And he says, real sassy, 'Brillig!' Like it was shit in his mouth. Then he says—this is where he made his mistake—he says, 'That's the shittiest name for a airplane I ever heard of.'"

"And that's when you hit him with the pipe?"

"No, Cap'n, not right then. I was real reasonable. I wanted to give 'im a chance 'cause I figured he was jus' plain stupid. So I tol' him about how Brillig was the god of victory in war a long time ago, so he'd un-nerstan' how come our plane is Brillig."

"Go on."

"Well, Cap'n, after I 'splained it real keerful, y'know what that asshole says?"

"What?"

"He says, 'That's still a shitty name for a airplane.' That's exactly what he said, and that's when I coldcocked him with that piece of pipe."

Robb stared through the hole in the door. "You can't go around damn near killing people, regardless of what they say!"

Hoyt looked away for a moment. He turned back, a puzzled look on his face. "Cap'n Robb, I don' think you heard me when I tol' you what he said 'bout Brillig."

Robb turned and walked the full length of the aisle before he turned around and started back for Hoyt's cell. It occurred to him that Hoyt or Boo would kill Monk Bradley, his co-pilot, if they found out Bradley had made up that cock and bull story about Brillig as the Greek god of victory to get them to cast their votes for the name "Brillig." The vote was tilting in favor of "Piccadilly Commando"—after the Piccadilly prostitutes—until Bradley made up the Brillig story. Bradley's story swung the vote to the nonsense name from Lewis Carroll's "Through the Looking Glass".

He stopped and turned to the little square hole and Hoyt's eyes. Robb said, "He shouldn't have said that, Sergeant. He made a big mistake, all right."

"That's right, Cap'n. He made a big mistake. And so I jus' did what I had to do." Hoyt peered at him through the little hole.

Robb paced back and forth in front of the door, rubbing the day's stubble on his chin. He returned to Hoyt's eyes. "All right, Sergeant. You did what you had to do. But from now on if anybody insults our plane or anything else you come and tell me about it and I'll take care of it. Do you understand?"

"I understand what you're saying, Cap'n, but I ain't sure I could wait that long."

"If you had killed him they'd have taken you to Litchfield and put you in front of a firing squad. Now Sergeant, you listen to me and you listen very carefully. When and if I get you out of here, the first thing we're going to do is have a long talk about how to deal with matters like this. You don't have to let the guy get away with it, but you don't have to damn near kill him. Do you understand that, Sergeant?"

Hoyt didn't respond, but Robb didn't expect him to. He turned and walked down the aisle toward the MP at the rear of the building. The MP showed him to Boo's cell. Robb made no attempt to hide his anger. He repeated the lecture he had given Hoyt. He was about to leave when he heard a stage whisper from the next cell. "Captain Robertson!"

Robb moved toward the voice.

"Captain Robertson?"

"Yes?"

The man spoke softly through a crack in the wall. "I'm Lieutenant Quist. You don't know me but I'm in Dagger Squadron, on Lieutenant Carter's crew. I'm his bombardier. I mean I was his bombardier."

"What are you doing in here?" Robb spoke softly, his mouth two or three inches from a crack between the boards.

"I got sick and couldn't fly missions any more."

He'd seen this kind of situation many times. "In what way are you sick?" He knew he shouldn't have asked.

The voice replied softly. "I get panicky when I get into my compartment on the plane. I can't breathe. My heart beats real fast and I get so dizzy I don't know where I am."

Damn! Robb cursed himself for stopping to listen to this guy. What are they going to do with him? Send him to jail? But some men who refuse to fly get grounded on medical grounds and are simply sent back home. But why is this guy in the stockade?

"How exactly did you refuse to fly?"

"One morning before a mission when I was getting ready to get into the plane I just kind of broke down. My legs kind of gave out under me and I sat down on the hardstand by the waist door and started crying and I couldn't stop. Then Lieutenant Carter called the tower and asked them to send an ambulance to the plane. They took me to the base hospital."

"When was this? I mean when you got sick?"

"Five weeks ago."

"How old are you?"

"Twenty."

"What's happened since?"

"They sent me up to Scotland for rest and recuperation for three weeks. When I got back they sent me to psychiatrists at Division. They reported to our flight surgeon that I was all right. He certified me for flying again and sent me back here. I was back on my crew again."

"Then what happened?"

"About two weeks ago at briefing, when they announced the Merseburg mission, I panicked right there in the briefing room. I was sort of paralyzed. When briefing was over I just couldn't get up and go to the equipment room. My navigator—who's my best friend—stayed with me, trying to get me to go to get my equipment. But I just couldn't go. So he finally left without me and went on the mission. But I stayed in the briefing room. I . . . I was crying. I cried like a baby. Christ! You have no idea how humiliating it was."

"What happened then?"

"Two MPs arrested me and hauled me here."

"Just like that? I don't get it."

"Uh . . . uh, there's something else . . ."

"What?"

"Well, I was kind of out of my head all through briefing. I was scared. I didn't really know what I was doing. They tell me I tried to talk my friend, Burt Livingston—our navigator—into not going on the mission. I told him he was crazy going to Merseburg. Some other guys heard me and reported it to the brass."

Robb closed his eyes. "Damn!" He knew this was a far more serious matter than refusing to fly. Encouraging someone else not to go smells like mutiny. The army will come down hard on that. "That's awfully serious, Lieutenant."

"But I was out of my mind. I didn't know what I was doing. I just didn't want Burt to get killed. I wanted him to stay with me. Believe me, Captain, I was out of my head, blubbering like a little kid. I'd never have done that in my right mind."

Robb pressed his fingers against his forehead again, his head bowed, his eyes closed. "What is it you want me to do?"

"I don't know. I guess I was hoping you might be able to talk to someone. You're one of the leading pilots in the Group. I've seen you with the C.O. and the other brass in the club. I thought maybe they'd listen to you."

"I've got to . . ." He stopped short, his voice drowned out by the roar of a plane that seemed as though it was coming through the roof of the building. How did that guy go right over our heads? This building is at least a half mile from the main runway. It could be someone in trouble. The whole Group should be on the ground by now. He shook his head quickly, bringing himself back to the stockade, to the plight of this kid. "I've got to go now. I can't see now how I can do you any good, but I'll think about it. Don't get your hopes up. I'm sorry." He started to leave, but he stopped short. "I meant to ask you. How many missions do you have to your credit?"

"Twenty-eight."

My God, only seven away from the magic number. He'd damned near made it! He simply wore out too soon. And only twenty years old. Damn!

Robb looked up as he left the stockade. The lights around the high stockade fence were shielded, but he could see the ceiling was even lower than a half hour earlier—less than 100 feet, possibly 50, and the mist-drizzle-fog had reduced horizontal visibility to a hundred yards at best. He brushed his shoulder with his hand: his trench coat was already soaked. He raised his coat collar and pulled his garrison cap lower over his eyes as he walked toward Operations.

He heard the drone of a lone B-17, probably the last one to return from the mission. The poor bastard didn't get in before the ceiling dropped to where it was now, maybe as low as fifty feet. How many attempts had he already made? He's got to be damned near out of gas by now.

Judging by its altitude and position in relation to the base, the plane had to be on the base leg of the landing pattern. The pitch of the engines lowered suddenly. He's on his final approach now. Robb stopped and waited for the guy to cut his power. The engine-sound ceased abruptly. Good! He made it! There was a sudden full-bodied engine roar. Damn! He missed it! He's going around again.

He walked along rapidly. He kept his eyes on the asphalt immediately in front of him, but his ears were tuned to the engine sounds of the B-17. The sound increased gradually and then faded behind him as the plane passed him on its downwind leg. The pitch of the engines lowered again as the pilot began his letdown on his final approach. He stopped again to listen. The engines slowed further, to less than half power. Good. He must be close to the runway now. The pitch of the engines increased slightly. He must figure he's coming in short. In his mind he was in the plane's cockpit, adding a little power. The guy is coming in on the beam, but the beam is so damned crude he could break out two or three hundred feet off to either side of the runway and not even see the runway lights.

The sound grew louder. He's approaching the runway now. He's got to chop the power right about now! Now! The engines died suddenly. Good! He must see the runway. Thank God! He had no more uttered his two-word prayer when the engines burst into life again with a deafening roar. Damn it to hell! He missed it! He missed it again! He's going around again. Damn!

He reflected on what he would do if he were in that fix right now. He'd climb southeast, toward the coast, and when he got up to 5000 feet—or as high as he could before the first engine quit—he'd put it on automatic pilot, nose slightly down, pointed toward the sea. And he'd order everybody to bail out and then he'd bail out himself. Somebody in that tower should order that guy to do the same thing! Maybe the Officer of the Day in the tower is having a hard time making up his mind. By God, I'll help him make up his mind!

He started to run for the tower. He heard the drone of the plane getting louder. Now the sound was opposite him, the half-way point on his downwind leg. The tower was still about a half mile away. He heard the pitch of the plane's engines decrease slightly. About three-quarters of cruising power; he's on his crosswind leg and starting to let down again.

He heard an abrupt decline in the pitch of the engine's drone. He's at half-cruise power now, on his final approach. The tower was still about 500 yards away. That plane will be at the runway in less than a minute. He yelled out loud. "Damn! I'll never make it!" He stopped abruptly. He stood in the middle of the road blowing clouds of steam into the drizzle and mist. He turned toward the head of the runway, his chest rising and falling heavily. It won't be long now. God help this guy! The engine sounds grew louder. "Now," he screamed. "Now! You've got to cut the goddamned power now!"

The sound of the engines ceased abruptly. Good, he made it. He made it! He yelled like a madman, "He made it!" But then, the sudden, full-throated roar of four Wright Cyclone engines cut through the mist and hit him like an avalanche. Before he could think of what was happening, he sensed the roar was coming directly at him. He ducked instinctively. The silver underside of the huge plane flashed over him, missing him by no more than ten or twenty feet. The prop blast knocked him over backwards. His ass hit the asphalt first, taking most of the blow. He raised himself to one knee, his hand grasping his forehead. He scarcely breathed as he waited for the sound he knew would come. He prayed a short, inept plea. Then it came. The ground shook. The explosion sounded like a thousand pound bomb going off. Echoes of the blast faded in diminishing waves across the black English countryside. Silence enveloped the air base, a silence more complete than any he had heard in his two years in England. Not a sound from the repair shops, from the engine test-stands, from a jeep or truck. Nothing. He knew then that everybody on the base had stopped doing whatever they do. They had stopped to sweat this guy out. Now it was over and there was nothing left but this silence. It was as though everyone on the base was standing silently, acknowledging that ten men who were alive seconds ago were now dead.

The silence was suddenly shattered by the screams of sirens as fire trucks and ambulances sped to their hopeless task. Robb numbly heard their wails, now diminishing in the distance. The plane must have hit the ground on the far edge of the field, maybe even beyond the perimeter track. He was vaguely surprised that it got that far before hitting the ground, or a tree, or whatever it was it hit.

He resumed walking, no longer with any destination, past Operations and the tower. He wanted no part of that scene. He walked for a half hour on the asphalt road that ran parallel to the flight line, behind the repair hangars and the aircraft maintenance huts along the flight line. Enveloped in the steady drizzle, he walked on into the blackness. The last B-17 in the line was now a mile behind him. He walked until the road ended at the barbed wire-topped chain-link fence that marked the edge of the airfield. He turned to retrace his steps.

"Halt where you are! Raise your hands and identify yourself!"

The guard's flashlight beam blinded him momentarily. Then he saw the rifle barrel pointed at him.

Robb spoke firmly, "Captain Robertson. Amber Squadron."

"Sir! May I see your identification!"

"Get that goddamned light out of my eyes and I'll find my ID card!"

The military policeman directed the beam downward. Robb took his billfold from his inside coat pocket and held it open in front of him.

"Sir! May I ask what you are doing here at this time of night!" Strange. He'd heard this guy's voice before. Where? Ah, yes. The voice of the MPs in the stockade. Of course, they all sound alike after a while. Good God! That was this evening, less than an hour ago!

"Sir?"

"What was that you said?"

"Sir. I asked you what you are doing here this time of the night."

"Ah yes." The MP fidgeted as the strange captain stared into the night. At last Robb said softly, "Walking, soldier. Just walking."

They stood in silence. Finally the MP spoke, his voice now modulated, conversational. "I understand, sir. That was a bad one. Do you know which plane it was, sir?"

Robb answered softly, absently, "No." He stood silently for a time, then he repeated, "No." He turned to leave.

The MP said, "Goodnight, *sir!*" He snapped to attention with a click of his heels, and with a lightning quick motion, brought his rifle to "present arms." It all seemed like a crazy dream, he and this MP standing in the rain and blackness way the hell and gone in the night performing this nutty ritual. Perhaps he had dreamt about the B-17 and the explosion that shook the earth. Robb touched the visor of his cap, nodding absently like an old man. He turned and began his long walk back.

Robb sat in a chair in the officers' club. but he had no recollection of how he got there. He was still wearing his sopping trench coat. Drops of water fell from the visor of his garrison cap onto his chest as he slouched in the chair. The room was very quiet even though most of the chairs and sofas were occupied and men stood shoulder to shoulder at the bar. Robb played the record in his mind yet another time: what other options did that pilot have tonight?

Sam, Kovacs, and Bradley entered the room. They headed for Robb.

"Tough one," Kovacs said.

Robb said, "Why didn't Operations tell the guy to climb to 5000 feet and bail everybody out?"

Sam said, "Colonel Strang got on the horn and ordered him—his name was MacDonald—to climb to 5000, put it on auto headed for the North Sea, and bail everyone out. But his receiver wasn't working."

"Oh no!"

"But he could transmit. He kept asking for instructions."

"Of all the lousy damned . . ."

Sam said, "Maybe that's why this one hit the whole Group so much harder than other crashes like this."

Bradley said, "And it went on so long everybody on the base became a witness to it."

Kovacs said, "By the time he was making that last attempt, we were all in the cockpit with him and we knew he was going to crash. And we were with him when he crashed." Kovacs stared vacantly."It's always a hell of a lot worse when it's a green crew."

Robb looked up quickly at Kovacs. "What mission was this for them?"

"Didn't you know?"

"Know what?"

Kovacs said, "It was their first."

Robb pressed the fingertips of each hand against his forehead, his head bent downward. Nobody had anything more to say.

8

As Robb trudged toward the squadron orderly room on Sunday morning, he acknowledged to himself that this was a "morning after" that ranked with some of the more memorable and horrible mornings after he'd known since he first joined the Eighth. It was the morning after he called on Hoyt and Boo in the stockade, the morning after Quist, the bombardier, poured out his tragic story to him, the morning after Mac-Donald, the rookie pilot, flew into the ground, the morning after he tried to escape these realities by numbing his brain with alcohol. He never was much of a drinker and he knew it, but Stosh, a real drinker, did the pouring. He had a headache, his mouth felt dry and fuzzy, and he was very tired.

A rush of warm air greeted him as he opened the door to the orderly room. He closed the door quickly behind him to conserve the precious heat from the small coal-burning stove that glowed in the middle of the large room. First Sergeant Kermit Kerrigan sat tall behind his desk, guarding the entrance to the office of Major William F. Sandell, Amber Squadron's Commanding Officer. Sergeant Kerrigan remained seated, yet he seemed to come to attention as Robb approached.

"Has Captain Kovacs been in this morning?"

Kovacs' voice boomed out from the Squadron Commander's office. "In here, Robb!"

With an almost imperceptible sideways nod of his head, Kerrigan indicated, "You may go in now". As he stepped around the First Sergeant's desk, Robb marveled at Kerrigan's ability to assume and communicate power.

Major Sandell, bull-necked and ham-fisted, continued signing documents as Robb entered. Kovacs said, "Hi, pal."

Robb lowered himself gently into a chair.

Kovacs said, "You don't look so good."

Major Sandell buzzed Sergeant Kerrigan. "Sergeant, would you please have the orderly bring in the coffee pot and some cups."

Sergeant Kerrigan must have been expecting the order and obviously didn't intend to have the orderly carry it out. Kerrigan himself appeared almost immediately at the door, tall and lean in his crisply pressed uniform. He placed the tray on the corner of the desk and departed. The major signed the last paper in the stack and looked up at Robb. "Now, what can I do for you?"

"Sandy, I want my gunners out of the stockade. I need your help with the C.O."

The Squadron Commander made a neat stack of the papers before him. He shook his head. "You and Stosh have as much influence with Colonel Strang as I do. He'd do anything for you he'd do for me."

"I was hoping you'd help me make my case, you know, emphasize to the colonel that these guys are the best gunners in the squadron. It would mean more coming from you."

"The Colonel knows how good Hoyt and Bohall are. There's really nothing I could say to him that would help. By the way, has the victim filed charges against Hoyt?"

"Sam Prentice told me that the guy asked to have a legal officer come to the hospital to see him. He'll file all right."

"That puts it into the hands of the Eighth Air Force Judge Advocate's office. If he doesn't file, then either Colonel Strang or Colonel Crick can handle it administratively."

Kovacs said, "If Colonel Prick had his way he'll have these guys shot!"

Sandell glared at Kovacs. He got up and closed the door, glancing out through the crack just as the door closed. If Sergeant Kerrigan saw his commander close the door, he gave no sign. He was writing something on a page of a small loose-leaf notebook.

Sandell sat down and leaned toward Kovacs. He whispered intently. "Don't ever use that name for Colonel Crick where Kerrigan can hear you! Don't you know that he's Crick's pipeline from this squadron? I can't go to the latrine without him reporting it to Crick!"

"Look, Sandy, you worry too much. I know all about Kerrigan and Crick and I couldn't care less. In fact, I hope he does tell Crick I called him Colonel Prick."

Sandell hissed, "But *I* care! I've got to run this squadron and I won't be able to if I make an enemy of Crick. So don't you ever run Crick down in my presence!"

Kovacs said, "Sorry, Sandy."

Sandell stood up. "I'm awfully sorry I can't help you, Robb. I'm afraid I'm going to have to assign two new gunners to your crew."

"Green ones, from the replacement pool?"

"Yes."

"Damn! There goes my crew!"

"I know how it is but there's nothing I can do about it." The major moved to the door. "I'm going to the mess hall. Can I give you men a lift?"

Kovacs said, "We could use a ride to Headquarters." Kovacs held out his hand to Sandell. "No hard feelings, about what I said about Crick. Okay, Sandy?"

Sandell smiled and shook hands with Kovacs. "You know me better than that."

Kerrigan closed the notebook and put it on his lap when the Squadron Commander's door opened. As the three officers passed Kerrigan's desk, Kovacs said, "Thanks for the coffee, Sergeant."

Kerrigan stiffened. "You're welcome, sir." As the outer door closed, Kerrigan put the notebook far back into a desk drawer and locked the drawer.

Major Sandell pulled the jeep to a stop in front of Group Headquarters. As Robb and Kovacs climbed out of the jeep, Sandell said, "Oh, I meant to ask you, Robb, what did that mechanic do that made Hoyt so mad he wanted to kill the guy?"

Before Robb could answer, Kovacs replied, "He said Amber Squadron was the shittiest squadron in the whole Eighth Air Force."

Sandell's mouth dropped open. Robb turned and started up the gravel path.

Sandell said, "Did the guy really say that?"

"Yep. That's what he said, and that's why Hoyt coldcocked him with that piece of pipe." Kovacs turned and started up the path to Group Headquarters.

Headquarters of the 990th Heavy Bombardment Group consisted of several oversized Nissen Huts connected by hallways constructed of concrete blocks. Robb and Kovacs entered the largest of these huts and walked around the desks of the clerk-typists and up to the desk of Corporal Susan James, secretary and receptionist to Colonel John Strang, Commanding Officer of the 990th Heavy Bombardment Group, and his Executive Officer, Lieutenant Colonel Horatio Crick. Kovacs said, "Is the boss in, Suzie?"

"Yes, sir, but Colonel Crick is with him now. I don't think he'll be long."

"We'll wait in Lieutenant Vandivier's office. Give a yell when Colonel What's-his-name gets out."

Corporal James covered her mouth with her hand to stifle a laugh. "Yes, sir."

Robb followed Kovacs between the clerk-typists' desks to the cubicle in the far corner of the large room. A sign on the wall, to the right of the open door, said, "Lieutenant Evelyn A. Vandivier, Administrative Assistant".

Kovacs leaned into the doorway. "Let's you and me go dancing tonight, beautiful."

Lieutenant Vandivier, a strikingly attractive young woman, smiled warmly at him. "Come in, Stosh. Take any chair you like." There was a single empty chair across from her desk. Robb appeared a moment later with a chair from the outer office.

Kovacs turned to Robb. "I was just telling Evelyn that you and I would like to take her out dancing tonight."

Robb grinned. "That's right."

"I'm honored, even though I know you're here to see the C.O."

Kovacs said, "And what makes you think that?"

"I heard you ask Susan if the boss is in." She leaned toward Kovacs and whispered, "And I heard you ask her to call you when Colonel What's-his-name leaves the Commander's office."

Robb was surprised. "You heard that all the way over here?"

"The walls in here are made of cardboard. I hear everything, and so does everyone else." She turned to Kovacs and said softly, "I'm afraid Colonel Crick heard you too."

"I don't care if he did."

"Please, Stosh," she whispered, "keep it down! You're talking about one of my bosses, who has power of life and death over me."

"We'll watch out for you," Kovacs said. "Just let us know if he gives you a hard time."

"He won't if you don't visit me here any more, and if what you said here today doesn't get to him. You had better check to see if he's left the C.O.'s office."

Robb leaned back and looked out. Corporal James motioned for him to come. He stood up. "Come on, Stosh. The coast is clear."

Colonel Strang was on the phone when they entered his office. He motioned for them to sit down. He spoke into the phone. "There's no point in seeing me about the matter, Paul. I delegate all personnel matters to Colonel Crick, as I've done since the Group was formed. I'm not about to change the arrangement now."

He listened for a moment.

"Yes, I'm quite familiar with Lieutenant Quist's case. You'll have to talk to Colonel Crick about him. I'm sorry. Goodbye." He hung up. "What can I do for you men?"

Robb said, "Forgive me for eavesdropping, John, but I couldn't help but hear you talking to Father Miller about the Lieutenant Quist thing. It's a very special case. It would be a tragedy to handle it routinely."

"What do you know about Quist?"

"He stopped me last night in the stockade, when I went to see my gunners."

"I see. Well, let's not get into that. Colonel Crick handles all refusals to fly—as he has since the Group got here."

"Quist didn't refuse to fly."

"What do you mean?"

"He wanted to go on that mission, even though it was to Merseburg. He wasn't cowardly. He folded emotionally in spite of himself, in spite of wanting to go."

"Every man who refuses to fly could say that."

Robb said, "It's stupid to punish some guy who really folds. It's not his fault."

The Colonel bristled. "Now listen to me, damn it! I feel like hell about Lieutenant Quist, but the psychiatrists and flight surgeons certified him to fly. If you want to pursue this further you'll have to talk to Colonel Crick. Now, what was it you came here for?"

Robb sighed. "So that's it then as regards Lieutenant Quist?"

"Yes. The matter is closed. Why did you come here this morning?"

"Two of my gunners, two of the best gunners in the Group, are in the stockade. I've got two other gunners in the hospital. I need Hoyt and Bohall back on my crew.

"I know about Hoyt and Bohall. They damned near killed one of our mechanics. As I understand it, the victim is filing charges. That takes it out of my hands and puts it under the jurisdiction of the Judge Advocate's Office. Was there anything else you wanted to talk about?"

Kovacs said, "You sure as hell got a short fuse this morning, Colonel."

"Look, Stosh, I feel like hell about Quist, and I'm concerned about your gunners, Robb. I know what this is going to do to your crew. It just happens that both of these matters are clearly defined under military law, and I'm not about to obstruct justice." He looked at his watch. "I have a meeting at Wing in exactly forty-five minutes." He stood up and walked to the door and opened it.

Robb paused in the doorway and said to Strang, "I'm worried about Quist."

Strang said, "Hell, Robb. So am I. I'm very worried about him."

The three officers walked out of Headquarters together. The C.O.'s driver held open the back door of the staff car. Kovacs said, "Before you go, don't you want to know what made Sergeant Hoyt so mad that he hit that mechanic over the head with a piece of pipe?"

Robb started for the mess hall. Strang looked up. "Yes, now that you brought it up. Why did he get so mad?"

"That mechanic said the 990th was the shittiest Bombardment Group in the whole Eighth Air Force."

The Colonel pulled in his chin. "Did he really say that?"

"Hoyt said when the guy said that he did what he had to do."

"I'll be damned!"

"See you, Chief." Kovacs turned and hurried after Robb.

It was mid-morning. The powdered eggs, now scrambled, were more rubbery than usual. Kovacs had the powdered egg man pile his plate high nonetheless. When they were seated, Kovacs held up a piece of toast that was, like every other piece in his stack, black around the edges and perfectly white in the middle. "You gotta admit this takes talent and training. They send those guys to cooks' school to learn to do this. There's no way you or I could do this no matter how hard we tried. Right? "Right."

"Take these eggs. There's no way you or I could get them to bounce like this." He held up a forkful of eggs and let them drop to his plate. "See that action? Could you cook powdered eggs that could do that?"

"No, Stosh." He watched Kovacs shovel in the powdered eggs. He made himself a Spam sandwich.

"They haven't learned to fuck up the Spam yet, but give 'em time. Right?"

"Right."

As they got up from the table, Kovacs said, "I gotta go over to the tower. Some asshole over there put me down for Officer of the Day for next Saturday. I gotta let him correct his mistake."

Robb said, "I think I'll go and see Colonel Crick. I'm worried about Lieutenant Quist."

"You're wasting your time talking to Crick."

"I've got a theory that deep down inside every person, no matter how rotten he looks on the outside, there lurks a human being."

Kovacs said, "And I've got a theory that beneath that prick-shell of Colonel Prick's there lurks a prick."

They parted in front of the mess hall. Robb headed for Group Headquarters and Kovacs started for the tower, but once Robb was out of sight he altered his course and picked up a heading for the base hospital.

Corporal James buzzed the Executive Officer and announced Captain Robertson.

"Send him in." Crick's tone was gruff.

"Make it fast, Robertson. I'm busy."

"I talked to Lieutenant Quist in the stockade last night."

"And what, may I ask, were you doing in the stockade last night?"

"Two of my gunners are there."

"Ah yes, your two wild men. They're in big trouble this time. The guy's filing charges and that means it goes to the Judge Advocate. Your man who tried to kill one of our mechanics is going to do a stretch in Litchfield. Serves him right. But you didn't come here to see me about that, did you?"

"I came about Lieutenant Quist."

"What about him?"

"He's not a coward."

"And how, may I ask, did you arrive at that diagnosis?"

"He wanted to go on the mission. He simply collapsed."

"He's collapsed more than once. He collapses conveniently. I suppose you could call it a severe case of Merseburgitis."

"He couldn't help it. Some people are made differently than others. I'm convinced Lieutenant Quist shouldn't have been a combat flier in the first place. He's too sensitive a person, and now as a result of combat he's emotionally ill."

"Are you a psychiatrist or a psychologist?"

Robb was tempted for a brief moment to admit to Crick he had in fact attended graduate school in psychology, but he thought better of it. "No, sir."

Colonel Crick leaned back in his chair and twirled a pencil between his fingers. He was sitting down while Robb stood before his desk, yet he seemed to be looking down at Robb. "The Army Air Forces' psychiatrists and flight surgeons say he's not sick. And that leaves us with but one conclusion, which is that the guy is yellow. Just plain yellow. Now, if you'll excuse me, I've got work to do."

"Sir, could you go over to the stockade and talk to him and make your decision about him on basis of actually talking to him?"

"Look, Robertson. You may have time to run around playing social worker. I don't." Crick got up and walked to the door. His flat, steel-gray eyes stared into Robb's as he held the door open. Neither man spoke as Robb passed through the doorway. Colonel Crick closed the door firmly.

9

The temperature was well above the freezing mark when Kovacs walked up the gravel path to the front door of the base hospital on the afternoon of Wednesday, November 1, but the wind out of the northwest bit sharply into his cheeks. Clearly, winter was on the way.

The base hospital was a sprawling, flat-roofed, one-story wooden building sided with dull-gray asbestos shingles, an undersized replica of the military hospitals that could be seen on any Army Air Forces base in the States. Captain Stanley Kovacs entered the double entrance doors and walked quickly across the large vestibule and through the doors to the main hall that led to the wards on either side of the main entrance. A nurses' station stood in the hall opposite the hospital's main entrance, guarding the passages to the wards. Second Lieutenant Meredith Cameron, U.S. Army Medical Corps, sat behind the counter of the station. Kovacs couldn't see her because the counter was about four feet high.

He stopped at the nurses' station, rested his arms on the counter, and looked down upon Lieutenant Cameron. He was pleasantly surprised, but it didn't show. Beautiful! Bright eyes with dancing light. Pug nose but not too much pug—just enough to give her an upbeat flair. Brown hair done in a short hairdo and a complexion on the near side of healthy-ruddy with a few freckles on each cheek. And all of it wrapped neatly into that crisp, white, nurse's dress. What a package! Whooh! He smiled broadly. "Hello down there."

"May I help you, Captain?"

"I'd like to see one of my mechanics who's in here with a head injury. Got it in a fight. I'd like to see him, please."

"His name please, sir?"

He was shocked at his stupidity. Man, you really fucked up this time! You said the guy was one of your mechanics and you don't know his name! Then, suddenly, a glimmer of light appeared. He smiled. "How many PFCs you got in here who were hit on the head with a piece of pipe?"

"Oh, you mean Private First Class Stills."

"That's right, PFC Stills." He exhaled audibly. "That guy's going to get himself killed one of these days. Always fighting." He was talking too fast. Slow down, damn it! "How's he doing, Lieutenant. . . uh . . . I didn't catch your name."

"Lieutenant Cameron. Private Stills is making a good recovery. He has a severe concussion and a laceration that required quite a number of stitches. We'll have to keep him here for at least a week for observation. The concussion could be serious."

She placed a loose-leaf notebook in front of Kovacs. "Would you sign in, please."

Kovacs scribbled his name, making sure it was completely illegible. Lieutenant Cameron led him down the hallway marked "Enlisted Mens Wards".

"Nice hospital you got here, honey."

She stopped and turned toward him. "I want to make something very clear. *No one,* Captain, *no one,* regardless of rank, calls me 'honey'."

"Sorry."

She smiled. "I'm sure you meant no harm." She turned to open the fire door that blocked the hallway.

Kovacs said quickly, "Hold it a minute, please. Before we get into that ward I need to ask you something. How about you and me going dancing in London Saturday night? That's if I'm not flying this weekend. The Grosvenor House has a good orchestra."

"You don't waste time, do you?"

"You have to skip the preliminaries when you're fighting a war, if you know what I mean."

"I know exactly what you mean. No thanks."

"You got me all wrong. I'm an officer and a gentleman. They come in the same package, by an act of Congress, remember?"

"Still 'no thanks', Captain Kovacs. "

"How'd you know my name?"

"Let's say I saw it when you signed in."

"No way. Not the way I . . . "   She reached for the door handle again. "Wait a minute. Private Stills isn't going to die if we talk a cou- ple of minutes. How did you know my name?"

"You're famous."

He smiled, "Let's have it. How did you know who I was?"

"All right then, let's say you're not famous, but you have a reputation."

"Good or bad?"

"No comment." She laughed. The effect was flirtatious.

"I'll admit I've been misunderstood by some of the fairer sex around here."

"Like by one WAC Lieutenant who works in Group Headquarters?"

"Oh, you mean Evelyn Vandivier. Old Evelyn and I are good friends. You know, pals, like brothers and sisters."

"Not like brothers and sisters where I come from." She reached for the door handle.

"Wait a minute. My God, you're in a hurry."

"It seems to me you're the one in a hurry, Captain."

"Evelyn's my pal. She wouldn't say anything bad about me."

"You don't take your sister out anymore, do you?"

"I've been flying a lot. Otherwise, I'd be seeing more of her. Ask her."

"I will. She's my roommate."

"Well, how about that! Small world."

"Small air base." She laughed again.

"My God, I love to hear you laugh. I'd like to go out with you just to hear you laugh. How about it? Seeing how we're comrades in arms on the same small air base."

"I don't know. I'll have to call up your sister to see how she feels about it."

"You don't have to do that. I haven't been taking her out, remember?"

"But only because you've been too busy flying, remember?" She tried to suppress a smile. "I just want to see if she'd mind, and if not, does she have any warnings for me."

"Warnings? What am I? Some kind of a gorilla?"

"That's what I want to find out, before I say yes or no."

"So when does the gorilla find out the verdict?"

She opened the door. "Today, if I can get in touch with her before you leave here. Otherwise you may call me tomorrow during the day, here at the hospital."

"Just one more question. What's your first name?"

"Meredith. My friends call me Merrie, but you may call me Lieuten-ant."

She turned into the first door on the right. There were eight beds in the room, four on either side of an aisle. "Just my luck," Kovacs said to himself. "Eight fucking beds and all of 'em full."

Lieutenant Cameron stepped to the side of the nearest bed. She grasped the young patient's wrist with one hand and deftly stuck a ther-mometer into his mouth with the other. "Go and visit your mechanic. You have ten minutes, Captain."

"Thanks." He surveyed the room. Shit! Three guys with bandages on their head! Okay, which one is the fucking mechanic? He walked up to the nearest head-bandage, carefully studying the man's fingernails as he approached. He tried to see the hands of the other two head-bandages on the other side of the aisle. Damn it! They all got clean hands! He looked back at Lieutenant Cameron. She looked down quickly. He addressed the man in the bed in front of him, "How are they treating you here, sol-dier?"

"Just fine, sir. Been here a week and I hope they keep me another week."

Kovacs smiled. One down, two to go. He turned to the nearest bandaged head across the aisle. "How're they treating you, soldier?"

"Cain't tell yet. I only got in here last night and been sleeping ever since. "

Kovacs' eyes lit up. He spoke loudly. "Well, Private Stills, you don't seem to be in too bad shape." His voice boomed as he pronounced his medical verdict.

The soldier sneered, "That's what you think, buddy. You ain't the one what's hurt."

Kovacs dropped into the chair beside the bed and leaned forward, his face within a foot of the soldier's. He spoke in a whisper, a hiss. "How long you been in this man's army, Private?" The soldier looked away. "Answer me!"

"Three years."

"Now you listen to me and you listen real careful." He pointed his forefinger an inch from the man's nose. "Don't you ever, as long as you live, call an officer 'buddy' or anything else familiar! Do you under-stand?"

The soldier's lower lip protruded. "Shit, man. If you had a headache like I got you wouldn't know which way was up, let alone how to talk to a officer."

"Look, soldier. One more insubordinate remark and you go to the stockade as soon as they kick you out of this hospital." His finger was still in the man's face. He looked to where Lieutenant Cameron had been. She was going out the door. Good! Now he can go to work on this fuck-off!

He fixed Stills with a stare. Stringy, blond sideburns hung down from under the bandages. He looked unwashed though Kovacs figured he must have had a bath since they brought him here. Stills' eyes darted furtively about the room. Kovacs nodded. If there ever was a guy who looks like he's in on the black market, this is your man.

Stills began to fidget. He reached for a pack of cigarettes on the bedside table. When he extended his arm, Kovacs saw on the inside crook of his arm what he had hoped he might see. "Closed case," he said to himself.

He began to play his cards. "Look, Private. I've been checking up on you. You got a lousy record. You know that, don't you?"

The private avoided Kovacs' eyes. "So nobody's perfect. What do you want with me?" His eyes fell to the silver pilot's wings on Kovacs' tunic. "You're a pilot, not no lawyer or no judge."

"I want you to drop charges against the guys who put you in here."

Stills sat up suddenly. "You gotta be crazy!"

"Watch it. You're getting over the line again."

He turned away from Kovacs. "I mean it's a nutty idea. Shit, I'd like to see both of them sombitches rot in jail for the rest a their lives."

"There's no way that's going to happen. The worst they'll get is a fine. And they'll be grounded for a month or two."

"Grounded! Sheeit! They'll like that. Some punishment!"

"They *won't* like it, but you wouldn't understand that."

Stills' face twisted in disbelief. "Those two nuts your gunners?"

"That's right. And I want them back, flying. Understand?"

"You want me to drop charges and they get off free like nothing happened. And here I'm stuck in this hospital with my head busted."

"You're not going to be stuck in here. They're letting you out tomorrow."

"What? I just got here! Shee-it!"

"You aren't hurt bad enough to stay longer, but I can talk to the nurse and insist that they keep you in here for a week. For observation. But you got to cooperate."

"Cooperate? Like how?"

"You got to tell that nurse you're one of my mechanics in case she asks, and you better get my name right. I'm Captain Kovacs. Just in case the nurse brings it up and I'm not here. It's spelled K-O-V-A-C-S. And don't you forget it."

"What else you want me to do?"

"You sign this sheet of paper which says you aren't going to file charges against the two guys who put you in here." Kovacs reached into his inside coat pocket and took out an envelope. He removed a typed statement and handed it to Stills. Stills recoiled. Kovacs grabbed his wrist and forced the paper into his hand. "Now read it!"

Stills' lips moved slowly as he silently formed each word. He finally looked up. "Ah ain't sure Ah'm gonna sign this piece a paper. They ain't enough in it for me."

"There's a lot more in it for you than you think. Some bad things that are going to happen to you won't happen."

"Like what?"

Kovacs leaned over and grasped the soldier's right arm and turned it palm up. There was a rash of needle marks on the inside crook of the soldier's elbow. He took the man's other arm and turned it over. More needle marks.

Stills folded his arms so that his hands covered the marks. "These marks is from them giving me shots here in the hospital since I came in last night."

Kovacs walked slowly to the foot of the bed, turned, and walked back to the chair, never taking his eyes off Stills' eyes. "The pilots are real mad about their wounded guys having to suffer bad pain all the way back to England because the morphine is missing from the kits. We're doing our own investigation. Anyone who gets caught gets a quick trip to the front line infantry in France. That's if he's lucky. If he ain't so lucky he ends up in the prison here at Litchfield. After your first week in Litchfield you'll wish you were dead." He stood up and walked slowly to the foot of the bed.

"If you don't sign that paper right now, I'm going to send the flight surgeon in here right away to take a look at that rash on the inside of your arms, and I'm going to have him give me a written report on it, and

I'm going to take that report to the Provost Marshal, *and* to Colonel Strang." Kovacs stood up, his eyes locked on Stills'. He put a foot on the chair and leaned forward. "You ever been in France, soldier?"

Stills looked one way and then the other, his small head perched on his long neck moving jerkily, like a chicken strutting in a barnyard. "Shit. You don't give a guy no room at all."

Kovacs sat down and crossed his legs, his eyes still drilling into Stills' eyes. "You got exactly one minute to make up your mind."

"All right, goddam it! Gimme a fucking pen."

"Now you're getting smart, but I don't want you to sign it yet. I'm going to get Lieutenant Cameron in here to witness your signature. Now, if she asks you why you're signing it, you tell her it's because the 990th needs good gunners. You fuck up on that and the whole deal's off, and it's the front lines in France for you. Or Litchfield."

"I ain't gonna fuck up."

"Good. I'm going to tell Lieutenant Cameron that you got a bad headache and you aren't seeing things right, and maybe they should keep you here for another week."

"I already told her I got a bad headache and I'm seeing double."

"That's what I figured, but she'll believe it if *I* tell her." He stood up. "You change your mind and you'll be in France so fast you won't know what happened."

Kovacs looked at his watch as he moved quickly down the hall to the nurses' station.

"Well done, Captain. Ten minutes exactly." Lieutenant Cameron continued writing on a sheet of paper attached to a clipboard.

"I need your help on a little matter, if you don't mind. I need you to witness Stills' signature on a document. He's decided to drop charges against the two gunners that put him in here."

"What made him decide to do that?"

"I explained to him how the gunners who beat him up told me to tell him how sorry they are they hurt him, and I told him those two gunners are the best gunners in the Group and how badly the Group needs those guys out of jail and flying again. You know, Lieutenant, old Stills may not look it, but he's really a patriotic guy when you get right down to it. He really wants to help the Group.

She studied Kovacs' face for a time. Finally she said, "You didn't threaten him in any way, did you? He is signing this document of his own free will?"

"Hell, yes. Excuse me, I mean heck yes. I forgot to tell you, he belongs to one of them holy roller churches and he takes it real serious. You know, about forgiveness."

"I'll be with you in a minute." She finished her writing and hung up the clipboard. "We'll have to make this quick." She got up and started down the hall.

"Just a minute please, Lieutenant. There's something else I got to tell you."

She stopped.

"Did Private Stills tell you he has a bad headache and blurred vision."

"He told me."

"Maybe you should keep him here another week if he's still got the vision problems and the headache after this week."

She faced him squarely. "Captain, let's come to an agreement. I won't tell you how to fly your airplane and you don't tell me how to diagnose and treat my patients. Agreed?"

Kovacs shrugged. "Sorry."

She put her hand on his arm. "I'm sorry. I'm afraid I was a bit blunt."

They moved into the ward. Stills' bed was cranked down flat. He had a hand on his forehead and wore a pained expression. Lieutenant Cameron placed her hand on his forehead. "Are you feeling any better?"

"No ma'am. Cain't say as I do. But I'm all right, 'cep for this headache and seein' sorta double when I look straight ahead."

"We may have to keep you here longer than we planned, to make sure you don't develop complications." The soldier's eyes opened to narrow slits. He looked directly at Kovacs. Kovacs nodded ever so slightly. "If you don't think it would make your headache worse, I'd like to raise your bed just a little so that you can sign the document Captain Kovacs told you about. All right?"

"All right, ma'am."

Lieutenant Cameron cranked the lever, raising his head. She leaned across his face, reaching around him as she fluffed up his pillows. Kovacs cursed to himself, "Goddammit! His nose is touching one of her boobs! I'd like to kill the slimy son-of-a-bitch!"

"May I have the document, please?"

Kovacs handed her the sheet of paper. She picked up a tray from the bedside table and turned it over and placed the paper on it in front of Stills. "You sign right here, above your name." She reached around behind him, supporting him as he signed the document. Stills peered at Kovacs through hooded slits. Kovacs stared back impassively, his lips a thin line under his black moustache.

She turned to Kovacs. "I see where I'm supposed to sign, Captain." She signed her name and handed the paper to Kovacs.

"Thank you, Lieutenant. Thank you, Private. We sure miss you down on the flight line. Be seeing you." He turned and started for the door. He paused in the doorway and looked back. Lieutenant Cameron was lowering the bed. Stills had his hand on his forehead, his eyes closed.

He waited for her at her desk. As she approached, he said, "Did you get hold of Evelyn on the phone?"

"Yes. I talked to her.

"Are we going dancing in London this weekend?"

"I can't give you an answer right now."

"What's the matter? I'm sure old Evelyn gave me a good report card."

"Quite frankly, I'm not comfortable with the idea of spending a weekend in London with *any* man, no matter how good his references. Evelyn thinks highly of you, and she told me I ought to go out with you. But I'm not ready to spend a weekend with you"

"I just asked you to go dancing with me in London."

"But that means leaving here Saturday afternoon and going out Saturday night, and staying in a hotel overnight because we can't very well get back to the base late Saturday night, or in the wee hours of Sunday morning."

"That's no problem. I reserve a room for you and another one for me."

She blushed. "Of course. I didn't mean I thought of anything else."
"Neither did I."

"But even so it would be a lot like us taking a trip together, and I'm not ready for that. After all, I really don't know you, do I?"

"I see what you mean." He stood silently, a puzzled look on his face. He brightened suddenly. "Hey, I got a great idea. What would you think of a double date? Say, you and me and Evelyn and a friend of mine? Robb and I could go in to London on Friday because we got business to attend to, and you and Evelyn could come in on Saturday after you get off work. That way it wouldn't be like you taking a trip with me."

"Robb who?"

"Robb Robertson, my best friend in the Group, actually my best friend in the whole world. Everybody likes Robb, especially the women. But Robb is kind of a quiet guy. He doesn't take the initiative with women."

"How do you know he'll take the initiative with Evelyn?"

"I'm going to supply the initiative."

"As you can well imagine, Evelyn gets asked out an awful lot, but she rarely accepts. She may not accept your friend."

"You're going to have to trust me on that. I've got a nose for this kind of thing. She'll say yes, flat out, right away. But don't tell her I said that."

"All right, then. If you can arrange for—uh—Mister Robertson . . ."

"He's a captain."

"If you can arrange for Captain Robertson to ask Evelyn and if she accepts, I'd like to go to London with Evelyn." She smiled brightly.

"Great! I'll talk to Robb, Robb will call Evelyn, and Evelyn will call you. I'll call you back this afternoon after everything is all set, just to nail everything down. What time do you get off on Saturday?"

"At noon."

"Good! The two of you can meet Robb and me in London at 2:00, Saturday afternoon."

"We get off at 12:00. There's no way we could make it to London by 2:00."

"Let's say 2:00 anyway. We'll enjoy waiting for you, regardless."

"I wouldn't be so sure about Evelyn accepting your friend's invitation."

"It's practically all set. I guarantee it." Kovacs held out his hand. A Saint Bernard extending a paw. "I'll be calling you this afternoon. Sure has been swell meeting you, Merrie. Maybe Stills got hit on the head with a piece of pipe just so we could meet."

She studied his face carefully. His expression was serious.

"Goodbye, Captain."

She watched as he pushed his way through the inner doors, her expression puzzled as her eyes followed the shy-sincere, devil-may-care-serious, happy-sad man whose hulk now filled the outer doorway.

Kovacs hurried to the officers' club He had agreed to meet Robb at around mid-morning. It was now 10:45.

There was a scattering of men in the club. A second lieutenant picked out a one-fingered rendition of "When the Lights Go On Again All Over the World" on the old piano. Kovacs spied Robb and Bradley in the corner to the left of the bar. He made for the corner in rapid strides. He handed the statement to Robb. "Take a look at this, pal."

Robb stared at the document. "I'll be damned! Here, Monk. Take a look at this."

Bradley read the statement. He looked up at Kovacs. "Is this on the level? Did the guy really sign this statement?"

"He sure as hell did. That statement is as legal as can be."

Bradley said, "Including the part that says he signed it of his own free will, with no coercion whatsoever?"

"Leave us not get technical."

Robb said, "However you got it, we're grateful to you. I can't tell you how much."

Bradley said, "That's right. Now tell us how you pulled it off."
Robb said, "Who wrote up this document?"

"I copied it out of a book on how to write things like that."

"You did a good job of it," Robb said. "Monk and I and all the guys on the crew are in your debt. Let us know if we can ever do anything for you. No matter what, we'll do it."

"Right," Bradley said.

Kovacs smiled. "Funny you should say that, because I was just about to ask you to do me a little favor."

"You name it," Robb said.

"Look, I want you to say 'no' right away if you don't want to do it. I know how you feel about. . . uh. . . Lady X."

"About Cynthia Allsford."

"That's a new one on me," Bradley said. "Is this a Cynthia Allsford as in Allsford Lynn and Allsford Hall?"

"The very same," Kovacs said. "Class, pal. Class."

Bradley said, "You've been holding out on me, Robb."

"I don't really know her. I'll tell you about her some time. Better yet, ask Stosh or Sam when I'm not around." He turned to Kovacs.

"What's the favor you want me to do?"

Kovacs lit a cigarette and blew out a thick cloud of blue smoke.

"Well, when I was at the hospital just now I met the most terrific woman in the world."

Bradley said, "The new nurse over there, Lieutenant Cameron. I know about fifteen guys who've tried to date her. No dice to all of them."

"Anyway, I met this beautiful nurse in the hospital, so I asked her to go out dancing with me this weekend. She said 'no thanks' right off the bat." Kovacs leaned back in his chair, his cap tilted forward so that his eyes peered out from under the visor. "Well, it sounded to me like her 'no' had a little bit of 'maybe' in it, so I told her to think it over for a little while, you know, while I had my little conference with Stills."

Bradley said, "Those other fifteen guys thought 'no' meant 'no'."

"When I went back out to her desk after I talked to Stills I asked her if she had made up her mind, and she said she didn't like the idea of going off to London with me. You know, just me and her. So I said maybe she'd feel better if we made it a double date, especially if the other woman was a friend of hers."

Bradley grinned at Robb. "I'm beginning to see where you come in. Okay, Stosh, we know who the other guy is. Who's the other woman?"

Robb watched Kovacs carefully. Kovacs peered out from under his visor. "Well, pal, it turns out that Merrie—that's this beautiful nurse's name—has a roommate by the name of Lieutenant Evelyn Vandivier."

Robb smiled.

Bradley said, "Not bad. Not bad at all. In fact, damned good. If Robb doesn't want to do you this favor, I know someone who can be talked into it."

"What do you say?" Kovacs studied Robb's face.

Robb said, "There's no one I'd rather go out with—except for one other person, of course."

"So what do you say, pal?" Kovacs picked up his package of Luckies, took one out and tossed the package to Robb. Kovacs snuffed out the cigarette he had been smoking and lit the fresh one.

"It's fine with me, although I'm not sure it would be fair to her. You know, with the reservations I have."

"Nobody's asking you to marry her. Just to go out together, do a little dancing, have dinner, take in a show. Things like that."

Robb shrugged. "Okay. It's fine by me if she's willing to go with me."

"She likes you, pal. I can tell. Why don't you take this paper Stills signed over to the C.O. right now, and stop in and see Evelyn at the same time? Tell her the plan is for her and Merrie to meet you and me in London Saturday afternoon."

Robb picked up the envelope and stood up. "Okay. I'll stop to see her after I give the C.O. this document of yours."

"I missed breakfast," Kovacs said. "I'm going in to get some chow now. I'll hang around here until you get back. Then I'll have lunch with you."

Bradley said, "You'll be having breakfast and lunch within an hour of each other."

He ignored Bradley. "She's going to jump at the chance to go out with you, but I thought I'd wait until it's official before calling Merrie to tell her it's all set."

Robb smiled. "I think that would be a good idea. We're talking about going to London this coming Saturday, three days from now?"

"Right."

"What if we're flying, or alerted?"

"I checked it out with Gib Hawkins before I went over to the hospital this morning. He said the continent is going to be solid crap through the weekend but it's going to be sunny in England. Of course he's wrong half the time, but I figure the ladies will give us a rain check if we gotta fly."

Kovacs stood up. "I just thought of something funny. If it rains hard enough in England we fly sure as hell, and so Merrie and Evelyn give us a rain check, which really fits. I'd really like to see an honest headline about us in the London newspapers, like 'U.S. Eighth Air Force grounded by a week of sunshine.'"

As Kovacs turned to depart, he raised his hand in a benediction of sorts. "Pray for good flying weather over England, so we don't have to fly."

Colonel Strang nodded as he read Stills' statement. "This is great, Robb. I'm remanding both of these gunners to your custody. This means they can fly as of now, but I'm expecting you to work out punishment that will impress upon these two wild men the seriousness of their actions. Whatever you decide to do to them has to be consistent and long-lasting. We don't want them to forget this thing, or to make light of it."

"Thanks, John. This takes a load off my mind. I'll try to think of something in the way of punishment, something that will impress them without alienating them." Robb stood up and moved to the door. "One question before I go, sir. Stosh and I are planning something for this weekend in London. How does the weather forecast look?"

The colonel pondered for a moment. He crossed the room and stood close to Robb. He said softly, "Now keep this under your hat. Right now it looks like we won't be going anywhere before Monday at the earliest."

"Do you mind if I tell Stosh?"

"You can tell Stosh, but absolutely no one else. Have a good time in London."

Robb walked quickly between the typists' desks to Lieutenant Evelyn Vandivier's cubicle. He stuck his head into the tiny office. "Got a minute?"

She stood up. "Come in, Robb."

As he looked at Evelyn he saw why so many men wanted to date her. Her bearing was dignified yet warm. She was fairly tall, five feet six or seven perhaps, and slightly on the buxom side. She seemed on the edge of overweight, but perhaps it was just her breasts and the thick wool uniform. Or maybe it was her cheeks which still had enough of that undergraduate baby fat to give her face an attractive fullness. Her dark blue eyes, now smiling at him, were accentuated by an unusually fair complexion and relatively short, brushed-back ash-blonde hair.

Robb was charmed by the subtle suggestion of restraint in her smile, a restraint insufficient to keep her cheeks from dimpling. As he studied her he forgot to respond to her.

Evelyn said, "I said 'Come in, Robb', and you were about to say. . ."

"I'm sorry. I came here to ask you if you'd go out with me this weekend."

"Well, this is a pleasant surprise. I'd love to."

"Thanks. I hope we can show you a good time."

"We?"

"Stosh and I. Lieutenant Cameron—who I understand is your room-mate—has agreed to go with Stosh, provided you agree to go along with me. Since you've agreed, I guess it's safe to say Stosh is taking your roommate on this little outing."

"What will we be doing?"

"A little dancing, go out to dinner, take in a show, things like that. In London, pal."

She laughed. "You're pretty good at that Stosh imitation. Let's see now. What shall I wear?" She pretended to be wrestling with a decision. "I think I have just the thing. I'll wear my forest-green suit coat and my beige skirt. Do you think you'd like that?" She described the dress uni-form she was wearing, the only dress outfit she could wear legally in London, or anywhere else.

Robb smiled. "I'd like it fine." He stood up. "Well, Evelyn, it looks like we're all in Stosh's hands for this weekend. I plan to relax and go wherever he leads. It should be fun. He really knows how to have a good time." He looked at his watch. "Time to meet Stosh for lunch."

"Thanks, Robb. I'm really looking forward to this."

"The plan is for you and Lieutenant Cameron to meet us in London on Saturday afternoon. Stosh didn't tell me the exact time."

"Two o'clock." She put her hand quickly over her mouth.

Robb said, "What's so funny?"

"Don't you know?"

It didn't occur to Robb that she must have already heard from Merrie about the London plan, and that her pleasant surprise at his invitation was put on. He simply said, "No, but my sense of humor isn't what it used to be."

"It isn't important. I'll tell you about it some other time."

"All right. I'd better get going." He turned in the doorway and faced her. "I'm looking forward to going out with you. I wish I had thought of it myself."

*   *   *   *   *   *   *

Kovacs and Bradley were well into their second helpings of Spam, hash-browns and bacon-greased green beans when Robb joined them in the mess hall. "Old Evelyn said she'd be delighted, right?"

"Right."

Bradley said, "Congratulations. I'd faint if she agreed to go out with me."

Kovacs reached out and placed his hand on Bradley's shoulder.

"Be patient, Monk. You're just a boy, fresh out of adolescence. Your time will come."

Bradley said, "A twenty-two year old adolescent, going on twenty-three."

Kovacs said, "I'll bet she's excited about it."

Robb grinned. "So am I."

Bradley said, "This conversation is getting me down. What did Colonel Strang say about Stills dropping the charges?"

"He was pleased. He expects me to work out a really tough program of punishment for them. But he really was pleased."

Kovacs said, "Of course he was pleased. After all, old Hoyt and Boo stood up for the honor of the good old 990th."

Robb frowned when he recalled Kovacs' bare-faced lies. "I'm still worried about those two. Monk, did you ever stop to think what would happen if Hoyt and Boo found out that your story about Brillig as the god of victory was a lot of bullshit you cooked up?"

Kovacs smiled. "He thought of it all right. They'd kill you. Right, Monk?"

"They sure as hell would kill me. So I've got a plan worked out in case someone comes along and shows them 'Twas Brillig' in 'Through the Looking Glass'. I'm writing a book called, 'Brillig, God of Victory in War.' Stosh is helping me on it. Actually, it was Stosh's idea."

"What?"

"I got a copy of The Iliad. I'm typing out a condensed version in which I change all the really big gods' names to Brillig. Each page is quadruple-spaced with two-inch margins all the way around. Stosh is going to pay to have a print shop in Cambridge set in Old English print and bind it between fancy hard covers."

Robb said, "That could cost a bundle."

Kovacs said, "It's only play money, pal." Kovacs always referred to his poker winnings as play money. "Besides, it's only going to be a six copy edition. One each for the three of us and Sam, and a copy each for Hoyt and Boo." Kovacs grinned, "With 'Brillig, God of Victory in War,' in big gold letters on a fancy cover, that other guy's book doesn't stand a chance. We'll tell Hoyt and Boo the guy who wrote the first book stole the name Brillig from our book." He looked to Bradley. "Just to play it safe you'd better put a copyright date on our book about a hundred years before the other guy's book came out."

"Good idea. We'll make Lewis Carroll a plagiarist. Hey, Robb, I might even autograph your copy for you."

"Kee-riste!"

——10——

Every seat in the Old Timers' Corner was occupied on the evening of Thursday, November 2nd. Among those gathered around the low, round dining table with the sawed off pedestal were Colonel Strang, Lieutenant Colonel Crick, the four squadron commanders, and Captains Kovacs and Robertson. All of theim were flyers except for Crick. They were talking about the rookie crew that augered in.

Colonel Strang said, "What could we have done last night , or earlier, say in our training program, to have made that tragedy less likely?"

Kovacs said, "Nothing."

Colonel Crick said, "What the devil do you mean by that?"

"The MacDonald thing was bound to happen, because of policy. If the target is clear, the word is 'go'. They don't care nearly as much about what the weather will be like in England when we get back."

Colonel Strang said, "Who are the 'they' who give these orders?"

"Eighth Air Force Command, but they're just taking orders from Washington to put up as many planes as possible on any day we can see the targets in Germany."

Crick looked incredulous. "Are you saying it's policy to send us out regardless of what the weather is like in England? That they give us the go sign knowing that the weather might be socked in to the ground when we get back?"

"No, Horatio, they won't send us out if they *know* the ceiling will be zero, but you know damned well they'll say 'go' if the target is clear even when the forecast says the ceiling might be down to a couple hundred feet when we get back."

Crick stiffened when Kovacs called him "Horatio". No one called him by his first name except Kovacs. "You're talking nonsense, Kovacs."

Robb said, "Look at the situation from the perspective of the policy makers in Washington. Germany is staggering, so they say the quicker we knock Germany out and end the war, the fewer Allied lives will be lost, including Eighth Air Force lives."

"And they're right," Colonel Strang said. "And that's precisely why we can't wait for perfect weather over England. Now is the time for the knockout blow."

Robb said, "I'm not arguing with the policy, not that I like it. Our factories are delivering something like a thousand bombers a month to the Air Forces, and the Training Command is grinding out a few thousand pilots a month—each of them coming off the production line after a year and a half in training, along with thousands of bombardiers, navigators, and gunners. We've got an almost inexhaustible supply of crews and bombers."

Crick said, "You're starting to sound as foolish as Kovacs."

Colonel Strang said, "Are you implying Washington would squander men, simply because we have a good supply of planes and crews?"

Robb said, "No, sir. What I do mean is that their perceptions of what's acceptable in the way of risks and losses are bound to be influenced by their knowledge that we've developed an unbelievable capacity to produce bombers and crews. And losses are relative. Compared to the losses in the early days, they see today's losses as quite acceptable. The upshot of this is we're going to fly in some pretty crappy weather, and we're going to lose a certain number of planes to the English weather."

Kovacs looked at Crick. "And that's why there's nothing can be done about cases like MacDonald last night."

"Perhaps you think we should fight the war according to what's convenient for you."

Several officers in the circle, all of them flyers except for Crick and Prentice, exchanged glances. Robb suspected that everyone was thinking pretty much the same thing: Crick, a ground officer as safe as any civilian at home in the States, was accusing Kovacs, the Group's most decorated flyer, of recalcitrance.

Kovacs sighed. "Horatio, I don't think you understood anything I said. Maybe we *should* shoot the works. I don't like it, but I accept it. But we shouldn't kid ourselves by saying when someone crashes, 'How could such a thing happen?' It happened before, many times, and it's going to happen again. I don't mean the loss of MacDonald's crew is any less awful because it was to be expected. I mean we shouldn't bullshit ourselves."

Captain Aaron Standing, the base Provost Marshal, appeared at the entrance to the club. He hurried across the room when he spotted Colonel Strang. He bent down and whispered into the Colonel's ear. Strang closed his eyes and squeezed the arms of his chair until his knuckles turned white.

Crick said, "Anything you can tell us?"

Strang said, "Lieutenant Quist is dead. He hung himself in his cell."

Crick broke the silence. "It was bound to happen. Only the weak commit suicide, and in war only the cowards."

Robb stood up, his fists clenched. Kovacs stood up and took Robb by the shoulders, trying to turn him away from Crick. Robb continued to glare at Crick but made no effort to free himself from Kovacs' grasp. Crick stared wide-eyed at Robb. Kovacs, Robb's shoulders still firmly in his grasp, turned toward Crick and said, "Come on, Robb, let's get the hell out of here and get some fresh air."

As Kovacs and Robb left, the others, all flyers, stood up and one by one left the seating circle. Finally only the Group Commander and his Executive Officer remained.

Crick said, "I'm going to charge that smart ass Robertson with gross insubordination. We'll see how cocky he is when he faces a Board of Inquiry."

Colonel Strang shook his head slowly as he looked at his second-in-command. "That would be a mistake. Robertson might be punished, as indeed he should be, but when the board hears what provoked his insubordination the biggest loser will be you."

Robb and Kovacs walked in silence through the veil of drizzle-fog. They felt their way along the gravel path with their feet as they made their way toward Amber Squadron Area. Robb was still seething. Kovacs sensed it. "Don't waste your steam on Crick. It's like arguing with an asshole. Only assholes argue with assholes."

Robb said, "Quist was a brave man. Just as courageous as Wister. Both of them flew more than twenty missions, and both of them went on missions long after their nerves were shot to hell."

Robb cringed as he recalled Bill Sandell's words when he came to his barracks to tell him about his radio operator. "Aarvid Wister blew his brains out last night. In his bunk, with his forty five."

"I sort of saw it coming with Wister. Even though he was able to do his job, I sent him to the psychiatrists at Division and they sent him back, saying he was okay, just like Quist. In a way, I saw it coming with Quist, too. Merseburg finally did him in, just like Quist. Maybe the Eighth Air Force psychiatrists are the real assholes."

"Wrong, Robb. The psychiatrists know exactly what they're doing. If they grounded every Eighth Air Force flyer who shows signs of folding, they'd end up grounding half the Eighth. The system wouldn't work, and the psychiatrists know it. So they say 'Give 'em a little whiskey when they land and lots of phenobarbs when they hit the sack.'"

Robb said, "I wonder how they decide who's crazy. The guys who fly bomb runs on Merseburg or the guys who can't." Robb momentarily lost the path. He had to feel his way back to the gravel surface with his feet. "I turned Wister in for a posthumous Distinguished Flying Cross. Crick blew his stack, but Colonel Strang knew what I was saying. I don't mean he thought Wister should have gotten a DFC. I mean he knew as well as I that Wister was a brave man who simply went beyond the limits of his endurance. He gave his life, just as Quist gave his life."

Kovacs said, "Did *you* think he had a DFC coming to him?"

"No, but that has nothing to do with it."

Kovacs nodded. "So when you wrote to Wister's folks your regrets that their son had been killed in action, you told them that you'd recommended him for a DFC, even though you knew there was no chance he'd get it. Right?"

Robb seemed lost in thought. Finally he said, "Yes."

"Look, pal, maybe we can work out something like that for Quist. I'd like to see his folks get a letter like that. I've got some friends in Dagger Squadron. Some of them are lousy poker players who owe me some real money." They walked in silence for a time. "Know something, Robb? I'm the asshole. I don't have to lean on my friends in Dagger. Quist was one of their guys. They feel worse about him than we do. All I have to do is plant the idea."

——11——

The meteorologists were dead wrong again. Late on Friday morning, November 3, the day before the big London weekend Stosh had so carefully engineered, dark, threatening clouds appeared on the western horizon. A cold drizzle began falling shortly after lunch, and by 2:00 P.M. the drizzle had given way to a heavy rain. When Stosh and Robb went to Headquarters to pick up their weekend passes they were told all passes had been canceled. No explanation was proffered. They knew, as did every flyer on the base, that an alert was in the offing. It became official at 9:00 P.M.. Robb had never seen Stosh more angry, but it didn't show when he phoned Merrie and asked her for a rain check for the following weekend. Evelyn gave Robb a rain check too. Stosh's anger reached the boiling point when both Saturday's and Sunday's missions were scrubbed at the last minute, after hours of preparation. As they climbed back into the sack after Sunday's scrubbed mission, Stosh declared, "Goddamn it, Robb, if we didn't have assholes for meteorologists we'd be in London right now with Merrie and Evelyn!"

At precisely 01:58 A.M. on Monday, November 6, 1944, Private Swovik put on his waterproof parka and went out into the driving rain. He followed the beam of his flashlight to the barracks where the squadron commander, Major William F. Sandell, slept. He stepped quickly into the barracks and stood next to the major's bunk, his flashlight beam on his watch. When the sweep hand of his watch reached 2:00 A.M., he spoke in a loud stage whisper.

"Sir. Time to get up."

The major mumbled in his sleep.

Private Swovik gently nudged the major's mound. "Sir! It's 0200 hours." The major's mumbling became a moan.

Private Swovik slowly, carefully turned back the blankets from the major's head. The back of his hand brushed against the Major's hair. His hand came away wet. The major's hair was soaked with sweat. Swovik gently placed his hand on the major's forehead. It was very hot. He stood next to the bunk for a time, flashing his light on his watch from time to time. He whispered softly to himself, "The Major's burning up with a fever and don't know where he's at!" He replaced the blankets over his commander's face and rushed out of the barracks. He ran to Kovacs and Robertson and awakened them, even though his orders were to awaken them at 2:30.

"Captain Kovacs! Captain Robertson! The Major's real sick and he's supposed to lead the mission today!"

Kovacs pushed the covers away from his face and said "Shit!"

Robb threw back his covers and reached for his pants. Kovacs sat up quickly and regretted it. He reached under his bunk and brought forth an opened can of grapefruit juice. He poured vodka into the can and swirled it around. He put the can to his lips and drank thirstily. Robb looked up from tying his shoes to see Kovacs with the can raised to his lips. "Goddamn it! We haven't got time for that. Get dressed!"

"Look, pal. Sandy ain't gonna die in the next couple of minutes, and from what I can tell by what Swovik says, you and I are in for one hell of a long day. So take a swig."

Robb took the can and took a quick pull on it. He pulled on his rain parka. "We'd better hurry. I'll run over and check on Sandy while you get dressed."

Robb was turning to leave the squadron commander's barracks as Kovacs entered. "He's in bad shape. I'm going to call Tony Rizzo and the C. O. You stay here with Sandy. Get some water and see if you can get him to drink it."

Robb hurried to the orderly room and called the flight surgeon. Rizzo said he'd be on his way immediately. He called Colonel Strang and told him Sandell was in bad shape. The colonel asked him to hold the line for a minute. Robb could hear voices in the background.

The C. O. came back on the line. "We've got a problem here. Sandy's down not only to lead Amber Squadron, but Amber Squadron is leading the Group. We can't change the position of the squadrons because the radar jamming frequencies in the planes are all set according to today's squadron positions and it's too late to change them. So Amber has got to lead. I'd take Amber lead myself but I'm Task Force Control

Officer at Division today. I'm all briefed for that so that can't be
changed. If Sandy can't fly, then Stosh leads Amber Squadron today—
and the Group—and you fly deputy lead. I want both of you guys over
here right away, and each of you bring your navigator and bombardier."

Kovacs came in the door of the orderly room.

"Here's Stosh now, sir." Robb handed the phone to Kovacs.

"John, there's no way Sandy can fly today. He's got one hell of a
fever and he's delirious. Doesn't know where he's at. Better send the
ambulance now."

Kovacs stood listening to the colonel on the phone. "Yes, sir. . . I
got it . . . yes, sir. Okay, John, we'll be right over."

Kovacs stared at the phone after he hung up. He looked like he had
the weight of the world on his shoulders. He did in fact have the weight
of 360 men—their lives—thrust upon him He exhaled loudly. "Shit!"

❋   ❋   ❋   ❋   ❋   ❋   ❋   ❋

They met Colonel Strang in his office. Kovacs said, "Let's have it,
Colonel."

"Let's have what?"

"The target. I could tell by your tone on the phone it's a bad one. Is
it Merseburg?"

"No."

"Thank God for that."

"It's Berlin."

"Shit!"

Strang said, "I'm sorry to lay this one on you on such short notice,
but nothing in war ever goes according to plans. Let's go to G-2 now and
go over the details."

Sam Prentice, Colonel Crick, and the other two squadron leaders and
their deputies were leaning over the large map table. Sam's eyes met
Stosh's and then Robb's, but with Colonel Crick standing at his side, he
said nothing. Sam outlined the route, the flak corridors, the points at
which fighter opposition could be expected, and the coordinates at which
Eighth Air Force fighter Groups would join the bombers. He said that
substantial flak could be expected at the target.

Kovacs said, "The Reichstag?"

Sam said, "Tempelhof Airdrome."

"Same thing," Kovacs said. "The target Hitler knows may soon be his only way out. They'll protect Tempelhof plenty. Bet on it."

Robb's heart fell at the word "Tempelhof". He knew Tempelhof Airdrome was surrounded by residential districts. What if we should miss! Quit kidding yourself. You know damned well a lot of our bombs are going to hit the neighborhoods around Tempelhof. What a dirty rotten business! He shook his head violently, dismissing the thought.

Kovacs said, "Look Robb, it's only Berlin, not Merseburg."

Robb said, "I'm not worried about Berlin. Tempelhof is surrounded by residential neighborhoods. What if we should miss?" Colonel Strang studied Robb for a moment. Kovacs said, "We're not going to miss, pal. So forget about it."

Sam quickly stepped in and passed out maps and charts. He stopped before Kovacs. "You're handling final briefing today, Stosh. Good luck."

As Colonel Strang was about to leave for Division, he called Kovacs and Robb to one side. He reiterated his regret that he had to stick them with this one on such short notice "Are you sure you got everything straight?"

Kovacs put his hand on the colonel's shoulder. "Look, John, this thing is duck soup. Just another mission. You worry about the whole Eighth Air Force and Sam and Robb and me will take care of Templehof." The Colonel smiled and shook hands with Kovacs and Robb.

Lieutenant Colonel Crick remained bent over the large map table, but his eyes were on the three men at the other side of the room. He saw the display of camaraderie among the three pilots. He frowned as he forced his eyes back to the map. Now, as always where flyers gathered, Crick was an outsider who could never know the flyers' silent understandings and closeness to each other.

※　※　※　※　※　※　※　※

Sam Prentice, ordinarily soft-spoken, had to yell to make himself heard over the din of the rain on the tin roof of the briefing room. His voice was strained as he pulled back the curtain and announced, "Today's target is Berlin!"

A loud, collective moan echoed through the corrugated metal tunnel, gradually subsiding into a rumble of comments, some bitter, some hostile, some resigned, but all of them negative. Kovacs, now seated in the chair ordinarily occupied by the C. O. at the front of the briefing room, stood up and said, "Quit your bitching. Look at it this way. It's not half as bad a target as Merseburg. Hell, not even a fourth as bad. It's just the name, Berlin, that gets you. Forget it. It's no big deal." More rumblings.

Sam continued his briefing. Robb thought, how ludicrous! Gentle, scholarly Sam Prentice telling these hardened, cynical flyers when to expect attacks by Messerschmitts and Focke-Wulfs. He sounded strained, unnatural, as he tried to make himself heard over the clatter of the rain. Sam, Robb mused, had a gentle upbringing, an only child in a well-ordered family. He never really learned to yell.

Robb's reverie was shattered by the booming voice of Stosh Kovacs. "Okay, men. Synchronize our watches! Coming up to 0443 . . . six, five, four, three, two, one, mark!"

Robb smiled. What a contrast to Sam! Loud, brash, commanding Stosh. A picture of Stosh's home flashed through his mind. Stosh had told him how his father ruled his roost with loud commands, threats, and blows. Stosh had had good yell-training.

"Okay, men. Remember, anyone fucks up it's everyone's ass. One final thing. Every pilot in this outfit has got to check each man on his crew to make sure he's got his Russian kit with him, just in case you get shot up over Berlin and have to head for Russian territory in Poland— which is just about due east from Berlin at its closest point. If you or your guys have to bail out over Russian territory, remember the Russians shoot first and ask questions afterwards. And be sure to tell your men not to reach for their Russian kits first thing if they come across Russian soldiers. We got reports some of our guys got themselves shot reaching for their Russian kits. The Russians thought they were reaching for their gun. So tell your guys if they come across Russian soldiers to just hold up their hands and yell, 'Americanski Soldat!' Okay, lets hear it all together. Americanski Soldat!"

"Again, everybody now, let's hear it, 'Americanski Soldat!' Okay, everybody now, one last time. Let's hear it!" The hundred or more men all yelled out in unison, laughing, "Americanski Soldat!"

Kovacs waved his hand at the group of flyers, a benediction of sorts, as he yelled, "Dismissed!"

Robb whispered to himself, "Good job, you big lout! And you call yourself just another dumb football player who didn't learn anything in college!

*   *   *   *   *   *   *   *

The Group took off near-blind, directly into the driving rain. It seemed to Robb such takeoffs were becoming Standard Operating Procedure. But they broke out of the top of the overcast at 13,000 feet with each squadron at full strength, twelve planes each. No mid-air collisions, a victory in itself.

The Task Force took its final form over the North Sea off the east coast of England, joined the bomber stream, and began its long grind upward and eastward just as the sun broke above the horizon. Robb had no idea how large their particular task force was, or the size of the bomber stream itself. He was relieved, though, to discover that the 990th was the third Bombardment Group in the entire bomber stream. A rare piece of good luck! Or was it luck? Perhaps it was Stosh's bitter declaration to the C. O. that after flying Tail End Charley to Merseburg, the 990th had paid its dues; perhaps the colonel did in fact relay Stosh's bitter message to the generals at Division. To discover one's Group practically at the head of the bomber stream on a raid on Berlin was a pleasant surprise indeed. Third place: a good omen! First and second might catch the worst of the fighter attacks. But in third place, while not as vulnerable to fighters, one might still get across the target before the German anti-aircraft gunners got their fuse-lengths set properly.

The undercast began breaking up as they crossed the Dutch coast, and by the time they reached the Dutch-German border, at 21,000 feet, there was but a scattering of clouds below them at around 10,000 feet. There was, however, a solid layer of cirrostratus above them, an unfortunate circumstance for the bomber stream, but fortunate for German fighters, providing cover for them on hit-and-run strikes.

Sam said at briefing that the Germans had some five hundred fighters at eight or ten airfields in an area extending one hundred miles westward from Berlin, precisely along their route. Robb knew the Luftwaffe would show up as soon as "Task Force Uber Alles" splits off from the bomber stream at Lukenwalde and makes its sharp turn north, straight for Berlin. Task Force Uber Alles! Robb wondered who the hell picked these childish names. Stosh, when he heard it this morning, had called it "TFC"—too fucking cute. Robb thought it was too much like World War One "Johnny Get your Gun" bullshit.

By the time they reached Lukenwalde the American P-51 Mustangs had become as thick as B-17s along the bomber stream. Robb had never seen so many American fighters on any single mission. When the bombers made their abrupt turn northward towards Berlin, he was glad to see that most of the P-51s stayed with Task Force Uber Alles.

Every pair of gunners' eyes in the Task Force strained for the first sight of the German fighters that were sure to come now that the Luftwaffe Command knew that the massed B-17s were headed straight for Berlin. They should appear any minute now, dropping out of the cirrostratus layer above them. Robb repeatedly reminded his gunners to keep their turrets and guns moving, but especially their eyes!

They waited, the intercom silent except for an occasional, "Come on you bastards," from Hoyt or Boo. But, miracle of miracles, the German fighters didn't show up, even though the bombers were headed directly for Berlin. Robb couldn't believe it when, by the time they started the countdown to the Initial Point on which they would turn sharply onto their bomb run, not a single Messerschmitt or Focke-Wulf had appeared. Apparently the massive display, indeed the challenge, of P-51s had done its job.

Although the high cirrostratus layer remained above them, there were only thin, scattered clouds below them as they approached the IP at 31,000 feet. Off and on, Robb could see Tempelhof Airdrome clearly between the scattered clouds. The bombs of the first Bombardment Group in the task force were hitting now. He could see the pock marks walking across the airfield, like the first isolated drops of rain hitting the surface of a dusty road on a summer's day.

The anti-aircraft shells exploded below them as soon as they turned on the IP and opened their bomb bay doors for their bomb run on Tempelhof. As they reached the halfway point of their six-minute run, Brillig, like the other planes of the 990th, began bouncing violently as the German gunners corrected their fuse settings. Though closer, they were still short, producing stronger   concussions—hard kicks in the ass—rather than actual damage to B-17s.

Ten seconds until bombs away. Kovacs counted out loud over the command channel in unison with his bombardier who was counting to him over his plane's intercom: ". . . six . . . five . . . four . . . three . . . two . . . *bombs away!*" All twelve planes of Amber Squadron began releasing their five hundred pound bombs simultaneously. The bombs, each released a second apart, would walk across Tempelhof, soon to be followed by the several hundred more five-hundred and one-hundred pounders of the Bombardment Groups behind them in the Task Force. Tempelhof would be turned into a no-man's land in a matter of minutes. Robb closed his eyes for a second, even though he had control of the plane. What if our bombs keep on walking beyond the boundaries of Tempelhof? How many old people, how many women and children would die? Pray we don't miss! What a rotten business!

Released of its heavy burden, the plane was now light in his hands, the controls easy, responsive. But the flak was heavy now. He yelled out loud to himself, "Come on, Stosh! Let's get the hell out of here!"

The sky, so clear at their altitude a minute ago, was now a dirty gray, mottled with black patches. The red-orange flashes of exploding shells became brighter as the atmosphere darkened with each explosion. Brillig shook violently with each flash as the concussions of the exploding shells slammed into its wings and fuselage. Shells exploded above and below them now; the German anti-aircraft batteries had them bracketed but they still hadn't found the 990th's level.

Robb's eyes were glued so tightly to Kovacs' plane that he scarcely dared blink, lest he miss the sudden evasion maneuver Kovacs should be making right about now. Goddamn it, Stosh! Let's get the hell out of here! What are we waiting for?

Kovacs wasn't reading Robb; he was yelling precisely the same thing at the leader of the Bombardment Group in front of him. He was boiling mad. What the hell was the matter with that guy? Why is he holding the bomb run heading and altitude when he should have been diving off to the right by now?

Kovacs yelled out loud into his mask, but his transmitter button wasn't down. "What the hell are you waiting for?" The explosions below were getting closer. The kicks of the concussions on the underbelly of his ship were bone-jarring.

"Okay, you son-of-a-bitch! If you don't make your turn by the time I count three, I'm turning without you!" The Group ahead finally began its evasive action. It swung to the right in a gradual, descending turn. Kovacs yelled to no one. "It's about time!"

The dreaded call rang out over the command channel: "Amber Squadron. Watch for 'chutes!" One of Amber's planes had bought it! Kovacs saw red. He pushed his transmitter button and yelled, "You son of a bitch! You cost us that plane! To hell with you!" He banked his plane steeply and violently to the right. For a moment the entire 990th Heavy Bombardment Group stood on its edge. Kovacs pulled back on his control column and Amber Squadron, followed by Dagger and Camelot squadrons, swung into a diving, turning wingover, well inside the gradual descending turn of the Group in front of them, the Group they were supposed to follow in the bomber stream. Kovacs leveled off momentarily to kill off some of their speed. They were well out of the flak now, but when his airspeed indicator dropped off to 250 miles per hour he put his nose down again, this time straight ahead on a generally westerly course, the course of Task Force Uber Alles, now off to the left of the 990th.

The Group that had been ahead of them was now some ten or fifteen miles behind them. Kovacs knew he'd have to slow down and let that chickenshit lead pilot pass them to get back into their assigned place in the Task Force. As the offending Bombardment Group pulled gradually past them, Kovacs yelled into his mask, "You son-of-a-bitch. If you hadn't been so damned chickenshit that plane of ours would still be fly-ing!"

Robb called to Hoyt and asked him who went down.

"Wayell, Cap'n Robb, looked to me like our Number Ten caught a shell in the bomb bay. He musta had a five-hundred pounder hung up that didn't drop, cuz he blew up like nothin' you ever seen, and took Number Eleven with him. Over."

"Roger, Tailgunner. Were there any 'chutes? Over."

"Hell, Cap'n. There weren't nothing left of them planes 'cep pieces of tails and wing tips. Everything else 'cep the engines was blown into little pieces. Some of the crew got out all right, but like little pieces of hamburger. Over."

"Roger, Tailgunner. Over and out." Robb's voice was steady, but as soon as he released the intercom button he screamed aloud into his oxygen mask. "No! No! Nooooo!" He took several deep breaths. He put his gloved fingers under his goggles and rubbed his eyes. Finally, he shook his head back and forth vigorously.

He motioned to Bradley to take over. He ran his finger down the formation chart taped to his left leg. Number ten: Hendrickson. Damn! Hal Hendrickson, quiet, studious, Hal Hendrickson. Number eleven: Costello. Costello? He couldn't place him. He must be new. But if he's new, what the hell's he doing flying squadron Tail End Charlie? What was Hendrickson's co-pilot's name? I can see his face now. Dark complexion, dark hair. Moustache. Good-looking guy. Lawless. That's it. Dean Lawless! Nice guy. Damn!

He scanned his instrument panel. They were on a direct course for home, altitude 24,500 feet, half-throttle, rate of descent 200 feet per minute, near optimum readings for trading off precious altitude for distance westward with minimum use of fuel. It suddenly hit him that if Number Ten and Number Eleven blew up together, how come Number Twelve, flying on Ten's other wing didn't blow up too? "Pilot to Tailgunner. Over."

"You got him, Cap'n Robb."

"Tailgunner, what happened to Number Twelve? Over."

"Ah cain't figure it out, Cap'n. He had two planes blow up right next to him, one with a five-hundred pounder still in it, and he's still flying. Middle of his fuselage is all ripped to hell, and his nose is full of big holes, but his wings is in pretty good shape and all of his props is turning. But I reckon it's pretty much a butcher shop in his nose and waist. Over."

"Roger, Tailgunner. Over and out." Robb released the intercom button and swore out loud to nobody, "Christ! A butcher shop!" Things were bad enough without Hoyt's descriptions. He checked his formation chart. Number Twelve was a Lieutenant Coleman in T-Tom. Strange. He didn't know a Lieutenant Coleman. Must be another new crew. He switched back to command channel. He was about to check on Number Twelve when Kovacs' voice crackled forth. "Amber Leader to Amber T-Tom. Over." T-Tom didn't respond. Kovacs repeated, "Amber Leader to Amber T-Tom. Do you read me, Amber Tom? Over." Still no answer.

Robb called Kovacs. "Amber Deputy to Amber Leader. Do you want me to drop back next to them and hand-signal them to switch to command channel? Over."

"Roger, Deputy."

Robb put his hand over Bradley's on the throttles. Bradley nodded and relinquished the controls. He banked sharply to the right, easing back on the throttles. When the rear of the formation was opposite him on his left he pushed forward on the throttles and swung back into formation on Coleman's right wing. The maneuver took less than ten seconds.

T-Tom was in worse shape than even Hoyt's lurid descriptions conveyed. There was a jagged, gaping hole, some six or eight feet long and three or four feet high along the near waist side of the plane. The honeycombed floor of the plane could be seen in cross-section. The waist window and waist gun were gone. There was another hole on the far side of the fuselage. Whatever hit them had gone right through the plane. Robb could see a large patch of daylight through the hole. A crewman was holding an oxygen mask on the face of a prone figure on the floor.

The plexiglass nose of T-Tom was blasted away. Surprisingly, the chin turret was intact, as far as Robb could discern He could discern no movement in the nose section. The near wing was shredded, its skeleton exposed at the wing tip, but it appeared serviceable. Incredibly, all props were turning. No smoke, thank God!

Robb saw at once that only the co-pilot was in the cockpit. Coleman may be wounded, or dead. The co-pilot did not see Robb. He kept looking back and to his left, away from Robb, now and then taking a quick glance forward to check his position. Robb could only wait until he happened to look his way. Apparently something was happening below and behind the co-pilot's seat, below the top turret.

There was a space of perhaps a hundred feet between T-Tom and the echelon in front of him. Robb decided to try to get the co-pilot's attention by pulling slightly ahead and in front of him. He added power until his wing was opposite Amber Tom's nose. He then nudged Brillig in close to T-Tom. He noticed for the first time the name painted on the front quarter of the crippled Fortress: "Lucky Lady".

The co-pilot turned his head forward and did a double-take. He waved Robb away frantically. Robb tapped his left earphone. The co-pilot nodded. Robb pulled over some twenty feet farther from the damaged plane. He saw the co-pilot reach out to switch channels. Robb motioned for Bradley to take over. He pushed his button. "Amber T-Tom. This is Amber Deputy on your right wing. Do you read me?"

A weary voice responded. "Roger, Amber Deputy."

Kovacs' broke in. "Amber T-Tom, this is Amber Leader. What's your situation? Over."

The weary voice again, this time with a noticeable tremor. "We have seven dead or wounded."

Kovacs came back, "Pilot wounded? Over."

"This is the T-Tom co-pilot. Pilot wounded. Both waist gunners dead, bombardier and navigator wounded or dead . . . we don't know. Radio operator and ball gunner wounded. Engineer and Tailgunner okay."

"Roger, T-Tom," Kovacs responded. "Report condition of your plane. Over."

"All engines working for now. Hydraulic system's probably gone. We took a shot in the cockpit and the gyro instruments are gone and most of the engine instruments. The only reading I've got on the engines is the cylinder head temperatures. I'm guessing on the throttle and prop settings. Number one is running very hot. I've got mixture full rich on it and cowl flaps wide open but the head temperature is still climbing, getting close to the far end of the redline. I'm feathering it right now."

Robb saw the co-pilot reach forward and hit the feathering button. Number one prop slowed and eventually stopped as its blades turned to match the longitudinal axis of the plane.

"Good idea, T-Tom," Kovacs interjected.

T-Tom broke back in, "My engineer and Tailgunner are taking care of the wounded. They've got some of the wounded on emergency oxygen bottles because their oxygen connections are out. The bottles aren't going to last long. I've got to get down to 15,000 feet damned fast. If my navigator and bombardier are still alive they'll be needing oxygen too, and if their heated suits are out they'll freeze to death pretty quick with the nose open. Request permission to break formation. Over."

Kovacs' reply was immediate. "Amber Leader to Amber T-Tom. Permission denied."

Robb closed his eyes momentarily. Christ! What a heartless sound, a denial of life itself. But the right decision. That layer of cirrostratus above could be full of German fighters, and if T-Tom breaks formation the piranhas will get him within minutes and be gone before our P-51s can respond. Besides, their P-51 escort had left them to take up positions with the Bombardment Groups still headed toward their targets. Stosh was right. T-Tom would be a sitting duck if he broke formation now. The scattered cloud-layer below was gradualy closing, but still not solid enough for protection.

T-Tom hadn't responded to Kovacs' denial of permission to break formation. Kovacs' voice again, "Amber Leader to Amber Tom. Did you read my transmission? Over."

"I read you. Permission denied, over." The voice sounded even more weary.

Robb shook his head. Dear merciful Christ! What a hell of a spot that guy is in! His pilot is dead or dying. His navigator and bombardier are dead or dying. Most of his gunners dead or wounded. Only two guys able to tend to the wounded and both of them hamstrung by portable oxygen bottles and the need to keep their heated flying suits connected to keep from freezing to death with the plane full of big holes. Some of the wounded won't be getting oxygen and their blood will have shorted out their heated flying suits. With the plane torn open they'll be freezing to death. Robb doubted they'd be able to do much for the wounded under such conditions. And then to be told "Permission denied!" A sudden thought struck him. He pushed his command button. "Amber Deputy to Amber T-Tom co-pilot. Are you yourself wounded?"

"Affirmative."

Oh Christ! We didn't ask and he didn't tell us! That guy's got guts! Robb's right hand moved involuntarily to his goggles, his gloved fingers pressed his forehead through his leather flying helmet. Kovacs cut in, his voice was soft now, almost gentle. "T-Tom, this is Amber Leader. Tell me exactly the location and severity of your wounds. I mean exactly. Over."

"Hit in upper right arm and upper right leg. No way of knowing how bad. I put a compression bandage on my leg while the autopilot was still working when I turned it on right after we got hit. I put a tourniquet on my right arm. Over."

"Are you still bleeding? Over." Kovacs' voice was soft, concerned.

"I think I've got the leg stopped. My arm is still bleeding some. Over."

"What's your name?" Kovacs was solicitous.

"Lieutenant Rossi."

Robb was astonished at Kovacs' quick assessment of the situation. Here he was, flying as Group Commander, violating one of the primary rules of communication on the command channel by asking this guy to give his name over the air. Clearly, Stosh figures it's more important to let this guy know right now that he's a real human being with friends around, not simply a disembodied voice that answers to T-Tom.

"Lieutenant Rossi. This is Amber Leader. Is your heated flying suit working?"

"Roger."

"Good. Now turn it down to 50 degrees."

"Roger. Fifty degrees."

Robb marveled at Kovacs' quick thinking in emergencies. He's telling Rossi to turn down his suit temperature in order to slow down his bleeding. But what about shock? Shouldn't he be kept warm?

Apparently Stosh thought about that too. Kovacs came on, "Lieutenant Rossi, is your first-aid kit handy?"

"Roger."

"Good. Has the seal been broken? Over."

"Negative."

"Good. Take your left hand off the throttles and break open the kit. Take out the morphine syringe and break off the tip. Place the syringe on the throttle pedestal. If the pain gets too bad give yourself a half-shot. I repeat: a half-shot. Over."

Robb could see Rossi trying with one hand to break the seal on the small plastic box. He finally succeeded. Robb saw him put the box down on his lap and break the glass tip of the syringe against the instrument panel.

Kovacs said, "Lieutenant Rossi, can you reach your engineer on intercom? Over."

"Roger, I can reach him."

"Good. Is your pilot still in his seat? Over."

"Negative. Engineer pulled him out of his seat and is working on him on the flight deck behind the cockpit, under the top turret."

Kovacs said, "Is your pilot on oxygen?"

"Roger. He's unconscious but he's on a bottle."

"Okay, Lieutenant Rossi. Order your engineer to leave your pilot and get into the pilot's seat right away. Then have him follow you on the controls so that he takes most of the weight of the plane out of your hands. If he corrects too much you straighten him out, but don't go taking on all of the controlling yourself. Acknowledge."

"Roger."

"We'll give you further instructions after you get the engineer to the cockpit."

Robb noted that Kovacs had decreased the rate of descent. They had slowed to 200 miles per hour with a rate of descent of only 50 feet per minute. Altitude 23,000 feet. This could mean only one thing: Stosh has gotten word that the crap was piled high over Allsford Lynn. If Stosh lets down to an altitude lower than the top of the overcast over the base, he'd have to climb back up before they got home to get above the top of the crap over Allsford Lynn. Some of the guys would sure as hell run out of gas.

"Amber Leader to Amber Deputy. Over."

"This is Amber Deputy."

"Amber Deputy, when the engineer gets into T-Tom's cockpit, let me know. When Gib Hawkins' usual conditions return below, I want you to eed-lay om-Tay own-day oo-tay ee-thay eck-day. Ast-fay! And then on to Broadway. Acknowledge. Over."

Robb pushed his button. "Loud and clear." Gib Hawkins' conditions meant lousy flying weather, in this case a solid undercast, below. Kovacs spoke the rest in pig-Latin because German fighter pilots might be listening in. Kovacs wanted him to lead T-Tom down to the deck as soon as the undercast closed up below, and then on to the big wide emergency runway, "Broadway," on the southeast coast of England. Without gyro instruments Rossi couldn't fly blind through the undercast. He'd spin out within a minute after he lost sight of the horizon. His only hope was to fly close formation with Brillig as they let down through the soup. If he drifted more than twenty or thirty feet from Brillig when they went through the cloud layer he'd lose sight of Brillig and that would be the end of T-Tom and all those still alive on board. And even if he got down to the deck he'd never find the emergency runway without a navigator.

Robb saw the engineer slip into the left-hand seat and grasp the wheel. He nodded from time to time as, apparently, he received verbal directions from Rossi. The plane wove gently from side to side and up and down. The corrections were slow and orderly. Good! No panic in that cockpit.

Robb studied the undercast as Bradley flew the plane. He looked back at T-Tom. Rossi was working the throttles with his left hand while the engineer wrestled with the wheel. The undulations, though continuous, were steady now, predictable.

The strange teamwork in T-Tom continued for the next half hour. They were now at 22,000 feet. The top of the undercast, now about 80 percent closed, was about 12,000 feet below them. Robb figured it would be closed up solid in a matter of minutes. He caught Rossi's eye and tapped his earphone. "T-Tom, this is Amber Deputy. Over."

"Roger." The voice was not strong but the despair was gone.

"I want you to move in close to me now. And no matter what I do, stick close. I want you to take the controls by yourself now. You and I are going to do some close formation flying. The closer the better. How are you feeling right now?"

"I'm all right."

"I'll give you a hand signal when we ive-day oo-tay ee-thay oud-clay ayer-lay. Do you read me? Over."

"Roger."

"Okay, Lieutenant. Keep your eyes on me and stay on the command channel. Amber Leader, did you get all that?"

"Roger."

Robb switched to intercom. "Pilot to crew. We're going to lead T-Tom—the plane on our left—to a lower altitude and then on back home. We're going to dive for about 10,000 feet to the undercast below. Then we're going to let down slowly through the soup and go home on the deck. Keep your eyes peeled for bandits. Over and out."

Robb kept studying the development of the undercast. It was almost solid now. Good! He took over the controls. He caught Rossi's eye and pointed downward. Rossi nodded and moved in closer. Robb banked sharply to the right and pushed forward on the control column, never altering his throttle settings. Rossi stayed right with him in perfect, close formation. That guy's all right! He's wounded, his plane is shot to hell, and he's flying perfect formation in a dive. Robb recalled Hoyt's phrase, "butcher shop". It must be a butcher shop in that cockpit right now, as well as in the nose and waist.

They were still over Germany. Robb recalled bitterly the most glaring mistake of his flying career. They were going it alone for home, on the deck, on his first tour. He had failed to get back into the overcast on time and lost both of his waist gunners to a single blast from a Messerschmitt 110. He wasn't going to let anything like that happen again. He was determined to negotiate the distance between themselves and the protective clouds below in record time. His airspeed indicator climbed to 300 miles per hour. Rossi remained glued to his left wing. They were now midway between the formation above them and the cloud layer below. Robb switched to intercom. "Pilot to crew. Keep your eyes peeled. We're in bandit country."

Brillig's airspeed indicator held at 300 miles per hour. One more minute and they'd be safe in the clouds below. Safe? With a battered Fortress flown by a wounded pilot with no instruments a few feet from him? Yes, safe, by God! That guy Rossi is all guts and he's a damned good pilot!

As they approached the cloud layer Robb began pulling back on the control column. He assumed straight and level flight at 11,400 feet. Wisps of cloud flashed over their wings. He tapped Bradley on the shoulder and pointed to the exterior light switches. Bradley switched on all of Brillig's exterior lights, including her huge landing lights. Robb thought ruefully that if this undercast was as dense as it seemed his lights would be visible to Rossi for all of twenty feet when they got into the soup. He looked back towards T-Tom's cockpit. Rossi nodded and waved at Robb with his left hand. Robb pressed the command button.

"Way to go, Rossi. Stay on the command channel. We're going to mush down through this crap at air speed 140, rate of descent 1000 feet per minute. But before we start down, let's do a quick check list. Have your engineer switch to command channel." "Engineer, I want you to do this checklist. Close cowl flaps so they're all just slightly cracked. We don't want your carburetors icing up when we start down."

The engineer reached for the panel. "Cowl flaps almost closed. Over."

"Good. Now lean out your fuel mixture on your three good engines until you see the cylinder head temperatures start to rise. Then enrich the mixture slowly until the temperatures settle down." It was a damned lucky break that the engineer was one of the survivors. He could do most of these things with his eyes closed.

"Mixtures lean and temperatures holding. Over."

"Okay. Now if your intercoolers are still on, turn them off."

"Intercoolers off."

"Now turn off your superchargers." The engineer reached forward without hesitation.

"Superchargers off."

"That about does it. Engineer, what's your name?"

"Sergeant Willis, sir."

"Good job, Sergeant Willis. Are you wounded in any way?"

"Negative."

"Good. Now, when we descend through the clouds I want you to turn on the carburetor heat every thirty seconds. Keep it on for 10 seconds and then turn it off again. Get that?"

"Roger, sir.

"Good. Now, Lieutenant Rossi. Leave your throttles set just where they are and increase your prop pitches to the maximum—high pitch, low RPM."

"Roger. All props high pitch, low RPM."

Rossi sounded business-like. Good! "Okay. Get ready to back off on the throttles. We'll mush down with a straight and level attitude. No matter what your senses tell you, remember that we're flying straight and level." Robb knew that the most dangerous enemy they faced right now was the vertigo Rossi would inevitably experience as soon as they entered the cloud bank. He would have neither flight instruments nor an actual horizon to orient himself in space. He would have to trust his intellectual conviction that they were flying straight and level even though all of his senses and his emotions would scream that they were turning, diving, or slowly rolling over and over.

"Okay, Lieutenant. Now we go into the soup. I'm backing off on the throttles." Brillig settled into the cloud layer immediately. The thick gray-black shroud enveloped them. Beyond the windshield the gray shroud slowly turned to black. Robb leaned forward, straining to see Brillig's nose. He couldn't make it out. Christ! This crap is thick! How the hell is Rossi going to be able to stick with me? He looked out his side window, back and to his left. There, not more than 15 feet from his fuselage was the green light at the tip of T-Tom's right wing. The aluminum skin had been blown away from his wing tip yet that light was still working! It was as though a tornado had blown the roof off a house without disturbing the place-settings on the dining room table. Robb felt a surge of optimism as he watched the light.

He had looked at the light too long. He began to feel the rolling sensations of vertigo. He quickly turned back to his instrument panel. The rolling sensations persisted but his intellect accepted the message from the artificial horizon: they were flying straight and level, by God! Poor Rossi! He must be rolling over and over in his mind by now.

"Lieutenant Rossi, remember now, we're flying straight and level. Straight and level. We'll soon be breaking out of this crap. I'm watching my artificial horizon right now. It shows straight and level. Picture my artificial horizon in your mind but don't take your eyes off my lights. Think of it as being on your own instrument panel. It shows straight and level. Straight and level. Straight and level."

He let up on the button. Better watch it. I might hypnotize him. Make it conversational. "Remember Lieutenant, we're flying straight and level. The artificial horizon shows straight and level. Picture it in your mind. Straight and level. It's on your panel but don't take your eyes off me. It shows absolutely straight and level. You and I are mushing downward at a good rate, but your plane is flying straight and level."

"Roger, Amber Deputy. Keep up the chatter! I'm rolling over and over and so are you right now! Keep it up!" He spoke too fast. There was desperation in his voice.

Robb pressed the button and repeated in an easy sing-song. "Straight and level. Air speed 140. Rate of descent 1000 feet per minute. Straight and level. Straight and level. You're looking real good. Straight and level."

They were actually letting down at 1500 feet per minute and the planes were in a slightly nose down attitude, but it was better to let Rossi imagine his own plane and Brillig as flying straight and level. The throttles were nearly all the way off, the props windmilling slowly in high pitch. They were mushing near the stalling point of the B-17's wings, given the near level attitude of the planes and the modest thrust of the propellers. Their air speed was actually 130 miles per hour, not 140. No need to have Rossi start worrying about stalling out. They had to get through the soup quickly and it was best for Rossi to mush down as close to straight and level as possible. His controls felt mushy and no doubt Rossi's did too. But this way the planes respond more slowly, more forgiving to movements of rudder and ailerons, so Rossi's flying formation in slow motion, in a sense. He looked back again. T-Tom's green wingtip light was now less than ten feet from Brillig's fuselage. Good man, Rossi! You've got what it takes, by God!

"Straight and level, Lieutenant Rossi. Our wings are absolutely level and we're mushing downward at a rate of 1000 feet per minute. Our wings are level but we're now flying in a slightly nose-down attitude to maintain speed. But your wings are level. Your wings are level. Air speed 140, rate of descent 1000 feet per minute. We should be breaking out of this stuff any minute now. Your wings are perfectly level. My artificial horizon shows wings level, with a slightly nose-down attitude. We're going downhill but your wings are level. Engineer, don't forget about the carburetor heat."

Robb peered into the blackness beyond the windshield. Damn! We could as easily be in a pitch-black tunnel or cave for all we can see. Poor Rossi! "Lieutenant Rossi. Don't take your eyes off me but we're getting close to the bottom of this stuff. You're flying perfectly straight and level. We're now passing through the 2000 foot mark. It's getting lighter outside your plane. You're flying straight and level."

The interior of the cockpit gradually brightened as though someone were slowly turning up a dimmer switch. Robb peered downward through the last wisps of the undercast. Where the hell's the ground? He was startled to see a large object pass below them. Oh hell! That was a ship! He laughed out loud into his oxygen mask. We're over the North Sea!

"Lieutenant Rossi. We're out of the crap now, over the North Sea. Add power and re-set prop pitches to assume level flight. Acknowledge."

"Roger. Adding power and setting prop pitches."

Robb pushed forward on the throttles and re-set his prop pitches. His altimeter held steady at 1300 feet; his airspeed increased to 200 miles per hour. He turned his head and was surprised to see Bradley's face. No oxygen mask. No goggles. Christ, I'm still on oxygen and we're down to 1300 feet! He motioned to Bradley to take the controls. He pulled off the mask and goggles he had been wearing for the past seven or eight hours. He unplugged his oxygen mask mike and plugged in his throat mike and fastened the garter-like band around his neck. He looked back at T-Tom. Rossi had backed off a bit. He was now about twenty-five feet away. We made it by God! We made it!

"Amber Deputy to T-Tom. Lieutenant Rossi, you did one hell of a job on the let-down! Hang in there. The toughest part's behind us now."

"Roger."

Robb took off his heavy gloves and liners and rubbed his face vigorously. The circulation gradually returned around his mouth where the mask had dug in. His hands and face were wet with perspiration. "Hell! I've still got my suit plugged in!" He quickly unplugged his suit and indicated to Bradley to turn off the cabin heat.

Bradley leaned over and yelled into Robb's ear, "Better check on T-Tom's gas supply."

"Amber Deputy to Amber Tom. How's your gas holding up?"

"I've got a quarter on each engine tank. All other supply tanks are empty."

"Good. That will be enough. We'll be going straight in to the big one. Acknowledge."

"Loud and clear."

Did he sound weaker or was he imagining it?

They were flying just under the layer of clouds, so close to them that the lower hanging puffs of cumulus occasionally obstructed their vision. Robb recalled again the sneak attack by the ME 110. He switched to intercom. "Pilot to crew. Keep a close watch for bandits." He switched to command.

"Is your arm or leg still bleeding?"

"I don't know. Not much anyway."

"Does your leg or arm hurt?"

There was a pause. He spoke very slowly, softly. "Arm's numb. Leg hurts like hell."

"Take your feet off the rudder pedals. You can fly a B-17 with ailerons only. You know that, of course. Back off to about fifty feet from me. Try to relax and let Sergeant Willis do as much as possible."

"Roger." His response was barely audible.

"Have Sergeant Willis call your Tailgunner up to the cockpit."

"This is Willis. Corey is up here taking care of Lieutenant Coleman."

"Tell him to get into the cockpit right now, and to stand between you and Lieutenant Rossi! I mean right now!" Robb switched to intercom and asked his radio operator for a report on the weather at the base and an altimeter setting. Brain Child reported a ceiling of 100 feet over Allsford Lynn with the top of the overcast at 16,000 feet and rising. Just as he thought! The Group is in for a long letdown through the crap over the base and they're going to be damned low on gas. Stosh should have taken the whole outfit under the stuff while they were still over Holland. Hell, maybe he did.

Robb called his navigator for a heading to the emergency field on the coast. Carlson gave him the heading and reported they would cross the coast of England at 1846 hours and should be on the emergency runway at 1851, assuming they maintain their present speed of 205 miles per hour. Robb wished he could slow down to 150 miles per hour to make it easier for Willis to control the plane, but even at their present speed they'd be lucky to get to the emergency strip before dark, and there's no way those two would make it onto the runway in pitch dark. They'd have to hold their speed at 200 minimally even though T-Tom's three remaining engines must be crowding the redlines.

He looked at his watch. Only about one more hour. If only Rossi can hold together that long! He looked across the 75 feet that separated him from Rossi. He's still wearing his oxygen mask. Good. He saw the Tailgunner move into position between Rossi and Willis. "Amber Deputy to T-Tom. Sergeant Willis, there's a syringe of morphine on the throttle pedestal. The tip's been broken off and it's ready for injection. Tell Sergeant Corey to give the lieutenant a half shot of it in his left forearm."

Robb saw the Tailgunner pick up the syringe. He rolled back Rossi's left sleeve and gave him the shot without Rossi's hand leaving the throttles. Robb said, "Good job. Now, Sergeant Willis, I want you to keep both hands on the wheel except when you have to switch channels. And keep your feet off the rudder pedals even though the lieutenant has his feet off the pedals too. You can steer a B-17 with ailerons only if you don't try to make any sudden turns, and I can guarantee you there won't be any sudden turns. If the Lieutenant feels like taking his hand off the throttles, that's okay too. Leave the throttle settings where they are. Tighten up the friction knob on the throttles so they don't wander. Acknowledge. Over."

"I read you, sir. Both hands on the wheel. Feet off the rudders, hand off the throttle, tighten friction. Over."

Better have them loosen the tourniquet or Rossi's liable to end up losing his arm. "Very good. Now tell Sergeant Corey to reach around the Lieutenant and loosen the tourniquet on the Lieutenant's right arm. Have him loosen it for a half minute or so. Tell him that if his arm starts bleeding again to tighten it up. Lieutenant Rossi, you tell the Sergeant right away if you feel your arm start bleeding again. Take your left hand off the throttles and hold the wheel with your right hand. I'll match my throttle settings to your speed or any changes in your speed."

"Roger." The voice was stronger. It must have been the engineer who answered. Robb could see the Tailgunner leaning over Rossi. The engineer's voice came back over the air. "Captain, this is the engineer. Corey loosened the tourniquet but he could see the arm start bleeding bad right away through the hole in his flight jacket, so he tightened it up again."

"Roger, Sergeant. Lieutenant Rossi, how are you feeling now? Over."

Rossi didn't respond. My God! What if Rossi passes out! Robb spoke very loud. "Lieutenant Rossi, do you read me?"

"Roger." His voice was very weak now.

It occurred to Robb that Rossi hadn't had anything to eat or drink for fifteen hours or more. "Now Sergeant Willis, tell Sergeant Corey there should be K-Ration packets in the cockpit, probably under the seats. Tell him break out the chocolate bar and shove it into the lieutenant's mouth in small pieces, one at a time. Tell him to put the lieutenant's

mask back on between pieces. Sergeant, do you have any coffee or water on board?"

"We've got some coffee in a thermos, but it's cold by now."

"Tell Corey to give the lieutenant a cup of the cold coffee. Lieutenant, you drink it. Did you read me, Lieutenant?"

"Roger." A whisper.

Bradley had the controls. Robb could watch all the goings on in the
cockpit of the battered Fortress. Corey had unsnapped one side of Rossi's
mask and was placing a piece of chocolate in Rossi's mouth.

Robb pulled off his leather helmet and wiped his forehead with the
helmet's liner. He unplugged his helmet earphones and clamped the
regular earphones over his head. He wondered if he was doing the right
thing with Rossi. Should he eat? Should he drink? Should he be kept
warm or cold? He pushed his button. "Sergeant Willis, how goes it with
the chocolate and the coffee?"

"He's got the chocolate in his mouth and he's taking a little of the
coffee.

"Roger, Sergeant." Damn it! Willis and I are talking about Rossi as
though he's not there, as though he no longer has his faculties.
"Lieutenant Rossi, this is Amber Deputy. Do you read me?"

No answer.

Oh God! Now what? "Lieutenant Rossi, do you read me?" Robb
was almost shouting. Still no answer. He took hold of himself by a conscious, determined effort. Okay. Get ready for the worst in that plane.
Keep them calm. Keep Willis calm. "Sergeant Willis, I want you to . .
."

Willis screamed hoarsely, "Captain! The lieutenant's passed out!
What do I do? I don't know how to fly an airplane!"

Robb could see Rossi slumped forward, hanging from his shoulder
harness. He took two or three deep breaths, deliberately delaying his response. When he responded, his tone was even, measured. "Amber
Deputy to T-Tom. Sergeant Willis, you and Sergeant Corey aren't alone
in that cockpit. I'm right here next to you. I can see everything that goes
on in your cockpit, and I can see your plane better than my own. All you
have to do is do exactly what I tell you. Right now all you have to . . ."

Willis gasped frantically, his voice full of terror. "I . . . I don't think
I can do it! What should I do?"

Christ! He's panicking! Robb pushed the transmission button on the wheel until his knuckle turned white. But he spoke evenly, firmly. "Sergeant Willis. Please shut up and listen to me! And don't interrupt! You're flying that airplane right now and you've been flying it for the past hour. So just keep doing what you've been doing." He exerted all his will to keep his tone matter-of- fact.

"Don't touch the throttles and keep your feet off the rudder pedals. All you have to do is keep your wings level with the ailerons and your nose level with easy, slow pulling back and pushing forward on the control column. Don't make any quick corrections or changes. Do everything in slow motion and you'll get along just fine. Did you get that, Sergeant Willis?"

"Roger." He sounded like a child forced to do something against his will.

Robb snapped back, "Roger_what, soldier!"

"Roger, sir." He sounded defeated.

"That's better, Sergeant. Now try it again, goddammit, like a soldier!" Get the son-of-a-bitch mad! Kick his ass! "Let's hear it again, soldier!"

"Roger, *sir!*"

"That's better. Now I want to talk to Sergeant Corey. Sergeant Corey, do you read me?"

"This is Corey. I read you, Captain."

"I want you to unplug the lieutenant's mask mike and helmet earphones. Take the earphones and mike off the hook behind the lieutenant and to put them on yourself. Plug them in the lieutenant's outlets." Robb was barking orders now. "You got that, Sergeant Corey"

"Roger, sir!"

Robb could see Sergeant Corey's quick movements. Throat mike and earphones now in place, Corey reached over and around Rossi to push the transmitter button. Corey said, "Sir. Do you want me to pull the lieutenant out of his seat and lay him down on the floor? There's room if we push Lieutenant Coleman to one side. Then maybe I could help more in the seat. Over."

"Leave the Lieutenant where he is so we can keep him on oxygen. Tighten up his shoulder harness so he's not leaning forward, but not too tight. Then I want you to loosen his jacket and flying suit and his shirt collar, and anything else that might interfere with his breathing. Now I want to talk to Sergeant Willis. Sergeant Willis, are you reading me? Over"

"This is Willis. I read you, sir. "

"You're doing a good job. Keep everything just as it is. You're making your corrections just right. Slow and easy. Don't start worrying about how you're going to get down on the runway, in case you're worrying about landing . . . "

Willis said, "Captain, uh, sir. I can hardly keep this plane flying let alone land it."

"You're interrupting again, Sergeant. Now just listen to me. You've probably seen the big emergency runway on the coast of England. In case you haven't I can tell you that it's wide enough for a half-dozen B-17s to land side by side in formation. That's where we're going. I'm going to lead you, in formation, right down that runway. We're going to land side by side, with you just about as close to me as you are now. I'll tell you and Sergeant Corey exactly what to do as we land. You won't have any problems. Did you get that too, Sergeant Corey?"

"Roger, sir, I read you loud and . . . "

Willis interrupted. "But sir, we don't have any hydraulic pressure so we don't have any brakes and we don't even know if the flaps are going to work or if the landing gear's going to come down."

"Even if they don't, I can still get you down all right. So stop worrying!"

"One other thing, Captain, uh, sir. I've been feeling pretty bad the last couple of minutes and right now it's getting real bad. Like I'm going to faint. And my face is turning numb around my mouth. I can't help it, sir."

Damn! Now what do we do? Robb pounded his right fist into his left palm repeatedly. If Willis faints that's the end of T-Tom and everybody in it. Better back off on Willis. Encourage him. Better get Corey into the other seat. Robb looked back at T-Tom's cockpit. Then it hit him that he had really screwed up. He yelled out loud to himself. "How stupid can you get! Willis is still on oxygen! He's hyperventilating! And it's because of my goddam stupidity!"

"Sergeant Willis." Robb spoke softer now, a note of concern in his tone. "You'll be all right. You're just getting too much oxygen. Now don't take off your mask. Just shut off the oxygen and take long, slow breaths into the mask. You won't smother. I want you to breathe your own air, the air you're exhaling. But keep both hands on the wheel except to turn off the oxygen.

"Sergeant Corey. Pull the mask away from Willis' face every fifteen seconds so he can get a breath of air. But you, Sergeant Willis, you keep both hands on the wheel."

"Now Sergeant Corey, I want you to take that morphine syringe on the throttle pedestal and give the remainder of the shot to Willis in his right forearm or wrist. Sergeant Willis, you keep both hands on the wheel. Corey can loosen your sleeve. As soon as you get the shot your numbness in the face and your faint feeling will be gone. Go to it, Sergeant Corey."

"Roger, sir." Corey had Willis' sleeve rolled back before Robb finished his transmission. He was now injecting the needle into Willis' forearm. "Now I want Sergeant Corey to push pieces of chocolate bar into your mouth, Willis, but I don't want you taking your hands off the controls when he does it."

Willis said, "Roger, sir."

Good! He's calming down. We might make it yet! Corey was already pulling Willis' mask away from his face and shoving pieces chocolate into his mouth. After two or three minutes Robb pushed his button. "How are you feeling now, Sergeant Willlis?"

"A lot better, sir."

"Good. Now Corey, pull off Willis' oxygen mask and snap on his throat mike."

Corey executed the maneuver quickly. "His throat mike's on him, sir."

"Good. Now I want you to lift the Lieutenant out of his seat. Be sure to unfasten his shoulder harness, seat belt, oxygen hose, and heated suit connections. Take off his Mae West and remove his .45 and his shoulder holster. Unsnap his parachute harness too. Now, when you lift him out of the seat do it very gently, slowly. Try to keep his tourniquet and leg bandages in place. Check to see if he's bleeding after you get him on the floor. Okay, Sergeant, go to it."

Robb could see the Tailgunner quickly disconnecting the straps, hoses, and wires that connected Rossi to the plane. Corey didn't appear to be a big man, and Robb had no idea how big the lieutenant was, yet the Tailgunner was up to the task. He already had his arms around the lieutenant and was lifting him through the space between the co-pilot's seat and the throttle pedestal.

—13—

The sea was calm. There was no way an untrained eye could discern where sky ended and water began. They had been descending at approximately fifty feet per minute for the past twenty or thirty minutes as the ceiling forced them ever downward. They were now three hundred feet above the surface of the North Sea. Robb was certain that Willis, without an altimeter, had no idea how low they were flying. And they'd be even lower by the time they crossed the coast. He pressed his button and was about to warn Willis not to be surprised by their altitude, or lack of it, when a long, gray-black object flashed under them. In the split second he saw it he recognized it for what it was: a small warship, either a destroyer or a corvette.

Sergeant Willis' voice crackled frantically in Robb's earphones. "Captain! Did you see that plane we just missed? Was it one of ours or a German fighter?"

"Nothing to worry about, Sergeant. We're flying quite low now, around three hundred feet above the surface of the North Sea. That was a warship you saw. One of ours. They didn't shoot at us because they're reading our IFF signal. That was probably a coastal patrol ship, so we're getting close to the English coast. Do you read me, Sergeant Willis? Over."

"R . . . Roger."

Robb looked at the clock on the instrument panel: 1841. He checked the time against his watch: 1841. Okay. Five minutes until we cross the coast. Better warn Willis. Robb looked back at T-Tom. The tailgunner was now in the co-pilot's seat.

"T-Tom, this is Amber Deputy. Acknowledge. Over."

"Roger. You got 'em, Captain."

Listen to that guy! He's acting like he belongs in that seat. Good enough! "Sergeant Corey. Good job with the lieutenant. Is he breathing all right?"

"He's breathing okay and he ain't bleeding right now."

"All right, then. I want to tell both of you what to expect and what to do." The altimeter now read 125 feet and they were still brushing the underside of the overcast. Damn! Fifty feet lower and we'll hit the trees when we cross the coast.

"Sergeant Willis. We're now down to 150 feet, which is just fine for us. It will make our approach to the runway that much easier. My co-pilot and I will be watching for church steeples and the like. You just watch us. When we cross the coast you're going to think we're flying right into the ground. We're not, but we will seem very, very low. Which is okay because we'll be on our landing approach. You got that, Sergeant Willis?"

"Roger."

Bradley was holding at 100 feet now. He had turned on all exterior running lights because they were now back in the bottom of the overcast. T-Tom's lights were still on. The bottom layer was thin enough that Robb could see T-Tom and they him, but they could see nothing below them because they were still over the North Sea where mist and water became one in their eyes. They dare not go any lower, but Robb knew, as did Bradley, that even though they would be in the overcast from time to time they would be able to see the ground through the bottom of the overcast once they crossed the English coast. The sun had set but there should be enough after-light to make out the trees and the ground. Or so he hoped. "Sergeant Corey, you'll see a toggle switch marked 'flaps' on the central control panel forward of the throttle pedestal." There was an incredible maze of switches, knobs, dials, and gauges on the panel. Would he find the right switch?

"Roger, Captain. I got my hand on it."

By God, he's quick! "Don't touch it yet, Sergeant. First, I want Willis to push all four throttles forward about half an inch. Slowly. Very slowly. You got that, Sergeant Willis?"

After a pause, Willis responded softly, "Roger."

Better reassure him. "There's nothing to it. You have to add a little power to make up for the added drag when I have Sergeant Corey lower the flaps a little. Are you ready? We've got to test them out for landing. Okay. Now push the throttles forward slowly."

T-Tom pulled abreast of Brillig but veered farther from Brillig as the two engines on the right side of T-Tom pulled against the single functioning engine on the left. Robb said nothing to Willis about his changed position, and Willis made the required correction with the ailerons, as Robb hoped he would. He motioned to Bradley to add power.

"Now, Sergeant Corey. When I say 'down', push down on the flap switch. And when I say 'stop' put the switch back to the neutral position it's in now. This is only going to take a couple of seconds so be ready to stop right away. Ready? Acknowledge."

"Ready when you are, Captain."

"Okay, Sergeant Corey. Get ready. Now, *down*! Now stop! Good!" The flap on the near wing had lowered about 15 degrees. Better check the other side. "Sergeant Willis. Look out your window. Is the left wing flap lowered about fifteen degrees?"

"Captain, it's not down at all. It's still even with the trailing edge of the wing."

"Are you sure?"

"I'm sure."

"How does the plane feel?"

"That's the funny part of it. The plane's flying easier now, not always trying to pull to the left, away from you."

Robb nodded to himself. Of course! They've only got the flap on one side working but it's on the side with twice as much power so it's balancing the thrust, adding drag to the side with more thrust. Good! Well, good for now. But what happens when they try to land with one flap down? This means that he really can't add even half flaps on landing, to say nothing of full flaps. If he lowers the one flap any more than now he'll increase lift on the flap side and the plane could flip over on its side. They're going to have to leave the flap setting as is and come in dammed fast, with no brakes. I should say that *we're* going to have to come in fast, with no flaps, or 15 degrees at best. Willis doesn't know how to come in nose-high at near stalling speed, hanging it on the props for a short-field landing. All we can do is make the approach at about 140 miles an hour and chop the power when we see the runway.

"Okay, Sergeant Willis. We're in luck. The one flap working is on the good side. It's compensating for the extra power on the right side by adding drag on that side. When I tell you to cut power when we're over the runway there'll be a tendency for the left wing to stall out first. So I'm going to have Sergeant Corey raise the one good flap, the right side one, at the same time we cut the power off. You got that, Sergeant Corey?"

"Roger, Captain. I got it. You give me the word and I raise the flap the same time we cut off the power. Who cuts off the power? Me or Willis? Over."

"*You* do. You cut the power when I tell you. You got that?"

"Roger. I'll cut it off right when you say so. And raise the flap at the same time."

"Good. Now Sergeant Corey, there's a switch to the left of the flap switch marked 'Landing Gear'. Do you see it?"

"Roger, Captain. I've got my hand on it."

"Take your hand off of it for now. Now, Sergeant Willis, I want to talk to you. We're going to try letting down the wheels now. Push the throttles another half inch forward."

Robb motioned to Bradley to add a half inch of power. Their position in relation to T-Tom remained unchanged. "Now, Sergeant Corey, flip the landing gear switch down and hold it down."

"Roger, Captain. Gear coming down."

The wheel on the near side came down all the way, slowly and evenly. The farther wheel descended about a foot and stopped. "Damn!" Bradley leaned forward to get a look at T-Tom. He couldn't quite get a line on it but Robb held his hands palms down in front of him, the left one higher than the right. Bradley nodded, and made an upward motion with his left hand. Then he leaned toward Robb and yelled, "Let's hope they go back up!"

Robb pointed to the loop antenna switch and yelled, "Time to tune in Broadway. Tune them in and get a fix on the loop right now. Then get them on the horn and get an altimeter setting and tell them to clear the runway. Be sure to tell them that there's two of us coming in side by side!"

Bradley switched on the loop receiver to tune in Broadway. He hit the directional switch and the needle on a large dial in the center of the instrument panel jumped to life. The beam tone increased in volume and when the sound began to diminish he reversed the switch, returning it to neutral when the beam sound reached maximum volume. The needle stopped on a heading two degrees to the left of Brillig's present heading. Bradley made the two degree correction in their heading.

Bradley pushed his intercom button as he gently corrected two degrees left to a heading of 272 degrees. "Good job, Fritz. Your course and the loop just about match. If your ETA is as accurate as your heading, we should be crossing the coast within a minute".

Robb pushed his button. "Sergeant Corey. I've decided you'll have an easier time landing if you go in with your wheels up. So push the landing gear switch upward and hold it there until I tell you to put it in neutral. Okay, push it up."

"Roger, sir. Gear coming up." The wheels disappeared into the underside of the plane.

"Okay, stop." Robb breathed a sigh and made an upward gesture with both hands as he looked at Bradley.

Bradley nodded and then pointed down suddenly, yelling, "We just crossed the coast."

Robb saw the trees flashing under their wings at 200 miles per hour. It seemed he could reach out and touch them. He pushed the command button. "Amber Deputy to . . ." Willis' yell stopped him short.

"Captain! Do you see those trees? We're damn near hitting 'em!"

"Sergeant Willis. I see those trees just as I've seen them dozens of times like this. They seem closer than they are. Listen carefully. We're three minutes from touchdown. The runway is straight ahead of us. I'm going to start backing off on the throttles now to slow our speed down a bit. I want Sergeant Corey to handle the throttles from now on so you can keep both hands on the wheel.

"Sergeant Corey, start pulling back on the throttles very slowly when I give you the word. Sergeant Willis, you'll have to pull back slightly on the wheel as we reduce power. Ready?"

Corey came back, "Roger, Captain. I've got both hands on the throttles now."

"I don't want you to have *both* hands on the throttles. Grab the top bar that controls all four throttles with your left hand. You'll be needing your right hand for other things."

"Roger, Captain. Left hand on top throttle bar."

Christ, he sounds cheerful. "Are you ready, Sergeant Willis? Remember, you have to pull back on the wheel as Corey eases back on the throttles. Acknowledge."

"Roger."

He's sounding scared again. Kick his ass! Give him hell! "Roger what? Soldier!"

"Roger, *sir*!"

"That's better! Now, Sergeant Corey, start easing back on the throttles. Slowly, slowly. Keep your nose up, Willis!" Christ! He lost twenty feet! Okay. He's pulling it back up now. Their airspeed decreased gradually . . . 180 . . . 160. The needle moved through the 150 mark. At 140, Robb commanded, "Okay. Hold the throttles right there. That's perfect. Good job! Good job, Sergeant Willis. Hold it right there. This is the speed we're going to land at. You're going to land wheels up so you won't even need brakes if you had them. You'll stop fast enough.

"Keep your hand on the throttles, Corey, and you, Willis, keep both hands on the wheel." He took a deep breath and exhaled slowly. "Now, Corey, when I yell '*cut*', you pull all throttles all the way back and raise that right flap at the same time. And then I want you to immediately hit all four of the big red feathering buttons on the instrument panel just forward of the control pedestal. Do you see the big red feathering buttons?"

"Roger, sir. I got my hand on 'em."

"Take your hand off them! Now then, when the time comes and I give you the word, hold the feathering buttons down until the props stop turning. Then take your hands off the feathering buttons and hit all four of the 'engine on-off' ignition switches right below them. Switch them off as soon as the props stop turning. You got that?"

"Got it, Captain. When you give the word I make like a one-armed paper hanger. Cut the throttles, raise the flap, hit the feathering buttons, and when the props stop, hit the off switches. How come I hit all the buttons when we already got one feathered?"

"Don't worry about it. Just hit all four feathering buttons."

"Roger. No sweat, Captain. Over."

"Very good, Sergeant." Robb couldn't help grinning. That guy obviously always wanted to be a pilot. He's actually enjoying all this! Another Hoyt or Boo! Too bad they didn't have an engineer to shut off the gas to the engines right after feathering. But they shouldn't explode if the engines aren't turning when the props hit the runway. In wheels-up landings fires usually start when the turning props hit the runway and the engines are twisted loose on their mounts and the gas lines break, shooting gasoline over the hot exhaust manifolds. Robb's heart fell as he admitted to himself that the engines could be wrenched loose on their front-to-back axis if a prop blade hits the runway squarely in the down position. God, don't let them burn!

Bradley hit Robb on the arm, indicating that he wanted him to raise his right earphone. "Broadway says we can't land there! There's two B-17s piled up on the runway! They said we should go to our own base!"

"Son of a bitch!" He looked wild-eyed around the cockpit. "No! No, damn it! No! No!" He suddenly felt numb. He slowly turned his head and looked around the cockpit as though seeing it for the first time. He was surprised to be back in the world of here and now. He had been so completely absorbed in the plight of T-Tom and their approach to the emergency runway that he found it difficult to adjust to a new set of realities. He looked at Bradley, almost surprised to find him sitting there, flying the plane.

He gave his head his quick back-to-reality shake. He closed his eyes as he tried to figure what to tell those two men trying to fly an airplane they didn't know how to fly, a plane carrying their dead and dying comrades. A flying butcher shop! What can I possibly say to Willis? Any more bad news could tilt him over the edge. What would Stosh tell him? The solution came to him immediately. Lie! That's it! Lie to him! "Amber Deputy to Amber Tom. Over."

"Go ahead, Deputy." Corey's jaunty voice. Ignore Corey. Talk to Willis.

"Sergeant Willis. I just got word that the ceiling is better at Allsford Lynn than at Broadway and it's only ten minutes farther, so I've decided to take us on home. You'll have an easier time of it landing at Allsford Lynn. Do you read me, T-Tom?"

"Loud and clear, sir. We go to Allsford Lynn. No sweat. Over."

"Engineer, respond please."

"Roger, sir. We go to Allsford Lynn." Willis sounded tentative.

"We're in luck, Sergeant Willis. The ceiling is a lot better there."

Bradley switched the loop antenna receiver to Allsford Lynn's navigational frequency. As Bradley worked the directional control, the needle finally settled on a heading eighteen degrees south of their present course. Bradley eased the plane to the new heading so slowly Willis didn't realize he had made a turn. As the direction finder needle approached zero, Bradley eased out of the turn, again imperceptibly. He then switched to the Allsford Lynn tower frequency.

Robb could see Bradley's lips moving as he talked to their home tower. He seemed to be speaking forcefully. He turned and tapped Robb's arm. "Operations wants us to find some other base to land on! The Group just crossed the cone of silence and they're peeling off over the base. He says we're going to get to the main runway at about the same time they do. He says we can't block the runway with T-Tom's crash landing even if we could squeeze in between them. He's right, Robb. We can't block the main runway!"

Robb yelled out loud to no one. "Christ! No!" He pounded his fist into his hand. "No, goddamn it! No!" He rubbed his eyes. "I don't believe this!"

Bradley stole a one-second glance at Robb. He reached out to put a hand on Robb's arm, but he thought better of it. He continued weaving gently around the higher trees, even though he would have probably cleared the highest of them by ten or twenty feet.

Robb shook his head violently. Get with it, goddamn it! What do we do now? He kept pounding his fist into his hand. They could look for a runway of some other outfit, Eighth Air Force or RAF, and hope to fly straight on in. No, Willis couldn't do the sudden maneuvering he'd have to do to get lined up on a strange runway, and even if he could there'd be no way of knowing if the runway was long enough. Besides, how are you going to find another airfield from 100 feet up, half the time in the soup? Robb yelled to his co-pilot. "Who's the OD for Operations today?"

"Hammersmith."

"Okay, Monk. You switch to Command and monitor T-Tom and I'll switch to Allsford Lynn. I want to talk to Hammersmith!"

"Amber Deputy to Upshaw Tower. Over."

"This is Upshaw tower. Over."

"Upshaw Tower, we've got one hell of an emergency here. I'm leading T-Tom home in formation, in and out of the soup at a hundred feet.

T-Tom's engineer and a gunner are flying the plane and it's shot to hell and they've got a lot of wounded people. Either we come into Allsford Lynn or its curtains for them. I mean all of them! Over."

"Roger, Amber Deputy. I understand your situation, but the Group just started its letdown. You can try to find some other base or you can go into a holding pattern. Over."

"No way, Operations. T-Tom has no flaps so we're coming in hot. We can't go anywhere other than home. There's no way T-Tom could do the maneuvers we'd have to do to get lined up on a strange runway. They're just able to keep it flying straight ahead. If we make a sudden turn they'll hit the ground. You know that as well as I do. Over."

"Upshaw Deputy. I read you loud and clear. But the Group's on its way in so you'll have to do the best you can. You can go somewhere else, or you can go into a holding pattern. Over."

"A holding pattern! At less than 100 feet in and out of the soup with two non-pilots flying the plane and no instruments—even if they could read them! Come on, Red! I don't think you understood one fucking word I said!"

"Amber Deputy. I do understand your situation. We simply can't wipe out the other planes to save T-Tom. It's as simple as that. Over."

"From what height did they start the letdown? Over."

"Eighteen thousand feet."

"Okay, Red, here's what I'm going to do. I'm going to land on the main runway but I'm going to have T-Tom land wheels up on the grass next to the runway. This way the wreck won't block the runway. I think I can beat the first planes in. Over."

"Sorry, Amber Deputy. I can't authorize that. You'll be getting to the runway about the same time as the first planes from the Group. *I specifically forbid you to land on the main runway.* Acknowledge! Over."

"I read you, Red. I'll be touching down on the main runway in seven minutes, with T-Tom beside me on the grass. Warn all planes in the letdown and have the fire trucks and ambulances standing by. Over and out." He switched off the tower.

He turned to Bradley and yelled wildly, "Find a runway somewhere else! Go into a holding pattern! Hah!" Robb looked manic, his eyes glassy. "Can you see those two non-pilots flying a holding pattern? Even if they had instruments?"

Bradley hardly dared blink for fear he'd run into a tall tree or a church steeple, but he stole another glance at Robb. Robb took command of himself. He leaned toward Bradley and yelled, "We're going straight on in to the main runway! Put us down at the very left edge of the runway. We'll put T-Tom down on the grass!"

Robb switched back to command. He instructed Corey to move his throttles forward a full inch and cautioned Willis to put forward pressure on the control column to compensate for the ship's tendency to climb with added power. The airspeed indicator climbed back up to 200 miles per hour. Willis' vertical undulations and horizontal weaves were amplified by the higher speed. They were flying eighty feet above the ground and barely clearing the tallest trees.

Robb suddenly experienced one of his moments of deadly rationality. He grinned mirthlessly. We're going like hell at treetop level, flying formation with a plane that's weaving and bobbing because the guys flying it have never flown a plane before. One guy's got the wheel and the other guy's got the throttles. Their plane is all shot to hell and full of guys who are dead or dying, the weather's shitty, it's damned near dark, and they're heading for a crash landing in formation with me, and we'll be getting to the runway at the same time as a bunch of planes whose pilots have just one idea: get it on the ground now, no matter what! He shouted out loud, each syllable long, the beat measured, *"I-don't-believe-this!"*

Bradley raised his left earphone. "I didn't get that, Robb! What did you say?"

Robb yelled, "Nothing!" He suppressed his rationality by an act of will. He turned to T-Tom. "Amber Tom. You're looking real good." His tone revealed none of the turmoil churning within him. They flew for five minutes with no communication between the two planes other than an occasional encouraging word from Robb .

"Sergeant Corey, you can start backing off the throttles slowly to where they were before we speeded up. Sergeant Willis, you'll have to add a little back pressure on the wheel as the power is cut. Okay, Corey. Back the power off, slowly. Starting *now*." Robb pointed to the throttles and yelled to Bradley to slow down to 140.

"Sergeant Corey, hold the throttles there." Willis and Corey made the change but their plane wandered as though flown by a drunk driver. Robb yelled to Bradley, "Call the tower. Tell them we're a minute from touchdown. Don't *ask* them. *Tell* them!"

He turned his attention back to T-Tom. "Okay, T-Tom. Everything's on schedule. We touch down one minute from now." He steeled himself to keep his tone level, confident. "T-Tom, I've decided to have you land on the grass on the left-hand side of the runway. It's been raining and the ground should be soft and muddy. This will make your landing softer and will avoid sparks which could cause a fire."

Bradley lowered Brillig's landing gear and cracked the landing flaps fifteen degrees.

"Sergeant Corey. Do you remember exactly what you're supposed to do with the throttles, the flap, the feathering buttons, and the engine-off switches?"

"No sweat, Captain. I know exactly what I gotta do."

"Okay, men. Get ready. Willis, do everything in slow motion. Take your time. Don't make any quick movements." Robb's pulse was thumping in his ears but his voice was steady, authoritative. "Okay, Willis. I see the runway lights dead ahead." He turned to Bradley and yelled, "Remember, put us down on the very left edge of the runway. I'll take over the throttles so I can keep us ahead of T-Tom." Bradley nodded.

The beginning of the runway lights was two hundred yards ahead, rushing at them at 140 miles an hour. "Okay men. Get ready. Here we go! *Cut power!*" Robb pulled all the way back on his own throttles as he barked the order to Corey. "Okay, Willis, push your nose down a little. That's good. Now start pulling back. Easy! You're pulling back too much!" The huge airplane shot abruptly upward, out of sight into the overcast some seventy feet above the runway.

"Push forward on the wheel, slowly, gently!" The battered plane reappeared at the underside of the overcast, flying level now, its momentum still well beyond stalling speed although its props stood starkly motionless, feathered.

"Good. You're doing good now, Willis." He was sounding too excited. Settle down! "Ease forward on the wheel now. That's it. Your left

wing is a little low. Lift it up. That's good. A little more forward on the
wheel. Good! You're coming down nicely. Good!"

Willis held it level twenty feet above the ground.

"Ease the wheel forward a little. Just a little. Good! Now start
pulling back. Slowly. That's it. Pull it back a little more. Okay, hold it
right there. Hold it off the ground. The ground is six feet below you now.
Hold it off! Good job, Willis." T-Tom was now even with Brillig, thirty
or forty feet to the left, its momentum rapidly dissipating.

"Pull back a little more, Willis. A little more. Hold it off the ground.
That's it! Hold it off! That's good! Hold it off the ground!" When is
that goddamn plane going to stall out? T-Tom passed Brillig.

"Hold it off! Good! You're going to grease it in right now! Now!
You're on the ground. Hold the wheel all the way back into your guts.
Keep it there! In your guts!"

The big Flying Fortress slammed into the soft earth. Huge geysers of
rain-drenched sod, silt and mud cascaded in great arcs on each side of the
sliding plane. Brillig touched down simultaneously with T-Tom, fifty or
seventy five feet farther back, but on the runway. The mud hit Brillig
squarely across its windshield and left cockpit windows. Robb could no
longer see T-Tom but he kept barking out instructions. Bradley kept
Brillig on the left side of the runway by looking out his right side window, estimating his distance from the far side of the runway.

Robb yelled, "Willis! Keep it going straight with your rudder pedals! Steer it like a goddamn sled! With your feet! If it turns right, give
it a left foot. If it turns left, kick the right rudder. When it stops sliding,
both of you jump out your side windows and run like hell! Good!
You're looking good. Real good!"

His window and windshield covered with mud, Robb hadn't noticed
that Brillig had almost stopped rolling and that Bradley was turning to
the right onto a taxi strip.

"T-Tom. How are you?"

Corey's voice came back, "We're just fine, Captain. Just now stopping. Getting ready to jump out the window. Be seeing you! Over and
out!"

Robb ripped off his earphones and throat mike. "Good man! You
crazy goddamned tailgunner!"

Brillig stood still on the taxi strip just off the runway, its props ticking over slowly. Robb suddenly realized they weren't moving. He rubbed his face with his hands, slowly, firmly. His hands remained over his eyes, his chest rising and falling. The narcotic of relief, sudden and complete, surged through him. He turned to Bradley. Bradley was grinning at him. Robb suddenly realized he had barely given a thought to Bradley for the past several hours. Only a few near-automatic instructions. Bradley had flown the plane since they broke out under the overcast, and he had skimmed the surface of the North Sea and he had dodged trees and he had landed under incredibly adverse circumstances so smoothly that Robb hadn't noticed when they ceased flying.

He extended his hand toward Bradley. They shook hands. Robb said, "What can I say? No one could have done better." He studied his co-pilot's face. He looked much older than his 22 years. "How are you feeling, Monk?"

Neither Bradley's grin nor his laughing eyes could obscure the gray mantle of fatigue that lay upon his face like a mask. His cheeks seemed to crack as he grinned. "Just fine, Captain. Just getting ready to jump out the window!"

They began to laugh. uncontrollably, hysterically, until tears streamed down their cheeks. Bradley finally said, "Don't press that transmitter button right now or they'll give us a rubber room in Section Eight!" They started laughing again.

They were startled back to reality by Wieriman who now stood behind their seats. "Robb, the Group's coming in now. They'll need this taxi strip to clear the runway quick."

Robb shook his head. "Thanks, John. Monk, I'm getting out here to go to T-Tom. You taxi it in. Better tune in the tower." He got up stiffly. He climbed down into the nose compartment and unlatched the bottom escape hatch. He waved to his navigator and bombardier as he dropped through the hatch onto the asphalt taxi strip.

——14——

Robb moved quickly toward Brillig's tail, around her left wing to avoid her spinning propellers and on toward the rear of the plane. As he emerged from under the horizontal stabilizer he motioned to Sergeant Wieriman, now back in his top turret, to give Bradley the go sign.

The last faint light of day, the light that had been so reluctantly granted by the heaviest of overcasts, had given way to the blackest night. The driving rain they had taken off in thirteen hours earlier had become a gentle drizzle. He immediately saw T-Tom. The ravaged Flying Fortress was bathed in a blaze of ambulance and fire truck spotlights. T-Tom had come to rest in the mud about 100 feet on the other side of the runway and some 400 feet beyond the taxi strip upon which he stood. A huge, plowed scar in the grass and mud on the other side of the runway marked T-Tom's path to its resting place.

Robb looked to his left as he prepared to run across the runway. He stopped in his tracks. A B-17, its landing lights blazing, rushed at him at a high rate of speed, followed by another plane a scant 200 yards behind it. A third B-17, having overshot on its approach, was touching down closely behind the two now rushing at him.

The first plane roared past followed closely by the second, both of them with power on to give the guy who overshot as much room as possible. Robb knew Hammersmith would be screaming at those first two guys to lay the coal on. The third B-17 flashed past, its brakes squealing deafeningly and its tires screaming. Robb was about to dash across the runway when he saw yet another on-rushing B-17. He waited, ready to make his dash as soon as it passed, but it didn't pass him. Instead, its pilot hit hard right brake and right rudder and gave his left outboard engine a full shot of power and swung his still fast rolling ship into the taxi strip where Robb stood. Robb dove headlong, face down, into the mud next to the taxi strip as the blasting outboard propeller whirled over his head.

"You dumb son-of-a-bitch!" He cursed his own stupidity, not the pilot of the plane that had damned near chopped him up. He knew that guy had to get off the runway fast. No doubt the tower had warned him of another plane behind him. He pushed himself up to a kneeling position in the mud, his back to the runway, and tried to shake the slimy silt from his hands. Just as he stood up the sudden full-throated roar of yet another set of engines struck him with the force of a physical blow as another plane swung wildly into the taxiway. He hit the mud again, face down. The outboard prop of a second B-17 roared over his head and was gone in a blast of prop wash as quickly as it had appeared.

Robb dashed across the runway, barely making it ahead of another plane. He slogged his way at a trot to T-Tom's side. A floodlight was focused on the gaping hole where T-Tom's waist window had been. Her interior was lighted by emergency drop cords. A medic, flashlight in hand, peeled back the eyelid of a crewman on a stretcher being passed through the hole in the side of the ship.

"No rush with this one, men. He's dead." Robb recognized the voice of Tony Rizzo.

"Tony! How many made it?"

Rizzo turned his flashlight to Robb's face. "Robb! What the hell you doing here?"

"I led these guys in. The engineer and a gunner flew it in. How many made it?"

"We've taken out four. All dead. But the guys who flew it in have to be alive. They haven't come out yet."

Robb turned around and yelled, "Sergeant Willis! Sergeant Corey!" A man in muddy, bloody, flying clothes appeared at the hole in the ship.

"Sergeant Willis?"

"I'm Corey."

"I'm Amber Deputy who led you in. Why didn't you jump out the window when I told you to?"

"I did, but I came back when I saw she wasn't going to burn. To check the crew. They're all dead except Lieutenant Rossi and Willis. Looks like Lieutenant Rossi's damn near dead." Corey's tone was matter of fact, much as Boo's or Hoyt's would have been.

Rizzo demanded, "Where's Rossi?"

Medical corpsmen appeared with another stretcher. A corpsman held a plasma bottle over the prone figure.

Corey said, "This one's Lieutenant Rossi, sir,"

Rizzo pulled off Rossi's helmet and goggles and focused his flashlight on the pilot's face. Rizzo turned back Rossi's eyelid and focused his flashlight on his eye. "Get this one to the hospital on the double."

Robb turned to Corey. "Where's Willis? Did he come back to the plane?"

"No sir. He never jumped out. I yelled for him to get out but he just sat there staring, holding the wheel in his guts."

"You did one hell of a good job, Sergeant." He climbed through the hole in the fuselage and made his way through the bomb bay to the flight deck, now eerily lighted by bare bulbs on extension cords. He stepped around a prone crewman as he passed beneath the top turret. He knew it must be Lieutenant Coleman.

Sergeant Willis sat in the pilot's seat. The cockpit was a shambles, a jumble of wires and tubes and broken gauges hung from where the instrument panel had been. The floor of the flight deck was covered with blood, bandages, the contents of medical kits and the remnants of airplane instruments, all smeared helter skelter by the flying boots of crew members as they struggled to save Lieutenants Coleman and Rossi and the plane itself.

Willis sat perfectly still staring blankly ahead, the control wheel pulled tightly against his belly. Robb was astounded. This guy had been holding up the huge, heavy tail elevator foil all this time! He leaned over and placed his hand on Willis' shoulder. He gently removed Willis' right hand from the wheel, grasping the wheel with his own right hand. He reached across him and removed his other hand from the wheel and eased the heavy control column forward until it rested in full forward position. He was shocked to see that Willis' jacket was covered with dried blood. Oh my God! Not him too! Then he remembered that Willis would have been the one to lift his pilot, Lieutenant Coleman, out of his seat.

"I'm Captain Robertson, Sergeant Willis. I'm Amber Deputy, the person who talked to you all afternoon. You did one hell of a job, Sergeant." Willis continued staring into the blackness beyond the windshield.

"Sergeant Willis, stretch your arms straight ahead, in front of you. Slowly." He knew Willis' arms must be cramped from holding up the dead weight of the huge elevator airfoil for such a long time. "Stretch your arms forward, Sergeant."

The Sergeant's arms moved slowly toward the instrument panel.

"Good. Stretch them all the way forward. Hold them there. Open and close your hands. That's fine. Keep it up. Good. Now reach up and pull your helmet and goggles off." Willis did as he was told. He turned his head slowly and looked up at Robb. He seemed dazed, his eyes glassy. The gargoyle mouth outline left by his oxygen mask was deeply imprinted into the bridge of his nose and the skin of his cheeks. His skin was pale white where the mask and goggles had been but sooty, near black where his face had been exposed—an open-mouthed, wide-eyed apparition. Willis turned slowly back to the blackness of the windshield.

Robb guessed Willis to be three or four years older than himself, maybe thirty or so. He was very thin, his thinness that of one who had flown a lot of missions. His naturally narrow features gave him a cadaver-like appearance, a dirty-faced cadaver with sandy hair matted against its head. "Sergeant Willis. You've been overseas quite a while, I can tell. You're not a from a new crew. How come you're flying with the 990th? I don't remember seeing your crew before."

Willis answered softly, "We joined you yesterday. We're from the Hundredth, on loan to you while they put our outfit back together again."

Robb spontaneously put his hand on Willis' shoulder when he uttered the fateful Group designation. The Hundredth! The 100th Heavy Bombardment Group, the Group wiped out repeatedly by the German fighters, the Group whose very number connoted disaster, destruction, death. Robb's heart went out to the skinny, defeated creature in the pilot's seat. Oh Christ! The Bloody Hundredth! This guy has been through the worst kind of hell over and over again. And now this!

Robb half-sat with his rump on the edge of the throttle pedestal. "Sergeant Willis, would you like to stand up now? You'll feel better if you move around a bit."

Willis turned slowly. "How many made it?" A hoarse whisper.

"Do you mean on your crew?"

Willis nodded.

He wondered how to soften the blow. He could think of nothing to say.

"How many?" Almost a croak.

"Sergeant Willis," he gripped the engineer's shoulder firmly, "three made it."

"That makes only five, counting me and Corey." Willis put his knuckles to his lips, pressing hard.

"No, Sergeant. Three of your crew made it, including you and Sergeant Corey."

"Only three? Seven dead? Pepper? Ringer? Kenny? Oh my God!" He stared open mouthed, slack-jawed, at Robb. "How awful! How dirty, stinking, rotten awful!" He was sobbing now, his head in his hands against the wheel. "Everybody! Everybody! The whole Hundredth! Again and again! I wish . . ." His words became unintelligible. His body jerked spasmodically.

Tony Rizzo appeared behind Robb. "Can I help?"

Robb squeezed Willis' shoulder. "I'll be back in a minute."

He looked into Rizzo's eyes and nodded toward the rear of the plane. They made their way through the bomb bay. Robb turned into the radio operator's compartment. The floor was slimy with blood. The human odors and the powerful smell of gunpowder were overwhelming. Robb said, "Let's get out of here."

They went to the waist. The waist was worse than the radio compartment. Robb knew the blood-soaked lumps on the floor must surely be lumps of flesh. Hoyt was right: a butcher shop! He climbed out of the plane through the jagged, gaping opening in the ship's side. With the plane resting wheels-up on its fuselage, the ground was only a couple feet below the bottom of the opening. Rizzo followed.

The spotlight that had been focused on the hole in the ship had been turned off but the generator truck remained on the taxi strip a hundred yards away, its motors humming as they fed current to the temporary lights strung inside the plane. A lone ambulance stood beside the truck.

A soldier approached Captain Rizzo. "Excuse me, sir. I kept one ambulance back. Are we going to need it here, or should I take it back?"

"I'll let you know in a minute, Corporal." Rizzo turned to Robb "That man in the cockpit should be put to bed in the hospital for tonight.

My men will take him to the hospital, so you can leave now. I have my jeep here. I'll drop you off at the whiskey tables."

"I'd like to take him to the hospital. I was pretty rough on him to-day—to keep him from folding in the cockpit. He must think we're a bunch of ghoulish bastards, insensitive to what he was going through and what he's been through. Did you know that he and his crew were on loan to us from the Hundredth, while the Hundredth re-groups?"

"Shit!" Rizzo's eyes widened incredulously. "And those other seven? They all survived the last wipeout of the Hundredth?"

"That's right. Rossi, too."

"Oh hell! Rizzo sighed. "I think it would be a good idea if you took the man up front to the hospital. Use my jeep. I'll go back with the ambulance."

Robb raised his leg over the bottom of the opening and pulled himself into the plane. He looked down on the flight surgeon. "Don't you think this guy Willis has had enough? Couldn't you simply declare him to be physically and psychologically exhausted and send him back to the States?"

Rizzo shook his head sadly. "That's not the way it works. You know that."

A scowl darkened Robb's face. He started toward the front of the plane. He didn't look back when he spoke. "Thanks for the use of the jeep."

Willis was sitting erect now, still staring at the windshield. "Sergeant Willis, I want you to come with me. I'm taking you to the hospital." Willis gave no sign of having heard him. "Sergeant Willis, I said you have to come with me now. To the hospital." The sergeant remained transfixed.

Robb leaned against the co-pilot's seat. He felt weak with fatigue. I should have had Rizzo stay. He could have handled this. He grasped Willis' shoulder and shook it firmly. The soldier's trance remained undisturbed. "Sergeant Willis, believe me, I want to help you. But if I have to get tough with you for your own sake I'm going to do it. Now stand up! That's an order!"

Willis stood up stiffly and stepped slowly into the space between the two seats. He didn't look at Robb. He walked slowly, slightly bent, toward the rear of the plane. He walked on the floor of the flight deck, still slippery with the blood of Lieutenants Coleman and Rossi, on through the bomb bay, the only unsullied part of the ship, past the bloody radio room and into the waist, the butcher shop.

Robb studied the back of the thin, slightly bent figure. Is he aware he's walking on blood? Does he have an image of the men whose lives it sustained this morning? Willis raised his left leg to step out of the hole in the side of the ship. His right foot slipped out from under him. Robb caught him, but too late. His feet slipped backwards and he landed on his face with Willis half on top of him. Neither man said a word as they got to their feet and wiped their hands on their clothes.

Robb kept a firm grip on the Willis' arm as he led him to the Rizzo's jeep. As they drove to the hospital, Robb decided not to try to jar him back to reality. He smiled mirthlessly. Reality?

He led the engineer up the gravel path to the hospital entrance. He sat Willis down in the vestibule and went to the counter and hit the little bell. The fire doors in the hall swung open and a nurse hurried through, her eyes focused on a clipboard. She looked up. "May I help . . . My God! Are you hurt?"

"I'm all right."

"But you've got blood all over you! Are you sure you're all right? Why are you here?"

Robb looked down at the front of his jacket and flying coveralls. He had forgotten his slip in T-Tom and his dives into the mud. He rubbed his hand across yesterday's stubble and saw the flakes of caked mud and blood on his fingers. "I'm all right. I just look like hell. I brought over Sergeant Willis, the man over there." He spoke very softly. "He flew a shot-up B-17 back from Germany today and he's not a pilot. And he lost most of his crew today. He's on loan to us from the Hundredth."

The nurse closed her eyes. She nodded toward Sergeant Willis. "Is he wounded?"

"No, but he's sort of in a trance. Tony said to bring him here."

She whispered, "Is Lieutenant Rossi from his crew?"

"Yes."

"And the other seven in the morgue?"

He nodded. "Is Rossi going to make it?"

"We don't know. It's touch and go right now."

Robb nodded. "I've got to go now. I'm late for debriefing." He turned to leave.

"Before you go, Captain. Uh . . . did Captain Kovacs come through this all right?"

"He's okay. At least he was when I left the Group over Germany. That was after the target so I'm sure he's all right." He studied her for a moment. "Are you Lieutenant Cameron?"

She nodded.

"I'm Robb Robertson."

"I . . . I hardly know what to say." She seemed to avoid looking into his face, her gaze now fixed on his mud-smeared and blood-caked flying suit. "How different all of this from what we'd planned for this weekend. I mean for you, and Captain Kovacs. How awful."

"We took one unlucky shot today. Just one. It's bad for the planes it hit and all of us feel sick about those men. But even so it's not nearly as bad as it used to be. I've got to go now. I'll tell Stosh you asked about him."

"I'll tell Evelyn you're all right."

He hurried to the jeep. The whiskey tables had been carried away by the time he pulled up in front of the debriefing room. He looked at his watch: 9:00 P.M.. He did a quick calculation: exactly nineteen hours since Swovic woke them up this morning. He needed a drink. He *really* needed a drink.

Kovacs was coming out of the debriefing room as Robb approached. "Robb! Where the hell you been?" He threw an arm around Robb's shoulders. "Good job with T-Tom. Too bad they lost so many guys. But they woulda lost 'em all if it hadn't been for you, pal."

"Knock it off. Would you mind coming back in with me while I go through debriefing? Then we can go to the club and have a few. I missed the whiskey line tonight."

"No sweat, pal. Debriefing won't be long. Monk and I told Sam everything he needs to know." He looked at Robb's flying clothes and made a sour face. "You look like you fell in a slit trench latrine."

"How was the letdown?"

"Same old crap. Long letdown, everybody running out of gas. But we all made it back except for those guys we lost over the target and in

T-Tom. Was that your plane sitting on the taxi strip across from T-Tom when I came in?"

"I got out there and ran over to T-Tom. Monk taxied on in."

"So you're the one that Pete DeLong almost chopped up! He told me there was some idiot standing on the taxi strip when he swung off the runway." Kovacs grinned. "He saw you take your dive."

"Tell him to keep his mouth shut about it." He put a hand on Kovacs' shoulder. "I saw Lieutenant Cameron—Merrie—at the hospital. I took one of T-Tom's guys over there. She asked if you got back all right. I could tell she'd been worrying about you."

Kovacs didn't say anything, but Robb saw a sudden softening of his expression.

They entered the debriefing room. All the other flyers had come and gone. They walked quickly to the table at the rear of the room where Sam was writing. Sam stood up and reached out to shake hands as Robb approached.

"I was beginning to worry about you. My God, you look awful! What happened?"

"I'll tell you some other time."

"Good job with T-Tom. I'm proud of you."

"Not much to be proud of. We lost twenty-seven men, and of the three survivors in T-Tom, one is near death and another one out of his mind. Ask me the questions real quick. I need a drink and so does Stosh. You're invited to join us."

"I can't. I've got to put together the intelligence report on the mission. I think I've got everything from Monk and Stosh. Are there any personal observations you'd like to make about the mission?"

"The leader of the outfit ahead of us in the task force fouled up. Bad. Very bad."

"Stosh told me about it. I'm including it in my report. Well, that's it, then. You're the last one in, so now I can start putting together my report. I can't tell you how glad I am to see both of you safe and sound." Sam shook hands with each of them.

As they walked in the drizzle toward the club and mess hall, Kovacs said, "Sam always seems surprised we made it back."

Robb having missed the whiskey tables, they decided to get a quick drink in the club before going into the mess hall. They stopped dead in their tracks a couple of paces inside the entrance. The place was deserted. The mug with the face on it on the back bar was turned to the wall behind the bar. The bar was closed. The 990th was alerted.

The two pilots stood silently staring at the darkened bar. Robb swayed as he stood there. Kovacs must have noticed; he put an arm around his friend's shoulders. Robb's shock gradually gave way to resignation. "I don't believe it! I just don't believe it!" He sounded very, very tired.

"What do you mean, you don't believe it? You new around here? When we walked over here it was raining. Right? And the ceiling was down to about 50 feet, and the horizontal visibility was down to about two hundred yards. Right?"

Robb nodded, his mouth half open. Waves of fatigue engulfed him. Kovacs' arm was strong, assuring.

"Okay. So this is the worst damned flying weather possible. So what's so surprising about us flying a mission tomorrow?"

They went into the mess hall. Some of the privates working the serving line made no effort to conceal their anger at having to work late. The mess sergeant was required to keep a close check on the debriefing room by phone to make sure all the flyers were through before shutting down the chow line. The soldiers working the line knew these two captains were the last two for the night, and they knew that if these two hadn't been so late they could have had the line shut down and been back in their barracks by now, or the enlisted men's club. Some made an obvious display of turning down lights and carrying out trays as soon as Robb and Kovacs passed their section of the line.

Kovacs seethed, as he always did when ground pounders complained about their lot, or if they simply looked unhappy. But he didn't show it. He simply said, "Scrambled eggs, please." The private in charge of the rubbery powdered eggs made no effort to conceal his anger as his eyes met Captain Kovacs'. His eyes held Kovacs' eyes as he dumped the eggs on Kovacs' plate without looking down, as if to say "Take that!"

Robb saw the private's defiant gesture, and he knew the man had just made the mistake of his life. Captain Stanley Kovacs could be remarkably patient at times, and it seemed to Robb his patience increased with his anger. Robb knew that this man with the shallow, gray eyes would yearn for the days when he served scrambled eggs to the flyers late at night in the warm, dry mess hall. Robb knew that by this time next week this man would be somewhere in France in the rain and mud, in the front lines with artillery shells whistling overhead, not knowing if the shells were coming in or going out. He knew that this man, now safe, warm, and dry, would soon be up to his ass in water in a foxhole in France. Too bad he couldn't have taken a lesson from Private Swovik.

Almost twenty hours had passed since they had last eaten. Kovacs shoveled down the rubber eggs and cold squares of Spam. Robb wasn't hungry but he made himself a Spam sandwich and washed it down with thick, black coffee. He wished it were a stiff whiskey and soda.

Kovacs picked up his and Robb's coffee mugs and walked back to the urn on the chow line. A private was wiping the steam table near the urn. "Soldier, is there a mess sergeant on duty back there?"

"Yeah. I mean, yes sir."

"Tell him I want to see him, please."

The mess sergeant appeared at Kovacs' table within a minute. "Sir, did you want to talk to me?"

"Yes, Sergeant. What's the name of that soldier over there? The blond guy with the tattoos and the cigarette in his mouth."

"Jack Crandall, sir. Actually, Private John Crandall."

"Thank you, Sergeant. That's all."

* * * * * * * *

It was a few minutes before 11:00 P.M. when they entered their barracks. All the other men had turned in. Kovacs poured vodka into a grapefruit juice can. Each man took a long pull on it.

Two minutes after they turned out the lights and climbed into their bunks. Private Swovik appeared as if by magic. They knew they had been in the sack for exactly two minutes when the door opened and the flashlight beam appeared next to their bunks. You could set your watch by it.

"How many tonight, sir?"

They each took two.

Three hours later, at precisely 1:59 A.M., Private Swovik appeared again at the barracks. He stood just inside the door. He stood there for exactly one minute, his flashlight beam focused on his watch. The rain pounding on the corrugated steel arch made a deep, resonant rumble. Private Swovik moved quickly toward Captains Kovacs' and Robertson's bunks.

———15———

On Friday morning, November 17, 1944, Robb contemplated London through the window of a boxy London cab as he and Sam rode from the railroad station to the hotel. The city's battle scars were obvious: a corner of a building missing here, a wing of another building gone; boarded-over windows in buildings otherwise intact; broken statuary and fountains, and innumerable other scars you scarcely noticed unless you looked for them. Yet, it seemed to Robb, London still had an air of stateliness and normalcy, even beauty, that was surprising after five years of a war in which it had been the Luftwaffe's primary target. It occurred to him that London itself was as resilient as its people.

And then the cab passed a moonscape, a square mile or more in which nothing remained but heaps of rubble. He knew there were many areas such as this, whole sections of the city obliterated by the German bombers earlier in the war and, more recently, by V1 buzz bombs and V2 rockets. He looked away and put his hand over his eyes. He knew that this is what he himself and the whole Eighth Air Force and the RAF were doing to Hamburg, Leipzig, Cologne and a hundred other cities. The whole bloody, ghoulish goddam business is a complete abandonment of civilization, on both sides of the war, and he himself was in the middle of it, as guilty as anybody on either side! How many schools, hospitals, churches, old peoples' homes had his own bomb loads hit when they missed a railroad yard smack in the middle of a city? He gave his head the quick shake. Get off it! Look at this beautiful day!

Sam said, "How do you figure Stosh's inviting me along on this outing of his?"

"Maybe he needed a treasurer so he wouldn't have to handle all his poker winnings."

Sam tightened his grip on the suitcase on his lap. "That's my best guess."

"I think he wanted you in on the fun. It's as simple as that."

The cab pulled up to the main entrance of The Grosvenor House. The driver placed their two B-4 bags on the sidewalk. A porter appeared and reached for Sam's small suitcase. Sam hung on to it tightly. The porter relinquished his hold and picked up their bags. Sam placed a hand on the man's arm. "Thank you. We'll carry those."

Robb said, "You're sure chintzy with Stosh's money considering he gave you a suitcase full. He'd have given that driver a pound tip and another pound to that porter."

"I'm sure he would have, and in the process confirmed the English stereotype of American soldiers. I'm working in the opposite direction."

"You're doing a good job of it."

They crossed a broad hall which opened on an area of interconnected lounges. Robb was this morning, as always, impressed by the Grosvenor's elegant yet carefully understated decor and furnishings: chairs and sofas of rich leather, thick carpets with intricate yet subdued Oriental patterns, dark walnut paneling, heavy tapestries and draperies, huge oil paintings in gilded frames, polished brass knobs and handles and railings, crystal chandeliers, sparkling yet muted.

Robb was also impressed, as before, by the number and variety of attractive women on the arms of American colonels and generals. He knew most of these lovely women were members of the "companion corps", and he knew the top brass showered gifts (never cash) lavishly upon these beautiful young women of taste, grace, and discretion. The woman, for her part, was expected by the giver to remain loyal to her swain for a period of time. As they approached the front desk, an immaculately tailored clerk looked up and addressed Sam. "May I help you, sir?"

It was clear to Sam that the young man was less than enthusiastic at the prospect of dealing with two mere captains. Sam looked at the man for a moment, noncommittally. Finally he said coldly, "We have a reservation in the name of Captain Stanley Kovacs."

The clerk thumbed through a card file. "Ah yes, here it is, Captain. . . uh. . . Kovacs."

"Prentice. Captain Kovacs made the reservation."

"I wonder if you would come with me, please. It is necessary that we confer with the Assistant Manager about this reservation."

"Do we have a reservation or don't we?"

"Oh yes, but this isn't our usual, everyday sort of arrangement."

"All right, then," Sam grumbled.

"I'll wait here," Robb said.

The clerk knocked at an open doorway. "This is Captain Prentice, sir. He is here to pick up this reservation." He handed a card to his superior.

"Ah, yes. Very good." He dismissed the clerk with a nod. "Won't you be seated, sir."

Sam remained standing. "What seems to be the trouble?"

The Assistant Manager glanced at the card. "Oh, on the contrary, sir. No trouble at all. You see, your colleague, Captain . . . uh . . . uh . . . Kovacs . . . has reserved our most exclusive suite." The thin, balding Englishman made a church steeple with his forefingers. "This suite, sir, is designed precisely for the needs and tastes of high-ranking diplomats, dignitaries who may upon occasion entertain even heads of state. We are, as you know, in the heart of the embassy district."

"What, precisely, is your point?"

"Well, sir, in unusual circumstances such as these it is customary for us to request fifty percent in advance for these accommodations."

"How much do you get for the suite?"

The church steeple returned. "One hundred and twenty-five pounds sterling."

"Per week?"

"Per day."

Sam took a deep breath. "We'll take it. And we'll pay the entire bill in advance. For two days." Sam unlocked his suitcase and withdrew one of several stacks of five-pound notes. Sam counted out a stack of five-pound notes and placed them before the assistant manager. He snapped shut his suitcase. "Now, if we're through with this foolishness, I'd like the key to our room." He turned and walked out of the office. The assistant manager hurried after him.

The assistant manager switched on his smile. "Thank you again, Captain Prentice. I do hope you enjoy your stay with us. If there's anything we can do, don't hesitate to call me *personally*."

Robb and Sam stepped out of the elevator into a broad hallway. The number on the double doors across from the elevator corresponded to the number on the brass tag on the key. Sam unlocked the door and stepped into the darkened room. He felt along the wall until he found a switch. He flipped it. A blaze of light momentarily blinded them. They stared in awe at the huge crystal chandelier hanging from the ceiling of the spacious foyer. The light from a hundred tiny bulbs hidden in a maze of cut glass danced and sparkled, ricocheting across thousands of crystalline facets. Robb pushed his garrison cap forward so that the visor shaded his eyes. He scratched the back of his head and said, "As our friend and benefactor might say, that is one hell of a light fixture."

Sam moved on into the main room. He flipped a switch. Again dazzling light blazed forth from crystal chandeliers augmented by the light from numerous floor lamps and table lamps, all controlled by the single switch Sam had thrown. Robb said, "Kee-riste!"

Sam said, "I agree. This place is damned near half the size of the officers' club. Now I know why Stosh invited me. He needs people in here."

Sam surveyed the room. There were several furniture groupings. A single arrangement around one of the fireplaces was the only concession to the modern era—actually the 1930's—with deeply cushioned sofas and chairs. The other seating circles were furnished according to periods. Sam said, "It looks like we've got several rooms in one here. Take your pick. What'll it be? Louis Quinze? Chippendale? Hepplewhite?" He gestured toward the turgid, white, modern grouping. "Perhaps you prefer late Mussolini?"

"I couldn't care less."

Sam said, "Come on. Let's go see if this place has any bedrooms."

Robb didn't move. "You check on the bedrooms. I'd like to check out that concert grand piano. " He sighed. "But if I go over there, I'm going to want to play it."

"Why not? I'm sure that's one of the privileges that go with paying more than four hundred dollars a day."

"If I play it I may start caring too much about things we abandoned, like that navigator in our barracks with the savings account." He sighed. "To hell with it. Let's go take a look at it."

Robb stood for a moment appraising the magnificent instrument like an art lover studying a piece of fine sculpture. Sam was pleased at his friend's renewed interest in his world. Moments ago he had seemed alienated from everything.

Robb sat down on the piano bench and raised the fallboard. He raised his hands slowly to the keyboard and began the adagio movement of the Beethoven Sonata Pathetique. His fingers moved slowly, with control and sensitivity. The sonorous melody and the lower accompanying notes filled the spacious room. His eyes were closed as he played.

Sam Prentice sat in a nearby chair listening attentively, watching the figure at the piano.

Robb sat with his eyes closed for a time after the last notes of the adagio faded. Finally he shook his head, his quick back-to-reality shake.

Sam stood up. He said quietly, "You're a much better musician than I ever suspected."

Robb carefully closed the fallboard and stepped to the side of the piano and lowered the heavy lid. He turned to Sam and said, "Let's go have a five hundred dollar lunch on Stosh."

❋   ❋   ❋   ❋   ❋   ❋   ❋

After lunch they took a cab to the University of London. They arrived at the building that housed the University of London's Anthropology Department at 2:30 in the afternoon. They found the office door with the legend "Charles M. Williams-West, Ph.D., Professor of Anthropology", and under it the more recently painted words, "Office of the Journal of Social Anthropology".

Professor Williams-West's secretary picked up the phone and announced their arrival. The professor rose from his desk chair as the American officers entered. He was a portly man of medium height, late fifties or early sixties, Robb guessed. His complexion was ruddy, his face round, his chin double. A few strands of sand-colored hair were combed carefully over the top of his head, which was otherwise bald. His smile was genuine; his eyes smiled with the rest of his face.

Robb said, "I hope we're not interrupting your work."

"You are, of course, but it's a delightful interruption, I must say. It's not often I have an opportunity to talk to American flyers. You have no idea how good it is for us to read about you chaps giving the Huns what they gave us here in London."

Robb felt uncomfortable. He hated to read about the damage they inflicted on German cities. And he was bothered by the term "Hun". He hadn't heard that since junior high school when their music teacher made them sing childish World War I songs, including "Johnny get your gun/ Johnny show the Hun you're a son of a gun." Robb forced a smile. "I'm trying to find Cynthia Allsford."

The professor's eyebrows raised ever so slightly. "Ah yes. Cynthia Allsford. A strange young lady, I must say, but very bright and talented."

"Do you know where she lives, or how I might get in touch with her?"

The professor shook his head. "I'm afraid I'll not be much help to you on that. Miss Allsford left without leaving a forwarding address."

Robb closed his eyes.

"I'm so sorry." The professor's regret was genuine. "I wish I could help you."

Sam said, "Did you know her very well? Perhaps she might have said something at some time or other, something that might give us a clue to her whereabouts."

"I'm afraid I can't help you there either. I suppose you tried her family home in Cambridgeshire."

Robb said, "There's only an old servant there. He says he knows of no such person."

"A strange situation, I must say! She simply phoned one day to inform me that she was resigning her position immediately. A few days later I received in the post all of the journal's materials she had. That's the last I heard from her. I tried to get in touch with her by phone and by post, with no success whatsoever. I suppose you've been to her Cambridge address? That was her residence as well as the office of the Journal."

"We made inquiries there. That's how we found out about the Journal, and you."

Professor Willliams-West rose from his chair and walked to the window and looked out over the top of his glasses. He turned and looked at Robb. "Please tell me if I'm prying, Captain." He studied Robb obliquely. "In what context did you know her?"

Robb studied the backs of his hands. He spoke without looking up. "I don't quite know how to put this. Let's say that I developed a strong emotional attachment to her."

"But surely you must know a great deal about her—where she might run to, what she is running from, that sort of thing—if you knew her well enough to form such an attachment."

Robb looked helplessly at Sam and back to the professor." I really don't know much about her at all. This must sound strange but all I can say is that's the way it is."

"Oh, I quite understand. I was young once myself, hard though my students find that to believe. We have a song here in England, a song by Purcell. The words go, 'There is a lady passing by, 'twas never face more pleased my eye. I did but see her passing by, and yet I'll love her till I die.'"

Robb was acutely embarrassed. Sam interjected quickly, "Did you see her in person very often? Enough to get to know her?"

"Rarely. She did her work for the journal in Cambridge and I did mine here. Of course, I talked to her on the telephone quite often. The only time I talked to her about anything other than the purely professional was on that one occasion when I took her to lunch, not too long before her disappearance."

Robb leaned forward. "Do you recall anything about your conversation? Other than business matters?"

"Let's see now. Hmmm. Ah, yes. We talked about chamber music in Cambridge. Hmm . . . hmmm . . . Let me see now. Yes, we talked about music in Glasgow, too. She mentioned going to concerts in Glasgow."

Robb said. "Had she been to concerts in Glasgow recently?"

"Hmm. Let me see now. Yes, it would seem so. She said that the chamber music in Glasgow wasn't quite up to the level she had become accustomed to in Cambridge. I'm sure she must have been in Glasgow recently, and on several occasions. She wasn't the kind to make a generalization based on a single case. Hmm. Let me see now. Hmm. . . ah yes! She did say she loves Scotland. Spent a good deal of time there as a child."

"What about Doctor Allsford, Cynthia's father? It seems he disappeared too. Do you happen to know the reason for that? Or do you have any guesses?"

The professor's expression darkened. He stood up and walked to the door and opened it. "Captain Robertson, I really can't think of anything else that would be of any use to you. I'm sorry I can't be more helpful."

Sam stood up and said, "You've been very kind to give us so much of your time."

Robb stood up and walked quickly to the door. He said, "Thank you." His tone was flat, cold. He didn't look at the professor as he passed through the door.

"Good day, gentlemen." The professor closed the door.

The autumn day was fast approaching twilight when the two Americans emerged from the building. They stood on the steps of the building. Robb said, "What the hell was that all about? Why the bum's rush?"

"I can't figure it out. All I know is that when you mentioned Cynthia's father he became a different person."

Robb hissed, "He turned into a first class prick."

"You know, Robb, we might learn something about Doctor Allsford, and possibly Cynthia, by examining Allsford's writings."

"Good idea. Let's find this university's library."

Sam studied his friend's face. "I think it would be a good idea if you went back to the hotel and slept for a few hours. I'd forgotten that what with missions and alerts, you must have averaged less than four hours sleep a night during the past week."

Robb hesitated. "You talked me into it. Thanks, Sam."

＊　＊　＊　＊　＊　＊　＊　＊

Robb stopped at the front desk to pick up a key to the suite. The neatly tailored young man who seemed this morning to have been offended by his very existence now seemed to rejoice in his coming.

"Ah, Captain, have you been enjoying London today?"

"May I have my key, please."

"Captain Kovacs checked in a half hour ago, sir."

As Robb entered the main room from the foyer, he called out, "Stosh!" He was about to yell again when he caught sight of a man sitting on a sofa off to one side of the room, a small, middle- aged man, impeccably dressed in a dark suit and a camel colored vest with a club cravat. He held a derby on his lap. He sat erectly as he spoke into a telephone.   He said, "Excuse me a moment, please." He covered the mouthpiece with his hand and said to Robb, "The gentleman is in his bath, off the far end of that corridor sir." He smiled pleasantly as he indicated the direction.

Robb said, "Thank you." He kept looking back at the man as he walked toward the hallway. The man had resumed his telephone conversation.

There was a single door at the end of the hall. He entered the room and found himself in another entry hall. As he entered the bedroom itself he was stunned: twin beds covered by counterpanes of rich brocade and satin throw-pillows, a sofa and two lounge chairs facing a fireplace. The glowing coals in the grate added a final touch of luxury that Robb found unbelievable. He exclaimed loudly, "Kee-riste!"

"In here, Robb!"

He entered the bathroom.   There in a huge bathtub lay Captain Stanley Kovacs, only his head and knees visible above billows of thick, frothy bubbles.

"Kee-riste!"

"I say, old man, what are you 'Kee-riste-ing' about?"

"Who's the guy in the living room?"

"First off, you slob, what you call the living room is the salon. And the guy, as you so crudely put it, is our valet."

"What! What in the hell do we need a valet for? To put on the dog?"

"Nothing like that. For one thing, Fred unpacked . . . "

"Fred?" .

"Yes, Fred. He said to call him 'Riggins', but I thought that sounded too much like Jeeves, so I asked him his first name. As I was saying, Fred unpacked our bags and sent our uniforms to be pressed. Hand me that bottle of shampoo, pal."

"Now that he's taken care of our uniforms, get rid of him. What do we need him for?"

"Mostly for inside dope. Old Fred used to work for big shots who are on the inside of this London scene."

"Crap!"

He told me he used to be a 'gentleman's gentleman'—that's how he said it—for one of the most powerful men in all England. Until 'His Lordship'—that's what Fred called him—fucked up and got dropped from the social setup in England. That's why old Fred had to take the hotel valet job. Nobody would hire anyone connected with Lord So-and-So who fell into the shithouse."

"Get rid of him."

"Hell, he's already earned his wages. He made a reservation for us at the Ritz after they told him they were full for Saturday night. He just told whoever answered the phone that he wanted to talk to Mister So-and-So. So he gets us a reservation for six people."

"Okay, so now you can lay some of your five pound notes on him and let him go."

"After he fixed us up at the Ritz, I asked him what the best show running in town is. So he tells me—forget what it is—and then he calls them for reservations, and again he gets the 'sold out' routine, and again he says let me talk to Mister So-and-So, and bingo! We got us six box seats that practically hang over the stage, he tells me."

"Good for him. Now pay him off and get rid of him. I can't stand this valet crap!"

Kovacs looked penetratingly at Robb for a moment. "Look, pal, you're slipping. You're starting to care about shitty little things. So let's have some fun and not get so damned serious. Nothing counts but *now*! So fuck all! Right, pal?"

Robb shook his head vigorously, his back-to-reality shake. He broke into a broad smile. "Right, pal!" he declared. "You're right. I was slipping. I can take Fred or leave him, for all I care. Same goes for this nutty hotel setup. Who cares? Fuck all!"

"Way to go! Now you're talking!."

"You keep talking about reservations for six people. Who's the sixth person?"

"Old Fred. I invited him to come along."

"Kee-riste!"

"He's a nice guy. Besides, we need him. He's already made all kinds of other arrangements for us."

Robb was looking more dour by the minute. "Where did you find him?"

"Easy. I called downstairs for some valet service, to get our uniforms pressed. I somehow got the Assistant Manager and he sends me Fred, to be *our* valet for as long as we like. Well, pal, I know a good thing when I see it, so I latched on to Fred and put him to work. Funny thing about that assistant manager. He's sucking me up one side and down the other." Kovacs stopped rinsing his head to observe Robb's reaction.

"I know. Sam told me."

Kovacs' eyebrows raised slightly. "Oh? Sam talked to him?"

"They weren't going to give us the royal suite, or whatever they call this setup, until they checked you out. They insisted Sam talk to the assistant manager."

Kovacs nodded. A broad smile spread his moustache into a thick horizontal line across his face. "So old Sam put that assistant manager in his place. Right? Probably laid some of that Harvard-looking-down-the-nose routine on him." He grinned. "That's what I figured might happen." He broke into a popular song of the moment in a deep baritone, slightly off key. "And there were angels dining at the Ritz, the nightingales sang in Baarkeley Squaare!"

"Look, Robb. I got some business to do here in London today. I might not get back until pretty late tonight. So you and Sam do something without me, okay? But the most important thing is we all got to meet the women in the lobby tomorrow at two o'clock."

"Don't worry, we'll be there."

Kovacs stood up in the tub.

Robb could see he had lost weight. He figured he was down to two hundred and twenty pounds or thereabouts in a rawboned way. As Robb looked at his friend—tall, hairy, thick-wristed and thick-ankled, deep chested, narrow waisted—he mused that no one could doubt that this is a very, very strong man. He'd still make one hell of a fullback.

Robb stood up. "I'll see you tomorrow, if not sooner." He reached over and turned the cold water tap on the shower full open and quickly hurried from the bathroom. He could hear Kovacs yelling "You son-of-a-bitch" all the way into the "salon", as Stosh called it.

He introduced himself to Fred and asked him where he might find a good record shop. Fred asked what kind of music he'd like. When Robb told him chamber music, he asked if he had specific compositions in mind. Robb named two Haydn Quartets and a couple of other works. Fred was quite familiar with the compositions, and recommended highly the London String Quartet's recordings of the Haydn works. He called up the store and ordered the records and asked them to deliver the records to their suite at the Grosvenor. "Now, if you don't mind, please." He showed Robb to the library where he demonstrated the operation of the record-player console. Robb stretched out on a sofa while waiting for the records. He fell asleep within minutes.

It was seven-thirty when Sam Prentice returned to the suite. He, like Robb before him, was surprised to find the little man with the derby on his lap sitting in the main room of the suite, talking into a telephone. The man covered the mouthpiece. "Sir, Captain Kovacs has departed for the evening. Captain Robertson is in the library."

Sam awakened Robb and asked who the man in the living room was. Robb told him that the erstwhile valet was now Stosh's private appointments secretary, arranger of events, and general factotum. "Did you find out anything about Cynthia's father?"

"Only one thing, but very important. I read the preface to every book by Allsford. You know how authors put down the date and place where they wrote the preface, at the end of the preface?"

"Go on."

"He put down 'Allsford Hall, Cambridgeshire, England' on the prefaces of most of his books—he's written a lot of them—but in the prefaces to three of his books he put down 'Shelbourne, Scotland'."

"I'll be damned! I think we've found her! All we have to do is find Shelbourne, Scotland, and we'll find Cynthia. I'm sure of it!"

———16———

Robb Robertson and Sam Prentice sat in soft leather chairs in the main first floor lounge of the Grosvenor House. It was 1:45 on Saturday afternoon. Sam and Robb agreed there was no way Merrie and Evelyn could make it to London by 2:00 if they got off work at 12:00, but, at Stosh's insistence, they kept an eye on the broad hallway that opened on the lounge from the outer foyer and the street beyond. Stosh had said, "You never know. They might hit the connections just right and get here pretty close to 2:00."

The lounge was crowded. A hundred people, more or less, milled about or stood in little knots chatting animatedly in what had all the appearances to Robb of an oversized cocktail party. The crowd was indistinguishable from the throng they had encountered upon their arrival yesterday. In fact, they seemed to Robb to be the same people, or perhaps they were interchangeable. The latter hypothesis seemed the more tenable.

Sam said, "Stosh really hit it big in poker last night. *Really* big. I found a knapsack crammed full of money next to my bed this morning, next to my suitcase, which was already crammed full of money. The only thing Stosh lost last night was his gas mask."

"How did he lose that?"

"He must have chucked it somewhere. He still has the gas mask bag, though. It was next to my bed too, packed with money."

Sam watched for Robb's reaction. None was forthcoming.

Sam said, "How does he do it? It can't be luck. Not that consistently."

Robb said, "He told me he has three rules: Only play the odds, never hunches. Never drink when you play, and always bring enough reserve funds with you to outlast the rest as the game wears on and the booze does its work on the others."

"Sounds reasonable. And it works," Sam said. "You're not going to believe this. Stosh won over fourteen thousand dollars last night. Counting the six thousand he won at the club on payday, that makes at least twenty thousand this week alone. With the money we brought with us we have over twenty-four thousand dollars on hand!"

"Oh."

"Just 'Oh'?"

"Come on, Sam. It's only money."

"I keep forgetting that. I'm going to have to get rid of my old fashioned notions about money. I'm going to keep saying to myself, 'It's only money, it's only money'."

Robb was amused at Sam's attitude toward money. Sam's family had lots of it and they'd had it for a long time. Robb said, "You'll be dipping into capital a lot this weekend, Sam. You're going to go straight to hell when you die."

"That's pretty good. You sound just like my grandfather." Sam studied his friend for a moment. "I was going to tell you about a problem we have with all this money, but I'm afraid you'll continue your little game."

"Try me."

Sam looked wary. "All right, then. I didn't know what to do with all these oversized five-pound notes. My suitcase is chock full of money, and the overflow is in a knapsack and Stosh's gas mask cover. We can't go around carrying all that money around in a knapsack and a gas mask bag."

"Why not?" Robb remained completely impassive, immobile. He stared straight ahead, occasionally glancing toward the entry hall when someone entered.

"Why not! You ask why not?"

"Yes. I ask why not."

"Because you can't. That's why."

Robb smiled and put his hand on Sam's arm. "So what are you going to be about this big problem of yours?"

"I've already done something. I opened a bank account for Stosh this morning."

Robb sat up suddenly, a look of shocked incredulity darkened his face. "You what?"

"I opened a bank account."

"That's nuts! What in hell did you do that for?"

"We simply can't go around carrying all that money with us."

"You could leave it in the goddamned bridal suite."

Sam shook his head. "We couldn't do that."

"Why not?"

"Someone might steal it. The chambermaids or someone."

"So what?"

"I give up." Sam brightened suddenly. "Here comes Stosh!"

Robb looked toward the elevators. Captain Stanley Roman Kovacs strode toward them. Robb said, "Do you want me to break the news to him about the bank account?"

Sam said gloomily, "Might as well get it over with while he's riding high."

"Cheer up. He can't do any more than kill you."

"I know." Sam tried to be cheerful. "Look at him. He's really spiffed up. He looks like Clark Gable or Errol Flynn in one of those movies about the Eighth Air Force."

Robb said, "He's better looking than either of those guys."

Kovacs was within earshot. "What was that you were saying, Robb?"

"I was saying that in your brand new uniform you looked better than Mickey Rooney in those war pictures."

"Thanks, pal." He glanced toward the entrance. "I was afraid I might miss the womens' arrival. I had a lot of last minute arrangements to make."

"You look so sharp today someone who didn't know you might say, 'There goes a man with a bank account.'" Robb smiled cheerfully at Kovacs. Sam shifted uneasily in his chair.

"No way, pal." He opened a pack of Luckies, took one out, and tossed the pack to Robb.

"I've got news for you. You *do* have a bank account."

"What the hell you talking about?"

"Just that. You have a bank account. As of this morning." Robb began to laugh the wild laugh Sam had noticed recently.

Kovacs said, "I think Robb's cracking up."

Robb wiped the tears from his eyes. "Sam opened a bank account for you this morning."

Kovacs turned to Sam. "Is that true?" His stared at Sam.

"It's not a regular savings account or anything like that. It's just one of those places you put money in till you blow it. You know, a temporary checking account."

Kovacs glared. "Why in hell did you go and do a crazy thing like that for? Of all the crazy things! Why, Sam? "

"I'm sorry. I just didn't have any place to put all those oversized five-pound notes."

"Hell, we got your suitcase, a knapsack, and three gas mask covers to put it in, and we can always pick up a barracks bag somewhere."

"Stosh, listen to me. It's just a checking account, not a savings account. I put in fifteen thousand dollars. I've got between nine and ten thousand crammed here and there in the suite, just to make you feel comfortable. It's not as though I blew the whole wad on a bank account." Sam reached into an inside pocket of his tunic and brought forth a checkbook. "Here's your checkbook." He held it out to Kovacs.

"You keep it." He stared into space, slapping his palm absently against the arm of his chair. He turned suddenly to Sam. "Can you yourself write checks against that account?"

"It's in your name, and Robb's and mine. Any one of us can write checks."

Kovacs smiled for the first time. "Good. You write 'em then. I don't ever want to see that checkbook. If we work it right, maybe we can clean out that account by this time tomorrow."

Sam nodded sadly. "I'm sure you can."

Robb said, "I'll try to help."

Sam was obviously upset. Kovacs got up and held a hand out to Sam. "No hard feelings, pal? I know you did what you thought was right. Still good friends, okay?"

Sam shook hands with Kovacs. "It's all right."

"It's just a thing I have about bank accounts. I don't expect you to agree with it. Each to his own, live and let live, it takes all kinds, and all that kind of shit. That's my philosophy."

Robb said, "Matter enough to mind one's own soul and all that kind of shit. Right?"

"Anyway, Sam, you go to your church and I'll go to mine. Right?"

Sam smiled wanly. "I got the point way back at 'each to his own.'"

"Did you catch that, Robb? Pretty smooth, huh? I'll bet that's the way he let that assistant manager have it. I forgot to thank you for that, Sam. I really appreciate it."

Sam didn't respond.

"You're not mad at me, are you, Sam?"

"You know me better than that."

"Thanks, pal." Kovacs pulled his uniform coat out away from his shirt and sniffed inside. "Old Fred put me on to this deodorant." Kovacs jumped up. "Look what just came into the lobby! Did you ever see anything more beautiful in your life? Come on!" He started for the entrance. Robb and Sam followed closely behind. About half way to the entrance, Kovacs pulled up short. "Look, you guys go first and I'll follow you, okay?"

Robb approached Second Lieutenants Cameron and Vandivier, pert and proper in their forest green uniform coats, beige knee-length skirts, and dark green overseas caps. He thought they looked like two girl scouts newly arrived in the big city from rural Indiana or Iowa. They stood in the entryway, surveying the lounge.

Robb had seen Merrie on the night he took Willis to the hospital, but he hadn't really seen her. Stosh was right. Merrie really is the girl next door. And Evelyn looked great. Robb said, "Hello, Evelyn." He took her right hand in his and placed his left arm around her shoulder, the half-embrace of good friends. He turned to Merrie. "Hello, Merrie. I'm Robb Robertson. We sort of met, in the hospital."

Before she could respond, Kovacs said, "And I'm Stosh Kovacs." Kovacs shook hands with Merrie, awkwardly. Robb was astonished. Stosh Kovacs, the coolest of the cool, embarrassed!

Sam knew both of the women well. He greeted them warmly. "I'm surprised you two made it on time. I thought Stosh was dreaming when he said we were meeting you here at 2:00, when both of you work until noon on Saturdays."

Merrie looked at Kovacs out of the corner of her eye, although she addressed her remark to Sam. "It just happened that Captain Rizzo told me I could quit at ten this morning, and Colonel Strang told Evelyn exactly the same thing! Now isn't that the strangest coincidence?"

Robb and Sam had difficulty keeping a straight face. Kovacs said innocently, "Well, these things happen sometimes, like filling out an ace high inside straight."

Sam compressed his lips in a mighty effort to keep from laughing. He exploded into a howl. Everyone except Kovacs broke up. Robb wiped tears from his eyes.

Kovacs said, "What's so funny?"

Merrie smiled. "We really do appreciate your thoughtfulness, Captain, and your influence."

Kovacs grinned his self-deprecatory grin. "Hey, let's get going up to our room. We got big things planned for this afternoon."

Merrie touched Kovacs' arm. "Hold it please. Correct me if I'm wrong. Did I hear you say 'our room'? 'Our', like us, and 'room', like singular?"

Kovacs hesitated. "Like Robb says, it's a figure of speech."

She turned to Sam. "We trust you. Is it room, singular, or rooms, plural?"

Sam adjusted his glasses on his nose. "I don't quite know how to answer that. It's plural, in a singular sort of way. All I can say is that you won't feel crowded."

They were standing waiting for the elevator when Kovacs noticed the porter, a middle aged man, with the two bags in hand. He turned to the man and said, "I'm sorry. I didn't see you. Put the bags down. I'll carry them."

The man put down the bags and Kovacs handed him a pound note and picked up the bags. The porter stared back and forth between the pound note and the bags in Kovacs' hands. "Are you sure you don't want me to carry those bags, sir?"

"I'm sure," Kovacs replied.

In the elevator, Merrie turned to Kovacs and said, "Wasn't that a pound note you gave that man? You know, like a four dollar pound note?"

Robb said, "To Stosh a pound is a dollar. He can't figure out the exchange system, so he decided to regard pounds as dollars. Don't confuse him."

Merrie said, "I'll bet that's the biggest tip that man ever got for not carrying someone's bags." She looked up and down the hallway as they stepped out of the elevator "Only one door here, so that word 'room' must have been singular."

Kovacs unlocked the door and opened it. He stood aside as the women entered. They stopped short, looked around wide-eyed and then looked at each other.

Merrie said, "I don't believe this!"

They stood and stared, much as Robb and Sam had the day before, even though Kovacs didn't—on Fred's advice—turn on the chandeliers. Kovacs moved to the double doors to the main room. He opened the doors.

Evelyn whispered, "I don't get it."

Merrie looked at Evelyn. "Do we run, or do we stay?"

Kovacs looked bewildered. "Run from what?"

"This place. It's so huge and. . . and palatial."

"It's a hotel suite," Kovacs said.

Merrie said, "Are you planning a big party? Who else is coming?"

Kovacs was crushed. "I'm sorry. I thought you'd like it. I guess I made a big mistake."

"No, you don't understand. It's beautiful. It's just that I can't figure it out."

"It's a suite. Your bedrooms are down that hallway over there, and ours are down this hall over here, at the opposite end of the suite."

Both women relaxed, so obviously that everybody but Kovacs burst out laughing. Merrie saw Kovacs' anxiety. "It's beautiful, Stosh, really. But overwhelming. You didn't expect us to walk in here and just say 'How nice!' Did you?"

"I sort of expected you to say something like that."

Merrie said, "All right, then. How nice!" She wandered about the near side of the room, examining furniture, oil paintings, tapestries. "This must cost a fortune!"

Sam smiled. "Stosh has an independent income."

"Which he's trying to get rid of," Evelyn said.

Sam grinned. "Something like that."

Kovacs put in quickly, "Come on over to Mussolini's and have some refreshments."

"Mussolini's?"

"Sam hung a name on each area of the room." He pointed ahead of him. "That one there is Mussolini's."

Evelyn said, "That's Mussolini's, all right." There on a stand in the middle of Mussolini's was a large silver ice-bucket with the gold foil of champagne bottle-tops protruding from it, and on the oversized cocktail table were silver platters of hors d'oeuvres, enough for a substantial cocktail party.

Merrie said, "Here we go again." She picked up a caviar-covered tidbit. "How nice!"

"Now you're getting into the spirit of this thing! That's the way we're supposed to look at it. The whole thing is a game!" Kovacs beamed as he unwired a cork, popped it, and began pouring champagne into the forest of glasses that covered a table next to the ice bucket. He ceremoniously handed a glass to each person. He raised his glass. "Cheers, everyone!"

Merrie drained her glass in two swallows." She said, "I needed that." She turned to Stosh and said, "May we have just a peek at our room. Evelyn's and my room, that is."

"But of course. Yours is on the right. You're on the left, Evelyn."

"We each have our own room," Merrie said. "How nice. Come, Evelyn, if you please."

When they were out of earshot, Stosh turned to Robb. "I maybe overdid it a little, huh pal?"

"Let's say you didn't underdo it." Robb grinned, but he shut it off when he saw how worried Kovacs looked. "This is a wild setup and they don't know how to take it. But remember, we don't worry about little things like this."

"When it comes to Merrie, I worry plenty."

Sam said, "Just give them a little time. Then they'll have a ball, if you play it right. You did the right thing when you said the whole thing is a game. Stick to that."

"Hell, man, that's what it is. Everybody is too damned serious about this. And you know why? Because everybody is too fucked up about money. The women have the wrong attitude about money, just like Sam."

Sam grinned, "Just like Sam used to have. I'm rolling with it now."

"Way to go!"

Sam said, "Why don't you let me talk to them. Perhaps I can put them at ease."

"Good idea. What's the angle you're going to use with them?"

"I've got a great angle. It's called the truth."

"Good thinking, Sam! That's it! Tell them the truth. Tell them the money was donated by officers of the 990th. Oh yes, and by the United States Navy, especially some admirals last night."

Merrie and Evelyn returned. Merrie said, "I was right. It gets better. I'd like just one more glass of champagne, please. This is my last one."

Kovacs handed newly filled glasses all around. "Cheers, everyone."

Merrie said, "I don't want to hurt your feelings, Stosh, but I don't know how to take all this. I feel terribly uncomfortable."

Kovacs said softly. "I understand. I think we should abandon this crazy place and ask them for some regular hotel rooms. And we can chuck the other crazy plans I had for this game we were going to play this weekend. It was a dumb idea. Sorry."

Sam spoke up. "Before you go changing anything, Stosh, why don't you simply tell them where the money comes from."

"You tell them."

"All right then. Stosh is an expert poker player. He plays in big games where the stakes are very high. Tell them how much you won last night."

"I don't know. A lot, I guess."

"I counted it this morning. You won something like fourteen thousand dollars."

Merrie and Evelyn stared. Robb yawned. Kovacs didn't react.

Merrie said, "Forgive me, Stosh. But how could you possibly win so much? And could the people who lost it afford to lose that much?"

"You tell her, Sam."

"Stosh has been playing for money since his teens. He's got a system. Oh yes, and the people who lose can afford to lose it because they're . . ."

Kovacs said, "Like some admirals and generals last night."

Merrie looked at Evelyn. "What do you think? Do we help Stosh put his ill-begotten gains back into circulation?"

Evelyn said, "I think I could enjoy that, knowing it came from generals. When does the party start?"

Kovacs beamed. He walked around the sofa and stood beside Sam and put his arm around his shoulder and gave him a solid man-to-man sideways hug.

Merrie said, "All right, Captain Kovacs. Our fate is in your hands. We'll just let the tide take us wherever it will this weekend. You're the tide."

"Great, except I'm not exactly the tide. I've got help. I've got Fred."

"Fred?"

Sam said, "The Lone Arranger now has an Assistant Arranger, a Tonto, as it were. Old Fred just fell into our lap."

Merrie said, "I'm not sure I understand."

Kovacs said, "He's our ticket to the inside scene here in London. Anything you need, you just tell Fred, and presto, you got it. And he's got lots of influence, and lots of interesting plans for all of us. Just wait."

Kovacs went to the library and retrieved his assistant. Robb was fascinated by the Englishman's costume, a dark blue, formal-looking suit with a gray vest, starched, upstanding Victorian collar with tips turned down at the front, broad silk cravat, derby, and walking stick in hand. Robb noted that while he was about a foot shorter than Kovacs, the valet's carriage and manner minimized their difference in stature. Merrie had trouble keeping a straight face as they met the assistant arranger, who bowed to each woman as he was introduced.

Stosh said, "What's next on the program, Fred?"

Fred corrected him. "Rather, where next do the fates lead us."

"Or where does the tide carry us." Sam said.

"You got it, pal."

Fred said, "Why don't we simply venture forth and see what London has to offer?"

A limousine was at the curb in front of the main entrance to the Grosvenor, a chauffeur at the wheel. The hotel doorman held the door open for them. Fred handed the doorman a tip and took his place next to the chauffeur. Robb wondered if the doorman knew Fred in his pants-pressing role.

Evelyn said, "How nice."

Merrie said, "This is a first-class tide carrying us along."

The limousine moved along the edge of Hyde Park for a mile or so and then made a turn away from the park. It stopped before a large stone building with a long, dark green, arched awning that reached out to the street. A small brass plaque beside the massive door read simply, "Ste. Germaine". The place turned out to be a dress designer's emporium.

Merrie and Evelyn emerged an hour later dressed in highly unmilitary "tea costumes", and capes. Kovacs and Fred followed close behind, each carrying a stack of boxes containing evening costumes and temporarily retired uniforms. It seemed Kovacs couldn't get over the transformation of Merrie: he continued to stare at her as they got into the car.

Fred suggested that it was now time they went to tea. Stosh made a sour face but they went to tea, a "high tea" in a hotel where the tea room and dance floor were arranged like a formal English garden, with potted trees and shrubs and white lattice arbors, and even a glass conservatory set in an ambiance of varying shades of pale spring greens. They danced to a small string orchestra that played Victor Herbert and Sigmund Romberg operetta tunes and an occasional Strauss waltz. Evelyn invited Sam to dance with her, and Sam danced with uncharacteristic enthusiasm—born of champagne.

Merrie invited Mr. Riggins to dance with her, and Fred danced with skill born of training and experience. Merrie was surprised at his grace and confidence as he led her expertly about the dance floor. She looked over Fred's head and smiled at Stosh, but he didn't see her smile. He was staring, his mouth slightly agape, at her swirling, loose-flowing dress and her shapely legs as she twirled under the masterful guidance of the dapper little Englishman.

Afterwards they climbed back into the car and returned to the Grosvenor. They collapsed for a time before the women started getting ready for dinner and the show which was to follow.

Whoever it was who told Fred that the Ritz was fully booked had apparently told the truth. But they had an excellent table nonetheless, with a good view of the orchestra and dance floor. They had a dinner of many courses, and the Ritz proved that it was the Ritz. Robb was amazed that the Ritz could take the meager fare available during wartime and do such magical things with it. But, upon more mature reflection, he couldn't help but wonder if the poulets of the "Poulet du Chasseur" may well have found their way across the channel from Normandy or Brittany by small boats with cargoes specifically destined for the Ritz. After all, parts of France were now Allied Territory.

They had time for one after-dinner dance before they hurried to the theatre. The show was a revival of Noel Coward's "Bittersweet", a romantic interlude in which a Victorian English girl falls in love with her handsome Viennese music teacher. When the lovely ingenue in her Victorian gown sang in her sweet soprano, "I'll see you again, whenever spring breaks through again" , she looked up at their box—which, as promised, did in fact practically hang over the stage—and looked into Stosh's eyes and sang to him and him alone. At least it seemed so to Robb. Maybe she thought she was singing to Clark Gable, Robb mused.

Merrie held Stosh's hand all the while and in his mind it was Merrie who sang ". . . this sweet memory across the years will come to me . . ."

When the soprano finished her solo everyone applauded enthusiastically, except Stosh who was still recovering from his transcendental dream in which Merrie had sung to him and him alone.

It was after 1:00 A.M. when they stood under the theatre marquee waiting for their car. Merrie said, "Well, Mr. Riggins, we're much in your debt. The show was lovely and we did indeed have the best seats in the house. It's been a fantastic evening. Thank you."

"My pleasure, I assure you, Miss Cameron. But the evening isn't quite over yet."

"But everything closes in London quite early the night clubs and the hotels—at least that's what I've heard."

"Yes, Miss. That's the law. But perhaps we can find something."

The driver drove for some fifteen minutes, making many turns and finally stopping before a large townhouse mansion. Fred handed the doorman a card and the doorman pushed a bell button. A young man in a tuxedo escorted them into the inner recesses of the building. They followed a labyrinth of hallways and eventually climbed a set of stairs. They passed through a foyer and found themselves looking down upon one of the largest and most elegant night clubs Robb had ever seen.

Merrie said, "And I thought London had closed for the night!"

Fred gave the maitre d' a business card and a five-pound note. The man signaled a waiter. The waiter escorted them to a table near the dance floor.

Robb, as was his habit, assessed the jazz band in a glance: three saxes, two trumpets, two trombones, piano, string bass, and a percussion man who doubled on vibraharp. And a sultry looking woman singer. The musicians were of African heritage, but clearly American, judging by their haunting chords and subtle beat. Duke Ellington sounds, Robb reflected. Slow, late night jazz sounds, as poignantly and uniquely American as anything he had experienced since he arrived in England. He felt a moment of homesickness. He led Evelyn directly to the dance floor without stopping at their table. So also Stosh with Merrie.

Evelyn swished in her silk gown as she followed Robb smoothly, effortlessly gliding and turning to the slow beat of "Ain't Misbehavin".

Robb whispered, "I love your swish."

She placed her lips against his ear. "Thank you. It's been a long time since anyone praised my swish. I love swishing with you."

Robb said, "There's a poem, an English poem, something like, 'When as in silk, my Evelyn goes/ Then, then, methinks, how sweetly flows/ The liquifaction of her clothes.'"

"How lovely, Robb. Was it really about an Evelyn?"

"Yes," he lied.

Robb, not ordinarily one to notice such things, did in fact notice that many of the male dancers who passed them appraised Evelyn carefully, and that some of them obviously worked their way around to get a better look at her. Robb held her back from him for a moment and took a good look at her.

She smiled, "What are you doing?"

"I was wondering if you look as beautiful as you dance and if you are as lovely as you feel in my arms." He continued to hold her at a distance, appraising her. "You are even more lovely than that."

She moved back into his arms. "How delightfully out of character for the reticent Alvin G. Robertson. Tell me more."

"You called me 'Alvin'. That's it for tonight."

Evelyn smiled as she whispered in his ear, "Who knows where the tide may carry us." She placed her hand behind his head and drew his head down to her level and placed her lips against his cheek and her lips were cool and tender. She kept her hand behind his head and her lips against his cheek for much of the time as they moved smoothly about the dance floor to the slow, insinuating rhythm of "Sophisticated Lady". After a time the band modulated into "Body and Soul". When the last chord ended, Evelyn kissed him on the cheek and made a sound into his ear that sounded like "mmmm". He felt a physical force, whether within him or her, pulling him toward her. He drew her tightly to him. He suddenly felt a moment of confusion. An image of Cynthia flashed through his consciousness. He knew in his heart of hearts that he actually lived for the day he would see Cynthia again. Yet he felt this strong attraction toward Evelyn. Why did he so readily agree to ask Evelyn to go out with him? But this wasn't the woman he had, at Stosh's behest, asked to go dancing in London. How could he have known the second lieutenant in the little cubicle in headquarters would turn out to be so beautiful? And so deliciously warm and tender.

On the way back to the hotel, Merrie snuggled tightly against Stosh in one corner of the back seat. And in the other corner, Evelyn reached around Robb's neck and drew his face to hers. Sam sat on one of the little jump seats facing them. He pretended he had fallen asleep. Not one of the four people opposite him noticed.

✳ ✳ ✳ ✳ ✳ ✳ ✳ ✳

They entered the hotel suite shortly after 3:00 A.M.. The lamps in the large, main room were turned low. Fires glowed in two of the fireplaces, and the chandeliers, now darkened, caught the firelight and became alive with red and orange and yellow and white stars whose rays danced among the crystal facets before flashing about the room.

Kovacs stood in the middle of the room and looked down into the dark blue eyes of Second Lieutenant Meredith Cameron and said to himself that what he saw in that moment was the most beautiful thing he'd ever seen in his whole fucking life.

Without a word, Kovacs took Merrie by the hand and led her to the sofa at Mussolini's, now lighted only by the softly glowing fire in the fireplace that was its centerpiece. And Evelyn led Robb to Mr. Chippendale's at the other side of the room, where the sofa that faced the fireplace was also, like Mussolini's, lighted only by glowing embers.

Soft chamber music sounds—Mozart's "Hoffmeister Quartet", Robb noted—could be heard through the closed door of the library where Sam and Fred had retreated.

Evelyn lay on Mr. Chippendale's sofa, her head on Robb's lap, and as his eyes appraised her he remarked to himself on how completely an army uniform disguised her figure. He smiled as he recalled that he had thought her overweight. He now saw her as she really was: tall and as generously sculpted by nature as though Leonardo had collaborated on the design.

She moved upwards to a half-sitting position and reached around him and insinuated her warm, ample softness into his arms. He asked himself: how could I have known, how could I have guessed the joy of knowing Evelyn? He loved Cynthia as no other woman ever, and yet he felt himself on the edge of genuine love with this loving woman in his arms. He felt a strange sense of guilt about his infidelity to Cynthia, the Cynthia he hardly knew. He relaxed his embrace, turning his face from hers.

"What's wrong, Robb?"

"Nothing, really."

He felt a moment's disgust with himself. Why should he feel guilty about a woman who knew next to nothing about him and probably cared even less? He swore silently to himself. You horse's ass! This lovely creature is *now*. You could be dead by noon on Monday! He pulled Evelyn tightly to him. His mouth found hers. He kissed her, open-mouthed, almost savagely.

"Please Robb. Let's take things a bit more slowly."

"Sorry. I was having an argument with myself. I'm over it."

Evelyn set the tempo. Her first kisses were sweet, almost shy, her embraces soft, restrained. But in a matter of minutes they became increasingly warm. His mouth on hers all the while, he gently moved her downward until she was again prone on the sofa. He caressed the back of her head, her neck, her back and the roundness below. He told himself "This is now. Cynthia doesn't exist. Monday doesn't exist." He felt her quick, warm breath on his neck and he knew he had never known such completely fulfilling joy of love before. He corrected himself. No. The genuine joy of *an act of love* before. Not like this. And yet . . ."

He slid his hand lower, to the hem of her gown, now above her knees. His hand wandered upwards, beneath her gown, and he felt her warmth. Her breath quickened. She moaned softly, "Robb! Oh Robb! I don't know . . ." His mouth stifled her words.

She freed herself quickly from his embrace and sat up. "I'm sorry, Robb. I'm afraid we're a bit out of control. I'm not quite ready for this. What I mean is I'm too ready. But we shouldn't, should we?"

At Mussolini's, Merrie stretched out on the sofa, her head on Kovacs' lap. He brushed his lips lightly over her eyelids and pecked her softly on her nose. He drew her tightly to him and locked his mouth on hers. She reached around his neck and drew him even more tightly to her. He continued his embraces and caresses for several minutes. Her breathing became quick. He slipped his hand inside the low-cut neckline of her gown and inside her brassiere. A low moan escaped her lips now pressed against his ear. She grasped his wrist and removed his hand.

He whispered, "Sorry. I shouldn't have done that." He sighed. "Merrie, I love you like I never loved anybody else in my life. I fell in love with you that first day, by the fire doors in the hallway in the hospital."

Merrie said softly, "It took me almost a week to fall in love with you."

A look of surprise crossed his face. "Say that again!"

"I love you."

He closed his eyes and remained silent for a time. Finally he spoke in an intense whisper. "I can't believe it! I've never been so happy in my whole fucking . . . . Sorry about that."

"It's all right." She held his hand up to her face and her lips lingered against the back of his hand. "I said I love you, and you were saying. . ."

"I was saying you made me the happiest guy in the whole world." He kissed her warmly. He started to caress her breasts but drew his hand away suddenly. "Sorry".

"Stosh, I'm sure you've had a lot of—uh—experience."

"You mean like sex experience?"

"Yes."

"I've been around, but not as much as you might think. I wouldn't take out a girl if I thought she was a bum, and I never made the first move—you know, below the waist—with any woman I knew was first class. You know, like somebody's sister. She had to make the first move."

"Aren't you curious about me? Don't you wonder about me?"

"You're the the woman I'd ask to marry me, if it weren't for the war."

"And I'm the woman who would say 'yes'". She smiled at him.

"I can't believe all this! I think I'm going to bust."

She whispered, her lips against his ear, "I've not been around much, almost not at all, but under our circumstances all the rules change."

"I know what you mean."

"You don't understand. I'm somebody's sister. That is, I've never known a man completely. But I'm making the first move."

He bent down and kissed her, long and passionately. "I feel like I've been hit in the head with a baseball bat." He kissed her again. "There's something I don't get . Just a minute ago you didn't want me to touch your. . .uh . . . your. . ."

"Because I couldn't stand being aroused that much without . ." She buried her face against his chest again. "I'm embarrassed."

They remained silent for a time. Finally he said, "Did you really mean what you said about marrying me, if it weren't for the war?"

"I'd marry you tomorrow."

He placed her head softly on the sofa pillow and stood up. He bent down and picked her up, almost effortlessly, cradling her in his arms. He glanced quickly at Chippendale's as he carried her silently across the room. As he approached the door to her bedroom he whispered into her ear. "We're going to cross the threshold now. You can still change your mind."

She pulled his head down and kissed him.

He lowered her softly on to the bed and returned to the door and closed it and turned the key in the lock. A small lamp on a cocktail table on the far side of the room cast a soft light. He stood beside the cocktail table and took off his shirt and tie and undershirt. His broad chest and his muscular arms and shoulders seemed bigger unclothed and, in the half-light of the single lamp, the thick hair on his chest and arms gave his upper body a dark, Mediterranean look. His tight trousers made his waist seem remarkably slender for such a big man.

Her eyes opened as he approached the bed. As he eased himself beside her, she whispered, "Gorilla." He smiled as he drew her tightly to him and her mouth found his. And while she held him with her mouth he reached around behind her and unzipped the back of her gown. She raised herself slightly and he lowered the bright red gown and its red underslip. He reached around her again and unsnapped and removed her brassiere. "Please, Stosh. Let's get under the covers. I've never been undressed in front of a man before."

He moved his face to hers and kissed her as he eased himself away from her. "Not yet." He stood up and moved to the foot of the bed and stood looking down upon her for a time. "Not until I fix in my mind all of your beauty, just as you are now. I'm going to carry this picture of you in my brain until the day I die, and even if it's tomorrow or fifty years from tomorrow I'm going to die happy. I really mean it."

His eyes never left her as he unfastened his belt and slipped his trousers down over his hips. He stood at the foot of the bed in his undershorts, looking down on her for a time.

Finally she opened her eyes and her eyes met his. She lowered her eyes slowly. She turned her head slightly to one side as she continued to look at him. She looked up and held his eyes with hers. She held her arms out to him. He moved to the side of the bed, slipped out of his shorts, and slowly lowered himself beside her and then over her, carefully distributing his weight on his knees, shoulder, and the side of his head, fearful that the bulk of his body would crush her. But he was even more fearful that he might hurt her.

She moaned softly and buried her face in the hollow of his neck and shoulder. He placed himself against her gently and remained motionless. She gasped as she moved in her initial attempt to draw him into her. She uttered a soft cry of pain from time to time. And yet, despite her movements, he held himself near-motionless.   Her movements quickened and deepened and he knew she had abandoned her concern for herself as she suddenly released herself to the moment and to him, freely and without restraint. She cried out softly, until at last she grasped him suddenly and tightly and completely.

Finally he permitted himself to move, not against her but with her. At last they lay quietly in each other's arms, their breathing now regular, their minds and bodies completely at ease. They lay in silence for a length of time that had no measurable duration for either of them.

In the salon Robb and Evelyn lay stretched out in each other's arms on the sofa before Chippendale's last embers, sound asleep. One might have thought their embrace the contented culmination of a night of love. Actually, they fell asleep right after he finished telling her a long story, a story that began when he went fishing one day last August.

——17——

On Friday afternoon, November 24, 1944, Robb sat alone in a seating circle along the south wall of the officers' club. It had been a rough week. His face had the gray pallor and parchment stiffness of exhaustion, and his eyes were glassy and deeper set than a few weeks ago. He felt unsure of his place in space and time. He marveled on how completely the war and his immersion in it distorted his sense of time and place. Had only a week passed since their wonderful, crazy weekend in London? It seemed like a lifetime ago. Almost another life, another incarnation. Maybe it was all a dream. Maybe it never happened.

He mused on how the typical mission now differed from the missions of a year or two earlier. One's chances of survival were much worse earlier, even though the required number of missions was twenty-five, not thirty-five. German fighter attacks were much to be expected in those days before our P-51s escorts could reach as far into Germany as our B-17s and B-24s. Nowadays fighter attacks were the exception rather then the rule, though the flak was worse now, or so it seemed, especially over Merseburg. And the missions were much shorter back then. Now that they were bombing in support of the Russians, there simply wasn't enough time in a twenty-four hour day to fly day after day to the Eastern Front without exacting a severe toll on the flyers. If you went to the Eastern Front two days in a row, the most sleep you could hope to get between missions, when you added the lengthy preparation time to the twelve or more hours in the air, was four hours.

And now they sweated out the crazy instrument take-offs only twenty seconds apart, this too dictated by the length of the hauls to the Eastern Front. If, as a year or two earlier, you took off thirty seconds apart it was no big deal. You'd still have enough gasoline to get back from the target even if the lead planes of the lead squadrons had to circle for an hour waiting for everyone to join the formation. But now, with the long hauls to the Russian Front, every drop of gasoline counted: a ten-second shorter interval between planes at take-off meant as much as a hundred gallons of fuel saved for the lead planes in the lead squadrons as they circled above the crap waiting for their squadrons to form. And so the mid-air collisions increased, and the acres of crosses in the Eighth Air Force cemetery outside of Cambridge increased in direct proportion to the shortened take-off intervals.

Everyone was exhausted from the week's long hauls: three missions to the Russian Front, but they hadn't lost a single plane. Robb, like most of the others who had gone on this week's three missions, had three or four hours of sleep on Sunday night before they were awakened at 2:00 A.M. for Monday's long haul. They had three and a half hours in the sack before Tuesday's repeat of the previous day's mission to the Eastern Front. Wednesday, after his usual nightmare, he had slept until 1:00 P.M., with the benefit of two more phenobarbitals. Yet he was near total exhaustion when he went to bed at 8:00 on Wednesday night. Then Private Swovik awakened them at 2:00 A.M. yesterday for another trip to the Russian Front. They landed at 6:30 last night, hit the whiskey line at 7:00, finished debriefing around 8:00, got to the mess hall around 8:30.

He had made it to bed around 10:00 last night, numb with exhaustion, knowing they were alerted yet again. Swovik awakened them at 2:00 this morning and they went through the usual hours of preparations and were sitting in the planes, idling at the head of the runway, when the word came that the mission was scrubbed. Robb taxied back in, put the ship to bed, checked in his equipment and then trudged back to the barracks. He took two more capsules and climbed back into the sack and slept until noon today.

Robb sat on a 1930's overstuffed sofa paging absently through a dog-eared, month-old issue of Life Magazine. He stopped on a page devoted to a Rosie-the-Riveter story, a piece about people doing their part for the war effort at home. The article told of victories but didn't mention human costs. Just as all of their missions were defined as victories, no matter how many men they lost.

He recalled from his childhood a professional veteran who came to their school every Armistice Day and recited a World War I poem: "In Flanders fields the poppies blow/ Between the crosses, row on row, / That mark our place; and in the sky/ The larks, still bravely singing fly/ Scarce heard amid the guns below."

Robb paraphrased bitterly: "In Cambridgeshire the poppies blow, between the crosses row on row." He saw in his mind's eye the white wooden crosses undulating over hill and dale as far as the eye could see in the Eighth Air Force cemetery outside of Cambridge. White wooden crosses that mark the graves of the thousands of Eighth Air Force flyers who died in England—on take-offs, landings, mid-air collisions. These among others who made it back from Germany in the planes, some dead, some dying, and still others who returned perfectly healthy until their badly damaged planes crashed somewhere in England. The thousands in Cambridge were but a fraction of the total: the remains of most of the Eighth Air Force's dead were buried in Germany, thousands of them identified but other thousands unknown soldiers forever.

He stared unseeingly at the Rosie-the-Riveter person in the magazine. Where is his brother Ted's cross? In Normandy, near Omaha beach where he died on D-Day? And if the 990th and the other Bombardment Groups of the Eighth hadn't missed Omaha Beach by three miles inland when they were supposed to be softening it up—destroying German mothers' sons—for the American landing, would his own mother's other son still be alive? He still felt numb at the thought of Ted's death. He couldn't accept it then; he couldn't accept it now. The lump was always there in his chest when he thought about Ted, yet he knew he had never been really close to his brother. Surely not as close as he was to Stosh and Sam. But he was never so close to anyone as he was to his brother and sister and his mother and father when they played chamber music together. They were in those moments one with each other and one with Mozart and Haydn and Beethoven.

They weren't that close at other times. Ted used to beat him up when they were growing up. And when he grew bigger than Ted he banged him around on more than one occasion. Yes, Ted was a feisty, combative sort of guy and fiercely competitive. But what a musician! He and Ted were the best musicians in the family, a fact his father quickly acknowledged. But his father also declared to anyone who would listen, "Ted's twice the violinist Robb is a cellist." But, what the hell, his father was right. Ted was damn near a musical genius. Not quite, but close.

Kovacs entered the room and circled past the bar where he picked up a bottle of rye and two glasses. He sat down silently on the chair nearest Robb. They sat in silence for a minute or two, Robb unaware of Kovacs' presence and Kovacs reluctant to disturb his friend. Robb finally sensed someone's presence. He opened his eyes. Kovacs smiled. "Hi, pal." He spoke softly.

Robb gave his head a shake. "How did you get here without me noticing it?"

"You weren't here when I came."

"I guess I wasn't."

"You seem down in the mouth. Is there anything you'd like to tell old Father Kovacs, your friendly peasant priest?"

"No. I'm just glad you're here."

"Would you like to kiss my ring?" He held out his left fist with the big silver ring with the large blue, oval stone on it.

Robb wore a similar ring. It signified their graduation from Advanced Flying School and their commissioning as second lieutenants. Robb looked at the ring. How young they were then. How important that ring had seemed. What glorious flying feats lay ahead.

Kovacs smiled broadly as he filled the glasses. "Now you're supposed to say 'How'd you like to kiss my ass'. Cheers, pal." They threw down the doubles in a single motion.

"How's the hunt for Cynthia going?"

"I'm up against a stone wall."

"I thought that professor in London told you and Sam she was in Glasgow."

"Not exactly. He gave us some clues that suggest strongly she's in Scotland, quite likely in the Glasgow area. Sam went to the London University Library and found that some of her father's books were written in a place called Shelbourne, Scotland. . ."

"Great! All you got to do is go to Shelbourne and find her. That should be easy. It's got to be a small town, right?"

"That's what I thought, but when Sam tried to find Shelbourne—we figured it was a town—he drew a blank. It's not on any map or chart, and it's not in any Scotland atlas. Sam's friend in Air Force Intelligence at Prestwick went to a government bureau in Scotland that would know about every town and hamlet in Scotland, and he was told there's no such place. We've come to the conclusion Shelbourne is the name of the Allsfords' place up there, either a house or an estate. The Prestwick Intelligence people drew a blank on that too. All we can say now is she's probably in the Glasgow area, but Sam and I can't figure out how to find her."

"Glasgow's pretty big, about the size of Detroit from what I've seen of it. Right?"

"That's about right." Robb sighed.

"Don't act so gloomy. We got it narrowed down to Glasgow, which is pretty good."

"So where do we go from there?"

"How do you see the probabilities she's in Glasgow or somewhere around there?"

"Let's say that it seems very likely she's in Glasgow or nearby."

"Like nine chances out of ten?"

"At least that good. We know her father wrote some of his books in Scotland, and we know she spent a lot of time in Scotland as a child, and we know she had been attending chamber music concerts in Glasgow as recently as a few months ago."

"Those are really good odds. Look, let me think about this for a while." Kovacs picked up his drink and walked over to the old piano. He sat down and began picking out "A Foggy Day in London Town" with one finger. He got up and walked quickly back to Robb. "Look, I've got it worked out how to find Cynthia in Glasgow or around there if that's where she's at. She's as good as found."

"You're crazy."

"Wait till you hear Father Kovacs' sure-fire plan for trapping beautiful women in Glasgow who are nuts about chamber music."

"Let's have it."

"Okay. There's no way we're going to find her in a big city like Glasgow if she doesn't want to be found. You know, with no telephone, no address listed anywhere, and no clues. She's a needle in a haystack. Right?"

"Right."

"So maybe the best way to look for a needle in a haystack is with a magnet. A real powerful magnet. Right?"

"Go on."

"What I mean is, all we got to do is to attract her to us."

"That's right. That's all we got to do."

"Do I detect a note of sarcasm, pal? That's not like you."

"How do we attract her?"

"We put on a real first-class chamber music concert in Glasgow. We hire the best outfit we can get and send 'em up to Glasgow. What do you think it might cost?"

Robb studied the ceiling. "I suppose if they happened to have an open date you could get them for around two thousand dollars plus expenses. For one concert."

"Two thousand dollars for each fiddler?"

"No. For the whole quartet. Expenses might run another five hundred."

"Twenty-five hundred bucks? Hell, that's easy. We still got around ten thousand in Sam's account plus whatever Sam's got left from the cash we kept out last weekend. And I've got other funds here and there. It's duck soup."

Robb grinned. "Okay. I'll play along with you on this wild scheme. So we've got the money. Now all we have to do is find a good quartet and go up to them and say, 'If you're not doing anything next week how about running up to Glasgow and giving a little concert for us?' Is that what you had in mind?"

"Something like that."

"I was afraid of that. Do you realize that any major musical organization has its concert schedule set up for two or three years in advance? They'd think we were crazy if we were to ask them to perform for us on a week's notice. We're talking the big leagues, like the Budapest String Quartet or the London Quartet, I gather?"

"Only the best. The magnet's got to be strong."

"I was afraid of that."

"You worry too much. When do you think we should put on this concert?"

"I can play games, too. Make it the second week in December."

"I think we should leave the day of the week open. A good outfit probably has a job about once a week. But if we let them choose the day of the week they'll be able to make it up to Glasgow one day, play that night, and go back home the next day. Does the day of the week make any difference?"

"Make it Sunday afternoon. But if your little band has a job Sunday, make it Saturday. Otherwise, any evening. You know something? I'm starting to believe that we're talking about the real world."

"Your trouble is you don't have enough faith."

"Do you mean faith in God?"

"I mean faith in money. You know, in gold we trust."

"I really appreciate what you're trying to do. It's just that I'm in awe of musicians of the kind we're talking about."

Kovacs remained silent. Robb was afraid he had hurt Kovacs' feelings. "Let's say you're able to pull this off. How would we find Cynthia if she does come to the concert? I'm the only one who knows what she looks like, and if she sees me she'll take off again. When I see her I've got to have her cornered in her home or some place where I can force her to hear me out. Another thing, what if we have to fly on the day of the concert?"

"You worry too much. Those are details we'll have to work out." Kovacs stood up. "I gotta meet Merrie in fifteen minutes. Think about this concert idea. See you in the morning. Pray it's not Swovik who wakes us up."

"I pray every day I won't see Swovik tomorrow. It's the only prayer I know. Thanks for trying to help."

Kovacs waved a benediction of sorts as he departed. "Bless you, my son."

"Thanks." Robb fell asleep before Kovacs left the building.

Evelyn's soft voice awakened him an hour later. "Robb."

He opened his eyes and stared dumbly ahead for several seconds. Her smile came into focus, then the rest of her face. "Oh. Hello, Evelyn. I must have dozed off." He was embarrassed, as though caught in bed in the middle of a working day.

"Hello, Robb."

"I must have dozed off." He was still out of it. "I think I already said that."

"Would you like a cup of coffee?"

"No, thanks. Sit down and let me look at you." He rubbed his face vigorously.

She sat down on the sofa and took his hand in hers. She quickly released his hand when she realized several men at the bar had their eyes on her.

He shook his head and rubbed his face again. "I'll be all right in a minute or two."

"Let me get that coffee." She was on her way to the mess hall before he could protest. He went into the latrine and splashed cold water on his face. When he came out Evelyn was back with the coffee. Robb stopped at the bar to get her a whiskey and soda.

Robb took a big drink of the coffee. He smiled. "Thanks, I needed that."

She smiled and raised her glass. "Cheers."

He studied her as she drew on her cigarette. Was there ever a woman in a cigarette poster more lovely than Evelyn? Could it be that she is even more lovely than Cynthia? Then he thought of Cynthia lying on her back on the sunlit platform.

She looked up at him suddenly. "What were you thinking?"

"I have no right to tell you."

"Tell me anyway."

"I was thinking that you are one of the most beautiful women I've ever known."

"Thank you. I'm glad I asked." He felt a strange sense of déja vu as he looked at her. He experienced again long treasured, dimly felt scents he had first known in late adolescence when so much of what is beautiful was new. The smell of the gardenia corsage he gave to a girl for the high school prom returned to him. But somehow, the image of Cynthia intruded. Cynthia's face in repose, her body bathed in sunlight on a summer's day.

"There's more," she said. "You were thinking more than that."

"I shouldn't tell you what I was thinking."

She looked at him for a time, her expression wistful, yet inquiring. It became apparent no further response was forthcoming from him. She stood up suddenly and reached down and took his hand, apparently forgetting her all-male audience. "I came to invite you out to dinner. At the fish and chips place in the village."

Robb brightened. "Thank you. I accept your invitation. But how do we get there?"

"I have a jeep."

"How nice. Do all second lieutenants have jeeps?"

She continued to hold his hand as they made their way to the vestibule. He held her shoulder bag and gas mask while she put on her trench coat. She made a show of holding his coat for him to slip into. "After all, Captain, you're my guest."

He opened the door. The sunny winter day had turned into a dismal night. A steady rain pounded the corrugated roof over the door and cascaded to the concrete stoop outside the door. He took off his trench coat and held it over them as they made their way around the main stream. They huddled together under the coat as they hurried toward the jeep. "The Eighth screwed up today!" He yelled as he pulled the coat closer around their heads. "We should have gone to Germany today! "We'd be landing right about now!"

She yelled over the din of the rain, "Nobody's perfect."

Robb settled back in his seat and watched her as she leaned toward the windshield, straining to see through the torrent. The rain beat noisily on the canvas top and side-curtains. The smell of canvas and water-proofing mixed with the delicate scent she wore. For a moment he was camping with the beautiful woman he now studied in profile.

His eyes became accustomed to the darkness and he made out the "G-2" stenciled in white letters on the olive drab dashboard. He broke into a broad grin. "Does Captain Prentice lend you his jeep often, Lieutenant?"

"All the time, Captain. All the time."

*   *   *   *   *   *   *   *

They were in a jovial mood as they drove back from the village of Allsford Lynn. They had re-discovered what they already knew from their wonderful weekend in London. They laughed at foolish things most adults would find childish and enjoyed playing with words. They anticipated each other's responses with remarkable accuracy.

It was 9:55 P.M. when they entered the outer door of the officers' club. To anyone who might have seen or heard them they would have seemed high, on the near side of inebriation. Actually, they had each had a single glass of English beer.

They shed their wet coats in the vestibule and went into the club, They didn't notice the club was empty until they were well into the room. Robb stopped short. Evelyn looked quickly at him, then toward the bar. The sign on the bar said CLOSED. The Toby mug on the back bar had its face turned toward the wall. The 990th was alerted.

Evelyn closed her eyes. "Oh no!"

He put his arm around her shoulders. "Don't make too much of it. It could be a milk run to the submarine pens at Brest or St. Nazaire."

"But you're dead on your feet."

They turned and walked toward the door. As he helped her with her coat, she turned and reached up and pulled his face down to hers. Her cheek was moist against his face.

He embraced her. "Please. It's all right. Things seem much worse from the ground."

She remained silent, drawing him tighter to her, as if to forestall the inevitable by the strength of her will.

—18—

Swovik awakened Robertson and Kovacs at 2:00 A.M. on Sunday, November 26, 1944. After three or four hours of preparation and another hour of waiting at the head of the runway, the word came from the tower, "Bring 'em back. The mission is scrubbed." Exactly as yesterday.

Robb met Kovacs in G-2 when he went to turn in his maps. As they started out the door for their Squadron area—and their bunks—Sam called them back. He asked if they would be up in time to join him for Sunday dinner in the mess at 2:00.

They crawled back into the sack at 8:30 A.M., six hours after Swovik had awakened them. They fell asleep immediately without the aid of Swovik's capsules.

They were late in joining Sam in the mess hall, but there was still a good supply of wings on the chicken trays on the line. The word must have gotten around about the quick trip to France of the powdered egg server who smarted off to Kovacs. A mess attendant went back and got a fresh steam tray of chicken as soon as he saw Kovacs. He piled choice pieces on Kovacs' plate. He tried to give Robb the same treatment, but Robb restrained him. Sam settled for a single drumstick.

They sat at a table in a remote corner of the mess hall. Kovacs attacked his plate of chicken with gusto. Robb looked at Sam. "I don't suppose anyone ever died from eating too much chicken, do you?"

Kovacs attacked a piece of chicken. "No problem. I took final absolution this morning and it's good for all day."

Kovacs went back for seconds. When he returned he noticed that Sam still hadn't eaten his piece of chicken. "You know what my old lady would say if she saw you picking at that one little piece of chicken and that measly spoonful of mashed potatoes?"

"What would she say?" Sam asked politely.

"She'd say one word. Eat! In my house, if you only took one piece of chicken, it was a crime against God, America, the chicken. God knows what all. My old lady never talked much and she almost never talked loud except when she said 'Eat!'

"My old man talked a lot and he really talked loud and he'd yell 'Eat', too. Sometimes, when we were younger, if you didn't eat everything on your plate he'd get up and give you a slap across the side of the head. Then he'd go and sit down at the head of the table. Nobody would say anything after that but we sure would eat whether we felt like it or not. After a few years of that you learn to want to eat. Probably got our stomachs stretched. Sam, your head would be lop-sided if you had been raised in my family. You'd weigh over 200 pounds and you'd have a lop-sided head."

Sam smiled. "That was a good bit of family history. You'd have made a good writer."

Robb said, "Speaking of writing, I subsidized a pretty good story yesterday."

Kovacs said, "What story?"

"Brain Child's Peace Plan."

Kovacs said, "Oh yeah, I heard about his peace plan. It's pretty good. My gunners told me it really went over big when Brain Child gave his speech on it in the NCO Club."

Sam said, "What exactly is this peace plan of his?"

Robb said, "As I recall, all B-17s and B-24s would have one extra seat, what Brain Child calls a 'potbelly seat', in the nose compartment, and all American congressmen, cabinet members, millionaires and generals would be required by law to take a ride over enemy territory in one of these potbelly seats from time to time. Brain Child says we've got thousands of bombers so we'd have enough potbelly seats to accommodate all the politicians and generals and millionaires. He says if you had such a law in force in peacetime you'd never have war declared, but if you didn't and it were set up in wartime, you'd have an armistice tomorrow. That's the gist of it. It's really quite elaborate."

Sam said, "That's a nice bit of satire."

"A lot of the guys who heard his talk on it in the NCO Club wanted a copy of it. Brain Child asked me if I could get it typed and mimeographed for him here on the base. I gave him ten pounds and told him to have some secretarial service in Cambridge do it."

Kovacs said, "Enough of this small talk. I've got some big things to talk about, Robb. What I mean is there's going to be a big concert."

"What concert?"

"The one in Glasgow."

"Oh, that one. Will the king and queen be able to make it?"

"I don't know about that, but the Lord Mayor of Glasgow is coming."

"That's nice."

Sam said, "Is this one of those silly games we used to play in college, where one guy makes a nonsense remark and the next guy follows with another one?"

"I'm not sure," Robb replied.

"There really is going to be a concert in Glasgow. I went to London yesterday and got things rolling. Before the poker game."

Robb looked at him quizzically. "You got things rolling?"

"I had a little business meeting with old Fred yesterday."

"Fred?"

"You remember Fred, our valet?"

"Kee-riste! *That* Fred. More wild doings!"

"Wait a minute, pal. Old Fred's all right."

"Okay. Old Fred's all right. Go on."

Sam looked back and forth from one to the other.

"I didn't tell him about you and Cynthia. I just told him there was this woman who's hiding out in Glasgow we have to find who's crazy about chamber music."

"She's not exactly hiding out. She just doesn't want to see me."

"Same thing." Kovacs started on another piece of chicken. "And you know something? Right off the bat Fred says, 'Let's set up a concert in Glasgow'."

"Two nuts are better than one." Robb's tone was drab, humorless.

Sam was excited. "I'll be damned! I'm beginning to see what this is all about!" He slapped his fist into his palm. "Yeow! Go on, Stosh!"

Kovacs smiled at Sam. "First time I ever heard you say 'yeow', pal."

"You've never seen me in a yeow situation. Go on. Let's hear about your concert."

"Okay. I was thinking this concert ought to be a charity thing, where we pay for the music and the hall, with the gate going for the charity outfit."

"What's the lucky outfit?" Robb asked.

"War orphans. I figured war orphans would be best. I like orphans and it would be tough for those big time fiddlers to turn down orphans, if you know what I mean."

"I know what you mean. You have a devious mind. Do you know what I mean?"

"I know what you mean, but I really do like orphans."

"Everybody likes orphans. Do you like orphans, Sam?"

"Yes, I like orphans, but let Stosh get on with this. I'm getting pretty excited."

"Me too," Robb said. "It's just that I don't know how to react. It's exciting, but I have this feeling we're getting mixed up in a big con game."

"It's all on the up and up. Fred liked my idea about the orphans, too."

"I'm sure he did. He likes orphans, too. Right?"

"Right. So we talked about the wages for these guys and the expenses and the dates we'd like and all that. You know, everything we talked about."

Sam looked at Robb, surprised. "You were in on the planning of all this?"

"Not really. When I first heard about it was just a gleam in Stosh's eye. I never thought anything would come of it. Let's get to the good part. What quartet did we get?"

"Wait a minute. We got to take these things in order." Stosh smiled, obviously enjoying telling the story. "Yesterday, right away after I talked it over with Fred in the hotel he picks up the phone and gets the number of the main Glasgow newspaper and calls them up and asks if they can find out the name of the war orphan outfit in Glasgow. He told them we wanted to make a big contribution.

"The newspaper guy asks where Fred's calling from. Fred says London and the guy says why do you want to help Glasgow orphans? Why not London orphans? It looked right then and there like old Fred had walked into a trap, right?"

"Right."

"You guys aren't going to believe this. Old Fred tells the guy he was once an orphan in Glasgow himself, a long time ago."

Robb frowned. "I don't like the turn this thing is taking. It really is starting to sound like a con game."

Kovacs held up his hands, palms out. "Wait a minute. That's how I felt too, and that's what I told Fred myself after he hung up. And do you know what he said? He said it was the truth. He said he'd swear on a stack of bibles he was an orphan in Glasgow."

Robb looked at Sam. "What do you think? Do you believe our friend, old Fred?"

"Why not? He has as much right to be an orphan as the next guy."

"Okay, Stosh. Go on."

"The newspaper guy says he'll call Fred back when he finds out something."

"Get on with it. Skip the details."

"Settle down. I want you to know exactly how things are set up. Okay. The newspaper guy calls back and gives Fred the name of the director of the orphans and the chairman of the board. A Lady somebody or other. So Fred calls up Lady So-and-So."

Robb's eyes widened. He looked at Sam.

"Fred tells this lady that there's a group of American flyers who want to do something for the war orphans in Glasgow. So she asks why Glasgow if you're calling from London. Why not London orphans? So Fred tells her the American flyers have their flak leaves in Scotland and they really like the Scotch people because the Scotch people have always been so good to them. I had told him about the flak leaves, just in case."

"Kee-riste! He changed his story. Why?"

"He told me the newspaper guy seemed suspicious. He said sometimes people find it harder to believe the truth than a good lie. But hell, it's no lie. We do have our flak leaves in Scotland and the Scotch people always knock themselves out for us, right?"

"Right. Go on."

"Getting back to this old lady, she says that's awfully nice of the flyers. Then she asks just what exactly it is we'd like to do. Fred says we're getting the London Quartet to. . ."

Sam and Robb exclaimed, "The London Quartet!"

Robb said, "You got the London Quartet?"

"Nothing but the best. Right?"

Robb and Sam stared at Kovacs, then at each other.

"So Fred tells her our contribution will be to pay for the quartet and the hall if they'll make all the arrangements for the hall and the publicity. And that all of the gate goes to the orphans."

Sam leaned forward. "What did she think of the idea?"

"Well, this old lady—I figure she's old, but how the hell should I know. Maybe . . ."

Sam said, "We don't care how old she is. Go on, please."

"All right. She really flips. It turns out this lady's not only big on orphans, she's nuts about chamber music. Right away she asks Fred if he and I could come up there to her place for dinner this Sunday."

"Kee-riste!"

"Don't worry, Robb. We're not going."

"Go on."

"Fred had told her about me being there when he was talking to her. I forgot to tell you Fred told her his name and mine, but he told her we got to be anonymous. He told her the program should only say that this is a benefit given by her association and a group of American flyers serving in England, and that the flyers themselves insist on remaining anonymous. She really went for that."

"Go on," Sam said.

"So Fred told her he'll call back when we get the date set with the London Quartet."

Robb stared at Kovacs in disbelief. "What if the London Quartet says no?"

"Fred knew they'd be in London through January because he has tickets for their London series this winter. And both of us were sure we'd get them because we got the magic combination."

"What's that?" Robb looked suspicious.

"Money and orphans."

"Go on."

"Okay. So Fred calls up someone in London to find out who the agent or manager of the London Quartet is. Then he calls their manager."

"Just like that," Robb said.

"You know Fred. He doesn't screw around when you put him in charge. He has a lot of faith in money, too. You know, in gold we trust."

"I remember that from last time. Go on."

"Well, he didn't get the manager right away but he asked whoever he was talking to have the manager call him back. He told this guy that he's calling for Lady So-and-So of the war orphan society and that we had a big donor who would pay whatever the Quartet asked for if they'd play for the orphans with all the take going to the war orphans."

Robb glanced at Kovacs. "Good old Fred wanted to make sure he'd call back. Right?"

"Right.   So the manager called back about a half hour later. Fred told him about how he was calling for Lady So-and-So and the Glasgow war orphan society and how they have this anonymous donor who'd pay anything they require—that's how he put it—if they'd play a concert series in Glasgow."

"A series?" Sam was incredulous.

"Just wait. You'll see why we wanted a series."

"Go on," Robb said.

"Fred told him the expenses and the hall arrangements and publicity would be taken care of by Lady So-and-So. Then he told him that he himself would go up to Glasgow to take care of the advance details."

"Fred's going up there?" Sam asked.

"Yep. He's taking a leave from valeting."

"Kee-riste!"

"You got to hand it to Fred. He told the guy that because the donor wants to remain anonymous he'd go over himself to this guy's office and pay the Quartet in advance, in cash, when he gets the word from him that the Quartet will play for the orphans.

"Go on,"

"Okay. The guy says he'll have to take it up with the members of the Quartet. Fred told him the first concert would have to be on a Sunday afternoon. I already told Fred to shoot for Sunday afternoon because Lady X . . ."

"Cynthia."

". . . because Cynthia is more likely to go to a Sunday afternoon concert."

Robb said, "You guys aren't shy, are you? You're laying down terms to four of the world's greatest musicians."

"The way I look at it, they're dealing with two of the world's greatest pilots."

"Cut the crap."

"Okay. They put their pants on one leg at a time like the rest of us. How's that?"

Sam was grinning from ear to ear. Robb said, "Go on."

"The guy tells Fred he'll call back on Sunday at noon. Then Fred says to the guy right away, 'I better call you at noon tomorrow because I'm all over London on Sundays'. What was going on was Fred was afraid to have the guy call him at the hotel—Fred has to work on Sunday—and Fred was afraid the guy would call the hotel and the hotel would give the guy Fred's hotel number, then someone would answer, 'Valet service'."

Robb started to laugh. "Wouldn't that be something, Sam?" They both laughed. Robb's laugh turned into his wild, crazy laugh. Kovacs gave him a sharp punch in the shoulder. "Settle down, Robb. It wasn't *that* funny."

"The hell it wasn't." He wiped the tears from his eyes with his fingertips.

"After Fred hung up we had a little business meeting. I gave him the cash for the Quartet and the expense money for himself when he goes up to Glasgow. I hired him for his leave period. He's taking one week off now and three weeks when the series is on."

Sam was really enjoying the whole business. He said, "I'll bet he'll get a lot more than he makes pressing pants,"

Robb said, "One problem, Stosh. What if the London Quartet says no? Do you guys have some sort of backup plan to present to your friend, Lady So-and-So?"

"You worry too much. They're not going to say no. You can count on it. "

"I wish I had your confidence."

"You would if you had this." He reached into his inside pocket and pulled out a yellow sheet of paper. "This was in my mail box at Squadron Headquarters when we went to get Swovik to give us a ride over here today. Sergeant Kerrigan took the telephone message for me. I bet Kerrigan thinks I'm some kind of spy. This is from old Fred." He read the neatly typed message. "'To: Captain Stanley Kovacs. Re: Operation Glasgow. Main events as follows: Number One: 3:30 P.M. Sunday, November 26; Number Two: 3:30 P.M. Sunday, December 3; Number Three: 3:30 P.M. Sunday, December 10.' Then he says at the end: 'Lady A ecstatic. Insists we come to dinner. Signed F'".

"I'll be damned! I can't believe it!" Robb reached out and shook hands with Kovacs.

Sam shook hands with Kovacs. "Congratulations, Stosh. You never cease to amaze me!"

"Knock it off, guys. Actually, Fred's a genius at things like this. How do you like that little touch, 'Lady A ecstatic. Insists we come to dinner.' ?"

"You know," Robb said, "Fred is a bit like you. He doesn't take things seriously, particularly people in high places, and he has complete confidence he can make things happen."

Sam said, "What's he doing pressing pants?"

"That's the way the dice rolled for him. You know, being an orphan and all." Kovacs eyes shot quickly from Robb to Sam and back to Robb.

"All Fred needs in this world is a little seed money. Then look out."

Sam said, "I'll bet he gets it."

Robb put his hand on Kovacs' arm. "This really is fantastic. Even if it hadn't been cooked up to find Cynthia, you're giving Glasgow a great concert series and it should raise some money for a good cause."

"What gets me is how easy it was. Fred started on this yesterday about this time. What I can't figure out is why don't people do this kind of thing all the time? You know, outfits trying to raise money for charity. It's like falling off a log."

Sam said. "All you need is lots of play money that happens to be real and two stout-hearted men who don't know the meaning of daunt or cawn't. That's a rare combination."

Robb smiled. "That's pretty good, Sam. One thing's been bothering me. Suppose we draw Cynthia out of her. . . uh. . ."

"Hiding place," Stosh said. He gave Sam a sly look out of the corner of his eye.

"Suppose she comes to the concert. Who's going to pick her out?"

Kovacs smiled. "You."

"No way. She'd disappear as soon as she saw me. I've got to get her cornered at home so she'll hear me out and at least tell me what this is all about."

"Quit worrying about it. Remember I said a little while ago you'd see why we wanted a series. We have your problem all figured out. We worked out a setup where a person can buy tickets for the second and third concerts by filling out a card they get in the program for the first concert. They fill out the card with their name and address and put it in one of the boxes Fred sets up in the lobby. Then the orphan society sends out the tickets to the next concert to the people who filled out the cards, inviting them to make a contribution if they like. So all Fred has to do is look through the cards until he finds Cynthia's name and bingo! We got her address."

Robb stared at Kovacs, his stare gradually shading into a grin. "I'll be damned!"

Sam was ecstatic. "That really is ingenious. And they'll probably get bigger donations this way, sending out the tickets before they get the money. The honor system."

"That's what Fred's going to tell Lady So-and-So, and he's going to tell her nobody gets to buy tickets for the whole shebang at once. He's going to tell her that in his experience he found you raise more money if people are asked to kick in two different times instead of just once."

"Not bad," Robb said.

Sam said, "He did say 'in his experience', didn't he? Can't you see Fred delivering a suit he's pressed for someone at the hotel? First he delivers the coat, then later the vest, and finally the pants, collecting a tip each time."

"Hey, Robb, old Sam's got quite a sense of humor once he starts letting it out."

It was now 3:30. They had the mess hall to themselves. The mess people were mopping the floor, staying as far away as possible from Captain Kovacs and his friends. The news must have gotten around about the reason for their colleague's quick trip to France.

"I'm really excited about this, Stosh," Robb said. "You've gone through an awful lot of trouble for me. Thanks."

"Forget it. I'm having the time of my life with this thing."

Sam looked at Kovacs. "Are you going to the concerts?"

"No way, but I think I can get you a couple of tickets."

"I wouldn't miss it for the world, but I'll buy my own tickets. Just out of curiosity, how much is all this going to cost you?"

Kovacs smiled. He took out the yellow sheet of paper again.

"There's a P.S. on the note. I've been saving it to spring on you guys. Get this. It says here, 'P.S. London Quartet insists on offering their services gratis to this good cause. Will require expenses only'."

Robb and Sam stared at each other.

"So you see, guys, you don't need a lot of money for this kind of thing. Of course we'll throw into the orphans' pot the money we would've had to pay the fiddlers. Maybe a little more, depending on how drunk those admirals and generals are in London when they play poker over the next few weeks, if you know what I mean."

Sam smiled, "I know what you mean."

Robb looked at Kovacs, "I wonder if we'll find her. What do you think?"

"Hell, yes, we'll find her. It's all set."

The 990th Heavy Bombardment Group stood down on Monday, November 20th, one of the clearest, brightest autumn days Robb had seen in England. Fog and drizzle made their first appearance just after dark as Robb, Bradley, Kovacs and Stew Adams, Kovacs' co-pilot, began their walk from the Squadron Area to the mess hall. By the time they reached the mess hall the fog was quite thick.

Bradley said, "Real Hounds of Baskerville, Wuthering Heights, Brennan on the Moor weather."

Kovacs said, "That's exactly what I was thinking."

Stew Adams asked, "Were you really thinking that, Stosh?" Adams' complete failure to appreciate Kovacs' wry humor never ceased to amaze Robb. Adams was very intelligent—he had been a mathematics student at Purdue—but his imagination was minimal and his sense of humor almost non-existent. He was a literal-minded person who, ironically, shared a cockpit with one of the least literal-minded of men. Adams was a good pilot, cool and with an extra measure of courage born of lack of imagination, but he and Kovacs, while respecting each other, would never be close.

"Something like that, Stew. I was also thinking this is real Eighth Air Force flying weather. I got a hundred says we're alerted tonight."

"You're on," Bradley said. "Pounds or dollars?"

"Who cares?"

"Right." Bradley could afford to be casual about it. Kovacs was always dumping money on him, just as he was on Robb. As Robb listened to the banter between Kovacs and Bradley, it occurred to him that Kovacs was closer to Bradley than he was to Stew Adams, his own co-pilot. How much happier Kovacs' life would be if Bradley were his co-pilot. But how much poorer he himself would be. He wondered if he could make it without Bradley.

Kovacs won the bet. The 990th was alerted at 9:30 P.M.

The string on the mission map wasn't too long on Tuesday morning. The target: the railroad marshaling yards at Frankfurt on Main. Robb knew that compared to some targets Frankfort on Main wasn't bad. Not bad, but definitely not good, especially if the skies were clear and German anti-aircraft gunners fired visually rather than on radar.

Strike time: 1222.

As he ended his briefing, Sam said, "Be glad it's not Frankfort on Öder." Frankfort on Öder, on the far eastern boundary of Germany, was twice as far as Frankfort on Main. Sam's attempt to end his briefing on a light note was a failure. No one even smiled.

As they walked through the mist-drizzle-fog on their way to the trucks to take them to their planes, Kovacs said to Bradley, "That was a sucker bet you made last night, but then you're new around here, right?"

"Right. I'll pay you off when we get back."

"No hurry. I don't think I'll be needing the money."

* * * * * * * *

The first echelon of Amber Squadron stood poised at the head of the runway, their propellers turning over slowly in the fog-laden, pre-dawn blackness as their pilots waited orders to roll. Kovacs' plane, Dogbreath, was at the head of the Squadron. Brillig was in the Deputy Leader position.

As Robb leaned forward, straining to see Kovacs' lights, he suffered another one of his attacks of rationality. He ruminated on the fact that if this runway were a four-lane, undivided highway—which was exactly what it looked like—and if this airplane were a tractor-trailer highway rig, and if he were to do what he was about to do right now with this truck, he would be certified as totally insane by any psychiatrist. Yet here he sat, ready to roar down this highway in this 64,000 pound vehicle, more than twice the size and weight of the biggest highway truck, loaded with 20,000 pounds of 100 octane gasoline and 8,000 pounds of TNT. He will be speeding down this highway at well over 100 miles an hour in the pre-dawn blackness and near-solid fog with nothing more to guide him than a gyrocompass and the little runway lights, which he'll only be able to see one by one on the left side of the highway as they flash past the periphery of his vision. And, oh yes, he'll be steering this monstrous machine, never meant to be a ground vehicle, with his feet.

If the man ahead of him in this wild, blind race—in this case Kovacs—lets a wheel slip over the edge of the runway it will sink into the soft mud and his plane will pile up in an exploding inferno, and Brillig, twenty seconds behind, will roar smack into that inferno. And the guy twenty seconds behind will join the pile-up, adding his thousands of gallons of 100 octane and his tons of TNT to the inferno. Add to all this the ever-present possibility that he might run out of runway before he gets off the ground. Loaded as he was, the slightest loss of power on a single engine on the takeoff run would make the runway too short, and they'd all end up permanent residents of Cambridge. It happened now and then. He thought about the good old days when they took off thirty seconds apart.

The props continued ticking over at 800 RPMs. Why was he dwelling on such gloomy possibilities today? He tried unsuccessfully to drive the answer from his awareness. Visions of a concert hall in Scotland kept intruding.

Kovacs' voice jarred him, "Okay, men, here we go. Keep it tight!"

Kovacs' exhausts flashed brightly through the fog and disappeared. Bradley counted the last seconds to take-off. ". . . eight . . . seven . . . six . . . " Robb advanced all throttles full forward at the count of "five". Both pilots exerted full pressure on their foot brakes as the plane strained and shuddered at the thrust of four Wright Cyclone engines. Bradley yelled out, ". . . two . . . one . . . go!" They released their brakes and Brillig lurched into the night.

They had been climbing in the soup in their seemingly endless, monotonous pattern for nearly a half-hour when Robb heard the yell over the command channel: "Mid-air! Mid-air! Mid. . . " and an abandon-ship bell ringing in the background. Then silence. Robb listened for a call from the other ship in the collision. Nothing.

Robb held his gloved hands over his goggles. He knew that twenty young men, most of them in their early or mid-twenties, some of them in their late teens, were about to be drilled by gravity into the English soil. They'll have minutes to think until at last their moment of hell ends in a blinding flash, or sudden darkness, or sudden nothingness. He always thought of it as a red flash. He looked at his watch. Right about now. A minute later he breathed easier. Their torment was over by now.

He stared numbly into the blackness beyond the windshield. Monk Bradley, now monitoring intercom, executed the procedural turns precisely, unaware of the tragedy.

Robb looked upward constantly. Still no sign of light. As they continued the upward grind, he wondered how far ahead of him Kovacs really was. A thousand feet? Five hundred? Fifty? Or was he directly above them, almost close enough for Brillig's props to cut off his tail?

Robb's spirits rose as light gradually illuminated the cockpit as they approached the uneven top surface of the cloud layer.

Bradley saw Kovacs' flares and swung into an intersecting turn to the left. Robb saw Barnstorm and Dagger squadrons flying in formation a thousand feet above them. The lead squadron, Dagger, had twelve planes. His eyes moved to Barnstorm. He saw it immediately: a lone plane at the rear flying as an echelon of one. Barnstorm had lost the two planes. He felt a moment's relief that the losses weren't Amber's, but his relief was immediately smothered by the thought of those twenty men.

Robb took over the controls. Bradley pointed at Barnstorm Squadron and held up ten gloved fingers. He shrugged his shoulders. Robb smacked his hands together in a glancing clap and pointed downward. Bradley nodded slowly .

They had made a half circle to the left when Robb nudged Bradley and pointed off to their left. Two of Amber's planes were emerging from the undercast, one exactly above the other with no more than ten feet separating them. How long had they been flying this close to one another? If the top of the crap had been a few hundred feet higher, would they have collided? Every pilot and co-pilot half way through his tour had emerged from the undercast in such proximity to other planes at one time or another. Strange, Robb reflected, no one ever talked about it.

They joined their Wing and the bomber stream at 27,500 feet over the North Sea and climbed eastward for the next two and a half hours, reaching mission altitude two and a half hours later. Robb was relieved to see that not a single gauge exceeded its redline, even though they were at 31,000 feet and only minutes from the Initial Point. A good sign. Chalk up another good job for Sergeant Yoder, their new crew chief.

Robb was glad to see that the undercast that had been developing four or five thousand feet below them had filled out to about seven-eighths cover. The Germans would be aiming on radar, not remotely as accurate as their visual shooting.

At 1221.30 Carlson warned Robb to get ready for Kovacs' turn on the IP on to the bomb run, yet when Kovacs made his turn Robb was surprised by the sudden violence of it. Robb whipped Brillig into a vertical bank to the right and pulled back on the control column with all his strength to keep from overrunning Kovacs. He yelled to himself, "Stosh, you crazy son-of-a-bitch!" Richards hit the bomb-bay door switch as they rolled out of the turn, now on their run on the railroad yard at Frankfurt.

Robb pushed his intercom button. "Pilot to waist gunners. Start throwing the chaff, but be sure to save some for after bombs-away so the guys behind us get some benefit from it. Over and out."

The flak was moderate to heavy, but as he looked ahead to the black mottled gray sky over the target he could see the chaff was doing its job. The concentrations of flak were a thousand feet below the formation now releasing its bombs ahead of them. They began to feel the usual bumps, but the shells were still exploding well below. The kicks in the ass were hard, but not enough to knock them out of the sky. Richards began his count. "Ten . . . nine . . . eight. . . " Shells began exploding at their level but two or three hundred feet off to the left. Richards droned, ". . . three . . . two . . . one. *Bombs away!*" At that precise moment Robb felt a blow to his left calf as if someone had whacked him with a baseball bat. He shook his head and leaned towards Bradley and hit him in the arm, motioning to him to take over. He reached down and grasped his lower left leg. He then felt the pain for the first time. He looked at his thick outer glove. It was covered with blood. He looked down again and saw the hole in the side of the fuselage just above and behind the left rudder. Damn! Of all the lousy luck!

The initial shock gave way to mind-searing pain, all concentrated in the calf of his left leg. He felt the warm blood running down his ankle and into his flying boot. He wiggled his foot and he felt a sloshing sensation. He was surprised by the intensity of the pain more than by the fact that he'd been hit. He had never imagined pain could be like this.

He nudged Bradley, indicating to him to raise his ear flap. He pulled his mask away from his face and yelled, "I've been hit! In the leg!"

Bradley raised his mask and yelled, "How bad?" He dared not take his eyes off Kovacs' plane for even a second. Kovacs would be starting his evasive maneuvers any second now, violently and without warning.

Robb took a deep breath and pulled his mask away again and yelled, "I'm bleeding quite a bit! I'll put a tourniquet on it! Call Stosh and get permission to go home alone, in the soup!"

Kovacs' plane tilted suddenly into a diving, vertical bank to the right. Bradley held perfect formation with Kovacs. Kovacs rolled out of his turn and leveled off at 28,000 feet on a westerly heading.

Bradley pushed his button. "Amber Deputy to Amber Leader. Over."

Kovacs came back, "This is Amber Leader."

"This is Amber Deputy. Pilot wounded. Much bleeding. Request permission to go solo, high speed, in the soup. Over."

"Permission granted. Turn his heated suit down and give him a half shot. Over."

Robb switched to command channel. He pushed his button. "Fiddler to Polack. I'll be okay."

"Roger, Fiddler. Turn your suit down to fifty degrees, *now*. And give yourself a half shot. Then set a speed record. Stay in the soup. Did you get that, Ape?"

Monk responded, "Roger."

Robb pulled the tourniquet strap tighter. It seemed to be doing the job. He felt weak, heady. The pain was unbelievable. He looked for the morphine syringe in his kit. Gone. He nudged Bradley and pantomimed a syringe shot. Bradley pulled his kit from his knee pocket, broke it open, pulled out the syringe, broke the tip against the throttle pedestal and motioned to Robb to pull up his sleeve. Bradley worked quickly with his left hand, wrestling the control column with his right. His eyes darted back and forth between Kovacs' plane, now twenty feet on Brillig's left, and Robb. He gave Robb the shot and immediately pulled back on the throttles to keep from overrunning Kovacs.

Robb switched to intercom. "Pilot to crew. In a minute now we're going to be diving into the cloud cover below. I've been slightly wounded in the leg." He stopped to take a few breaths. "Not serious, but we're heading home on our own. We'll be exposed for a minute in our dive, so keep a lookout for bandits. Ready, Monk? Okay, let's go!" He let up the button and sat still, breathing hard. He pulled his mask away from his face and vomited down the front of his Mae West life-preserver.

Bradley executed a wingover to the right. He headed downward for ten seconds before he pulled the ship into a sloping descent on a course slightly north of due west. He easing back on the controls to keep their speed from exceeding 300—about 50 miles per hour beyond redline speed. Brillig disappeared into the undercast.

Bradley picked up a heading directly for home, indicated airspeed 275, rate of descent 50 feet per minute. He had to pull substantial mani-fold pressure to maintain their speed even in their slightly downhill attitude, but Wieriman assured him that their fuel supply was adequate, provided they didn't have to do an elaborate instrument letdown.

They crossed the Dutch coast at 1415 hours at 12,000 feet, still sol-idly in the soup. Carlson called Bradley, "Robb, ETA for Allsford Lynn is 1532 if we hold present speed."

Brain Child reported Eighth Air Force was reporting a ceiling of 300 feet at Allsford Lynn with the top of the crap at 16,500 feet.

"Roger." Bradley pulled off his oxygen mask and yelled, "Good weather setup at home, Robb!" He was shocked to see Robb's head slumped to his chest, his upper body hanging forward in his shoulder harness.

"Co-pilot to Engineer. Come to the cockpit."

Wieriman stepped out of his turret. Bradley yelled, "See if he's sleeping or if he's passed out!"

The Engineer shook Robb's shoulder. No response. He lifted the pilot's mask and put his ear against his mouth. He replaced the mask and turned up the supply on the oxygen line. He leaned towards Bradley. "He's unconscious but he's breathing."

"Check his left leg, at the calf. If it's bleeding put another tourniquet above his knee." He lowered Brillig's nose and added two inches of manifold pressure to each engine. Their speed built up to 300 miles per hour. He tuned in Allsford Lynn just as they crossed the English coast.

As always on a mission day, officers began wandering into the Operations Room about an hour before the Group was scheduled to return. Sam and Evelyn arrived a few minutes before Bradley's first transmission crackled forth over the loud speaker. They, like everyone else, had expected the first transmission to be from Captain Pete Peterson, today's Group Leader.

"Amber Uncle to Upshaw Tower."

"Amber Uncle. This is Upshaw Tower."

"Upshaw Tower. This is Amber Uncle co-pilot. My pilot is wounded. He's breathing, but he's unconscious, probably from loss of blood. Over."

Evelyn closed her eyes tightly. Sam grasped her hand.

The men in the room looked toward Evelyn as Bradley's announcement blared forth. Her face was buried against Sam's chest. Sam's eyes were closed as he embraced Evelyn.

"Amber Uncle. Do you have mechanical problems?"

"Negative."

Hammersmith gave Bradley instructions in the strange Air Force sing-song that acquired bored overtones at the first sign of an emergency. "Amber Uncle. Are you under the overcast?"

"Roger. I'm at 300 feet."

"Roger, Amber Uncle. You have clearance to come straight on in. Runway 31. Ceiling 300. Altimeter setting 29.28, winds out of the northwest zero eight. Use end taxi turnoff. Stop as soon as you clear runway. Ambulance and medical personnel will meet you there. Acknowledge. Over." Hammersmith could have been reading baseball scores to Bradley.

"Roger, Upshaw Tower. Loud and clear. Will stop on end taxi turnout. Touchdown in approximately seven minutes. Over and out."

The number of people in the Operations Room increased. People started moving toward the stairway to the roof of the tower. Sam and Evelyn joined the others on the roof. Sam trained his binoculars to the east. "I see him now."

Bradley came in hotter than Sam had ever seen a B-17 land. He touched down at the beginning of the runway, but didn't start slowing down until he passed the halfway mark on the runway. Sam kept his binoculars on Brillig. Finally he saw the smoke from the tires as Bradley hit the brakes. Sam breathed at last when he saw the plane swing into the taxi turnout and stop, its bomb bay doors already opening. As soon as the props stopped turning, the ambulance backed up to the plane.

Sam wormed his way between Hammersmith and the C.O. at the railing. He asked Hammersmith how long it would be before the Group landed. Hammersmith said, "A little over an hour."

Sam turned to Colonel Strang. "Sir. Would you mind if Lieutenant Vandivier and I made a quick trip to the hospital? I can make it back a half hour before the Group lands."

"All right, Sam. Tell Lieutenant Vandivier she may take the rest of the day off."

Lieutenant Colonel Horatio Crick overheard the exchange. He frowned.

The ambulance was backed up to the emergency door when they got to the hospital. Neither Sam nor Evelyn knew the nurse on duty at the nurses' station. "Captain Rizzo and Lieutenant Cameron are with Captain Robertson now. I'm afraid that's all the information I have."

Evelyn said, "Is he alive? Do you know for a fact that he's alive?"

"I don't even know that. If you'll wait in the vestibule, I'll keep you informed. I wish I could be more helpful." She placed her hand on Evelyn's arm. "You're Merrie's roommate, aren't you?"

Evelyn nodded.

"I know how this is for you, not knowing anything. I'll be back as soon as I find out anything."

They sat for ten minutes or so in the vestibule. Sam looked at his watch. "I have to get back. Call the Officer of the Day as soon as you hear anything. His orderly will relay the message to me." He embraced her and kissed her on the cheek.

Sam was interviewing Kovacs' crew when the orderly handed him Evelyn's message. "Robb's condition is officially listed as critical, but Tony says—unofficially—that Robb is going to make it."

Sam said softly, "Thank God."

He handed the note to Kovacs. Kovacs read it and crossed himself.

On Tuesday afternoon, November 28, seven days after the mission to Frankfort on Main, Sam and Kovacs were at lunch when Kovacs was called to the phone. He came rushing back. "Merrie says they just brought Robb back from the big hospital. She says we can see him any time now. Let's go."

Merrie met them at her station. She came around the end of her counter and embraced Stosh and kissed him on his mouth. "Evelyn is with him now. Give them a few minutes. You may want to talk to Tony. He can fill you in about Robb."

Rizzo was in a good mood. "We should have a drink to celebrate Robb's survival, but this is a U.S. Army hospital and drinking isn't allowed." He withdrew a bottle of Scotch and glasses from his desk drawer. "Have some medicine." He poured three double shots.

Sam said, "How is he?"

"Surprisingly well. We came within minutes of losing him. Monk setting a speed record saved him, without a doubt."

Sam said, "How's his leg?"

"That piece of flak sliced his left calf as neatly as if someone had pulled a sharp butcher knife across it. The surgeons couldn't have ordered a neater wound, which made it easier to put everything back together. The flak missed the bones completely."

Kovacs asked, "Any permanent damage?"

"The Achilles tendon could be a problem. When you sew an Achilles tendon back together it often ends up slightly shorter than it was. Robb's tendon got sliced above the hard tissue, above the point on the calf where the tendon splits in two and joins the softer muscle tissue, so it should heal pretty fast. Another good thing, only one side got sliced."

"Will he limp?" Sam asked.

"He's in a foot to thigh cast to keep him from bending his knee and putting a strain on the tendon. He'll limp for a while after he gets the cast off, but if he does his exercises properly after he gets out of the cast he'll be all right."

Kovacs said, "How long before he'll be able to walk okay?"

"He should be all right by the first of the year, barring complications. You guys can go see him now if you like."

They checked with Merrie. Evelyn had gone back to work. Merrie led them to Robb's room. He looked better than he had in some time. The gray fatigue and the dark circles under his eyes were gone. His bed was set at a half reclining position. He was reading a book, his cast propped up on pillows.

Kovacs said, "Pretty fucking soft."

Robb smiled, "Right."

Kovacs said, "You cooperate, soldier, and I can arrange to have your vacation here extended for another week."

"No thanks. I hope to be out of here by this weekend."

Kovacs reached into his pocket. "I've got a little present for you." He handed him a note. "A little message for you received at squadron headquarters by your buddy, Sergeant Broomstick." Kovacs often commented that Kerrigan sat at attention like he had a broomstick up his ass.

Robb read the message: "Captain Stanley Kovacs: Strategy successful. Have party's specific location—thirty miles from Glasgow. Interviewed postmaster in area and have determined party is in residence. F".

Robb beamed. "I'll be damned! You did it!"

"I thought that would pick you up."

Robb handed the note to Sam. Sam nodded, "Stosh showed this to me. Congratulations."

Robb said to Kovacs, "Put yourself down to fly the next crew due for flak leave in Scotland. I'll go along."

Sam shook his head. "You won't be going anywhere for a while." Robb rolled over and picked up a set of crutches from the floor on the far side of his bed. He stood up next to the bed. "Want to bet?"

Sam said, "Pounds or dollars?"

Robb and Kovacs had hoped to get to Cynthia's place in Scotland early in the evening of Friday, December 8th, but such was not to be. When Kovacs filed his flight plan at 3:00 P.M., Red Hammersmith, Group Operations, refused to clear them for takeoff in The Colonel's Lady. The base was shut down. "In case you haven't noticed, Stosh, it's snowing like hell and the ceiling is damn near zero. Besides, what difference does it make if Tad Turk's crew start their flak leave in Scotland today or tomorrow? What are you so antsy about? Big poker game in Glasgow tonight?"

Finally, at 7:15 P.M., four hours after they filed their flight plan, Hammersmith gave them clearance to take off. "The snow's let up a little and the crews have got the runway pretty clear." Robb was surprised that Hammersmith made such a fuss about the weather but said nothing about the fact that he, as co-pilot, couldn't possibly work the rudders or brakes with his left leg in a foot-to-thigh cast.

They took off from the short runway into a 30 mile an hour headwind, the snow blowing directly into the windshield. Visibility was poor to nil, but they had the runway all to themselves and the Flying Fortress lifted itself into the air in less than a half mile on its run into the wind. Stripped of its armaments, the Flying Fortress was grossly overpowered, extremely responsive to its throttles and light to the touch on the controls. Kovacs leveled off at 250 feet above the end of the runway and held straight and level until the airspeed indicator read 275 miles per hour. He hauled back suddenly on the control column and they shot upward to fifteen hundred feet in seconds, the sensation heightened by the fact that they were flying blind. They climbed to 8,000 feet and held that altitude.

Robb felt a strange contentment as he surveyed the cockpit: Kovacs hunched over the controls, silhouetted in the green phosphorescent light from the maze of dials on the instrument panels; the pungent smell of ozone produced by myriad electrical relays; the subtle, almost indiscernible smell of gasoline that was often present in the cockpit of high performance military aircraft. He was where he belonged, here in this cockpit, and beneath this surface awareness was the knowledge that this cozy cocoon was speeding toward Scotland, toward Cynthia. At one moment he thrilled at the thought that perhaps he would, at long last, see her tonight, but in the next moment he plunged into deepest despair at the thought that she might reject him.

The outside temperature was well above freezing when they touched down on the main runway at the international airport at Prestwick, Ayrshire, Scotland, the port of entry for most of the heavy bombers that arrived in Europe by the North Atlantic route. A "Follow Me Jeep" led them between endless rows of high-tailed B-17 Flying Fortresses and huge, double-tailed B-24 Liberators, finally pulling up to a parking space on a broad concrete apron near Operations. A U.S. Army Air Corps bus met them and took Tad Turk's crew off to their flak-leave hostelry. As Kovacs put The Colonel's Lady to bed, Robb filled out the forms. He was concerned that they were without transportation to Largs, some thirty miles north of Prestwick, but he figured Stosh would make whatever arrangements were necessary.

As they left the cockpit Kovacs grabbed Colonel Strang's B-15 flight jacket that the C.O. always kept on a hook on the bulkhead behind the top turret. He took off his own jacket and put on the Colonel's with its bright silver eagles on the shoulders. As they approached Prestwick Operations, he slipped on his trench coat—with its captain's bars on its epaulets—over the colonel's jacket. They completed the required forms at Operations and proceeded to the U.S. Army Air Forces Motor Pool at Prestwick Air Base.

As they approached the motor pool office, Kovacs removed his trench coat, turned it inside out, and carried it over his arm. Kovacs cautioned Robb, who had no insignia on the shoulders of his trench coat, to button up his coat collar to cover the insignia on his shirt collar. "You don't want this guy to see you're a captain in case you come up sometimes without me and you want to use the C.O.'s jacket to get transportation."

Kovacs approached the sergeant at the counter and demanded a staff car. The sergeant told him there were none available. Kovacs responded with the cold, controlled ire expected of an angry colonel. The sergeant beamed when Kovacs agreed to accept a jeep. Kovacs signed the form "Stanley R. Kovacs, Capt. A.C." but the letters the "C" in "Capt." were quite illegible. They might even have been confused with "Col. A.C."

✳   ✳   ✳   ✳   ✳   ✳   ✳   ✳

Fred had been more or less correct. They drove some three to five miles north from Largs when Kovacs saw the two stone pillars marking the driveway to "Shelbourne". No name or address at the entrance, but this was the place Fred had described.

Wisps of powdery snow made their first appearance, blowing horizontally across the winding asphalt driveway as the jeep whined in second gear upward and inland for a half mile or so through the darkly wooded hillside. The drive leveled off suddenly as they broke into a clearing at the top of the hill. The house loomed massive and dark in the shadows on the far side of the driveway circle. Kovacs said, "They're not exactly poor, seeing this is their summer cottage." As the jeep's headlights struck the facade of the house, Robb could see that although the house was huge, its architecture was strangely reminiscent of the Cotswolds: gray, hand-split limestone now near-black, windows of small, leaded panes set deep into thick stone walls, steep slate roof with many dormers, and a broad, deep entry alcove.

Kovacs stopped the jeep opposite the main door and turned off the motor and lights. The house stood thirty or forty feet from the drive on a slight rise.

Robb said, "I'm nervous as hell."

"Look, we never get nervous or scared! Not for nobody!"

"I can't help it."

Kovacs' tone softened. "Maybe I should go to the door first."

Robb said, "I can handle it." His tone lacked conviction.

"Still, it might be better if I went up to the door first, maybe get inside to tell her what's up. She could close the door in your face. Then what you going to do? Break the door down?"

"I hadn't thought of that."

"I'll just tell her it would only be fair for her to see you, to hear you out."

"You're right. You go first."

"Wish me luck."

The wind had picked up considerably since they left Prestwick. Kovacs had to exert pressure to open the jeep door, its side curtains catching the full brunt of the cold wind that swept across the Irish Sea and the Firth of Clyde. He pulled the colonel's collar up around his ears as he approached the massive oaken door. He raised the heavy wrought iron knocker and let it drop. It hit the door with a resounding bang. Kovacs said "Shit!"

He took the knocker firmly in hand and tapped lightly. He looked at his watch. 10:10 P.M.. He shrugged. Pretty late to be calling but, what the hell, there's a war going on.

The door opened and Cynthia stood in the dimly lighted doorway.

"Miss Allsford?"

"What do you want?" Her tone was cautious, on the edge of un-friendly.

"Miss Allsford, I need to talk to you about a serious matter concern-ing our air base which is on your land." Kovacs was much taller than Cynthia Allsford, his shoulders well above her eye level. "You'll want to see my identification, of course." He reached into his pocket and pulled out his wallet. It slipped out of his hand and fell to the stone surface of the stoop. He turned sideways and bent down quickly to retrieve it, but he rose slowly, pausing ever so slightly as his right shoulder was even with her face. The bright silver colonel's eagle on his shoulder caught the light from the interior of the house.

"Come in, please."

She turned and led him through a vestibule and a large entry hall, across another hall and into a drawing room. Kovacs surveyed the room, clearly the main room in the house. Spacious, yet warm, intimate. Huge exposed beams of dark walnut supported the ceiling. Heavily laden bookshelves were set deep into walnut paneling on either side of the massive fieldstone fireplace. Most of the books were of large format and thick, their spines dulled by much use. A long, dark brown leather sofa faced the fireplace. Two easy chairs, also leather, were placed at either end of the sofa to form a seating circle of sorts around a large, knee-high, round oak table. Neat stacks of books, journals, and filing folders covered the table except for a small area immediately opposite the center of the sofa. Whoever worked with these books and journals obviously preferred this sofa and this low table to a conventional desk.

A fire radiated warmth and welcome. Small, cut glass, beveled windowpanes caught the orange-red and yellow flashes of firelight and sent them dancing back into the room. Kovacs' eyes swept the room. He said to himself: "Class!"

"Won't you be seated, Colonel." She motioned to the chair to the right of the sofa. She sat in the opposite chair. The big low table with its books and journals lay between them. "Are you from the American aerodrome on our land?"

"Yes, Miss, I am."

"Before we get into the trouble, or whatever it is about our land, I'd like to know how you found me here."

"Well, Miss, my Bombardment Group has had a certain amount of correspondence with your family about the land. You know, getting permission to lengthen the runways, expanding the bomb storage area, that sort of thing. Well, we found this address here in Scotland on a letter in the file—actually on the envelope—when your father answered one of our inquiries."

She looked at him curiously. "Really?"

Kovacs remained silent.

"So it was as easy as that?" It became obvious no response was forthcoming from Kovacs. "Be that as it may. Now, about our land, just what is the problem?"

"The problem isn't about the land. It's about one of our lead pilots, a man who's probably the best pilot in our entire Bombardment Group. His health's been declining. You can help. I guess you know who I'm talking about."

Her eyes opened wider. She hesitated before she spoke. "You say this man has been ill?"

"He's been wounded."

"Oh my God!" She whispered the words. Finally she said, "How badly? Is his life in danger?"

"Oh no. I didn't mean that. He's going to live all right."

"I'm so glad."

"But he's not recovering as well as our flight surgeon had hoped. Actually, we were worried about him even before he was wounded. He hadn't been eating much to speak of and he was sleeping poorly. Then he was wounded and in his weakened condition he's not recovering very well." Kovacs seemed sad, reflective.

Cynthia reached for a box of Players and took one out. Kovacs whipped out his Zippo and had the flaming lighter in her face before she had finished tamping the cigarette against the box. She seemed surprised as she accepted the light. Kovacs said to himself, "Too damned fast! Slow down!"

"How does this concern me?"

"What's that?"

"Captain Robertson's . . . uh . . . your colleague's illness . . . whatever it is . . . and his slow recovery from his wounds."

Kovacs eyes narrowed when she mentioned Robb's name. He pulled out a package of Luckies. "Do you mind if I smoke?"

She didn't answer. She looked at her own cigarette.

What a dumb fucking question! Slow down and get yourself organized!

"Sir. I asked you how your colleague's illness concerns me."

"I think you know the answer to that." Kovacs waited but she didn't say anything. "Well, maybe you don't." He lit his cigarette and drew heavily on it, inhaling deeply. "Let me put it this way. Robb is real concerned about you. Ever since you sent him away that time in that pub in Cambridge."

"I'm still not sure what you are saying, or perhaps I should say I understand your words but not your purpose."

"He's been worried about you. A lot. You know, leaving you like that in that pub, with you so unhappy. He hasn't been the same since, you know, from worrying about you. I'll bet he's asked me a hundred times, do I think something's happened to her."

"Now you can go back and assure him that I'm all right."

Kovacs shook his head, sadly. "I don't think that would do it. He doesn't trust me. I lie to him a lot, especially about bad news. You know, to make things sound not as bad as they are."

She smiled. "Crying wolf in reverse, one might say."

"That's right. It would be a lot better if you'd see him."

"I'm afraid that's quite impossible. I have a publisher's deadline to meet."

"It won't take much of your time."

"It would take one day going, one day there, and one day coming back."

"Could you spare a couple of hours?"

"In what hospital is he?"

"He's out of the hospital, temporarily. For his morale. Would you see him for an hour? Up here?"

"I'm not sure that would serve any purpose. How badly is he wounded, really?"

"Worse than he knows." Kovacs studied her reaction out of the corner of his eye.

"Am I to understand he'll not be able to fly again?"

"Not for quite a while, I'm afraid."

Cynthia stood up and moved around her chair. She put her hands on the back of the chair. "I'm afraid I've been a poor host, sir. May I get you a drink?"

"No thank you. I'm flying a plane back from Prestwick tonight." He crushed out his cigarette in an ashtray on the table. "I'd like to ask you a question, if you don't mind. If it had been him at that door tonight instead of me, would you have invited him in?"

"In what way is he wounded? I mean, does it show?"

"It's his leg. He's on crutches."

"Well then, of course I would have invited him in."

"I'm glad to hear you say that, Miss Allsford. Right now I'd like to tell you something about myself."

She looked at him curiously.

"I want you to know that I'd do anything for Robb. I'd steal. I'd cheat. I'd lie. I'd even mislead someone like you for his sake."

She pulled in her chin and stared at him. "So he isn't wounded after all."

"I didn't mean that. He's wounded all right."

"What *did* you mean then?"

"You assumed he was down in Allsford Lynn, or near there, and I let you assume that. The fact is, he's here."

"Here? In Scotland?"

"I mean here. Out on your driveway. In the jeep."

"What! He's here? Right out there?" She pointed to the front door.

"Yes."

Kovacs watched her carefully as she walked to the fireplace and poked at the fire. He watched her as she looked into a mirror and gave her hair a push upwards. He nodded almost imperceptibly. She returned to her chair and stood behind it.

She stared at Kovacs for a long time. "Sir. You tricked me. I'm inclined to ask you to leave." She continued to stare at Kovacs.

Kovacs remained impassive, staring blankly at the books on the table before him.

Finally Cynthia spoke, her tone now modulated. "But that would be quite unkind to Captain Robertson out there, would it not?"

"Yes. And it would be unkind to you, too. I can tell you want to see him."

She tightened her grip on the back of her chair. She turned her head to one side and looked obliquely at Kovacs. "Can you tell that I also *don't* want to see him?"

"I can tell that too." Kovacs nodded sadly.

She walked back to the fireplace. She poked at the embers again. She stood up suddenly and turned toward Kovacs. "Have Captain Robertson come in, Colonel."

Kovacs stood up immediately and started for the door. Not too fast, dummy! You look bad enough as it is! When he reached the door to the main hall he stopped and looked back toward her. "I'm sorry I deceived you."

Kovacs walked around to the driver's side of the jeep and climbed in, closing the door quickly behind him. "You all right, Robb? It's colder'n hell out here."

Robb was crouched low in his seat. "Bad news?" He spoke without turning his head, shivering, his teeth chattering.

"Hell no. I just need to talk to you before you go in."

Robb sat up quickly. "Don't joke about this!"

"Relax. No way I'd joke about it. She's waiting to see you."

"I'll be damned! I gave up long ago, when it took you so long!"

"Before you go in there's something I got to tell you. I misled her a little. I told her how you're wounded and how you're grounded. I think she thinks it's for a long time."

"What else?"

"I was wearing the Colonel's jacket. I think she thinks I'm the C.O."

"Damn!"

"Look, it's no big deal. You can go in there and tell her right off I'm wearing the Colonel's jacket and that you're only grounded for a couple of weeks and you can fuck up everything in two minutes. Or you can play it smart and make your confession next week or whenever you see her again. There's no way she'd have let me in if she hadn't seen these colonel's chickens on my shoulders, or if she didn't think you were seriously wounded."

"That's all the lies, then?"

"Well, there's one other thing. She asked how we found her and I told her we had a letter on file at the base from her father with this Scotland address on the envelope."

"That's one lie I'd have to go along with. If she knew how we found her she'd think we were nuts."

"That's what I figured."

"Thanks, Stosh. I must sound ungrateful. It's just that I'm nervous as hell."

"Get over that crap! It's stupid!"

"Sorry. Well, here goes." Robb opened the door. "Aren't you coming?"

"No. I think she expects you by yourself. Good luck."

Robb covered the distance between the jeep and the house as quickly as he could have with two good legs. He raised the knocker and tapped the door lightly. He could hear his heart pounding in his ears.

The door opened. He stood for a moment looking into her eyes. Cynthia looked at him intently but her expression told him nothing. She stepped to one side. Robb moved through the vestibule and into the main hall. He stopped. She walked past him and into the drawing room. He followed.

She stood behind her chair. She looked to the chair Kovacs had occupied. "Won't you be seated."

He leaned his crutches against the sofa and lowered himself into the chair. She watched him closely. He looked up at her when he got his cast situated comfortably. Her face and her hair reflected the firelight. Her dark brown hair, auburn perhaps, was as he remembered it: short, brushed back, a suggestion of waviness. Her features were even, the eyes dark blue, set apart, a slight flare to the nostrils. There was a sadness about her. She turned her head to one side as she looked at him.

He studied her carefully. She isn't a creation of my imagination. She is beautiful, *and she is real, and she is here*! But the longer he looked at her, the less sure he became that he was actually in her presence.

He had sat in the jeep in a stupor, freezing, imagining what she looked like, imagining for one moment her acceptance of him, and in the next moment her total rejection of him. The silent soliloquy begun in the jeep continued now in the warmth of Cynthia's house. Again, as in the worst nightmare-realities he had known in combat, he became unsure of where his nightmare of the moment ended and the reality of now began. And, as so often in combat, where his nightmare-realities were so bizarre they exceeded his capacity to accept them as knowledge, he became increasingly unsure of his location in time and space. He shook his head. He tightened his grip on the arms of the chair, declaring to himself, "This chair is real and she is real. She is real, standing there behind that chair."

As if to test his assumption that this moment he had dreamed of so long was in fact real, he spoke to her. "I've waited a long time for this moment."

She didn't respond. He felt himself drifting back to the jeep again. Freezing. Say something else to her. He was about to speak when she spoke. "I'm terribly sorry you were wounded." Her voice, soft, soothing.

He heard himself saying, "It's nothing." He rubbed his face vigorously. He felt dizzy. Cold. Very cold. Shivering.

"Are you all right?" Her voice again. Sotto voce.

"I'll be all right in a minute."

She moved quickly to the fireplace. She poked at the fire and placed several pieces of wood on the embers. She stood up and turned toward him. "Excuse me a minute, please." She left the room through a door behind him.

He closed his eyes. He knew he was in Cynthia's house and yet he was freezing. His feet and hands were numb. The cold penetrated his tunic and his flesh and settled in his bones.

He was aware of a scent, childhood flowers dimly remembered. He opened his eyes and he knew he was in her house and she was next to him. If he leaned his head an inch to his right his face would touch her shoulder. She was reaching past him to clear a space among the books on the table. And then she was gone again.

He closed his eyes. The scent of flowers returned, the scent of long ago. He saw them, roses, their vines interlaced through a white trellis against a porch on a house in another life. He opened his eyes. She was leaning past him again, placing a tray on the table in the space she had cleared. No, not roses. Lilies of the valley on the north side of a white frame house.

He saw a tea pot, cups and saucers, bottles and glasses. She filled a cup with tea, dark and steaming. His hands shook as he took the cup and saucer from her. The cup rattled against the saucer. He put the saucer back on the tray and took the cup in both hands and sipped the tea.

"Would you like a bit of cognac?"

He nodded. He drank the cognac in one swallow and he felt its warmth surging through him. He could feel her eyes on him. "I'm all right now."

"Does this happen often? Have you had malaria?"

"It never happened before. I guess I got chilled in the jeep."

"Doesn't it have a heater?"

"It doesn't work." The thought struck him suddenly. "I can't leave Stosh out there. May I ask him to come in?"

"I'm sorry. I should have thought of that. I'll go and ask him to come in."

He reached for his crutches. "I'll go."

"Are you sure you're all right?"

"I'm fine. I'll get him." He picked up his crutches and started for the door. He stopped short. "Will you mind discussing personal matters in front of him?"

"He can have a cup of tea in the library."

"He'll want something stronger than tea, especially when he sees those bottles."

"He said he can't drink tonight. He's flying your aeroplane back from Prestwick."

Robb's eyebrows raised slightly. He turned quickly toward the door.

Robb opened the door on the passenger side. Kovacs sat huddled behind the wheel. He was wearing his trench coat over the Colonel's flight jacket. "You cold, Stosh?"

"Get in and close the door."

"She wants you to come in. She knows it's cold and the heater doesn't work."

"I'll stay here. You have to talk to her alone. If I go in there I'll fuck things up." His teeth were chattering.

"They've got a library. She says you can go in there and warm up with a cup of tea."

"Fuck the tea. I just got to get where it's warm." He opened the car door and started to get out. He turned to Robb. "Is she still pissed off at me?"

"She's over it."

As they entered the drawing room Cynthia extended her hand.

"We've really not been introduced. I'm Cynthia Allsford."

Kovacs smiled brightly, "Stosh Kovacs. Nice to meet you."

"I'm sorry we left you out there in the cold. I didn't know your heater wasn't working. You must be frightfully chilled."

"I'm quite all right, really." Kovacs unconsciously slipped into an English accent of sorts whenever he talked to an English person.

"Really? I'd have thought you'd have been as cold as Captain Robertson. I just made a fresh pot of tea." She reached for the tea pot. Kovacs eyes were on the bottle of Scotch.

"Actually, Miss Allsford, I *am* a bit chilly. A bit of that Scotch would go quite well."

"I thought you were flying an aeroplane tonight?"

Kovacs smiled. "I think we should be big enough to rise above our convictions once in a while."

Cynthia laughed. It was the first time Robb had heard her laugh."Why don't you fix your own drink? Shall I get a soda siphon?"

"This is fine just like this." He poured himself a third of a water tumbler.

"I'll show you to the library."

When she returned she resumed her place in the chair some twelve feet away from Robb with the stacks of books and journals between. "You were saying that your wound isn't serious, yet your entire leg is in a cast. I must say that seems quite serious to me."

"The big cast is to keep me from bending my leg. The wound is small, but it won't heal if I bend my leg."

"Your Colonel told me it was serious. He said you will be grounded indefinitely."

"He lies for me. He's good at it. My wound isn't serious and I'll be flying again in a few weeks."

She compressed her lips.

"And he's wearing our commanding officer's jacket. He's not a colonel. He's a captain."

"Why would he do a thing like that? Isn't that a serious violation of your law?"

"He was afraid you might not let him in the house without the Colonel's eagles."

She nodded. "He's quite right about that. When I answered the door he asked me if I was the Cynthia Allsford whose family owned the land the American aerodrome is on. He then said there was a problem he needed to discuss with me."

"He implied there was a problem concerning the land?"

"That's why I let him in. Is he always this devious?"

"He's very honest, in his own way."

"Then why all this?"

"For me."

"You must have known about his impersonation of your Colonel. He must have put on the jacket in your presence."

"The jacket was in the Colonel's plane."

"He took the Colonel's aeroplane, too?"

"The plane is legal. The jacket is illegal."

"Don't you worry about such things?"

"No. Actually, we don't worry about anything."

"But you and your friend still fly sorties over Germany, don't you? And you lose a certain number of planes, do you not?"

"Yes"

"And yet you don't worry about anything?"

"Not really."

"Are you telling me the truth?"

"I'd never lie to you."

"Then tell me now, truthfully, how you found me here."

"Stosh told me what he told you about that. He lied to you."

"I thought so but I wasn't quite sure. We have a complete file on all of our correspondence with your people. Your friend said he found a letter from my father in your aerodrome's files. It so happens that, to the best of my knowledge, neither my father nor I ever corresponded with the Americans directly. All of our correspondence was—and is—handled by our agent. And we don't give out our Scotland address. I was almost sure Colonel Kovacs was lying."

"Captain Kovacs. Yes, he lied to you because he knew that if you knew how we found you you'd think we were crazy, and that you might reject me as some sort of nut. That's the way Stosh had it figured."

"How, then, did you find me here?"

The question caught him off guard. How much should he tell her? He couldn't think of anything to say. "It wasn't easy."

"How did you find me?"

He sighed resignedly. "I hope you won't be angry with the people who helped me. I told them I'd keep them out of it."

"I'll not be angry and I'll not say anything to anyone."

"It's a rather long story. I'll skip the details."

"I want the details."

"All right, then. I told my other good friend on the base, Sam Prentice, our intelligence officer, that I had seen you on the stream twice, that I had become obsessed with you, and that I had seen you, by accident, in Cambridge at the concerts. I told him about our meetings in the pub in Cambridge. I told him I thought the pub keeper knew more about you than he let on. Sam went to Cambridge and squeezed a confession out of the pub man."

Her eyebrows raised slightly. She studied his face carefully.

"The pub man refused to tell me anything on several occasions when I went back there. He was my only hope of finding you. He was very upset when finally he told Sam your name and where you lived, or had lived, in Cambridge." He paused. "Are you angry with Mr. Mosely?"

"No. Go on, please."

"A few days later Sam went to your flat over the drug store—the chemist's—and talked to a woman who now lives there. She knew nothing about you, but she had a letter addressed to you, a letter she hadn't yet returned to the postman. The letter was addressed to you as manuscript editor of the Journal of Social Anthropology."

"The trail was warming fast, was it not? I think that's the expression they use in Sherlock Holmes stories." She seemed more animated now.

"Yes. We were now on our way, but we had a long way to go. Sam went to the Cambridge library and looked at recent issues of the journal and found that the primary editor was at the University of London."

"So you went to see Professor Williams-West."

"Yes. But this is ridiculous. We should be talking about more important things right now. We could talk about this another time."

"This is important to me. I can't imagine what the professor could have told you that would have helped you find me."

"We—Sam and I—asked him if he could remember anything you had talked about, anything that might provide a clue. He finally remembered something you said when you had lunch with him in London."

Cynthia cocked her head to one side. Robb was pleased to see that she was smiling.

"He remembered that you had remarked that you didn't think the chamber music in Glasgow was up to Cambridge standards. It struck the professor, and Sam and me, as a generalization, and the professor knew you weren't one to make generalizations based on a single case. It seemed to all of us that you had probably been to several chamber concerts in Glasgow."

"So on that flimsy bit of evidence you decided I was in Scotland?"

"Yes."

"But Scotland is huge, and Glasgow too. How did you ever locate me in Scotland?"

"This is where the story gets awkward, sort of crazy and . . . " He fell silent.

"I find this fascinating. Please go on."

Robb had never seen her in good spirits before. He felt his spirits rising.

"You're going to find this hard to believe."

"Go on, please."

"We didn't find you. You found us."

"Oh?"

"We put on a concert series in Glasgow."

"I don't understand."

"You went to concerts by the London Quartet, didn't you?"

"Yes. They were wonderful. Among the finest I've ever heard."

"We put those on."

"I'm sorry. I'm afraid I don't understand what you are saying."

"We, Stosh and I, sponsored those concerts."

"Sponsored them?"

"We—actually Stosh—hired the London Quartet and made arrangements with the charitable organization in Glasgow for the concert series."

She stared at him. She stood up and walked to the fireplace and turned her back to the fire. "Captain Robertson, I really don't know what to say to you now. First of all your colleague arrived at my door late this night, disguised as a colonel, and lied that he was here because of some sort of difficulty regarding your aerodrome on our land. And then, having gained access to my home on basis of his initial lie, he proceeded to present a whole series of further fabrications to get me to admit you to my home. I, quite gullibly, went along with all that. I'm afraid, Captain, that I've reached the limits of my gullibility. I really don't know what to say or what to do . . . about you, or about us."

"Please come here and look at me. I swear I'm telling you the truth. We, actually Stosh, sponsored that concert series."

"Surely you're joking, or kidding, or whatever it is you Americans do."

"I'm telling you the truth."

"You really are quite serious now, aren't you?"

"Yes."

"I really don't know you that well, do I? But it doesn't seem like you to make up anything this—what's the word?—this wild. You *are* serious, aren't you?"

"Yes."

She bent down and picked up the poker and seemed about to use it on the fire. She put it back in its bracket without using it. She walked back to her chair and stood behind it.

"Are you saying that those concerts were organized—that the London Quartet came all the way to Glasgow—just to help you find me?"

"Yes. Of course the people in the quartet didn't know that."

"And you're saying that those huge audiences came to the concerts, in a sense, because you wanted to find me?"

"In a sense, yes."

"And that you got Lady Margaret Ashton to organize the Glasgow community to get behind these concerts and the Lord Mayor of Glasgow to speak to the audience because you wanted to find me?"

"Yes. But remember, none of those people knew anything about our motives. Actually, the whole thing was Stosh's idea and he was the prime mover. I simply agreed to it. And I didn't know about the Lord Mayor. I do recall Stosh mentioning the Lord Mayor of Glasgow, but I thought he was joking."

"I can't believe this!" She picked up her glass and walked to the table behind the sofa. She picked up the Scotch bottle, looked at it, and put it down again. She left her empty glass on the table and returned to her chair. She stood behind the chair.

"I really don't know what to say. If it were your friend in there"— she motioned toward the library—"who was telling me all this I'd think it was one of his lies. But you don't lie. I know that."

"Stosh rarely lies and never for his own personal gain."

"So this is the truth."

"Yes."

"I'm sorry I accused you of lying."

"I told you it was crazy."

"This must have cost you a fortune."

"Not really. I'd rather not go into that now. Another time, perhaps." He looked up at her. "I hope there will be another time. But right now can't we talk about us?"

"But I still don't know how you found me here, how you found this house. Did you see me at the concert hall and follow me home? But you couldn't have. I stayed with friends in Glasgow."

"Do you recall filling out a card so that the charitable organization could send you tickets to the next concert?"

"Good heavens! So that's how you did it! I put my name and address on that card!" She was excited now. Robb could see she could be vivacious when her mood permitted.

"Yes."

"I still don't know how to react to all this, but I must say it's the most ingenious thing I ever heard of. It beats anything Sherlock Holmes ever did. Whose idea was it?"

Robb pointed toward the library. "Of course he won't admit it. He gives someone else credit for the idea. But the idea is standard Stosh Kovacs ingenuity."

"He's really is quite a clever chap, isn't he?"

"Yes. He tries to act dumb, but he's as smart as they come."

"Imagine what a political leader he would make! Can't you see him sitting down with Mr. Churchill and Mr. Roosevelt and Mr. Stalin!"

"They'd lose their socks."

"I can see now why you were reluctant to tell me about all this. I agree. It *is* crazy."

"When this thing was brewing, I felt like crawling into a hole and hiding."

She walked around to the table behind the sofa and picked up the bottle. "Would you care for another?"

"No, thank you."

"Then I'll not have one either." She returned to her place behind her chair. "I can accept all of this cognitively," she said, "but I think it will be days before I accept it emotionally. This concert series and all the trouble so many people went through."

"It's been a long time since I heard that."

"What?"

"Cognitive versus emotional."

"Did you study social anthropology?"

"Psychology."

"Where?"

"Graduate School. The University of Chicago."

"A fine university. Did you take a degree?"

"Let's not get into that. Can't we talk about us?"

"Unless we get into that sort of thing how shall we know who 'us' are?"

"Are you saying we should know more about each other?"

"Yes."

Robb said, "I find that encouraging."

"It's just that I'm curious about you. That's not surprising, is it?" She studied his face for a time. "Why did you come here?"

"I don't know how to. . . " He stopped short. " I couldn't get you out of my mind. I hardly know you at all, yet I love you. Maybe I should say I think I love you."

She seemed not to have heard him. Her eyes were fixed on a stack of books on the table in front of her. The wind sweeping across the Firth of Clyde struck the cornices of the house, sending a moan through its interior spaces. The sharp reports from the fireplace grew louder as the silence between them lengthened.

She spoke, just above a whisper. "Love is for other people, not for you or me."

"I don't understand."

"You do your duty. Your duty is to fly your aeroplane . . . until you die."

Neither spoke for a minute or two. She continued to look at her hands. He watched her carefully.

"I loved one other man in my life. He looked much like you. He did exactly what you do . . . and he died."

Robb closed his eyes. "I can't tell you how sorry. . . "

"I had to tell you this."

Robb said. "I guessed that you put me out of your life because you had lost someone and that he was a flyer." He was saddened by her loss, and yet he was thrilled by her phrase, " I loved one *other* man in my life."

Her eyes remained downcast. He couldn't see the tears that welled in her eyes. She closed her eyes and he saw the tears on her cheeks.

"This is ridiculous, us sitting so far apart. We need each other." He rose from his chair and reached for his crutches.

"Please stay there." She spoke quietly but firmly. "I'll be all right."

He settled back in his chair.

"He was a pilot in the Royal Air Force. Wellingtons. His friends saw his aeroplane explode."

"I can't begin to tell you . . ."

"It happened two years before I saw you. Two years to the day I saw you on the stream."

"Christ, I'm sorry."

She stood up and walked around the end of the sofa. "Would you like a drink?"

"Yes, but let me fix my own." He rose quickly and worked his way around the end of the sofa, supporting himself against the furniture. She moved three or four feet farther down the table.

"Are you going to have a drink?" he asked.

"Not right now."

"I don't think I'll have one either." He was about to return to his chair when, on impulse, he held his hand out to her. She didn't take his hand. She simply stood there, looking down at the table. He worked his way back to his chair.

She returned to her chair. She took a cigarette from the box on the table and lit it, inhaling deeply. "If you don't mind, I'd like to get back to what you did before the war. Did you take a graduate degree in the University of Chicago?"

"I was working on a dissertation for the Ph.D. I never finished it. But let's not get into that. Can't we talk about us?"

"I'm a social anthropologist. That makes us rather close relatives, academically. "

"Cynthia, I know by what you said that you care about me, and you know that I care about you. We should be sitting together on that sofa. You should be in my arms. This is ridiculous."

"There is no way of knowing what we should or should not do now. Besides, I don't think we'll ever see each other again." She stared into the fire.

"Don't say that. Circumstances determine the choices we make, not inner convictions or hopes or fears. I had hoped you might look carefully with me at the circumstances we're in."

She stood up. "I'd better take your friend another drink. When I return we can talk more about you, and us, and our circumstances."

It occurred to Robb that perhaps he was going about things wrong. She might find it more difficult to send him away for good if they knew each other better.

She returned with the drink still in hand. "Captain Kovacs is sound asleep, sitting up."

"Stosh can sleep anywhere, in any position."

"Stosh is a strange name. Where does it come from?"

"He's of Polish descent. His name is Stanley. Stosh is short for the Polish form of Stanley. His last name is Czech, although he's mostly Polish."

"He really is a charming fellow in his own way. It's unfortunate he has such difficulty with the truth."

"Anytime you want the truth from Stosh just look him squarely in the eye and tell him to tell you the truth. You'd get it if you were a judge and his life were on the line."

"You think a lot of him, don't you?"

"I'm closer to him than I was to my own brother."

"Was?"

"He's dead. Last June. D-Day."

"I'm terribly sorry."

He closed his eyes for a moment. He sighed. "Don't you see, nothing we choose to do can make this war any better or any worse. The only thing we can control is *now*. We—you and I right here—have control over *now*. That's all we have."

He stared at the embers in the fireplace. She stirred herself suddenly. "We really don't know one another, do we? I'd like to know more about you. Did you study psychology for the baccalaureate?" The brightness of her tone was clearly the result of a conscious effort.

"No. Music for two years. Then I quit music and switched to psychology for my last two years."

"Why did you abandon music?"

"I knew I wasn't good enough to get a job with a good symphony orchestra, and I didn't want to be a music teacher. You become a mediocre musician very fast. There's no time for practice and pretty soon you're second-rate. My father is a music teacher in a small college in Indiana. He was once a good musician. Now he's mediocre. And tired."

"What is your instrument?"

"Cello. I used to play the cello. Do you play an instrument?"

"I play the piano."

"Somehow I knew you were a pianist. That makes me very happy. Do you—I should say, have you—played the Goldberg Variations?"

"I have played them."

"Would you play them for me?"

"Now?"

"Oh no. I didn't mean now. I don't even know if you have a piano in this house."

"It's in the library."

"I meant another time."

She studied him carefully out of the corner of her eye. "Your friend's way of influencing events is contagious."

"I wasn't trying to trick you. I was expressing a hope."

"I'm sorry. I shouldn't have said that." She looked into his eyes. "May I ask you a personal question, Captain Robertson?"

"Yes, but call me Robb."

"Are you married?"

"No."

"Engaged?"

"No."

But for the moan of the wind and the crackling and hissing emanating from the fireplace, there was no sound in the house. She stared at the box of Players on the work table. He studied her profile. Then he saw the tears on her cheek. He swung himself from his chair to the sofa. He leaned toward her and took her hand. She withdrew her hand and moved farther from him.

"Tell me you'll see me when I come back here in a few days. We'll celebrate each day as the greatest of God's gifts."

She did not respond.

"You have no idea how happy we could be. I would gladly trade weeks with you for years without you, carefree weeks in which we celebrate the *now* of our lives."

"I don't know what to say." She sounded tired.

"Don't say anything now, except that you'll see me again when I return here, and that you'll talk with me about this after you've had time to think about it."

"What exactly am I to be thinking about? Just what are you proposing?"

"That you'll agree to see me again, in a week or two, or whenever Stosh is free to fly me up here, and that in the interim you'll decide whether you and I should have an ongoing relationship, taking life one day at a time, with all the joys and risks that go with it."

She stared at the fire for a long time. Finally she said, "All right."

"I can't tell you how happy that makes me." He picked up his crutches and started to move toward her.

She stood up. "Don't you think it's time we awakened your friend? You really ought to be going if you intend to fly back to Allsford Lynn tonight."

BOOK II

Scottish Idyll

O what can ail thee, knight-at-arms
Alone and palely loitering?
The sedge is wither'd from the lake
And no birds sing.

John Keats, "La Belle Dame Sans Merci"

21

In the week following his reunion with Cynthia, each day for Robb became a week, each week a month. The four days when the Group went out were the worst. He had the officers' club practically to himself for days at a time, crutching himself aimlessly about the club, occasionally reading dog-eared magazines and books, grasping little of what he read. He practiced for hours each day on the old upright piano, concentrating on a set of Bach Two-Part Inventions he had played quite well years ago. His thoughts jumped from the music book in front of him to Cynthia in Scotland to the Group over Germany and back to Bach again in an unending cycle.

He needn't have worried about the Group. The 990th, on its four long hauls to the Russian Front encountered no fighter opposition, and the flak at the targets was light. They lost but one plane, and that one to the English weather.

Robb hardly saw Stosh during the week, beyond exchanging mere grunts as Stosh came and went from the barracks in the middle of the night between missions. Robb was elated when, at lunch on Thursday, Gib Hawkins told him that a big weather system was moving in on the continent, enough to obliterate all targets for days. Robb caught Colonel Strang as he was leaving the mess hall and asked him what the chances were that Kovacs might get a three-day pass this weekend. Strang said "good". He smiled knowingly when he said he and Stosh might use The Colonel's Lady to go to Scotland "if they liked". Robb hadn't said anything about Scotland.

It seemed to Robb the fates did not intend for him to arrive at a decent hour at Cynthia's place in Scotland. Last Friday it was Red Hammersmith's peremptory imposition of peacetime flight rules that delayed them. This Friday morning, December 15, 1944, it was Colonel Crick. Crick commandeered The Colonel's Lady and two pilots and didn't get back until 7:15 P.M., by which time Robb "was having a baby," as Kovacs put it.

Kovacs, Robb, and Bradley, who had offered to come along to serve as co-pilot on the return trip should Cynthia invite Robb to stay on in Scotland, waited on the hardstand as Colonel Crick and his pilots disembarked. Bradley saluted Crick as he passed; Kovacs and Robb just happened to be looking the other way. Kovacs gave Robb a boost through the waist door and handed him his crutches.

Kovacs and Bradley followed patiently as Robb slowly worked his way through the plane and into the cockpit. Though now out of its cast, Robb's leg was still quite unusable.

As Robb slowly lowered himself into the co-pilot's seat, Kovacs said, "Could you fly this plane if you had to tonight?"

"Not tonight, but give me a week or two of Dr. Rizzo's exercises and then ask me that. "

It was after 8:00 P.M. when Kovacs pulled the war-weary B-17 to a stop on the taxi strip at the head of the main runway. They took off into a driving rain. Kovacs kept his climb gradual. They broke out above the clouds at 10,300 feet, just north of Manchester. He had climbed from dismal night into glorious moonlight a hundred times on a hundred night flights, yet he was no less awe-struck tonight as they, without warning, burst upon the vast, blue-lit Arctic scene.

Robb glanced at his watch and did a quick calculation of their Estimated Time of Arrival at Cynthia's. Around midnight, provided they get transportation from the Prestwick Motor Pool. A dissonant thought struck him. He glanced quickly back at the rear bulkhead of the cockpit. "We're in trouble, Stosh. The C.O. has taken his jacket."

Kovacs said, "You worry too much. We'll think of something."

"I'm sure we will," Robb said.

Bradley, perched on a wooden stool immediately behind the pilots on a piece of plywood laid over the hatch to the nose compartment, looked from Robb to Kovacs and back to Robb again. "You guys going to let me in on what we're talking about?"

Robb turned and put his hand on Bradley's arm. "We discovered it's easier to get a jeep from the Prestwick motor pool if you're a colonel. The C.O. left his jacket in the plane last week, and Stosh borrowed it. But now the colonel's taken the jacket."

"I'm worried," Bradley said.

Kovacs looked back at Bradley. "We'll get us a car or a jeep. Just wait and see."

"I'm worried about you two ending up in the concentration camp at Litchfield."

Kovacs said, "You worry too much."

Bradley shook his head slowly, his lips pursed. "There are a lot of crimes you might commit, like mounting a Piccadilly Commando in front of the crowd at the changing of the guard at Buckingham Palace, or exhibiting yourself in Westminster Abbey at high noon on a Sunday, or . . ."

Kovacs smiled. "Out of uniform, huh?"

"But these are nothing compared to impersonating a colonel. They could lock you up for a long time for that. God knows what else they might do to you."

Kovacs said, "Would what they might do to us be worse than sending us on a bomb run on Merseburg?"

"Hell no," Bradley replied.

"Okay, pal. So what's there to worry about?"

Bradley remained silent for a time, brooding. He suddenly brightened. "Yeah! So what's there to worry about?"

A light drizzle was falling as The Lady's wheels met the Prestwick runway. A "Follow Me Jeep" awaited them at the taxi turnout at the end of the runway. They followed the jeep closely. Blackout rules were in force; there was little artificial light to relieve the blackness of the starless, moonless night. The Lady's running lights didn't help much, and the occasional drop-cord lights of mechanics working on airplane engines punctuated the darkness more than they illumined. The Follow Me Jeep led them to a hardstand close to Prestwick Operations.

As they disembarked, Bradley carried Robb's B-4 bag along with his own. Kovacs carried not only his B-4 bag, which seemed overstuffed, but also a bulging canvas barracks bag.

As they walked toward Operations, Bradley said, "What's in the barracks bag?"

Kovacs said, "A little present for a Scotch lady I know here in Scotland."

"And your B-4 bag looks like you packed for a week," Bradley continued.

"Just an extra dress uniform, in case I spill a Brussels sprout or a spot of tea on the one I got on."

Robb phoned Cynthia while Kovacs filled out the operations form. He made an effort to keep his tone steady, controlled. He told her to expect him in about an hour to an hour and a half. He studied her tone of voice carefully. He could detect no sign, one way or the other, to indicate the direction of her choice.

Kovacs stopped suddenly as they approached the Motor Pool office. "Wait a minute." He reached into his overcoat pocket and produced a jeweler's box. He opened the box and handed Robb a pair of colonel's eagles. "Here. Pin these on my shoulders."

Robb grinned. "See, Monk? Stosh said we'd think of something." He removed the captain's bars from the epaulets of Kovacs' overcoat and pinned on the silver eagles.

"Congratulations, sir," Bradley said.

"Thanks." Kovacs reached into his pocket and came up with another jeweler's box. "Here, Robb. I bought you a set too, for a rainy day when you need a jeep."

Robb put the box into his overcoat pocket. "You shouldn't have done it."

"You can say that again," Bradley said.

"Hold it, pal. You don't want those in your pocket. You got to put them on now so that if that same motor pool guy is on duty on that rainy day, like next month, he won't remember you as a captain. You'd have a hard time making him believe you got promoted from captain to colonel in one month."

"Good thinking." Robb handed the box back to Kovacs. Kovacs pinned the eagles on Robb's shoulders in place of his captain's bars.

Bradley said. "Were they all out of general's stars?"

"That would violate one of my rules. When the cards are falling your way, don't get greedy. And if something is working, don't change it."

"That's two rules," Bradley said.

"Leave us not quibble. Let's see if these eagles get us some wheels."

The sergeant on duty behind the counter was the man who had issued them the jeep a week ago. "Need another jeep, sir?"

Kovacs stared coldly at the man for a moment. Finally he spoke, softly, but there was steel in his voice. "No, Sergeant. I need a staff car. And I don't want to hear about you being out of staff cars."

"Yes, sir. We have a staff car available. But, sir, I'm required to ask all transient officers if they'll be using the vehicle on official business."

"Sergeant. Would I be using an army car if it wasn't on official business?"

"Sorry, sir."

"I'm going to try to overlook that you asked that."

"Thank you, sir." He placed a form on the counter. Bradley watched out of the corner of his eye as Kovacs signed the form.

"The car's out front, sir." He handed the car keys to Kovacs. Kovacs handed them to Bradley.

＊　＊　＊　＊　＊　＊　＊　＊

It was 11:35 P.M. when the olive drab Ford sedan turned into the driveway between the two stone pillars and began the long climb. Bradley kept the car in second gear for the entire climb, negotiating the narrow spaces between huge, encroaching tree trunks. The car dropped suddenly from a twenty degree climb to straight and level as it crested the brow of the hill where the heavy forest gave way to the sweeping lawn at the front of the house. The headlights struck the vast stone facade of the house.

Bradley said, "They're not poor."

Kovacs said, "Good line, Monk."

"I thought you were sleeping. Welcome to Shelbourne, old boy."

"Thanks."

Bradley parked the car where the jeep had stood a week ago.

"Two things about this spot, Monk. It gets colder than hell here, and Robb gets very nervous here. How you making out, pal?"

"Don't ask." Robb opened the door and stepped out into the drizzle. Kovacs handed him his crutches. "Wish me luck."

"Right, pal. Good luck."

He swung himself up the walk on his crutches. He couldn't remember when he had felt déjà vu so strongly. No, it isn't déjà vu. Everything happening now happened this way the last time. He raised the knocker carefully.

The door opened and his eyes met hers. She said nothing, nor did her eyes tell him anything. She stood aside and he moved through the vestibule and into the entry hall and on into the main hall. As before.

"May I take your coat, Captain?"

He looked quickly to see if her formality was mock or genuine. She was serious. She said nothing as she took his coat. He warded off despair by telling himself he still didn't really know her decision.

She stood beside the chair she had sat in last time. Her eyes indicated the chair he had sat in before, the chair opposite her. The low oaken table with its stacks of books and journals would be between them again. As before. A bad sign.

Robb maneuvered himself into the chair. He looked up at her. She was dressed much as she had been last week: calf-length wool skirt of dark green, muted plaid; forest green sweater with crew-neck over a white blouse open at the collar. Her hair, sometimes brown, sometimes auburn, depending on the light, was short, brushed back.

As she stood before him she looked exactly as she had last week, exactly as he had carried her in his mind since then, her head held high and turned slightly to one side as she looked at him. It occurred to him she never lowered her head, not even when she had cried last time. He could see how one could easily see her as cold, aloof, but all one had to do was to look into her eyes. He recalled Stosh's observations last time in the plane on the way back. Stosh had said that she had that high mucky muck way of standing and looking at you, but that underneath there was a warm and loving woman who was scared to death of showing it. He said he could see it in her eyes, "Just like a beagle hound's eyes." He had said that with those nice cheekbones and that smile that goes sort of down at the corners of her lower lip showing her lower teeth, she looked kind of like a young Katharine Hepburn, but with beagle hound's eyes. As Robb looked at her he agreed that Stosh's description was pretty good. But why, he wondered, why the hell is she so determined to hide the real Cynthia?

He smiled at her. She smiled in response, but her smile was restrained. "Would you like a cup of tea, or a drink?"

"A drink."

She handed him his drink She half-sat against the arm of her chair, almost standing. In his deep chair he felt as if he was sitting in a hole, looking up at her.

He raised his glass. "Cheers." She nodded and took a sip from her glass. Robb drank half of the contents of his glass in one swallow. He wondered why she didn't say 'Cheers', and why she remained half-standing. Does this mean she doesn't plan on him staying very long tonight? Why doesn't she say something? He was relieved when at last she spoke. "How is Captain Kovacs?"

"Fine. He's out front, in the car."

She stood up. "We must ask him to come in!"

"Not now. Not yet."

"We can't let him freeze again, can we?"

"We have a closed car this time, and the heater works."

She sat against the arm of her chair. "As you wish."

Robb smiled at her. She smiled, but she was still holding back. He gave his head the quick shake.

"Why did you shake your head like that?"

"It's a habit I have, almost unconscious. I seem to do that when I want to change my thoughts from things I shouldn't be thinking. I was telling myself I should act as though I expect the best, even though I'm afraid that you might reject my proposal."

They sat in silence for what seemed to him an eternity. She took a cigarette out of the box on the table. Finally, she spoke, softly. "Just what exactly was, or is, your proposal?" She lit her cigarette and exhaled, watching his face.

"Anything you want it to be."

"That's not very specific."

"The only specific thing I had in mind, or have in mind, is that we be with each other as much as possible, that we grab as much of life as we can. And that we rejoice in that, forgetting about the future. And the past, if you like."

"Go on."

"Whatever you want, I want. Just being with you is enough for me. I guess the only thing I'd hope for is that you'd join me in living in the *now*."

"The present tense."

"The present tense isn't present enough. I mean the *now*, in the sense that we be aware of each moment." He picked up his glass and drank the remainder of his drink. "Just as I consciously feel this whiskey's warmth coursing through me." He withdrew a new package of cigarettes from his pocket and began opening it. "Just as I'm aware right now that I'm tearing this cellophane wrapper off this package of cigarettes, and this silver paper off the corner of this package." He struck the package against his palm and pulled out a cigarette. "And now I'm very aware that I'm lighting this cigarette and taking a puff on it. I feel the smoke in my lungs and it feels good. I feel a subtle elation, euphoria, as the smoke, this smoke, fills my lungs and enters my bloodstream. It feels very good. That's what I mean by living *now*."

He fell silent.

"Please go on. I know this is how I must learn to live. I've thought about it constantly this past week."

He caught the softening in her tone. His spirits rose.

"I have a feeling you were going to say more. Please go on."

"You're wearing a certain fragrance tonight. I'm very aware of it and it takes me back to flowers—lilies of the valley—along a walk on the north side of a white frame house in the spring in a small town in Indiana." He smiled. "I'm also aware that I'm starting to sound pretty corny."

"Don't become self-conscious. Go on as you were."

"That's it. That's what *now-living* means to me. I'm alive in a way I never thought possible before. I want this for both of us."

She walked to the fireplace, poked the embers and returned to her seat on the arm of the chair." That's what I want. I want that too."

"I'm so glad . . ." He stood up and took a step toward her. He forgot his injured leg. He caught himself on the arm of the sofa.

She rushed to him. He pushed himself to a standing position. He grinned. "I'm all right. I forgot about my leg."

He reached out to her but she stepped backward quickly. He picked up one of his crutches and followed her as she moved toward her chair.

She turned quickly. "Please stay where you are."

He returned to his chair. "I thought you accepted my proposal."

"I accept your proposal, as best I understand it."

"Then let me hold you. Let me . . ."

"Not now. Everything in its own time."

He sighed.

After a time she said, "What are our immediate plans? Immediate plans are all right, are they not?"

He smiled. "Of course. We—Stosh, Monk, and I—had to plan from one hour to the next today to fly to Prestwick."

"You mentioned a Monk. Who is he?"

"My co-pilot. He came along with us tonight. He's out in the car with Stosh."

"He's out there too? I must say we're being terribly inconsiderate. We must have them in for a drink, or a cup of tea, in case Captain Kovacs isn't drinking tonight. I'll get them now."

"Not yet, please. You asked about plans. I really don't have any."

"None whatsoever?"

"Just that we be together as much as possible."

"When must you return to Allsford Lynn?"

"A week from tomorrow."

"Does that mean you can stay here?"

"Whatever you want."

"That's what I want. I want you to stay here."

He took a deep breath. "Thank you."

She stood up suddenly. "That's settled, then. Now I'm going out to get your colleagues before they freeze."

Robb picked up his crutches and stood up. "I'll get them."

"I'll put on some tea."

He smiled. "Ah yes, tea for Stosh." He swung himself toward the door on his crutches.

The car's motor was running. Robb got into the back seat beside Kovacs. The car was warm and stuffy. Kovacs said, "How'd it go?"

"She invited me to stay for the week's leave I have left. She wants you guys to come in for a drink."

"You must be pretty happy right about now."

He put his hand on Kovacs' arm. "She's putting on some tea for you right now, Stosh. In case you're flying tonight."

Kovacs made a sour face. "Let's each flip a coin. Odd man drinks a cup of tea. Okay?"

"Just tell her you're not flying tonight."

"Okay. Just so she won't mind. You know, after her making that tea for me."

"It's all right."

"I hope you're right. Give me the keys, Monk. I need something out of the trunk."

Robb and Bradley stood behind the car and watched as Kovacs opened his B-4 bag. He took out a paper sack, its contents apparently heavy. Robb said. "What's in the sack?"

"A little present for the lady. Sort of."

Robb led the way into the house. Cynthia was standing beside the table at the back of the sofa. She held out her hand as they approached. "Captain Kovacs. How nice to see you again."

Kovacs took her hand and smiled his warmest smile. "Hello, Cynthia."

Robb said, "Cynthia, this is Monk Bradley."

She shook hands with Bradley. "How do you do, Lieutenant."

"Pleased to meet you." Robb was surprised that Monk, ordinarily so extroverted, could be so shy.

Kovacs placed his sack on the table. "I brought you something." He withdrew three pinch-bottle fifths of Haig and Haig Scotch whiskey.

"How thoughtful of you, Captain. You're very generous, I must say."

"I just thought of something funny. Here I am bringing Scotch whiskey to Scotland. Just like bringing kielbasa to Hamtramck."

She looked puzzled. "Like bringing what to what?"

"Kielbasa is Polish sausage, and Hamtramck, where I used to live before we moved, is a one hundred percent Polish town inside of Detroit. In Michigan. In America."

"Oh, I see. Rather like bringing coals to Newcastle."

"Something like that, if Newcastle has already got a lot of coal."

Kovacs picked up one of the bottles of Haig and Haig. "Do you want me to break open one of these bottles?"

"Yes, please. And would you pour the drinks please?"

Cynthia smiled. "You chaps do seem to have a good time together. Are there others in your little circle of friends?"

Robb said, "There's Sam Prentice, and Merrie and Evelyn. Merrie is Stosh's girl friend."

"She's more than my girl friend. She's the love of my life. She's my fiancée. What I mean is she would be my fiancée if it wasn't for the war."

"You are a lucky man, Captain." She turned to Bradley. "Is Sam a pilot?"

Bradley said, "Sam is our intelligence officer. All of us feel very close to Sam. And Evelyn is an administrative officer."

"Is Evelyn your lady friend, Lieutenant?"

Robb said, "Evelyn is my friend. She and I go out together now and then."

Cynthia's eyebrows raised ever so slightly. She turned her head slightly sideways as she looked at Robb. "Oh, I see." She turned to Kovacs. "I can see you are a man of impeccable taste. I would imagine Merrie is a lovely person."

"Tell her, Monk."

"Cynthia —I mean Miss Allsford—I must tell you in all honesty that when Merrie walks into the officers' club everything stops. A hundred pairs of admiring eyes watch her every movement. When she. . . "

"That's enough, Monk." He turned to Cynthia. "He's right. Merrie is a knockout."

"What about Evelyn, Lieutenant? How would you describe Evelyn?" She smiled pleasantly at Bradley.

Bradley looked at Robb.

Robb said, "Tell her."

"She's pretty special." Bradley's tone was strangely soft in contrast to his declarations of a moment earlier. He didn't elaborate.

"Go on, Monk," Kovacs said. "I never saw you at a loss for words."

"She's beautiful . . . she . . ." He stopped short. There was an awkward silence.

Cynthia reached for Kovacs' glass. "Let me fix another drink."

Kovacs said, "No more for me, please. We're running late." He stood up.

"Before you go, I have a question I've been meaning to ask Robb. I've recently been to three wonderful concerts by the London Quartet, here in Glasgow. Before each concert—they were benefit concerts for war orphans—the Lord Mayor of Glasgow gave a little speech of appreciation for the sponsors of the concerts. It seems these concerts were sponsored, and paid for, by the flyers of the American Eighth Air Force. Did you know about this?"

Kovacs said, "Well, I'll be damned. Excuse me, I mean darned. How about that, Robb?"

Robb shifted uncomfortably, but he said nothing.

Kovacs continued, "I mean how about our public relations department in the Eighth?

Cynthia said, "Do you mean this was a public relations gesture?"

"Heck yes. You got to hand it to them. They know their stuff. The way they figured it, sometimes the American soldiers over here look like a bunch of slobs, so they get the London Quartet to make us look like we got some class too. Like the English."

Cynthia said, "In any event, it was a wonderful gesture, and I'll always remember the Eighth Air Force fondly for it."

Kovacs said, "Thanks. Well, Monk, we better get going. Glasgow will be closed before we get there."

"I'll look forward to seeing you again. I do so enjoy your visits, Captain."

"And I look forward to coming back."

Kovacs opened the trunk and pulled out Robb's B-4 bag and the barracks bag. Robb reached out for his B-4 bag.

Kovacs shook his head. "No way you can carry two bags and yourself on those crutches." He started for the door. Robb followed. Kovacs set the bags down just inside the front door.

"What's in the barracks bag?"

"Grub from the mess storeroom. Her family may be rich, but they all get the same food rations, like a couple of tea bags and a Brussels sprout a week. You can't eat here for a week with no ration card."

Robb shook hands with Kovacs. "Thanks, Stosh. I don't know what I'd do without you. I mean it.   Good luck in Glasgow."

Kovacs smiled. "Good luck in Shelbourne, pal."

Robb left the barracks bag in the vestibule. He hobbled into the drawing room on one crutch, lugging his heavy B-4 bag. Cynthia sprang to her feet. "Let me have that. I could have carried that bag for you." She took the bag from him. "Please sit down. I wonder what your doctor would say if he could see you carrying that heavy suitcase."

"Tony Rizzo would be pleased." He sounded weary. "He told me I could start using my leg a little at a time."

"But surely 'a little at a time' doesn't include carrying heavy objects. I find it hard to understand why you should want to rush your recovery." She softened her tone. "Would you like a drink before turning in?"

"Yes, thank you." He hadn't thought about turning in. He glanced at his watch. It was after 1:00 A.M.. He suddenly remembered the barracks bag. He stood up.

"Please sit down. You're hurting yourself. There's perspiration on your forehead."

"I forgot something in the vestibule. Something for you from Stosh."

"I'll get it. Now please sit down before you collapse. You're in pain. I can see that."

She took him by the arm and steered him toward the sofa. "Perhaps you'd like to stretch your leg out on the sofa." She smiled warmly at him. "I'll be right back."

He was on the edge of falling asleep when she returned with the heavy barracks bag.

"I don't understand Captain Kovacs' penchant for giving gifts."

"That's what he does. He flies airplanes and he gives gifts."

"But can he afford such expensive gifts?"

"Yes, easily, but the gifts in the barracks bag are from Uncle Sam, not Stosh."

She opened the bag and looked into it. "Good heavens!" She reached into the bag and came forth with a variety of canned goods and dried food packages. "This is a year's rations!"

Robb grinned. "That's Stosh. If a thing is worth doing, it's worth overdoing."

"Did he steal it from your storerooms?"

"He probably had the mess sergeant fill the bag for him. "

"Do you think I can accept all this in good conscience?"

"Unless you do I can't eat your rations in good conscience."

She laughed. "All right, then. I'll keep it if you promise to eat heartily. I must say, your Captain Kovacs is one of the most interesting people I ever met. He's bigger than life in everything he does, isn't he?"

"That says it exactly. "

"Does your leg require any sort of treatment?"

"I'm supposed to stretch the Achilles tendon and muscles while sitting in a hot bath. Three or four times a day."

"I'm putting you in a downstairs room. There's a bathroom close by, across the hall from the library. It's getting on towards 2:00. Perhaps we should get to bed soon so we can get up at a decent hour. What would you like to do on the first day of your holiday?"

"Anything you'd like to do is fine with me."

"With your leg, I don't suppose we can do anything out of doors. Can you think of something we might do indoors that would interest you?"

"I'm sure I could think of something if I put my mind to it." He held her eyes for a brief moment. She blushed. He continued quickly, "I'd like to hear you play the piano."

"We could have good indoors fun at the piano, couldn't we? Perhaps we can play something together. You did say you played, didn't you?"

"Very little. Do you have the Mozart Sonatas for Four Hands?"

"I'm sure I have them somewhere. I'll try to find them."

"I'd like to try them with you, if you'll try to remember that I don't play the piano."

"With whom did you play those sonatas?"

"My brother."

"The brother who died?"

"Yes. He could play the piano quite well, but he was a first-rate violinist, the best musician in the family by far. He'd play the primo with great delicacy, and I'd whack away at the secondo. He called them Mozart's sonatas for hands and fists. He said I was better than no one, but he wasn't sure."

"I get the impression he was older than you."

"A year and a half older. A younger brother can be a pain in the neck. I remember deliberately banging those bass notes just to irritate him."

"Did you get along well after you were grown?"

"We didn't see much of each other after he went off to New York on a scholarship to Julliard, and when I finished high school I went off to the state university."

"He must have been a good musician indeed to win a scholarship to Julliard."

"He really was. All of us, my family and I, went to his senior recital in New York. He was very good."

"You must have been very proud of him."

"I was."

"And envious?"

He answered quickly. "No!" He softened his tone. "No. I was very proud of him!"

Cynthia looked at him curiously, her eyebrows raised slightly as she studied his face. Robb stared at the fire.

"Couldn't he have gone into some branch of service that would have made use of his talents? Surely there was a place for good musicians, indeed if they have to go at all, which I dare say I wonder about."

"He was idealistic. He was in love with a Jewish girl, and she with him. She was involved in Jewish causes, and Ted became involved too. They were very aware of what was happening in Germany, even before our own government admitted it. There was no way he'd have fiddled, even in an army uniform, while that was going on." He drained his glass in one gulp. "They were going to be married after the war."

She moved to the sofa and took his hand. "I'm sorry I brought this up. This must hurt terribly."

"You should bring it up. That's the only way to deal with these things."

He placed his arm behind her along the back of the sofa. His hand touched her shoulder. She looked at her watch and stood up quickly. "I had no idea it was so late. We really should get to bed so we can get up at a decent hour tomorrow. I'll show you to your room." She picked up his bag as she started down the hall. He followed on his one crutch.

As they entered the hall he said, "I'd like to see your piano if I may." He had seen the piano in there last week when he went to wake up Stosh. He wanted a better look at it.

"Of course." She put down the bag and stood in the doorway to the library.

He stepped into the room. It was a genuine library, and a big one. The walls were covered by book-shelves, all fully laden with books. The top shelves were at least twelve feet from the floor. A dark oak step ladder, the kind one saw in Victorian public libraries, hung from a track that ran around three sides of the room. The wheels on the bottom of the ladder had worn a groove in the oak flooring in the space between the Persian rugs and the bookshelves. As in the great room, a sofa and two chairs formed a seating circle of sorts facing the fireplace and, again, a low, heavily laden work-table was the centerpiece immediately in front of the sofa. The grate in the fireplace was cold.

An ebony concert grand piano stood before the heavily curtained French windows on the west wall. He moved across the threadbare Persian rugs and looked under the propped-up lid. Steinway. He stuck his head farther under the lid. A hundred year old German Steinway with bright red felts on the action and unsullied white felt sandwiched into the hammers. The piano of a serious pianist.

He turned and hobbled toward the door on his single crutch. He picked up his B-4 bag and lugged it down the hall. Cynthia caught up with him and grasped the bag's handle, but his grip remained firm. He stopped. He looked into her eyes and then down at her hand. She relinquished her grip. She opened the first door on the right beyond the library. He moved toward the bed. He hadn't quite reached the bed when he began to sway. He dropped the bag and grabbed a bedpost. He gripped the bedpost firmly, waiting for the dizziness to pass.

She grasped him around the waist. "What's wrong?

His eyes were glassy. He shook his head quickly from side to side. The dizziness persisted and he gripped the post tighter. She turned back the bedclothes in a single motion. She took his arm and led him a few steps and turned him around opposite the middle of the bed.

"Sit down on the bed, please." He lowered himself slowly to the edge of the bed. "What's wrong?"

"I'll be all right." He began unbuttoning his tunic. He fumbled awkwardly.

She unbuttoned the remaining buttons and helped him out of his coat. She removed his tie and unbuttoned his collar. "Lie down, please."

The pillow was cool and soft against the back of his head. She removed his shoes and pulled the sheet and bedspread over him. He felt her hand on his forehead. Her hand felt wet. He knew it was his own sweat. He was vaguely embarrassed at the thought of her getting her hand wet with his sweat.

She turned out the light and he perceived the sudden darkness through closed eyelids. The bed was smooth and soft, a bed from another world, another life. He felt the softness of her lips on his eyelid, but this too he experienced as from another world and time. He didn't know who it was, or when.

He didn't know she left the door ajar. Nor could he know that she took blankets and a pillow from a closet and made a bed for herself on the sofa in the library. Nor could he know that, toward daybreak, she heard him screaming, "Shut up Hoyt! Shut up, Boo! For God's sake shut up, Boo!" A hard, grating man-scream. But his voice no longer cracked when he shouted, "They'll hear you!" It was more a wail than a scream.

22

Robb awakened shortly before 9:00 A.M. on Saturday morning. He lay on his back for a minute or two, staring at the ceiling in the half-light that penetrated the heavily curtained windows on the west wall of the room. He remembered holding on to a bedpost, but he wasn't sure that wasn't part of his nightmare. His eyes darted about the room. He saw the tall bedposts. Ah yes. Cynthia had helped him to bed.

He hobbled to the bathroom. He shaved quickly while the water ran into the tub. He sat in the hot bath and performed the exercise Tony Rizzo had prescribed, pushing the ball of his foot against the front of the tub, bending his foot upward as far as possible. When the pain became acute he relaxed the pressure. It seemed to him he reduced the angle between the bottom of his foot and his leg from slightly obtuse to approximately 90 degrees during these few minutes. He must have gained a half inch. He was encouraged. Rizzo had said he wouldn't certify him to fly until he could bend his foot upwards at least an inch beyond ninety degrees. He had until next Saturday to achieve that inch.

He returned to his room where he dressed quickly. He hobbled to the library and sat down at the piano. He tried the right hand part of one of the Bach Two-Part Inventions he had worked on last week. Good enough. He tried the left hand part. He frowned. Not too bad if you ignored the missing notes in the left hand. He played it with both hands, this time trying to re-create the broader brush strokes rather than merely replicating lines of notes. Not bad. Not good, but not totally lousy.

"Very good, Captain."

He looked up at Cynthia. "What's very good?"

"The improvement between your first and last attempts at the Bach invention. You deserve a star on your book for improvement." "For a minute I was afraid you meant I played it well. I didn't play it well."

"I agree. But I have hopes for you."

"Surely not as a pianist. I'm beginning to doubt your judgment again."

"As one who plays the piano, and who might do a creditable job on the secondo of the Mozart Sonatas for Four Hands."

"They'll become the sonatas for hands and fists again."

"We'll see. It's time for breakfast now. If you will follow me please, Captain." Her formality was mock. He didn't like it.

They passed through the great room and into the opposite wing of the house. The breakfast room had a western exposure, and though the sun was still east of its zenith, the room was bright with natural light. "If you'll sit here, please, I'll get the coffee."

The breakfast table was in an alcove with multi-paned, floor-to-ceiling windows on three sides. He looked to the west as he was in the process of sitting down. He froze in a half-sitting position. He was astonished. He slowly lowered himself to the chair. The vast expanse of land and water was totally unexpected. It was a rare, crisp December day, and it seemed he could see a hundred miles to the west, to northern Ireland, perhaps, a little south of west. He stared at the panorama for several minutes, unaware that Cynthia had joined him at the table.

"Coffee?"

"Thank you" He seemed mesmerized. He continued to stare westward.

"I would have thought such views would be old hat, given your occupation."

"I'm used to looking at a flat world from very high up, with nothing between us and the ground. Here you have the slope of the hill, the trees, and the water and the islands. And more water and more islands. You get a tremendous feeling of height and depth. I can see why whoever built this house picked this spot."

"My father's people had it built. About a hundred and fifty years ago."

"I'd like to look around outside after breakfast. Maybe we could take a walk."

"I'd like that. But what about your leg?"

"It feels much better today."

They followed a lane that ran in a southerly direction along the crown of a ridge. The lane was apparently used by farm vehicles; gravel showed through the grass where wheels had traveled, and there were cleat marks now and then. How long had wheels traveled this lane? Since the American Revolution? Possibly.

He stopped as the lane entered the woods. A soft breeze rustled the sparse, dead leaves that clung to the branches overhead. Brown and russet leaves skipped along over the closely cropped, flaxen grass, now dappled light and dark at the center of the lane. He blinked. Suddenly it was autumn in a small college town in Indiana. Saturday football autumn.

She studied him as he leaned on his crutches. "Schoolboy."

"You're psychic. Come on. Let's see if you can keep up with this invalid."

They had walked a quarter of a mile when he stopped. He was breathing hard.

Cynthia said, "I'm afraid this was a mistake. You're not quite ready for this."

"What's at the end of this lane?"

"The farm. A farm house and farm buildings, and sheep."

"I'd like to see it. I'll make it all right if we stop now and then for a breather."

"It's more than a mile, and I daresay you are almost beyond the point of no return."

"A good choice of phrases. I bow to your choice of phrases." He leaned against the massive trunk of an oak tree.

"Perhaps you can meet Blaze and Ginger another time."

"Blaze and Ginger?"

"My horses. Hunters. I rather think we should start back now."

"All right. I hope I'll get to meet your horses before I leave."

They were half way back when Cynthia suggested they stop for him to catch his breath. They sat on a large oak log which lay beside the lane. It seemed to Robb the log had been left there years ago for precisely the purpose for which they were now using it. They smoked their cigarettes in silence for a time. "I somehow get the impression this place was, or perhaps is, more your home than the place at Allsford Lynn."

"Your impression is correct. My mother was born and raised in Scotland, and she much preferred Scotland to England, and Shelbourne to Allsford Hall. So I spent most of my first eight years here. And after my mother died I was still here much of the time when I didn't go with my father on his digs. Mrs. Campbell became my mother for all practical purposes."

"Mrs. Campbell?"

"Our housekeeper. Mr. and Mrs. Campbell run the house. I gave them this week off."

It occurred to Robb that she may have planned on having him stay on. "Would the Campbells have disapproved your having a man as a house guest?"

"I have no idea."

He decided not to pursue the coincidence. "You must have jumped back and forth between schools."

"Actually, I never went to public school."

"By which you mean a private school."

"I had tutors all my life. I entered university by examination."

"Isn't that unusual?"

"Yes, but not unheard of. It was an especially good arrangement after my mother died. My father and I needed each other, so it made no sense for me to go off to boarding school, and because I had no fixed school schedule I could go off on archaeological expeditions with my father whenever he went."

"And so you became a child archaeologist."

"I did develop strong interests in archaeology quite early. Of course my father was my tutor in archaeology and anthropology."

"So you never went to school with other children."

"Yes. It goes without saying, doesn't it, that I was a very lonely child. I wish I could have gone to school with other children, just for their company. And of course one does learn a good deal from other children, doesn't one?"

"Yes. A lot of things they don't teach in school or at home. Weren't there children to play with up here?"

"The Campbell children and I played together. I'm somehow embarrassed to admit they were the only children I knew during my entire childhood." She stood up suddenly. "Perhaps we had better start back now."

Robb stood up. "Would you be good enough to carry this for me? In your left hand." He handed her one of his crutches and put the other one under his right arm. He draped his left arm over her shoulders. "Lead on, MacDuff. It's still a glorious day."

"The line is, 'Lay on, MacDuff.'"

"Ah yes, but you must remember, I come from a country where we're still learning the language."

The sun, now at the zenith of its winter arc, cast its rays directly along the lane as they trudged northward. Their shadows were long in front of them, even though it was mid-day. Cynthia seemed small as she walked along with her arm around his waist, his extra crutch swinging horizontally in her free hand. He put very little weight on her shoulders.

23

On Sunday evening Robb sat in a hot bath, stretching his Achilles tendon and reflecting on the day. It had been, if anything, even more idyllic than yesterday. The weather was perfect and they tried the hike to the farm again. Again, they failed to reach their goal, the farm, but Robb was able to walk twice as far as yesterday, and although he one-crutched his way back, he put almost no weight on Cynthia's shoulders.

As he stepped out of the tub it seemed he could bend his foot slightly beyond ninety degrees. Tony Rizzo had said he'd have to exceed ninety degrees before he'd certify him to fly again. By way of celebration, he decided to abandon his crutches. He dressed quickly and headed for the Great Room, crutchless.

He leaned against the door to the Great Room. There were beads of perspiration on his forehead but he was grinning. Cynthia turned when she heard his heavy breathing. "Robb! Where are your crutches?" She hurried to his side.

"In the bedroom." He was panting like a runner who had pushed himself beyond his endurance. "The crutches are in the bedroom."

"Oh Robb! Stop to think what you're doing to yourself! Put your arm around my shoulders. I'll help you to the sofa." She held him tightly around the waist as she guided him slowly across the room.

He smiled. "This is the way I want to get around."

She eased him down on to the sofa. "Why on earth do you want to rush your recuperation? The sooner you recover the sooner you'll have to return to your special . . ." She didn't finish her sentence, but Robb knew she was about to say his "special hell".

"I'm not eager to return to flying." He smiled ruefully. "God knows that. But if I'm not certified soon my crew will be turned over to another pilot."

"Would that be all that bad? Surely their new pilot would be quite capable. "

"I can't abandon my crew, any more than any one of them would abandon me, or our crew."

"I still can't understand . . ." She stopped short. "I'll get you a drink."

Robb watched her as she poured Haig and Haig. She handed a drink to Robb and sat down beside him.

Robb looked at the drink. "One thing the flyers agree on—those who've had flak leaves up here—and that's that the Scottish people aren't Scotch with their Scotch." He frowned. "Now, let's talk about something beside the goddamned war." He put his arm around her shoulders. She moved farther down the sofa.

After an awkward silence, he turned the conversation to musical esoterica. Her mood gradually improved. She replenished their glasses from time to time, almost automatically, without interrupting their dialogue. Robb began to feel whiskey-induced vertigo. Cynthia mistook it for fatigue. "You'd better get to bed, Robb. You've had rather a large day."

He stood up, crutchless. "I agree. But firsht . . . excuse me, first I would like to play something for you on the piano." He draped his arm over her shoulders and she grasped him tightly around the waist and guided him carefully down the hall to the library. He grinned as she released her hold when they reached the piano bench. "I've abandoned the crutches for good."

He sat silently for a time looking at the keyboard, his mood suddenly somber. He raised his hands and began playing a piano transcription of the sonorous andante, baroque yet strangely romantic, from the Bach A-Minor Suite for Unaccompanied Violin. They sat in silence after the last chord faded. Finally Cynthia spoke. "That was lovely."

"I shpecialize in adagios and andantes. I make it a rule never to play anything faster than an andante. People who've heard me play agree it's a good rule."

"You're far too modest. That was perfectly lovely. That suite is one of my favorites. I'd never heard it on the piano before. I must say that's an awfully good transcription. Did you transcribe it?"

"My brother Ted. I don't have that kind of talent."

"He must have been gifted."

He nodded absently as he closed the fallboard over the keys. "And so endeth another lovely day with the loveliest woman in Scotland. Thanks, Thinthia." He laughed softly. "Thinthia. Someone called you Thinthia. Who was that?"

She looked at the clock on the mantle. "Time for bed, my love."

"The atmosphere is pregnant with time-to-go-to-bedness, Thinthia. Someone called you Thinthia. Who was that?"

He stood up. He swayed slightly.

She hurried to his side. "Let me help you." She held him tightly around his waist and he draped an arm around her shoulders. He put almost all his weight on his injured leg as they made their way slowly down the hall.

She pulled back the bedclothes and sat him on the edge of the bed. He said, "I don't want to ask you to do anything that you don't want to do, but the time has come when I must. I want you to do me a big, big favor. Will you do me a big favor?"

She stepped backwards.

"Would you please get me a glash of water from the bathroom to drink, please?"

"Of course." She smiled.

"I can see you are pleasantly surprised by the modesty of my request, Sssynthia."

"You see well for one who has had too much to drink. I'll be right back."

When she returned with the glass of water, Robb was sitting on the edge of the bed, opening an aluminum soap container. She stared at the soap tray filled to the brim with yellow capsules. "What are those capsules?"

"These capsules are capsules."

"Robb! What is in those capsules?"

"These are Achilles tendon capshules. You take one for each Achilles tendon." He tossed two capsules into his mouth. He took the glass of water and washed them down.

"Did your doctor prescribe them?"

"Yesh. I got them from Doctor Swovik."

"I didn't know there was a Doctor Swovik. I thought your doctor's name was Rizzo."

"A lot of people don't know Doctor Swovik. He's invisible. He blends into backgrounds."

"What does he do?"

"He's a shpecialist. He passes out these pills. That's all he does."

"To whom?"

"To the flyers of Amber Squadron at bedtime before a mission. Each squadron has its own Doctor Swovik."

"So those are sleeping pills."

"Would you care for a couple? I have a goodly shupply."

"Robb, you shouldn't be taking barbiturates after all you've had to drink. They could kill you!"

"If what you say is true we've lost the war."

"It's very dangerous!"

"They're only dangerous in peacetime."

"Why did you take them now? You're not flying a sortie tomorrow."

"I can't sleep at all without them. C'est la guerre, I guess."

She sighed. "I understand. Goodnight, Robb."

He stood up. He held his arms out to her. "Come. I want to squeeze you."

She stepped forward into his arms. He held her tightly. She put her arms around him and held him. He realized this was the first time he'd felt her drawing him to her rather than pushing him away.

"I love you, little English girl."

"I love you, big Yank."

He kissed the top of her head. "That's the name of some overalls."

"What?"

"Big Yank. It's like saying I love you, big Oshkosh B'gosh."

"What's an Oshkoshbagosh?"

"An American Indian chief."

"What tribe?"

"Wisconsin."

The side of her face was against his chest. He touched his lips to her hair and he remembered her fragrance from his first night at Shelbourne, when he was shivering and she made tea for him. He wanted her then, but now he wanted her as he had never wanted any woman in his life.

She suddenly released her hold, but he continued to embrace her. She pushed against him gently. "Time to say goodnight." She continued to exert gentle pressure against his chest. He squeezed her harder. "Robb. It's time to say goodnight."

He released her from his embrace, but he held her with his hands on her upper arms. He smiled as he looked down at her. "I wonder if I'll love you just as much when all the Cynthia Allsford mysteries have been solved."

She closed her eyes tightly.

He said, "Don't look so worried. I'll always love you. There's a line in Grieg's 'Ich Liebe Dich'. 'Ich liebe dich in Zeit und Ewigkeit.'"

She translated, "'I love thee now and for eternity.'" She stood on her toes and kissed him on his mouth. He put his hand behind her head and drew her tightly to him. She pulled away. She stopped and turned in the doorway. "Goodnight, my love."

He sat for a time staring at the wall in front of him. He took off his clothes and draped them over the chair between the bed and the dresser. He lay on his back, naked, staring at the light fixture on the ceiling. He was convinced that if he could get a good grip on the light fixture with his eyes he could roll the bed out of its steep left bank. Get that left wing up! Keep it straight and level!

He raised himself and pulled up the bedclothes without taking his eyes off the light fixture. He had managed to cover one side of himself up to his waist, but his left leg and his groin remained uncovered. He fell asleep staring at the light fixture.

Fifteen or twenty minutes later, Cynthia rose from her makeshift bed on the sofa in the library. The embers in the fireplace cast a faint, reddish light as she put on her robe over her silk nightgown. She walked silently out of the library and down the hall, now dimly illuminated by the light from Robb's room, remaining in the shadows on the far side of the wide hallway. She walked beyond his open doorway until she could see into the room. She entered the room and stood for a time beside the bed, looking down at him.

She knelt next to the bed and sat back on her heels. She sat thus for several minutes. From time to time her eyes moved up and down the length of his body, but for the most part she looked upon his face. The tension that was always evident at the corners of his mouth had disappeared in the relaxation of sleep. He seemed younger, and strangely vulnerable for such a big person.

Without rising from her kneeling position she carefully lifted the bedclothes and pulled them up and lowered them over him so that his legs and chest were covered. She turned out the bed lamp and returned silently to the library.

It was nearly 4:00 A.M. when she heard his screams. She lay for a time, wide-eyed, in the dark. He was yelling now. She heard the names she had heard him scream last night. "Hoyt" and "Boo".

She sat up and groped for her robe. She moved silently toward the door, her fingers brushing the books along the wall. She moved slowly down the hall, still guided by her fingers against the wall.

She stood for a time beside him. It was pitch dark in the room, but her knees, now barely touching the bed, gave her a sense of where she stood. He was shouting now, over and over again, "Shut up, Boo! Shut up, Hoyt! They'll hear you! Shut up!" His voice trailed off into a soft, low pitched moan.

She slipped out of her robe and let it drop to the floor. She pushed the shoulder straps of her nightgown off her shoulders and it too fell to the floor. She lifted the bedclothes slowly, just enough to slip under them. She let the blankets fall behind her and eased her body slowly toward him. He was still lying on his back, moaning softly. Her body touched his. She put her arm slowly across his chest and drew herself gently to him until her breasts pressed firmly against his side. Her legs embraced his left leg. She began to move her body rhythmically against his side, ever so slowly, gently.

His moaning suddenly ceased. She stopped her movements. He turned toward her suddenly, throwing an arm and a leg around her in one quick motion, pulling her tightly to him.

"Cynthia, I..." His words were muffled immediately by her mouth. Soon he felt himself engulfed by her arms and her legs. The moans that escaped his lips were immediately smothered by her mouth on his. Her moans became one with his. She seemed bent on taking him into herself with all of her person, her mouth, her lips, her thighs, and finally, her body. At last her movements ceased. His heavy breathing eased gradually into the breathing of sleep.

The light of dawn was visible around the edges of the draperies when she began to ease herself out of his arms. She slipped out from under the bedclothes and put on her robe. She carried her nightgown over her arm as she moved noiselessly from the room. She picked up the pillow and blankets from the sofa in the library and carried them over her arm as she made her way up the central staircase.

24

Robb awakened at 9:20 A.M. on Monday. He opened his eyes and closed them quickly. He felt a piercing pain behind his eyes. His mouth was dry and his tongue felt swollen and thickly coated. He remembered his nightmare: Hoyt and Boo yelling at the German fighter pilots, challenging them to attack, and the Germans accepting the invitation. He closed his eyes and he remembered even more vividly his dream of Cynthia and her searing passion. He tried to recapture the details of the dream.

He lay very still, staring at the ceiling. He quickly turned to one side and pulled the pillow to his face. "I'll be damned!" The scent was unmistakable. Cynthia's fragrance, whatever it was she used. He held the pillow against his face for some time.

He turned back to the ceiling. He rubbed his face to check on his assumption that he was awake. His dreams and reality—whatever that may be—had become increasingly mixed together these past few weeks, but the confusion was never more complete than now. The dream was so real he could smell her presence, even now!

Cynthia was sitting in the breakfast alcove when Robb appeared a few minutes before 10:00. His one-crutch performance had improved remarkably, but he moved slowly so as not to jar his head. She turned as he approached the table. "Good morning, Robb." She stood up and kissed him. A quick peck on the mouth. She placed a cup of coffee before him. "This will help. Excuse me for a minute, please."

He eased himself into a chair. He studied her as she approached with a fresh pot of coffee on a tray. He stared out at the Firth of Clyde as he sipped his coffee, still wondering about his dream, yet reluctant to face Cynthia with such imagery in his mind. Cynthia, for her part, watched him out of the corner of her eye. She turned her eyes quickly away whenever he turned his eyes toward her. He turned to her suddenly, before she could avert her gaze. Their eyes met for a moment. She blushed a deep crimson. She gazed out the window, her head held high.

"Do you have any aspirin in the house?"

"I'll get them." She left the room.

He studied her carefully as she departed. If only she were as warm and loving as the woman in his dream! But, damn it, it was more than a dream! Or was it?

Cynthia returned with the aspirin. He swallowed three tablets with a gulp of coffee. He kept looking at her, scrutinizing her every move.

"Perhaps you'd feel better if we were to take a walk this morning."

He seemed not to hear her. He continued studying her.

"I'm beginning to feel self-conscious. Please look at this lovely day."

"Cynthia, I wonder if you'd do something for me. Don't ask any questions. Just do it."

She cocked her head, her eyebrows raised.

"Please lean forward, and kiss me squarely on my mouth, and hold it. The table will be between us, so you needn't fear any serious breach of social order."

She leaned forward and kissed him. The thought flashed through his mind that this was the first time she had really kissed him. Her kiss was tender, strangely cool yet warm.

Cynthia said, "Why did you do that? I mean why now, at this moment?"

"I wanted to compare reality with a dream of you I had last night."

"And which do you prefer? The dream or reality?"

"Reality. Your kiss was the loveliest thing that ever happened to me." He took a sip of coffee and looked at her intently. "But the dream was almost as real as that kiss."

The color rose in her cheeks. "What would you like to do today?"

"Have you ever had a dream where the effects of the dream survive the dream?"

She blushed fully. She turned her face to the window.

"Are you all right? You seem flushed."

"I'm fine, but I do feel warm. Perhaps it's this wool sweater and skirt."

"The dream was so vivid I could still smell your presence when I woke up."

Her face turned crimson. "Robb! Why on earth don't you answer my question?"

"What question?"

"What would you like to do this afternoon?"

"Let's do whatever happens. Did you hear what I said? I experienced your presence in bed this morning in my sense of smell, after I was awake."

"I'm going to play the Beethoven A-Flat Major for you this afternoon. Perhaps I had better practice now."

He reached across the table and placed his hand on her arm. "Please, don't leave yet. This is one of the most amazing things I've ever experienced. It was like a visual after-image after the object is gone."

"I really should practice."

"I had an olfactory after-image, long after the dream, and it wasn't a fleeting thing, like a visual after-image. It lasted. I could smell that lovely fragrance you use."

She exhaled audibly. She suddenly relaxed. "You could smell my perfume this morning? I must say that is interesting indeed."

"I thought you'd think so. Please kiss me again, just like you did a minute ago."

She leaned forward and kissed him. He put his hand behind her head and drew her to him. Her kiss became warmer, her lips fuller. Her mouth opened and she began to roll her head from side to side. She made a low moaning sound. She withdrew from him suddenly and stood up. "I really must practice."

"Please don't leave. Don't leave now just when I've discovered how warm and loving you can be!"

She hesitated for a moment. He saw her chest rising and falling, as though she had run up a hill, or a long flight of stairs. "I really must practice." She hurried from the room.

Robb's hangover persisted throughout the day. His head ached and he was consumed by fatigue. Finally, while they were listening to records in the library in the early evening, he excused himself and returned to his bedroom. He took off his shoes and stretched out on the bed. He fell asleep within minutes.

He awakened some three hours later and hurried to the Great Room. He could hear radio sounds coming from the kitchen. He arrived just as the BBC's Nine O'clock News was beginning. Cynthia greeted him with her eyes as he stood in the kitchen doorway. She nodded toward the radio.

"This doesn't sound good."

The broadcaster, his voice ominously stentorian, intoned:

". . . what had been feared yesterday has become a fact today. The German attacks on British and American positions in the Ardennes Mountains of Belgium which began on Saturday were a harbinger of a major German offensive on the Western Front."

She looked to Robb. "I don't like the sound of this."

The broadcaster continued:

"Allied forces have been driven back several miles on a broad front. German forces in division strength have broken through Allied lines in what has been called by informed sources the largest scale German offensive in the West since the blitzkriegs of 1940. It is estimated by informed military spokesmen that the German High Command has thrown upwards of twenty armored divisions into this offensive. Allied air support has been negligible since the German offensive began on Saturday due to adverse weather which has blanketed the entire European continent. The American 82nd and 101st Airborne Divisions, still regrouping after their victory at Arnem, have been sent to the Ardennes to reinforce Allied troops."

She turned off the radio. Robb said, "Well, now we know what the Eighth Air Force will be doing for the next week or two—or months, perhaps. We'll be bombing everything for miles behind those advancing German divisions. It will be very much like before and after D-Day."

"When do you expect all this to start?"

"As soon as the weather in that area clears."

Cynthia shuddered. He put his arm around her shoulder. She looked up at him. "What are the likely consequences of all this?"

"The Germans will be driven back eventually, but this could prolong the war by a year or two."

Cynthia swayed slightly. Robb grasped her around her waist and led her to a chair in the alcove. She sat with her eyes closed.

"Are you feeling sick?"

"I'll be all right in a moment." She took a deep breath. "Do you realize that England has been at war for five years? I can hardly remember what life was like during peacetime, it seems so long ago. I hate this war to the very depths of my soul! And now it seems it might go on another two or three years!"

"I was speculating. That was stupid future-thinking. I should know better!"

"Oh Robb! I want peace so terribly! I dream of it, I yearn for it all the time, yet in my heart I've come to believe that this war will never end. Oh God, how I hate it!"

"Let me get you a drink."

"I'm really quite all right now. I'm sorry I'm such a . . ."

"I feel exactly as you do about this war. I'm sick of it too."

She stood up suddenly. She took a deep breath and assumed an erect posture, her head held high. "Shall we get on with the business at hand?"

To Robb she suddenly became an Englishwoman self-consciously slipping back into a role she had momentarily slipped out of. She said, "I will now serve the most non-gourmet repast you've ever suffered. Creamed chipped Spam on toast." Her tone was bright, brittle.

"I've got a confession to make. All American soldiers are required to hate Spam. If you don't hate Spam you must act like you hate Spam. Actually, I like Spam. So there. Now you know. I'm beginning to feel better already."

She laughed. "Oh Robb, I do so like it when your mood is light!"

Robb finished his Spam and wiped his mouth on his napkin. "I've got a surprise for you." He stood up and walked slowly across the room without his crutch. He turned his right foot outward but he didn't limp. He grinned as he returned to the table.

"Robb! That's wonderful!" She started for the door. "I'll be back in a minute."

He glanced at the front page of a two-day-old copy of The London Times. Cynthia appeared in the doorway with an armload of canes and walking sticks.

Robb smiled. *"That* is a supply of canes."

"Take your pick." She stood the collection in a corner, spreading them out. "No one who ever lived here discarded a cane or walking stick. A family tradition, one might say."

He selected a heavy black cane with a crook handle. He strolled back and forth across the room, using the cane with a flourish.

"I say, old Robb, you look terribly English."

"Thank you. Please sit down again for a minute. I have a proposition to make." He sat opposite her at the table. "How would you like to run down to London for the remainder of my leave? We could go to concerts, and maybe a show or two."

She took a cigarette out of her box of Players. "That's a bit of a surprise. Give me a minute to react."

He gave her a light.

"When would we leave?"

"What about the day after tomorrow? Wednesday, I guess. I've lost track of time."

She took a deep pull on her cigarette. "Whatever you prefer is fine with me."

25

Early on Wednesday morning Robb called Largs for a cab to take them to Glasgow to catch the train for London. Cynthia overheard him. She was shocked. "That's terribly extravagant. The Glasgow bus picks us up at our gate when we go to Glasgow. No one takes a cab all the way to Glasgow. I never heard of such a thing!"

"It's only play money."

"What do you mean, 'play money?'"

"It's a long story. I'll tell you later. I have to get my things together now."

The cab appeared over the brow of the hill in less than twenty minutes after Robb's call. They rode to Glasgow in the solid comfort of a boxy, high-roofed English taxi cab. Robb told Cynthia about Stosh's poker playing and his money accumulation problem. They arrived at the railroad station with plenty of time to spare.

The train was precisely on time. They found an unoccupied first-class compartment. Not long after the train was under way, Cynthia leaned her head against Robb's shoulder. He put his arm around her and she turned her face up to him and kissed him. He was encouraged. After all, it was *she* who took the initiative just then. Before he left last Friday, Stosh had told him, "Get her away from her territory where she's in charge." Right you are, Stosh!

The wind that had been gathering force in the North Atlantic, beyond Cynthia's beloved Isle of Arran, and beyond Kintyre, drove the rain sharply against the windows of the compartment. And in the warmth of their compartment his face brushed against her hair. Her subtle fragrance, the dream fragrance, touched an olfactory nerve ending and sent a thrill up and down his spine.

The train picked up passengers at cities along the way. All of the seats in their compartment were occupied by the time they left Manchester, and long before they reached London there were people standing shoulder to shoulder in the corridor that ran along one side of the car.

Robb offered his seat to a middle-aged woman who was forced by the crowd to stand in the doorway of their compartment. She started to move toward the seat, but she stopped abruptly when she saw his cane. She said, "You're very kind, sir, but I really don't mind standing."

He sat down again and slouched in his seat, pushing his cap forward so that the visor covered his eyes. From time to time Cynthia, after carefully checking the eyes of her fellow passengers, leaned over and kissed him on the cheek. He sensed she was checking to see if he was awake. He squeezed her hand each time. The train pulled into the station in London at 7:40 P.M..

Robb gave the porter a pound note and asked him to carry their bags to the front of the station and to find them a cab. When the cab got under way Cynthia put her lips against Robb's ear and whispered, "No one, not even the king and queen, gives one- pound tips!"

"Stosh is my role model," Robb said aloud, "not your king and queen."

"You're debasing the king's currency."

"Sorry. I thought it was Stosh's."

"I love you, Robb."

The cab moved slowly through London's wartime blackness. Only the smallest signs, their lights carefully shielded, indicated major intersections, hotels, and restaurants. The cab finally pulled into the line of cabs discharging passengers at the main entrance to The Grosvenor House. "Do you want to eat at our hotel, or would you like to go out to a restaurant, the Ritz perhaps?"

"The Ritz, perhaps. Just like that, off the top of your head. I must say, old Robb, *that* is style. I'm impressed."

"Stosh likes the Ritz."

"I'm sure he does, and I'll bet the feeling is mutual."

"Pari-mutual. Stosh would say the feeling is pari-mutual, if you start with 'I bet'. Where would you like to eat?"

"The closest, quickest place possible. I'm dying of hunger."

"All right, then. We'll keep it simple. We'll eat here at the hotel."

Cynthia looked out the cab window. "I don't know how much you know about London, but eating at the Grosvenor isn't exactly slumming. This is one of London's finest."

The porter deposited their bags in front of the main registration desk. Robb frowned when he saw the clerk on duty was the immaculately dressed sycophant who had received them so disdainfully until he got a sniff of Stosh's money. "Ah, Captain Robertson! What an unexpected pleasure! It's so nice to see you again. And how is Captain Kovacs?"

"May I have the key." The man already had the key in his hand. "And would you reserve a table for two for dinner, please. For nine o'clock."

They waited for the elevator with their porter. Cynthia pulled Robb to one side. She spoke softly, between her teeth so that her lips hardly moved. "Here I thought I was running around with a shy country boy from Indiana, and now I find he's a big man about town. That clerk greeted you like you were the Rajah of Punjab. And you actually acted like the Rajah of Punjab. Do you have any Punjabi in your background?"

"I come from an old Hoosier Punjabi family."

"Hoosher? That *is* what you said, isn't it?"

"Yes. They're people in Indiana who trace their ancestry back to the Norman Conquest. I'll tell you about Hoosiers some other time. It's complicated."

"Whatever, I was proud of your hauteur, as it were."

Robb smiled. "Hoosier hauteur. Wait till they hear about that in Terre Haute, dear."

"What on earth are you talking about?"

"Nothing, actually. I was wondering what's happened to the elevator."

"Perhaps it doesn't know you're a friend of Captain Kovacs."

The elevator finally arrived. The porter, a middle-aged man, seemed bent on making up for the elevator's recalcitrance. When they entered the suite, this one much smaller than the "royal suite" Stosh had rented a month earlier, the porter made a great show of turning on lamps and opening ventilators. Robb gave him a pound note.

After he left, Cynthia said, "I daresay the next time you arrive at this hotel that porter will be as delighted to see you as the chap behind the front desk." She stood in the middle of the sitting room and did a 360-degree turnaround. "If I may say so, the man about town from Indiana certainly knows how to pick accommodations. This suite is lovely." She walked across the sitting room and disappeared down the hallway to the bedrooms. She reappeared, smiling brightly. "Two bedrooms and two baths. An ideal arrangement under our circumstances, don't you think?"

"I pass."

She glanced quickly at him. "I was going to say something, but your clever retort made me forget what it was. You are a clever retorter at times. Did you know that?"

"Robb Robertson, Boy Retorter."

"I say, old Robb, you *are* in a clever mood tonight. I'm so glad we got away from that gloomy old house in Scotland. I see a new side of you, and I must say I like it." She strolled about the room examining the oil paintings. She turned to him. "When you proposed this little expedition you made it sound as though the idea occurred to you just then, yet I see compelling evidence of advance planning, as it were."

"Stosh has a long-term reservation on this suite, paid up ahead. Almost like a lease."

"A lease! For how long?"

"The duration of the war, or the duration of Stosh, whichever comes first."

"Please, Robb. Please don't talk like that."

"All right. What were we talking about? Oh yes. Stosh's paid up suite. Not too bad an idea, is it?"

"Not if one has an accumulation problem."

"Would you like to do something before we go down to dinner?"

She looked at him quickly.

"Would you like to freshen up a bit?"

She crossed the room and threw her arms around his neck and pulled his head down roughly and kissed him. She turned and walked toward the bedrooms. She stopped and faced him. "I'll be a while. I heard you make that dinner reservation for 9:00. We have lots of time."

Robb took a hot shower and did some quick tendon stretching exercises. He broke into the baritone solo, "O du mein holder Abendstern" from Tannhauser. The tiled walls gave his baritone a depth and richness it didn't ordinarily have.

Cynthia was sitting on the sofa smoking a cigarette when he returned to the sitting room. He stopped short when he saw her. "Stand up, please. Let me see you." She stood up and smiled at him. She clasped her hands in front of her and turned around slowly. She was wearing a form-fitting, black velvet dress with a neckline that was very decollete´. A necklace of small diamonds sparkled against her throat. She seemed taller in her spike-heeled, black leather pumps. Robb noted with surprise the diamond bracelet around her left ankle. He'd seen such ankle bracelets on many of the "companions" in the Grosvenor. The thought that she might be taken for his "companion" excited him. In fact, Cynthia, severely black-velveted, her eyes sparkling like the necklace against her throat, excited him incredibly. "As our benefactor would say, you, Cynthia, are a knockout!"

"Thank you, sir. I like your costume too. I heard your 'O du mein holder Abendstern'. You really have a good voice."

"Only if it bounces off tile. If there's a rug in the room, there goes my voice."

"I wish I had packed a stole, or something to throw around my shoulders. I don't relish the thought of wearing my damp raincoat to dinner."

"Come with me, fair lady." He led her to the bedroom she had, by default, assigned to him. He opened a closet door. Hanging along the closet rod were evening gowns, dresses, two fur stoles and two capes.

"Take your pick."

"These are beautiful! But what are they doing here?"

"They belong to Merrie and Evelyn."

Cynthia looked at the labels on some of the dresses. "I say, these are very expensive clothes. Merrie and Evelyn must come from families that are very well situated indeed."

"These things were bought with play money."

She shot a quick glance at him. "Oh, I see. You and Captain Kovacs bought them."

"Stosh, actually."

"But why are they here, in this closet in this suite?"

"They're illegal. They can't take them back to the base. No soldier— officer or enlisted man—is allowed to wear civilian clothes or even have them in his possession during wartime. Merrie and Evelyn are lieutenants."

She closed the closet door abruptly. "Come back to the sitting room with me." She led the way. "Sit down and talk with me for a few minutes."

Robb sat on the sofa. He moved over to make room for her.   She took a chair facing him, with the cocktail table between them.   "I don't know how to put my feelings into words without impugning the character of two fine young women.   I must tell you I feel like an interloper, like I don't belong here."

"I don't understand."

"Take my role for a moment.   I arrive here and find a beautiful leased suite.   I find women's clothes, expensive clothes, in one of the closets.   Imagine you are I.   What would you think?"

"I guess I'd think I'd walked into a philanderer's den."

"How would I feel if I used one of those garments?"

"Do you mean you'd feel like. . .uh. . .what shall I say? Like another kept woman?"

Her eyes were fixed on the cocktail table.

Robb continued, "It seems to me the only way you might feel like another kept woman passing through this den of iniquity would be if I'd slept with other women here.   I haven't, nor have I ever slept with Evelyn, here or anywhere else."

She looked up at him without moving her head.   Her features seemed to soften.   "You told me she knows about me.   Is she in love with you?"

"Yes."

"What happens to Evelyn now?   What are your options?"

"I guess we just go on like now.   I'd never hurt her.   I couldn't do it, no matter what the consequences.   I love you, but I wouldn't hurt Evelyn. Not for anything."

"It would seem you're stuck with two women."

"She knows I'm in love with you and not with her.   I'm going to tell her that you and I have a commitment to each other, a life-long commitment.   We do, don't we?"

She studied his face carefully.   "Yes."   She took a cigarette package from her evening bag.   "How do you think she'll respond to that?"

"She'll go on as now.   She has no intention of saying goodbye to me."

"I wonder if she might not be optimistic about the future."

"She's learning to live without a future.   She's not thinking along those lines."

She looked at him quickly, studying him intently for a time.

Robb smiled. "I'm glad you're an anthropologist."

"Why do you say that?"

"You know there are infinite ways humans solve their problems, none right for all people at all times. Most women wouldn't settle for the deal I'm handing you, keeping my friendship with Evelyn. It would drive some women crazy." He looked up at her suddenly. "You *are* willing to settle for this arrangement, aren't you?"

She lit a cigarette and took a long pull on it, inhaling deeply. She exhaled slowly. Finally she spoke, just above a whisper. "Yes." She stood up suddenly. She spoke quickly, brightly. "We had better be leaving. We're going to be late for our dinner reservation."

"You would agree that the fact that Evelyn doesn't sleep with me gives those clothes in the closet a different meaning. Isn't that so?"

"Yes."

Robb stood up slowly, placing his left leg behind his right, stretching his tendon. "Then why didn't you simply ask, right off the bat, if Evelyn was sleeping with me?"

"That would have been terribly rude of me. I'd never do that." She walked around the table and put her arms around him. She gave him a quick, tight hug. She turned and walked to the closet in the entry hall. She took out her rain coat and put it on.

———26———

The maitre d' escorted them to their table. They had a good view of the dance floor and the orchestra on its raised platform beyond. Almost all of the tables were occupied. There were perhaps two dozen couples dancing.

Robb noted that the orchestra produced a full-bodied, American dance-band sound. As he watched the musicians, the sax players traded their saxophones for clarinets, and the trumpet men put wah-wah mutes into the bells of their horns. The color of the sound changed dramatically. "They're good, Cynthia. Did you notice that switch just now from a Tommy Dorsey sound to Glenn Miller?"

"I would say they sound exactly like Glenn Miller," she smiled pleasantly at him, "if I knew what Glenn Miller sounds like."

"I keep forgetting you're English."

"I'm sure most English men and women know what Glenn Miller sounds like. It's just that I lead rather a sheltered life, so to speak." She indicated the waiter's presence with her eyes. The waiter placed an over-sized menu in front of each of them. Robb looked up at the man. "Could you recommend something?"

The waiter leaned forward. "I understand you are Captain Kovacs' guests. That is correct?"

Robb looked at Cynthia. She smiled. "Plead guilty." Robb nodded to the waiter. " Yes."

"I believe I could prevail upon the chef to prepare two servings of veal scallopini."

Cynthia brightened. "Veal scallopini!"

The waiter raised his hand quickly and looked over his shoulder. "It's not on the menu, madam," he said softly. "We must be discreet."

"With real veal?" Cynthia whispered.

The waiter nodded solemnly.

Cynthia closed her menu. "Well then, the issue is settled as far as I'm concerned."

Robb said, "Fine. I agree."

The wine steward arrived as soon as the waiter departed. He placed the wine list in Robb's hand. Robb looked at the list for some time. Finally he turned to Cynthia. "Is there something you'd like?"

"It's your party, Robb, or Captain Kovacs'."

The steward said, "Perhaps you'd like the champagne Captain Kovacs prefers."

"That's a great idea. Bring us two bottles, please." As soon as the man was out of earshot, Robb leaned over and kissed Cynthia on the cheek. "Name dropper."

"I was simply being discreet," she said. "In any event, I'm sure he'd already been told we are Captain Kovacs' guests."

The wine steward returned and opened one of the bottles and filled their glasses. Cynthia took a sip. "This is very good indeed." Robb clicked glasses with her. "Cheers." He drained his glass in two gulps. "We're polishing this stuff off like it was Haig and Haig." He refilled their glasses.

A waiter arrived with a tray. Oysters on the half shell, followed in order by Vichyssoise, a fresh green garden salad, the veal scallopini with real veal and with dark brown wild rice and fresh asparagus spears with Hollandaise sauce. The waiter later appeared with a multi-colored ice and, finally, pears zabaglione.

Cynthia leaned toward Robb and whispered, "This is the best meal I've had since 1939." She sat up straight and smiled. "I must confess I feel more than a little unpatriotic. I shall, however, follow our benefactor's advice and upon this occasion rise above my convictions."

"I'll tell Brain Child I have further support for his theory of sacrifice in wartime."

"Who, may I ask, is 'Brain Child'?"

"My radio operator. He's a genius."

"I can already surmise the tenor of his theory. I wish you hadn't brought it up."

"Sorry. Let's have some more champagne."

Robb asked Cynthia to dance, and Cynthia said that surely he was joking, and Robb said that until she'd danced with an American soldier with a game leg she had never really danced. "You'll love our dip."

Robb used his cane as they made their way between the tables to the dance floor, but when they began dancing he hung the crook of the cane over his left arm.

"I say, Robb, this is truly remarkable! You dance better than you walk!"

"You've heard the old Hoosier saying, you have to dance before you can walk."

"Oh, those Hooshers again."

They glided smoothly about the floor. Robb became increasingly confident. He found there were movements he could execute while dancing that he couldn't have ordinarily with his bum leg, sideways movements that went well with his particular affliction. Cynthia put her cheek against his chest. Robb glided and pivoted about the floor, oblivious of his leg and the amused glances of the dancers who happened to see the cane hanging from his arm.

Four saxophones intoned in the lower register the popular melody, "Together". Muted trumpets provided an obligatto, and the baritone sax, trombones and string bass gave it all a deep foundation. The beat of the rhythm section was sure, inexorable, and Robb felt as though he and Cynthia were impelled by a force external to themselves. For a moment he was outside of himself, watching himself and Cynthia. She looked lovely from behind as she danced. Rounded calves moving smoothly above spike-heeled pumps, rounded-slender hips undulating subtly beneath black velvet.

Cynthia said softly, "What are you thinking right now?"

"I was admiring how lovely you look from behind when you dance."

"Thank you. But how do you know that?"

"I'm developing an English talent for watching myself, and you with me, from the outside. It's an important part of now."

"Come back inside for a while."

The band's vocalist, a youngster of seventeen or eighteen, sat primly on a straight-backed chair to one side of the band's leader. She smiled a shy little smile from time to time as a passing dancer caught her eye. Her baby-fat cheeks dimpled, no matter how slight her smile. Her diminutive size and her pageboy hairdo with Dutchboy bangs made her seem even younger than Robb guessed her to be. Robb contemplated her through a champagne haze. Watch carefully this creature of an hour! Her beauty will pass and all of you dancing here will miss it! Then she stood up to sing. She brought her elbows back and thrust her breasts forward, challengingly, and looked along her left shoulder. She looked squarely into Robb's eyes. He felt a pang for her suddenly lost adolescence as she assumed the classic girl-singer-in-front-of-band posture.

He had once known a girl who stood exactly thus before a jazz band. And she had looked into his eyes, often at times when he had been her only audience in her apartment in Chicago. It occurred to him that he could have as easily written her the Dear John as she to him. He was now glad she had spared him the awkward moment.

The youngster who had suddenly jumped out of adolescence into womanhood began to sing. She sang in a sotto voce that was totally unexpected after the harp's lavish announcement. Her tones pure, her intonation flawless. Robb squeezed Cynthia and kissed the top of her head. Cynthia squeezed back. The yet unspoiled, adolescent voice yearned,

"We strolled the lane, together,
Laughed at the rain, together,
Sang love's refrain, together,
And we both pretend, this will never end..."

Robb bent his head down so that the side of his forehead brushed against Cynthia's cheek. The corner of her eye was damp. He put his hand under her chin and raised her face to his. "What's wrong?"

"Nothing's wrong." She pulled his head down so that her lips touched his cheek. "It's just that I'm so frightfully happy!"

Little page-boy belted out the last verse, Judy Garland-like: the same wide-open style, the studied non-vibrato for the first part of the long notes with the now anticipated, hoped for, finally delivered vibrato at the end of the note. When finally she let go of the last note, Robb exclaimed softly, "Wow!" Cynthia pulled his head down and placed her lips on his cheek.

It was a few minutes before midnight when they emerged from the elevator. Robb carried a paper bag containing two bottles of chilled champagne. He asked Cynthia to hold the champagne while he searched his pockets for the key to the suite. "Thish may take a while. They put about fifteen or twenty pockets in these uniforms."

"I say, Robb, how do you keep track of those myriad dials and switches in the cockpit of your aeroplane?"

"I pray a lot. Actually, Shynthia, I'm not afraid of this hotel crashing if I forget where I put the key. Ah, here it is! Oh thou of little faith!"

They collapsed on the sofa in the sitting room. "Whooh!" Robb exclaimed. "Whoohee!" He put his arm around her shoulder.

She stood up quickly. "Would you like a glass of champagne?"

He sighed as he stared at the cold grate in the fireplace. "Why the hell not?"

"You seem angry. Why are you angry?"

"One guesh. I mean guess. I'll give you one guess."

"Will you pop the cork, please."

He began angrily working the cork out of the bottle. "Watch this. See that little goddamn lamp on that table in the entry hall?" The cork exploded out of the bottle and hit the little lamp.

Cynthia said, "You have talents I never dreamed of."

"And you have talents I dream of all the time. For all the good it does me."

She studied him for a time. "Perhaps we should go to bed soon so we can do wonderful things tomorrow, just as we did today."

"As you wish, if I may borrow one of your favorite phrases." He stood up, chug-a-lugged his glass of champagne and put his glass down firmly. He turned and walked unsteadily toward the bedrooms. He turned abruptly. "Ssynthia. I want to fuck you. I love you and you love me, and I want to fuck you and you want to fuck me. It's as shimple as that. Sweet dreams." He turned and walked toward the hallway. He hardly limped although he turned his left foot outward slightly as he walked.

Her look of shock metamorphosed gradually into bemusement. "And sweet dreams to you," she whispered to herself. "I really mean it, my love."

He waved his arm in her direction as he closed his bedroom door. He took two capsules out of his aluminum soap container and placed them on the bed table. He took off his clothes and slipped into the cool smoothness between the sheets and turned out the bedside light. The capsules remained on the bedside table. Some twenty minutes later Cynthia walked silently to his bedroom door and opened it very carefully, perhaps six inches or so. She returned to her own room. She left her door ajar.

She awakened to his yelling shortly past four. She got out of bed, slipped into her robe, and made her way silently to his bedside. After a time his yells modulated into a low moan. She let her robe and nightgown fall to the floor and slipped into the bed beside him. His moans ceased, and soon only the heavy breathing of two people could be heard.

He was lying on his back when first she insinuated her warm softness against the length of his body. His arms closed about her and she drew him tightly to her, embracing him with her arms and legs. She buried her face against his upper chest and neck as she moved her body rhythmically against his.

His left arm ceased its embrace and moved slowly away from her, toward the switch at the base of the lamp on the table beside the bed. He switched on the light and threw the bedclothes back in a single, sudden movement.

She tried to push herself away from him but he held her firmly. She was still half on top of him. In her initial attempt to separate herself from him when the lights went on, she had pushed herself away from him but he had grasped her firmly in both his arms and pulled her back to him. In the process she had slipped farther down. Her legs embraced his left thigh, now involuntarily, and her face was buried against the side of his chest, below his arm. After a time she ceased pushing against him.

"Cynthia. It's all right. It's wonderful, really. I didn't want to miss it. I didn't want to know it only as a dream mixed with other dreams, bad dreams, nightmares." He stroked her back, slowly, softly. He kissed the top of her head, but she buried her head deeper under his arm.

"It was the perfume. I couldn't believe the fragrance could remain after the dream. And when you kissed me that morning in the breakfast alcove, I knew I already knew that kiss and I wondered how I could have known it simply from a dream. And you had that fragrance about you that morning. The two things made me wonder if I had really only dreamt it all."

He pulled her upward quickly along his body. She was unprepared for his quick move. She was very tense. He continued stroking her back, reaching ever so slightly lower with each stroke of his hand.

For a moment he saw himself pulling a helpless, naked girl to him against her will. He felt a wave of self-loathing. He told himself she had come to his bed of her own free will. The moment of self-recrimination passed.

He felt a slight movement of her breasts against his side. He continued stroking her back, his strokes now extending along the small of her back to the roundness below. Gently, slowly. He could feel the tension subsiding. "I'm not going to do anything you don't want me to do. We're in a holding pattern." He continued to caress her.

"I'm holding you now, but not to keep you from getting up and leaving this bed. I'm holding you because I love you." He stroked the back of her head, the near-auburn hair with flecks of red and gold, and he stroked the smooth contours of her back. The tension was gone. She was again warm and soft and supple against his chest, his abdomen, his thigh. He sensed a slight movement of her body against his side, a movement toward him, not away from him. He felt the movement again. He reached over and switched off the lamp.

He continued stroking her back and her thighs. She started to move slowly. He felt her lips against his chest. He pulled her upwards so that her face was even with his. Her mouth found his and she became again as he had known her in his dream-nondream. She was at the height of her passion immediately, and she stayed there. She seemed bent on drawing him totally into herself. She made strange vocal ejaculations, primordial sounds long extinguished by the daylight of civilization.

He had experienced her passion before, but now in this unbelievable moment he knew it, and he knew he knew it. He became as abandoned as she and for a brief time it all became the wild, crazy dream again.

Finally her movements began to slow and her strange vocalizations grew softer, finally ceasing.

"I love you, Cynthia."   She didn't respond. She lay there, content in his arms—or so it seemed to him—but she didn't speak.

He wondered if by some strange schizoid process her mind could still be angry with him while her body remained responsive. She never uttered a sound, but he felt a contentment that seemed to ooze from her to him by some mysterious osmosis as he held her warm softness against himself. Sleep soon overcame his concerns.

Robb awakened at 9:20 the next morning. He lay on his back for a time trying to reconstruct his dream of the night before. Dream? Hell no! Reality, by god! He gave his head a quick shake and rubbed his face with his hands.

He and Cynthia had made love! He closed his eyes and re-lived her warmth, her softness, their closeness, her unbridled passion. How incredible! He saw her as in the picture he had fallen in love with: Cynthia on the stream, naked, lying on her back in a patch of sunlight on a summer's day. Who would have thought then that this would ever come to pass? He hadn't imagined in his wildest dreams that she would one day give herself to him. And so completely. And yet it happened. It happened last night.

He remembered his earlier "dreams" of love. How amazing. She had managed to merge her nocturnal visits into his dreams. He sat up suddenly and turned on the lamp. There they were, the two sleeping pills. If he had swallowed those pills he'd have missed it again.

He took a shower, flexing his leg as the hot water splashed against his calf. He shaved and dressed quickly. He put on his shoes and walked back and forth across the bedroom. He turned his foot outward slightly, but he hardly limped.

Cynthia was sitting on the sofa paging through a magazine when he entered the sitting room. He walked quickly around the end of the sofa and bent down and kissed her on the mouth. "Good morning, lovely lady." He straightened up and looked down at her. She turned away from his gaze. "I've never seen you more beautiful."

She refused to meet his eyes as she spoke. "Well, now you know."

"Know what?"

"My problem."

"I don't know what you're talking about. I know it has to do with our making love last night. You were wonderful. Childe Roland scaled another peak last night."

"Please, Robb! Please don't make light of it."

"Believe me, I have no idea what you're talking about."

"Are you serious?"

"I've never been more serious."

"Surely it's obvious to you now that I'm not normal sexually."

"If you mean your responsiveness, all I can say is hooray for your problem."

"You still don't understand."

"I do understand. You are responsive. All right, extremely responsive, but as far as I'm concerned that's a blessing. You act as though it's a curse."

'It *is* a curse. That's exactly what it is. A humiliating, incurable curse!"

"In what way?"

"I can't just kiss you, or let you take me in your arms. Can't you see why I've avoided contact with you? I can't stop! Can't you understand that? *I can't stop!*" She burst into tears and hurried toward her bedroom.

He followed her. She threw herself face-down on the bed, sobbing. He sat on the edge of the bed and stroked her shoulder gently. He stroked her hair. "You're making something bad out of something good. You have to learn to rejoice in what you are."

"You have no idea how humiliating this is!" Her face was buried in the crook of her arm, her voice muffled.

"If you feel humiliated about anything that happened last night, then we live in a world in which most people should feel humiliated, including me." He turned her over gently. He stood up and took her hand. "Come with me now. We need to have a talk." He led her to the sitting room. He sat beside her on the sofa and picked up the phone and ordered breakfast. "Any breakfast for two that occurs to you will be fine."

He studied her face. "Will you forgive me if I ask some very personal questions?"

She nodded.

"Did your mother or your father, or Mrs. Cameron, or the Cameron children, or anyone else ever talk to you about sex when you were growing up?"

"No, nor did anyone else, but I must tell you I've read extensively on the subject."

"Did you read about passion? Did you read about the degrees of passion that are possible—and often characteristic—in humans?"

"I've read a good deal about nymphomania."

"I hate to ask you this, but I must." He looked at her quickly but her eyes were averted. "How many men have you been with. . . sexually?"

She remained silent for a time. "One . . . not counting you."

"How many times . . . with the other person?

"Once. A few days before he died." She turned her back to him. "I know you're trying to tell me that I'm unsatiated and that this is why I'm so pathologically responsive. It's really not that simple. Do you know that if a man, even a strange man in a public place, so much as brushes against my shoulder I'm sexually aroused immediately, almost uncontrollably. Please don't try to tell me that's normal. I'm not a child."

"How many men have touched you? Hugged you? Kissed you?"

She stared at the cold fireplace. Robb had concluded that she had no intention of answering when finally she said softly, "Two, counting you."

"Don't you realize you really *are* actually starved? That, along with your natural responsiveness, would make you very sensitive to a man's touch. But if you were really a nymph, you'd have been with a hundred men by now, no matter how sheltered your life."

"I wish I could believe you."

"Give me a week or two of love-making with you. I'll prove it."

"Oh God! How I wish I could believe that!"

"I'm going to prove it. I want to make love with you after breakfast, and again before dinner, and again when we go to bed tonight. And I'm going to touch you and caress you and fondle you as often as I can in between. I'll prove my case." He smiled. "I think I'm going to enjoy this experiment."

"I wish it were that simple. I must say at this point I'm terribly confused."

There was a knock at the door. He smiled at her. "Breakfast. The major problem we have at the moment is breakfast. I consider myself the luckiest man in the world at the prospect of having breakfast with you on this beautiful day that the Lord hath made."

"Did you look out at this day? Go to the window and look out"

"I'd better let in the breakfast first."

Robb opened the door for the waiter. He walked to the window while the waiter laid the table linen and silverware. He pulled the drapery aside and looked out. It was late morning and it seemed as though night was falling. The fog blocked out the light from the sky and obliterated the street below. They were on the fifth floor and yet they were above today's ceiling, solidly in the soup. The near-black nothingness beyond the hotel window became the black nothingness beyond his plane's windshield. His hands became rigid on an imaginary control column and throttles and he felt himself climbing endlessly through the blackness. Now he was on the bomb run and he saw a thousand B-17s release their thousands of tons of incendiary bombs in a single salvo, and he watched the city below become an inferno in an instant and as he watched the flames die he saw the city metamorphose into a dead, gray-black, treeless moonscape of burned out remnants of buildings and trees, a lifeless place inhabited by the living dead. Moaning women with dead babies in their arms, children writhing and crying, the elderly and infirm wandering and groping, all of them naked and forever locked in a gray near-dark eternity through which a cold wind blew unceasingly. Robb felt the cold wind and for a moment he saw himself in that place naked and writhing among his victims, all of them staring at him with large, round, accusing eyes set deep in skeletal sockets. The cold wind seemed to blow through his very heart and soul. He let the drapery fall, but the coldness remained in his heart and he knew for a moment terror such as he had never imagined.

"Robb. The food is going to get cold."

He rubbed his face with his hands, as though awakening from a deep sleep. "Sorry." He walked briskly to the table. He lifted the cover from a plate. "Look at this, would you. Fresh eggs!" His tone was bright, brittle. "When I see that weather out there and these fried eggs smiling at me, I'm absolutely positive I'm going . . . " He stopped short.

Cynthia served the eggs and bacon. "What were you about to say?"

"I don't know. You know absent-minded me. I forgot what I was going to say, right in the middle of a sentence."

"That's the first time you've ever lied to me."

He reached across the table and placed his hand on hers. "It's not lying when we accidentally wander into the future and have to extricate ourselves."

"You were about to say you felt you were about to leave on a sortie."

"Yes."

"What do the eggs have to do with it?"

"They give us two fresh eggs each, fried, before a mission. Americans have great faith in the power of eggs and milk. The Eighth Air Force runs on eggs and milk."

"I've never seen you drink milk."

"We're not allowed to drink English milk. The Eighth Air Force is afraid their rosy-cheeked boys will catch something from unpasteurized English milk. It's a well kept secret because one nation must never besmirch another nation's milk, especially its own motherland's milk." He smiled his closed-mouth smile.

She smiled. He smiled back, again his closed-mouth, ear-to-ear smile. She burst out laughing.

Robb laughed too. "What are we laughing at?" He smiled the smile again and she started to laugh again. "I wish you could see your smile. Did you know you have a funny smile? Not all your smiles. Just the one where you keep your lips together."

"I know. Ted used to call it my village idiot smile. When I was in junior high school I used to stand in front of the bathroom mirror practicing smiling with my mouth not closed. I wasn't completely successful." He attacked his breakfast with uncharacteristic gusto.

"I'm glad you weren't successful."

"I can wiggle my ears, too. I used to take a break from smiling practice and wiggle my ears for a while."

"Oh Robb, let's stay here in the hotel after breakfast and you can tell me all about your past. I'd love that."

"All right, but I think we ought to get out into the world for a while first. Would you like to go Christmas shopping? Today is Thursday, the twenty-first, so that leaves just Friday and Saturday."

"Christmas shopping is a future thing. Why don't we have them build a fire in the fireplace and stay here in the suite today? And you can tell me about Hooshers and ear-wiggling and other wonderful things."

Robb placed his napkin on the table. "All right, but first come to your bedroom with me. It's time for a training session." He smiled and reached for her hand. She held out her hand and smiled warmly at him. The phone on the end table rang and her smile froze.

Robb picked up the phone. "Stosh! How did you know I was here?"
Robb nodded. "Yes . . . yes. . . uh-huh." He sighed. "It's about better."
He nodded. He shot a glance at Cynthia. She was listening carefully,
watching his every move, every detail of his facial expression.

"Okay. Put him on." He smiled at Cynthia. Her face remained a
mask.

"Hello, Tony." He listened for a moment. "It's all right. Yes. You
can certify that I have full use of it." He bent his foot upward. "Okay,
put him on."

"Hello, sir." He listened for a moment. "Yes sir." He shot another
glance at Cynthia. "I understand, sir. I assure you, there's no problem.
Would you do me a favor, Colonel? Have someone tell Monk right
away so he can tell the rest of the crew. I'll catch the first train I can.
Yes, sir. Good bye."

He put down the telephone. Cynthia stared at him but it seemed to
Robb she was staring through him at something behind him. He took her
hand. "Today is still today. Now is still now. Let's not ruin it. I have to
catch the earliest train I can. We won't be flying today. Perhaps you
could go to your home in Allsford Lynn and maybe I can get over there
early this evening after my meeting."

She sat as in a trance.

"I have to pack now." He stood up and held his hand out to her. She
didn't react. He sat down again and put his arm around her and drew her
head to his chest and kissed the top of her head. "Please, Cynthia. We
still have today. We'll be together in the cab and on the train, and we'll be
together this evening at your place at Allsford Lynn."

He stood up again and held out his hand. "Come with me now."
She remained as in a trance. He bent down and kissed her gently on her
mouth, but she didn't kiss him in return. He stood before her looking
down at her. She stared blankly ahead, unaware that he had kissed her or
that he was standing there.

"I've got to pack now." He turned and walked slowly toward the bedrooms. His foot turned slightly outward as he walked. Other than that
he walked perfectly.

——28——

It was a few minutes past 1530 hours when Robb hung up the phone in the sentry booth at the main gate to the United States Army Air Force Base at Allsford Lynn. Sam said he'd be right over.

He leaned against the sentry booth as he waited. It was four hours since he had first looked upon this dark, dismal day through the hotel window. The fog seemed to smother the world itself, and with it all light and life and hope. He contemplated the lonely MP, the squat, stocky man now standing at parade rest in the middle of the road, legs apart, chin tucked in, rifle at the ready, his posture declaring, it seemed to Robb, "Let's see you get past me!" His paratrooper boots were polished to a high shine that even this day couldn't dull.

He heard the approaching sound of the jeep's motor long before its headlights penetrated the fog. When the jeep emerged from the fog, the soldier snapped to "present arms" as though the jeep were a thing of flesh and blood with some sort of power over him. Robb touched the visor of his cap as he opened the door of the jeep.

"Thanks, Sam."

Sam contemplated Robb for a moment. "Why the long face?"

"Cynthia didn't make the adjustment."

"To what?"

"My job. The thing she's been so afraid of all along. Her reason for hiding. I wish for her sake she had never met me. It hurts like hell to see her suffering so, when I'm the cause of her suffering."

The fog seemed to be getting thicker. Sam crawled along at five miles an hour, his nose almost touching the windshield as he peered into the fog through the thick lenses of his glasses. Sam said, "It takes some people longer than others to adjust."

Robb nodded. "Maybe her mood will improve by the time I see her tonight."

"The base is closed. No one is allowed in or out."

"Goddamn it, Sam! I've got to see her, even if I have to climb the..."

"Don't do anything rash. You'll soon see why security is so crucial."

Robb's mood remained dark, but he felt himself relaxing gradually as the jeep rumbled on. Sam stopped in front of the hospital. "Here we are, at Tony Rizzo's place of business."

Robb smiled ruefully. "I'm really screwed up today. I feel awful about not being able to see Cynthia tonight, and yet I feel better now than I have all day."

"Maybe this is the only home we have now."

"No. That's not it. It has to do with a really weird experience I had this morning. We were on the fifth floor of the hotel in London. I looked out the window and the fog was so thick I couldn't see the street below or the buildings across the street, or anything above. I suddenly felt like I was in the cockpit, climbing in that soup. That was when it happened." He stared at the dark gray nothingness beyond the windshield.

"What happened?"

"I know it sounds crazy, but I saw beyond where any human should—a wasteland of burned remnants of trees, of forests, buildings, cities, the whole landscape laid waste. The sun forever blotted out, and bitter cold. Everything gray or black. Crying children, mothers and fathers holding dying babies, and everyone naked and dying and moaning and not wanting to die. The clinging, cringing, dark, cold, dying of all humans and the very earth itself." He stared into the fog beyond the windshield.

"Christ, that's awful, Robb." Sam sighed. "You'd better go on in to see Tony."

"I've had this cold terror in my guts all day, yet now that I'm back on the base I feel almost safe. I'm here where I belong. I don't have to face death anymore. It's behind me now . . . it's all over with . . . where it has been for a long time."

Sam said, "I've got to see the C.O. before the meeting. The meeting is at 1700 hours. You'd better get moving, too."

"I can't tell you how much better I feel, even though I'm sick about not being able to go to Cynthia tonight when she needs me so badly. Does that sound crazy?"

"No."

"That terror, that death-terror I felt when I looked out that hotel window, is the worst thing that can happen to anybody. Worse than death itself. Much worse. Do you believe that?"

"I don't know, Robb."

Tony Rizzo had a hard time making up his mind. Under ordinary circumstances he would have recommended Robb take another week off, but apparently he knew more than he should have about the upcoming military operation and the Group's peculiar needs. He decided to toss the ball into Colonel Strang's court.

Colonel Strang tapped a pencil on his desk as he carefully regarded the man across from him.

"Get up and walk back and forth across the room a couple of times."

Robb walked swiftly across the room, his face carefully composed. His limp was hardly noticeable.

"Does it hurt?"

"Not much, sir."

"All right. Sit down. Tony Rizzo called just a minute ago. He said your case is borderline. He's leaving it to me to decide whether you fly or not, depending on how much we need you. Well, Robb, we need every lead pilot in this outfit. Now look me in the eye and give me an answer. Can you do the job?"

"Yes."

"Don't lie to me. You have to be as good as you ever were."

"I am."

"That's good enough for me." He spoke softly, confidentially. "We've got fifteen minutes until the meeting. There are a couple of things you need to know before then, things too sensitive to talk about in the meeting. One slip to the wrong person could cost the lives of thousands of our troops, and even prolong the war."

Robb knew full well what the Colonel was driving at. If the Germans got wind of how the bombers would be guided by Allied ground forces fighting at "the battle of the bulge"—as the newspapers were calling it—and how the drop zone markers were to be set up, they could send up fake signals and in effect command the bombers to drop their loads on their own ground forces. This was indeed a situation where a slip of the tongue could be disastrous.

"As you've already figured out, I'm sure, we're scheduled to lay a carpet behind the German lines as soon as the weather clears over the Ardennes." He paused for a moment and looked Robb in the eye. "The 990th is leading the Task Force."

Robb nodded.

"What I'm about to tell you is top secret. I'm telling you this because you have to know about a new strategy we've set up for this operation. This is why I've decided to send you out in spite of that limp."

"The limp is nothing."

The Colonel appraised him carefully. "All right. We'll be using every lead pilot in the Group on this operation. We're going to have three lead planes in each squadron. The lead and deputy lead in number one and number two position, and a backup lead plane hidden well back in the formation, ready to move up front should anything happen to the lead and deputy lead."

Robb knew all too well the ominous connotation of the Colonel's words. The Luftwaffe would be going for the Lead Group in the Task Force, and within the Lead Group they'd concentrate on the lead plane and the deputy leader.

"Is that clear? You'll not hear anything about this again, either in the meeting today, or in briefing on the morning of the mission."

"I understand, sir."

"You're going to be the backup lead in Amber Squadron, hidden back in the pack. Amber Squadron is going to be the 990th's Lead Squadron, so that means Amber leads the entire Task Force on one of the biggest and most important raids of the war. We can't fail, Robb. Our worst possible failure would be dropping our loads too soon and wiping out our own guys."

"I don't have to be reminded of that. I remember Saint-Lo all too well." Robb cringed at the thought of the biggest Air Force fiasco of the war, the time the Eighth Air Force, near Saint-Lo, in France, wiped out God only knows how many American troops, including their com- mander, General McNair. They'd never flown in close support of the ground forces since. Until today. He felt a momentary wave of nausea at the thought of the possibility of another Saint-Lo. Rumor had it that General Eisenhower decided right then and there that that was the last time he'd ever use the big, strategic bombers in close support of ground troops. Could it be that this Ardennes breakthrough is so important that General Eisenhower is willing to take a chance on the high altitude . . .

Strang said, "We've got a much bigger margin for error this time than we had at Saint-Lo, but even . . ."

"Thank God."

"But even so, we've got to more careful, more accurate than we've ever been. Above all, we must not drop too soon. But remember, if we drop too late we end up missing the German support systems and that too could cost thousands of lives of our guys on the ground."

Robb said, "Like at Omaha Beach on D-Day."

The Colonel frowned at Robb's reminder of their other big screw-up, when they missed Omaha Beach by three miles inland, a foul-up that cost untold thousands of American lives. "Look, Robb, we're not going after front-line German troops this time. Our object in laying this carpet is to wipe out their support systems—ammunition dumps, fuel storage tanks, supply convoys, roads, railroads, communications systems and anything they have well behind the lines in the way of support for their armored divisions that are leading this breakthrough."

"Good. That makes another Saint-Lo unlikely."

"But not completely out of the question. We've still got to be more careful than we've ever been." He looked up quickly. His tone softened. "Hell, Robb, I know you're as worried about another Saint-Lo as I am." He quickly resumed his command tone, as though he regretted slipping out of role if only for a moment. "Now, get this. Nobody will know you've been readied to step in as leader. Nobody except you, me, the other officers on your crew, and Sam Prentice." Strang stood up. "It's good to have you back, Robb." He reached across his desk and shook hands with Robb. "That's it for now."

Robb turned to leave.

"Oh, one final thing. No one may leave the base, and no one may call out."

"Goddamn it! If that isn't a hell of a note!" He didn't care if his anger showed. "The call I have to make tonight . . ."

"The call you *were* going to make tonight." He raised his eyebrows as he looked at Robb. "Lady X?"

Robb wondered if each human life was merely a series of random events, or if there was some sort of plan, often diabolical. "Lady X," he said softly.

"Sorry, Robb, but that's how it has to be." Strang glanced at the huge clock on the wall. He stood up. "That's all for now."

29

On Friday evening Robb sat alone at the deserted end of the club, as far as possible from the Old Timers' Corner. Only one day had elapsed since his return from his week in Scotland and London with Cynthia, yet it all seemed so long ago, almost as though he had dreamt it all. He stared into space as he thought of Cynthia, as he had constantly since his return, yet with the passage of each hour the events of the past week became increasingly vague impressions lacking in visual substance. And when he tried to reconstruct their lovemaking, it all became an incredible dream again, so much so that he for a moment doubted he was awake. He shook his head and looked around the club and he knew he was awake and that he was back, safe and secure in the world of death.

The Group had been alerted last night. The Swoviks awakened their squadrons at 0300 this morning, and the flyers were again swept along by the inexorable tide of military organization, through the myriad preparations for "The Big One." They were poised at the head of the runway, minds and machines ready to go, when the word came from the tower, "Bring 'em back. The mission is scrubbed."

Robb was in a foul mood. Cynthia, right at this moment, was less than two miles from where he sat, but she might just as well be on the moon. He couldn't as much as phone her. Perhaps he could focus all of his powers of concentration on her like those Ouija Board people and send her a telepathic message. "Bullshit!"

"Shame on you. And you an officer and a gentleman!"

He looked up quickly at Evelyn. He grinned. "You sure are a sight for sore eyes."

"You just left a sight for sore eyes yesterday."

"Yes, and yet I can't tell you how glad I am to see you."

"Thank you. I'm encouraged." She took a chair next to him, at right angles to the sofa he was sitting on. She placed her hand on his hand and gave it a quick squeeze.

"I was as low as I've ever been, until I heard your voice. Now my spirits are in a vertical climb, and I feel guilty as hell."

"Why so low?"

"Cynthia can't take it . . . the realities of my job."

Evelyn took a package of Chesterfields out of her shoulder bag. She studied Robb's face out of the corner of her eye as she lit her cigarette. "Would you like a drink?"

"The whiskey lamp is out. Beer only. We're on the edge of an alert."

"Oh Robb!"

"It's all right. C'est la guerre, C'est la vie, C'est la morte, et cetera."

"I don't know French. What was that last one?"

"I don't know."

"Liar."

"I believe in lying, ever since I discovered lying is normal in wartime, especially the Eighth Air Force's news releases to The London Times. Someone said the first casualty in war is truth. Remember?"

"I'm a lot like Cynthia, Robb. Maybe I can't take it either. When you said the whiskey lamp was out, my heart stopped. I can't imagine anyone feeling worse."

"That was just the initial response. We all feel like that when they spring an alert on us. It's a momentary thing."

"Did you get an alert when you were with her?"

"In effect. I was called back to the base suddenly, on an emergency basis."

"She didn't get over her initial reaction?"

"She was overcome by the deepest melancholy I've ever seen. She just stared into space. When I left her all she said was 'God help us'."

"I know it's a funny question, but tell me anyway. Did you kiss her goodbye?"

He looked at her quizzically. "Yes. But it was like kissing that post there." He nodded toward one of the pillars that supported the club's roof.

"Kiss me, Robb."

"Here? Now?"

"Who cares?"

He smiled. "That's right. Who cares?" She leaned forward, her eyes closed, presenting herself to him. He kissed her. Her kiss was warm, and tender. And loving.

"I love you, Robb."

"Please don't say that. Not now."

"All right. Not now." She sighed. "Anyway, we just beat the system."

"How?"

"That kiss. They can't take that away from us no matter what happens. Their scare tactics didn't keep us from stealing it from them."

"Something's screwy here. Those are my lines."

"I've been working on making them mine, remember? I'm getting the hang of it."

"You just said you were like Cynthia. That maybe you couldn't handle it either."

"I changed my mind. It was the initial scare. I'm in great shape now."

"All along I had thought you were incapable of guile. Now this."

"You can't waste time when there's a war on, if you know what I mean, pal."

They laughed harder than her imitation of Stosh merited. Robb took a deep breath and wiped his eyes with his handkerchief. "I'd forgotten you went out once with Stosh."

"Twice. Once dancing and once dining, when he insulted the head waiter and the Brussels sprouts. Speaking of Brussels sprouts, does Cynthia know about me?"

"Yes."

"What did you tell her?"

"That I love you."

"My morale is improving too. Just like yours. We're good for each other, Robb. How did she take all that?"

"She said she likes you too, or that she would like you if she knew you."

"You did say she's very intelligent, didn't you?"

Robb suddenly noticed that the club was deserted except for him and Evelyn. The Group was alerted. "Evelyn, look around."   She closed her eyes tightly. "Oh Robb!"

He put his hand on hers. "I'd better be heading for the sack."

She sighed. "I've got Sam's jeep tonight. I'll give you a ride to your squadron area on one condition." She reached out and took his hand. "That you'll kiss me goodnight when we get there. I mean really."

He looked absently across the length of the room, to the deserted bar at the far end.

She sighed. "It's all right. I'll give you a ride anyway."

He put his arm around her and gave her a quick squeeze. He held out the crook of his arm and she took it and they walked arm in arm toward the vestibule. His foot turned outward as he walked, just a little more than it had when he walked into Tony Rizzo's office yesterday.

* * * * * * * *

The mission scheduled for Saturday morning, the day before the day of Christmas Eve, was scrubbed at the last minute. The Group had been locked up for several days even before Robb's return. They hadn't flown a mission, but they had sweated out several which, after hours of preparation, were scrubbed at the last minute. The effects of confinement were beginning to show. The base had taken on the nuances of a detention center.

On Saturday evening Robb sat in the officers club, completely immersed in the book he'd been carrying around for the past two days, an exegesis on Bach's, "The Art of the Fugue". Sam Prentice had borrowed the book from one of his Cambridge friends. Robb had devoted most of yesterday and today to studying this analysis of Bach's tour de force on counterpoint in general and the fugue in particular. He was grateful for the intellectual challenge during the Group's strange state of limbo.

Stosh, on one of his visits with Robb between poker games, claimed the lock-up was another ingenious scheme cooked up at the very top. "Make 'em bored as hell for a week and at the end of that time guys who damn near faint before every mission will be ready to give the Germans hell. You got to give 'em credit. They sure as hell know what they're doing." Robb no longer bothered to ask just who the all-powerful, nebulous "they" were.

But the club wasn't the least bit crowded. Robb knew that most of the men, like good soldiers anywhere, were in the sack. Stosh saw this inordinate love of sleep as the product of yet another ingenious scheme

emanating from the top. He said the plan was to keep everybody exhausted for their first year in the army. This way the GI's learn to hit the
sack at every opportunity, if only for five minutes between tasks. Then,
in combat, when the dogfaces need to grab whatever sleep they can,
they're ready. Stosh maintained that that's why any good soldier can fall
asleep immediately, whether lying, leaning, sitting, shitting, or standing.
He said a lot of the guys who bailed out over Germany grabbed a few
winks on the way down, and those who got hung up in trees had to be
awakened by the Germans.

Robb took his book over to the battered upright piano to work out a
particular example of counterpoint. He just about had it worked out when
a pair or hands covered his eyes. "Guess." The voice was deliberately
deep but unmistakably feminine, and the hands were smooth and slender.

"Private Swovik."

"No."

"Colonel Horatio What's-his-name." He announced the name loudly.

The hands moved from his eyes to his mouth, clamping it shut.
"Robb!" Evelyn whispered intently. "He might hear you!"

He pulled her down beside him on the bench. "Who cares? Remember?"

"I do. He's my boss, remember? Please, please don't ever do that
again."

"Come, let's go sit in our appointed place." He led the way toward
their usual chairs at the far end of the club. When they were half way
there, he stopped to allow her to go ahead of him. She stopped too.

"Please," he said. "Ladies first."

"Captains first, lieutenants second. That's why we're called second
lieutenants."

He grabbed her around the waist and propelled her along beside him.
They were still laughing when they sat down. Robb said, " I'll get us a
drink."

He returned from the bar with two shots of Irish whiskey with two
small glasses of soda on the side. They raised their glasses and said
"Cheers" in unison. And grimaced in unison, even though he took only
a symbolic sip before placing his glass on the table.

"Irish," Evelyn said.

He nodded. "Liquified peat."

"Why didn't you drink your drink?"

"They shut down the bar just as I picked up the drinks. We're alerted."

She stared at the nearly full glass in her hand. Finally Robb said, "Anything going on in there, or is it blank?"

"I was praying. Is it wrong to pray with a glass of whiskey in your hand?" She didn't smile. She put the drink down on the table.

He picked up her glass and handed it to her. "Down the hatch." She drank all of it.

"I should get going. Do you have Sam's jeep?"

She nodded. "I'll take you to your barracks, but first we ought to pick up Stosh at the WAC BOQ. He's there with Merrie."

When they stepped out into the night they found the fog that had enshrouded the base all day was lifting. A star could be seen here and there. Neither of them spoke as Evelyn drove the quarter of a mile to the Womans Army Corps Bachelor Officer Quarters.

The WAC BOQ was indistinguishable from the other corrugated steel, arch-roofed huts that served as barracks throughout the Eighth Air Force, but the inside was a pleasant surprise to those men fortunate enough to be invited in. By partitioning off the front one-fourth of the Nissen hut, a large sitting room had been created. Sofas and chairs scrounged in Cambridge had been re-covered in warm shades of beige, tan and brown. An autumnal warmth was achieved by a few calculated shots of red, yellow and orange here and there in small pillows, throw rugs and wall hangings. When Robb and Evelyn entered this room at a few minutes past ten o'clock, they found Merrie stretched out on the sofa with her head on Kovacs' lap. She sat up immediately.

"Don't get up," Evelyn said, "it's just us."

Merrie stood up. "What a pleasant surprise. Two of our favorite people."

"Right," Kovacs said.

Merrie said, "Make yourselves at home while I fix something to drink. I think I can find some battery acid and vodka around here somewhere."

Robb said, "No drinks, Merrie, please."

"Speak for yourself, pal. I'd like a drink, Merrie."

"We're alerted."

"Shit!" He looked at Merrie. "Pardon my French."

"It's all right," Merrie's smile was brittle, forced. "Do you want a drink, Stosh?"

"No thanks, beautiful. We better get going." Kovacs held out his arms to her. "Come to papa, funny face." He enfolded her in his arms and began what seemed to be the beginning of a very long goodnight kiss. It occurred to Robb that the way he was kissing her you'd think he was going to the moon. And then it struck him: Stosh might be going much farther than that. He turned away.

Evelyn held out her arms to Robb. "Come to mama, funny face."

He stood there for a moment, uncertainly. He smiled at her but she didn't smile back. Her eyes held his. He sighed, almost imperceptibly. He stepped forward and she took him into her arms and drew him tightly to her and kissed him warmly. But soon the initiative became his as much as hers. She interrupted their kiss and murmured into his ear. "I noticed the hesitation, but c'est la guerre."

"I'm a rat," he whispered. "Rats hesitate."

"Not real rats," she whispered. She placed her hand behind his head and drew his face to hers.

Evelyn dropped them off at Amber Squadron Area. As the two men walked to the Squadron Orderly Room, Kovacs said, "Look at this sky. Not a cloud in sight. Want to make a bet?"

"Why not?"

"I've got a hundred says there's fifteen or twenty thousand feet of crap between us and those stars about three hours from now when Swovik wakes us up."

30

Amber Squadron, the lead squadron of the 990th Heavy Bombardment Group, crossed the Dutch coast at precisely 0958 hours on Sunday, December 24th, the morning of the day of Christmas Eve, 1944. Exactly as planned. And also exactly as planned, Robb noted, the formation reached the 29,000 foot mark, bomb-run altitude, just as the last planes in the Group crossed the coast. Robb acknowledged to himself that Bill Sandell was doing a bangup job leading the Group—and the Task Force. Of course Sandell had Colonel Wilson, the Task Force Commander from Division, in his co-pilot's seat, but Wilson wouldn't be doing much of the flying today. Colonel Wilson would be more concerned with the larger picture as transmitted to him from Eighth Air Force in England: weather over the target, likely enemy air opposition and—most important of all on this support mission: troop movements at the "bulge".

The ponderous monster that was Task Force Foxfire had come into being at 10,000 feet over East Anglia with the assembly of Bombardment Groups into Wings and Wings into a single body. The armada, some 350 planes strong, with the 990th Heavy Bombardment Group in the Lead, had been climbing eastward for the past hour and a half. Bradley flew the plane as Robb lolled back in his seat, bone-weary, his eyes closed. The strained roar of the engines lowered suddenly to a steady drone as Bradley pulled back on the throttles to assume level flight.

Robb assessed the situation. The German high command knows we're coming. The Luftwaffe has been ordered to stop us no matter what the cost. And they know that the situation *right now* is ideal for them, with the sun in our eyes and that layer of cirrostratus above us for them to hide in and our P-51s nowhere to be seen. The Luftwaffe also knows this sitting duck setup will last for only the next ten or fifteen minutes, until the sun climbs behind that cloud layer, or less than that if our P-51s show up. The time for the Luftwaffe to attack is *now*! He pushed his intercom button. "Pilot to crew. Keep a sharp lookout. They'll be coming out of the sun any minute now."

As he surveyed the 990th's formation from his Number Eight position—right-wing man of the third echelon in the squadron—he knew the Group was ready. The planes were tucked tight into what the C.O. called proudly, if ingenuously, the "990th Special." He continued his internal soliloquy. The Luftwaffe will be coming at us any moment now. That is certain. And in large numbers. The Luftwaffe will pay a huge price when it flies into the 990th's massed firepower. But so will the 990th. That too is certain. The 990th will catch it first. The Germans know we'll have difficulty bombing in close support without a Lead Group, and they know that without lead planes the Lead Group is in bad trouble. So the lead plane of the Lead Group in the task force is undoubtedly the Luftwaffe's Candidate Number One. That's Sandy and his co-pilot for today, the task force commander from Division, Colonel Wilson. Next in line is the Lead Group's deputy leader—Stosh. Stosh will catch it, but good. That's for sure. Where the hell's our P-51s? They should have joined us when..." He never finished the thought. The Luftwaffe struck!

Within seconds an inferno erupted in the sky. Bombers and bombs exploded. Attacking fighter planes, their wings torn away by fire-hose streams of fifty caliber tracers, hurtled onwards toward their prey, tumbling end over end. In a split second Robb's chronic nightmare had become reality, a reality that in its violence exceeded his wildest dreams. He knew in a flash of insight that this was real, and *now*. The sudden realization that he was not dreaming was devastating.

The German fighters kept coming, screeching out of the sun, an avalanche of wildly abandoned fury, spewing machine gun bullets, cannon shells and rockets. The on-rushing Messerschmitts and Focke-Wulfs seemed as huge, blinking cannon shells themselves as they streaked toward Brillig's cockpit. They seemed bent on a suicidal explosion, with Brillig's nose as the immovable object that would explode attacker and victim alike. But they pulled up at the last second, miraculously missing Robb's cockpit and Wieriman's top turret by a few feet as they flashed past like streaking meteors.

He watched in horror as Bill Sandell's—and Colonel Wilson's—left wing burst into flames. The wounded plane swung into a steep, left bank, away from the formation. It hung for a moment on its side before its swung nose-down. He pushed his intercom button. "All gunners. Watch the plane in a dive to our left. Watch for 'chutes and where they come from."

Boo's voice: "They leveled off for a li'l' bit way down below. A few chutes, but they ain't gonna be no more. They just blew up."

The attack was over as quickly as it had begun, and in that first moment of relative silence Robb was sickened to the core of his soul, sickened by the obliteration of Bill Sandell and Colonel Wilson and those other men from the face of the earth. He was on the verge of throwing up, and in his queasiness he knew he had lost his perception of the hell around him as *having been*, and with it his detached objectivity, his spectatorship. Oh how he wished he had never met her!

Kovacs was now flying Task Force Lead in a two-plane echelon, the deputy position now vacant. Robb wondered if he should pull up into the deputy lead position now? The Colonel's instructions hadn't covered this contingency. He decided to lay back a little longer. Someone yelled out hoarsely, "Another bunch coming, straight ahead high!" The attackers flashed over the cockpit amidst a cacophony of outgoing machine gun fire and incoming bullets and cannon shells.

They kept coming, wave after wave of infuriated hornets bent on the destruction of the monsters who had stirred their nest, waves of crazed, venomous creatures bent on destroying the invaders, wildly attacking creatures defending their territory, oblivious to the fact that they themselves would die in the very stinging of their adversaries.

Cannon shells exploded in the middle of the tail assembly of Plane Number Five, directly ahead of Brillig. Robb and Bradley ducked instinctively as pieces of airplane flew past their cockpit. The tailless B-17 did a snap roll, and in an instant its roll became a series of bizarre forward somersaults as it plunged earthward.

Wieriman's top turret guns, a few feet behind the cockpit, barked deafeningly as the flight engineer pumped burst after burst of fifty caliber machine gun bullets into each screaming phalanx as it flashed past. Hoyt—or maybe it was Boo—screamed into the intercom, "Come on, you bastards Come on! Come on! Take that, you bastard!"

Robb yelled into the intercom: "Hoyt! Boo! Get off the intercom!" His voice nearly cracked as he yelled. He took a deep breath and continued in a firm tone, loud but even, trying to make himself understood amidst the staccato explosions of their own machine guns which echoed deafeningly through the length of the plane. "Pilot to all gunners, keep the intercom open for necessary calls. And keep your bursts short. Remember, short bursts! That's better, Top Turret."

"Wait until each wave is well within range." His tone was even, firm. "Don't waste your ammo. Tailgunner, get them going away, but let up when they're out of range. Nose-gunner, top turret, you're shooting too soon. Hold your fire until each wave is well within range. Ball turret, watch for attack from below. It will be coming any minute now." All the while he spoke the ear-shattering staccato of Wieriman's top turret guns blasted off and on, amplified within the long, bare metal tube that was the interior of a B-17 Flying Fortress. The plane shuddered as round after round of 20 and 30 millimeter cannon shells hit the wings, fuselage and tail.

Wieriman called out. "Number one engine on fire!"

Bradley responded, "Roger, John, I see it."

"Pilot to crew. Snap on your chute packs but don't leave your position until I give the order."

Even as Robb spoke, Bradley hit the cowl flap switch, opening them, and hit the fuel shutoff to number one. He hit the big red feathering button. Robb pulled the mixture control to idle cut-off and snapped off the ignition switch. Bradley turned the fire extinguisher selector to number one and hit the CO_2 button. He pushed his intercom button. "Hitting number one extinguisher, Robb. Feathering number one." They had performed the emergency procedure in four or five seconds. Robb increased power to the remaining three engines.

Wieriman yelled, "Engineer to pilot. I think you got it out."

Robb looked out at number one, its propeller motionless, its blades turned to feathered position, its thin edges facing the windstream. No sign of a fire. Not even smoke. Just white, steamlike vapors forming a wispy condensation trail behind the engine. He reached across the throttle pedestal and nudged Bradley's shoulder and gave him the okay sign. Bradley nodded.

"Pilot to crew. The fire is out. I repeat. The engine fire is out. Over." Thank God!

The call rang out over the intercom, "Bandits three o'clock low!" Again the explosions of a half-dozen fifty caliber machine guns bounced off the bare metal walls and floor of the plane. The plane shuddered, whether from the recoil of its own guns or from cannon shells passing through it—or exploding in it—Robb couldn't tell.

On the intercom, a blood-curdling scream cut through the clatter of machine gun bullets coming and going. Someone was hit. Who?

On the intercom, a soft, gurgled plea, "Help me Robb. I . . ." The voice faded out.

Robb knew it was Brain Child. He pressed his button. "Hang in there, Billie. I'll send someone to help you. Acknowledge, please."

He waited for the response he knew would not be coming.

"Waist to Pilot. Should I get on a bottle and go help Brain Child?"

"Not now, Waist. Stay with your gun. I'll let you know when you can go to Brain Child. Get ready, everyone! There's another bunch coming from twelve high right now!" Robb heard the excitement in his voice. Settle down, goddam it! He spoke calmly, his voice lowered, "Here they come. Hold your fire until they're in range. Remember, short bursts."

He watched with fascination as a phalanx of fighters came swooping down on them from out of the sun. He pushed his intercom button and said calmly, "Nose and top turret get ready for the bunch coming from twelve high. Concentrate on the planes on your right—their left. They're the ones that will be going after us. They'll round out below us. Nose gun take the one on the right end. Ball take the second one from the right as they round out. Top turret take the third one as they pull up to go over us. Hold your fire until they're well within range. Hold it." The attackers rounded out their dive slightly below them as he had predicted. "Hold it. Hold it. Fire!" The first tracers to strike home came from Boo's guns in the ball turret. He caught the Focke-Wulf—the second plane from right—dead center. Black smoke erupted as the plane hurtled toward the bomber squadron. The tracers from the bombardier's nose gun and Wieriman's top turret met their targets a split second later. The second plane, Boo's target, blew up less than 200 yards in front of the bombers, taking his left wing-man with him. Boo screamed, "Whooee! Hey, Hoyt! I just got two in a bunch, bah gawd! Whooooeeee!"

Wieriman yelled, "Shut up Boo! Another bunch coming from four o'clock low!"

They were coming from the right and slightly behind—a bad mistake on their part, Robb noted with wide-eyed wonder—exposing themselves to every right waist gun, top turret and ball turret in the squadron. Brillig's guns went off as one, as though on command. Streams of .50 caliber tracers from a dozen B-17's merged at the oncoming phalanx. The attackers came apart like the clay targets on a skeet range. Four fighters blew up in succession. A Messerschmitt lost a wing and went into a wild, unbalanced cartwheel straight at Brillig. Robb saw the hurtling plane out of the corner of his eye. He pushed his control column forward hard, but the cartwheeling fighter's remaining wing struck Wieriman's top turret and ricocheted on into Number Seven plane—the plane on Robb's left wing—hitting it broadside and ramming it into Number Nine plane beyond it. All three planes, the Messerschmitt and the two B-17s, exploded in a single ball of fire.

Robb swung off to the right to avoid the debris flying in all directions. Something—a large piece of debris—landed on his left wing, near its end, and hung there for a moment. He glanced quickly to his left. Two eyes, two eyes in a shocked, tortured face—helmet and goggles and parachute harness blown away—two still seeing, terrified eyes met his eyes for a fleeting moment. He watched as the man fell free.

He looked back to his instruments. He reflected on what he had just seen even as a spectator at a magic show reflects on a remarkable feat of sleight-of-hand. How strange! The man who had just fallen from his wing had been barefoot. He had been blown out of his shoes and socks!

The shock of seeing the doomed man on his wing did the trick. At that moment he felt it coming on, a warm, soothing balm insinuating itself into the depths of his being. He felt the calm of acceptance settling in his guts, the incredible peace in the midst of chaos that seemed to course through his veins like a narcotic when things got rough. He was amazed. He still had it, by God, in spite of Cynthia! The pre-Cynthia calm. He felt the burden of fear lifting from him like a veil. His fear gave way to fascination. He was again a spectator to one of the most bizarre dramas in human history. Its strength—the strength of whatever it was—seemed to be proportional to the degree of violence around him, the degree to which his death was imminent. He felt as he had when they gave him shots of morphine when he was wounded, but this feeling of well-being, this feeling of peace which penetrated the very marrow of his bones exceeded anything the morphine had induced. Thank God!

He looked back at his left wing. The wingtip was bent downwards where the man had hit it. He worked his ailerons slightly. Still good control. He added full take-off power to the remaining three engines to regain the fifty feet of altitude he lost when he pushed forward on the column to avoid the cartwheeling plane. His quick push on the column had saved them from the tumbling fighter, and it had put them farther away from the three-ship explosion. Even so, if the bombs in either of those two B-17s had gone off, Brillig wouldn't be flying now, nor would any other plane in the squadron.

Wieriman's guns were silent. Bradley looked back at Wieriman's turret. He turned back quickly. He lifted his oxygen mask from his face and vomit gushed forth onto his lap. Robb didn't see Bradley throw up. "Better call roll now, Monk."

"Roger."

"Where the hell are our P-51s?" Someone yelled.

"Who needs 'em?" Hoyt yelled. Or maybe it was Boo.

Robb pushed his button. "That's enough chatter. Keep the intercom clear for essential calls. Lieutenant Bradley is going to call the roll now. Answer 'all right', if you are in fact all right."

"Little friends at three o'clock high!" someone yelled into the intercom. Someone else called out, "More little friends at nine high!"

Robb breathed a sigh of relief into his oxygen mask. He looked up out his left side window. He saw fifty or more P-51s a thousand feet or so above them. He knew there would be a comparable number on their right. That should end the Luftwaffe's . . . A sudden barking of machine guns. Another wave of fire-spitting German fighters came streaking in from head-on. A scream on the intercom. A desperate scream for help. Boo's obscene monologue rattled on, as though he hadn't heard the death-scream. "Come on, you bastards! Woooeeee! Got him! Got the fucking Jerry! How you doing, Hoyt?"

"Shee-it! I'm losing count, Boo! Come on, you bastards! Let's have some more of you. Come on! Come on, you yellow-livered som-bitches!"

"Pilot to all gunners. Keep the intercom open for essential calls."

Silence. The Germans had broken off the attack. Then he saw it. Kovacs' plane: white hot flames on the inboard side of number three engine, between the engine and the fuselage. Bare wing framework starting to show. He switched to command channel and pushed the button. "Stosh, you've got a bad fire on your right wing, on the inboard side of number three engine. Do you read me?"

"Roger, Robb."

Robb watched in horror as in an instantaneous flash Kovac's right wing burst into flames. Robb pushed his button. "Hit the alarm, Stosh!"

Kovacs' plane moved to its right, away from the formation, and then, in a blinding explosion, its right wing disintegrated along with the near side of the cockpit and forward fuselage; the plane plunged downward in a grotesque, uncontrolled twisting tumble. Robb looked backwards and downwards out his left window—a reflex rather than a conscious act—hoping to see parachutes, but knowing there would be none. Bradley looked down and back and shook his head. If Robb could have seen downward and behind his plane, he would have seen the remainder of Kovacs' one-winged plane hurtling downward followed by smaller pieces of debris and the remnants of human bodies.

Robb put his right hand over his goggles. He gripped the wheel with all his strength with his left hand. He switched to intercom. "All gunners. Watch carefully for 'chutes from the plane that just went down. Tailgunner and ball gunner, keep your eyes on all debris. Follow it all the way down. Then report to me. Over." Bradley slapped Robb's throttle hand sharply and took over the controls.

He knew there would be no parachutes. Stosh had moved to the right before hitting the bail-out alarm because he knew if he hit it immediately his men would have bailed out smack into the propellers of Number Four plane flying close behind and slightly below him. The plane must have blown up a second before Stosh would have hit the bail-out bell, or maybe even at the precise moment he had in fact hit the alarm.

The clatter of guns stopped as quickly as it had begun. The drone of the engines, ordinarily so loud, now seemed a hushed hum. He waited for the message he knew would come.

"Cap'n Robb?" Hoyt's voice.

"Go ahead, Sergeant."

"That plane that just went down, that was Cap'n Kovacs', wasn't it?"

"Yes. Did you see any "chutes?"

"No 'chutes, Cap'n. The rest of his plane just blew up. No 'chutes. Over."

"Roger, Tailgunner." He let up on his button. He whispered into his mask, "No! Oh dear merciful Christ no! Please! No, no, no!" And then he screamed at the top of his lungs, "*Nooooooooooooo!*" The scream trailed off into a moan, a moan of ultimate anguish.

He stared unseeing out the windshield. No! It didn't happen! He's in bed in Scotland, at Cynthia's. He drank too much. He's dreaming. He'll awaken any minute now!

Bradley reached across the pedestal and gripped Robb's upper arm firmly. He looked at Bradley and he saw Bradley flying the plane and knew he was in the cockpit and that he was awake and that what he had seen had in fact happened. "Dear Christ No! Goddam it, no! *Nooooooooooooo! Nooooooooooooo!*"

For a time he lost all sense of where he was. He stared dumbly through the windshield. After a time his consciousness returned to the cockpit. He shook his head. He looked at Bradley. He took a deep breath. Put Stosh out of your mind! It's your turn to lead now. So lead, goddamn it!

He slapped Bradley's throttle hand and took over again. He pushed full forward on the throttles. In the rarefied atmosphere, the manifold pressure on his three remaining engines climbed to forty-six inches, far beyond the redlines. He decreased the prop pitches, increasing the speed of each engine to 2500 RPM. His engines were now at maximum power, power ordinarily allowable only for a minute at the very most, on take-off. The B-17 slowly, painfully, passed Number Four and Number Six, now flying in an echelon of two planes since Number Five bought it. He was flying exactly as in his nightmare: the plane sluggish, throttles full forward, engines hot and ready to blow.

It was then, precisely then, when he knew the engines might explode, that he felt the narcosis of shock coming on again, the narcosis born of Stosh's death. It re-surged through him, the calm, the peace, the *at-one-ness* with all time and space, with all that ever was and is and ever will be. He felt an *at-one-ness* with Stosh's death itself. Stosh's death had already become an abstraction, an abstraction devoid of valuation, an irrevocable *is-ness* that always was and always will be. His engines might blow themselves to bits at any minute, but he was in no way terrified as he watched himself acting his part.

Bradley pointed to the cylinder head and oil temperature gauges, their needles now at their ultimate limit beyond the redlines. Bradley made an exploding gesture with his hand. Robb nodded, but he kept the throttles full forward. It seemed to him he had abused the engines for ten or fifteen minutes—but the clock on the panel told him it was two or three minutes—before he finally pulled into the squadron-lead position, ahead of and to the right of Number Three who until now had been flying lead by default. He pulled back on the throttles. The cylinder head and oil temperatures began dropping. Bradley pointed to the gauges and did a mopping-his-brow gesture. Robb nodded. He was pleased that Monk was relieved.

"Pilot to navigator. Give me a check on our heading. Over."

"Navigator to pilot. You're on the money for the Initial Point, Robb. Hold her steady as she goes and we'll hit the IP on the nose. Over."

Their heading would carry them on an easterly course roughly parallel with the northern boundary of the Ardennes bulge, five to five and one-half miles inside the friendly side of the front line. Sam had repeated his instructions so much he had sounded like a broken record: When they hit the Initial Point they would turn south to a heading of 162 degrees, and they would cross the smoke-flare line—the "bombs away" line—one minute after their turn on the IP on to the bomb run on a course more or less perpendicular to the front.

He pushed his intercom button. "Pilot to crew. We're now Group Leader." He consulted the formation sheet taped to his upper leg. "Tailgunner, give me a rundown on Amber squadron. How many planes do we have in our squadron?"

Hoyt came back, "Cap'n Robb, Amber's got seven planes left... so far."

He gasped into his mask, "Oh God!" He gripped the wheel with all his strength. He pushed the button. "Thank you, Sergeant." He spoke very calmly. "Now give me a rundown on the other two squadrons. Over."

"They didn't get it as good as us, Cap'n. Number Two squadron lost two. Number Three squadron lost two too."

Robb nodded to no one. We lost five and each of the other squadrons two. Nine planes lost. Ninety men. Oh God! He pressed the button. "Thank you, Sergeant."

He had forgotten momentarily that he was Task Force Leader. He pushed his intercom button. "Pilot to Tailgunner. How many Bombardment Groups can you see behind us? I mean clearly. Over."

"Wayell, Cap'n. I kin see three or four of 'em real good."

"Tailgunner. Did you happen to see how many other Bombardment Groups were hit by the enemy fighters?"

"We was the only one, Cap'n. I was watch'n for it. I could see way back in the bomber stream, maybe seven or eight Groups back and I didn't see nobody else the bastards hit. Looks to me like they was after just us, Cap'n, on account of us leadin' the whole Air Force. Over."

Hoyt's job was to give the facts, not interpret them, but Robb decided this was hardly the time to get on him. "Roger, Tailgunner. Over and out."

He switched to command channel. He pushed his button but he let up on it without transmitting. He reflected that his plane now had four code designations: Amber Uncle as an individual plane, Amber Leader as Squadron Leader, Upshaw Leader as Group Leader and Foxfire Leader as Task Force Leader. Better keep them straight. He pushed his button again. "Amber Leader to all Amber aircraft. Close ranks forward. Over and out." He switched back to intercom. Bradley was speaking. "Right waist gunner. Get on a walkie oxygen bottle and go to the radio room and see if you can help Brain Child."

Robb pushed his intercom button. "Monk, maybe you'd better send Wieriman back with the big medical kit."

Bradley unsnapped his safety belt and shoulder harness and stood up. He leaned toward Robb. When Robb saw Bradley stand up, he pulled his helmet's right flap and earphone away from his head and leaned toward his co-pilot. Bradley pulled his oxygen mask a couple of inches away from his face and yelled, "Don't look back!"

Bradley clamped his mask over his mouth and took a couple of breaths. He lifted his mask again and yelled, "Wieriman's dead! The top turret's gone! Don't look back!" He sat down and strapped himself back into his seat.

Robb had been too preoccupied with the attack to have noticed when Wieriman's guns went silent. He didn't respond to the crash when the ME 109's wing hit because it was simply another explosion and jolt to the aircraft among many jolts and explosions. And he had been too busy to notice how cold the cockpit had become since the Messerschmitt 109 sliced off the top turret. His preoccupation had spared him the sight, or so Bradley thought, that would be branded forever in Bradley's brain: the decapitated body of Sergeant Wieriman hanging from his harness, swinging back and forth only four or five feet behind the cockpit below the gaping hole where his turret had been. The flight engineer's feet dragged back and forth across the turret platform in a distorted posture of death.

He would have known about Wieriman earlier had they been at lower altitude and the temperature in the plane above freezing. Given the tail-high attitude of the ship, Wieriman's blood would have run along the flight deck, under the pilots seats and into the cockpit. Instead, with the outside temperature somewhere around 60 below zero, and the interior temperature not much higher, Wieriman's blood had frozen on the floor next to his turret's platform into a stalagmite, an upside down red icicle, several inches wide at its base, pointing upward toward its source.

Robb gestured to Bradley to take over. He looked back. He blinked several times until the image on his retina registered in his brain. His eyes swept the flight deck, beyond and to each side of Wieriman's feet There were no traces of Wieriman's head. It was simply gone.

Robb raised his goggles and rubbed his eyes vigorously with his gloved hands. He lowered his goggles and pressed his intercom button. "Pilot to Tailgunner. Are the planes closing ranks?"

Hoyt's twang: "Roger, Cap'n Robb. Amber's looking real good now."

Looking good! Fifty men in the squadron dead and the rest of us all shot to hell and we're looking real good! He pushed his button, "Pilot to navigator. Give me an ETA for the IP, please." He spoke very calmly and, as always when the narcosis set in, he became formal in his relations with the crew. Calm, formal, polite.

"Roger, Robb. Give me half a minute. Over and out."

"Waist to Pilot. Over."

"Go ahead, Waist."

"I'm here in the radio room with Brain Child." Marconi's voice quavered. "He's in real bad shape. What should I do, Robb?"

"Is he conscious?"

"No sir."

"Is he breathing? Is his oxygen mask working?"

"Roger. He's breathing and he's got oxygen. But he's bleeding pretty bad."

"Where from? Where are his wounds?"

"He's wounded all over. I can't tell where all he's bleeding from."

"Turn his heated suit down. Make him as comfortable as possible and give him a shot of morphine. Then get back to your gun and stay there until we turn off the bomb run. As soon as we start evasive action go back to Brain Child and see how he's doing and report to me, Tony."

He wondered if he was doing the right thing, but he wasn't really worried. He had made a rational decision as best he could tell. He hoped Brain Child's bleeding would be stopped by the near-freezing temperature. But another part of his brain told him that when a person is in shock you're supposed to keep him warm. But he'd most certainly die if his bleeding isn't stopped. He closed his eyes momentarily, debating whether to keep Brain Child cold or warm. Okay. We'll keep him cold now to stop the bleeding. We'll turn up the heat on his suit after the bomb run if the bleeding is stopped by then.

He put aside his concern for Brain Child. He looked at his watch. In his mind, he calmly ran through the details of the operation, the details hammered into his head by Sam this morning.

31

The visual Initial Point for the 990th's bomb run was the intersection of a main road and a double railroad. The Groups behind them were to ignore the IP taken by the Task Force Lead Group; each Group had its own Initial Point. The IPs and timing were calculated so that each Group in the bomber stream would reach its IP at the same time and make its ninety degree turn to the right at the same time as the others, the bomber stream itself thus making a massive "by the right flank" turn, as in close-order drill. Thus the Bombardment Groups would approach the front side-by-side, each Group bombing a different stretch of territory behind the front.

Robb figured the intersection should be visible about now, straight ahead. "Pilot to bombardier. Keep your eyes peeled for IP visual referent. You should be able to see it about now."

"I see it, Robb. Our heading is right on the money. Hold her steady as she goes. Starting countdown at fifteen seconds to IP. Hold her steady now. Fifteen ... fourteen ... "

Will Richard's voice droned, "... four ... three ... two ... one ... *mark*!"

Bradley banked the plane smoothly to the right. Robb looked out his left window. Number Three was above them now in the bank, sticking in close. Bradley rolled out of his turn. The gyro compass read 162 degrees as the plane leveled out. Richards hit the bomb bay door toggle switch. Bradley immediately added power, anticipating the added drag of the gaping opening in the bottom of the ship. With one engine out, he had to push the throttles to within an inch of the forward stop to maintain the prescribed bomb run speed of 150 miles per hour. The cylinder head temperatures started climbing immediately.

Robb unhooked his shoulder harness and leaned forward and looked out the right window of the cockpit. Off his right wing-tip, he could see the Group immediately behind them, now square on 990th's beam, about a mile away. They could be dropping their loads a fraction of a minute before or after the 990th, depending on the zig-zags of the front and in turn the wiggles in the smoke-flare line. He could see several other Bombardment Groups flying side by side, just about even with the 990th. The bomber stream's "by-the-right-flank" turn had been negotiated successfully: the single file of Bombardment Groups had suddenly become a monumental, wingtip-to-wingtip phalanx, many miles wide.

He wondered, what will those American and British ground soldiers in the most forward positions think when they see the bombers begin releasing their bombs over them! They'll think this is a repetition of the Saint-Lo tragedy. Many of them won't realize that the planes' momentum—and thus the bombs' momentum—will carry the bombs well beyond the front. "Pilot to navigator and bombardier. Navigator, give me a countdown to smoke release."

Fritz Carlson's voice: "We'll be seeing it in fifteen seconds. Countdown to smoke-flare line. Twelve ...eleven ... ten . . ."

Robb wondered, what do I do if the smoke line doesn't appear? Damn it! Just call out over the command channel to all Wing Commanders to lead their Wings to targets of opportunity,   but to be sure to pick up a heading of due east, ninety degrees, and to be damned sure to wait three minutes after their turn before dropping any bombs. And he'd warn all Wing Commanders to make sure their Groups are staggered to the right and out of the path of any Group ahead of them.

" ... five... four ...three ... two ... one ... *mark!*" The line of smoke flares appeared as if by magic, as if triggered by Carlson's countdown. Robb was relieved.

Will Richard's voice now: "Countdown to 'bombs away': Thirty ... twenty-nine ... twenty- eight ... twenty-seven..."

Boo's sudden yell overrode the bombardier's countdown. "Wayell, look at that line of smoke, by gawd!"

Robb snapped angrily, "Get off the horn, Boo!"

The plane shuddered violently. He looked up and saw a huge black ball of smoke. Damn! He'd only once seen bigger shell explosions in the air—when they bombed that battleship, the Prince Ruprecht, at Kiel with its big naval cannons. The plane shook violently again. Another big explosion. Still high, thank God! The German heavy artillery at the front was letting them have it with their really big stuff! Now regular ack-ack fire began bursting around them along with the big explosions from the heavy artillery. The plane bounced as if they had suddenly encountered rough weather.

"... nine ... eight ... seven... six ... "

The bombardier's platform was far from steady. He might miss! Robb reached out and gripped the back of Bradley's hand on the throttles. He pushed Bradley's hand and the throttles all the way forward. The extra speed would cause them to err—if they erred at all—on the long side. Their airspeed, and that of the squadron, increased by two miles per hour. There were no violent bounces for the moment.

"... three . . two ... one ... *bombs away!*"

Richards hit the bomb release switch and the plane began disgorging its 8000 pounds of bombs, one 500 pound bomb every two seconds. Progressively freed of its heavy load, Brillig became increasingly buoyant, as though a giant hand had suddenly released its downward pressure. Immediately after their last bomb was released, there was a powerful slam against the bottom of the aircraft. The plane jumped again, this time much more violently than before. Robb saw the altimeter needle jump. It now read 29,890 feet. They had jumped ninety feet!

The plane shuddered violently again. The huge red flashes of the heavy artillery shells were at their altitude now, the closest of them some fifty yards or so off to the left, and getting closer by the minute. "Pilot to Tailgunner. Let me know when the other squadrons finish dropping their bombs."

"Roger, Cap'n. Both of 'em is finishing droppin' rah't now. You kin git hell outta here rah't about now."

"Have the Groups to our right finished dropping?"

"Roger, Cap'n. They's all finished droppin', 'cep one Group which is droppin' rah't now. Hang on a minute, Cap'n, and I'll tell you when they's finished." There was a moment of silence. "Okay, Cap'n. They's finished. Closin' their bomb bay doors now. Over."

"Roger, Tailgunner." He turned and gave Bradley's throttle-hand a quick double pat. Bradley relinquished the throttles. He started a turn to the left, slowly at first, but when his left wing dropped about 20 degrees, he whipped the plane sharply into a nearly vertical bank, at the same time pushing forward on the control column. He pulled back on the column as their speed approached 250 miles per hour. The Groups to his right were instructed at briefing to make a left, descending turn with the

Group immediately to their left, thus re-forming the single file of Groups, the bomber stream. He leveled out 25,500 feet, on a heading of 88 degrees—as prescribed on the mission map. When his speed dropped to 200 miles per hour he backed off on the throttles and pushed forward on the column until the indicator registered a rate of descent of 100 feet per minute, still maintaining 200 miles per hour.

"Pilot to Tailgunner."

"You got 'em, Cap'n."

"Did the Groups behind us turn with us? Did they re-form into a bomber stream?

"They sure as hell did, Cap'n. Prettiest thing you ever seen. Jus' like a goddam air show. You shoulda seen it, Capn. All of 'em followin' Brillig, jus' like they should, by gawd, with Brillig leading the whole damned bunch!"

"Roger, Tailgunner. Over and out."

They were well out of the range of the German heavy artillery, heading almost due East, away from home. He began a very gradual turn to the left, to the North. He was painfully aware that he was leading an armada of several hundred airplanes into the turn. Nothing created by man, it seemed to him, turned more slowly, more gradually, than an air armada.

He called Carlson and asked him to call out their heading-changes as they approached turning points, as laid out on the mission map. Robb had taped to his left leg the pilot's reduced version of the mission-map with its specific routes, but he needed his navigator's instructions on when to make his turns. As always in flying across enemy held territory, their homeward route would be zig-zag and indirect, a path that scrupulously avoided German anti-aircraft gun emplacements. At times the corridors between the flak emplacements were very broad, at other points quite narrow. His biggest task now was to get the Bombardment Groups home safely and efficiently. A missed flak-corridor could spell tragedy: Task Force Foxfire was a very large target and an ever-lowering one.

He found his position strange: He was responsible for the Task Force, so huge it was almost an abstraction, yet he had to stay on top of specific events within his own plane. He pushed his intercom button. "Pilot to Right Waist. Tony, get back to Brain Child. Take an extra oxygen bottle with you. Report to me on his condition as soon as possible. Over."

"Roger."

He wondered about the big explosion. He hadn't experienced anything quite like it before. "Pilot to Ball Gunner. Over."

"You got him, Cap'n."

"Ball Gunner. What was that big explosion? Did you see anything? Over."

"Ah sure did. It was one o' them big German artillery cannons hit one of our bombs, maybe two or three hundred feet under us. That's what made the blast." Bohall's voice sounded strange, constrained, almost like someone trying to imitate Boo.

"Bohall. Are you all right?"

"Got a little flak in mah ass is all. It's no big deal." He sounded weak.

Hoyt chimed in, "How's the family jewels, Boo?"

Robb snapped, "Get off the intercom, Hoyt!" He closed his eyes and took a deep breath. "Sergeant Bohall. I'm sending Bruno to open your turret for you. Do you think you can climb out?"

Silence.

"Sergeant Bohall, do you read me?" Robb waited a few moments. "Bruno. Did you read my transmission to Bohall just now?"

"Roger, Robb."

"Get on a portable oxygen bottle and see if you can help Boo. Take an extra bottle in case he needs one. Then get him out of the ball and try to stop the bleeding. Then give him a shot of morphine. Did you get all that, Bruno? Acknowledge. Over."

"I got it, Robb."

"Report to me as soon as you get to him. Put on your throat mike before you leave your position, in case you have to stay with Bohall until we descend to below-oxygen altitude. For now you can hook your mask mike into the ball turret outlet. Over and out."

He checked all systems while he waited for Marconi's report on Boo. He looked out his left cockpit window. Brillig looked like she shouldn't be flying. Number One propeller stood starkly still; the wing that supported the dead engine was blackened and completely peppered with bullet and flak holes. A large segment of aluminum skin was missing from the top of the wing and its tip was bent downward about a foot. Yet the plane handled reasonably well. Thank God for self-sealing gas tanks! And thank Boeing for those oversized wings! "Pilot to Tailgunner.."

"You got him, Cap'n Robb."

"Tailgunner. I need a damage report. How does tail look to you?."

"All tail looks good to me, Cap'n, but this tail on this here airplane looks good, too. It's full of holes, but it's all here, far as ah kin tell."

He pushed his button, ready to jump on Hoyt for his smart-ass remark. He decided to wait until they got back on the ground.

The three surviving engines were performing smoothly, their temperatures now down to normal as they turned over at a mere 1800 RPMs with the plane in a nose down attitude, losing altitude at 300 feet per minute. Better check on the weather over England. He pushed his intercom button to call Brain Child to get him to pick up the weather report from England, but then he remembered he had neither a functioning radio operator nor radio room. He switched to command channel. "Upshaw Leader to Barnstorm Leader. Do you read me, Barnstorm? Over."

"Roger, Upshaw Leader."

"Is your R.O. and his equipment okay?"

"Roger."

"Barnstorm Leader. Have your R.O. pick up the weather report from the base. Then report to me. Over."

"Upshaw Leader, we just got the report. Base is reporting solid overcast with ceiling six hundred feet and going down. No reading yet on how high the top of the stuff is. The crap just moved in. Over."

"Roger, Barnstorm. Have your man monitor U.K. weather and let me know anything new. Over and out." He switched to intercom.

Bradley was speaking into his mask-microphone, "Go ahead, Waist. The Captain's on intercom now. Over."

Robb pushed his button. "Hold it, Waist. Monk, take over the controls now. And monitor the command channel. I'll be on intercom for a while."

Bradley hit Robb's throttle hand, assuming control.

"Pilot to navigator. Monk 's flying the plane. He's on command channel. Override on command so we get your heading changes quickly. Some of these flak corridors are damned narrow."

"Roger, Robb."

"Pilot to Right Waist. You can go ahead now with your message, Tony."

"Robb, Brain Child is dead."

"No." He spoke softly into his mike, but his thumb wasn't on the intercom button. "Brain Child too? No. Dear God in heaven, no! No! No!" He told himself to wait. The worst shocks bring on the narcosis. Wait. He took a deep breath. He waited. But he should respond to Marconi. He felt it coming on. Thank God!

"Pilot to Right Waist. Tony, please check Brain Child again to make absolutely sure he is in fact dead."

"I'm sure. He's not breathing. His eyes are open, but he's dead ... sir." The "sir" was an afterthought. It seemed ridiculous under the circumstances. Poor Marconi. Next to Broz he was probably the closest man to Brain Child.

"Roger, Tony," he said firmly. "Bohall is wounded. Bruno is helping him. See if you can help Bruno get him out of his turret. Acknowledge."

"Roger, Robb. I got it." He sounded exhausted. Exhausted and resigned to his special hell five miles up in the sky.

"Navigator to Pilot. Course change coming up in thirty seconds."

"Roger, Navigator. I'll tell Monk to get on intercom." He poked Bradley in the arm and pointed to his map, the nose compartment and tapped his earphone. Bradley switched to intercom."

"Pilot to TailGunner."

"You got 'em, Cap'n."

"How does the bomber stream look. Are there any Groups out of position, or lagging?"

"Everybody's in good position, Cap'n, neat as kin be."

"Roger, Tailgunner. Pilot to Left Waist. Report on Sergeant Bohall."

"Left Waist to Pilot. Boo's unconscious, but he's breathing. He's got his mask on and I checked it and he's getting oxygen. Over."

"Roger, Bruno. Tony will be joining you about now to give you a hand getting Bohall out of his ball. Report back to me as soon as you get Bohall out. Over and out."

He switched to command. "Upshaw Leader to Barnstorm Leader. Over."

"Go ahead, Upshaw."

"Barnstorm. Have you received a report on how high the top of the cover is over base?"

"Roger, Upshaw. We just got the word. Top of the crap is at 21,000 as of now. Bottom holding at 500 feet. Over."

"Roger, Barnstorm. Over and out." He switched to intercom. He remembered Colonel Strang's non-stop, broken-record message to his lead pilots: Don't ever, repeat, don't ever lead your outfit back in under the overcast except in the most dire emergency! Robb also knew that the risk of the loss of one life did not justify exposing hundreds of other lives to the possibility of mid-air collisions.

Marconi's voice broke in, "Right Waist to Pilot."

"Go ahead, Tony."

"Boo's jammed in and Bruno and I can't get him out. He's going to freeze to death because his turret is full of holes. We can't crank his turret up because it's jammed. And his heated suit isn't working and it's cold back here, and a lot colder down in that ball. He's going to freeze to death. What should we do, Robb?"

"Stand by, Tony." He knew they had to get Bohall down to a warmer level fast. But what could they do now to help him?   "Tony.   Can you lift him up at all?"

"Roger. We can lift him a few inches."

"All right. Hang on a minute, Tony." He nudged Bradley and tapped his earphone. Bradley switched to intercom.

"All right. Tony. Now listen carefully. I'm going to bring a couple of Mae Wests and two extra 'chute packs back to you. Don't inflate the Mae Wests. Just lift Bohall up and place the Mae Wests under him. Then I want you to pop the 'chute packs and stuff the silk all around him. Make sure you get him wrapped as completely as you can. Before you wrap him see if he's bleeding. If he has wounds you can reach, do what you can to stop the bleeding. Did you get all that, Tony?"

"Roger, Robb."

"I can go back there, Robb." Bradley spoke over the intercom.

Robb shook his head. He pushed his button. "I want you to fly the plane and to monitor command and intercom. Keep switching back and forth so you don't miss any messages from other Groups. I'll be back as soon as possible." He didn't want Bradley to have to look at Wieriman again. They were over friendly territory now. The chance of a fighter attack was remote. The Germans were bent on stopping the bombers on the way to the bulge, not on the way out. Anyway, Bradley could handle any situation that might arise, and they weren't likely to miss the flak corridors with Fritz navigating.

He unbuckled his seat belt and shoulder harness and unplugged his flying suit, earphones, and microphone. He reached behind his seat and retrieved an oxygen bottle. He disconnected his mask from the plane supply and hooked up the bottle to his mask, strapping the bottle against his leg. He lifted his Mae West off over his head. He raised himself stiffly out of his seat. Bradley passed his own Mae West to Robb.

Robb turned toward the rear of the plane, the two yellow, uninflated rubber life preservers in hand. Bradley didn't see Robb pick up his own 'chute chest-pack from under his vacant seat. Without looking up at Wieriman, he picked up the big first-aid case and Wieriman's chute chest-pack from their usual place on the floor, against the bulkhead behind the top turret. Without looking up, he sensed that the hole in the top of the fuselage was sucking air out of the plane. At least air wasn't blasting in.

He worked his way carefully around Wieriman and the frozen blood at his feet. His hands full, he carefully placed one foot in front of the other on the narrow catwalk as he passed though the bomb bay. As he stepped out of the rear door of the bomb bay, he looked into the radio room. Brain Child was stretched out on the floor in a spot Marconi must have cleared in the jumble of smashed radio equipment, oxygen bottles, charts, and the mute evidence of his comrade's efforts to save him: bloody bandages and medical supplies strewn among the wreckage. There was blood everywhere on the floor, smeared about by Marconi's boots as he tried to keep his friend alive. There was a jagged hole the size of a bushel basket in the aluminum wall of the ship where the radio console had been. Through the hole he could see the midsection of Number Three plane, gently undulating as it flew on Brillig's left wing.

He moved toward the rear section of the plane. The floor was covered—ankle deep in some places—with spent fifty caliber shell-casings.

The two waist gunners were on their knees above the ball-turret opening. They stood up and stepped aside as he approached. He held little hope for Boo when he saw Marconi's blood-covered flying clothes.

He handed the Mae Wests and the two parachute packs to Marconi. Robb lay down on his chest among the shell casings. He took off his thick outer glove and his thin, inner leather glove, but kept his silk innermost glove on. He reached down and ran his hand around Bohall's buttock, thigh and side. He repeated the procedure on the other side. He pulled his hand out and examined his glove. No blood. Apparently the extreme cold had stopped the bleeding. It occurred to him that the blood on Marconi was Brain Child's blood. He stood up and showed his glove to the two waist gunners, indicating to them that the bleeding had stopped. They nodded. He turned and started back toward the front of the plane.

As he strapped himself into his seat, he pondered his dilemma. The temperature in the back of the plane must be around thirty or forty below zero. He had to get Bohall down to a warmer altitude as fast as possible. But the rule for Group Lead pilots was rigid: you come in under a low overcast only as a last resort in an emergency. There were good grounds for the rule. If on a thousand plane raid the whole Eighth were to come home under, say, a two hundred foot ceiling—obviously with no altitude separation—the mid-air collisions would rival the losses suffered on a typical Merseburg raid. He pushed his intercom button. "Pilot to Tail-gunner. Give me a rundown on the condition of the other planes in the Group. I want to know about the planes that appear to have serious damage. Over."

"Hell, Cap'n Robb, easier to count ones what ain't damaged bad. Everybody's shot up, some pretty good. There's one guy only got half a tail, and another guy ... "

"Thank you, Sergeant. You've told me what I need to know."

He had two formation charts taped to his right leg: the Group chart and the Task Force chart. He placed his finger on the Task Force Chart. The 882nd Heavy Bombardment Group, code name Phoenix, was directly behind them, in second place in the Task Force.

He switched to command. "Foxfire Leader to Phoenix Leader. Over."

"Foxfire Leader. This is Phoenix Leader. Over."

"Phoenix Leader. Are you able to assess Foxfire Lead Group's condition from your position? Over."

"Foxfire Leader. Roger. I see you clearly and I saw the action clearly. I read you loud and clear. Over."

"Phoenix. Is your Group's condition comparable? Over."

"Foxfire. Negative. Condition A.l. Foxfire, I read your intention loud and clear. We are prepared. We have personnel, equipment, and Triple-A road map. Do you read me, Foxfire?"

"Roger, Phoenix. Loud and clear. Does your Joe-where-to-go have current fix pinpointed? And do you have U.K. weather, top and bottom?" He rolled the phrase, "Joe where-to-go", air-crew slang for "navigator", quickly into a single, foreign sounding word.

"Foxfire. I read you loud and clear on both questions. Answer affirmative on both. Over."

"Phoenix. Except in emergency all Groups must do procedural letdown. No deck. Acknowledge. Over." Robb knew there were other Eighth Air Force Task Forces out today, attacking other targets. Even if there weren't, a whole Task Force couldn't be taken in on the deck without great risk.

"Roger, Foxfire. I'm with you on that. No deck. Give us the word when you're ready."

"Foxfire to Phoenix. There will be no further word. On't-day ollow-fay. Acknowledge. Over."

"Ogeray, Foxfire. Loud and clear. This is Phoenix over and out."

He reached under his goggles and rubbed his eyes. He took a deep breath. He pushed the command button. "Upshaw Leader to Barnstorm and Dagger Leaders. Did you read my transmission with Phoenix? Over."

"This is Barnstorm. Loud and clear, Upshaw. We're ready. Over."

"Dagger to Upshaw leader. Loud and clear. I'm with you all the way on that. We're ready. Over."

"Upshaw to Barnstorm and Dagger. *Now!*" He took over the controls. He banked left and eased forward on the column. Their indicated airspeed built quickly to 240 miles per hour—rate of descent 2000 feet per minute. He switched to intercom. "Pilot to Tailgunner. Are any Groups in the bomber stream following us? Over."

"Negative, Cap'n Robb. You gave 'em all the slip but good. But ah shore wish you hadn'ta. I was really enjoyin' leadin' the whole damned

Air Force like that. That's right where old Brillig belongs, Cap'n. Right at the head of the whole goddam pack. Over. "

"Roger, Tailgunner." Robb shook his head slowly. Hoyt was getting out of hand on the intercom, but there were more important things to deal with now. He called his navigator for a heading that would take them directly over the emergency field on the English coast. Anyone in serious trouble could drop out at that point.

They were at 500 feet when they crossed the English coast, flying in and out of the lowest wisps of the solid overcast. Robb was glad he had decided to bring the Group in under the crap. He switched to command and pushed his button. "Upshaw Tower, this is Upshaw Leader. Over." He knew the tower would be crowded right now with the Group's ranking officers and any other officers who could squeeze in, all of them waiting for the first transmission upon the Group's return.

Major Red Hammersmith's voice came back immediately. "Upshaw Leader. This is Upshaw Tower. Over."

"Upshaw Tower. This is Upshaw Leader." He did a quick calculation. "We'll be crossing the cone of silence in approximately twenty two minutes. Over."

"Roger, Upshaw Leader. Altimeter setting twenty nine point five. Ceiling 400 feet and dropping. Winds West North West six miles per hour. You are cleared for Runway Three One. Upshaw Leader. Are you above or below overcast? Over."

"Upshaw Leader to Upshaw Tower. We are below overcast, altitude four hundred feet. You'd better line up all fire-fighting equipment and all ambulances and medical personnel, and any other vehicles that can serve as ambulances. Over."

"Upshaw leader. This is Upshaw Tower. Message received, loud and clear. Upshaw Leader, identify your own aircraft. Which plane are you? Over."

"Upshaw Tower. This is Upshaw Leader. I am Amber Uncle. Over."

"Roger, Upshaw Leader. Upshaw Tower reads you loud and clear. Over and out."

He knew that Hammersmith was telling him, by his last "loud and clear," that he knew Sandell and Kovacs had gone down. Robb also knew that everybody in the tower would be in a state of shock at the news he just delivered. Would Evelyn be in the tower? What about Merrie? No. Merrie would be on duty in the hospital.

Robb homed in on the loop antenna. They were at 350 feet when the direction finder needle spun 180 degrees as they passed through Allsford Lynn's cone of silence. Robb pulled up thirty or forty feet and, after checking to make sure Number Three plane hadn't pulled up with him, peeled off sharply to his left.

Not since his return from the bloody Schweinfurt raid a year and a half ago had he seen the sight that met his eyes as he made his final approach: Every plane behind him in the landing pattern was shooting off flares, indicating wounded on board or serious damage to the plane, or both.

A thought flashed through his mind as he cut his throttles and held the plane off the runway, waiting for it to stall out: Is Cynthia counting planes as we come in? Does she see the flares and does she know what they mean? He forced the thought from his mind as Brillig's tires hit the runway with a loud squeal.

32

Robb landed well down the runway, giving the planes behind as much room as possible. He was still rolling fast when he swung off to the right onto the taxi-strip turnout at the end of the runway. He taxied toward his hardstand faster than ever before. "Upshaw Tower. This is Amber Uncle."

"Go ahead, Amber Uncle."

"Upshaw Tower. Get an ambulance to my hardstand immediately. My ball gunner is wounded and jammed in his ball."

"Roger, Amber Uncle. Over and out."

An ambulance was pulling up to Brillig's hardstand when Robb, with a full blast on engine number two, swung the plane around into its parking position. He and Bradley performed the shut down procedure in record time.

He leaped from the flight deck into the nose compartment and dropped out of the plane through the front hatch. Three medical corpsmen were placing Bohall, mummy-like in white silk, on a stretcher. Robb watched as they unwrapped Boo's head and removed his oxygen mask, goggles and helmet. His heart fell when he saw Boo's pale, waxen face. He was sure Boo was dead.

A corpsman put his ear to Boo's mouth. "He's breathing!" Another corpsman inserted a plasma needle into Boo's arm while the third man placed a transparent oxygen mask over his nose and mouth. Robb and his crew watched in silence as the corpsmen lifted the stretcher into the ambulance. They were about to close the door, when someone called out, "Wait!"

All eyes turned to see Sergeant Bruno Broz walking slowly toward the ambulance, the lifeless body of Brain Child cradled in his arms. The little man known as a child in life seemed even more a child in death, reduced now by the sheer bulk of the gunner who held him in his arms. A corpsman placed a stretcher on the ground and Broz placed his friend's body on it. One of the men flashed a light into Brain Child's face. He looked up quickly at Robb. "He's dead, sir."

"I know."

"Sir, can you step around to the other side of the ambulance please."

The man spoke softly, glancing back to make sure he was out of ear-shot of the crewmen gathered behind the ambulance. "We can't take dead people, sir. It's against orders. We have to take care of the living first. I'm sorry, sir."

"You'd better take him anyway." His whisper was a near-hiss. "If you don't, that big man back there who carried him to the ambulance will shoot you, and I don't think I could stop him. Tell Captain Rizzo I ordered you to take him to the morgue, or wherever you take them to get them ready for the morgue. You'd better hurry, for our Ball Gunner's sake."

"Yes, sir."

As the ambulance started rolling, Broz turned and walked down the flight line in the general direction of the squadron area. Clearly, he had no intention of going to debriefing, and Robb had no intention of ordering him to go, despite the standing order that all able-bodied crew members must go through debriefing.

Bradley called Robb aside. "We've got a problem. Hoyt and Marconi won't let anyone in the plane until they remove Wieriman's body. The crew chief tried to get past Hoyt and Hoyt told him he'd blow his fucking brains out with his forty-five."

"I'll take care of it."

Hoyt was standing guard at the rear door of the plane. Bradley, Carlson and Richards hung back while Robb talked to Hoyt. Robb placed his hand on Hoyt's shoulder. "I'm sorry about Boo."

"Ole Boo'll be all right, Cap'n. He's a tough sombitch."

"If anyone tries to get into the plane before they remove Wieriman, you tell them you have orders from me not to let anyone in until the medical people remove Wieriman. I don't care who it is."

"Don't you worry about it one bit, Cap'n. Nobody gets in. Not even Colonel Prick."

Corporal Weatherholt, Sam's orderly from G-2, came rushing up. "Sir. Captain Prentice sent me here to get you with his jeep. Colonel

Crick is about to blow a fuse. He's waiting for the strike report from you. Division's waiting for it."

"I'll be with you in a minute, Corporal. Sergeant Hoyt, I'll be back after debriefing to check if they've taken care of Wieriman."

Sam's orderly dropped the four officers off on the flight line, opposite the debriefing room. The whiskey tables formed a bar, some thirty or forty feet long, directly in front of the de-briefing room. As they walked around the end of the tables, each of them reached across the table and picked up a double shot from the array of filled glasses the Red Cross women had set up. Each of them threw back a double shot, and each carried off a second glass—a violation of the one-double-per-man rule—but nobody was going to enforce the rule under the circumstances. They continued on to debriefing, each with a full glass in hand.

The room was packed and noisy as some half dozen crews recounted the events of the day to interviewers from G-2. Lieutenant Colonel Horatio Crick stood, hands on hips, behind Sam's table at the back of the room. Sam stood at his side. Robb and his officers were half way across the room when Lieutenant Colonel Crick's voice boomed out, "Where the hell have you been, Robertson! You landed fifteen minutes ago!"

The silence was instantaneous and complete. All eyes turned to Robb. The four officers stopped directly across the table from the Group Executive Officer. Crick glared at Robb. He roared, "Don't you know better than to stand around drinking whiskey while Division is waiting for a strike report?"

Robb said nothing. His look was clearly a deliberate non-response.

Crick's voice was strident. "Do you know who's waiting for Division's report? Do you? Air Force! And do you know who General Doolittle has to relay our report to? Do you?" He walked around the end of the table, his eyes glued on Robb's. "Do you know who?" His shallow, steel gray eyes glinted. "General Eisenhower! That's who!" He stared at the glass in Robb's hand. "So General Eisenhower has to wait while you stand around drinking whiskey! Now correct me if I'm wrong, Robertson. You did lead the Task Force on the bomb run today, did you not?"

"Yes."

"Then where the hell have you been since you landed?"

Robb remained silent for a moment. He looked down at the full shot glass in his hand. Then he looked Colonel Crick squarely in the eye and drank the shot in one quick motion, his eyes still locked on Crick's. "I was *not* standing around drinking whiskey!" His tone was as loud and assertive as Crick's. "I was looking after my dead and wounded."

The eyes of every man in the room moved from Robb to Crick. Crick seemed taken aback, either by his subordinate officer drinking his whiskey before answering a direct question—an act which bordered on insubordination—or by his tone, which was definitely insubordinate. Crick suddenly noticed that all eyes in the room were following the confrontation.

He exploded, "Goddamn it!" He waved his arm wildly. "Get on with your interviews! Division's waiting for your reports!"

The bustle of voices resumed, however subdued.

"Did you hit the target, Robertson?" Crick's tone remained combative.

"I think so."

"You *think* so! You *think* so! Don't you *know*?"

"Sir, the target was an area, not an identifiable landmark."

"What do you say, Lieutenant Richards? You were the lead bombardier today. You should know whether or not you hit the target. Did you hit the target?"

"We dropped the bombs within the area we were supposed to, sir. I have no way of knowing what, or who, we hit, sir." Richards kept looking down at his whiskey glass.

"What is General Doolittle supposed to tell General Eisenhower? We *think* we hit the target? The 990th Heavy Bombardment Group, the Group that was chosen by Air Force to lead the Task Force on one of the most important missions of the war, *doesn't know if it hit anything*? He yelled, "Is that what Air Force is supposed to tell General Eisenhower?"

Robb said, "You may say we hit the target."

"Am I to understand that you, Robertson, are giving me permission to say that?"

"You misunderstood me. I mean that one may say with a reasonable level of confidence that we hit the target."

"At last I get an answer that's worth something." The Exec turned to Captain Prentice. "You may continue your interrogation. I'm now going to call in a preliminary report to Division that we hit the target. The strike photos better match your claim, Robertson!"

As Crick turned away, Bradley, Richards and Carlson, as though on command, threw down their whiskey simultaneously. Colonel Crick had taken no more than three or four steps when he stopped and turned around. "One other thing, Robertson. You came back on the deck again, as usual. Who gave you permission to come back on the deck?"

Robb stared dully at the Group's Second-in-Command. "Sir. I found myself in a position of command. I commanded. I gave myself permission. Commanders who fuck around trying to get permission in emergencies kill people. Their own people."

Crick's face reddened. "What if everybody did that?" His voice boomed. "Do you have any idea of the chaos there would be over England? Do you? The mid-air collisions? Did you consider that?" The room grew silent again.

Robb remained silent.

"Answer me, goddammit! Answer when you're addressed by your superior officer!"

"I have nothing to say, sir."

"I'll deal with your insubordination later, Robertson!" Colonel Crick turned abruptly and made for the hallway to Group Headquarters.

Sam said. "Sit down men, please," He spoke softly, embarrassed. "I'm awfully sorry about all that, Robb."

"It's not important. You know me well enough to know that nothing he could say or do makes any difference to me. And especially today."

"I'm terribly sorry about Stosh..." Sam spoke just above a whisper. "... and Sandy and Stew Adams ... and the rest."

No one spoke for a time. Finally Robb said, "We knew it was going to happen sooner or later. Stosh knew it too. So did Sandy. We lost Wieriman and Brain Child too."

"Oh my God!" Sam turned pale.

"And we may lose Boo. He's still alive, but barely."

"Christ, I'm sorry, Robb." Sam took off his glasses and started wiping them.

No one said anything. Finally Robb said, "Better get on with the debriefing."

Sam put his glasses back on. "All right. I have to take things in their order of importance—from the Air Force's standpoint. I want to know all about what happened with Stosh and Sandy and Colonel Wilson, but first I have to ask you about the bombing. Did you mean what you said to Colonel Crick? Are you really that confident that you hit the target?"

"I can't see how we could have missed."

"Is there any chance we bombed any of our own troops?"

"No. Not the way we did it."

"How can you be so sure?"

"Everything went perfectly, down to the last second. The only way we could have hit our own troops would be if they screwed up on the placement of the smoke line, and you can be damned sure they didn't do that. Not with their lives on the line." He decided not to mention the two-mile-per-hour insurance margin he invoked just before "bombs away".

"What do you think, Will?"

"Nothing is certain in this business. We did everything according to plan. If the planners didn't screw up, we were on target. I mean about the 990th. Even though we led the Task Force we have no way of knowing whether the other Groups hit their targets." Sam nodded thoughtfully. "I know. Each of the other Groups will file their own strike reports." Sam closed his notebook. "That's it for now, men. Thank you." The crew headed for the door. Robb hung back.

33

Sam, his countenance infinitely sad, watched Robb's crew as they departed. He turned to Robb. "He was a presence such as no one else I've ever known. I'll never be able to accept his absence. Ever."

Robb nodded absently. He stared at Sam's table, nodding slowly.

Sam said, "I wish you and I could go off somewhere together now. Just to be together now, with Stosh ... in a way. But I have to interview some more crews."

Robb nodded slowly. "I have to get to the hospital to check on Boo."

Sam said, "You had better stick around until the C.O. returns from Division. He interviews the Group Leader personally after each mission. He should be getting here any minute now. We could also get a call from Division or Air Force from someone high up who might want to talk to you about today's mission. Crick was right. This was a big one, possibly one of the most important missions of the whole war. You did a fantastic job, Robb, taking the lead of the whole Task Force."

Robb frowned. "Is the Group still incommunicado? I'd like to call Cynthia."

"You may call her, but don't say anything about the mission. You can use the phone in my office." He handed him a key.

Robb went to Sam's office and sat behind Sam's desk. He retrieved a scrap of paper from his wallet and gave the base operator Cynthia's number. He recognized the butler's voice, and his lisp.   "Thinthia is in, but she is indisposed. She really can't come to the phone."

"Please tell her that Robb called. It's very important."

"I know. I will most certainly tell her. You may be sure of that, Captain Robertson."

"Thank you." As he hung up he reflected that the strange butler had, just now, admitted Cynthia's existence for the first time, and he had even acknowledged his own existence by calling him by his name.

He returned Sam's key and joined Bradley, Carlson, and Richards at the whiskey tables. Bradley told him they had taken Wieriman away. Robb hadn't yet had a drink when Corporal Lynn found him.

"Sir, Colonel Strang is back. He wants to see you."

Strang and Sam were poring over aerial photos. The Colonel reached out and shook Robb's hand, clapping him on the shoulder. "Great job, Robb, taking the lead. I'm proud of you." Robb didn't respond. The Colonel studied him for a moment. "And you should be proud of yourself. Here. Take a look at these photos."

Sam said, "We hit the target on the nose, and we didn't hit any of our troops. See this very faint line of smoke flares here? These tiny flares mark our ground forces' most forward position. As you can see, our bombs cleared our troops by two or three miles, but they started hitting within two or three hundred feet behind enemy lines. Of course, this means we were maximally effective."

Sam handed Robb a magnifying glass. "See what we hit! These are big artillery pieces, and these here are—or were—tanks, and these were trucks, a few hundred of them! And here's a fuel dump going up in smoke! We hit an armored division and some big artillery!" He looked up. "Well, Robb. How do you like that?"

"I'm glad we didn't hit any of our own people."

Sam continued enthusiastically, "See here, Robb..."

Robb's eyes, while they looked into the magnifying glass, saw nothing. Sam continued pointing with his pencil. "With two-second intervals between bomb releases at 150 miles per hour—which is 220 feet per second—the bombs should hit in a string of impacts 440 feet apart. With each plane dropping sixteen 500 pounders, each plane's string of craters is about 7000 feet long. If the other Groups were as accurate as we were, the Task Force laid a solid pattern several miles wide by more than a mile deep."

Robb was infinitely saddened as he watched his friend, this gentle schoolmaster who would avoid walking on a cricket, enthusiastically describing a pattern of death as though the craters were mere holes in a Chinese checkerboard.

"Here, you can see the patterns clearly!" Sam pointed with his pencil. "See the craters marching along the ground!" Robb no longer pretended to look through the magnifying glass. "Look! Look what you fellows did today!"

He refused to look. "I believe you, Sam."

Sam shot a quick glance at Colonel Strang. Strang's eyes communicated nothing.

"Congratulations, Robb," Strang said, again shaking his hand. "You couldn't have done better. They'll be ecstatic at Eighth Headquarters. Eighth Air Force will have these photos at General Eisenhower's headquarters within a few hours."

"Another Pyrrhic victory," Robb said absently, looking at the photos but not seeing them. "Like Schweinfurt or Regensburg, or any Merseburg mission." Without looking at his commanding officer, he said, "Who won today, John?"

Colonel Strang stiffened. "Stand up, goddam it! Now look me in the eye! Now you listen to me, Robb! You know damned well Sam and I feel as bad as you do about Stosh and Sandy, and all of us are sick about the hundred other guys. And your two gunners. And Colonel Wilson. But you know it's a hell of a lot better this way, hitting the target on the nose, than missing the target and losing all these men for nothing. You know as well as I do that if this German breakthrough in the Ardennes succeeds it will lengthen the war by another year at least, and that means tens of thousands of men lost—including thousands of Eighth Air Force men. Now, with this mission and others like it to follow, our ground forces can turn things around pretty quick. We lost Stosh and Sandy and Colonel Wilson and the others and nothing can make up for that, but we saved a lot of lives, too. Thousands."

Robb stared at Sam's table.

The Colonel's tone softened. "You know as well as I do that the loss of Stosh and Sandy is no surprise. Stosh expected it, Sandy expected it. You expected it and I expected it. And I still expect it for you and me. Sure, it hurts right now. It hurts like hell. But it's built into this business. You and I have known it for a long time now, longer than anyone else in this room." He put his hand on Robb's shoulder. "Come with me to my office. I want to talk to you."

Colonel Strang took a bottle of Scotch and two glasses out of his desk drawer. He poured two substantial drinks. He handed Robb a drink and raised his glass in silent toast. Robb nodded and raised his glass. Each drained his glass in a single gulp.

They stood in silence for a moment. Robb opened his mouth—twice—to say something, but each time he failed to utter a sound.

"John, I ... " His voice broke. He turned suddenly and left the office.

He walked rapidly around the corner and down the hall to the door to the men's latrine. He went in and entered a stall and closed the door and leaned his shoulder against the door, his forehead against the side partition. He covered his face with his hands.

And he wept.

Silently. His body shook as in a seizure. If he made any sound it would have been hardly audible to anyone in the next stall.

When finally he came out of the stall he had no idea if he had been in there for five minutes or a half hour. He rinsed his face with cold water. He rubbed vigorously the area around his mouth, but the gargoyle-mouth impression left by his oxygen mask remained as sharp as before.

He saw Evelyn as soon as he opened the door to the hall. He was shocked. He felt that somehow she had witnessed the events in the men's room. He was embarrassed, yet warmed by the sight of her. She was standing against the far wall, smoking a cigarette. Beyond her, the main office appeared to be deserted.

He stared at her dumbly as she walked toward him. She embraced him quickly and kissed him on his mouth. She took his hand and led him back to the main office and to the Colonel's office door. She put a key into the lock and opened the door, closing it and locking it behind them. She turned and took him into her arms and he held her tightly and they swayed together for a moment. And they wept, he silently, and she near-silently. He could not have said how long they stood thus, but he felt her grief become one with his and in the sharing he felt the sharp pain in his chest easing.

Still holding her tightly, her face pressed against his chest, he spoke. "Does the Colonel know we're in here?"

"He came to my office and gave me his key as he left for Division with the strike photos. He told me where you were."

He released his grip on her and walked to the window and looked out at the winter darkness. After several minutes, she went to his side and took his hand. He turned to her and he saw for the first time the redness around her eyes. He took her into his arms again and he wept again, spasmodically, muffled. Evelyn cried openly, uncontrollably. He held her head tight against his chest.

After a time they held each other quietly. Robb said, "Do you have a handkerchief?" He wiped her eyes and then his own. He turned to the window and stared at the blackness. "Have you seen Merrie?" He spoke without looking at her.

"I went to the hospital as soon as it was definite. I caught her in the hall and she stopped and embraced me and said something like, 'I know. It's all right.' Then she went back to her work. She seemed wooden, vacant, like another person."

"Thank God she's got her work."

Evelyn nodded absently. "It's a madhouse over there. They had people lined up on carts in the halls, with more coming in. She'll be all right until they get all the serious cases shipped to the big hospital. I'm worried about when the lull sets in."

"She'll be exhausted. She'll sleep. I hope you're with her when she wakes up."

"I thought of that. I'm sure I can arrange it with Colonel Strang." She looked up at him, lovingly, but he didn't see it. "Would you like a drink? Colonel Strang told me where he keeps his whiskey when he gave me his key."

"All right." He sat down next to the desk and watched her pour the drinks.

"The C.O. told me to tell you you're now on a twenty-four hour pass—if you like."

He threw back the drink. "Were you in the tower when I called in?"

She nodded. "I recognized your voice. So did Sam. It was no longer a secret that each squadron had a hidden leader. We knew Stosh and Sandy had gone down when we heard your voice. Everybody else knew it when you identified your plane."

"I know."

"Sam told me he would send someone to tell me once he found out if it was definite, so I could call Tony and he could tell Merrie. Sam got confirmation from the first crew he questioned. His orderly came to my office and I called Tony and asked him to tell Merrie right away, before she heard it from one of the wounded. Then I went to the hospital."

"I've got to get to the hospital right away."

"To see Merrie?"

"I want to see her, but I don't think I should bother her now."

"Was someone on your crew wounded?"

"Boo. My ball gunner."

"Is it serious?"

"Yes."

"One of the invincible ones. How awful."

He was glad she didn't know about Wieriman and Brain Child.

She lit a cigarette and handed it to him. "Would you like another drink before you go?"

"All right." He emptied the glass in a single swallow. "I'd better go now."

"You really should eat. You haven't had anything since three or four this morning."

"I'm not hungry."

"Please, Robb. Come with me to the mess hall."

He hesitated for a moment.

"Please."

He sighed. "All right."

They stepped out into the main office. Someone had turned off the lights, except for the lights on a small Christmas tree on a table in the center of the room. He stopped when he saw the tree. He stared at it dumbly.

She took his hand firmly. "Come, my love. Time to eat." She led him outside. A strong, cold wind blew ice crystals out of the north, crisp, sharp and biting. Robb stood for a moment looking toward the flight line. He heard the wind as it shrieked angrily through the battered empennages and fuselages of the ships arrayed along the line. He couldn't see them in the blackness, but he saw them in his mind. Dead creatures, deserted in the winter night, ghoulish monuments commemorating this day. He looked up out of habit. The sky was still overcast. There wasn't a star to be seen on this Christmas Eve.

34

Robb left the base hospital shortly after 9:00 P.M. on Christmas Eve. Tony Rizzo's news was good: Boo had regained consciousness, and even though he might lose two or three toes to frostbite, his vital signs were surprisingly good for one who had suffered so many wounds and lost so much blood. But then, Robb reflected as he climbed into Sam's jeep in front of the hospital, Boo was a tough son of a bitch. Rizzo said Boo would be transferred to the big hospital tomorrow where he would suffer the scalpels of a corps of surgeons highly practiced at removing foreign bodies from human bodies, and equally experienced at removing toes irreparably damaged by freezing. Rizzo said the folds and layers of parachute silk had saved the gunner's limbs, and most likely his life.

As he put the jeep through its gears, Robb said a silent prayer of sorts, thankful that at least one of his wounded men would survive, but he stopped short: he was thanking the same God who let Stosh, Sandy, Brain Child, and Wieriman die, and Stew Adams and a hundred other men! Some people would say that God had reasons humans weren't meant to fathom. He couldn't buy that. That was the kind of thinking that made it so difficult for him to live with his religious sentiments. He wondered why, in face of so many religious explanations he couldn't accept, his religious sentiments persisted, breaking through to the surface, as now, like a deep fistula finding its way to the outer skin of its victim. Why, he wondered, did his rational attempts to dispel such sentiments always fail? He said a silent prayer for Merrie.

Merrie weighed heavily on his mind. He felt a pang at the thought of Merrie's courage in the face of her unspeakable loss. When, minutes ago, he encountered her in the hospital hallway, she embraced him and said, "Thank God that you came through all right." But her tone, like her face, was devoid of feeling. And then, without another word, she went on quickly with her work, just as Stosh had said she would. And in that moment Robb knew she would never get over her grief, just as he knew he would never get over his. He yelled, "God damn you Stosh! Why did you have to be so different from everyone else!" Oh God how Merrie's heart must be breaking, or will break as soon as she stops! He took a deep breath and took hold of himself.

As he passed through the main gate, the military policeman on duty saluted him—or the jeep, perhaps. As Robb touched his cap, he saw it was the same man in the shiny boots who had challenged the fog last Thursday. Last Thursday? Today was Sunday. Was it really only four days ago that he stood next to that booth waiting for Sam? He had lived a lifetime in those four days, and Stosh had lived and died in those four days. And in that interlude the upbeat, sparkling personality that was Merrie died also. Oh Christ!

He turned into the mile-long drive that led to Cynthia's house. Did Cynthia count planes today? Should he tell her about Stosh? How could he avoid it? It suddenly occurred to him that he couldn't tell her anything if he wanted to. The mission, including Stosh's death and everything else about it, is classified.

Allsford Hall loomed dark in the winter night, as forbidding as its butler and as dark as the mysteries its master, Cynthia's father, had wrapped around himself. The house—he felt strange calling it a house— was as large as the main buildings of some of the colleges of Cambridge University and, it seemed to him, every bit as old as most of them. It had darkened with age, but in no way mellowed. Its massive facade, surely once bright and sharp-edged, was near-black, its limestone blocks rounded at their edges by time, wind and weather. Or perhaps it was the cold gray lichens that had softened the crisp-cut edges. How appropriate Gray's line, he thought, in this graveyard-like place.

The house may well have been patterned after the architecture of the older Gothic buildings in Cambridge University's colleges, or perhaps it was the other way around. But Cambridge's colleges, in their age, beckoned one come in, come share the excitement of learning, come share the warmth and certitude time has given. But Allsford Hall, in its cold, bloodless senescence, said "Go away". Or, Robb mused, maybe it was only the butler.

As he stepped out of the jeep opposite the front door of the house, the tiny ice shards stung more sharply than before, driven by a wind that seemed angry at the edifice before him. He pulled up the fur collar of his flight jacket and pressed it tightly against his ears.

He tapped the oaken door with its heavy iron knocker, shivering as he waited. He thought of Stosh and of his remains, unidentifiable, ungatherable, now scattered in some winter field in Belgium. "O all the instruments agree, the day of his death was a dark cold day." He had committed these words to memory, long ago in Bloomington, Indiana, but he had never really shared Auden's feelings. Until now.

The sound of an engine running up on the flight line cut through the wind. He turned toward the source of the sound, the sound of a B-17 engine challenging the wind for a brief moment, spinning its propeller, creating a pebble-in-the-ocean wind of its own. Could it be that Sergeant Yoder and his crew were already trying out a new Number One engine on Brillig, getting the plane ready for more of the same? When? Tomorrow? No, not tomorrow. The C.O. had given him a twenty-four hour pass. Maybe the day after tomorrow, Boxing Day, as the English call the day after Christmas. No, that would be too soon; they lost twelve planes today and twelve crews, and assorted other people who came back dead or who were now in the hospital, not quite officially dead. Yet. They lost more people and planes than could be replaced by pirating Camelot Squadron, the squadron that had stood down today. But the supply of planes and crews is endless. He knew that right now, on this Christmas Eve, there was a stream of B-17s and B-24s flying northeastward across the Atlantic, an endless string stretching from Maine to Labrador to Iceland to Northern Ireland and Scotland. There might at times be several hundred miles between the beads on the string, but it was there.

And he knew that there were yet unsullied replacement crews on the base right now, green crews awaiting their initiation, newly terrified by today's grisly forebodings. Their six or eight hours of pre-mission practice would be stepped up now. They would be shooting practice takeoffs and landings all day tomorrow, getting ready for Russian roulette by the day after tomorrow. Do they know that they may be numbers on a formation chart already prepared and mimeographed for the Group's next mission?

He was looking toward the base, and in his reverie he didn't see or hear the door open. He was startled at the butler's voice. "Won't you come in, please, Captain Robertson." The butler seemed to have been expecting him.

The butler's features were indelibly written in Robb's mind. He was a tall man, as tall as Robb, but large-framed and thin. His face, naturally long, was further lengthened by his receded hairline. He appeared to be in his middle sixties. As Robb looked at this man, he acknowledged to himself that there were only three people in this world he genuinely hated: Lieutenant Colonel Crick, First Sergeant Kerrigan, and this butler. He knew from his past encounters with this man that he was a cruel man who, like the other two, enjoyed his cruelty.

"If you will follow me, please."

They passed through a vestibule into a large entry hall and on into a huge main hall. It was as large as some of the sanctuaries in churches his family's string quartet had played in. The great hall was early Gothic, its floor and walls of stone, its window and door openings pointedly arched, its vaulted ceilings soaring upwards, some three or four stories at least. Walls, floors and ceilings were darkened, blackened at many points, by centuries of open fires in the huge fireplace, a cold, black cavern at the far end of the hall. The stones of the floors were worn smooth, with depressions in doorways and along more traveled routes within the large hall. It seemed as cold in this cavern as outside. The butler now shuffling along before him produced clouds of vapor as he breathed.

Oriental rugs, now threadbare, and dull wall tapestries may have been an effort, a failed effort, it seemed to Robb, of past generations to soften the cold hardness of the cavern. The oil paintings, huge portraits of people in the costumes of distant eras in English history, were nearly as dark as the walls they graced, or once graced before they blended into their backgrounds.

He wondered at original function of such a vast space. Obviously, it nourished the ego of whomever caused it to be built, and undoubtedly the egos of countless generations since, but what was its original, ostensible purpose? Clearly this great hall served no purpose now. He found it incredible that Cynthia, or anyone, could live here. How could she retain her sanity living in a place like this?

He was relieved when the butler turned down a hallway to the left of the great hall. The man opened a door and with a nod of his head beckoned him enter. He was astounded. He found himself in a library that was a duplicate of the library in the house in Scotland—the bookshelves with their rolling ladder hanging from its track, the fireplace and its seating circle and the low worktable covered with books, file folders and journals. And the identical black, concert grand piano. The room was warmed by a fire burning brightly in the grate.

He began to understand how Cynthia survived in this dreadful house. This room was as warm and intimate as the great hall was cold and re- mote. It occurred to him that if this horse-faced butler weren't here, he'd feel at home in this room.

"Won't you be seated, Captain." The butler indicated a chair with his eyes. "Would you care for a drink, perhaps?"

"No, thank you." He felt a softening of his attitude toward the butler and he was angry with himself. Why should I feel anything less than contempt for this sadistic bastard? Simply because he offered me a drink?

He was surprised to see the butler preparing a drink despite his re- fusal. But instead of serving him, he sat down on the sofa. He raised the glass in his hand, said "Cheers", and took a healthy pull on the drink. He picked up a box of Players and offered one to Robb, which he refused, and then lit one for himself.

They sat in silence for a time. Robb studied the strange butler's face. He seemed to have more teeth, large teeth, than his mouth could accom- modate. Keeping his lips pulled over his teeth seemed to require constant effort. Perhaps this explained his slurred, sometimes lisping speech. Whatever, he couldn't have been cast into a better role than the one he filled as gatekeeper to this manor. Finally Robb said, "I'd appre- ciate it if you'd tell Miss Allsford I'm here."

The man took a long puff on his cigarette. He looked squarely into Robb's eyes. "I am Thinthia's father."

Robb heard the words. He thought he heard the man say he was Cynthia's father, but his brain couldn't process what he heard. He hadn't fully appreciated how tired he was. He knew now, as he tried to com- prehend this man's words, that he was physically and emotionally exhausted. He decided he didn't know what the hell the man was talking about, and he didn't care.

"Sir, I'm afraid you missed what I just said. I am Miss Allsford's fa- ther."

Robb stared at the man. He shook his head quickly, as if to awaken himself.

"I rather thought this would come as a bit of a surprise to you."

"I don't understand."

"I am Thinthia's father."

"I don't understand the butler act, or the father act, whichever one is the act."

"Perhaps I can clarify matters for you. I value privvacy very much. Complete, absolute privvacy. As far as the public is concerned, I don't exist. Only the butler you met—on a number of occasions, if I may say so—exists. I daresay you must have found him rather an unfriendly chap. But, then, his function is to keep people away from me, and from my daughter. I must say he's rather good at it, or I should say he was, until you came along."

Robb noted that Dr. Allsford was highly proficient in his mastery of the Colonel Blimp mumble, the slurred speech with its suggestion of condescension and disdain, the kind of talking that reduced the listener to a hat-in-hand petitioner hanging on each word trying to catch what in hell the speaker was talking about. Robb told himself he was immune to such bullshit. He had no higher opinion of this man than he had had of the butler, and he didn't care in the least what this man thought of him. In fact, he really didn't care what in hell the man mumbled.

"Is Cynthia all right?"

"I am coming to that. Are you sure you wouldn't care for a drink? I can see you've had rather a long day." The words were mumbled together into a single, sustained line of sound, without rests between the notes. But Robb knew he had asked him if he would like a drink. He also knew the man had been counting airplanes today. Cynthia too, most likely.

"No. Thank you."

"As you wish. And now, about Thinth ... er ... my daughter. I must tell you my daughter is not well. Indeed, she has not been well since she came home this Thursday past." He turned his head away but his eyes remained locked on Robb's. "I don't suppose this comes as a surprise to you." He peered down his long nose as he waited for a response.

Robb said nothing.

"In fact, one could fairly say my daughter is quite ill."

Why the hell does he have to stretch this out like this?

"I must tell you, Captain, you ... you are the cause of her illness."

He was exhausted. He'd felt physically sick from the time Stosh went down. Now this!

"Sir, I can see you are exhausted. I don't wish to add to your burdens, but I must talk to you about these matters before you see my daughter this evening."

"Does she know I'm here?"

"No. Nor does she know I intended to talk to you about her."

"Did you give her my message?"

"Yes, of course. She was elated at ... uh ... at your call."

They've both been counting airplanes today. They know about today.

"We have a serious problem, Captain. My daughter very nearly went out of her mind today. I doubt she could survive many more such days. She's been through too much of this sort of thing. There's a limit, and I daresay she has gone well beyond that limit. I am terribly worried about her, Captain. Indeed, I'm afraid, sir. I'm afraid for her survival."

"What do you propose?"

"That my daughter return to Scotland. The situation here is quite untenable ... with us ... her ... living practically on your aerodrome. I should say, rather, with you and your people living on our estate. She's too close to it here, yet almost totally in the dark, as it were."

Robb said nothing.

"Forgive me, but why didn't you call her Thursday evening as you had planned, or Friday, or Saturday? That went hard with her. Very hard."

"I can't respond to that. I'm very concerned about Cynthia, and I was very concerned about her every hour of those days, but I can't answer your question."

Dr. Allsford got up and walked to the liquor cabinet. He poured a substantial drink. Robb recalled his own drinking in Scotland. He found the recollection unpleasant.

Dr. Allsford sat down. "I quite understand, Captain." He drank half the contents of his glass. "As regards my daughter's return to Scotland, I should tell you I suggested it to her, but she wouldn't hear of it. She wants to be near you. Yet, if I may repeat myself, I don't think she can survive many more days like today, indeed any." He turned his head

away from Robb again, studying him sidelong." I want you to suggest to
her that she return to Scotland, and you may tell her, if you wish, that
you will visit her up there as often as you can. I have no objection to
that."

Robb said nothing.

"Captain, I don't know how to interpret your silence. I should tell
you her life is in danger. She's hardly slept since she came home, nor has
she eaten anything to speak of."

"I don't know what to say."

"I was hoping for more of a response than that. You must reflect
upon the fact that it's not as though I were insisting that you never see
her again. I'm sure many fathers would do precisely that under the circumstances."

Robb knew that Dr. Allsford was far too intelligent to think sending
him away for good was a viable alternative, or expecting him to believe
it. Robb said, "If I were to suggest to Cynthia that she return to Scotland, would you object to my telling her that you talked to me about the
matter, and that it was your idea?"

"I would not want you to tell her I talked with you about this. That
would make it seem I was scheming behind her back, would it not?"

Robb said to himself, "Which is precisely what you are doing."

"She would be furious with me." Dr. Allsford's speech had become
surprisingly clear.

"If I were to suggest she leave here, without telling her it was your
idea, there are interpretations she might put on that that could be far
worse than her thinking of you as scheming behind her back."

"Then where does that leave us?"

"Let me think about this, after I've seen her. In any event, I won't
bring up the matter tonight. I can come back here tomorrow. Perhaps
we can talk about this then."

Dr. Allsford's eyes appraised Robb coldly. "As you wish." He stood
up. "My daughter is upstairs in her apartment. I will tell her you are
here. Good evening, Captain."

35

Robb felt chilly even though he was wearing his flight jacket. He warmed his hands before the fire, contemplating the strange man who had just left the room. What sort of man was he really, apart from his harsh butler role and his role as Cynthia's keeper, or protector, or whatever?

He heard her footsteps on the stone floor of the hallway. He turned towards the door. She stopped in the doorway and looked at him curiously. She broke into a broad smile and hurried to him. He met her half way and took her into his arms. She kissed him and her kiss was warm and without reservation. He was overwhelmed—and surprised. Surprised because he had come to expect reticence, forgetting for the moment the short, ecstatic chapter that began and ended so suddenly in the London hotel suite. Still in his arms, her face pressed against his chest, she began to cry, near-silently. He felt her body shake spasmodically as he held her tightly and stroked the back of her head.

She whispered intently, her voice muffled against his chest. "You are alive! You are alive and you are here! And I still can't believe it!" Her sobbing was more controlled now. He led her to the sofa. "I'll get you a drink." He went to the cabinet where he had seen Dr. Allsford put his bottle of Scotch. He poured two drinks and returned to the sofa with them. He sat down next to her and took her into his arms.

Her voice quavered when she spoke. "When the aeroplanes returned and nearly half were missing, I was certain you were dead. But you are alive and I am here in your arms!" She reached around his chest and pulled him tightly to her as if he might vanish if she should let go. She whispered, "Thank God!"

She released her hold on him and leaned back and looked at him intently, as though seeing him for the first time. "You look awful! You're completely worn out!" Worried furrows appeared between her eyes. "It was bad today, wasn't it?"

"That's history," he said softly. "It doesn't exist anymore. Here, let me look at you." He held her away from him, his hands gripping her upper arms.

She smiled wanly. "I daresay I'm a bit of a mess."

"You are the most beautiful person I've ever seen."

"Thank you for your lovely lie. You're almost as good at lying as Captain Kovacs."

His grip on her arms tightened, but almost imperceptibly. He spoke softly. "And I can see that you are very tired too."

"I'll not argue with that. Aren't we the pair though? In love and exhausted."

He smiled. "We'll be good as new tomorrow."

The fire had burned down to embers. He poked the fire and placed several pieces of wood on it. He stared into the fire and soon he was back in Scotland with her again, as though he had never left. Would God that he hadn't! He returned to the sofa and she handed him his drink and raised her glass and whispered, "Cheers." She smiled wistfully.

"Cheers," he whispered. He had thought of her constantly in their separation, yet he had forgotten how completely enraptured he was by the very sight of her, particularly by her smile. She slipped out of her shoes and drew her legs up under her and leaned her head against his chest. He said, "Home again. We've come around full circle. I was back in Scotland when I was fixing the fire. It was as though we had never left."

"That's how I feel now."

"I was shocked when I entered this room tonight." He spoke softly, absently. "For a moment I was sure I had lost my wits completely. I knew I was in Allsford Hall, and yet my eyes told me I was in your library in Scotland. Why the exact duplicate?"

"My grandfather was an historian. He found he wrote much better in the library in Scotland than in his library here, so he had an exact replica of the one in Scotland built here." She wriggled against his chest, as though trying to get closer to him. The firelight, her fragrance, her warmth and the Scotch whiskey carried him back to Scotland and the four happiest days of his life. Their Scottish Idyll. Or iddle. "Iddle." He said it out loud.

"What did you say?"

"I was thinking this, being here with you like this, recaptures our Scottish idyll. We say 'idyll', you say 'iddle'. So I said 'iddle', out loud. Inadvertently. Sorry".

She squeezed his hand. "You're starting to sound like your old self. I love it when you sound like your old self."

They were silent for a time, perhaps as long as four or five minutes.

"Robb. How is Captain Kovacs?"

He stiffened.

She sat up quickly. "Oh Robb! No! Dear God no! Tell me the truth! Captain Kovacs was killed today, wasn't he? Please tell me the truth!"

"Please, Cynthia, I'm not free to comment on the mission in any way."

"How is Lieutenant Bradley?"

"He's fine." He knew immediately what he had done. Damn!

"Oh Robb!" Her voice was filled with despair. "Oh Robb! Not Captain Kovacs! Not that beautiful, wonderful man! Dear God no!"

"Please, Cynthia. Sit close to me." He put his arm around her and drew her to him. "This is now. There is no past, no future. Just now. This is all we have." She wept silently, her face buried against his chest. Finally she spoke.

"Oh Robb. What a hell on earth this day has been for you—this Christmas Eve. Your dear, dear friend, and God only knows how many others you've not told me about."

He took her in his arms again. After a time he felt her relaxing, but just when he was sure she was asleep, she got up abruptly. She knelt in

front of him and pulled off his shoes. She loosened his tie. "Stand up."
She placed two sofa pillows against the arm of the sofa, then reclined
on the sofa. She reached up and took his hand. "Come."

He lay down beside her and worked his arm under her and around
her. His lips touched her hair and he smelled her fragrance and the
smell of hard wood burning, just as before. And he felt her warmth and
breathing against his chest. When he was sure she was asleep, he permitted himself to fall asleep.

Only the faintest embers glowed in the fireplace when he awakened.
Her breathing was heavy and even. He pulled his arm slowly from under
her. He looked at his watch. Six thirty A.M. He sat up slowly.

It was cold in the room, almost as cold as the barracks on a morning
like this. He put wood on the fire and blew on the embers for several
minutes until the wood ignited. He explored his pockets for a piece of
paper. He found yesterday's formation sheet, the sheet that had been
taped to his leg. He tore off the bottom margin and wrote in a very
small, neat script on the narrow strip: "*Cynthia—I will be back this afternoon. I love you. Robb.*"

He placed an end of the strip of paper under the whiskey bottle so
that it hung over the edge of the table. She was wearing a heavy wool
sweater and skirt, and knee length wool stockings, but he knew she must
be cold. He took off his heavy, fleece-lined flight jacket and placed it
over her. He studied her face in repose, free from the tortures of yesterday.

He picked up his shoes and silently left the room. He put on his
shoes in the vestibule and let himself out of the house. The house was on
a rise so that when he put in the clutch the jeep coasted slowly along the
driveway around the perimeter of the lawn. He was a hundred yards
from the house when he let out the clutch and the jeep roared its jeep
engine sound.

He stopped at the gate and presented his I.D. card to the MP His
teeth chattered as the MP looked at the I.D. card, and then at his face and
then at the card again. The MP returned his card and saluted. "Merry

Christmas, sir!" Robb was startled. He tried to control his shivering as he returned the salute.

The MP stared after the jeep as it faded into the pre-dawn darkness.

＊ ＊ ＊ ＊ ＊ ＊ ＊

It was 2:40 in the afternoon of Christmas Day when again he raised the knocker on the oaken front door of Allsford Hall. Dr. Allsford answered the door, almost immediately, as though he had been expecting him.

"Good afternoon, Captain. My daughter has left for Scotland. She gave me this to give to you." He handed him an envelope. "And this." He handed him his flight jacket.

Robb stared dumbly at the envelope in his hand. The door closed, but he didn't notice it. He continued staring at the envelope. He turned slowly, absently, and walked towards the jeep. His left foot turned outward as he walked, much more than it had in Tony Rizzo's office four days ago. He sat behind the wheel and opened the envelope and took out the note.

December 25, 1944 (8:30 A.M.)

Dearest Robb,

I must seem an awful coward, running from Allsford Hall, yet I know - I cannot stay here. I am certain beyond all doubt that were I to remain here I would go completely out of my mind. I am devastated by the loss of dear Captain Kovacs. I have no business saying this, knowing that a part of you—and especially of Merrie—died with him, but the loss of that wonderful, incredible man is— I'm sorry, I don't quite know what to say without sounding foolish. Yet I must say what is in my heart. The death of Captain Kovacs is one of the great losses of my life even though I hardly knew him. He had a being, a vivid being such as I have never seen in any other human. His non-being is impossible to accept. He was, as we agreed, bigger than life. He is, in some strange, indefinable way, big-

ger than death. Accepting his death at any depth of knowing is impossible.

I feel guilty writing this, knowing that for Merrie the light of the whole world has died. I was going to ask you to tell her how awful I feel for her, but that wouldn't make sense. I hardly knew Captain Kovacs and I don't know Merrie at all. At the moment nothing makes sense to me. When will this monstrous war end? When!!! When will all this senseless killing stop? When? Dear Robb, when???

I just read what I wrote and I'm confused and embarrassed and sorry I'm so weak and I'm sick of this world and I'm angry at God only knows what—perhaps God himself! I'm tired of pretending to be strong. Please love me as I am.

I took a moment away from writing this note and I have a better grip on myself now. You are in my heart and prayers constantly. With all my being, I love thee now and for eternity. I hear Grieg's melody as I write these lines and I love you with that melody in my heart and wrapped around you in my vision of you, the vision I have carried in my mind since first "I did but see you passing by"—in Cambridge. Please come to Scotland soon, if only for an hour. I shall live for that hour.

Cynthia

He stared unseeing through the windshield and into the dark mist, repeating the words, softly, "I love thee now and for eternity". Grieg's melody, once so happy when they had repeated those words to each other in Scotland, resonated in his mind. He folded the note and put it carefully into the envelope. He started the engine and drove slowly around the circular drive.

The edge of the drapery in one of the front windows of the house fell back into place just as the jeep disappeared into the woods at the far edge of the lawn.

—36—

Much of Germany was socked in for three weeks following the Christmas Eve massacre. The 990th flew only four missions, yet the flyers were awakened in the small hours on eight other mornings. The crews suffered the long, depressing mornings of exhaustive preparations for the hated twelve to fourteen hour hauls to the Russian Front, knowing the chances were two-to-one against them taking off. Some men who wanted to complete the magic number of missions—thirty five—as soon as possible, cursed when word came from the tower, "The mission is scrubbed."

Robb didn't care one way or the other. What would be would be. And though he lived for the day he would see Cynthia again, he told himself, again, what will be will be. He hung around the officers club most of the time, often studying esoteric books on Baroque or Renaissance music that Sam managed to find in Cambridge.

Evelyn appeared in the club each evening after dinner. On several occasions she suggested they go into the village for fish and chips, but each time Robb declined. She knew why he declined, and he knew that she knew why. Finally, after dropping the subject for a week, she gave it another try. Much to her surprise, he accepted her invitation.

It was a few minutes past 7:00 P.M. on Wednesday, January 17, when Second Lieutenant Evelyn Vandivier stopped the jeep at the curb in front of the Fish and Chips Parlour in the village of Allsford Lynn. Robb looked upwards as he stepped out of the jeep. He couldn't tell how high the bottom of the overcast was, but his nose told him it was still there like a huge canopy locking in place Allsford Lynn's atmosphere heavy with the smoke of a hundred chimney pots—and getting heavier by the minute as villagers carefully placed on their grates the last precious handful of the day's ration of coal.

Fish and chips in Allsford Lynn had been their standard date for some time before the tragic Christmas Eve. They had become such regular customers that the proprietor or his daughters began preparing their order, which never varied, as soon as they entered the place, and they were greeted almost as old friends.

Evelyn knew that through some strange calculus Robb had determined that the fish and chips thing wasn't really a date in the ordinary sense, and thus he spared himself whatever guilt he might otherwise have felt. But that was before Christmas.

Robb followed Evelyn into the establishment. The proprietor called out, "Good evening, Lieutenant! Good evening, Captain!"

They took their regular table in the rear corner of the room. They were served immediately. They ate in silence, Evelyn having learned some time ago that neither Robb nor Sam cared for small talk, and that they were in no way embarrassed by long silences. Robb, never a big eater, nonetheless ate his last slice of soggy potato with the gusto with which he had consumed the first. Evelyn folded the remains of her meal—more than half her order—into its newspaper, tapped her mouth and fingertips with a handkerchief, looked up at Robb and smiled brightly.

He said, "Is that a 'that's that' smile? Or a 'where-do-we-go-from-here' smile?

"It's an 'I-love-you' smile."

He started to speak but he changed his mind. He seemed to be trying to read the greasy newspaper the fish and chips had been wrapped in. At last he said, "Please don't say that."

"But it's true."

"All the more reason why you shouldn't say it." He twirled his glass of ale round and round on the table, producing a set of wet rings which he appeared to be studying closely. "I've been meaning to ask you, have you and Sam been on any dates lately?"

"Not really on dates."

"I know you've gone to movies together. And out to eat. That's a lot like a date."

She studied him critically for a moment. "Are you trying to pass me off on Sam?   You know, to solve the triangle?"

He sighed. "I don't know what I'm trying to do."

The silence between them lengthened. At last Evelyn spoke. "I've been wondering about something." She took a package of cigarettes out of her shoulder bag and removed the cellophane wrapper. She turned the package over and over again on the table top, her eyes on it. She looked up at him suddenly. "Did Cynthia ever ask you if we, you and I, uh . . . how shall I say this . . . mmm . . . let me see now . . . did Cynthia ever ask you if we ever shared a bed?"

His eyes were again glued to the fish and chips newspaper. He opened his mouth as if to speak, then he apparently decided not to. Her eyes followed his every movement, every blink, every breath.   Finally he said, "No."

"Just 'no'?"

He nodded.

She smiled. "That's the most carefully considered 'no' I ever heard."

"I was reconstructing the situation where that subject came up. Actually, I told her I hadn't gone to bed with you, but she hadn't asked me that."

"Did she ask you if I *would* go to bed with you?"

"No."

She took a cigarette from the package on the table, tamped it against the back of her hand, put the cigarette between her lips and lit it. She watched the thin column of smoke ascending from the end of her cigarette. She looked up, locking her eyes on his. She said softly, "I would."

He took a deep breath. He reached across the table and took her hand. He studied the pale, slender hand he held in his. "You're really quite small-boned, aren't you?"

Her eyes never left his, even though he was looking down. Finally he looked up at her. He smiled wistfully. "I don't know what to say. Anything I say would be wrong."

The ash grew long on her cigarette, but she remained absolutely still, her eyes on his, though his remained downcast. Finally he looked up. "Your saying that makes me more confused than ever. More than is healthy for the triangle."

"That makes me happy."

They sat in silence for several minutes. Suddenly he smiled. "How would you like to live in Salt Lake City?"

"Now there's a non-sequitur."

"See! I'm corrupting you. You're starting to use stupid academic words."

"What about Salt Lake City?"

Robb said, "Salt Lake City is full of Mormons."

"Oh, I get it! Sometimes Mormon men have more than one wife. Right now I'd settle for that. Check it out with Cynthia."

He looked at his watch. "We better get going. It's nine o'clock. We could be alerted right now."

Robb held open the door on the driver's side for her. As he climbed in on the passenger side, Evelyn said, "I just thought of something. Do you realize you've never once driven this thing on our little outings. How come I do all the driving?"

"Sam lends the jeep to you, not me."

"No good. Try again."

"Every time we go out together there's always a good chance I'll be doing a hell of a lot of airplane driving the next day."

"That's it. We only go out together when neither of us has any real time off. Only an evening pass. I'd like to go out with you sometime when we don't have to think about an alert. You know, with nothing to worry about."

"That would be nice."

She started the engine, pulled the gear shift lever into low, opened her door and looked back, and whipped the jeep expertly into a "U" turn. They were out of the village when next she spoke. "Don't misunderstand me, Robb. Fish and chips with you in the village is a really special occasion for me. I mean it."

"I've been meaning to ask you, do you like fish and chips?"

"Dearest Robb, love of my life, I don't know what to say." She reached up and turned on the windshield wiper and wiped the steam off the inside of the windshield with her glove. "I don't know how to answer that without hurting your feelings."

"Go ahead. I'm a big boy. I can take it."

"All right, then. Remember now, you asked for it. The answer is 'no'. I do not like fish and chips. When the war is over and I get out of the army I will never eat another fish or another chip as long as I live."

"You don't pull any punches, pal."

"We promised to be completely honest with each other, remember?"

"Know something, Lieutenant?"

"What?"

"You're a hero."

37

By the time Robb banked the P-47 Thunderbolt on to the final approach to the main runway at Prestwick, his frustration at the events of the day, Sunday, February 11, had given way to high excitement.   As the lights of the runway rushed up to meet him, he was engulfed by a rush of happiness at the thought that Cynthia would soon be in his arms.

He cut the power and eased back on the stick of the monstrous flying machine. He was keenly aware of the moment, of the feeling of exhilaration that coursed through his veins, of the intoxication of speed as the runway lights became streaks at the outer edges of his goggles. The moment of awareness persisted as he held the plane inches off the runway until at last, with only the slightest squeal, it ceased flying and became a ground vehicle, a 10,000 pound ground vehicle racing down the runway at more than one hundred miles per hour. It was twenty minutes until midnight. He raised his goggles and rubbed his eyes as he turned off the runway on to the taxi strip where the "Follow Me" jeep executed a U-turn in preparation to leading him to where Prestwick wanted him to park.

The jeep slowed and pulled into a space between two B-24s. The driver stopped and waited while Robb completed his shut-down procedure. He was grateful for the jeep ride; Prestwick Operations was some two miles from where he parked the P-47.

It was after midnight when he left Prestwick Operations and started for the Motor Pool. One whole day of his precious three-day pass was gone, and he still had to get to Cynthia's from Prestwick! Now, if he was unable to get a vehicle from this Motor Pool, he might well use up a good part of the second day of his leave just getting to Cynthia's from here. Only then did he remember he hadn't pinned on the colonel's eagles

Stosh had given him. He turned around and walked back to Operations. He went into the latrine and removed the captain's bars from his shirt collar and pinned on the colonel's insignia in their place. He pulled up his flight jacket collar so that it covered the insignia.

He started for the motor pool again. As he walked up the gravel path to the Motor Pool office, he unzipped his jacket and turned down his jacket collar so that the colonel's insignia on his shirt collar were plain to see.

The sergeant on duty in the Motor Pool office remembered him. "How are you, sir?"

"Just fine, Sergeant."

The sergeant ran his finger down a list on a clipboard. "Haven't seen you here for a while. Haven't seen the other colonel either—the one who travels with you—Colonel . . . uh, let's see now. . . "

"Kovacs. He's dead." He felt a wave of self-loathing as soon as he uttered the words. Why did I say that? What business is it of this man's? What's the matter with me, telling a stranger about Stosh? Ah, to hell with it! What's done is done.

"Jesus, sir, I sure am sorry to hear that. I sure am. Was it in combat, sir?"

"Yes."

"I sure am sorry to hear that. Uh, I guess you're here for transportation, sir?"

"Yes." He thought angrily, why else would I be here? To tell you about Stosh?

"Sir. I'm supposed to ask you the nature of your business, to see if I'm allowed to assign you a vehicle."

"I'm not free to divulge that."

The man hesitated. "Oh, I see. Well, then, let me see what we have." He ran his finger down a list. "We're in luck, sir. We can spare a car, depending on when you can bring it back. How long will you be keeping the car, sir?"

"Two days. I'll return it around 1800 hours, on Tuesday." He gave himself a two hour margin for weather. He had to check back in at

Allsford Lynn at 2100 in case the Group was alerted. He signed the form, "A.G. Robertson, Col. A.C." He didn't have Stosh's talent for blurring his signature or his alleged rank.

As he drove northeasterly into the blackness along the narrow asphalt road, he ruminated on the strange way things worked out whenever he planned to visit Cynthia in Scotland. He had waited for six weeks for this three-day pass, counting the days like a prisoner marking the days on the wall of his cell. They were all set to take off in The Colonel's Lady this morning when the call came from the tower, "Bring it back. Colonel Crick will be using The Colonel's Lady today." Robb couldn't believe it. Would Crick cook up trips in The Lady just to frustrate him? Or am I getting paranoid? But twice in a row? A coincidence, no doubt, but damned ironic. Robb went directly to Colonel Strang and asked if he could use The Bolt, Strang's personal plane. Strang said okay and Robb suddenly found himself better off than before. The single engine, war-weary fighter was faster than a B-17 and he'd not be dependent on another pair of pilots to drop him off and pick him up in Scotland. But when he ran up the big radial engine on the P-47 it wouldn't develop takeoff RPMs, and so he had waited like some tourist whose car had broken down along the road on the first day of his vacation while the mechanics tore down the engine. They got it back together at 2230 hours. The mechanic in charge suggested he take it easy on his flight. He did. For the first ten minutes. Then he pushed it hard. His tires met the runway at Prestwick only fifty minutes after his departure.

He looked at his watch as he turned between the pillars marking the lane to Shelbourne. One fifteen A.M., as usual a ridiculous time of arrival. But Cynthia knew about the delays. He had asked Bradley to call her as soon as he got airborne, and he called her himself from Prestwick operations.

She greeted him brightly. There was none of the gloom of Allsford Hall about her that had colored his remembrance of her these past six weeks. Her kiss was warm and without reservation. And again he was surprised, as he had been a month ago in Allsford Hall, still expecting reticence. And after her kiss she continued holding him tightly, her head pressed hard against his chest. When at last she released him, she looked up at him and smiled. She took his hand and led him to the library. There was a fire in the grate and the silver tray with its bottle of Scotch, siphon, and glasses was on the low table before the sofa. His eyes fell on the familiar tray.

He said, "Let's see now. Where were we?"

She turned to him and pulled his head down and kissed him.

"This is where we were," she murmured.

He marveled at his surprise at her intimacy. He had spent so much of their Scottish idyll trying to get close to her that he couldn't quite get accustomed to—what's the word?—by her unabashed willingness. As if to test again this new reality, he pulled her tightly to him and kissed her again.

She led him to the sofa and sat down beside him. She looked at him intently. "How have you been, Robb?" A look of concern darkened her countenance.

"I'm fine. I missed you every hour of every day since last I saw you." He studied her for a moment. "You're looking much better. You've been able to sleep, haven't you?"

"I work on my manuscript until I'm physically and mentally exhausted. Then I can sleep, provided I have enough to drink before bed. But I must tell you, Robb, *you* look tired. I think we should go to bed now." She stood up and reached out for his hand. "Come, my love. I'll see you to your bed."

"It's your turf, pal."

"I'm glad you're able to talk about Stosh, and to imitate him."

"He's alive as long as he comes up in our conversations, and any one else's. Everyone who knew him will be telling Stosh stories for the rest of their lives."

She held out her hand. "Come. Bed time." She led him to the bedroom. She stood on her toes and kissed him. "Goodnight, my love." She started for the door.

He grasped her hand and drew her back. "Where are you going?"

"To the library, to change into my night clothes."

"Why? Why not in here?"

"I couldn't do that! Now really, could I? Besides, my night clothes are in the library."

"Cynthia. It's time we developed some good habits. Now, if you'll stand here, I'll sit here." He sat on the edge of the bed and began unbuttoning the top buttons of her cardigan.

She closed her eyes and gasped, "Robb! Please don't! I'm terribly embarrassed, and . . "

"And excited. Which is great. But that's precisely what you must get over, or what you said you wanted to get over. That and your embarrassment." He unbuttoned two more buttons.

She grasped his hand. "Please Robb!"

"We're in love, remember? And we've made love with each other, several times. Surely we can undress in front of one another, or even undress each other."

She backed away from him. "I'm sorry. I'm afraid I'm not quite ready for this."

He smiled, genuinely but wanly. He sighed. "All right, then." He reached out and grasped her arm and drew her back to him. He turned out the light on the bed table. He removed her sweater and blouse and slipped the straps of her slip over her shoulders. He fumbled with the clasp of her brassiere.

"Please hurry!"

"We have all night, my love."

He decided not to remove her underclothes. Instead, he lowered her skirt and slip to the floor. "Now I'm going to take off my clothes except for my underwear, and we're going to climb into this bed and go into a holding pattern for a while. I'm going to hold you in my arms and we're going to talk, while we enjoy simply holding each other."

"I don't think I can wait."

"And I think you can. Now, if you'll throw back the covers and climb into bed, I'll join you in just about ten seconds. As he stepped out of his trousers he said, "Please forgive me for being so bossy, but this is an operation on which I think I should be in command, for a while anyway. Later on, after a few more visits to Scotland, I'll gladly turn the command over to you." He slipped under the covers beside her. The sheets were cool against his skin, but she was deliciously warm and soft as she enfolded him in her arms and drew him to her. He ran his hands up and down her back and discovered she had taken off her underclothes. "You cheated. You ruined the training. . . "

Her mouth smothered his words. As in London and as in his "dreams", she was immediately at the height of her passion. Her strange, low-pitched vocalizations, sounds he knew so well, excited him hugely.

38

The western sky on Monday morning was a dark slate-gray, cold and ominous. At breakfast the only landmark they could make out in the Clyde Estuary was the Isle of Arran, and it no more than a black, horizontal blur under clouds that seemed to touch the sea.

After breakfast Robb suggested they try another assault on the farm, up to now as elusive to him as the peak of Mount Everest. As though in celebration of the return of his leg to normalcy, he jogged part of the way, and when they slowed to a walk as they approached the farm, his breathing was more labored than hers. They went directly to the barn where he at last made the acquaintance of her horses, Blaze and Ginger. He confessed that he couldn't distinguish a fetlock from a wither, but that even his untrained eye could see that Blaze and Ginger were fine horses.

They called on the Hendersons, the tenant family that managed the farm. Robb noted that Cynthia and the Hendersons were close yet distant from one another, the relationship clearly that of the mistress of the manor to her old, loyal retainers. They were genuinely pleased to see her, but he could see they didn't relax for a moment in her presence. They had known her from the time she was born, yet they called her Miss Allsford and she addressed them formally. Robb saw that while she was freer than they to respond with warmth, her warmth was measured, precisely rationed as only women of life-long high position can ration their warmth in their dealings with people more humbly placed. Robb had never seen this Cynthia before, the mistress-of-the-manor Cynthia, gracious and charming yet unmistakably in charge. He didn't like it.

Cynthia had prepared an all-Bach recital for the afternoon. She played preludes, inventions, partitas, fugues and other shorter pieces with no apparent pattern to her selection. She didn't announce her final presentation, but he knew as soon as she played the first notes that it was Bach's "Capriccio on the Departure of a Beloved Brother". He was much moved by her thoughtfulness as well as by her performance of the composition. She placed her hands on her lap after the last notes died, and sat looking at the keyboard for a time. Finally she turned and looked into his eyes. He went to her and put his hand under her chin and raised her face to his and kissed her. He whispered, "Thank you".

He took her hand and led her to the sofa. Neither spoke for several minutes. After a time she reached up and placed her hand behind his head and drew his face to hers. She kissed him passionately, greedily. She lay down upon the sofa and reached up and took his hand and drew him beside her. She began to move her body rhythmically against his.

"Not quite yet, Cynthia. Just lie still here in my arms, for just a little while." She stopped her movements and lay still for a time. He kissed her forehead from time to time, and when she began to move rhythmically, he restrained her. After a time she settled contentedly in his arms and they talked of an imaginary concert in which all of their favorite performers would participate, much as two gourmets might verbally create the ultimate meal. After a time she fell silent. He soon fell asleep. When he awakened, an hour later perhaps, he felt the warmth of her body and the even rise and fall of her chest against his."

"Are you awake, Robb?"

"Uh huh."

"I'm improving, aren't I? Perhaps there's hope for me after all."

"I love you as you are. But yes, you showed remarkable restraint."

After dinner they retreated once again to their lotus land, the library, where again Cynthia turned the conversation to her favorite subject: his growing up in a small town in mid-America. "I must say, Robb, I envy you. You grew up under ideal circumstances, with so many friends."

"That's how it seems to me now, but it didn't particularly at the time."

"But nothing is ever perfect, is it? There was always that conflict between you and your brother, wasn't there?"

He looked at her quickly. "That was never serious! Sure, we teased each other, and we fought, and we competed, but Ted was really a wonderful person. He was the finest brother in the world!" He seemed angry.

Cynthia drew her chin in suddenly. She looked at him curiously, her eyebrows raised. "I used to say the same sort of thing about my father, that he was the finest father in the world."

"Knowing your father, I find that hard to believe." He caught himself. "Please forgive me. I shouldn't have said that."

"Not at all. He is, after all, rather difficult."

"But you just said he was the finest father in the world."

"You misunderstood. I said *I used to say that*—when I was in university, when I was still lying to myself. That was before I admitted to myself—I should say before my psychological counselor got me to admit—that I hated my father."

"Why do you hate him?"

She closed her eyes for a moment. "The answer to that question requires that I let a skeleton out of the family closet, a rather large skeleton." She sighed. "I've only talked about this with one other person, even though it all happened nine or ten years ago."

"You don't have to tell me anything."

"But I need to tell you about this." She paused for a time. "I came to hate my father because he is a bitter, nasty man. He wasn't always like this. His bitterness came on suddenly, with a monstrous error he made . . . the mistake of his life." She looked up at him for a moment. "My father published, in 1934, in collaboration with his research assistant, one of the most celebrated articles in the history of archaeology. The article presented proof that the early Saxons, during the reign of Alfred the Great, in the late Ninth Century, were the first Europeans to set foot on the North American mainland, long before Columbus, of course, and even before Leif Ericsson. My father became instantly the most celebrated archaeologist of his time."

"I remember my high school science teacher telling us about the discovery."

"My father's heady celebrity lasted exactly one year. One year after the monumental article was published, his world crumbled. On one day in 1935 my father was a lionized archaeological hero, a candidate for the Royal Academy, and the next day he was the most celebrated scoundrel in the history of scholarship." She glanced at him, apparently waiting for some sort of response.

He remained silent.

"The evidence for the claim that our forefathers discovered America was in the form of artifacts extracted from an archaeological dig in Labrador. . . well-preserved weapons, tools, and utensils that were without a doubt Saxon, artifacts that could be dated precisely on basis of established archaeological and historical knowledge of the artifacts of the Saxon period here in England.   The press made much of our British forefathers as the discoverers of America. The proof was conclusive." She looked up at him. "And false."

His gaze remained fixed on the fire. He said nothing.

"The person who fabricated the findings—my father's hired assistant, who was himself a professional archaeologist—actually took the Saxon relics from England to Labrador, established an archaeological site there along the coast, and then returned to England with these same artifacts after spending the better part of a year ostensibly digging at the Labrador site. "

"Did your father know this man cooked this thing up?"

"No. He thought the findings were genuine."

"Then I don't see how he can be blamed for the hoax."

"He made one fatal error. He manipulated the truth. Moreover, because my father was an established archaeologist with considerable stature in the profession, his name appeared first on the momentous article, as senior author of the famous piece."

"But did he make any claim that he himself had been in on the finding of these things?"

"Only by implication. The article uses 'we' throughout: 'We found this and we found that in Labrador'. If one were extremely charitable, one might say perhaps the 'we' was the 'editorial we'." She smiled ruefully. "One would have to be extremely naive as well as charitable."

"I see."

"It seems the chap who perpetrated the fraud was ill-qualified for such nefarious acts. He had a conscience. A year later he published another article, unbeknownst to my father until it appeared in print. In the second article he confessed that the celebrated findings reported in the first article were fraudulent, that he had carried the artifacts to Labrador, established a dig, and salted the dig with the artifacts, making sure the workmen on the site saw the artifacts as he extracted them."

"Did this man, in the second article, state that your father had no knowledge that the findings were fake?"

"That's the strangest part of it. He said nothing about my father. He didn't mention my father's name in the article."

"And by this omission conveyed the impression that your father knew they were fake."

"Exactly."

"Why didn't your father publish a denial, declaring he too had been duped by this man?"

"Who would have believed him? You must remember, in the original article my father had in effect stated, by unquestionable implication, that he had participated in the discovery in Labrador. Such a demurrer on his part would have been believed by no one, and he would have seemed even more scurrilous than he already did, if indeed such were possible."

"Be that as it may, it would still have helped if he could have gotten the guy to tell the world that he conned him. Your father's crime is a relatively minor crime of vanity, but left as it is it leaves him the worst possible charlatan."

"Exactly. And that is where my father stands now, and always will."

"He could have sued this other man and forced him to declare he duped him."

"He intended to do just that, but the man disappeared after he published his confession, and by the time the detectives my father hired established the man's whereabouts—in America some two years later—the man was dead. He had committed suicide."

"Christ, that's awful. Not only for your father, but for the man himself."

"Yes, of course. And so my father's fate was sealed, almost as irrevocably as that of his poor assistant. My father became, and remains, an outcast, a pariah whose name by common agreement is not even uttered in any university in this land."

"Was your father a professor at Cambridge?"

"No. He was an independent scholar, although he used the resources of Cambridge and any number of other universities."

"I can see how he came to hate the world, and why he holed up behind that butler facade." He took her hand in his. He said softly, "And the disgrace was yours, too."

She stared at the fire. "The disgrace *is* mine, and will always be mine . . . as well as my father's. So you see why I hate my father. He destroyed himself and me. But he also destroyed our family. What was left of it. We were a proud family, a very old family. The entitlements to our lands were given to my family by William the Conqueror. Allsford Hall has been our family's seat since the Dissolution of the Monasteries"

He suddenly knew what the function of that cold cavern, the main feudal hall in Allsford Hall, had been. He wondered how many monks were bloodied as well as dispossessed in the usurpation of that monastery by Cynthia's ancestors.

Cynthia said, "A family eight hundred years old destroyed by the vain act of one man!"

It occurred to Robb that he knew of no family that wasn't eight hundred years old. It also occurred to him that the gains distributed by William the Conqueror were ill-begotten in the first place, booty distributed to his collaborators by a murdering plunderer. "I don't like your father, and I don't like what he did, but I don't think it's that serious, or that important. Not anymore."

"It is very important if it is important to the people who are important to me. None of our relatives will even utter my father's name, to say nothing of having anything to do with us. Even if my father weren't misanthropic he'd not be less lonely than he is now. This way he makes it seem a matter of his own choice, like a grossly unattractive person going out of his way to make himself even more unattractive and in the process saying, 'You can't reject me, I've already rejected you'."

"How old were you when all this broke?"

"Sixteen."

"Why did you tell me all this?"

"It was the most crushing event in my life. I had to tell you about it. I feel much better about it now that I've told you and you don't seem to mind."

"Mind?"

"When you've hidden something like this as long as I have, you come to think that everybody in the world would be concerned about it, and outraged."

"It means nothing to me, and it wouldn't have meant anything to me even if I liked your father, which I don't." He held out his hand to her. "Sit here before the fire while I put on an album I discovered in your collection today. For us there is no past, and the future will take care of itself. This is *now* and nothing is more beautiful than now."

Robb went to the record player and put on Bach's "Suite for Unaccompanied Violin in A Minor", the composition Ted had transcribed for piano and which Robb had played here in this room so long ago. So long ago? Less than two months ago, but actually a lifetime ago. He was enraptured by the heavenly sounds created by Bach some two hundred years ago. How was it possible that any mere human could have conjured this perfect blend of notes, harmonies, and melodies and combined them into a poem so ethereal.

Cynthia said, "Are you religious?"

"You read my mind. I had just said to myself, as I listened to this suite, that I'd find it easy to deny the existence of God were it not for Bach." He smiled ruefully. "A lot of people try to believe and fail. I'm always trying not to believe, and it seems I always fail. I think it's Bach. Knowing Bach, I know that all things are possible under the sun. I should say under the suns, suns without number in infinite universes. When I hear that suite, I know that I know nothing, and that if we add together all of the knowledge of all the human beings who ever lived, we still know nothing."

"You haven't really answered my question. Are you religious?"

"I don't know what I am. I guess you could call me a non-disbeliever."

She smiled. "I've always thought of myself as a believer, but perhaps your term describes me more adequately. I suppose I could be called a deeply committed non-disbeliever. I think it's the Gregorian chants and the boys' choirs. The pure, vibrato-less tones of a boys' choir singing Gregorian chants in unison yet in harmony with its own after-ring in a huge cathedral. The candle glow in the faces of little boys in crisp, starched white and blazing scarlet. And of course, the ritual, the ceremonies, and the beautiful churches and cathedrals."

Robb said, "Those are as good reasons as I can think of for joining the vast multitude of non-disbelievers."

"It seems we're non-disbelievers for similar reasons. "

He nodded thoughtfully. "The Gregorians hooked you with their chants, and old Sebastian Bach wouldn't let me go." He shook his head slowly in disagreement with himself. "Here I go again. I'm lying, to you and to myself. It's not just Bach. I know it's Christ—especially the Sermon on the Mount—who became a part of me as a child in my Quaker family, who will not let me go, even now as an adult. And yet I wish I had no religious feelings whatsoever. God knows I've tried to emancipate myself. It's no use."

"Why are you so determined to dispel your religious sentiments? I should think you'd find comfort, even hope, in your religious feelings. Especially at this phase of your life."

He remained silent for a time. Finally he said very softly, "I feel strange talking about these things. I've never talked about this to anyone.

I've got a crazy sort of embarrassment about admitting to anyone that I have any religious feelings at all."

"But why on earth would you want to be irreligious?"

He smiled absently, without humor. "It would make my job a whole lot easier. Did you ever stop to think of what happens when our bombs explode . . . what happens when we miss a military target in a big city?"

"But Robb, please stop to think of what they did to us, to London, Southhampton, Coventry, Bristol and so many other cities. And remember, they started this modern form of Carthaginean slaughter. Indeed, they *invented* it."

He remained silent.

"Please say something, Robb."

"We hear this 'they started it' argument all the time. It doesn't help. In fact, for me it makes the whole bloody business worse." He looked down at his hands.

She took his hand. "I wish I could say something that would help, but anything I might say would sound foolish, just as a moment ago."

Robb stared at the wall before him. Finally he spoke, softly, absently. "There aren't any justifications that aren't shallow or foolish or stupid. I wish I could wake up some morning and find out that Hitler and the Nazis hadn't murdered those hundreds of thousands, perhaps millions, of Jews. That they weren't bent on exterminating a whole people on fanatical racial or religious grounds, that it was all ugly war propaganda, that it never really happened."

"What would you do then?"

"I'd become a pacifist."

"In uniform?"

"Yes."

"No more trips to Germany?"

He repeated her words slowly, just above a whisper. "No more trips to Germany."

"You'd refuse to go?"

"Yes."

"What would they do with you?"

"They'd shoot me." He spoke softly, absently. "That's the specified punishment in the Articles of War."

"Robb. Look straight into my eyes."

He turned towards her.

"Now tell me the truth. No matter what their other crimes, if the Nazis hadn't committed their mass murders in the name of race and religion, you would prefer to be shot than drop bombs on Germany? Look into my eyes. Now answer me."

"Yes. I swear it."

"Oh Robb! Robb! It's so awful! Look what this war is doing to you!" She pulled him tightly to her, pressing her face against his chest.

He said, "Look what this war has done to you. Look what it did to you long before I showed up to add to your burdens."

———39———

At 1535 hours on Tuesday afternoon, Major Red Hammersmith called Colonel Strang and asked if he thought they should shut down the base to all air traffic. Visibility was down to a half-mile, and the snow was getting heavier by the minute. Hammersmith said all the Group's planes were present and accounted for except The Bolt, which Robb Robertson had flown up to Scotland. The Colonel told him to shut the base down, but to tell the tower people to make an exception for Robb when he got back, unless conditions were impossible.

Strang called Lieutenant Colonel Crick and asked him to call Prestwick Operations to see if Captain Robertson had left for home yet in The Bolt and, if he hadn't, to call Sam Prentice to see if he knew a phone number where Robertson could be reached. He told Crick he should then call Robertson and tell him to get started back right away. "Tell him the base is shut down but we'll let him land if conditions hold as they are now."

Colonel Crick called Prestwick Operations and they told him Robertson hadn't left yet. His P-47 was still on the ground at Prestwick. No, they had no clue to his whereabouts.

Crick called Sam Prentice's office but got no answer. He asked Susan James to call the club to see if Captain Prentice was there. He wasn't. Crick decided to call Prestwick motor pool against the chance that Robertson checked out a vehicle. He knew the motor pool forms require one to state his destination when using an army vehicle. Sergeant Stuart Schary, the soldier who had assigned a staff car to Robb two days ago, answered the phone. "Motor Pool".

"This is Colonel Crick of the 990th Heavy Bombardment Group. To whom am I speaking?"

"Sergeant Stuart Schary, sir!"

"Sergeant, I want you to check to see if a Captain Robertson checked out a vehicle from your pool within the past two or three days."

"One moment, sir. I'm checking the list now, sir. No sir. No Captain Robertson on the list, but a *Colonel* Robertson checked out a staff car, at midnight Friday, sir."

"Did I hear you correctly? Did you say a *Colonel* Robertson checked out a vehicle?"

"Yes sir."

"Please give me Colonel Robertson's full name."

"I don't have his full name, sir."

"How did he sign the form?"

"A.G. Robertson, Colonel, A.C., sir."

There was a long pause. "Sir, are you there?"

"Tell me, Sergeant, was Colonel Robertson wearing a colonel's insignia?"

"Yes sir."

"Do you have his serial number on your form?"

"Yes sir. O dash 452869, sir."

"Now tell me if I have this correct, Sergeant. Colonel A. G. Robertson's serial number is O dash 452869. Is that correct?"

"Yes sir. That's correct."

"Did he enter his unit on the form? His Bombardment Group?"

"Yes sir. The 990th Heavy Bombardment Group, sir."

"What is your name again, Sergeant?"

"Sergeant Stuart Schary, sir."

"State your full name, serial number and unit!"

"Staff Sergeant Stuart NMI Schary, sir! Serial number 32422365, 405th Ground Support Squadron, USAAF, Prestwick, Scotland, sir!"

"Tell me, Sergeant, what rank must an officer have to qualify for a vehicle?"

"Rank makes no difference, sir, if he's a permanent party officer here at Prestwick. The only thing that counts is that he needs the vehicle for official business, sir."

"What about transient officers?"

"They have to be a Major or higher, sir, unless the vehicle was requisitioned for a lower ranking officer ahead of time by a higher ranking officer, sir. And they have to need the vehicle for official business, sir."

"Did Captain. . . er . . . did Colonel Robertson indicate to you that he needed the car for official business?"

"Yes sir. Well, he didn't exactly say it. All he said when I asked him was that he couldn't answer that. He said his business was secret, sir."

"Did Colonel Robertson indicate his destination on the form?"

"He just wrote down 'Largs, Scotland', sir."

"Did he put down a phone number where he could be reached, in case of an emergency?"

"No, sir."

"Tell me, did Colonel Robertson check vehicles out on previous occasions?"

"No sir. When he was in here before it was always with the other colonel who checked out the vehicles for them, sir."

"What was the other colonel's name?"

"Colonel Kovacs, sir. The one who got killed in combat."

"Colonel Kovacs, did you say?"

"Yes sir. Colonel Kovacs, sir."

"How did you know he was killed?"

"Colonel Robertson told me, sir."

"Colonel Robertson told you that? Why did he tell you that?"

"I don't know, sir."

"Do you have the forms there that Colonel Kovacs signed?"

"No sir. That was some time ago that he checked out vehicles. I'll have to dig in the files for the forms, sir. Do you want to wait while I look for them?"

"No. Just find them and have them ready. What are your duty hours tomorrow?"

"I'm on the second shift tomorrow, sir, 1600 Monday to 0200 Tuesday, sir."

"I'll call you then. I want you to have ready all the forms you have that either Colonel Kovacs or Colonel Robertson signed. That will be all, Sergeant."

"Thank you, sir."

Crick called Sam Prentice's office. No answer. He buzzed Lieutenant Evelyn Vandivier's desk and asked her to come into his office. She appeared at his door almost immediately. "I want you to find Captain Prentice. Pronto."

"Isn't he in his office, sir?"

"Would I ask you to find him for me if he was in his office?"

"No sir.   But if he's not in his office, I have no way of knowing where he is, sir."

"I'm sure you have a better idea than any of the rest of us around here.   He *is* a member of your little club, isn't he?"

"I don't know what you mean, sir."

"Never mind. Find him."

"Yes sir." Evelyn left the office quickly, closing the door softly behind her. Just to be sure, she went to Sam's office and knocked on the door. She returned to her desk and called the club. No one had seen him. She called the Link shack. Sam answered the phone.

"Sam! I'm so glad to hear your voice! Colonel Crick has been trying to reach you, and he seems to regard it as my fault that he's not been able to contact you. He wants you to call him right away."

"Is something wrong?

"I have no idea."   She swiveled her chair so that she faced away from the main office. She spoke just above a whisper. "Colonel Crick seems excited about something."

"Good excited or bad excited?"

"I can't really tell. But he was hostile toward me. I don't know why."

"You must learn not to take anything he says too seriously. I'll call him now. Can you meet me at the mess hall for supper?"

"I'll meet you in the club at 1800."

"I'm delighted, Evelyn. I'll see you then."

Sam called Colonel Crick.   Corporal James answered the phone. "This is Captain Prentice. Colonel Crick wanted me to call him."

"Roger, sir."

Crick's tone was more aggressive than usual. "Yes!"

"Sir. This is Captain Prentice."

"Ah yes, Prentice. Look, Prentice, I need to get hold of your friend Robertson, pronto. Do you have a phone number where I can reach him in Scotland?"

"I'll have to phone various parties up there to see if I can locate him, sir." Sam squirmed inwardly as he lied.

"All right. You do that. Can you tell me why he goes to Scotland all the time?"

Sam tried to think of something he might say that wouldn't involve Cynthia.

"Prentice! Are you still there?"

"Yes sir."

"Then answer my question, damn it!"

"He has a lady friend in Scotland, sir."

"He's got a woman up there? I thought he and Lieutenant Vandivier were stuck on each other."

"He and Lieutenant Vandivier are just good friends, sir."

"They sure as hell are, the way they carry on in public in the club. Yessiree, they sure as hell are good friends! Your friend Robertson is quite a guy. Did you know that?

"I don't know what you mean, sir."

"He's one of these crazy kind of hot-shot pilots we have come through here now and then. He just puts on that intellectual front, but behind that smoke screen he's exactly like Kovacs was. Exactly. Two peas from the same pod."

"I don't know what you mean, sir."

"You know damned well what I mean! He's just like Kovacs was—hard-drinking, always on the prowl for a lay, a real cocks-man, devil-may-care, to hell with the rules. You know goddam well what I mean! Hot shots! Too big for their britches!"

Sam cradled the phone between his chin and shoulder and took out his handkerchief and began polishing his glasses.

"Are you still there, Prentice? Or did I offend you talking about members of your little club like that?"

"Yes, sir."

"Yes sir what?"

"I mean 'Yes, sir,' I'm still here."

"I asked you a question."

"I don't know what to say, sir."

"Don't say anything. Just get hold of Robertson, pronto. Now listen to me carefully. When you get hold of him I want you to quote me verbatim. Tell him I said for you to tell *Colonel* Robertson to get his ass back here to the base pronto. Verbatim. Did you get that? *Colonel* Robertson. Got it?"

"Yes, sir."

"That's all. Get going on it."

40

On Tuesday afternoon, Robb and Cynthia lingered long over their after-lunch coffee and cigarettes in the breakfast alcove. Robb glanced surreptitiously at his watch from time to time. His precious hours with Cynthia had dwindled down to less than three. He sensed she was steeling herself against his imminent departure, but she showed no signs of the melancholy that had paralyzed her the last time he left her to return to the war.

He would never forget the world-smothering gloom, the midday night of the day of their departure from London. He had hoped the day of his departure this time would be sunny. Instead, low, leaden, clouds scudded landward under a high solid layer of cirrostratus that reluctantly admitted to the world a cold half-light. As he stared westward, light snow flurries made their first appearance, bouncing off the window panes as the wind moaned low and soft in the bare branches of the thickly wooded hillside. Tiny drifts of white appeared outside the glass in the blackened limestone corners of the window openings. During the next fifteen minutes the flurries became a light snowfall and the force of the wind increased. It wasn't anything to worry about, but he welcomed Cynthia's suggestion that they go to the library, so insulated from the world and its weather by its heavy draperies.

Her planning was again much in evidence: a fire in the grate; a decanter of cognac and glasses on a tray on the table before the sofa; stacks of records neatly arranged on the cabinet top next to the record player. She put on an album, the Schubert Fifth Symphony, as Robb stretched out on the sofa. She soon joined him.

Robb had to exert all of his will to stay awake as they lay on the sofa, warm in each others arms. He dare not fall asleep and delay his departure. He roused himself when he heard the amplified scrapings of the phonograph needle on a record label. He tried to get his arm out from under Cynthia without awakening her.

"It's all right, " she said. "I'm awake."

The phone rang. Cynthia answered it. She turned to Robb. "It's your friend Sam. He seems to be in a bit of a hurry." Her countenance darkened as she watched him cross the room and pick up the phone.

"Hello, Sam."

"Robb, Colonel Crick's been trying to get hold of you to tell you you'd better start back right away. It's snowing quite heavily here. The base is shut down but the tower has instructions to let you come on in if it's at all possible. Crick tried to trace you through Prestwick but all he could find out was that you were in Largs. He asked me if I had the Largs phone number. I told him I'd try to find it and that I'd call you and give you the message. I didn't want to give him Cynthia's private number."

"I'll leave here right away. Hang on a minute. I want to look out the window at the weather here."

He pulled back a drapery. Sheets of powdery snow swept out of the north across the wooded hillside, borne by a gale-force wind. He sighed. He looked at his watch as he turned toward Cynthia. "I have to leave as soon as possible." He returned to the phone.

"It's pretty bad here, Sam. Almost a blizzard. I'm in trouble if Prestwick shuts down. Could you call Prestwick and get their weather. I'd call them but I'm sure their weather info is classified. Do you have their code? Good. Call me back right away. Thanks, Sam."

Cynthia was looking out a window. Robb! You can't possibly fly back in this!"

"That's not the problem. I can fly back in this with no trouble, but only if they'll let me take off at Prestwick. It could be shut down."

"Wouldn't it be dangerous to fly in a snow storm such as this?"

He smiled and gave her a quick sideways hug. "Sam is calling Prestwick now. He knows the code, so they'll tell him what I need to know. He's going to call me back."

"What would they do if you couldn't make it back tonight?"

"Don't ask."

"But it wouldn't be your fault that the weather changed and the Prestwick people closed their aerodrome, would it now?"

"Yes."

"Surely you're joking. They can't be that unreasonable."

"It's my responsibility not to get into situations like this. They're right, actually."

"But surely they'd regard these as extenuating circumstances."

"The only extenuating circumstance they might accept would be if I crashed on the way back, and if I survived they probably wouldn't even accept that."

"Please don't talk like that."

"I wouldn't have said that if I thought there was any danger involved in this peacetime sort of flying I'll be doing tonight. That's if I fly at all."

"I still must say they're terribly unfair. Robb, I. . ." She stopped and thought for a moment. She poured a glass of cognac and took a drink of it. "Robb, I know you're in a terrible hurry and I know this isn't the time to bring it up, but really I must, before you leave."

"What was it you wanted to talk to me about?"

"My problem."

"What problem?"

"The problem we talked about in London . . . just before that awful phone call."

"Oh, that." He bent forward and kissed her quickly. "It seems I was right about the solution to that, doesn't it?"

"Perhaps. In any event, I've come to accept your solution, as you put it. I have been living one day at a time, and I shall continue to live one day at a time. As long I have you, I can live with my. . . uh . . . how shall I say this? . . . let me see . . . my response problem." She compressed her lips. She refused to meet his eyes.

He smiled. "That sounds like something straight out of the University of Chicago psychology department."

"Please, please don't make light of this. I find it frightfully difficult to talk about this. Now, if I may continue. As long as I can count on a visit from you every month or so, I'll be fine. I daresay I . . . how shall I say this? I daresay I taxed your strength this weekend." She blushed deeply.

"I love to be taxed. In fact, I can't think of anything I like better."

"I was about to say that as long as you survive, I shall survive. And so I shall live one day at a time, and I shan't worry about what will become of me if you should die. I accept fully the simple fact that if your life ends, my life ends."

He leaned forward and looked at her intently. She turned away.

"Please look at me! What exactly do you mean?"

"I'd rather not elaborate."

"Do you mean that if I die your life will lose all meaning? Something like that?"

"I don't want to discuss it any further. Please let it go at that."

"I don't like the implications of. . . ."

The phone rang. "Excuse me, please. That will be Sam. I don't want to leave this like this. I'll want to pick this up where we left off."

"Please answer the telephone."

She listened to Robb's end of the phone conversation this time.

"Is Prestwick open?"

"They're shut down, but I talked to a friend of mine there who talked to the Prestwick Exec. Their Exec was a combat pilot himself. He knows your situation. He told their Operations Officer to let you take off if they can keep the main runway clear. When you report to Prestwick Operations they'll tell you if you can take off."

"Thanks. Wish me luck."

"Before you hang up—Colonel Crick said something strange. He said 'Tell Colonel Robertson to get his ass back here pronto.' He emphasized 'Colonel'. Do you have any idea why he called you 'Colonel'?"

Robb's heart skipped a beat. Damn! Damn! Damn! Sam had said Crick found out from Prestwick that he was in Largs. The only place he could have gotten that was from the Prestwick Motor Pool. The motor pool sergeant must have referred to him as 'Colonel Robertson'. Of all the lousy goddamn luck! Crick's got me where he wants me now!

"Robb. Are you still there?"

Better leave Sam out of it. "I don't know what Crick meant. I quit trying to figure out that guy long ago. Thanks for everything, Sam. If I'm unable to take off, please do what you can to smooth things over with the C.O. Tell him I did my damnedest to get back, that the storm blew in out of nowhere. Hell, you know what to tell him. He'll probably have me court-martialed anyway if there's a mission tomorrow and I miss it." Another pause. "All right. Wish me luck. I'm really going to need it. In more ways than one. I'll see you, tonight, I hope."

He walked rapidly back across the room. "I've really got to hurry. Please come with me to my room while I throw my things together."

She followed him as he hurried to his room. He unzipped his B-4 bag and laid it on the bed and began gathering his clothes.

"Would you like me to put your toilet articles into your case?"

"Would you please?"

She gathered his things from the dresser top.

"Sam checked with Prestwick and they told him I can take off, but I've got to hurry in case their weather gets worse."

She picked up his aluminum soap tray and shook it gently. The tightly packed sleeping capsules hardly made a sound. She turned her back to him and slipped the soap tray into the pocket of her skirt. She put the remaining articles into his shaving kit. She turned back to him.

"Would they really court-martial you if your squadron were going out tomorrow and you failed to return in time?"

"Yes."

"I thought Colonel Strang was your friend."

"That has nothing to do with it. He'd court-martial his mother if she missed a mission." He zipped his bag shut. She handed him his shaving kit and he put it into one of the side pockets of his bag. He put his arm around her and kissed her quickly. "I'll say goodbye properly at the door." He picked up his bag and hurried out of the room. She hurried after him.

She took his flight jacket out of the entry closet and held it up for him to slip into. He took her into his arms and he kissed her and as he kissed her he remembered how Stosh had kissed Merrie goodbye like he was going to the moon, and he wondered now if he himself might be going to the moon tomorrow. Or farther. And he wondered what she meant when she said that if he died she would die. But in his heart of hearts he knew what she meant.

He released her and held her away from him so that he could look into her eyes. "I know I shouldn't say this—it's future thinking—but I want you to know that I really don't have many more missions to go. Not many at all."

"Oh Robb! I can't tell you how delighted I am to hear that!"

"So please dismiss those gloomy thoughts of yours."

"I can't tell you how happy I am! I feel as though I've just heard a wireless announcement that an armistice has been declared, that the war is over!" She grabbed him around the waist and tried to swing him around in celebration.

He restrained her. "We really shouldn't celebrate yet."

She caught his meaning. Her expression changed abruptly. "Perhaps we shouldn't celebrate yet, but I must say my heart is full of hope." She smiled brightly up at him. "I daresay I'd forgotten what hope feels like. It is all right to hope, is it not?"

"I guess so." He brushed his lips against her forehead. "I'd just about forgotten how to hope too. Your hope is contagious." He looked out the window beside the door. "I better get going." He kissed her quickly. "I've got to go now."

She placed her lips against his cheek. "I love you," she whispered. "I love thee now and for eternity."

She watched through a window as he drove off in the olive drab sedan. The car hadn't traveled 200 feet before its tail-lights disappeared completely, swallowed by the wildly swirling, powdery snow that turned the last vestiges of day into night. It was twenty minutes past four.

✱ ✱ ✱ ✱ ✱ ✱ ✱

Robb looked at his watch as he pulled to a stop before the Prestwick Motor Pool office. The trip that should have taken little more than an hour took twice that long. He shut off the Ford's engine and sat for a minute looking at the silhouette of the Motor Pool office as it revealed itself intermittently through the blowing snow. The abscess that had been gnawing below the level of his consciousness broke through to the surface. He knew that the sergeant in there, or his counterpart, had referred to him as Colonel Robertson when Crick called. What rotten luck! He wondered what the punishment was for impersonating a colonel. Monk had said it was the most unspeakable crime imaginable in the eyes of the top brass. He had said it facetiously, but when you stopped to think of it, Monk may have been right. Ah, well.

As he entered the Motor Pool office, he pulled up his flight jacket collar so that it covered the captain's bars on his shirt collar. He was glad to see that the man on duty wasn't the man who had assigned him the car. He handed in the keys, filled out the form, and departed for Prestwick Operations. The sergeant behind the counter in Operations told him he was expected. The soldier hit an intercom button and said, "Captain Robertson is here, sir." A captain appeared from an office at the rear of the room. He introduced himself as the Prestwick Operations Officer of the Day. Robb noted the pilot's wings on the man's uniform.

"I have orders to clear you, but I have to tell you you're crazy to take off in this crap."

"I'd be crazy not to."

"I see." He studied Robb for a moment. "They've got the same snow storm at Allsford Lynn. You could have trouble getting in there."

Robb said, "How high is the top of this stuff?

"Twenty-two thousand feet at last report."

"Which one of your runways is open?" Robb handed him the completed form.

"None. But you can use three-one, if you insist on going. But check with the tower before you take off. The snow plows are still on the runway." The Operations Officer reached across the counter and shook hands with him. "Good luck."

As he climbed into the Follow Me Jeep, he reflected on the little military ritual that had just taken place. The Operations Officer wanted to be on record in front of a witness, his sergeant, as having advised him not to take off, just in case he crashed on takeoff. Now that he's covered his ass, he's probably back in his office reading his London Times, his mind already wiped clean of the matter of the nutty pilot from Allsford Lynn. That man will go far in the army.

The jeep driver leaned forward, his nose a few inches from the windshield, as he drove through the blizzard at five miles per hour. The soldier spoke without turning his head. "Not a very good night for flying, sir."

The north wind, now shrieking through the empennages of a hundred high-tailed bombers, had swept clean the wings and fuselage of The Bolt. Robb grasped the hand and foot holds and pulled himself up on to the wing, slid back the canopy, climbed into the cockpit, switched on the instrument panel lights, and went through the checklist. He made sure the switches were off and the brakes locked. He climbed down to the hardstand and with the aid of the Follow Me man pulled the huge prop through two or three revolutions. He climbed back into the cockpit and energized the flywheel until its spinning produced a consistent, high pitch. He hit the engage switch and the monstrous radial engine sprang to life with a deafening roar.

He warmed up the engine for ten minutes. He gave the Follow Me driver the thumbs up sign, and they began their five mile per hour trek to the head of runway three-one. When at last they reached the head of the runway it seemed he had been crawling behind the jeep for a half hour or more. He looked at his watch. It was more like ten minutes.

"Prestwick Tower, this is Upshaw Bolt. Request clearance for take-off. Over."

"Roger, Upshaw. Hold it there. We've still got a plow on the runway. Upshaw, have you had instrument take-off experience? Not Link. Real live experience. Over."

"Roger, Tower. Much. Over." Another bureaucrat covering his ass.

"Roger, Upshaw.   The plow is off. You're cleared for takeoff. Prestwick Tower, over and out."

The   tower man must have hit the runway light switch just as he cleared him for takeoff.   A runway light near his left wingtip came on and he accepted on faith the validity of his assumption that the lights on either side of the runway all along its length had also come on. He could see the light nearest him off and on through the blowing snow, but he couldn't see its mate on the other side of the runway, to say nothing of the lights farther down the runway.

He gave the engine a quick blast, and when the plane moved about fifty feet beyond the only visible light he swung its nose into the driving wind to a heading of 310 degrees, the direction of the runway. He re-caged and uncaged his gyro-compass and ran the engine up to half power, holding the foot brakes.

He sat still for a minute. The plane was ready, but he wanted to make sure he was ready himself. He pulled down his goggles and in the proc-ess erased from his mind all thoughts but the immediate task at hand. He knew that if he were fifty feet from the near edge of the runway, the other edge should be 100 feet to his right. He had decided to take off on one side of the runway so that he'd be able to see the lights on the left edge as they flashed past him on his take-off run. He'd make corrections as the lights got closer or farther from him, but he'd go with his gyro-compass more than the lights.

He pushed his throttle forward to three-fourths power, holding the brakes. When the plane began to shudder, he let up on the brakes and pushed the throttle all the way forward. He had to give the ship hard right rudder to counteract the powerful torque of the engine. The Thunderbolt shot forward into the strong headwind, as though catapulted, pinning his head backwards against the headrest. He kept his eyes glued to the gyro-compass but he half-saw, half-sensed the lights flashing past the periphery of his vision. He was surprised to find himself airborne in less than twenty seconds.

He smiled as he flipped up the landing gear switch. The take-off had been routine, much easier than any mission takeoff. No load and no one immediately ahead of him or behind him on the runway. As he climbed into the blackness he experienced a sense of relief, despite the fact that he was on a milk run. Those bureaucrats at Prestwick had managed to communicate their anxiety to him.

It didn't seem worthwhile to climb above the weather on such a short flight so he leveled off at 8000 feet and stayed on instruments all the way home. He called Allsford Lynn tower five minutes—twenty-five miles—before he would cross the base's cone of silence. He was told that there was "a blizzard in progress" (goddamn the army's miserable syntax!) and the base was closed, but that he had special permission to land. The tower gave him an altimeter setting and landing instructions.

The visibility turned out to be better than in Scotland. He saw the runway lights when he was still two hundred feet above the ground and perhaps two hundred yards from the beginning of the runway. As he cut the power and pulled back on the stick, the thought flashed through his mind that it was a lot easier to land a fighter than a bomber in this crap. He felt he proved his point as the plane ceased flying without even a squeal of the tires. But he soon realized, when he touched his brakes and nothing happened, that there had been no squeal because the runway was icy. He touched the brakes again and he felt the tires grip the runway, intermittently.

He was surprised to see that the jeep waiting for him at the taxi strip at the end of the runway wasn't a Follow Me jeep. Then, when his landing light hit the jeep squarely, he saw the "G-2" on the tailgate, and he knew it was Sam. He followed the jeep's tracks to The Bolt's hardstand. He climbed out of the cockpit and looked down. There stood Sam, his garrison cap and shoulders covered with snow, grinning like a kid in the first snowstorm of the winter. Sam yelled something, but he couldn't make it out in the wind. When he climbed down, Sam reached out and shook his hand. "Hooray."

"You can say that again. I couldn't hear what you said when I was up on the wing."

"I said you looked like an Indian mahout standing on his oversized elephant."

"That's about how I feel in that monster. Thanks for everything, Sam. I might have been facing a court-martial if it weren't for you, that's if the Group goes out tomorrow."

"We're alerted."

Robb frowned, but his frown gradually shaded into a smile as he looked at his friend. "Then I sure as hell would have been court-martialed. Thanks again."

Sam drove him directly to his squadron area. When he passed through the orderly room neither Kerrigan nor Swovik were there. He signed in on the list on Kerrigan's desk and went directly to his barracks. The barracks was dark except for the very small bare light bulb over the inside of the front door of the barracks. It seemed everyone was in the sack, at least everyone within range of the light's dim glow.

He undressed quickly and pulled on the woolen flying coveralls he used for pajamas. He wondered if he should wait for Swovik to show up with his bottle of pills and his canteens. To hell with Swovik. He'd take his own pills, without water. He pulled his shaving kit out of his B-4 bag and unzipped it. At precisely that moment Private Swovik appeared with his collection of canteens hanging by their straps from his neck, like some pots and pans peddler Robb remembered dimly from a cowboy movie of his childhood. The soldier held in his hand a pint-sized, square, dark brown bottle of sleeping capsules. He dumped two yellow capsules into his own hand and passed the capsules to Robb. Robb threw the capsules into his mouth and took a swig of water. As Swovik turned to leave, his hand formed its claw and the claw touched the klutz cap. Robb slipped under the mound of blankets and coats. He didn't see Swovik's salute.

BOOK III

Recessional

The tumult and the shouting dies;
*   The captains and the kings depart;*
Still stands Thine ancient sacrifice,
*   An humble and a contrite heart.*
Lord God of Hosts, be with us yet,
Lest we forget— lest we forget!

Rudyard Kipling, "Recessional"

41

In the early hours of Wednesday, February 14, 1945, Robb sat bent over on the bench opposite his locker in the equipment room, lacing his leather flying boots over his electrically wired, felt inserts. Something's wrong, damn it! What? He racked his brain as he tugged on the laces. What was it that brought on this gnawing feeling in his stomach? It came on during briefing. Someone—Sam, Colonel Strang, the weather man— had said something that pulled the scab off a sore deep within him. Damn! What was it? He gave the leather laces a hard, angry pull. A leather flying boot stepped on the boot he was lacing. "Happy Valentine's Day." Robb continued lacing his boot without looking up at Bradley.

"Why so gloomy? It's Dresden, way the hell and gone, but not Merseburg. The Germans aren't going to waste their fighters or flak protecting a second-rate railroad yard like this one."

Robb stood up and strapped on his shoulder holster with its heavy .45 caliber Colt automatic. He picked up his map case and parachute pack. "Let's go."

He stood and waited while Bradley knelt to take Communion with the others kneeling before Father Paul Miller in the vestibule. The priest dipped his forefinger into a dish and marked a cross of damp ashes on the forehead of each man in line. His task completed, the priest looked up at Robb and extended his hand. He said—as he had before almost every mission Robb had flown—"God bless you, Robb."

Robb said, "What do the ashes symbolize?"

"Penance. Today is Ash Wednesday. On Ash Wednesday each sinner publicly declares his sinfulness and his sorrow about it by the ashes on his forehead."

Robb pointed to his own forehead. The priest dipped his finger and made a cross on Robb's forehead. He shook Robb's hand again and repeated, "God bless you."

As they walked toward the canvas-covered trucks that would take them to their planes, Bradley said, "Why the ashes?"

"I don't know. An impulse."

As they walked from the truck to the plane Robb continued playing the broken record in his mind. What was eating at him? Was it Crick? He was plenty worried about what Crick and the C.O. might do to him for impersonating a colonel. To hell with it! Whatever will be will be. He could handle that, whatever the punishment. But whatever it was that was eating at him this morning was a different kind of worry, deeper, something worse. Much worse. What was it? It came on during the Colonel's briefing. Something to do with the target. He had been troubled from the day of his first mission by the thought that they might one day miss their target and hit a residential neighborhood, a hospital, a school. He was particularly troubled by such thoughts following briefing this morning. That's it. Something to do with today's target.

Robb climbed into the plane through the waist door. Strange. Whatever fear he felt at briefing always left him when he climbed into the plane. Yet here he was in the plane, where he belonged, and his anxiety hadn't moderated in the least. As he stepped onto the bomb-bay catwalk, he swept the bomb-bay's load with his flashlight. It hit him like the blow of a hammer: *Incendiaries*! That's it! That's what had been eating at him! He ran his gloved hand along one of the long, square-edged, silver-white sticks in one of the huge bundles of metallic sticks. Damn!

It came back to him in a rush. Sam had said that the target was the railroad marshaling yard at Dresden. But then, later, after the rest of Sam's intelligence report and the meteorology report, the C.O. had said, "We'll be dropping incendiaries today." Robb couldn't believe it. Fire bombs on steel rails and locomotives? He moved as in a dream to the cockpit. He felt sick as he eased himself into his seat.

He sat in silence for a time, his eyes closed. He wondered if maybe it was just the Crick thing that had him on edge. Hell, there's probably a military reason for the incendiaries. Maybe there are trains with highly inflammable cargoes in that railroad yard.

Bradley said, "Are you all right?"

"Start the checklists."

The clear skies below gave way to broken clouds as they crossed the Zuyder Zee in Holland. By the time they reached 31,000 feet, mission altitude, some two hours later, the holes in the layer had closed and they flew over a solid, unbroken, white undercast. In another hour the layer had thickened so that its top was about 5,000 to 10,000 feet below them, maybe at 20,000 to 25,000 feet.

He first saw the black cloud when they were about fifty miles from Dresden. By its distance and direction it had to be over Dresden. Damn it! Another Merseburg! The flak is so goddam thick the anti-aircraft explosions are merging into a single black cloud! And Sam had said they could expect the flak to be moderate!

Bradley had the controls. Robb kept his eyes fixed on the cloud as they droned eastward. But then, some ten or twelve miles from the IP, his mouth dropped open in astonishment. It wasn't a Merseburg cloud. The top of the black cloud was at least ten thousand feet below their altitude.

As they approached the Initial Point he slapped Bradley's throttle-hand and took over the controls. He stole quick glances at the target. He could see the flak bursting sporadically around the Bombardment Group now unloading over Dresden. The flak was moderate, not nearly heavy enough to produce a semblance of a Merseburg cloud. He stole a quick glance downward. He stared in amazement at the solid black pillar several miles wide churning upwards for thousands of feet above the top of the undercast before it bent, dispersed with the prevailing winds.

The outfit ahead of them was rolling out of its IP turn on to its bomb run. He warned himself: get ready for the sudden turn. The turn came immediately. Brillig was in Number Five position, on the tight side in a right-hand turn. He had to haul back on the column with all his strength to keep from running into Number Four.

As they rolled out of their turn Bradley hit the bomb bay door switches. Robb added power to make up for the drag of the open doors; one minute now to "bombs away." He stole a glance downward and ahead out his side window. He saw again the miles-wide black column churning upwards through the top of the sea of white clouds below. That's no cloud! That's smoke, by God! We're not bombing a railroad marshaling yard! Not with incendiaries! You don't destroy steel rails and steel locomotives with fire bombs! You use conventional heavy steel penetrating bombs on railroad yards. And we're bombing a railroad yard in the middle of a city *on radar*, and our radar is inaccurate as hell! We're bombing a whole city! We're burning a whole city with incendiaries! Oh God!

He thought of putting the plane in a sweeping dive to the right, away from Dresden. Should he? He could get his crew back home on the deck. Does it really matter what they'd do to him? Does it really matter when you think of what these incendiaries are going to do to that civilian population? Just then the plane jumped, the jump that comes when the bombardier releases the bombs. He saw the clusters of square-edged incendiary silver sticks tumble from the bomb bays of Number Four and the other planes in the squadron. "Too late!" He yelled into his mask. "Too late! Too late! Oh God!" His words trailed off into a cry of despair.

He felt dizzy and sick to his stomach. He gave Bradley a quick poke in the shoulder, indicating that he wanted him to take the controls. Bradley no sooner had the controls than the squadron banked suddenly to the right.

They were on a westerly course, losing altitude at 500 feet per minute, indicated airspeed 250 miles per hour. Robb looked upwards and to his right. He saw the unbroken line of B-17s, all grinding eastward toward the black column of smoke. A gargantuan silver freight train stretching across the map of Germany, a freight train laden with hundreds of tons of incendiary bombs, all destined for the inferno that surely Dresden had already become.

He began to feel strange. The plane seemed to tilt, even though there was a clear horizon formed by the smooth, level top of the cloud stratum below. Brillig seemed to be descending earthward in a long, sweeping dive to the left. He wondered if it was all another nightmare. He looked up and to his right. The stream of B-17s was still there, heading for Dresden. How the hell many B-17s do they need to destroy one railroad yard? No. Dear Christ, no! He wasn't making it up! He closed his eyes and he felt the plane rolling over and over, much as his bed had rolled at Cynthia's place when he'd had too much to drink. He fell asleep.

When he awakened, he lingered in the demimonde of half-wakefulness for a time. He shook his head the quick one-two shake and glanced at Bradley. Bradley was watching him, smiling. Bradley bare-headed, no helmet, no oxygen mask, no goggles. He glanced at the altimeter. Four thousand feet! They were over water. How long had he slept? He took off his mask, helmet, and goggles and took over the controls.

Not a cloud in sight. The sun was a dull red half-ball on the horizon, about 20 degrees to the left of their course. Strange. The weather had been socked in solid over the target, and now it promised to be absolutely clear over England. When was the last time this happened?

It was 8:48 when they completed their shut-down. He tried to stand up but he had to let himself down again. He stretched his bum leg forward between the rudder pedals for a time. He slowly raised himself from his seat.

Bradley said, "You're getting old."

He nodded. He had strapped himself into his seat before daybreak this morning. He looked at his watch. It was now 8:51. He'd had nothing to eat or drink since the two fried eggs and a piece of toast at 3:00 this morning, yet he was neither hungry nor thirsty. He looked down at Bradley. "Thanks for doing most of the work today."

Bradley said, "How do you figure that big black cloud? It could be we hit one of the biggest oil storage farms in Germany. Maybe that's why they sent so many planes to that one target today. Maybe they knew they had something big there."

Robb stared into the blackness beyond the windshield. Finally he said softly, "I don't know, Monk. I don't know."

Bradley watched Robb out of the corner of his eye. "I'll fill out the forms and I'll run the inspection with the crew chief as soon as I finish the forms."

He squeezed Bradley's shoulder. "Thanks, Monk."

Robb hadn't been at the whiskey tables for more than ten minutes when Bradley showed up with Fritz Carlson and Will Richards. Robb said, "That was a fast inspection." He picked up a double shot and handed it to Bradley.

Bradley's face had a bluish, greasy shine in the harsh light of the bare bulbs strung over the whiskey tables. "Not too bad a haul, all in all, was it?" Robb said nothing. He handed Robb a drink.   "Still down in the dumps, huh?"

Robb threw back the shot. "Let's go in and get debriefing over with."

Sam stood up and shook hands with Brillig's four officers. "How was it?"

Bradley said, "Not too bad."

"Anything in particular to report? Any one of you?"

"Nothing," Robb said quietly.

Bradley said, "Just the biggest black cloud of smoke you ever saw churning up through the undercast. Smack over the target and several miles wide."

"Anything else?" No one responded. Sam said, "That's it, then. Thank you."

Bradley said, "This has to be the shortest debriefing ever."

Sam again shook hands with Robb. "Welcome back. I already said that, didn't I?"

The dimly lit, sparsely populated mess hall had the barren, lonely aura of a cheap cafeteria in a big city at midnight. The air was heavy with the smell of steam-table food. Robb ate half of a Spam sandwich. Bradley consumed a can of Spam, a mound of fried potatoes and a half-loaf of bread. After dinner they went into the club for a drink. The club was deserted; the face on the mug on the back bar was turned toward the wall. The 990th was alerted.

—42—

Breakfast for flying personnel of the 990th Heavy Bombardment Group was at 3:15 on the morning of Thursday, February 15, 1945. Robb ate two pieces of toast and a square of fried Spam and drank five mugs of black coffee. He gave Bradley his ceremonial two fried eggs.

Robb and Bradley sat in the last row at briefing. The flying officers talked in muted tones while they awaited the announcement of today's target. All talk ceased when Sam Prentice stood up. All eyes followed him as he walked to the shrouded map. Sam pulled back the curtain and announced, "Today's target is the same as yesterday's! Dresden!"

Bradley stopped to take Communion, but Robb went on out the door without a glance. He caught a truck just as it started rolling. Bradley hurried out after taking Communion but Robb was gone.

Again, as yesterday, Robb climbed into the plane through the waist door rather than following his usual practice of hoisting himself up through the hatch in the floor of the nose compartment. He flicked his flashlight on as he entered the bomb-bay. Again the bundles of luminescent white sticks. He turned off his flashlight immediately. He felt his way along the catwalk to the flight deck. He slipped into his seat and closed his eyes. Bradley slipped into his seat five minutes later.

He was startled when Bradley spoke. "Shall I have them pull the props through now?"

Robb nodded. He put on his earphones and snapped his throat-mike garter around his neck. He lifted his right earphone and placed it against his head above his right ear so he could hear Bradley and still monitor the command channel. Bradley proceeded to call out the items on the pre-startup checklist. Robb perfunctorily tapped the various dials, switches and controls as Bradley called out each item. Bradley put his hand on Number One energizer switch. He looked at Robb. Robb nodded.

They completed the run-ups and final engine checks and ran through the remaining checklists. The engines idled smoothly at 800 RPM while they waited for orders to taxi. Colonel Strang's voice rang out from the tower. "This is Upshaw Command. First echelon, Amber Squadron, roll!"

Amber Squadron was the lead squadron today. Robb's position within the squadron was the same as yesterday: Number Five. A B-17 taxied past them on the apron, closely followed by the other two planes of the first echelon.

"Second echelon, Amber Squadron, roll!"

Number Four taxied past Robb's windshield. It was now Robb's turn to pull out on to the apron. He released the hand brake and placed his hand on the throttles, but he didn't advance them, and he kept full pressure on the foot brakes. Bradley looked at him curiously. Robb's face was impassive, eerily reflecting the green phosphorescent glow of the instrument panel. Robb made no move.

The C.O.'s voice snapped loudly in the ears of every pilot in the Group. "Amber Uncle! Get going!"

Robb sat still, his hand on the throttles, his eyes fixed on the tachometers.

"Amber Uncle! Acknowledge!"

Robb pushed the button on the control wheel. "Amber Uncle," he said.

"Amber Uncle. Do you have a problem? Report! You're holding up the Group!"

Robb pushed his button. "Upshaw Command. This is Amber Uncle. I'm not going today. I'm shutting down engines."

"Amber Uncle. Explain why you are shutting down. Quickly!"

"Upshaw Commander. I'm shutting down because I am not going to today's target. My reasons are personal."

"Amber Uncle. Are you sick?"

"Negative."

"Are your crew and plane all right?"

"Roger."

"Now listen carefully, Captain Robertson. This is Colonel Strang, your Commanding Officer." His words were measured, crisp. "I'm giving you a direct order to taxi now, and to take off and to fly to Germany to face the enemy with the other flyers in this Bombardment Group. Do you read me? Over."

"Roger."

"I'm giving you one last chance to start taxiing."

"I'm not going, sir."

"Captain Robertson, this is Upshaw Command. Do you appreciate the seriousness of your act? You will be charged with disobeying your commander's order to face the enemy."

"I understand. I'm shutting them down now. Over and out." He switched off his command transmitter.

Every pilot in the Group heard the exchange, and every one of them knew that according the Articles of War the punishment for refusal to obey one's commander's order to face of the enemy could be life in prison. Some thought it was death by firing squad.

Robb reached across the throttle pedestal and pulled Number One ignition switch to "off" and advanced throttle Number One to full open. Bradley reached for Number Two switch. Robb grasped his wrist and pulled his hand away from the switches. He proceeded to shut down the other engines.

He shut down the various systems, occasionally half-standing and reaching to the far side of the instrument panel beyond Bradley to reach a switch. Bradley reached for the intercooler controls but Robb reached across him and grasped his wrist and pulled his hand back.

The shutdown completed, Robb sat very still in his seat, staring into the blank wall of night beyond the windshield. Bradley watched him. He had heard the exchange and he still couldn't believe what he heard. "What's the matter, Robb? Are you all right?"

"I'm all right." He switched to intercom. "Pilot to crew. We're not going on today's mission. I'm ordering each one of you to return to the squadron area. I want each one of you to understand that you are being sent to the squadron area by direct orders from me. As of this moment I'm turning over command of this crew to Lieutenant Bradley. From now on you are to take your orders from him. Over and out." Robb remained in his seat, staring into the night.

Bradley finally spoke. "Do you want to tell me about it?"

"Did you hear me and the C.O. on the command channel?"

"I heard it."

Carlson and Richards emerged from the nose compartment. Robb turned to them. "Did you hear the transmission between me and the C.O?"

 Carlson said, "We're with you Robb, no matter what happens."

"No! You are *not* with me in this! Don't ever say anything like that again!"

Richards said, "We want to help."

"No! You can't help me and you must not even offer to help me! I'm all right. The two of you had better check in your kits and start for the squadron area."

Carlson said, We're with you, Robb, and I don't give a damn what you want." The two lieutenants dropped back into the nose compartment.

Robb turned to Bradley. "I'd appreciate it if you'd fill out the forms and put the ship to bed." He raised himself from his seat. "You're going to have to get used to filling out the forms."   He held out his hand. "See you, Monk. I'll never forget you."

"Damn it, Robb! Don't talk like that. You're not going to the moon!"

"I don't know about that," he said as he dropped through the hatch.

The four enlisted men behind the counter in the equipment room were in high spirits. There would be no more work for them until the Group returned late this evening. Robb could hear their boisterous banter as he approached the building. Their laughter ceased when they saw Captain Robertson in the doorway. The private who accepted his medical and escape kits avoided his eyes, and he seemed to look away when he handed Robb his receipt. Robb wondered, had the word reached these men already? But he really didn't care.

He went to G-2 to turn in his maps and charts. Sam stood up when Robb entered the office. He moved quickly around his desk and threw an arm around Robb's shoulders. "Sit down here, Robb." Robb remained standing, his face impassive.

"I heard about it. I'll do anything I can to help. I'll gladly take the rap with you."

"What good would that do? Don't do anything. Don't say anything. The subject is closed." His tone was flat, colorless.

"I'd rather be dragged down with you than watch you take this alone."

"That would serve no purpose. I know you'd help me if you could." He turned and left the office before Sam could respond.

"But Robb! Wait a minute!" The door closed on his words.

He started up the hall, toward the C.O's office. He didn't see Evelyn standing farther down the hall. He stopped and turned when he heard her call. She rushed up to him. "Oh Robb! Robb!" She embraced him, pulling him very tightly to her.

"It's all right," he said softly. "It really is." He stroked her hair gently.

He held her away from him and looked into her eyes. She had been crying.

"What is going to happen to you? What will they do to you?"

He drew her back to him. "I don't worry about the future, remember?"

"I want to help. What can I do?"

"I don't want you to do anything." He spoke just above a whisper. "The best thing you can do for me is to do nothing. I don't even want you to speak to anyone in my favor. I want you to promise me you'll not say one word to anyone in support of me."

"I won't promise that."

"Please. You must not say or do anything that would seem to put you in my corner."

"I can't promise that. Ever. I love you now more than ever." Her eyes filled with tears.

"I've got to go now. I'll always cherish what you just said to me." He held her head against his chest. He kissed the top of her head. She stood on her toes and kissed him on his mouth. He turned quickly and walked down the hall toward the C.O.'s office.

He didn't notice Corporal Susan James' astonishment as he walked past her desk. He simply opened the Colonel's door and walked in. Colonel Strang was on the phone. "Something has come up. I'll call you back." He stared wide-eyed at Robb.

"You're required to arrest me." His voice was flat, devoid of expression.

"Arrest hell! You're coming with me to the flight surgeon!" Colonel
Strang grabbed his trench coat and garrison cap and started
for the door. Robb hung back. "Damn it, Robb! Come on!"

Strang sat next to Robb in the back seat of the Colonel's car. The
C.O.'s countenance was grim, the muscles at the hinge of his jaw working. Robb sat calmly in his corner, looking out the window to the east
where the first light of day showed faintly above the trees on the eastern
perimeter of the airfield. The Group would be crossing the Dutch coast
about now. The people of Dresden would still be sleeping, unaware that
a force of several hundred bombers would hit their city again today.

No, he corrected himself. That's not right. The people of Dresden
aren't sleeping, except for those whose sleep is permanent. The people of
Dresden are fleeing the City of Ashes on this day, the day after their
Ash Wednesday. And those who remain will be fighting the fires and
digging in the rubble for survivors. Or for non-survivors.

Will they be shocked to see the massive formations approaching
their city yet again, after the night before last and after yesterday? Will
they be shocked? Or are they beyond shock? He wondered, did the
RAF go back again to Dresden last night? Will the weather be clear over
Dresden today? Will our crews see the Armageddon we and the RAF
created? No. Not Armageddon. Armageddon was the last battle between good and evil. The distinction no longer makes sense.

Why Dresden? Why did the finger on the map, the finger with the
power of life and death over hundreds of thousands, stop on Dresden?
Is Dresden a surrender to war-lust on the highest policy level—the lust
that inevitably grows in all wars as they wear on and death becomes
commonplace and palates become jaded? Is this giant step toward total
barbarism the first expression of a new Allied policy?

Why did the finger stop on Dresden rather than, say, Munich, Germany's other Paris? He nodded to himself as the answer occurred to him.
If Munich had been selected for total annihilation the Russians now
bearing down on Germany's eastern boundaries wouldn't see the massed
might of the West and its determination to use it. Now you know, Russian Allies, that neither you nor the Nazis have a monopoly on unbridled
savagery!

Colonel Strang said, "Robb." He spoke louder. "Robb?" No response. He ran his hand before Robb's eyes. Robb didn't see it. The Colonel sighed and shook his head.

The Colonel's hand had in no way obstructed Robb's view of the bomber stream, nor did it interrupt his dialogue with the Russians. And, Russians, try to remember Dresden when we start talking about who won this war and who gets what. Or maybe this is revenge, pure and simple, payment in kind for Coventry, London, Bristol, Southhampton and the rest. True, the Nazis started this wild, indiscriminate killing—hell, they *invented it* in its modern aerial form, but do you pay them back by killing their children? Has it come to that? Did it occur to you, Air Marshal Harris or whoever it was who called this shot, that thousands of those children who died in Dresden yesterday and who will die today weren't even born at the time of the Germans bombed Coventry?

Maybe the American or British leaders figure this annihilation of Dresden will shorten the war, that the German leaders will sue for peace. Hah! Don't you know that Hitler and his gang may even yearn for a Wagnerian Gotterdammerung, a twilight worthy of their exalted, god-like estate? Would Siegfried have grieved at the sight of Dresden's ashes? Or would he have gloried in those ashes in his mysterious Teutonic love-hate relationship with death?

"Robb."

No doubt the people on the highest level of command, the ghouls who called this shot, defended their decision by arguing "But they did it to us first to us!" An eye for an eye and a tooth for a tooth! A Dresden for a Coventry! But didn't we learn two thousand years ago that revenge is no longer ours?

"Robb."

Goddamn it! Don't they know that every rotten stinking war that lasts long enough becomes a contest to see who becomes the most barbaric?

"Robb! What the hell's the matter with you?" Colonel Strang's voice. Robb blinked and looked around. The car had stopped in front of the base hospital. Colonel Strang was standing on the ground leaning into the car. Robb slid across the seat and stepped out of the car. The driver closed the door behind him.

"Damn it, Robb! Get hold of yourself! Your mind is a thousand miles away!"

Colonel Strang walked rapidly to the entrance of the hospital, but Robb made no effort to keep up. Strang waited for Robb before he knocked on Rizzo's door. Rizzo stood up when his commanding officer entered the room.

Strang said, "I suppose you heard about this business this morning? I mean about Robb?"

Rizzo nodded sadly. "I heard about it." He shot a glance at Robb, now standing by the door. "Sit down, Robb, please."

"All right, Tony. Robb's one hell of a sick guy. He says he's not, but I know he is. He's been acting pretty nutty lately, but I guess you know that. On the way here his mind was a thousand miles away. I had to shake him to bring him back to life, even though his eyes were open. I ran my hand in front of his face twice on the way here and he didn't even notice. We've got a classical case of combat fatigue here, Doc."

"I'll examine him, Colonel. Let me walk with you to the outer door. I'll be right back, Robb." Rizzo turned back toward Robb as he opened the door. "Someone will be in to take a blood sample."

Robb stood up and walked to the window facing the front of the hospital. The gray-black dawn had modulated into another English winter day, a day that promised grayness and gloom. He saw the Colonel's driver sitting behind the wheel of the staff car, but the image didn't register.

As he looked eastward, his mind turned to the Group. For a moment he was at the controls of Brillig, droning steadily toward Dresden in the middle of a broad river of shining aluminum flowing across Germany. It occurred to him that right about now a German farmer might look up and see the endless, mile-wide flow of bombers stretching from west to east as far as he could see. What an awesome sight that must be! And if it's the beginning of a sunny day he'll see the vapor-trails of hundreds of huge airplanes, maybe a thousand, merge, creating a solid overcast that will blot out his sun for the rest of the day. What will he think when he sees that? What kind of sense can a simple farmer make of it? What kind of sense can anyone make of it? There was a knock on the door. If Robb heard it he gave no indication. The door opened and Merrie came in. She closed the door behind her.

"Robb! Dear Robb!" She threw her arms around him and hugged him tightly, burying her face against his shoulder. He embraced her. She backed away to appraise him. "I'm so sorry, Robb. I feel so awful about it."

"It's all right. Really."

"Why did you do it?"

He looked at her sadly, absently. "I can't talk about that now.   Not to anyone."

"I wish I could do something."

"You already have. Your friendship means more now than ever." He embraced her briefly again. "I think you're supposed to take some of my blood."

She sighed. "All right. Take off your jacket, please, and roll up your sleeve." She thrust a thermometer into his mouth and prepared to measure his blood pressure. "I just wanted you to know how bad I feel about it and . . ."

She stopped short as the door opened. Captain Rizzo came in.

Rizzo leaned back in his swivel chair, closely observing Robb as Merrie stuck a needle into a vein on the inside of his arm. Rizzo's face was long, and infinitely sad. He wore what Stosh used to call his "Basset hound look". Merrie wrote something on the form on her clipboard, picked up the blood sample, and left the room. Rizzo studied Robb's face for a time after the door closed. "Do you want to tell me why you did it?"

"There's nothing to tell."

"That's not much of an answer, considering what happened this morning." The flight surgeon pulled a pack of Camels out of the inside pocket of his uniform coat. He withdrew a cigarette and tossed the package to Robb. He stood up and leaned across the desk and gave Robb a light and then lit his own cigarette, inhaling deeply. "Well?" Rizzo looked at him intently, his eyebrows arched.

"I don't want to talk about it."

"Bullshit! Don't give me that I-don't-want-to-talk-about-it crap!"

"I mean it. I'm not going to talk about it."

Rizzo sighed. "All right. Have it your way." He took a deep pull on his cigarette. "How have you been feeling lately?"

"Fine."

"Sleeping okay?"

"Okay, under the circumstances."

Rizzo nodded thoughtfully. "Eating?"

"Same answer, pal." Robb's inadvertent imitation of Stosh reminded him of how close the four of them had been—Stosh, Tony, Sam, and himself—for almost three years. They had been together at Walla Walla when the Group was formed, and they had come over together when the air base was a single runway surrounded by army wall tents.

"Look, Robb. I'm not going to go through a long checklist with you. Just tell me this. Do you have any symptoms, physical or mental, I should know about?"

"I'm all right."

"Are you worried?"

"About what?"

"About what? You ask about what!" Rizzo's arms and eyes reached heavenward in entreaty. "You know fucking well about what! You're in one hell of a jam, the jam of your life, and you ask 'about what'!" Rizzo's hands continued to speak eloquently. "I'm beginning to think the C.O. is right. Maybe you *are* nuts."

"Look me in the eye and say that, doctor." Robb smiled genuinely.

Rizzo crushed his cigarette in the ashtray on his desk. "Tell me —no crap now, just as a friend to a friend—why did you do it?"

Robb stared absently across the room. "The question is, 'Why *didn't* I do it.'"

"All right, goddamn it. Why *didn't* you do it?"

"My reasons are personal."

"Get off it! Are you going to sit there and tell me it's too personal to tell *me*, one of your closest friends?" Rizzo got up and came around and sat on the front edge of his desk. "I could ground you for medical reasons, you know. After all, you're nearing the end of your second tour. If you're not suffering from combat fatigue, you should be."

"But I'm not, and you wouldn't fake it any more than I would."

"Don't be so fucking sure of that, pal." His imitation of Kovacs was pretty good.

"I know you too well. You're a man with a conscience and you're stuck with it."

"Let me ask you one more question. Now think about this carefully. I may have to testify under oath about the answer you give." Rizzo lit another cigarette. "If the Group goes out tomorrow and your squadron is scheduled to fly, will you go on the mission?"

Robb got up and walked to the window. The sky had turned ominous. Heavy gray clouds scudded low across the air base at right angles to the main runway. The first cold drops of rain spotted the asphalt stoop where the gravel began. Some of the raindrops glanced off the hard surface and bounced along the ground. Ice. He heard the sleet's tattoo on the window pane. He returned to his chair. He spoke absently. "It will be night when they get back and this weather could get worse. It's bad enough now but it could get worse. Much worse."

"Would you go on the mission tomorrow? Or whenever your squadron flies next?"

Robb said, "Maybe whoever is leading will get them under this crap before. . . ."

"Goddamn it, Robb! Knock it off and answer my question! Would you go tomorrow?"

Robb sat in silence for a time. Finally he said, "That depends on the target."

"What do you mean?" Rizzo's expression was wary.

"If the target is Dresden, the answer is 'no'. Or if it's another Dresden type of operation, regardless of what city, the answer is 'no.'"

"If the target tomorrow is Merseburg—the Leuna Oil refineries—would you go?"

"Yes."

"But if the target is Dresden, you'd refuse?"

"Yes." He closed his eyes. "I'd have no choice." He blinked and stood up and returned to the window and looked out. The sleet was blowing near horizontally now. He watched as the sleet accumulated at the edge of the walk. He remembered Martin Luther's words. He whispered them to himself, barely audibly, "God help me. I can do no other."

But Rizzo heard it. The Flight Surgeon walked slowly to the window. The two men stood side by side, mute spectators to nature's ominous promise for the men now climbing inexorably toward Dresden. Rizzo, still staring out at the day so rich with impending doom, put his hand on his friend's shoulder. "I understand, Robb. I wish I didn't. God how I wish I didn't."

Robb turned and walked to his chair. He rolled down the sleeve of his flying coveralls and picked up his flight jacket. He turned to Rizzo. "Is that it, then?"

Rizzo nodded, but as Robb opened the door he crossed the room quickly and closed the door before Robb could leave. He spoke softly, intently. "You know, don't you, that the position you're taking is the one position for which there is no defense. You calmly broadcast your refusal to fly, not only to your Commanding Officer but to every other pilot in the Group. You could lie kicking and screaming on the hardstand under your plane, and we could help you. You could scream over the command channel telling the C.O. to go fuck himself, that you've had it and you're not going on any more missions. That might be evidence of a breakdown, and we could all of us—the C.O., me, Sam, all of us—we could all of us stand behind you and not let them hurt you any more. God knows you've done your job so far beyond the call of duty that this nation could never adequately acknowledge it no matter how many fucking medals they gave you."

"I'm going now."

"No! Goddamn it! You're going to hear me out! I was about to say that history will eventually put you and every other man who went to Schweinfurt or Regensburg in the same class, for bravery, with the Charge of the Light Brigade or the Confederate soldiers who charged up the hill at Gettysburg, however ill-conceived the battles . . . "

"I'm getting out of here." He reached for the doorknob. Rizzo grabbed his wrist.

"Listen, Robb. This is very important. You declared to me just now that you're willing to bomb one target but not another, according to the dictates of your conscience. They can't let that go. They could cover up almost anything else, given your record, but not that. Incredible though it is, you will probably be charged with refusal to obey your C.O.'s order to face the enemy."

"I know."

"One more thing before you go. The C.O. told me to tell you you're under arrest. Confined to quarters. You're to go directly to your barracks or your squadron orderly room. I'm sorry, Robb." Robb put his hand on

Rizzo's shoulder for a brief moment. He stepped into the hall and slowly closed the door behind him.

Captain Anthony Rizzo stood in the window and watched Robb, collar up, hands in pockets, lower his shoulder into the wind as the driving sleet swept horizontally across his path. He watched until his friend disappeared over a slight rise in the road that led to Amber Squadron Area, a mile and a half down the road.

Rizzo sat for a long time with his elbows propped on his desk, the heels of his hands in his eye-sockets. After several minutes his right hand dropped to the lower right-hand drawer of his desk. He took a bottle of Scotch out of the drawer. He took a pull on the bottle and put it back in the drawer.

✻ ✻ ✻ ✻ ✻ ✻ ✻ ✻

If the interior of the barracks was warmer than the outside on this mid-February morning it was because the corrugated steel afforded protection from the wind and the driving sleet. But the temperature, both outdoors and in, hovered in the teens. The tiny stove at the center of the room was cold.

Robb climbed into the sack. Exhausted though he was, he couldn't sleep. The pain that would not let him sleep was not the pain of fear. He had no fear whatsoever of what the Army might do to him. His was the pain of melancholy, a sadness the depths of which he had never imagined possible. It was the sadness of total defeat.

The pain in his chest was as real as if someone had placed a blunt instrument against his chest, a shovel handle perhaps, or the blunt end of a pool cue-stick, and was pressing it with all his strength against his heart. He threw back the blankets and coats and went to the door of the barracks and opened it wide. The sharp ice slivers bit into his face as the wind blew straight into the doorway. There was relief in the very sting of the driving ice crystals. The pain in his chest seemed to subside a little.

He went to his foot locker and took out his shaving kit and reached into it. He knew he'd find relief now. He felt about inside the case. He took the case to the door and held the inside of it to the daylight. His aluminum soap tray wasn't there. A bewildered expression crossed his face, but only for a moment. A scene—Cynthia gathering together his

toilet articles—flashed across his mind. The meaning of what he had just
seen in his mind's eye was slow in coming. The meaning finally penetrated his dulled consciousness. Cynthia's words, "If you die, I die." The
pain in his chest ceased and the darkness of this day and the cold deserted ugliness of the barracks ceased and all that was left was numbness,
a near-nothingness of time, place, and being. He moved slowly to his
bunk and climbed into it and pulled the blankets and coats over his head.

Some two hours later Private Swovik stepped out of the orderly
room and climbed into the Squadron Commander's jeep to warm it up,
per orders from Sergeant Kerrigan. As he waited for the engine to warm
up, he noticed the door to one of the barracks was wide open. He got out
of the jeep and walked to the barracks. He saw the occupied bunk and he
studied it carefully. He saw at last a slight rise and fall of the mound. He
closed the door quietly and returned to the jeep.

✻ ✻ ✻ ✻ ✻ ✻ ✻ ✻

Sam Prentice and Colonel Strang left for Division shortly after
Strang left the hospital after delivering Robb to Tony Rizzo. They arrived at Division in time for the briefing for a mission that was planned
for the Eastern Front. The briefing, which should have taken no more
than a couple of hours, took all day. Plans had to be altered constantly as
newly developed weather information arrived. The gathered brass finally
agreed that the only available target for tomorrow was the German submarine base at Brest, on the Bay of Biscay, far from the crappy weather
on the Eastern Front.

Sam and the Colonel finally got back to Allsford Lynn at 2015
hours, just as the lights of the first planes returning from Dresden appeared low in the eastern sky.

Sam had lived through a schizoid day. On the surface his thoughts
had followed the business at hand, first the seemingly endless briefing at
Division and then, after their return to Allsford Lynn, the de-briefing of
the crews returning from Dresden. But on a deeper level his consciousness was constantly occupied with Robb's incredible life-and-death
predicament.

He began work on his mission report immediately upon winding up
his interview with the last crew from Dresden. It was 2348 hours when

he finished his report and handed it in to Colonel Crick for relay to Division. Too late to look in on Robb.

At 0630 on Friday morning Sam stood at the front of the briefing room as the crews, their morale sky high, departed for the equipment rooms. He still felt the warmth of their response to him when he announced today's target, the milk run of milk runs: the German submarine pens at Brest. His moment of good feeling was brief. His thoughts turned to Robb. He reflected that these men now leaving the briefing room had been to Dresden yesterday and the day before, and yet they were as happy as a bunch of schoolboys suddenly given the day off. Somehow they hadn't seen what Robb had seen at Dresden or, perhaps more correctly, they didn't interpret what they had seen in the way Robb had. How did it happen that Robb saw what he saw and interpreted it as he did, while all these others—surely almost all—apparently didn't see or interpret the events as Robb had? Perhaps it was Robb's perpetual preoccupation with the consequences of their bombing in general—the death and destruction they wrought—that sensitized him to what he saw, or thought he saw, at Dresden.

Actually, Sam himself had not been apprised of the overall Dresden strategy. There had been no briefing for him or the C.O. at Wing or at Division. The 990th's instructions for the Dresden raids had come from on high and had been terse and to the point. Sam still felt uneasy about the whole business, and doubtful about the effectiveness of incendiaries for bombing railroad yards.

As soon as the last plane cleared the runway, Sam hurried to his jeep and headed for Amber Squadron Area. The sun was shining brightly, the temperature hovering around ten degrees when Sam stepped into the barracks. He closed the door behind him quickly. He found the light switch and flicked it on. The two bulbs, one at each end of the barracks, cast forth their ugly, bare-bulb half-light. He stood for a moment surveying the oval-roofed, corrugated steel cave.

All but one of the bunks were covered with thrown back, disheveled piles of green army blankets, jackets, overcoats and other parts of uniforms called upon to serve as blankets. The mound of the first bunk on the left remained rounded and intact. He sat down on the chair next to Robb's bunk. "Robb," he said softly. No movement. "Robb! Are you awake?" He sat still for a time. Then the mound moved ever so slightly.

Robb pushed back the blankets and coats from his head and the upper part of his body. He looked at Sam, but he didn't speak. He was
wearing the flying coveralls he had worn yesterday morning. He was
unshaven and his eyes were bleary. His face was greasy with the unwashed shine of sleep and his hair was damp and matted against his
forehead.

"Have you eaten today?"

"I'm not hungry."

It occurred to Sam he may not have eaten since three o'clock yesterday morning, over thirty hours ago. "Did you eat yesterday?"

"What difference does it make?"

"I want to help you, Robb. Is there anything I can do?" Robb seemed
not to have heard him. "It's like an ice box in here. You should go to
your orderly room."

Robb shook his head. "Kerrigan."

Sam closed his eyes. He knew Robb would rather freeze to death
than go to the orderly room and have Kerrigan as his jailer. Sam stood
up. "I'll be back in a little while with something for you to eat." He
turned to leave.

"Sam. Call Cynthia. Tell her what happened."

Sam thought for a while. "I really can't tell her much. Everything is
classified. I can't tell her about the mission, or where it was to, and I
can't tell her you refused to fly, or why, because your refusal is probably
classified too. You can see why it would be." He sighed. "I'm sorry.
Robb. I'd like to do it for you. I can't, obviously."

"It's all right."

Sam opened the door. "I'll be back in a little while with something
for you to eat."

"Wait a minute, Sam. I just thought of something. My soap tray.
Whatever you do, don't call Cynthia. Don't tell her what happened."

Sam stepped back inside and stared at Robb. He suddenly realized he
was staring. He tried to soften his expression. "All right, Robb," he
said gently. "I won't call her. I'll be back soon with something for you to
eat." He closed the door softly.

Sam drove back to Group headquarters and went directly to the
C.O.'s office. "Suzie, please tell Colonel Strang I need to see him."

"Captain Rizzo is with him now, sir."

"Tell him anyway, please." She buzzed the Colonel. He asked her to send Sam in.

"Sit down, Sam. Tony and I have been trying to figure out what to do about Robb."

Sam said, "We have an immediate problem, sir. I was just over to check on him. It's below freezing in his barracks. He's been in his bunk since yesterday morning and . . . "

Rizzo said, "Doesn't he know he's allowed to go to his Squadron Orderly Room?"

"He won't go there. Kerrigan."

Rizzo slapped his palm against his forehead. "Shit!"

Strang sighed. "I forgot about Kerrigan,"

Sam looked at the floor. "He hasn't eaten since O three hundred yesterday morning."

Strang looked at Rizzo. "What do you think we should do?"

"I'll take food to him," Sam said, "and when I'm tied up one of my men can do it."

"But he can't stay in bed all day, every day," Rizzo said.

Colonel Strang shook his head slowly. "Let's quit kidding ourselves. He'd be better off in the stockade. It's warm and he'll be fed there."

Sam said, "May I make a suggestion, sir? Could you confine him to the Link shack?"

"Where would he sleep?"

"We could set up a bunk in the storeroom, and there's a latrine with a wash bowl off the main room. My orderly could take his food over to him. "

Strang turned to the Flight Surgeon. "What do you think,?"

"How does Robb get along with Lieutenant Thomas and his instructor, Sergeant. . ."

"Ted Frasker. He gets along fine with both of them."

Strang tapped his pencil on his desk. Finally he said, "Okay, Sam. I'll call Lance Thomas and tell him he has a boarder. You can get Robb and haul him to the Link."

Sam got up quickly. "I'll take him over there now."

——43——

Corporal Susan James brought the C.O. a second cup of coffee without him asking for it. The boss was in a foul mood, just as he had been for the past two weeks, ever since Robb Robertson refused to fly. She seemed sad as she placed the cup on the Colonel's desk. Colonel Strang had spent all of yesterday at Division, waiting to be called to answer questions by Colonel John T. Leonard and the other legal officers who had met from morning until late last night. The investigating board's function was to recommend to Colonel Leonard whether or not one Captain Alvin G. Robertson should be court-martialed for his acts of February 15, 1945, or whether there were extenuating circumstances that might justify some sort of administrative action to punish him for his crime.

Strang squirmed inwardly as he reflected on his testimony of yesterday. He knew he had talked too much, but perhaps some good had come out of it. He testified that while Robertson had been awarded a Distinguished Flying Cross for his deeds on the day of Christmas Eve, he had in fact considered recommending him for an even higher award, but that after reflection he decided that by awarding a higher medal he would be taking something away from the Distinguished Flying Crosses won by men both living and dead whose heroism couldn't possibly have been exceeded by any act or acts he could imagine.

He had gone on to maintain that every man who flew to Schweinfurt or Regensburg a couple of years ago—and Robertson was one of those—should have gotten a Distinguished Flying Cross. It was at that point that the board excused him. As he stood up to leave, he knew he had talked too much, but what the hell, he meant every word he said! When, last night, at 2200 hours, the board still hadn't appeared, Strang was sure the board would recommend a reprimand of some sort. There was no way they would court-martial a man with Robb's record.

Colonel Leonard, one of the Eighth Air Force's top legal officers, finally emerged from the meeting at 2230 hours. He had walked up to Colonel Strang and said in a matter-of-fact tone, "The investigating board recommends, and I concur, that Captain Robertson be tried by court-martial. We'll meet again on Tuesday to decide what the specific charges, of the several possible, will be. Thank you, Colonel Strang. Every legal officer in that room appreciates your strong loyalty to your men, as do I."

Strang felt at the time like he'd been struck in the groin with a rifle butt. He had sat down, dazed. Colonel Leonard had seemed at a loss for words. He hesitated as though he were about to say something, then he simply walked away.

Strang got back from Division at 2330 last night. He had been told before he left Division that his Group was alerted. His orderly awakened him at 0200 hours this morning, a scant two hours after he had hit the sack.

Briefing this morning had been tough on the C.O., what with the Robertson issue preying on his mind. Then, after all was in readiness for the long haul to the Russian Front—always a nightmare of preparations—two simple words had issued forth from Division: "Scrub it." No, Colonel John Strang's mood was not good at all when Corporal James announced over the intercom that there was a First Lieutenant Hagopian, from Division, here to see him, as counsel for Captain Robertson.

Lieutenant Hagopian entered the office with dispatch. He was a small man, fly-weight perhaps by boxing standards. His face was narrow, his dark, piercing eyes set close together. His hair, short even by U.S. Marine standards, was a dark, thick brush. He communicated remarkable strength for such a small man. He walked briskly to the front of the Colonel's desk and executed a snappy salute. Having performed obeisance to military regulations, his tone and style underwent a quick though subtle change. The chasm between a first lieutenant and a full colonel became a minor crevice.

The lieutenant told Colonel Strang he was here to meet with his client, and that he would need the use of a completely private office or room, perhaps for the whole day. Colonel Strang told him he could use the Meteorology Office without fear of interruption.

The lawyer listened as Colonel Strang called Captain Prentice and told him to bring Captain Robertson to Lieutenant Hawkins' office, where he was to meet with a lawyer appointed for him by the Army. And would he tell Captain Robertson that Colonel Strang expected him to be shaved and in his dress uniform. Sam was miffed by the Colonel's extreme formality, until he surmised the lawyer must be with Strang.

While they awaited the arrival of Captain Robertson, Lieutenant Hagopian said, "I would imagine, sir, that Colonel Leonard's decision came as a shock to you".

Strang nodded. "How do you yourself understand the decision, Lieutenant?"

The lieutenant took a document from his briefcase. "I get the impression, sir, that you weren't apprised of all the evidence the investigators dug up here last week."

"What evidence?"

"The other side of Captain Robertson's illustrious record. I have here the document that cooked Captain Robertson's goose yesterday, and which may hang him." He smiled apologetically. "That's a figure of speech." He handed Strang a sheet of paper. Strang's eyes widened as he read. He looked up at Hagopian. "You don't believe Robertson did all these things? Take this one here. It says Robertson impersonated a colonel. That's nuts."

"Robertson is innocent until proven guilty. But that list, and particularly the charge you zeroed in on, is why our hero couldn't simply be sent home. With that staring them in the face, Colonel Leonard had to indict him"

"Who made these charges? Who cooked up this list?"

"A Lieutenant Colonel Horatio Crick and a First Sergeant Kermit Kerrigan."

"Damn!" Strang pounded his fist into his hand as he walked to the window. He trembled as he spoke. "If Robertson did these things I'm going to kill the son of a bitch!"

"Sir. I'm here to do everything I can to see that no one kills Captain Robertson, or sends him to a federal prison for life."

Robb was standing at a window, his back to the door, when Lieutenant Hagopian knocked. He seemed not to have heard the knock.   The lieutenant knocked again. Finally he opened the door a few inches and looked in. "Captain Robertson?"

Robb remained immobile.

The Lieutenant entered the room. "Captain Robertson?" Hagopian stood uncertainly for a moment, then he moved quickly. He strode across the room and stood beside Robertson. "I'm Lieutenant Hagopian, Captain. From Division. I'm your lawyer, if you decide you want me."

Robb continued to stare out the window.

"I'm here to help you, Captain."

Without turning, Robb said, "No one can help me."

"Captain. You outrank me . . . "

"For the moment."

"Can we forget about rank distinctions as I deal with you?"

"I abandoned all that on February 15th."

"Good. Look, Captain, I'm not going to bullshit around. You're up to your ass in trouble. Big trouble. You need me. You need me bad."

No response.

"I'm a damned good lawyer, Captain. You have a right to accept me as your lawyer or to reject me. It's no skin off my dink if you don't want me. But there's a damned good chance the next guy they send over won't be nearly as good a trial lawyer as I am. I'm a hell of a lot better trial man than most of the army prosecutors I've gone up against."

Robb turned and walked to a chair in front of the desk and sat down. He took out a package of Luckies and lit one. "Do you want one of these?"

The lawyer nodded. Robb tossed the package to him. Hagopian pulled a chair around so that it faced Robb. He sat down and leaned forward. "First of all, Colonel Leonard, Division's head legal officer, has decided that you're going to be court-martialed."

Robb seemed not to have heard the ominous words.

"Did you hear me, Captain?" He spoke slowly, enunciating his words carefully. "You are going to be tried by court-martial."

"I've known that since February 15th."

"Well, now it's official. You're not surprised? Or disappointed?"

"No."

"You sure as hell ought to be. If the investigating board had recommended—and Colonel Leonard agreed—not to opt for court-martial, you could have gotten off with an administrative solution to all this—you know, where your colonel and Colonel Leonard agree that you've had it, that you've been in combat too long. You know, give you a one-way ticket back to the States where you'd get a medical discharge, or maybe fly a desk for a while. These things are often handled informally."

"When is the trial?'

"The trial date hasn't been set yet. You have to be arraigned first. That'll be in a week or two, but my guess is the trial will start a week or two after arraignment. Colonel Leonard and his people are meeting tomorrow to decide what the specific charges will be."

"I'm curious. What do you think they'll be?"

"You're curious! You sure as hell ought to be! We'll get to that in a minute. But let me proceed in an orderly manner. In the first place, this isn't like most cases where there is doubt that the accused did what he's charged with. That's not arguable, but some of the circumstances are . . . are circumstances that can exonerate you if we play it right or, if we screw up, hang you. Excuse me, that's a figure of speech."

"Do you think they'll shoot me?"

"No way!"

"There's no chance of that? I seem to remember when they read the Articles of War to us in the Aviation Cadet Corps that refusal to obey your commander's order in the war zone shall be punishable by death or whatever. . . "

"Hold it, Captain! That's not how it's going to work out. Okay. You're right about the Articles of War. In Article 75, called "Misbehavior Before the Enemy", even the slightest misbehavior is punishable by death or such other punishment as a court-martial may direct. And your other assumption—about the war zone—is true. There's an Annotation under Article 75 on 'Misbehavior Before the Enemy' that says you don't have to be in the presence of the enemy to be chargeable under this Article, but simply that your organization was so situated, quote, "as to indicate its involvement in an impending combat.""

"That means they can shoot me."

"No, godammit. Well, technically yes. You were in a situation, at take-off time on the morning you refused to take off, in which involvement with the enemy was much to be expected, but you've got to realize, damn it, that the Eighth isn't run by a bunch of ghoulish bastards who want you to die."

"But they might not have any choice, legally."

"That's how it looks, I know. Your public refusal to obey your commander's order to face the enemy is damned near as serious as cowardice in the face of the enemy. But they're not going to have you shot. So you can forget about that."

"What about life at hard labor?"

"Stop it! How the hell am I going to organize a defense if you insist on running ahead of me like that? Now stop and listen to me."

Robb swung his chair around so that he faced the window across the room.

"All right now. About the charges. There's no way they can lay on you a charge of cowardice in the face of the enemy. Even if they wanted to—which they don't—they couldn't make that one stick. I think the most likely charge will be refusal to obey your commanding officer's order to face the enemy in combat. They can make that stick easily, because they've got a hundred witnesses to the fact that that's exactly what you did."

"What's the punishment for that?"

"A damned long stretch in a federal . . . " Hagopian threw up his hands. "Stop it, damn it! Let's get on with your case."

Robb said nothing.

"Now, assuming that's the big charge, here's our plan for your defense. We build our case around the fact that you were approaching the end of your second tour. You've flown over fifty missions. You're suffering from combat fatigue the likes of which . . ."

"I've already told our flight surgeon I won't go along with that defense."

"I phoned Rizzo last night, right after I got the call that I had been chosen to defend you. He told me about your refusal to let anybody plead combat fatigue for you. But he told me he wouldn't disagree with the defense I'm planning, which is that while you showed no symptoms of combat fatigue, your actions on the morning of the second Dresden mission were ipso facto evidence of extreme combat fatigue. In fact, he said he thought the ipso facto argument *isn't something that could be dismissed lightly*! We're going to make damned sure it can't be dismissed lightly.

"We're going to plead that you're suffering from the effects of the wounds you suffered a few months ago, and the trauma of your outfit losing so many men on Christmas Eve, and that in spite of this you led the whole damned task force to the target and back to . . ."

"Knock it off, damn it!"

"Now wait a minute. This is no time for false modesty. Your life is on the line."

"There's no way I'll sit still and let you lay all that crap on the court. That has nothing to do with why I did what I did."

"Okay. Forget what I said. That was just an illustration. We hammer at the ipso facto combat fatigue angle. Given what you've been through, we can make it damned difficult for that court to convict you of deliberately, rationally, and with due consideration of the consequences, refusing to obey your C.O.'s order to face the enemy in combat."

"It wasn't a case of combat fatigue."

"Who cares? If I say it's combat fatigue, it's combat fatigue, and I'll prove it."

"I'll say it wasn't."

"Shit!" Lieutenant Hagopian got up. He stood in the middle of the room appraising his client. "I'm a lieutenant and you're a captain, but I've got to say something disrespectful."

"I'm getting used to disrespect."

"Do you know what's wrong with you, Captain? You're nuts. You really are."

Robb smiled. "Are you willing to testify to that under oath?"

"There's nothing funny about this. Your life is at stake. I mean literally."

Robb walked around the desk and sat down in Lieutenant Hawkins' desk chair. He opened the lower right hand drawer of the desk and withdrew a bottle of Scotch and two glasses. "Do you want a drink?"

"No thanks. How did you know that whiskey was there?"

"I didn't." He poured himself a drink and threw it back in one motion.

"Do you drink a lot? I mean do you have a drinking problem?"

"No."

"I was hoping we could say your job has driven you to alcoholism. I've gotten a few flyers off on that. Guys who refused to fly."

"Sorry."

"Now I want to ask you a question, one you're sure as hell going to be asked in court. You give the wrong answer and everything else goes down the drain. Now think carefully." The lawyer leaned forward. "Are you willing to fly missions again?"

Robb stared into space.

The lieutenant waited for a time. "Excuse me, Captain. I had thought maybe you were composing your careful answer to my question. Are you?"

No response.

"Captain Robertson!"

"What was that you said?"

"Shit! I said 'shit', Captain!"

"Oh."

"Goddamn it, we're fighting to save your neck! You've got to pay attention to what I'm saying. I asked you if you would fly missions again if given the opportunity."

"Yes, but not if I know they're a Dresden type of operation."

"When the prosecution asks you that on the stand, is that what you intend to say? Do you intend to say you'll only fly missions that you agree with morally? Is that it?"

"I'll fly on any mission they like, provided the target is a specific military target. But I won't go if I have any reason to believe it's a Dresden type of operation."

"That answer will hang you."

Robb poured another drink.

The Lieutenant exhaled loudly. "That answer is going to cook your goose because any army that lets its officers or men decide on moral grounds whether or not they'll participate in particular battles is no longer an army at all. The very thought is bizarre. You know that, don't you?" Hagopian walked back and forth in front of the desk, as though performing in court for a jury. He took a quick look at Robb from time to time. "Quite obviously you're not going to buy any of the kinds of defenses I had in mind. So what sort of defense do you yourself propose?"

"None."

"So in effect you plead guilty, and throw yourself at the mercy of the court."

"I don't intend to enter any plea in the arraignment or in the court-martial."

"They'll hang you."

Robb stared at the empty shot glass in his hand. Hagopian paced back and forth across the room. "You're a hell of a client, Captain. You give me absolutely nothing to work with. You get your ass in the worst possible jam by refusing a direct order to go into combat, and you do it publicly, broadcasting your refusal to every pilot in the Group as well as to your commander." He stopped pacing and looked at Robb. "And so you effectively tied the hands of your commander, who, incidentally, would do anything in the world to get you off, even if it means the end of his career. And he's an academy man."

"I know."

Lieutenant Hagopian paced some more. He seemed to be summing up the case, as though before a jury. "And you tell your flight surgeon you have no signs of combat fatigue, and that if he certifies you as worn out, you'll deny it." He stopped pacing. "Incidentally, your flight surgeon is also willing to sacrifice his career as an army doctor to get you off, by coming out and testifying that anybody who's flown two tours is *ipso facto nuts*, but you've tied his hands on that, too. And your Intelligence Officer, Captain Prentice—I called him up last night—and he's willing to do anything in the world, to sacrifice all, to get you off. He's volunteered to testify that you suffer from extreme absentmindedness, which he found in some psychiatry book is sometimes an autistic response, an irrational retreat from reality. He's willing to push this in the face of the opposite opinion of the psychiatrists, who say you insist that you are normal, and that you in fact are. Even the psychiatrists would like you to fake some symptoms for them, so they could help get you off, but you won't do that either. You really are nuts."

"What do you think they'll do with me?"

"Do you mean after they find you guilty? Do you mean the sentence?"

"Do you think they'll shoot me?"

"I already told you to forget about that."

"That was before I told you I'm not going to enter a plea."

"Even so, you don't have to worry about that."

"I'm not worried about it, one way or the other. I'm curious."

The lawyer looked at him steadily for a time. He sighed. "All right, goddamn it! Whether you're worried about it or not, there's no chance they'll shoot you. I already told you that I don't think your refusal qualifies as cowardice in the face of the enemy. Even if it did, they're not going to have you shot. Not with your record and all your medals and that sort of thing. Speaking of your record, it's not all to the good. In fact, there were several things introduced at the hearing that were damned serious in and of themselves." He took a document out of his briefcase.

"What did Colonel Crick and Sergeant Kerrigan tell them?"

"Ah! So you know who your enemies are!"

Robb continued staring into space.

"I have here a list of violations of military regulations, actually a list of crimes that are alleged to have been committed by you. Crick and Kerrigan gave this list to the investigators. Do you really want to hear all this?"

Robb shrugged.

"Your most serious crime by far, other than the primary one, is impersonating a colonel. This alone is enough to get you a stiff prison sentence. Did you know that?"

Robb walked around the desk and sat down in the chair he had been sitting in earlier. Hagopian sat down opposite him and leaned forward. "Now this one, the impersonation, is one you'll most certainly be charged with and tried on, in addition to your refusal to fly. It's an open and shut case. Crick gave the investigators a photocopy of the form you filled out at the Prestwick motor pool and which you signed 'A. G. Robertson, Colonel, A.C.' And he also presented a deposition from the motor pool sergeant which states that you wore a colonel's insignia at the time."

The lawyer stood up and stared at Robertson in amazement. "All of this just to get you a car! Just to get a car! Do you want to know something, Captain? That was dumb. I mean really dumb! Do you know that if you had stolen a car from some Scotchman up there it wouldn't have been nearly as serious a crime in the eyes of the army?"

Robb remembered Monk's soliloquy on the seriousness of impersonating a colonel.

"Crick told the investigators that he also has comparable evidence against your buddy, one Captain Stanley Kovacs, in whose company you were when he committed the same crime on a couple of other occasions. Of course that makes you an accessory to his crime, and of course he'll be tried for that one too, just as you will be."

"So Crick intends to drag Kovacs into this too." He shook his head slowly, almost indiscernibly, from side to side. "That man is totally devoid of humanity."

"Impersonating a high ranking officer is a very, very serious crime. The whole army system goes down the drain if they don't come down on that one real quick, and hard. I'll do all I can to defend you on this impersonation business, but I don't mind telling you privately that whatever they do to you and Kovacs for this one, you've got it coming."

"Kovacs too?"

"You're damned right!"

"Kovacs is dead."

The Lieutenant's mouth dropped open. "Shit!" He began pacing the room again. "Why the hell didn't someone tell me that?"

"Does Crick's statement identify Kovacs as one of my fellow criminals?"

"No. I read the transcript. He simply told the investigators that he has hard evidence that your best friend also pulled the same thing at Prestwick in your presence, and that he's prepared to enter that evidence at your trial."

"Lieutenant, do you believe that there is that of God in every man?"

"I don't know anything about such things. That's out of my line."

"I thought I believed that, but now, with this performance of Crick's, I can't help but wonder about it." A dreamy, absent look clouded his visage. He said softly, "I don't think I can let Crick do this to Stosh."

"There's not a thing in the world you or anybody else can do to keep him from doing it. He wants to show that your impersonating a colonel wasn't an isolated, impulsive thing, but a regular pattern. The introduction of incriminating evidence against your friend, even though he's dead, can't be quashed by any objections I might make. I'd be overruled, and the court would be right. I know how you feel about it. Hell, I feel the same way, but there's nothing anyone can do about it if Crick chooses to introduce it."

"I can't let him do that."

"That might not be as bad as you think. If Crick brings up Kovacs he could be walking into a trap. If he does I'll be able sooner or later to paint Crick with a brush full of shit. I'll show—indirectly, of course— that Crick was willing to besmirch the names of our fallen heroes and that . . ."

Robb hissed, "If you try to use Stosh in my defense I'll . . . I'll . . ." He was livid, at a loss for words, but his hands declared eloquently that he'd go for Hagopian's throat.

"All right! All right! Settle down. Let's let that go for now."

"Not for now! For good!"

Lieutenant Hagopian sighed. He appraised Robertson carefully for a time. Finally he looked down at the document in his hand. "Continuing now with the other side of your record. Here's the next charge. 'Drinking on mornings before missions.' Kerrigan says he's willing to testify under oath on this."

Robb thought of Stosh's eye openers—one or two swigs of a single shot in a half gallon of grapefruit juice. Just enough to alter the taste of the battery acid.

Hagopian continued, "'Abetting insubordination toward their superi- ors by lower ranking officers and men.' Kerrigan says you and Kovacs repeatedly allowed lower ranking officers and men to refer to Colonel Crick by an obscene name." He looked up quickly. "By the way, what's the obscene name?"

"Colonel Prick."

Hagopian smiled. "I'll buy that. Here's one that's more serious: Crick maintains you were 'grossly insubordinate' toward him in the pres- ence of a large number of officers and men on the evening of December 24, 1944. Were you?"

"Yes."

"You didn't call him Colonel Prick to his face, did you?"

"No."

"Thank God for small favors. Do you want to hear some more? Ex- cuse me. I keep forgetting you're masochistic. The next one is pretty serious. I quote: 'Jeopardizing the safety of his Bombardment Group while the Group was landing after a mission. Captain Robertson led a crippled B-17 to a crash landing adjacent to the main runway while the main body of his Bombardment Group was landing. He did this in direct violation of specific orders from the operations officer in the tower forbidding him to do so.'" Hagopian looked at Robertson. "What about that one?"

Robb recalled T-Tom's plight and Sergeant Willis' paralysis. He wondered what happened to Willis. He wondered. . .

"Captain, I asked you a question."

"I'm sorry. What was that you said?"

"What about this crippled B-17 business?"

"It's a long story."

"Did you in fact lead it in against specific orders from the tower not to?"

"Yes."

"Shit!" Lieutenant Hagopian shook his head slowly from side to side. He sighed. "Do you want to hear some more?"

Robertson shrugged.

"Okay, here's another one. 'Appropriation of government property without proper invoice or authorization.' In other words, stealing. In this case taking emergency oxygen bottles for your own use in your barracks.

"Here's another. Using Army Air Forces' airplanes for your own private purposes. Incidentally, Crick may get your C.O. in hot water on this one. Apparently he gave you permission to use planes for non-military purposes."

"So Strang gets pulled into it too."

"And a couple of other officers get pulled in on this next one. 'Aiding, abetting, and encouraging lower ranking officers in his presence to wear civilian clothes in the war zone during wartime.'"

"I don't remember that one. Do you know what that one is all about?"

"Crick submitted a picture of you and Captain Kovacs and two young lieutenants—women—in evening gowns in some fancy night club or some such place."

"Damn! The picture that photographer took of us in that London club! Stosh kept that picture in his foot locker. Kerrigan must have gone through Stosh's things immediately when he heard Stosh was killed, before I had a chance to go through them. Damn! So Evelyn and Merrie get sucked into the quicksand too."

"That's right. They're in it too."

"What'll they do to them for this dress thing?"

"Demotion, most likely. Maybe getting busted down to enlisted rank. Forfeiture of pay, a big blot on their record, that sort of thing. Of course, with that picture they're as good as convicted."

"Damn!"

"Here's another. 'Encouraging and abetting the dissemination of propaganda subversive to the mission of the army.'"

"I don't get that."

"It seems a member of your crew circulated a mimeographed diatribe on how unfair our country is to its soldiers. You helped him get it typed and mimeographed."

"Brain Child's theory of sacrifice in wartime."

"Brain Child?"

"Sergeant Blum. My radio operator."

"He may be in big trouble over that one. You too, of course, but it's all relative. You're in such big trouble that a lot of these things lose their meaning. But your radio operator could really be in hot water on this one. Spreading anti-military propaganda in wartime while in the service in a war zone is a major crime. Not like taking an oxygen bottle without a requisition. Your Brain Child could go to prison for this one."

"He's dead."

"What! Him too?" The lieutenant walked to the window. He returned to his chair and sat down facing Robertson. "Captain Robertson, I can't tell you how sorry I am about all this. I'd give up my goddamned career too for this case, just like everybody else around here. But I can't see how it would do any good. And I can't see how I can do you any good as a lawyer, given your position." His voice modulated to a lower pitch, and softer. "A position which, really, I understand. I understand it a hell of a lot better than you might think."

Lieutenant Hagopian studied Robb's face for a long time, but Robb seemed unaware of the lawyer's gaze. "I've never seen a case like you. I mean like yours. I'm beginning to wonder if the very wildness, the sheer volume of craziness of this case might not make the court throw up its hands like I'm throwing mine up. There's so much about this case that's so wild it's difficult to make heads or tails of it. Something's missing."

Hagopian got up and walked the floor some more. He stopped in the middle of the room and stared at Robb. "How in the hell did a guy like you manage to get into so much trouble? You, an intelligent, educated, sensitive human being? What's the missing piece in this puzzle? You say it wasn't combat fatigue, and I'm not going to argue that. But there's something hidden here that explains every one of these crazy things you did. What is it? That's not a rhetorical question. I'd like you to try to answer that."

"Was it crazy, my not going to Dresden after I figured out the first time what our side was doing? What we in this Group were doing? What I myself had in fact done the previous day? Was that crazy?"

Hagopian walked to the window. He turned suddenly. "I wasn't talking about Dresden just now. I was talking about all those other things. You know, impersonating a colonel. All that crap. I was look- ing for the missing piece that would explain all of that."

Robb looked up at the lieutenant. "Do those things seem important to you when you think of what we did at Dresden?"

"But you did these crazy things *before* Dresden. You and . . . you and your friend impersonated a colonel long before Dresden."

"Yes, but after several trips to Merseburg."

"What's Merseburg got to do with it?"

"Well, as one of my crew put it, I forget who, flying a bomb run on Merseburg is like playing Russian roulette with a four-shooter. You know, with only one bullet out of a possible four." Robb fell silent.

"So?"

"Stosh and I figured we were going to die one of these days anyway, so impersonating a colonel for five minutes on a few occasions didn't seem like such a big deal."

"You can be damned sure the court is going to think the impersona- tion of a colonel is a damned big deal! And so do I, goddamn it!" Hagopian resumed his pacing as he spoke without looking at Robb. "You know, I can usually make a pretty good guess what sort of judgment the court will make in most cases, but in this one I can't even make a guess. On the one hand there's your great war record, but on the other there's this impersonation of a high-ranking officer along with all those other crimes on the list." Hagopian started his courtroom-pacing again. "Military law doesn't give the court much leeway as regards the punishment for your big one, even though your case is unique. You, a veteran combat pilot going conscientious objector damn near in the face of battle. The Articles don't have a specific provision for your case. No Eighth Air Force court is going to have you shot, but no court can, under the law, give you anything less than a long prison sentence if you're convicted of what we think you'll be charged with."

"That's about how I had it figured."

Lieutenant Hagopian sighed. "I really need a drink, but I'd settle for a cup of coffee. Any way a guy can get a cup of coffee around here?"

"Hit the buzzer on the desk. Suzie will bring it."

He pushed the buzzer. "Suzie. This is Lieutenant Hagopian."

"This is Corporal James."

"Look Corporal. I need a cup of coffee. Okay?"

"Yes, sir."

He turned back to Robertson. "I thought this was the most buddy-buddy base in the whole Eighth, yet she doesn't want to be called Suzie." He shrugged. "We can forget about the rest of the things on this list. You don't mind if I skip the rest of them, do you? We've got one final problem we've got to deal with. This is kind of a sticky one."

Robb looked at him curiously.

"The investigators interviewed each member of your crew. They came up with two findings. One, your crew members think you're the bravest and coolest customer who ever lived. The greatest guy as well and . . ."

"Damn it! Knock it off!"

"All right! All right! The other thing the investigators found is that you've got two real, genuine, certifiable nuts on your crew. I mean real nuts."

"And the two best gunners in the Group."

"Let's see here." He looked at his notes. "A Sergeant Hoyt and a Sergeant Bohall?"

"Yes. They're not crazy. They're from the hills of Kentucky. They have their own codes of conduct and woe unto the man who doesn't understand that."

"That's what I was coming to. Each one of those two, each one separately, told our investigator he'd kill anyone who accused you of cowardice, and they 'don't care who the fuck it is'. Quote, unquote."

He waited for Robb's response. Robb said nothing

"I was asked by my superiors to look into that. What do you make of that?"

"They'll kill anyone who accuses me of cowardice. It's as simple as that."

"What! You actually think they'd kill anyone who accused you of cowardice?"

"I know they would."

"I feel like I'm losing my marbles. This is wild! Really wild! They can't go around threatening to do something like that. People just don't do that, damn it!"

"They're gunners."

"What's that got to do with it?"

"They're in the business of killing. They've been in it for years. Just like me."

"I really want a drink, but I better not take one. You know, Captain, you have an insidious way of making the breaking of laws seem normal." Hagopian lit a cigarette. "Look, we know you're not going to be accused of cowardice in the face of the enemy, but someone might bring it up as one of the alternative charges considered, and let's say these two nuts are called in to testify and happen to be in court at the time. What happens then?"

"You had better warn your court not to use the word cowardice in their presence."

"Come on! That's ridiculous! No two hillbillies can tell a duly constituted court, a panel of high-ranking officers, what they can or can't say in court!"

"I know that. All I'm saying is the members of the court and the prosecutors and the witnesses should be warned of the consequences of their use of that word."

"You almost sound like you agree with these two nuts."

Robb scrutinized the lawyer for a time. "Is it really necessary for me to tell you I disagree with them? That's what this whole trial is about. The killing of innocent people. I'm simply telling you that this is a matter of honor with them, something to be squared by blood vengeance. Once they've decided something like this, nothing can change it."

"Are they armed?"

"Every flyer is required to carry a forty-five caliber Colt Automatic."

"When you're on a mission, but not when you're running around England."

"Hoyt and Boo probably carry their guns wherever they go."

"They've gotta be locked up. That's all there's to it."

"That means the end of two very brave and devoted soldiers. You can't cage those two. They'll keep trying to escape until they're killed."

"What do you recommend?"

"Keep them as far as possible from this trial of mine. They're almost through with their second tour. As soon as they're through discharge them and send them back to eastern Kentucky. Let 'em go back to where they belong."

"I was asked to check if the threat they made was made seriously. I have to report that it was serious. They're going to be locked up, whether you like it or I like it."

"If you put them in jail that's the end of them and undoubtedly other innocent people as well. You can be sure of that."

"How did they survive this long?"

"That's a long story. Ask Monk Bradley about that. Or Sam Prentice. But whatever you do, don't involve them in the trial. Promise me you won't let them put them in jail."

"It's not up to me. They threatened the court, and it's a matter of record. Incidentally, they scared the shit out of our investigator."

Robb got up and walked to the window. He spoke without looking back. "Look at what I've done. Hoyt and Boo are going to be killed by you or your troops in the Judge Advocate's office. The C.O.'s career is seriously compromised by all this. Evelyn and Merrie are going to get busted. Tony Rizzo and Sam Prentice will sure as hell get dragged into this too. And Stosh's name and Brain Child's are going to be dragged through the mud. Did I leave anyone out?"

"Just one other person." He picked up his coat and cap. He studied Robb for a moment. "You." The lawyer walked to the window and stood next to his client. "That about does it, Captain. I'm sorry it turned out this way. What I mean is I'm sorry it's going to turn out the way it's going to, if you stick to your position. Before I go, I've got to ask you. Why won't you go the combat fatigue route? I really think we could win, and we'd take care of all those other charges in this one blanket defense. Please let me go for ipso facto combat fatigue."

Robb continued staring out the window. "I can't."

"I don't get it."

"I'm a witness." Robb whispered, but Hagopian heard him.

"Like hell you are. You're the accused!"

"Let's drop it."

"What do you mean, 'Let's drop it'! You can at least tell me why you can't."

"If you don't understand now why I did what I did, nothing I can say is going to . . ." He closed his eyes for a time. "Let's just drop it."

Hagopian sighed. "Okay. If that's how you want it." He started for the door. As he opened the door he turned to Robertson. "Don't give up hope. Who knows? Maybe something good will happen in the trial, something we haven't even imagined." Robb gave no sign of having heard him as he stared out the window.

Once in the hallway, Lieutenant Hagopian moved with his characteristic bounce. He headed straight for Colonel Strang's office. "Tell the boss I'm here, Corporal."

"I'll tell Colonel Strang you are here, sir." She buzzed the C.O.

Lieutenant Hagopian came right to the point. "Your Captain Robertson intends to remain mute at the arraignment, in effect throwing himself at the mercy of the court. The court may not be in a very merciful mood when they get through hearing the testimony on all those other crimes of his."

"What do you think the charge will be?"

"I'm not sure. As you know this case is unique. As far as I can tell, military law doesn't cover Robertson's type of crime, except in the most general sort of way."

"So now where does this leave us?"

"My guess is they'll charge him under Article 75—'Misbehavior Before the Enemy'—which is so general it covers just about everything from sleeping on guard duty to cowardice in the face of the enemy."

Strang nodded. "That's the way I had it figured. That's why I told Robertson on the tower radio that morning that he'd be charged with refusing his commander's order to face the enemy. Of course we're in a face-the-enemy situation. No one can argue that."

"Exactly, and that's what I told Robertson, but he's still determined to throw himself at the mercy of the court. Of course, when he stands mute at the arraignment I'll enter a 'not guilty' plea for him. I can do that legally, and that's obviously the position I'll take in court, whether Robertson likes it or not."

Strang frowned. "Let's assume he's convicted. What's the likely punishment?"

"As things stand now, we don't have to *assume* he'll be convicted. He did in fact refuse a direct order from you to take off and face the enemy, and the court has a hundred witnesses to his broadcast of his refusal to obey your direct order."

Colonel Strang said, "I know. I know. But what's the worst they'll do to him?"

"As you may know, all violations under Article 75 are punishable by, quote, 'death or such other punishment as a court-martial may direct,' unquote. Assuming he's found guilty of refusing to obey—or disobeying—his commander's order to face the enemy, which fits in a general way under Article 75 regardless of the phraseology of the specific charge, as far as I can see the court has no choice. You and I know they're not going to have him executed, but I think he's in for a long sentence unless we can get him to let me put up a defense."

"But you just said he's as good as convicted."

"I've got a plan, but it requires that I put up a defense that he's not going to like very much. By the way, Colonel, how do you understand his motives in all this? When I asked him why he wouldn't let me go for the combat fatigue defense he just said 'I can't'. When I pushed him to tell me why he can't he got kind of upset. Do you have any clue to all that?"

Colonel Strang stared absently across the room. Finally he said, "Sam Prentice, our intelligence officer, and I talked about this. Prentice is Robertson's best friend. Apparently they've talked about religion on occasion. Prentice told me that Robertson comes from a Quaker background, but that he describes himself as a 'back-sliding Quaker'. Prentice figures he hadn't slid back as far as he thought, so I guess you'd have to call this whole business a case of conscientious objection."

The lawyer exhaled loudly. "Hell! A guy is supposed to declare his conscientious objection *before* he's drafted, not in the middle of a war he's been fighting up to his neck. Besides, Robertson was never drafted. He volunteered to become a pilot. Hell, he even volunteered for a second tour." Hagopian sighed. "You know, Colonel, the more I think about it, the less this looks like an open and shut case. The plan I have in mind might just work. *Without* his approval."

"I don't like the sound of this, but what the hell, I'm grasping at straws."

"Here's what we do. I ask to address the court—which is my legal right—right after the judge advocate's initial presentation. I begin by stating flatly that Robertson is not competent to enter a plea. I ask the court's indulgence to permit me to tell them exactly why I don't think he's competent.

"First off, I tell them that he claims to his flight surgeon and to everyone else that he has no emotional problems, that he really believes that he's all right. Then I give them a real big 'but'. Legally, that's our object, to plant doubts all over the place, doubts that Robertson is as sane as he thinks he is.

"I tell the court—and I offer to testify to this under oath—that Robertson told me he doesn't care in the least whether he's convicted or not, or whether he's shot or sent to prison for life. And I tell the court that I believe him. I do believe him. Do you?"

"Yes."

"Good. Then you can testify to that too. That's the idea. All of us gang up in this—you, Rizzo, and your intelligence officer, who can throw in his absent-minded autistic stuff. Maybe we can get a psychiatrist to admit he may not be as sane as he first appeared. I'm going to talk to the psychiatrists and tell them about Robertson's total lack of concern whether he lives or dies or spends the rest of his life in prison."

"This sounds illegal to me—all of us getting together to cook up testimony like this."

"It's legal, provided we tell the truth. It's perfectly legal for you to maintain that you find his passive acceptance of his possible life imprisonment, as strange. You can also testify that he's been something of an oddball on his second tour. You did think that, didn't you? That's in the investigators' reports."

"Who did they get that from?"

"Your intelligence officer. Was he right?"

"Yes."

"Good! So you testify you saw he was becoming something of an oddball, and that's why you decided not to have him fly as a lead pilot any more."

"I was worried about him, even before the Christmas Eve mission. That's why I put him back in the pack, as a reserve leader rather than as a leader or deputy leader."

"Great! That's the truth and that's all you have to say. Just what you said just now."

"There's something else." Strang hesitated. "He really folded on Christmas Eve, after debriefing. He kind of came apart in here, right here in this office. He left in a hurry and went to the latrine down the hall. He was in there a half hour or more"

"Man! Excuse me, I mean Colonel. That's great! We can really use that!"

"But you've got to remember his best friend was killed a few hours earlier, and two members of his crew, one of them his flight engineer, who was decapitated and swinging from his harness a few feet behind him, all the way back from Germany. He had others who were wounded, and his plane was shot up even before he took over the lead of the Group—and the Task Force. Of course he was exhausted and he hadn't had anything to eat for eighteen hours. A lot of very normal men would have broken down. Maybe I would have."

"Don't say that. Just stop with the word 'exhausted'. Remember everything else you just said. This could save his ass. You tell all that along with the other good things about his record. Was that the night Colonel Crick says he was grossly insubordinate?"

"Yes."

"Good! I'll enjoy fixing Crick on that one!"

Colonel Strang stiffened. "You're not fixing anyone on that one, Lieutenant! I don't care what Robertson had been through that day. There's no excuse for insubordination! And you may be sure I'll testify to that effect, should it come down to that!"

"Okay, okay, Colonel. Sorry I brought it up."

"What about this long list of other crimes, including his impersonation of a colonel? By the way, do you think he really did that?"

"I think you can assume he did. The documentary evidence is irrefutable."

"I'll kill the son of a bitch!"

"All right. But wait until after the trial. They may do it for you. Let me get on with the plan. We argue that this monstrous crime—that's what we'll call this impersonation he did—we argue that this unthinkable act on his part. . . "

"Are you being sarcastic, Lieutenant?"

"Do I seem like the kind of a guy who would be sarcastic?"

"This isn't the time or place to start acting smart-ass. Watch it!" Strang's cold, piercing eyes and the set of his jaw communicated more than his words.

The lieutenant tried to look contrite. "Anyway, we argue that his impersonation of a colonel is the most obvious kind of evidence that he's badly disturbed, and that he has been for a long time. If I may say so, sir, without sounding smart-ass, this is an argument the court will buy, because they will in fact regard the impersonation of a colonel as an unbelievable blasphemy of the worst kind—like pissing on the floor in church in front of the whole congregation. Only a nut would do it."

"What about Kovacs? Crick claims he impersonated a colonel too."

"We maintain that Kovacs was nutty as a fruitcake too, ipso facto, just like Robertson, and for the same reasons. After all, he was coming down the home stretch on his second tour too. He'd been through the slaughterhouse days of Schweinfurt and Regensburg, and through the Merseburg meat grinder several times since, just like Robertson."

"If you bring up Stosh, Robb is going to blow his stack."

"I know. That's part of the plan. I'll say Kovacs was suffering from combat fatigue, ipso facto, like Robertson. I'll say that Kovacs was one of the great heroes of this war."

"Which he was."

"I know that, but let's get back to Robertson. When the time comes, I'll enumerate his medals one by one and I'll read the specific citation for each medal. Then I want you to take the stand and repeat exactly what you said to Colonel Leonard and his people yesterday about you considering him for the Silver Star for the Christmas Eve thing."

"How did you know about that?"

"Colonel Leonard got a copy of the transcript of yesterday's hearing to me before I left Division this morning. You can bet Leonard made some stenotype operator stay up all night getting that transcript ready for me. That in itself says Colonel Leonard doesn't want Robertson hung. He insisted I get together with Robertson immediately, and he wanted me to have all the necessary information to prepare the best possible case for Robertson. Last night Colonel Leonard told me he wanted me to get on it *now*, and when he says now, he means *now*. That's why I called Rizzo last night, and Prentice. Anyway, I really liked what you said about the Silver Star and the rest of that about the guys who went to Schweinfurt and Regensburg, including Robertson."

"I felt like crawling into a hole after I said all that. I meant what I said, but it was embarrassing as hell. I'd rather go to Merseburg again than to say all that again to the court."

"Which is more important, Colonel, your embarrassment or Robertson's life?"

"I didn't say I wouldn't do it. I would, of course. But I don't have to like it."

"Good! That will help a lot." Lieutenant Hagopian got up and paced the floor. "Hmmm . . . there's something else I wanted to ring into this plan, something Prentice told the investigators . . . ah! I remember now. This will really help. Robertson had a brother who was killed on D-Day. I bring this up as another contributing factor to our hero's jumping his trolley. And in my summary to the court, I ask those guys sitting in judgment how they like the thought of sending word to Robertson's old parents back in Iowa . . . "

"Indiana."

"Same thing. Anyway, I ask the Board how they like the idea of sending a message to his folks that not only did you lose one son on D-Day, your only remaining son is going to spend the rest of his life in jail. I can't ask them that in those terms, but what I'll do is work things so every one of those guys on that panel will have a picture in his mind of those old folks in Indiana getting the word that their only surviving son—the one who won all the medals—is going to spend the rest of his days in a federal penitentiary." He looked intently at Strang. "What do you think so far, Colonel?"

The Colonel drummed absently on his desk. "You make quite an impressive case, but you sure as hell make me feel like my hands are dirty."

"Don't worry about that. I promise you in court I'll come off like an eagle scout whose only concern is helping little old ladies across the street."

"You've damned near got me convinced that what you've described is what happened in fact to Robertson during his second tour here. But there's something about it I don't like. It's got a smell about it I don't like. I can't quite put my finger on it."

"You don't want to do too much soul-searching in things like this, Colonel."

"We'd be going smack against Robertson's wishes, but maybe there's no alternative, and you can be damned sure Robertson is going to decide right there and then—when you start the line of defense you just out-lined—to testify, to come back at you. You can't keep him from testifying himself if he wants to, can you?"

"No."

"There goes your case. If he testifies after he sees what we're up to, he'll throw it all into a cocked hat. He's going to blow his stack, right there on the stand."

"That's exactly what I'm hoping he'll do. And once he blows his stack he'll no longer be able to throw anything into any cocked hat. He'll have lost all credibility, and his blowing his stack is going to be prima facie evidence that he's nuts."

"You are a devious man, Lieutenant."

"Thank you, sir. And just to make sure he flips real good there in court—you got to remember, Colonel, he's liable to go passive on us—I'm going to bring up the fact, indirectly, of course, that two of the peo-ple Crick is making out as criminals—Kovacs and the Brain Child—are in fact dead, having died for their country in combat. That will make Crick come up smelling like a slit-trench latrine. Can you imagine any-one stooping so low as to besmirch the names of our fallen heroes? I'll see that the court gets the point."

"But how is this going to help Robertson?"

"I told Robertson I was going to paint Crick with a brush full of shit—indirectly, of course—by letting the court know that in order to make his case against Robertson Crick was willing to defile the memory of our now defenseless fallen heroes. Robertson blew his stack when I told him that. He said he'd kill me with his bare hands right there in court if I try to use Kovacs or Blum in his defense."

"So you'd like him to do just that."

"Exactly! No, not exactly. What I mean is I'd like him to try it. But if he goes for me, that gives us even more dramatic evidence that he's emotionally shot. That would tilt the court our way like nothing else. In fact, if he gets mad enough in court he may be promoted from ipso facto nuts to prima facie nuts. That way they could have Robertson locked up in Section Eight for a while and then, when the shrinks declare they've cured him, they could send him home with a medical discharge."

"There's something screwy about your argument." The colonel tapped his pencil for a time. "Ah. I see the flaw now, and those prosecutors are going to see it too."

"What flaw?"

"First you tell the court Robertson is crazy because of his passivity about whether he lives or dies or goes to prison. Then you use his aggression—the exact opposite kind of thing—as evidence that he's crazy. You can't have it both ways."

"I know it sounds screwy on the face of it, but it's okay. It really is. You can get away with it. I've done this before in court—not precisely like this, of course—and it works. We say Robertson is crazy because he's so passive. Then when he gets aggressive we say that too is evidence that he's nuts. That's the beauty of psychology, sir."

——45——

After Lieutenant Hagopian left, Robb returned to Lieutenant Hawkins' desk, withdrew the whiskey bottle from a drawer and poured a drink. He sat staring at the full shot-glass on the desk for more than an hour, as though mesmerized. When finally he stood up he had no idea how long he had sat there, but when he walked to the window he felt stiff. It was 4:30 P.M., but the gray winter day was already on the edge of night, a cold, wet, winter night.

He turned suddenly and picked up his cap and trench coat. He walked quickly down the hall to the main office. He stopped at Corporal Susan James' desk. "Is Crick in?"

"Uh . . . Captain Robertson, I really can't say." She seemed at a loss. Finally she said, "I'll buzz him, but he may not want to see you, sir."

Robb walked quickly past her and opened the Executive Officer's door. Crick's shout filled the outer office. "Get the hell out of here!"

Robb entered the office and closed the door behind him. "Sir. I'm here to ask you, to beg you, not to bring up Kovacs' name, or Sergeant Blum's name at my trial. No purpose will be served by that."

"I'll do anything I like! Now get the hell out of here!"

"I'm going to plead guilty to all charges. There's no point in bringing them up."

Crick stood up behind his desk, his hands on his hips. "What you plead doesn't mean a hill of beans. It's an open and shut case. You are guilty! Period! But cases like yours are reviewed automatically back in the States, so you can be damned sure I'm entering into the record every last shred of evidence I have against you, *Colonel* Robertson, so that it will be impossible for any court to overturn your conviction."

"Think of their families. They lost their sons. All they've got left is their pride in their sons. Don't spoil that."

"All I care is that you get the maximum sentence. One of two things is going to happen to you. Either you get the firing squad or life in a federal penitentiary. And if you should be unlucky and get life in prison, after a few weeks in the U.S. Army prison here at Litchfield you'll wish to hell you'd gotten the firing squad!" Crick walked around his desk and stood directly in front of Robb. "Another thing. I'm going to see that this Link Shack farce ends pronto. You belong in the stockade and I'm going to see that you get there pronto! Now get the hell out of here!"

Robb opened the door. He stepped into the outer office and was about to close the door behind him when he turned and stepped back into the doorway and faced Crick. He said softly, "God help you."

Crick leaned forward like a drill instructor, his face six inches from Robb's. "God help *me*? God help *me*! Hah! God help *you*! You're the one who's going to be convicted of cowardice! Did you get that? *Cowardice* in the face of the enemy! God help *you!*" Crick shoved Robb out the doorway and slammed the door shut.

Robb sensed the eyes of every clerk and typist in the outer office on him. When he looked up all eyes immediately averted to typewriters or desks. His embarrassment gave way to shock in a split second. There sitting in a chair opposite the payroll clerk was a gunner from Amber Squadron, and in the blink of an eye that it took for him to perceive and recognize the gunner, another image superimposed itself. He saw in his mind Colonel Crick bent forward, clutching his abdomen, staring at a Colt .45 Automatic in Hoyt's hand. And as Robb stood there dumbfounded, he gradually realized that Colonel Crick, by his words just now, had in fact pronounced his own death sentence.

He didn't know whose crew the man was on, but he was certain he was in Amber Squadron. He'd seen him in the Squadron Orderly Room many times. If that man goes back to the Squadron Area and tells what he heard just now, which he most certainly will, Crick is as good as dead.

Robb moved quickly to the gunner. "Sergeant, I need to have a word with you. Come with me for a minute, where we can talk."   "Yes sir."

The man followed him into the hall. Robb opened the door to the officers latrine and was about to enter.

"I'm not allowed to go in there, sir."

"All right. I'll talk to you here. You're from Amber Squadron, aren't you?"

"Yes sir."

"Do you know who I am?"

"Yes sir. Captain Robertson."

"Do you know my gunners?"

"Yes, sir."

"What's your name?'

"Sergeant Rod Hardardt, sir."

"Did you hear what Colonel Crick said just now, when I came out of his office?"

"Yes, sir."

"I have a big favor to ask of you. I want you to promise you'll never repeat what you just heard Colonel Crick say. Not to my gunners, or anyone else."

"I won't repeat it to anyone, sir."

"If you repeat what Colonel Crick said, someone's blood is going to be on your hands. Not my blood. Someone else's. Do you understand?"

"Yes sir. Loud and clear, sir."

"Thank you, Sergeant. How far along on your tour are you?"

"Twenty-six. Nine more to go, sir."

He reached out and shook the gunner's hand. "Good luck, Sergeant."

Robb returned to the main office. As he made his way between the desks toward Lieutenant Vandivier's office, he knew he was being followed by every pair of eyes in the room. He stuck his head into the little cubicle. He whispered, "Evelyn."

She stood up and held her arms out to him. They embraced, much as they had on the morning when his career as an Eighth Air Force pilot ended and his career as a criminal began.

She stood back and looked at him. She spoke in an intense stage whisper. "Robb! Oh Robb! What's going to become of you!" The redness around her eyes was not from a moment's weeping, but told of grief and sleeplessness. He kissed each eyelid and the tears overflowed and he tasted their saltiness.

Robb said, "I'll be all right. No matter what happens I'll be all right. Try to remember that."

She buried her face against his chest.

"Did you hear what Crick yelled as I left his office?"

"Yes," she whispered.

He knew then that at least a dozen people had heard Crick. Word of the incident would spread throughout the base within a matter of hours. He knew the promise he had exacted from the gunner had been an exercise in futility.

He took her into his arms again and he kissed her and she kissed him as they had kissed only once before—on the Saturday night of their weekend in London, before he found Cynthia. "I have to go now," he whispered. "I love you. I will always love you."

He turned and left before she could utter a sound. She sat down and buried her face in her arms on her desk. And she wept. She wept bitterly, even as Merrie had wept for days after last Christmas Eve. The clerks and typists in the outer office, their eyes fixed on papers, desks, or typewriters, pretended they didn't hear her.

Robb walked through the night toward the Link Shack. A foggy vapor rose from the ground as the cold drizzle met the warmer earth. His view of the world grew ever darker as he trudged through the smothering blackness. He told himself that on Ash Wednesday, 1945, England and America had succumbed to the very disease they had fought all these years. He was convinced that both England and America had been defeated completely and forever on Ash Wednesday. He experienced again the bitter taste of defeat, much as he had on the morning of his defection.

He was mildly surprised to find himself at the Link Shack. He had experienced no passage of time. He took out his key, unlocked his prison door and turned on the lights. He sat down at Sergeant Frasker's desk and retrieved the cognac bottle from its drawer and poured himself a drink. He withdrew a record from the file cabinet and placed it on the Link trainer turntable. He climbed into one of the Flight Simulators, put on the earphones, and turned on the set. He was soon fingering the cello part of a Haydn Quartet and in a matter of a minute or two he was oblivious to the myriad problems he and those he loved faced as a result of his refusal to return to Dresden.

Sam Prentice's orderly, Corporal Weatherholt, entered with Robb's evening meal on a mess-hall tray covered by a large, brown paper bag. The corporal placed the bag on the desk and walked to the Link trainer and reached up and touched Robb's shoulder, pointing to the paper bag. Robb turned and nodded, waving his bowing hand at him in thanks without interrupting his fingering the cello part with his left hand.

When the last note of the Quartet died, he reached up and shut off the set, removed his earphones, and climbed out of the Link cockpit. He sat down behind Sergeant Frasker's desk and pulled the tin tray of food out of the bag. He made a sandwich of the Spam and bread and dumped the cold mashed potatoes and army green beans with their inevitable aroma of bacon grease into the paper bag and rolled the bag into a ball. He looked absently at the ceiling. Who in the army decided, he wondered, that the flavor of green beans should be totally masked by the powerful smell of bacon grease? Stosh would have had a theory about that. Ah, well. He took aim on the wire waste basket in the corner across the room and let go with his makeshift basketball. A perfect shot. He took a big bite of the cold Spam sandwich.

He unscrewed the lid from the Mason jar and took a swig of the black coffee. Cold. He picked up the bottle and sloshed cognac into the coffee. He took another drink. Not bad. He took another bite of the sandwich and allowed that this was a damned good sandwich. It didn't occur to him that this was his first meal of the day.

＊　＊　＊　＊　＊　＊　＊　＊

Robb had been gone from headquarters no more than ten minutes when First Sergeant Kermit Kerrigan appeared at Corporal James' desk. "Corporal, tell Colonel Crick that I have an important message for him." She pushed the buzzer and announced Kerrigan.

"Send him in." Crick's tone was cheerful, friendly.

Kerrigan was with the Executive Officer less than two minutes. No sooner had he left when Colonel Crick called Corporal James and asked her to get a long distance number for him. The call went through rapidly. Corporal James placed her phone in its cradle. Some ten minutes later, Crick's voice boomed out over the intercom. "Corporal, get Captain Prentice on the horn and tell him I want him in here pronto. I mean pronto!"

Sam appeared at Corporal James's desk within a minute. "Go on in, sir. Colonel Crick is waiting for you."

Crick obviously knew Sam was standing in front of his desk, yet his eyes remained fixed on a document in his hand for a full minute after Sam's arrival. Sam Prentice, tall, skinny, and rumpled, assumed a posture that approximated parade rest. Crick finally looked up. He scrutinized Sam for a time. "Prentice, I want to know the last name of Robertson's girlfriend up in Scotland. She's a material witness to two of Robertson's major crimes."

"I don't understand, sir."

"She called the base today for Robertson and was put through to Amber Squadron. She told Kerrigan to have Captain Robertson call her—she said 'Cynthia'—at this number in Scotland." Sam turned pale. "Are you going to call her, sir?"

"I already did." Crick watched Sam closely.

"May I ask what you told her, sir?"

"It's not any of your business." He studied Sam for a time. "But maybe I just will make it your business." His mouth smiled but the rest of his face remained rigid. "Yes, by God, I'll tell you exactly what I told her! I told her her friend Robertson is charged with a number of crimes and is locked up, that he's coming up for trial on a charge of refusing to fly to Germany and face the enemy when ordered to do so by his Commanding Officer, and I told her that this is cowardice in the face of the enemy and that he's as good as convicted." His mouth smiled again. "You better believe it, that shook her up plenty."

Sam took off his glasses and began wiping them.

"She asked when she might see him. I told her not for a good many years, if ever."

Sam whispered under his breath, "Oh my God!"

"What was that, Prentice? Speak up!"

"Nothing, sir."

"I asked her if Robertson or Kovacs used Army vehicles to visit her, and I asked her if they wore colonel's insignia. She refused to answer my questions. I told her it made no difference, because the British legal authorities would be calling on her for a sworn deposition, so she might just as well tell me now. She still refused to answer my questions. I asked her her last name and she refused to tell me even that." He leaned forward, his eyes drilling into Sam's. "Here's where you come in, Prentice. We need her last name to file with our request to the British Government to get a sworn deposition from her for us. What is her last name?"

Sam stared through his thick glasses at the wall behind Colonel Crick. Crick stared at Sam. Neither man moved nor spoke

Crick finally broke the silence. "Look, Prentice. I'm giving you a direct order to tell me this Cynthia person's last name. I'm sure you're aware Army Intelligence can get it easily enough through this telephone number. But I need this information now! So I'm giving you one more chance to answer. If you don't you will be formally charged with gross insubordination."

Sam remained silent. Crick seemed to smile as he pushed the button on his desk. "Corporal James. Tell Lieutenant Vandivier to get her ass . . . er, to get in here pronto. And I mean pronto! And when she gets here I want you to come in here with your shorthand notebook."   Evelyn appeared followed closely by Susan James. Evelyn stood beside Sam.

"Sit down, Corporal James. I want you to take down every word spoken in this room from now until I dismiss you."

"Yes, sir."

"Lieutenant Vandivier, I need you as a material witness to an act of direct, gross insubordination." He fixed his eyes on Sam. Sam continued to stare at the wall behind Crick. "Now, this is your last chance. As your immediate superior officer, I order you, Captain Samuel Prentice, to tell me the last name of Captain Alvin Robertson's girlfriend in Scotland, this Cynthia person, whose telephone number in Scotland is Scotland 51205."

Evelyn turned to Sam. "What difference does it make? He can call her anyway?"

"He already has."

Crick said, "You have ten seconds to make up your mind, Captain."

Evelyn said, "Tell him, Sam. Please tell him! With that phone number Intelligence can find her name in a matter of hours."

Sam closed his eyes. He said softly, "Allsford".

Crick leaned forward. "What did you say? Repeat the name!"

"Allsford."

"Did you say Allsford, as . . . uh . . . as in Allsford Lynn? The same name as the family that owns the land this base is on?"

"Yes, sir."

"Is she any relation to this family here?"

"She's their daughter. She and her father own the land the base is on."

"Well, I'll be goddamned!" Crick was obviously perplexed. "Well how about that!" He tapped his pencil on his desk. He started to speak, "Well, now, that introduces complic . . . " He slammed his fist on his desk. "Well, goddamn it, they may be big shots in England, but that doesn't cut any ice with the United States Army Air Forces! We'll insist on a sworn deposition from her anyway, by God!" He turned to Corporal James. "Take out that part about big shots."

Sam said, "Is that all, sir?"

"That's all for now. I hope you realize you're still in trouble. All of this goes into your file. You're dismissed. "

Evelyn said, "Are you through with me, sir?"

"You may go. I'll want to see you in the morning to sign a memo as a witness to Captain Prentice's recalcitrance."

Sam heard the exchange as he opened the door. He seemed ten years older than when he entered the office. He held the door open for Evelyn.

❋ ❋ ❋ ❋ ❋ ❋ ❋

After his meal Robb lit a cigarette and picked up the tin tray and took it to the sink in the latrine and rinsed it. He placed the tray on the floor against the wall outside the door to the latrine, where Corporal Weatherholt would be sure to see it. He took his toothbrush and toothpaste out of his shaving kit. Sam entered just as he finished brushing his teeth.

Robb tried to smile but failed. "I was hoping you'd show up tonight."

"Cynthia knows everything."

"What do you mean?"

"She knows about your refusal to fly, and your arrest and the charges being brought against you."

"What!"

"She called the base to talk to you and left her number with Kerrigan, with a message for you to call her. The message said for you to call 'Cynthia". She didn't give him her last name. Kerrigan got the message to Crick, and Crick called her and told her everything."

"No! Dear God no!" He yelled wildly, "No, goddamn it! No!"

Robb's face suddenly went slack. He sat down heavily at the Link instructor's desk and grasped his head in his hands, his elbows on the desk. "Why? Why would he want to hurt her? Why in God's name, Sam? Why?"

"To hurt you. He says he wants her to provide a sworn deposition that you impersonated a colonel and that you used Army cars for your own purposes. She refused, but he told her he's going to get the British government to get a deposition from her for the U.S. Army Air Forces, whether she likes it or not."

"That dirty, slimy son of a bitch!"

"She asked if she could see you. Crick told her that it would be many years before she'd get to see you, if ever." Sam sat down. "Christ, I'm sorry, Robb."

Robb spoke with the heels of his hands in his eye sockets. "Every time I think Crick has hit bottom he manages to crawl even lower." He lowered his hands and looked at Sam. "A little while ago I was scared to death Hoyt or Boo might kill Crick. I had thought just now—Crick clutching his belly with Hoyt standing over him with a gun in his hand. And I was glad! Did you hear that, Sam? Glad! See how quickly we sink to the level of our enemies! Just like any goddamned war, it's a stinking race to see who becomes the most blood-thirsty the fastest! Now Crick and I are neck and neck."

"But that was a passing thought. You really don't want Hoyt to kill . . ."

Robb stood up suddenly and clutched the front of Sam's coat. His mouth dropped open and he stared in horror. "Sam! My soap tray! Cynthia took my soap tray!"

"What about it?"

"It was filled with sleeping pills!"

Sam said. "Maybe she's been sleeping poorly. Maybe she just needed them to sleep."

"Just before I left, the last time I was up there she said if I die, she dies! I didn't know then that she had taken my soap tray." He sat down heavily and put his head down on his arms on the desk. He pounded the desk with his fist. "Oh no! No! No! No! Dear Christ no!" His voice trailed off into a moan.

"Don't panic, Robb. All this doesn't necessarily mean anything." He saw Robb's shoulders shake from time to time, but he heard no sound. He stood up and put his hand on Robb's shoulder for a moment, and then he sat down again. Neither man spoke for five or ten minutes. Robb finally raised his head. "You'd better go, Sam. I'm going to bed."

"You go on to bed. I'll stay here for a while anyway."

"I want you to go."

Sam stood up and placed his hand on Robb's shoulder again. "All right, I'll look in on you in the morning." He closed the door quietly as he left.

Robb stared blankly ahead for a half hour or more. When finally he stood up his knees were stiff, his first steps toward the latrine were the steps of an old man. He took his toothbrush and a small penlight out of his shaving kit and put them into the inside pocket of his uniform coat. He saw he was wearing his dress uniform and he was vaguely surprised. Then he remembered his long meeting with Lieutenant Hagopian.

He rummaged around in his shaving kit until he found the colonel's eagles. He put them into the side pocket of his coat and started for the door. He stopped abruptly. He returned to Sergeant Frasker's desk and picked up the receiver from the phone. Before the operator could respond, he hung the receiver back on its hook. Better not call her. Just get there as fast as possible!

He put on his garrison cap and trench coat and went to the door and turned out the lights. He stepped out into the darkness and drizzle, carefully locking the door to his prison behind him. He pulled the visor of his cap low over his eyes and lifted the collar of his coat around his face. As he walked toward Amber Squadron Area he again experienced the strange feeling of lacking any location in space. He knew where he was and yet he felt like he was somewhere else. Where, he didn't know. His mind was filled with a jumbled, wakeful nightmare in which Cynthia repeatedly appeared, only to be blotted out by visions of Crick cornered by Hoyt and Boo. He was surprised when he arrived at the squadron area. He had experienced no passage of time since he left the Link.

He looked at the luminous face of his watch: 7:18. Kerrigan would be at his nightly billiards game in the NCO club until 8:00. Only Swovik to contend with.

He entered the Orderly Room by the side door and appraised the figure curled up in the wooden swivel chair behind the stove. It occurred to him it might be a good idea to send Swovik off to his barracks on an errand, any errand, but the longer he studied the little soldier the surer he became that he was sound asleep.

He moved quietly to the tall metal storage cabinet behind Kerrigan's desk. He turned the handle and pulled gently. The door was stuck. He gave the handle a firm pull. The door opened with a tinny clang. Damn! He was sure he had awakened Swovik. His mind raced until he settled on a solution. He'd tell Swovik he was looking for stationery, and then he'd send him off to his barracks for something. He turned to speak to Swovik, but the soldier's eyes were closed, his head lolling to one side.

Robb reached into the cabinet and withdrew a Colt .45 automatic and an ammunition clip. Swovik's left eye opened just as Robb slipped the heavy, snub-nosed gun into his right-hand coat pocket.

He closed the cabinet door until it touched its frame. He turned toward Swovik. Clearly, no sound had disturbed him. He took two slow paces toward the door and stopped. He returned to the cabinet and withdrew one of the square, pint-sized, amber bottles of sleeping pills. He opened it and poured out a generous handful of capsules and put them into his coat pocket. He capped the bottle, put it into the cabinet and closed the door silently. He turned and walked quietly to the side door. Two eyes, imperceptible slits below the front edge of the klutz cap, followed the captain as he stepped out the door and into the night.

Robb retraced his steps along the asphalt lane. Now and then he passed a shadowy figure walking in the direction of Amber Squadron Area , but it was too dark for them to recognize him or he them. When he was perhaps a half mile from Group Headquarters, he turned off the road, forty-five degrees or so to his left, and headed across an open area in the direction of the eastern reaches of the flight line. He passed between two storage buildings, now shadows only slightly blacker than the night itself, and on across the vast concrete apron toward the B-17s arrayed on their hardstands in an irregular row, a row he couldn't see but which he knew stretched a half mile or so farther east from the point at which he calculated he would intersect the row.

When he reached the first B-17, he turned to his left—east—and walked from one plane to the next, beneath the huge wings and fuselages. He stopped when he made out the vague outline of the plane he sought, the P-47 Thunderbolt. He took a few steps toward the fighter plane when he stopped short: there, at the level of the wing of the second B-17 farther down the line, a single light shone from a scaffold that embraced an engine nacelle. A shadowy figure, apparently a mechanic, moved about on the scaffold. He reached into his pocket and pulled out the Colt .45. He knew he wouldn't shoot anyone but he'd sure scare the hell out of anyone who got in his way. He stood for a moment indecisively. He put the gun back into his pocket and walked quickly past the P-47 and on under the wing and fuselage of the next B-17. As he approached the scaffold, he said loudly, "Soldier, I'll need a hand pulling the prop through on the P-47."

A flashlight beam shone down on him. "Yes, sir. Right away." The man came down from the scaffold.

Robb said, "I'll climb on up and make sure the switches are off, then I'll come down and give you a hand pulling the prop through."

"That won't be necessary, sir. I can do it myself." Only then did he notice how big the man was. He was as tall as Stosh—as Stosh had been—and as broad as Broz.

Robb grasped the hand-holds and climbed onto the wing. He pulled back the canopy and lowered himself into the cockpit. He turned on the panel lights, touched the switches, and yelled, "Switches off!" He directed the beam of his pen light forward and saw the blades moving slowly as the mechanic pulled the huge, four-bladed prop through.

"That's enough, Soldier."

The mechanic stood to one side, his flashlight beam focused on the engine. Robb did a hasty check of his instruments and controls and made the necessary adjustments. He reached behind the headrest and retrieved the colonel's leather helmet, goggles and earphones, which he donned in place of his garrison cap. He pushed the energizer switch upwards. The flywheel hadn't quite reached full whine when he hit the engage switch and the monstrous Pratt and Whitney engine exploded to life with a deafening roar. Robb knew the roar that could be heard not only by anyone in the tower and the Operations Office, but in every other building on the base. The thought occurred to him that everyone who noticed would think it was the sound of a mechanic doing a test run-up. He relaxed.

He signaled the mechanic to pull the chocks. The man disappeared under the plane. He emerged and waved his flashlight indicating the chocks were free. Robb gave the engine a quick, half-blast. The plane jumped forward into the open area of the concrete apron. He pushed hard left rudder and left brake and gave the engine another blast and the plane swung ninety degrees to the left and rolled rapidly toward the near end of the main runway.

He turned on to the farthest taxi strip. He had hoped to taxi without lights, but he found he had only the vaguest idea where the edges of the taxi strip were. He switched on his running lights but they were inadequate. He had no choice. He switched on his landing light. He was shocked. The P-47's powerful landing light cut through the drizzle for a half-mile or more. Damn! They're going to see me from the tower sure as hell! Nothing to do about it now. Just get the hell out of here fast! He advanced the throttle and taxied faster than he ever had. He had no idea if the base was open or shut down and, if open, what runway they were using and in what direction: he had no knowledge of the wind velocity or direction.

He lined up the plane on to the runway and pressed hard on the brakes. He locked his tail wheel and ran the engine up to three-quarters power. He was about to release the brakes when the cockpit was suddenly filled with a bright, eerie red light. Goddamn it! An Aldis light from the tower! It was focused directly into his cockpit. A red Aldis light in your cockpit means *"stop where you are!"* He jammed the throttle full forward and let go the brakes. The fighter plane shot forward, twenty-four hundred horsepower jamming his head hard against the headrest. The red light disappeared from the cockpit as he ran out from under the Aldis beam.

He was airborne in fifteen or twenty seconds and solidly in the soup immediately. He pulled up the gear and flaps and swung the plane in a climbing turn to a heading of 334 degrees. He looked at his watch: 7:46.

He climbed to 10,000 feet and leveled off. Not knowing how high the top of the crap was, he decided to hold at 10,000 feet and go all the way on instruments. As he flew blindly into the night at more than 300 miles per hour, toward Prestwick, he turned over in his mind a simple fact. The red light he had refused to acknowledge would come back to haunt him in his attempt to get into Prestwick unobtrusively—and to get to Cynthia's in time. A bad turn of events. Nothing to be done about it now. Except pray. But he had no faith in his prayers. But he wished to God. Oh God how he wished. For Cynthia.

The Tower would by now have reported to Operations, telling Red Hammersmith of the single engine fighter that just took off without filing a flight plan and without clearance or radio contact and, if that weren't enough, ignoring a red Aldis light. And Hammersmith would figure it was The Bolt. A call to Group Headquarters would determine that no one had permission to use the P-47 tonight, and once they found The Bolt was missing, they'd send someone to the Link Shack to see if their prisoner was there. They'd know then who it was who took off. They'd know within fifteen minutes.

He broke into the clear as he crossed the Scottish southern uplands. He could make out a light here and there on the ground. Good! If Prestwick had been socked in, he'd have been in trouble trying to land on instruments with an altimeter pressure set by guess. He could be off by four or five hundred feet if there was a marked difference in atmospheric pressure between Allsford Lynn and Prestwick.

As he approached Prestwick he tuned in Prestwick's loop frequency. His heading was almost on the money. He wondered if maybe he shouldn't simply call their tower for landing instructions and an altimeter setting and ask them to turn on their runway lights. He could make up a Fighter Group code name for his plane. Let's see. The Fighter Group near them at Hallstead Howard had the code name "Chippo." He'd call his plane . . . let's see now. . . "Chippo Charley". No. Too damned cute. Make it "Chippo Hawk." Fighter outfits lean toward birds of prey. He snapped on his throat mike and tuned the dial to Prestwick tower's frequency. He pushed the transmitter button, but he couldn't bring himself to speak. He let up on the button.

He was disgusted with himself; he was thinking wishfully. They're not going to buy the "Chippo Hawk" crap. Everyone on the Base at Allsford Lynn who knows him knows he's heading for Prestwick. Robb knew that Aaron Standing, the 990th's Provost Marshal, had already called the Prestwick Provost Marshal to be on the lookout for him and to place him under arrest. Of course Prestwick Tower's been alerted to expect his arrival. Robb knew that by now a reception committee of military policemen was waiting for him at the taxi strip turnoff at the end of the runway, and another committee most likely waiting at the sec-ond-from-the-end turnout.

He circled Prestwick Air Base at 10,000 feet, lights off, keeping about ten miles out from their cone of silence. He couldn't see Prestwick Air Base, but he knew he would be flying a perfect circle around it as long as he kept his direction finder needle pointing ninety degrees to the left and kept the volume of the signal constant in his earphones by turn-ing closer or farther from Prestwick as the volume of the signal varied in his earphones.

What to do? He decided to list in his mind all the alternatives open to him. He couldn't think of a single thing to list, at least not anything that made sense.

A solution hit him suddenly. How simple! He could land at some other base up here, on the other side of Glasgow. He reached into the map case beside his seat to retrieve the sectional charts from the chart box. Empty. "Damn! That takes care of that!" To find any other base up here he'd need either their instrument approach beam frequencies or their loop antenna frequency, and without a sectional chart or any other code book he was out of luck. And even if he should catch sight of another airfield, without their tower frequency he couldn't even call them for an altimeter setting or to ask them to turn on their runway lights. He then realized that if he hadn't known Prestwick's loop and beam frequencies by memory he'd never have found Prestwick.

It occurred to him that he could fly to someplace near Cynthia's and point the plane for the Clyde Estuary and bail out. He might get hurt or even killed. But then again, he might come out of it all right. But then a sudden thought struck him. He yelled out loud, "Kee-riste! How dumb can you get! You don't have a parachute!"

He continued circling at 10,000 feet. Actually, he could land at Prestwick without an altimeter setting if the runway lights were on. Maybe he could call Prestwick Tower and use the "Chippo Hawk" code name and get them to turn on the runway lights. Then he could slow-fly in on a short-field landing procedure, and if he hit the brakes hard as soon as he was on the runway, he could turn off on a turnout at the halfway mark on the runway, maybe even closer, and elude the reception committees, even though everyone down there would have guessed by then that "Chippo Hawk" was in fact Upshaw Bolt, the fugitive P-47. If

he could turn off the runway soon enough, he could park the plane before the MPs could react; he'd simply climb out of the cockpit and
disappear into the night in Prestwick's forest of B-17s and B-24s.

Just then Prestwick's runway lights came on. He knew immediately
what was happening. Somebody else was coming in to Prestwick,
probably a bomber from overseas. He scanned the sky below him, to the
northwest. He saw its lights immediately. A plane far below approaching
Prestwick from the northwest, at a forty- five degree angle to the lighted
runway.

He whipped the P-47 into a wingover and straight down into a dive.
He was down to 1500 feet in a matter of seconds. He leveled out and
circled at 1200 feet some three or four miles from the head of the runway. He saw the plane turning onto the base leg of the landing pattern.
He put The Bolt's nose down and pushed forward on the throttle. He was
about a quarter of a mile behind the other plane as it rolled out of its turn
on to its landing approach.

He could see by the flames of four exhausts that it was a bomber. He
knew no one could see his own exhausts—they'd have to be looking
squarely into his exhaust pipes—and he knew that with his lights off no
one in the tower or on the ground could see him at all. When he was
within one hundred yards of the bomber, he pulled back on his throttle
and matched his speed to the bomber's.

He began his slow-flying, short-field procedure. He dropped his
landing gear, opened his cowl flaps fully, dropped his wing flaps full
down, and rolled back his canopy. He raised the nose of the ship slowly,
adding power as he did so, but decreasing his air speed by raising the
nose of the plane to an angle of attack just short of stalling. His airspeed
dropped to eighty miles per hour. He kept easing back on the stick and,
though he continued to add power, his airspeed continued to drop. Now
seventy five miles per hour. The controls were mushy. He had to do a
balancing act with the rudders—with a lot of right rudder to counteract
the torque—to keep the ship from falling off on one wing or the other.
Now seventy miles per hour, slower than the P-47's normal stall-out
speed. He was pulling three-quarter power with the plane's nose sticking
upwards at a ridiculous angle, twenty or thirty degrees at least, hanging
from its prop as much as from its wings. That's it! Hold it there! He
could no longer see straight ahead, but he knew that the bomber, ap-

proaching the runway at over one-hundred miles an hour, was now at least a quarter of a mile ahead of him. Good. He couldn't stand much propwash with his plane threatening to stall off on one wing or the other at any moment. He yelled, "Don't turn off those runway lights!"

Now, with his plane in its incongruous, nose-high attitude, he could see neither the plane ahead, the runway, nor the ground. His altimeter read two hundred feet, but having set it by guess its reading was meaningless. He unbuckled his safety belt and shoulder harness and leaned his head out the left side of the cockpit. His heart skipped a beat. The ground! Ten feet or twenty feet below him! He hit full throttle and hard right rudder and eased forward on the stick. Too late! He knew he couldn't achieve level flight in time to avoid hitting the ground. Then he saw the runway lights. The plane hit the concrete with a bone-jarring slam. The five-ton airplane hit the runway like a five-ton lump of metal, within fifty feet of the beginning of the runway. No bounce. Just a slam on to the runway. Five tons of dead weight fell from the sky and met the runway with a deafening crash-sound, the sound one hears in the distance when two cars hit head-on.

The plane didn't bounce because it had no buoyancy, flying as it had been well below its stalling speed, hanging from its prop. When the tail wheel hit the runway the nose whipped down abruptly and the plane became dead weight in a split second. It felt like he had landed a brick. He looked out at the top of the wing to see if the landing gear struts had bent the wing upwards. No damage as far as he could tell in the dark, and the tires seemed to have survived the controlled crash.

He cut the power and hit his brakes full hard. He knew there must be a strong headwind, because he hadn't rolled more than 200 yards when he had slowed sufficiently to permit him to whip the plane into a taxi turnoff. The turnoff came so soon he wondered if it wasn't the second from the end turnoff for planes landing *from the opposite end of the runway.* He guessed there must be a strong headwind, maybe even twenty miles an hour. With his airspeed at seventy miles per hour, he may have in fact landed at a ground speed of only fifty miles an hour!

He taxied very slowly in the dark, all lights out, leaning out of the cockpit and squinting downward as he tried to make out the left edge of the taxi strip. The black asphalt taxi strip ended and he discerned the beginning of the broad concrete apron. He saw a row of B-24's and he knew it had to be the last row, the one farthest from the tower, the same apron he had taxied along behind the Follow-Me Jeep when he left here two weeks ago in that snowstorm. He decided to swing to the right, to taxi along the length of the broad apron, to get as far away as possible from the military police vehicles he was sure were gathered at the far end of the runway. Then he saw a pair of lights, close-together jeep lights, approaching from his left, a mile or so up the apron toward the far end of the runway.

Instead of turning to his right, he taxied straight ahead until he could see clearly the spaces between the B-24 bombers. He eased forward on the brakes and slowed the plane to a crawl. He guided the fighter plane between the high, double-tail empennages of two B-24s parked wing tip to wing tip. He had less than a yard to spare as his wingtips passed the vertical stabilizers of the B-24s. He stopped just before his prop would have chewed up the trailing edges of the B-24s' wingtips. He shut off his ignition and the idling prop stopped rotating in a matter of seconds. He turned off the panel lights and sat very still, fearful that even his slightest movement in the cockpit might attract the attention of whomever it was who was in that jeep.

The jeep lights grew brighter. Then he saw the running lights of the B-24 behind it and he knew it had to be the Follow-Me Jeep leading the guy who had just landed. Pray that the driver doesn't spot this P-47 in its strange parking place.

The jeep and the B-24 passed behind him. He had no way of knowing if he had been seen. If the jeep driver had seen him, he'd be calling the tower on his radio right now, and the tower would immediately call the MPs at the end of the runway.

He carefully put the plane to bed, executing each action required by the shutdown check list. He peeled off Colonel Strang's helmet and goggles and hung them on the hook behind the seat and put on his own garrison cap. He climbed out of the cockpit, closed the canopy, and eased himself to the trailing edge of the wing and lowered himself slowly down the side of the plane, placing his hands and feet securely onto the hand and foot holds until he could feel with his feet the concrete surface of the parking apron.

46

Robb walked rapidly away from the P-47. He walked in a southeasterly direction, away from the far end of the runway and the reception committees he knew were surely there, and farther away from Prestwick tower. He bent forward as he walked, his head down in an unconscious attitude of stealth as he moved beneath the wings and fuselages of the B-17s and B-24s in the outermost row of bombers.

He had seen the jeep a mile off, so he knew that, where there was light, visibility was quite good tonight. But there was no light. He could make out the huge airplanes only one at a time as he moved out from under one plane into the shadowy presence of the next. When he had walked a half mile or so, he turned 90 degrees to his left and began cutting across the rows of bombers and the taxi lanes between them. If he could make his way to the flight line and slip between the hangars and repair buildings, he could make it to the fence and then follow the fence to the main gate. He'd worry about getting through the gate once he got to where he could observe the gate and the situation there.

He could see lights ahead of him now, some shining steadily, others dimly and intermittently. He knew the steady lights would be from the maintenance hangars and the others the drop-cord lights of mechanics working on planes along the flight line. He moved more cautiously now as he approached the lighted area in front of the repair hangars. He stopped under a B-17 in the last row of bombers and stood in the shadow of one of its huge tires. He could see the mechanics moving about on scaffolds wrapped around the engine nacelles of bombers parked before the maintenance buildings.

Should he walk boldly out into the open area and head for the gate? Whom, really, was he hiding from? Even if the word were out that there was a fugitive running around loose on the air base, these mechanics wouldn't know about it. And even if they did know, from what he knew of mechanics they couldn't care less. But if an MP's jeep were to turn suddenly on to this apron? No. He'd better not chance it. He'd have to make his way across this concrete apron and between those buildings to the fence behind and then follow the fence to the gate. Maybe he should move farther down the flight line, farther from the tower before he crossed over.

He heard voices approaching from his right. Loud, young male voices in a group. Then he saw them emerge from among the bombers farther down the line, a group of eight or ten men, a bomber crew obviously. They were coming his way now, laughing and talking loudly— the celebration of terra firma after a long haul. It occurred to Robb that this could be the crew of the B-24 he had followed in.

He waited as they approached. When they were fifty feet or so from him he stepped out into the dim light of the open area and stopped. He took out a cigarette and his Zippo and went through the motions of lighting the cigarette, but he held his thumb over the wick of his lighter. When the group of men was within ten feet of him he said, "One of you got a Zippo that works?"

"Sure enough, Captain," a young second lieutenant said. All ten men stopped and waited while Robb lit his cigarette. He handed the lighter back to the lieutenant.

"Thanks," Robb said. "How's the night life in Goose Bay?"

They laughed heartily. Goose Bay, Labrador, a refueling stop on the long haul from the States, was one of the most desolate places on earth in winter. Robb joined them as they walked along. A voice in the crowd called out, "Goose Bay, Laybrador, the ayasshole of the universe!" There was a chorus of agreement.

A lieutenant said, "Are we on the right course for Operations, Captain?"

A lieutenant at the back of the group piped up, "He's our navigator, Captain. He navigates by the interrogation method."

Everybody laughed. Robb too.

Robb said, "Operations is straight ahead, Lieutenant. How was the flight over?"

The second lieutenant, the man who had given him the light, responded. "Strong headwinds on the last leg. Would you believe strong headwinds *out of the east*? Damned near ran out of gas. We're celebrating right now. Right guys?"

Another chorus of agreement.

"You finished your tour, Captain?"

"Yes."

"How was it?" A hush fell over the group. They moved closer to Robb.

"Not bad. Especially toward the end. It's a lot easier now than it used to be. You men are to be congratulated on your timing."

They laughed, almost too loudly, too readily. Robb had been asked this question dozens of times by green crewmen, and recently he had hit upon the answer he had just given, words that invariably evoked the response they got just now. But he had told them the truth. It was in fact a lot easier now than in the early days. If this were 1943 their chances of survival then would be lousy. Right now they're pretty good. Just stay away from Merseburg.

A 4X4 canvas-covered personnel carrier pulled alongside the group. "You guys want a ride to Ops?"

Again the youthful, affirmative chorus.

Robb felt a surge of poignant remembrance. His own crews, both his first crew and his second, had sounded like that. He was all too familiar with the change in spirit in individuals that came with combat, but he hadn't thought much about the collective, youthful spark in new crews and how quickly and permanently it was extinguished by the first rough missions. How will this little gang of happy warriors sound a month from now?

The rookie crew climbed into the back of the truck and disappeared behind the canvas flap. Robb walked around and climbed into the cab beside the driver.

"Drop me off at the bus stop, please. I'm going to Ayr."

The driver, a private, looked at his watch. "The last bus leaves to pick up the stragglers at 9:30, sir, two minutes from now. Maybe we can make it." He stepped hard on the accelerator.

"Thanks, soldier."

They were really rolling now, toward Operations, the tower, and—he found the thought disturbing—the Motor Pool.

"There's the bus now, sir. I'll see if I can catch it."

The bus, which had been coming toward them a couple of hundred yards ahead, swung left on to the road between Operations and the Motor

Pool, the road that led to the gate. The truck driver stepped harder on his gas pedal and leaned on his horn: a long blast followed by a series of short, frantic beeps. The bus stopped. The truck driver whipped his truck around the corner and pulled alongside the bus.

"Thanks, soldier."

"No sweat, sir."

As Robb walked past the rear of the truck, he said loudly, "Good luck, men." Again a chorus of jumbled, youthful enthusiasm. Someone yelled out, "Golden Gate in forty eight!"

As Robb entered the bus, his heart skipped a beat. The bus was empty. He'd be conspicuous as hell as they went out the gate. Damn it! He took a seat at the front of the bus.

He spoke to the driver, "Thanks, soldier."

"No sweat, sir."

The driver slowed down as he passed the sentry booth, but he didn't stop. The M.P. must have seen Robb. He sprang to "present arms" with his rifle. Robb muffled his sigh of relief as he touched the visor of his cap, returning the salute.

Apparently no one had seen him land behind the B-24. And they sure as hell hadn't discovered the P-47 nestled between the B-24's. The more he thought about it, the more likely it seemed to him that The Bolt wouldn't be found before daybreak.

As he stared through the bus windshield at the narrow ribbon of asphalt that wandered toward Ayr, he mused on the strange turns fortune took. He found it difficult to adjust to the ease and simplicity of it all. He felt as though he had put his shoulder to a locked oaken door and found it to be made of cardboard. It almost seemed as if it were all meant to be.

As the bus approached the outskirts of Ayr, the driver turned and said, "Where would you like to get off, sir?" He thought of saying "As far north as possible." Instead he said, "Your main pickup stop will be fine."

The driver made a U-turn and pulled up to the curb in front of a large stone building of nondescript architecture on the main street. A sign over the door of the building caught the periphery of the bus's headlight beam: *Service Club*. A small knot of soldiers stood ready to climb aboard. They moved to one side as Robb stepped down from the bus. He looked at his watch: 10:05.

He stood for a moment on the sidewalk near the doorway to the service club. He could smell coal smoke and the inevitable odor of fish and chips. Except for the group of soldiers and the bus, the town was deserted. No lights, no people, no cars. Only six or eight American jeeps and army trucks parked along the curb.

He walked to the jeep farthest from the service club. He opened the canvas and celluloid door and ran his hand about on the floor under the steering wheel and under the driver's seat. He moved to the jeep directly behind. He opened the door and groped about under the seat. His motions stopped suddenly. His hand closed on a set of keys. He climbed in and turned on the interior light and put the key in the ignition and turned it. He watched the gas gauge climb. He nodded slowly as he watched the needle pass the half-full mark. He started the engine and pulled slowly away from the curb, keeping the engine noise down as much as possible.

The jeep moved slowly up the road, its gear changes slow, unhurried as it climbed northward up the gradual grade, toward Largs. Its labored engine-sounds punctuated the otherwise absolute stillness of the night.

47

Sam Prentice returned to his office after telling Robb that Crick had called Cynthia. He hoped that by working on his monthly report he might get his mind off the events of the day, but he had difficulty concentrating. He had been at his desk for more than an hour, yet he was still on page one of his report when Monk Bradley burst into his office.

"Robb's gone! He took off in the P-47!"

"What?"

"Robb stole The Bolt and took off!"

"You're panicking, Monk. Robb wouldn't do a thing like that."

"Listen, Sam, damn it! The P-47 is gone and Robb's gone!"

Sam whispered, "Oh no!"

"Robb's an escaped prisoner now."

"Do you know what this means, Monk? Do you?"

"He's as good as convicted, if they don't shoot him trying to catch him."

"Exactly! But what will happen to him if he doesn't make it to Cynthia's, if he has to land somewhere else than Prestwick, or if he sees the MPs waiting for him someplace and goes into hiding?   Where will he go? Where will he sleep? Where will he eat? You know Robb, he'll forget to eat!"

Bradley said, "What makes you so sure he's heading for Scotland?"

"Crick called Cynthia and told her about Robb's arrest and that he was going to get life in prison or a death sentence. . ."

"That rotten son of a bitch!"

"And I told Robb about Crick calling her. Now Robb is scared to death that she's going to commit suicide. He told me she pilfered his supply of sleeping pills, a lot of them, when he was up there the last time."

"That doesn't mean she's going to kill herself."

"There's more to it." Sam pounded his fist into this hand. "Damn it! I shouldn't have told him about Crick's call to Cynthia."

"You had to tell him sooner or later."

"Did they actually see him take off in the P-47?"

"The tower saw The Bolt take off a little over half an hour ago, without a flight plan or takeoff instructions, and without radio contact. The tower gave him a red Aldis but he took off anyway, the wrong way on the main runway."

"Wait a minute! Did anyone actually see Robb at the controls of that airplane? Maybe it was someone else. Maybe he's somewhere on the base!"

"Come on, Sam. You're grasping at straws. Figure the odds. The P-47 takes off illegally, actually tries to sneak off. The tower spots it and tries to stop it. They check the Link right away and Robb is gone. And you just supplied the motive. It was Robb all right."

"No, damn it, Monk. No!" Sam paced the floor.

"I just talked to Aaron Standing," Bradley said. "He told me he alerted Prestwick himself. He says Prestwick has MPs all over the place waiting for him to land. They have orders to put him in jail immediately, and to transfer him to prison tomorrow to await his trial."

Sam looked at his watch. "Robb's still in the air right now, if it was actually Robb." He resumed his pacing. "Can you believe all this? One of the most civilized men in the whole damned army, or anywhere for that matter, running around like a fugitive from a chain gang." Sam stopped pacing and looked at Bradley. "What will Robb do when he sees the MPs waiting for him?"

"That's what worries me. He's liable to whip the plane around and take off in the opposite direction. And they're liable to start shooting. And even if he gets off again, where's he going to land? You can be damned sure that every Provost Marshal and MP on every U.S. Air Base in England and Scotland is alerted to be on the lookout for that P-47, and to arrest him on sight. I imagine every RAF base is alerted too."

Sam nodded sadly. "I know."

There was a soft knock on the door. Sam opened the door. Private Milan Swovik saluted Sam. Sam said, "Yes?"

"I'm sorry to bother you, sir. I'm from Amber Squadron. I need to talk to you, sir. It's real important."

Bradley recognized Swovik's voice. He went to the door. "Private Swovik, is it about Captain Robertson?"

"Yes sir, Lieutenant."

"Come in." Swovik took off his cap and stood awkwardly in the center of the room. Sam pulled a chair around to the front of the desk. "Sit down, please."

Sam and Bradley half-sat on the edge of Sam's desk, looking down at the soldier twisting his cap in his hands. He looked up at the two officers. He looked away quickly.

Sam said, "Now what's this about Captain Robertson?"

Swovik twisted his cap tighter. "If I'm wrong about this I could end up in France. I came here anyway, even when Sergeant Kerrigan wouldn't give me permission to leave the orderly room. I just walked out on him." Swovik looked upward and quickly down again.

Bradley said, "Don't worry about Kerrigan. We won't let him punish you. Now what about Captain Robertson?"

Swovik hesitated. "Well, sir . . . I . . . uh . . . uh. . . ."

Sam and Bradley waited patiently.

". . . uh . . . Captain Robertson, he came to the orderly room tonight when Sergeant Kerrigan was at his pool game at the NCO club." Swovik seemed to be debating with himself.

"Go on."

"I was sleeping behind the stove, but I woke up for just a minute and I saw him do something. I didn't mean to spy on him."

"That's all right," Sam said. "What did he do?"

"He went to the cabinet back of Sergeant Kerrigan's desk."

Prentice and Bradley leaned forward.

"I saw Captain Robertson take a .45 automatic and an ammo clip out of the cabinet and put it in his trench coat pocket."

Sam said, "Oh no!"

Swovik said, "There's one other thing. Captain Robertson started out toward the door after he took the gun, but then he came back to the cabinet and took out a bottle of happy pills and dumped like a big handful in his hand and put 'em in his pocket. Then he put the bottle back and left."

Bradley said, "Anything else?"

"No sir. That's it. I hope I did the right thing, sir."

Bradley stood up and put his hand on Swovik's shoulder. "You did the right thing, and a brave thing. You may go now."

Swovik stood up. "I don't know where to go, sir."

Bradley said. "Go back to the Squadron orderly room. Go back to your place behind the stove. It's against the law for Kerrigan to punish you physically, and we're not going to let him do anything else to you. Tell him what you did was an emergency."

"That won't help, sir. He carries a lot of weight with Colonel Crick."

Sam said, "Tell him that you had to see me on an intelligence matter that I said you have to keep secret. Tell Sergeant Kerrigan I said the Group Commander himself will explain it to him later. Tell him I told you to tell him to phone me tomorrow, and that I said that's an order."

"Thank you, sir."

Swovik got up and walked to the door. He opened the door and turned to face the two officers. He raised his hand to his forehead. Sam touched his forehead with his right hand, slowly, thoughtfully. Bradley returned the salute sharply. Swovik closed the door behind him.

"We've got to act fast," Bradley said, "but I'm damned if I know where to begin."

Sam grabbed his cap. "Come on. We've got to tell the C.O. everything. He'll do all he can to save Robb. Come on!"

Colonel Strang sat in shocked silence upon hearing about the gun and the sleeping pills. Finally he said, "I'm beginning to think Robb really is nuts!" He looked at his watch. He picked up the phone and asked the operator to get him the Provost Marshal.

"Aaron, I want you to call the Prestwick Provost Marshal and tell him to tell his men to be careful how they approach Robertson. Tell them not to gang up at the end of the runway waiting for him. and to stay out of sight and let him land and to nab him after he parks the plane and shuts it off and climbs down. Tell them he's armed but that he's very unlikely to use a gun on anybody, even if they have him cornered. But above all emphasize that the MPs must stay out of sight until he shuts down the plane. Is that clear? Good. Now, I want you to send your two biggest and toughest MPs to Operations right away, armed and ready to take a trip to Scotland. I mean right now. Good. One more thing. Tell the Prestwick Provost Marshal to tell their Motor Pool to have two vehicles, a staff car and a jeep, ready for our people. They'll be getting there in a couple of hours."

The Colonel hung up and turned back to Sam and Bradley. "All right. Robb could land anywhere in the U.K., but we have to proceed on the assumption he's going to Prestwick. Here's what we do. Monk, I want you to fly Tony Rizzo and one of his nurses and those two MPs up there. The Prestwick MPs may be waiting for Robb, but he's one hell of a smart guy. He could easily give them the slip. Have you been to her place, Monk? Can you find it?"

"I've been there. I know exactly how to get there."

"Good. I want you to go along too, Sam. Robb's most likely to listen to you. You've got to talk him into giving himself up to our MPs. Our MPs will be under my orders to deliver him to the Provost Marshall at Prestwick."

Sam said, "Are the MPs really necessary? Couldn't Tony give him something to knock him out?"

"That might not work. You'll need the MPs with you. That's settled. Remember, Robb is armed."

Sam said, "John, you know very well Robb would never shoot anyone."

"Then why did he steal the gun?"

"Maybe to scare off anyone who tries to stop him. Maybe to hold up someone up there to get a car to get to Cynthia's from Prestwick. But he wouldn't shoot anyone."

"Not ordinarily. But Robb isn't himself. He's liable to do anything."

Sam frowned. "So Monk and I are supposed to lead the police to Robb so they can put him in jail."

"In order to save his life. He'll understand in the long run. Now Sam, you call Tony and tell him the situation and to report to Operations with a nurse. Monk, you call Engineering and tell them to get The Lady ready. Then get hold of your co-pilot and engineer and tell them to report to operations. You're dismissed."

Bradley hurried from the office. Sam got up to leave.

Colonel Strang said, "Sam, before you go, why did he take off like this?"

"Have you talked to Colonel Crick this evening?"

"No."

"Colonel Crick called Cynthia this afternoon and told her Robb is locked up and charged with cowardice, and that he'll either be shot or put in jail for life. Robb found out about it."

Colonel Strang turned red in the face. Sam could see his jaw muscles working.

Sam said, "Robb has reasons to think Cynthia might commit suicide. Good reasons. She's got a lot of sleeping pills and she told Robb that if he dies, she dies. That's why he took off. To try to save her."

"Do you think he'll kill himself if he finds she's already . . . "

"Robb would never kill himself."

"Then why did he take the sleeping pills with him?"

"Robb can't sleep without the pills. He probably took them along in case he has to hide out for a while. You know, until he can get to Cynthia and get her straightened out. Then he'll turn himself in. Remember, he wants to stand trial, he wants to stand up and be counted, about the Dresden thing. What the Quakers call being a witness. For him to kill himself would be the same as going along with the combat fatigue defense, which you know and I know would have gotten him off with a medical discharge."

Strang said, "That's about the way I had his motives figured. I mean in his not going along with the combat fatigue defense. But don't be too sure about him not killing himself. If Cynthia has killed herself by the time he gets there that could change everything. That could push him over the edge and he might do it too, either with the gun or the pills. You've got to remember Robb's not himself anymore."

Sam closed his eyes and moved his head slowly from side to side. "Robb would never kill himself."

Colonel Strang walked around the end of his desk. "Sam, nobody knows what Robb might do. Not even Robb."

Everybody was aboard The Colonel's Lady by 10:15 PM—Sam, Tony Rizzo, Merrie, the two MPs and the plane's crew. Bradley taxied very fast to the head of the runway, but he took off as straight and steady as the most conservative airline pilot. The Lady disappeared into the solid overcast before Bradley's new co-pilot, Second Lieutenant Dave Lewis, got the wheels up. Bradley looked at his watch just as the wheels locked into the up position with their characteristic thump: 10:35. He figured Robb had an hour and fifteen minutes head start on them, more or less. He'd gain another hour on them in the air because a P-47 could make it to Prestwick twice as fast as a B-17. If Robb really pushed it, which seemed highly likely, he may have picked up as much as two and a half hours on them all told.

Sam Prentice, now sitting on the floor of the radio compartment with his back against the forward bulkhead, made precisely the same assessment. Tony Rizzo, sitting between Sam and Merrie, made the same sort of calculation, but he was considering certain chemical and physiological processes that could transpire within a period of a couple of hours.

When they reached 1000 feet, Sam, Rizzo, and Merrie, at Bradley's suggestion, moved from the radio room to the nose compartment. Merrie, the top of her head sticking out from the fleece collar of a leather flight jacket several sizes too big for her, sat on a parachute pack, her back against the curved aluminum side of the compartment. Sam sat beside her and Rizzo opposite them.

Rizzo and Merrie fell asleep almost immediately, or they gave the appearance of sleeping. Sam wished he could talk to them. After an hour or so, Rizzo stood up and stretched. He made his way to the hatch and climbed on up to the flight deck. Merrie opened her eyes and stretched her legs.

Sam said, "Merrie, how was Evelyn this evening?"

"Much as to be expected."

Sam said, "I wish I could be with her in this."

"Me too."

They remained silent for a time. When Merrie finally spoke, her tone was absent, colorless. "There's not much hope for Robb, even if he survives tonight, is there?"

"I don't know."

"How do you think all of this is going to turn out?"

"Do you mean tonight, when we get to Cynthia's place?"

Merrie said, "Let's say we get there in time, and you talk him into giving himself up. What do you think will happen to him?'

"I don't know. I'm trying to take all of this hour by hour."

Merrie smiled sardonically. "We used to try to take things one day at a time. Now we're reduced to one hour at a time."

Sam said, "Are you worried about Evelyn?"

"Yes."

The engines slowed and the plane assumed a slightly nose-down attitude. Merrie said, "Can you believe how happy we were the first time we were all together, on our wonderful weekend in London?"

Sam remained silent.

"That was the high spot of my life. That was only a little more than three months ago, but in a way it seems like years. And yet it seems like I saw Stosh just yesterday." She stared at the bare aluminum opposite her. Sam waited. "I knew him for exactly forty-four days. That was the sum of our lives. Forty-four days."

Sam took her hand in his.

Merrie said, "Have you ever known a more tightly compressed pair of lives? At least Evelyn had Robb longer—almost three times as long. I'm glad of that." She pulled the fleece collar away from her face and turned her head toward Sam. "But she really didn't have him at all, did she?"

The engines slowed to half power and the downward inclination of the plane increased. Rizzo dropped down from the flight deck into the nose compartment. "We're coming into Prestwick now. Our hard-nosed pilot says we have to go to the radio compartment for the landing." Rizzo smiled. "He's right, even if he is out of character."

Merrie nodded. "Doesn't it seem funny having Monk in charge? It's like taking orders from your kid brother."

Bradley called Prestwick Tower at 12:26 AM, five minutes from Prestwick. "Prestwick Tower. This is Upshaw Lady. Over."

"Upshaw Lady. This is Prestwick Tower. You are cleared to come straight on in on runway Three One. Altimeter setting 29.68. Winds out of North Northwest at zero eight. Over."

"Roger, Prestwick. Loud and clear. Over." That was quick, Bradley reflected. It seems like everyone is excited about catching the notorious outlaw, Robb Robertson.

"Upshaw Lady. This is Prestwick Tower. I have instructions to inform pilot of Upshaw Lady that he must report directly to Prestwick Provost Marshal in Prestwick Operations. There have been developments in the case you are pursuing. Over."

"Roger, Prestwick. Will report to Prestwick Provost Marshal. Over and out."

It sounded ominous to Bradley. Had they captured Robb? Had he been shot trying to escape? Had he crashed trying to land in the dark without an altimeter setting or trying to take off again after seeing the MPs waiting for him?

The Follow Me Jeep led The Colonel's Lady at a good clip, as though the jeep driver too was in on the act. Bradley wondered if everyone in the Eighth Air Force knew about Robb Robertson.

Bradley climbed out of his seat before the props stopped spinning. He instructed his co-pilot and engineer to put the plane to bed. They were to have the plane ready to go at a moment's notice. Bradley met his passengers on the parking apron. Rizzo and Merrie each carried a black medical case. The MPs stood to one side, one with a stack of blankets, the other with two large oxygen bottles. Bradley told them of the tower's message. Sam, Rizzo, and Merrie went directly to the Motor Pool, followed by the two MPs. Bradley broke into a jog as he headed for Operations.

48

The Provost Marshal was waiting inside the door to Operations.

"Lieutenant Bradley? I'm Captain Mel LaFleur, Prestwick Provost Marshal. Your man gave us the slip."

"Gave you the slip?"

"We found the P-47 squeezed in between two B-24s on the parking apron. We have no idea how he did it. We monitored every landing since 25 minutes after he took off from Allsford Lynn. That guy's a Houdini."

"How long ago did you find the plane?"

"About a half hour ago. We don't know how long it was parked there, but we know it must have been at least a half hour because the engine was stone cold. That means he's got at least an hour lead on you."

Bradley looked at his watch. It was now 12:40 AM. "More likely a two and a half hour lead. Thanks, Captain." He started for the operations counter.

"Just a minute, Lieutenant. We have to plan our strategy on how to apprehend the subject. All of this is going on in my jurisdiction. I'm responsible."

Bradley sighed. "Captain, could we talk about this after I fill out my Ops Report? We can talk about it on the way to the Motor Pool." Bradley hurried to the counter and filled out his report in record time. He walked rapidly from the building.

The Provost Marshal hurried alongside him. "Do you have any idea where he might have gone up here in Scotland, assuming he was able to slip off the base here?"

Bradley answered without slowing. "We have a very good idea of where he is."

"Good. I'll put together a strong police detail and we'll follow you there."

Bradley stopped. "Hold it, Captain. I don't think that's necessary."

"He might be dangerous. I happen to know he's armed, and I know from experience one desperate man can put up one hell of a struggle."

Bradley held up both hands, palms outward. "You've got it all wrong. Captain Robertson is a very civilized man. He's not in the least dangerous."

"You never know. Are you equipped to handle all situations you might run into?"

"We have a doctor, a nurse, and two big MPs."

"If he's not dangerous, then why the medical team, and the MPs?"

"We're afraid he might try to kill *himself,* not anyone else."

The captain pondered the situation. "I see. But my men and I will have to go up there with you anyway. Sort of a reserve."

"That won't be necessary, I assure you."

The Provost Marshal's tone changed abruptly. "Look here, Lieutenant. I want to make something very clear. Your friend gave me the slip here and that's going to look like hell for me. I'm up for promotion to major. Your man is sure as hell going to cost me my promotion unless I capture him myself. And that's what I intend to do. If he gets away again, it's my ass."

They approached the staff car. Sam, Rizzo, and Merrie were standing next to the car. The two MPs were sitting in the jeep. The jeep's motor was running.

Bradley said, "Robb landed here. They found the P-47 a half hour ago. Parked. No sign of Robb."

Rizzo said, "I'll be damned!"

Bradley said, "This is Captain LaFleur, the Prestwick Provost Marshal. He wants to send more MPs with us to make sure Robb doesn't get away again. Tell him what the chances are of Robb giving us the slip, or resisting our efforts to bring him back here."

Sam said, "Zero. The chances are zero."

"I'm sorry. I'm going to have to go along with you with a detail of my men."

Sam said. "And I'm sorry, but if you do that we're not going. We'll stay here until hell freezes over. Then you're really likely to lose him."

"I'm afraid I'm going to have to order you to lead us to him."

"You can order all you like," Sam said. "We've got all the people we need."

"You're guilty of obstruction of justice. I could put you under arrest."

Sam said, "I know this man very well. If he sees this army of yours coming you could bring about the worst possible consequences, and if that happens every one of us here is going to testify against you to that effect in the hearing."

Rizzo cut in. "And if we don't get going right now he may die while we're standing around here arguing."

The Provost Marshal hesitated. He started to speak but he changed his mind. He took a card out of his pocket. "All right. I'm turning the responsibility for this matter over to you, Captain." He looked at Sam. "What is your name?"

"Prentice. Sam Prentice."

"Okay. Our emergency number is on this card. If you have any trouble at all, I want you to call this number. We'll be standing by."

Sam put the card in his pocket. "Fine. Thank you, Captain. We really appreciate your offer to help." He reached out and shook hands with the Provost Marshal. He turned to Bradley. "All right, Monk. We'd better get going."

They got into the car quickly. Bradley put the car in motion just as Rizzo slammed the back door shut. He stepped hard on the gas pedal as he turned on to the highway. The speedometer soon read eighty miles per hour. The Ford sedan's grip on the road seemed tenuous as it rose and fell with each undulation of the narrow asphalt highway.

"Back off, Monk," Sam said. "No point in killing all of us, or those MPs trying to keep up behind." Bradley slowed down to seventy.

Rizzo said, "I'll bet that Provost Marshal's ass is in a sling, not being able to nab someone landing in a P-47, with all the warning in the world."

Bradley said, "He said Robb cost him his promotion to major."

Rizzo said, "Fuck his promotion."

Bradley shot a glance at Sam. Sam's eyebrows were raised in surprise. He glanced sidelong at Merrie. They rode along for five or ten minutes without anyone saying a word. Bradley broke the silence. "It just occurred to me. Robb may not have as big a lead on us as we think. It may have taken him quite a while to get transportation to Cynthia's from Prestwick. "Shit! Excuse me, Merrie. He could even be *behind* us!"

"I know," Sam said. "I thought of that."

Bradley was back up to eighty. Sam said, "Back off, Monk."

Sam looked back as they pulled into the outskirts of Largs. "No sign of the jeep. Better wait here for them."

Bradley pulled to the side of the road. The close-together jeep lights appeared in four or five minutes. Bradley pulled back on to the road.

Merrie said, "How much farther?"

"Three or four miles," Bradley said. "Maybe five." No one spoke until Bradley turned between the pillars marking the entrance to Shelbourne. Bradley stopped the car and got out and walked back to the jeep. He told the MPs to park at the bottom of the hill and that they would come back and get them if they needed them. The MP in charge gave him a walkie-talkie and told him to call if they ran into trouble. Bradley took the oxygen bottles from them and returned to the car.

Bradley kept the car in low gear as they climbed the hill, hoping to keep the sound down as much as possible. As they crested the hill, the jeep lights illuminated the massive facade of the house. Bradley pulled to a stop opposite the front door.

Sam said, "I'd better go in first. If anything has happened, to either of them, I'll come out to get you right away. If not, it would be better if we didn't arrive in a bunch. Tony, you and I will have to have a quick meeting with Robb and convince him it's in his best interest to get into this car and come with us to Prestwick." As Sam stepped out of the car, he said, "Pray."

Rizzo said, "I'm all prayed out."

Sam knocked softly. All eyes in the car were fixed on the door.

Sam knocked firmly. The door opened and Mrs. Campbell stood in the half light of the vestibule.

"I'm Captain Prentice from the American base on the Allsford land in Cambridgeshire. I need to talk to Captain Robertson if he's here. It's very urgent. Is he here?"

"I don't know, sir."

"I'm Captain Robertson's closest friend. What I have to see him about is in his best interest, and Cynthia's. Please trust me. Is he here?"

Mrs. Campbell hesitated. "Yes, he is here, but I'm afraid the Captain has retired for the night, as has Miss Allsford."

It's very important that I see Captain Robertson immediately."

"I really can't disturb them now, sir."

"Are you a relative of Cynthia's?"

"I'm the housekeeper."

"I'm sure you're concerned about Cynthia. This emergency concerns her too."

"I'm sorry, sir."

"Can you tell me where Captain Robertson is in the house? He won't mind if I disturb him. This is a very serious emergency. Please tell me where he is."

Mrs. Campbell hesitated. She sighed. "Come in, sir." She closed the door behind them. "They're in the library. If you'll follow me, please." She led Sam through the great room to the hallway. "The library is the first door on the right. Knock at the door, and don't enter until they ask you in."

"Yes. Would you mind waiting here for a few minutes? I may need to talk to you."

"Yes, sir."

Sam walked quickly to the library. He knocked on the door. He waited. He rapped very hard and called out, "Robb! . . . Robb! Are you in there?"

Sam opened the door a crack. "Robb? . . . Robb!"

He opened the door and entered the room. He stopped inside the door. He saw Robb sitting on the sofa facing the fireplace where a few embers glowed. He saw only the back of Robb's head. "Robb? . . . Robb?" He didn't move. "Robb!" Sam stood for a moment uncertainly. He took a deep breath and strode quickly across the room and around the end of the sofa. He stopped short and stared in disbelief. Robb sat stark still, staring blankly ahead. Cynthia, her face drained of all color, her mouth slightly open, her eyes closed, lay with her head on his lap. "Robb! Robb! Answer me!" He felt Robb's forehead. Warm. He put his ear to Robb's nose and mouth. Breathing. He felt Cynthia's forehead, knowing before he touched her what he would feel. Cold. He knew she was dead. He turned and rushed from the room.

He ran across the great room toward the front door. Mrs. Campbell stood in the hallway, fear written on her face.

Sam opened the door and yelled, "Tony! Come quickly!"

Rizzo yelled, "Come on, Merrie!" He sprang from the car. "Bring the oxygen, Monk!"

Mrs. Campbell watched in horror as Tony Rizzo, black bag in hand, followed Sam quickly toward the library. Merrie rushed after them, followed by Bradley carrying the oxygen bottles.

———49———

On Tuesday morning, February 27th, Colonel Strang called Lieutenant Evelyn Vandivier into his office as soon as she reported for work. The Colonel met her at his door. He asked her to sit down. "Would you like a cup of coffee?"

Evelyn said, "Robb's dead, isn't he?"

Colonel Strang sat down facing her. "Robb is going to be all right. He's at the Army Air Forces Hospital at Prestwick."

She burst into tears.

Colonel Strang left the office and returned with a cup of coffee. "Drink this."

She wiped her eyes. "I'm sorry, sir."

"There's something else I must tell you."

"Something's wrong with Robb!"

"No. Not that. He's going to be all right." He studied her face carefully. "His friend, Cynthia Allsford, is dead."

Her hand began to shake. Colonel Strang took the cup from her.

"Lieutenant, I assure you Robb is going to be all right."

"Why is he in the hospital? Did he try to take his own life too?"

"No. He made no such attempt. We think he went up there to try to save Cynthia. He got there too late. According to Tony Rizzo a few hours too late. He apparently went into a state of shock when he found her. A severe state of shock. He hasn't spoken a word since they found him. He doesn't respond at all, to anything." Strang came around the end of his desk and was about to place his hand on her shoulder. He withdrew his hand and sat back on the front edge of his desk. "We've seen this sort of thing here on the base now and then, after particularly rough missions. In almost every case they come out of it okay. Usually all it takes is time." The C.O. went to the door. "I'll be back in a minute."

After a time Evelyn stood up and left the room. When she came back from the restroom Colonel Strang wasn't there. She walked to the window and gazed eastward. A ray of sunlight appeared on the horizon beneath the overcast. In a minute it was gone and the morning became dismal gray again. Colonel Strang returned.

"Would you like to go up to Prestwick to see Robb this morning?"

She nodded. "More than anything in the world."

"I called Captain Peterson and made arrangements for him and his co-pilot to fly another pilot up there to pick up the P-47. I told him you'd be going up there with them. You're on a one-week leave as of now. You can stay up there in the WAC BOQ. You'd better go to your barracks and get your things together, and you'd better hurry. Pete Peterson and his people are probably on their way to Operations now. You're to report to Operations as soon as you can."

Susan James buzzed Colonel Strang shortly after Evelyn departed. "Lieutenant Hagopian is on the phone, sir. Do you wish to speak to him?"

"Put him on."

"Colonel, I just heard about Robertson going off his rocker."

"He didn't go off his rocker. He's in a temporary state of shock."

"I mean his stealing the P-47, taking off the wrong way on the runway under a red Aldis and flying up there like a goddamn maniac and all the rest of the nutty business."

"What did you want to talk to me about?"

"Well, sir, our Captain Robertson last night added another string of serious crimes to his already impressive list. What I'm saying is we gotta put these new crimes to work for us, along with the fact that he's a basket case up there right now."

"How?"

"I asked Colonel Leonard if he'd meet with you and me this afternoon, provided you were in favor of the idea and could spare the time. What do you think, sir?"

"Just what is your plan?"

"The same plan I had before. We go the combat fatigue route, without the help, or hindrance, of Robertson."

Strang pondered for a minute. "We'd be going against Robertson's wishes, while he's incompetent to speak for himself."

"Right you are, Colonel. You just said the magic word. *Incompetent*! He's incompetent to do a fucking thing. Excuse me, sir. What I mean is we don't have to worry about his wishes. Right now he's incompetent to have wishes, just as he's incompetent to enter a plea of guilty or nolo contendere or to remain mute or anything else!"

Strang cradled the phone between his head and shoulder and lit a cigarette. "I'm referring to his wishes before he went into this state of shock."

"He was incompetent even then. Stop to think of what he did last night on top of everything before that, and his indifference about whether he lives or dies. Shit, sir, you and I and everybody except Robertson himself and the investigators knew he had gone bananas. Oh yes, and except for the psychiatrists. Last night was the final plunge. He completed the jump off his rocker last night."

"Colonel Leonard has already rendered his decision."

"He can reverse himself at any time up to the trial. That's what we go for with Colonel Leonard this afternoon. We ask him to reconvene his people as soon as possible. We want them to meet before Robertson comes out of his trance and fucks things up."

Strang sighed. "I envy you, Lieutenant."

"What do you mean?"

Strang smiled ruefully into the phone. "Let it go. What do you think of our chances for a reversal?"

"First, we've got to get the board to meet again on the case."

"Let's say the board agrees to reconvene, what are our chances then?"

"A hell of a lot better than last time."

Strang snuffed out his cigarette. "They may say there's no way they're going to change their recommendation to Colonel Leonard just because Robertson committed an additional string of crimes."

"I know, but this time *I* go before the board, not you, to present Robertson's case. You gotta remember, I'm a pro at this kind of thing. I've been here before. I'm goddamn good at . . ."

"What, specifically, do you intend to tell the board?"

"I tell them all of Robertson's bizarre crimes are a result of the ravages of war on his personality. Here we have a guy who, as they can plainly see by his war record and personal history, was an intelligent, well-educated, sensitive, concerned human being who under ordinary circumstances would have been a model citizen. The war has done this to him. He's practically a psychopath, unable to distinguish between right and wrong, unable to accept society's rules or the army's rules on the level of conscience. There was a time he could, but he can't anymore. The sheer volume of his bizarre acts and wild crimes and his refusal to defend himself in the slightest, and his total lack of concern over whether he's shot by a firing squad or put in prison for life—all of this attests to the obvious fact that he's a very seriously disturbed man. I tell the board that the additional crimes he committed last night are further evidence of the fact that Captain Robertson is totally shot psychologically, a basket case. Which he is, by God! Hell, Colonel, I'm not going to settle for ipso facto nuts. Now, with the poor son of a bitch in a basket up there, I'm going for prima facie nuts!"

"Will the board buy that?"

"I'm not through, Colonel. I end up my presentation by repeating, by emphasizing all of this was done to him by the war in which he served like few others, *volunteering* for a second tour, mind you, and winning more medals than Hermann Goering gave himself."

"Let's say you win your argument and the board reverses its recommendation. Will Colonel Leonard reverse himself?"

"Hell yes. I could tell it by the way he's bothered by this whole Robertson thing. He's ordinarily tougher than hell when it comes to big crimes, but I got the impression he already thinks Robertson had been folding for some time, but he didn't want to go against the board's recommendations— especially in light of the impersonation thing."

"Let's say Colonel Leonard reverses himself. What happens then?"

"In that case it's all pretty much pro forma, automatic. Colonel Leonard drops the charges. The shrinks rubber-stamp Colonel Leonard's conclusions. They certify Robertson as nuts and he gets sent back to the States to Section Eight in some army hospital. A few months after he comes out of his trance, maybe even a year or so, the shrinks declare him cured— as they always do because they need the beds—and the army gives him a medical discharge."

"What are our chances for things turning out like that?"

"Good. Actually damned good."

"What time do you want me up there?"

Lieutenant Evelyn Vandivier entered the front door of the U.S. Army Air Forces Hospital at Prestwick at approximately 11:30 AM. She stopped short. There, in a corner of the vestibule that doubled as a visitor's lounge, sat Sam Prentice. He was sound asleep.

She approached him quietly. "Sam?"

Sam's eyes opened. He stared at her uncomprehendingly. Recognition dawned slowly. His face, gray with fatigue, cracked into a smile. "Evelyn!" He got up and embraced her. "Robb is going to be all right."

"I know, thank heavens. How is he now?"

"The same. He still hasn't spoken a word or responded in any way."

"What does Tony say? Did he say how long this is likely to continue?"

"He says he's seen this before, in men who've suffered a particularly rough mission. He says it's usually temporary."

"Usually? I don't like the sound of that."

"He says they all come out of the shock sooner or later, but sometimes the man is permanently damaged neurologically, never recovering his normal personality. He says he's not worried about Robb, but I can see he is."

"Where's Tony now?"

"In Robb's room, with a neurologist. We'll know more when the neurologist finishes going over him."

Tony Rizzo came into the vestibule. He embraced Evelyn warmly. Rizzo said, "He's going to be all right." Rizzo looked haggard. He needed a shave and there were dark circles under his eyes. "Things could have been a lot worse. He could easily have taken a handful of pills, like Cynthia. Cynthia's box of pills and wine bottles were right there on the table in front of him." He shook his head sadly. "We couldn't do anything for Cynthia. She was dead hours before Robb got there. She must have done it as soon as she got Crick's phone call."

Evelyn said, "May I see him?"

"Maybe all three of us should go in there now, to let him know his friends are pulling for him. Your coming is going to help a lot, Evelyn. Come on."

Evelyn said, "Where's Merrie? And Monk? Maybe they should come too."

"Sleeping. Monk was a zombie and he has to fly us back pretty soon now, and Merrie is in pretty bad shape over all this. I insisted she go to the WAC BOQ. Come on. Let's go see if we can breathe some life into Robb."

The three of them entered the room and stood next to the bed. Robb lay on his right side, his face to the wall. A tube ran from an I.V. bottle to his left arm.

Rizzo said loudly, "Robb. You've got company! Sam and Evelyn!"

"Robb, it's me, Sam."

The rise and fall of the side of his chest remained steady, as though he were asleep. Evelyn looked at Rizzo. "May we pull the bed away from the wall?"

Rizzo pulled the bed away from the wall. Evelyn walked around to the other side of the bed and took his hand in both of hers. She spoke softly. "Robb, I'm here. I'm going to stay here with you for a week. Please say something to me." She tried to open his hand so that she could hold it properly, but his fist remained tightly closed.

Rizzo shook his head. "Don't try to open his hand. It won't do you any good, and it's not necessary anyway." Rizzo came around the bed and bent over and focused the beam of his penlight into Robb's eye. He stood up and motioned for them to leave the room. He followed them out and closed the door behind him. They returned to the vestibule.

Rizzo said, "This is liable to take some time. He's awake but he's still out of it. According to the neurologist he's withdrawn from reality, a reality that was too harsh."

Sam said, "An autistic state."

Rizzo looked at Sam curiously. "Where the hell did you get that?"

"I read about it somewhere."

Rizzo said, "You happen to be right. That's exactly what the neurologist called it. He says this has nothing to do with autistic personalities. It refers to a specific response in this case, not an on-going personality syndrome. He'll come out of it. What I should say is the chances are good he'll come out of it. You've got to remember he suffered a hell of a lot of psychological trauma long before all this happened. From the standpoint of hindsight, it's easy to see he's been heading for an emotional collapse for some time now. The massive trauma of Cynthia's suicide pushed him over the line. Under normal circumstances, say in peacetime, something like this, no matter how horrible, wouldn't have sent a guy like Robb into shock like this."

Sam said, "How long before he'll come out of it?"

"Possibly today or tomorrow, or it could take weeks, maybe even months. But he'll come out of it. The big question is will he be an emotional wreck or will he bounce back." He turned to Evelyn. "I've been on the phone with the C.O. There could be a mission tomorrow so Sam and I have to leave with Monk as soon as possible. The doctors here will take care of him. Stay with him as much as possible. Keep talking to him. Let him know you care." He smiled and put his arm around her shoulder. "How could you do anything else?" He kissed her on the cheek.

"Come on, Sam. Let's go wake up Monk. Maybe we can squeeze in a shave at the BOQ."

Sam said, "You go ahead. I'd like to see Robb one more time, just to say goodbye. Well, actually I'd like to give it one more try, to try to get him to respond. I'll meet you and Monk at Prestwick Operations. May Evelyn and I go back in there now?"

"Of course. The more stimulation he gets, the better. Goodbye, Evelyn."

The bed was still at an angle to the wall. Robb hadn't moved. He lay on his side facing the wall. Sam walked around the end of the bed and stooped down so that his face was within a foot of Robb's. "Robb, It's me, Sam. Say something if you hear me." He clasped Robb's open, right hand. "Robb, squeeze my hand if you hear me." Robb's hand remained inert. Sam looked up at Evelyn and shook his head. He spoke again to Robb, loudly, directly into his face. "Robb. I have to leave for Allsford Lynn. I came to say goodbye for now."

"But I'm staying, Robb." Evelyn said.

He showed no sign of having heard them.

Sam stood up and moved away from the bed. He bent over and kissed Evelyn on the cheek. He raised his hand to her as he left the room, carefully closing the door behind him.

Evelyn could see the airfield from where she sat. She could see the B-17s and B-24s coming in now and then, touching down after their long journey across the sea. She spoke to Robb from time to time. She told him the time of day, and she told him of the weather and its gradual changes and the changing light as the day wore on. When she saw a plane land, she told him what kind of a plane it was. When she couldn't identify a plane she described it to him, hoping that if her descriptions were accurate enough he might say what type of plane it was.

She saw bombers taking off. She knew they were going to southern England, and she thought of their youthful crews flying into the unknown, not knowing what awaited them. She didn't tell him about the bombers taking off.

Toward sundown a nurse came in, a big, crisply starched, handsome young woman whose face communicated strength and competence. She placed her hand on Robb's forehead. She felt his pulse and measured his blood pressure and changed the I.V. bottle. As she departed, she asked Evelyn if she could bring her something to eat. Evelyn shook her head.

The nurse came again around 9:00 PM and repeated her ritual. She moved the bed farther from the wall so that Evelyn could move nearer to the head of the bed. As the nurse departed, she left the door open. The light from the hall outlined Robb's figure on the bed. Evelyn's eyes never left him. After a time her eyes became accustomed to the half-light and she could see his eyes, his open, unseeing eyes.

His arm hung over the side of the bed as he lay on his side facing her. His eyes remained open throughout the night. Toward morning, perhaps an hour or two before daybreak, she took his left hand, his fist, in hers. She kissed the back of his hand, and as her lips lingered she sensed a relaxing of the tight fist. She stroked the back of his hand softly, slowly. She kissed the back of his hand from time to time and continued her gentle stroking. She felt his fist opening, the fist that had been tightly locked for thirty hours or more. When his hand was half-open a small, crumpled ball of paper fell from his hand into hers. She grasped the ball of paper and his fingers and continued stroking his hand.

"Robb? Robb? If you hear me, please answer me."

He gave no sign of having heard her.

She carefully opened the ball and smoothed it against her lap. She held it up to the light from the hall and read the awkwardly scrawled, almost illegible words. She sat staring at the sheet of paper for several minutes. Finally she leaned forward, her face close to his, and whispered Cynthia's message. "How beautiful upon the mountain are the footsteps of the Messenger of Peace." He blinked and turned his eyes to hers. She thought she saw a glimmer of comprehension in his eyes.

End